RAVE
Sharleen

<u>LIVES OF VALUE</u>

BOOKS BY SHARLEEN COOPER COHEN

Love, Sex and Money
Marital Affairs
The Ladies of Beverly Hills
Regina's Song
The Day After Tomorrow

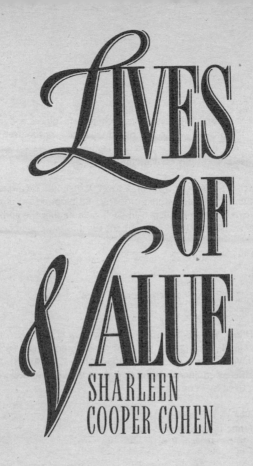

LIVES OF VALUE

SHARLEEN COOPER COHEN

WARNER BOOKS

A Time Warner Company

WARNER BOOKS EDITION

Copyright © 1991 by Sharleen Cooper Cohen
All rights reserved.

"All the Things You Are." Music by Jerome Kern and lyrics by Oscar
Hammerstein II. Copyright © 1939 PolyGram International Publishing,
Inc. (3500 West Olive Avenue, Suite 200, Burbank, CA 91505).
Copyright Renewed. International Copyright Secured. All Rights
Reserved. Used by Permission.

Cover design by Jackie Merri Meyer
Hand lettering by Carl Dellacroce
Cover photo by Herman Estevez

Warner Books, Inc.
1271 Avenue of the Americas
New York, NY 10020

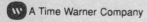 A Time Warner Company

Printed in the United States of America

Originally published in hardcover by Warner Books.
First Printed in Paperback: January, 1993

10 9 8 7 6 5 4 3 2 1

ACKNOWLEDGMENTS

I am grateful to the following people
for their time and expertise:

Penny Roberts
Carole Lees
Barbara Friedman
Sam White
Claretta White
Barbara Gordon, M.S.W.
Richard Kaplan
Charles G. Hutter, M.D.
Ernest Beutler, M.D.
Richard Ungerleiter, M.D.
Paul Markoe
Anthony Brand
Madelyn Kramer
Jerry Pierce
Forrest Elliot
Sandi Gelles-Cole
Charles Gordon, Esq.
Sam Birenbaum, Esq.

To my daughters,
Cambria and Dalisa,
who are so fortunate to be sisters

For Steffani

Don't speak evil to sad-seeming women
Leave them dream of blonder days
Or let the curse of some men touch them
Better win them with words and gentle ways
For tears will drown caresses
Melting memories sometimes proud
Of pink-lipped shadows and flowing tresses
And deny the urge to cry out loud

Some men stifle female thunder
Crushing her magic with a glance
Unable to accept the wonder
Committing crimes against romance
While others smile and whisper
All is well and oh so fine
Pouring wine into a slipper
Sipping dewdrops from the vine

So, she dances through the shadows
Smiling sunshine in the rain
Putting bouquets into flowers
Bringing good times back again
Kissing men with hairy arms
Huddled close in their embrace
As the tinkling of her laughter
Weaves a web of special place

Those that know enough to miss her
Search a thousand inner flames
Of candles flickering whispering softly
Smoothing memories of her pain
Hallowed truth more than required
Wrapped like hope in antique lace
Won't fade softly with a smile
But grabs fiercely with her nails
To leave a shiny mollusk's trace

PENNY ROBERTS AND SHARLEEN COOPER COHEN

LIVES OF VALUE

PROLOGUE

I grew up on fairy tales. Even before I was two, my grand-mother read them or told them to me. The sound of her voice filled me with wonder, a fascination with magic, and a belief in happily-ever-after. She came to this country from Romania when she was twelve, but I don't remember any accent . . . or maybe I do, just the faintest hint in the way she said certain things. She died when I was seven and I still feel a profound sadness at her loss. But her legacy was immense, for now I tell stories for a living and re-create the feeling of warmth and security I had when I sat in her lap with her arms around me, my head nestled against her soft breast, the picture book in front of us and her gentle voice lilting with emotion as it fired my imagination with enough fantasy for a lifetime.

Every princess had hair as black as coal or as golden as wheat. Their skin was as white as snow, their lips as red as cherries, their hearts as pure as the crystal water in a rushing blue stream. Writers of fairy tales, like the Brothers Grimm, or Hans Christian Andersen, happily used clichés. For with-out those cherry lips, snow-white skin, or hair as black as a raven's wing, I wouldn't have been so easily transported to fairyland. Those familiar words were signposts that shifted my base from the reality around me into what I now know was a state of alpha.

To me, my nana was the essence of beauty because she gave me pure, uncritical love. She had dreamed of being a writer but in those days few women fulfilled their dreams; family responsibility, lack of money, and—even more con-

fining—women's second-class standing in the world kept
them back. She had never been past grammar school, and yet
she did write a novel in which she transformed her mundane
existence into the romantic, as novelists do. Considering that
this woman never had any luxuries, her knowledge was amazing: the choosing of finest emeralds, the weaving of Gobelin
tapestries, the inlaying of marquetry tables. She could describe in detail the intricacies of a jewel-encrusted egg, the
majesty of a palace lined with marble, the magnificence of a
lapis lazuli basin, the exquisiteness of clothes of the finest
silk trimmed with handmade Belgian lace, and of course the
most romantic love. Her novel was a fairy tale, as naive as
the ones she read to me. Sadly, it wasn't publishable, but
perhaps it will find an audience when I complete it. I hope I
have the skills to bring it alive, and not lose its original charm.

Steffani was three when Nana died and didn't know her
the way I did, hadn't been privileged to hear all her stories.
I felt sorry for my sister because of that, but I also felt a touch
of smug superiority. That younger sister of mine, the usurper
of my spotlight in the family, hadn't been as close to our
grandmother as I was—after all, she was *my* nana, and nobody else's.

The novels I've written are not as blatantly romantic as
Nana's book. But I believe that people long for entertainment
that allows them to escape. If one wants to be depressed one
can read Joyce Carol Oates or Joan Didion, not Suzanne
Winston. My ultimate fantasy is to fly away through the night
sky with Peter Pan to Never-Never Land, that magic place
where elves and fairies dwell and trees can talk.

If it's true that the spirits of departed loved ones guide our
lives, Nana must be guiding mine. She gave me a love of
stories, the belief that I could make them up because I'd seen
her do it so many times, and even the legacy of a novel to
complete. The irony is that I was also given a sister who
desperately needed the distraction that stories brought. I know
now that those fictitious worlds into which my sister and I
escaped were as necessary for me as they were for her. Being
able to tell stories has always been my greatest joy.

In my early years as a writer, I'd reward myself by reading my chapters to Steffani. She preferred to read alone, but if I begged her, she'd listen, re-creating that time in our childhood when she was sick and I'd tell her a story.

"You tell better stories than Uncle Jules," she'd say. "His stories are too scary. I want the beauty, not the scary."

I'd come over to her bed and she'd be lying there, with her braids spread out on the pillow and the finger curls at the ends, her round blue eyes gazing up at me, two dimples playing in the softness of her cheeks even though her face was flushed with fever. Wincing with pain, she'd shift her weight over to make room for me as I climbed up and settled against the wall, feeling the cold wallpaper chill my back, keeping my voice low so our parents in the next room wouldn't hear us. And I'd say: "Once upon a time, a long time ago in a faraway land, lived a beautiful princess with long golden hair."

Sometimes we'd get halfway through the story before the pain would get so bad she'd be hitting her knee with her small fist, or pounding on her thigh, or her hip, or wherever the pain was throbbing, and she'd moan and toss in bed and say, "I've got to call Dad, Suze, I can't stand it."

There'd be tears in her eyes, which she fought to hold back.

"We're just getting to the good part," I'd say. "Where the prince and princess find the treasure and the wicked fairy queen locks them in the dungeon."

"Okay," she'd gasp, torn by her need to hear more of the story and the pain throbbing in her joints. I had a perverse control over her at those moments. It was true that I was sparing our father from getting up in the middle of the night, and I was keeping my sister from taking more doses of her medication, our euphemism for drugs, over too short a period, which we all knew wasn't good for her and ought to be avoided as long as possible. But what I was really doing was plying my craft, weaving my own spell, doing what I loved most in the world to do, tell a story.

SUZANNE WINSTON, *October 1976*

BOOK I

Baby Face

CHAPTER ONE

The enormous amount of mail jammed into the box would have made me laugh if it weren't so overwhelming. All those people shouting to be heard, and catalogs filled with useless items; who bought them? And who gave money to all those worthy causes? (Actually, I did, which may explain why I was on so many lists.) Being a writer of some fame had responsibilities. I believe in supporting worthy causes with donations, especially since I don't have time to work for them.

Tugging at the mail with both hands while juggling everything else I was holding caused the catalogs and magazines to unroll and pop open, scattering everything into the street. "Damn!" I muttered, keeping my purse under my arm and trying to hold my keys and the garage door opener ready as I bent to retrieve the fallen mail. That's when I saw my copy of the *New York Times Book Review* for this week, October 10, 1976, and my heart began to race. I threw everything into the passenger seat and opened the *Book Review* to the best-seller list, my heart beating so fast I felt as though I'd been jogging. There it was, my fifth novel, *Mortal Wounds*, number three on the fiction list. And the pub date was still two weeks away.

"Hey, world!" I shouted, honking the horn. "I'm number three and climbing." I wished the whole neighborhood could have shared my excitement, but there was no one around. I drove up the driveway into the garage grinning and pounding the steering wheel with excitement. *How about that!* Even though all four of my other books had made the list, it was still such a thrill. The first time it happened was months after the book was on the shelves; this time I'd gotten on before the pub date. Being on this list adds thousands of dollars to my contract, and staying there adds even more. Escalators, they called it. But even more than that, only a few out of the nearly forty thousand books published every year achieve this honor. Tears of gratitude came to my eyes. In moments like these, the years of hard work are worth it. I sacrifice a great deal for my success, though I'm not a workaholic. But writing demands enormous amounts of time, to plan, to outline, to research, to rework the plot, to create believable characters; and time just to contemplate what it is I want to say. And some of that time is spent feeling insecure, certain that I'm inadequate to complete this enormous task. I have to over- come those feelings every time I sit down to work, often in the face of cruel criticism from others and even harsher criti- cism from myself, not to mention the editorial demands that would daunt a person of lesser will and determination. For instance, *Publishers Weekly* and the LA *Times* gave *Mortal Wounds* excellent reviews, but Brett Slocum in the *New York Times* really trashed me. "Not a human character among them," she said. Now, seeing my name on the list took the sting out of her words. I felt proud of my accomplishments, something I seldom take the time to do.

The rest of the mail contained the usual catalogs, bills, invitations to charity functions, and a note from my sister, Steffani, attached to a review of someone else's book. "I loved this," she wrote. "The author digs deep and it shows." My sister is never subtle when it comes to her opinion of my work. She wishes I, too, would *dig deep*. I could hear Mother's voice saying, *She just wants what's best for you.* (And for me to be a *literary* writer so she can impress her pseudointellectual friends, who I think of as bums.)

I dumped the mail on the kitchen desk and dialed my answering service. My editor had called to tell me about the *Times'* list; my mother was inviting me and the children to dinner tonight—good, I wouldn't have to cook. My dad sent me his love (I'm surrounded by love, but at the moment have no love life). And there was also a request to be the featured speaker at an American Cancer Society luncheon in two months. I enjoy public speaking when it helps raise money for causes, and also because it allows me to meet my readers in person. Rarely do I get feedback from those who enjoy my books. Mostly I spend time alone in my office, struggling with my demons, though I love my work as much as I love anything in my life—sometimes more.

The last piece of mail was a manila envelope addressed to me, postmarked from New York with no return address. Inside was a photocopy of about ten pages of a book, clipped together with a cover letter. The letter, on plain stationery, was addressed to my current editor, Judy Emory, at Silver's Press, from someone named Sherry Fallon, who said she was formerly an assistant editor in the Young Adult division. I didn't know Sherry Fallon. The second paragraph said:

As an ex-employee of Suzanne Winston's publisher, I'm writing to you to inform you that she definitely plagiarized her second novel and may have plagiarized other ones as well. Please see the enclosed pages.

The word *plagiarized* leaped out at me, slammed me between the eyes. "What the hell is this?" I said out loud.

I read on. *Everyone in my division at Silver's Press when I worked there knew what Ms. Winston was doing. It's surprising how well that secret was kept, but no more. I thought it was time you in Editorial were told, in case the* real *writer of her books should decide to sue.*

My hands were shaking so badly I could barely hold the letter.

Even though the book S.W. plagiarized from was written a long time ago, the real writer or her heirs might still own the copyright and want to sue for damages. You can't fool all of the people all of the time, this crazy, vicious person continued; my heart pounded and my head felt light and empty as though I had just entered a nightmare.

The words blurred before my eyes and I blinked to clear
my vision.

*I have enclosed a Xerox of a Xerox of some of the work
Ms. Winston has plagiarized. I'm in the process of uncovering
copies of the original books, but since they are out of print,
they're difficult to find. Forgive me for informing you by letter
this way, I know it's cowardly. But I'll be glad to answer any
questions. Sincerely yours, Sherry Fallon, Former Assistant
Editor.* There was no return address but there was a phone
number. I recognized it as the general number for Silver's
Press. I glanced at the clock on the built-in oven, 3:45 here,
6:45 in New York. Silver's was closed by now. I couldn't
call them; I'd have to wait until tomorrow.

The feeling of horror, of disbelief, was overwhelming. My
eyes searched for the familiar, comforting sights of my house,
the blue-and-yellow-print cotton sofas in the family room, the
kitchen with the dark ash cabinets and the children's artwork
attached by magnets to the refrigerator door. All normal, yet
now off kilter, as if the whole room, and suddenly my life,
were at an angle. An evil presence had just entered here
making everything oddly perverse.

I was afraid to read what Sherry Fallon had enclosed in the
envelope, but I had to know. What possible proof could there
be that I had done such a heinous thing?

The photocopied material was from the pages of a book.
Whoever Sherry Fallon was, she'd gone to a great deal of
trouble and expense to create this lie; it wasn't that easy to
have something typeset. The pages numbered 131 through
135. They seemed oddly familiar. I read:

> Only his beloved flamenco music and the sound
> of his feet beating the rhythm of the dance could
> make him feel the way Jessie made him feel. And
> music was a lonely partner.
>
> But not as lonely as death. What was it like
> to be dead? Gone forever. Luis remembered stand-
> ing on that hill watching them lower his brother

Paco's coffin into the ground. Twenty-five years old and gone forever. No more heartache, no more searching for completion, no more loving Jessie, no more anything. Luis hadn't cried at the funeral, but he had cried later. God, how he'd cried. He hadn't wanted to give Jessie the satisfaction of seeing his pain, that twisting of a knife in his guts; his brother dead. Are you at peace, Paco? Have you forgiven me for taking your girl, your love, your Jessie?

He had hated Jessie that day as she stood in the wind, her hair flaming red against the blue sky, the dry, cracked earth of the cemetery beneath her feet, her dress clinging to her body whipped by the wind, as his lips remembered it, soft and yielding to his kiss. She was so beautiful. He remembered their love. Seeing her face streaked with tears made him hate her more. He'd wanted to scream across the grave at her, "It's too late to cry, now. You killed him, how dare you cry!"

For a moment I was caught up in the scene, seeing the people described, the two lovers, the dead brother. And then I remembered it. My second novel, *The Reunion*, about a rock group whose members hated one another and refused to have a reunion concert no matter how much money they were offered, or how much their fans longed for it to happen. Only my characters had been named Cord and Regina, not Luis and Jessie.

I ran into my office and pulled down a copy of *The Reunion* from the shelf. The passage was easy to find; after all, I'd written this book. My heart pounded as I read my own words. They were almost identical except for a few changes to allow for a difference in setting and to make a rock group into a troop of Spanish dancers. I felt as if I were about to explode. The unreality of it was terrifying, yet it was very real. For a moment I wondered if I'd actually read a book about Paco and Luis and Jessie at some earlier time in my life and unconsciously stolen it. But that was impossible! I would know if I'd copied someone else's work word for word, just as I remember almost every book I've ever read. Books are precious things to me. To be able to write them, to be included in that rare segment of society known as writers is a privilege I cherish. And besides, I remember the exact moment when I thought of the idea for *The Reunion*.

Alex and I were still married then, and we'd gone to a wedding of one of the members of Kiss. There were numerous celebrities milling about, adding to the wild atmosphere of the wedding being held high above Beverly Hills in a private home with a spectacular view of the city and ocean beyond.

I stood among the guests in their flamboyant clothes and outrageous hairdos and I sensed inherent drama. One of the guests caught my eye. An odd-looking black man with a slicked-up pompadour was surrounded by a group who were fawning on him. Dressed in a purple suit and silver shirt, he had them eating out of his hand.

Alex nudged me. "He's the pusher, the main man who supplies everybody with drugs."

But he's so obvious, I thought, watching the man smile, slap hands, kiss women's necks; I marveled at how a man like that had made it to the top, had all these famous faces gathered around him. Right then, I decided to write about how a group of wealthy entertainers, whom the public idolized, fawned on a low-life pusher because he got them drugs. And that led me to the task of creating my characters and discovering who they were. It was my idea. I hadn't copied if from anyone; how dare anyone say I had?

Suddenly, I felt terrified, invaded. Who was Sherry Fallon? Why had she done something like this, and in such diabolical detail? A deadly undetectable gas had seeped its way through the cracks in the doors and windows of my house and threatened to suffocate me. I was unaware of this nuclear fallout, until I'd been contaminated. If this could invade my world so easily, I was completely vulnerable. I recoiled, as if shocked by electricity, and trembled all over. *Why did she hate me this much? What had I done to deserve this? My God, what if Sherry Fallon wasn't even her name. It could be a fictitious name. That meant it could be anyone. Even someone I knew.* That thought was so threatening, I pushed it far away, leaving myself to deal with it another time.

My writing was the best part of me, second only to my children. Now, it had been sullied. I roared a silent protest, feeling the muscles in my back and shoulders clenching tightly against the black terror that yawned beneath me. I was familiar with terror, but always managed to keep it at bay before it engulfed me. All my life, whenever I felt it approaching, stealing toward me, bringing its numbing presence, my mind would focus on other things, other places, lovely fantasies; stories told to me or stories I would tell filled with happy moments. This time, I could barely keep it from swallowing me whole. I kept thinking, *How could something like this have happened to me?*

For some reason then, I did the strangest thing. I locked all the doors, closed all the drapes, and took the phone off the hook.

CHAPTER TWO

"Mommy, tell me a story about Nana and Papa," Jered asked, wiggling down under the covers. He would do anything to put off going to sleep, but tonight I welcomed his request; a story would get my mind off of that package I'd received this afternoon. We'd declined my mother's invitation to dinner and eaten at home. By rote, I'd prepared the food, acted as referee for my three children, answered their questions on automatic, while the neurons in my brain prodded the stinking mess that had been dropped into my life. Whatever it was I might be facing made me want to lower myself into a hole and hide.

Amy and Miles were in their rooms doing their homework and this was my time with Jered. My seven-year-old's sweet face looked up at me with such an anticipation of pleasure that I forced myself to set aside thoughts of an unknown tormentor setting about to destroy my life and identified with Jered's need to delay the inevitable bedtime for as long as possible. I, too, would do anything to put off dealing with what lay ahead.

"Okay." I smoothed the hair back from his forehead and climbed up on the bed. He scooted over so I could sit on the edge, his face framed by the Snoopy-patterned pillowcase. He yawned, making me want to yawn too. He was tired, I could see it in his eyes. He'd be asleep in no time. I wanted to bury my face in his innocent chest and breathe in his trust like ether, let it erase my realities. Instead, I prayed that the God who diverted thoughts from bad to good would be there for me again as I forced myself to concentrate on my story.

"Gorgeous," I began. "They were both so gorgeous when they were young. Lynnette Rosenberg from Kansas City looked like a brunette version of Rita Hayworth, and Burt Blacker from Chicago was an exact replica of Errol Flynn— blue eyes, black hair, and a mustache. People used to ask him for his autograph. And she had long dark hair, and white skin, and big brown eyes. She was small and slender, and she wore a red wool dress that her mother had made for her."

He smiled at me and I smiled back, both of us caught up in the memories of my parents' youth and their courtship, totally diverted. It was working!

"From the top, Lynnette," Mel Harrison said, raising his baton. "And one, and two."

On the downbeat she sang, "Embrace me, my sweet embraceable you," holding on to the microphone as the band played the song behind her and her soft, low voice filled the high school auditorium where they were rehearsing.

He was out there. The man who booked acts for a theatrical chain out of New York. A friend of Mel's, he'd come to watch the band perform. The moment she'd looked into his smiling gray-blue eyes, she'd felt an instant attraction.

At dinner (where she sipped tea while the others ate dinner because the restaurant wasn't kosher) she found herself sitting opposite Burt Blacker. He kept looking at her while she pretended not to notice. It made her nervous, an excited kind of nervous.

After dinner, he came up to her. "I enjoyed your singing very much, Miss Rosenberg. I wish I were looking for a female vocalist."

She smiled up at him, flirting. "Have you been wasting our time on a lark here in Kansas City?"

"Absolutely not," he kind of blustered, defending his sincerity. "Since we're now part of RKO, instead of the Orpheum Circuit, we need good acts, even though the biggest acts aren't playing variety theater anymore. But I used to book them all—Jack Benny, Burns and Allen, Fanny Brice, even Singer's Midgets." His smile mixed pride with regret. He seemed young to have done all that.

She touched his arm to reassure him. "The smaller acts need more exposure. Everybody has to start somewhere." The tweed of his coat felt alive beneath her hand.

"I'd like to take you out while I'm here, maybe to a nightclub?"

How lovely to dance with this handsome man, the most beautiful man she'd ever seen, so nice, refined. But her mother would never let her go out with him alone. "I don't mean to offend you," she said, trying to let him know she liked him while still turning him down, "but you're a stranger, after all. It wouldn't be proper."

His expression told her he rarely met girls in show business who cared about being properly introduced. Then he smiled again, dazzling her. "Suppose I come and introduce myself to your parents tomorrow night. Would that be proper enough?"

Lynnette's cheeks flushed hotly. This man was older than

the boys she'd grown up with, at least twenty-eight, with an important job. She couldn't believe that he really liked her.

"Would you like to come for dinner?" she asked, knowing they couldn't afford to make a fancy dinner for company on a week night, which would embarrass her mother. But she had to do something.

Thursday night when he rang the bell, the radio was playing a new Tommy Dorsey recording and she felt like dancing as she opened the door. She had helped her mother make cabbage soup with raisins, Romanian style, and the aroma filled the small house. But he didn't seem to mind. She introduced him to her father and brother and her mother. They sat down to dinner, everyone awkward, staring at him, trying not to.

"Mrs. Rosenberg, you're a wonderful cook," Burt complimented her. "I can't tell you what it means to me to have a kosher meal, traveling the way I do."

"You eat in restaurants? Tsk, tsk." Elizabeth Rosenberg shook her head with sympathy but her eyes were smiling. So, this young man of Lynnette's was Jewish. The auburn braids wrapped into a coronet on top of her head caught the light as she moved.

"I do miss my family when I'm traveling," he told her. "Two brothers and a sister, in Chicago. We're very close."

"Are your parents living?"

"My mother and father are both in good health." He knocked on wood for good luck and proceeded to tell her everything she was too polite to ask. "Mama is not as good a cook as you," he lied. "And though she's tiny, like you, every one of her babies weighed over ten pounds. My father is tall, you see. My brothers are both six feet, my sister, Sima, is five-seven, and I'm six-three." He sat up straight in his chair so they could tell.

Lynnette's mother liked him. Her father, Henry, inscrutable as usual, barely spoke, but studied Burt with sidelong glances that made Lynnette's heart skip wildly. It was hard to believe this vibrant, worldly man was here in her modest living room, seeming at ease at their dining room table, which

Lynnette had set with the hand-crocheted cloth her aunt Anna had made for her mama's wedding. Burt's blue-gray eyes were kind, but they didn't miss a detail; he appraised them as if they were auditioning as one of his acts.

Lynnette admired his beautifully tailored clothes, noted the hand-stitching around the collar of his open-necked shirt, probably of silk shantung—it had to be to look so creamy. And his tweed jacket with the leather buttons fit him perfectly, tailored to his tall frame; the slacks were of the finest brown gabardine. Lynnette's father sold men's clothing downtown at Leffler's store so she knew about quality fabrics. But nothing in Leffler's store looked like this.

After dinner, Burt asked her parents if he could take her for a walk in the neighborhood. She held her breath until her mother and father said yes. Her father raised his bushy white eyebrows at her brother, Sid, so he wouldn't laugh.

Burt draped a hand-knitted shawl, another present from Aunt Anna, around her shoulders to keep out the September chill, and they started out. The autumn night air was scented by the smell of wood smoke wafting from neighborhood kitchens.

"Do you plan to stay in Kansas City all your life?" he asked, taking her arm.

"No. I'd like to go to New York and become a singer."

"Not Hollywood?"

"Oh no. I want the challenge of New York where they recognize real talent. I plan to try out for the musical stage."

He nodded, impressed, yet surprised at her ambition. "And what about marriage and a family?"

Again, her heart thudded and then leaped about. "That's really the most important thing to me."

He sighed with relief. "I'm glad you said that." The two of them breathed in the sweet night air. Then he said, "I wouldn't want a wife of mine to be on the stage. It's too difficult a life. The hours, the travel, the insecurity of the job, hustling all the time, having to be nice to people you don't like so they'll hire you." He towered over her. She felt overshadowed by his strength, his magnetism.

"If I were married I wouldn't want to work. I'd stay home and take care of my family," she told him.

His arm crept around her shoulder and held her to him. Her feet felt light, as though they barely touched the ground.

"I'd like to know more about you," she said. "Though I can see you're good at what you do. People respect you."

He stood a bit taller from her praise. "I enjoy my work, except for the travel. It's lonely sometimes, and tiring. When I started booking acts, vaudeville was king. But then, it went on the decline. Radio and movies really killed it, you know. And it's a damned shame. Because where will the new talent get its training now? Except in the smaller theaters."

"How did you get into show business?"

He smiled down at her in the darkness; she could see his beautiful teeth in the moonlight. "I never wanted to stay in the family business. My father is in wholesale leather goods. Lately there's a lot of competition in the Midwest so he's thinking of moving to California." He sighed. "Dad's not a young man. It's hard to start over at his age."

"He wants you to be with him, doesn't he?"

"Yes," he admitted. "We've had some disagreements about it. But I have to follow my own dream."

"You know, I think you're handsome enough to be a movie star yourself," she said, her eyes flirting with him.

He laughed. "I'd rather be the one who controls the talent than the talent itself." His arm was still around her and she prayed he would leave it there. "You're so easy to talk to, Lynnette. It's an unusual quality in a girl who's so beautiful."

They walked along the tree-lined street without talking for a while and then he said, "You know, I'm leaving tomorrow for St. Louis. I won't be back this way for months."

She felt a deep kind of sadness. "I'll write to you, if you like."

He stopped on the sidewalk and turned to her in front of the Feders' house as though he was going to say something. But then they saw that Mr. Feder was on the front porch waiting while his dog, Tiger, did his business in the bushes, and he called out to them. "Who's there?"

"It's me, Mr. Feder," Lynnette answered.

"Who's that with you?"

And Burt answered, still staring into Lynnette's eyes, "I'm Burt Blacker from Chicago, Mr. Feder. I'm Lynnette's fiancé."

But before Lynnette could say anything, Mr. Feder said, "Didn't know she was engaged. Nobody tells me nothin'." And he called to his dog, Tiger, to get back here, and they went into the house.

Lynnette stared up at Burt, waiting for Mr. Feder to shut the front door. As he closed it they could hear him calling out to his wife, "Mary, why didn't you tell me the Rosenberg girl was engaged?"

"Tell him?" Lynnette laughed, "I think I should have been told first, don't you?"

"I'm sorry, Lynnette," he said. "I should have asked you. But I could tell from the moment I saw you that you were the kind of girl I wanted to marry. I've never been ready to settle down until now. I'm nearly thirty years old and I've had my fill of being a bachelor. I like your family and they like me. I promise to make a good life for you."

"But you don't love me," she said, wanting to cry with frustration, because she was already in love with him.

He smiled. "That will come in time. I just had to know if you'd consider my proposal of marriage before you go to New York, because some other man is sure to snap you up." He snapped his fingers as an example.

"Was Nana happy that he proposed?" Jered asked, interrupting the story.

"Yes, but she was also embarrassed as well as excited. 'It's going to be all over the neighborhood,' Nana told him. 'I don't know whether to cry or laugh.' It was funny to think Mr. Feder had been the first to know."

Jered's eyelids were drooping. "I thought Papa was an agent."

"He is, sweetheart."

"What's the Orpheum Circuit?"

"A group of theaters all over the country that Papa used to work for finding entertainers to appear before a live audience. And when the theaters closed he started representing many of those same entertainers, getting them other jobs."

"Why did they close?" Jered was so sleepy his eyes nearly shut, but he wouldn't give in.

I colluded in keeping him awake, relieved to be distracting myself as well. "They closed because people stopped going to see live comedy and musical acts in the theater when the musical movies got so popular and then television came along. And then, later on, Papa decided he wanted to represent opera singers and musicians."

"Did Nana marry Papa?" he asked.

"Of course she did, silly, you know that. And they had me and Aunt Steffani, and I had you and Miles and Amy. And we all lived happily ever after."

He turned over on his side and curled up into a ball, finally asleep. I leaned down and kissed his cheek and left the room.

It wasn't quite happily ever after with my parents, I thought as I closed the door behind me. Perhaps it might have been, if it wasn't for Steffani's illness. Her condition. I didn't have it. My bone marrow tests said so.

The phone rang and I hurried to get it, almost afraid to pick it up.

"Hi," Steffani said. "What's new? You okay?"

"No," I said, miffed because I'd called her this afternoon and she was just returning my call. "I really needed to talk to you."

"So? What's wrong? Isn't making the *New York Times'* best-seller list enough?"

"Yes, it's wonderful. You know how much it means to me. It's something else. Can you come over?" I couldn't hide the tension in my voice.

"Now?" Steffani said. "It's nine-thirty."

"I really need to see you," I admitted. Usually she was the one who needed me. "Nine-thirty isn't that late, is it?" I pressed.

"I've got a date, Suze, and papers to correct."

"Okay, forget it. I'll talk to my lawyer instead."

"Your lawyer? That sounds serious. What is it?"

My mouth felt suddenly so dry, I could hardly tell her. "Swear you won't repeat this to anyone, especially Mom and Dad."

"You've got the clap."

"No! Swear, or I'm hanging up." The whole thing seemed so dirty. I didn't want anyone to know about it. Maybe it would just go away. *What if people believed it was true?*

"What is it, Suzanne?"

"Someone's accused me of plagiarism."

Steffani paused. "You're kidding."

"No, I'm not." I couldn't help it, I started to cry.

"Suze, it's okay," Steffani said, "I'm on my way."

Lynnette and Elizabeth arrived at Grand Central Station in New York at noon, after taking the overnight from Kansas City. And for Lynnette it was the most exciting thing she'd ever done. Especially when she spotted him standing on the platform, taller than the rest of the crowd. He was looking for her, and in that moment she knew he was her destiny.

"You don't want him to see you so anxious, do you?" her mother cautioned. "Please, Lynnette."

But it was almost too much to bear, having New York City and Burt Blacker in her life all at once. "Do you think he still cares about me?" Lynnette asked.

"He's meeting us, isn't he?" Then Elizabeth sighed. "I hope your father and your brother are all right."

"We only left them yesterday," Lynnette assured her. The train was coming to a stop and she stood up and reached for her train case. This exciting moment almost made up for not being able to go to college. She had wanted to go ever since she could remember, but there was only enough money for her brother, Sid. As a consolation she was coming to New York.

"You'll find work as a singer," her mother insisted, "and

get to know Burt better, find out if he'll make a good husband.''

''But what about Sid and Daddy?'' Lynnette asked, wishing she could have come alone without a chaperone. ''Sid can't leave school in his senior year of high school, and Daddy can't leave his job.''

Lynnette hated the idea of breaking up the family, but neither did she want to spend another year in Kansas City and take a chance on losing Burt.

Burt waved and grinned when he saw them and Lynnette waved back. He was wearing a gray overcoat and hat and smoking a pipe. The sight of him took her breath away; he did look like a movie star. She'd forgotten that he had a high forehead, wore his hair parted on the side, that his nose was prominent, almost too prominent, and that it added to his looks just as his high cheekbones did. What she liked the best was his perfect, even smile above a cleft chin, and those blue-gray eyes.

She was wearing a red-and-gray checked suit that her mother had made for her, with a gray hat to match. Elizabeth made all of Lynnette's clothes. In her suitcase were four new outfits to wear at interviews, and a red fox stole with two fox faces biting onto each other's tails to drape over her shoulder. It was October and not yet cold enough for a coat. But soon it would be, and she'd need a fur. Her mother had designed one to be made out of a secondhand coat. It would be Persian lamb, and have a stand-up collar, wide bell sleeves, and a circular body. But first she had to earn the money to buy a used fur.

Burt had set up some interviews for her, and she'd written to some agents on her own.

''Hi, beautiful,'' he said, taking her hands and kissing her on the cheek. Then he greeted Mrs. Rosenberg with a dazzling smile. ''I've made reservations for us tonight at the Waldorf Astoria Hotel for dinner, and then we're going to the Stork Club.'' He motioned to a Filipino man in a brown uniform standing nearby to come forward. ''Reyes, see that the Rosenbergs' luggage is put into a taxi and taken to their cousin's house. You have the address. Then you and I will take the ladies for a drive around the city and show them the sights."

Usually, Elizabeth made all the arrangements, deciding what was best for everyone. But now she was smiling up at Burt, willing to put herself into his hands, obviously impressed by the respectful way he behaved, and the luxurious way he lived.

Lynnette's first day in New York was as wonderful as she'd imagined. After a whirlwind tour of the city, Burt took them to Cousin Alva's house—a relative on Lynnette's father's side of the family—where they were staying until they could find jobs and a place of their own. Burt had invited them to stay with him, but Elizabeth wouldn't hear of it.

Cousin Alva lived in a one-bedroom apartment on Fourteenth Street with a pull-down Murphy bed in the living room where her two children slept. She and her husband, Harry, shared the bedroom but she had offered to sleep on the box springs and put her mattress in the living room so Lynnette and Elizabeth would have a bed of their own. Elizabeth knew that Alva's generosity would not last long, and that she'd never let Elizabeth forget such a favor. But it would have to do for now.

Lynnette and Elizabeth were still exhilarated from their afternoon with Burt when they were dropped off at Cousin Alva's. Alva came running down the front stoop, her skirts kicking above her knees in her haste.

"So, Elizabeth, we've been frantic over you. One o'clock, two at the latest, we thought. Then we knew for sure your throats had been cut by hooligans, or worse, you were robbed or beaten. I almost called Henry in Kansas City, but I didn't want to tell him about a tragedy."

"We're fine, Alva," Elizabeth assured her, feeling guilty that she'd had such an exciting afternoon and made Alva suffer for it. But Alva had never been a favorite of hers, nor she a favorite of Alva's. Alva's children were *meiskites*, "homely children," while Elizabeth's were both as beautiful as angels. And if that wasn't bad enough, Alva's children were also stupid, while Elizabeth's were smart.

"Lynnette can work for Mr. Meyers who needs some help in the hardware store down the block," Alva began. "I told him you'd be there in the morning."

Elizabeth's lips were pursed together into her determined expression. "Lynnette will not be working in a hardware store for Mr. Meyer, Alva," she stated. "But I thank you for your concern."

"So, what's she going to do? Be a secretary? Can she type?" Alva wanted to know.

"How I would love a cup of tea," Elizabeth said, changing the subject. And Alva was chastised for not having offered her newly arrived guests some refreshments.

Elizabeth had come to America at the age of twelve weighted by a terrible secret that poisoned her soul and would haunt her for the rest of her life. Her father had died the year before, leaving her mother pregnant and penniless with four children to care for. When the baby died too, her mother became a laundress and sent Elizabeth to America, the land of promise, with a family who were friends from their town in Romania. On the way to America the ship was wrecked in a storm and Elizabeth nearly drowned. Separated from her foster family in the lifeboats, she didn't know if they were alive or dead. The foster family was taken to New York, their original destination, and she landed in Galveston all alone, a terrified child in a new world, unable to speak the language and homesick for her family. Eventually, through a Jewish agency, she met up with her foster family in Kansas City only to discover that they expected her to become their servant. From then on, she did all the cooking and cleaning for them just like Cinderella while they refused even to buy her medicine when she was sick, and ostracized her when she broke out in a rash from being bitten by mites while cleaning out their garbage and cinders. During the time that she kept house for her foster family, she also worked as a seamstress in a factory, making $1.50 a week to pay for her room and board.

It took her two years to save the money to send for her brother. And then, finally, she and her brother saved enough money to send for the rest of the family. What kept her from despair was imagining that she was indeed Cinderella, and someday her prince would come. She taught herself to read and write English, and spoke without an accent. Now, it embarrassed her to be in the debt of Cousin Alva, who claimed to be generous, yet wasn't. Alva didn't want Elizabeth's children to have more out of life than her own children were capable of having. And conversely, if anyone tried to tell Elizabeth that her children should lower their aspirations in life, she made ready for battle.

That night, when Lynnette got dressed for her evening with Burt in a beige satin gown and peach satin capelet trimmed with beige ruffles to match, Alva was both envious and resentful. "You're not having dinner with us?" she said, pulling in her chin, pursing her lips in disapproval. "I made flanken and roasted potatoes. I thought, on your first night, you'd at least eat with the family before starting to run around the city half-naked."

"Alva, Lynnette's young man has made arrangements for us," Elizabeth said. "It wouldn't be polite to say no to him. And besides, we don't expect you to feed us while we're here. We are in your debt. Tomorrow night while Lynnette goes to see the Rockettes, I will cook dinner for you."

"The Rockettes," Alva's son, Sam, said. "Boy, I've always wanted to see the Rockettes."

"And I've told you it's a waste of money to watch a bunch of floozies kicking up their legs. We don't have money to throw away on things like that in this family, not like some people." And she gave Lynnette a look.

"How about roast chicken?" Elizabeth said. "I could make that for dinner tomorrow night. Is there a kosher butcher in the neighborhood?"

"What do you think, this is Kansas? Of course there's a *shohet*, right down the block. And you never tasted chicken, until you taste his."

Elizabeth nodded to Lynnette that it was all right. And the two women left for their night on the town, Lynnette in her beige and peach, Elizabeth in her black crepe. But as soon as they were out the door, Elizabeth said to her daughter, "Tomorrow, first thing, we're going job hunting so we can move out of here right away. I forgot what a pain in the neck Alva can be."

Lynnette laughed at her mother's expression. "She is a pain in the neck, isn't she?"

As Elizabeth got dressed early the next morning, she weighed the pros and cons of Burt Blacker as a son-in-law. She could see why Lynnette found him appealing, but show business was too unsteady for her daughter. And here was Burt, encouraging Lynnette to be a singer. Why not, he was in show business too. With times as tough as they were in 1936, a steady job was something to be treasured, and Burt Blacker seemed to be doing quite well, making good money, living in his apartment with servants. But would that last?

Henry had never earned enough to support the family and Elizabeth had worked to put food on the table since Lynnette was in the first grade and Sid was still a baby. None of her friends in Kansas City worked, she was the only one. She walked to work in the snow and ice because she couldn't afford bus fare. But she was a clever woman, and her skill as a tailor was always in demand. She had an innate sense of style, entirely self-taught, the same way she'd taught herself to read and write English, and the ability to make a dollar stretch until it nearly broke.

So if Lynnette had nice clothes, it was because Elizabeth was an expert seamstress and knew how to buy a piece of fabric at a bargain price. If their home looked beautiful, it was because Elizabeth had stenciled the walls to look like wallpaper, and woven the fabric for her own draperies out of a bale of cotton flax someone had given to her for nothing; she even trimmed the drapes by tying red, green, and blue Tinker Toys onto the ends of the tassles. She restuffed and upholstered a castoff sofa in cotton chintz, she hand-painted and repaired an old set of chipped china so that it looked like new, and she knew how to turn a collar on a shirt so that it lasted for years without needing to be replaced. She even monogrammed her husband's initials on his shirt pockets so they looked like the ones at Wanamaker's.

By 7:00 A.M. the two of them were out of the apartment and by that night Elizabeth had gotten a job as a seamstress in a fashionable boutique on Park Avenue, making seventy-five cents an hour.

Lynnette's first stop was to see Jake Finberger, a talent agent, the cousin of a girlfriend from Kansas City. Jake sent her on an interview for a chorus dancer in a new Broadway musical, and a man in the elevator, Isadore Moskowitz, gave her his card to come and model furs for him during the day in his showroom. Mr. Moskowitz had a son, Milton, whom he introduced to her, and Milton invited her to go to a football game that Saturday with him and a group of his friends from Columbia. Just as Burt had feared would happen, the boys were after her already.

Through the fall and the winter and on into the spring, Lynnette went on dates with many young men she met through her work, or was introduced to by her friends. Burt didn't like her dating other people, but she had to be sure. And besides, this was the only time in her life she'd ever have the freedom to test herself in a single world. She had fun, went to interesting parties, met glamorous people, but no one compared to Burt. By March, she knew she wanted to marry him.

In the meantime, her career was thriving. She was in the chorus of first one and then another Broadway musical, which unfortunately ran only for a short time. But she appeared in a musical film made by MGM, shot in New Jersey, and had a speaking part in a historical film starring Clark Gable. But mostly she modeled furs and dresses in fashion shows and charity luncheons. Then she got a job singing with the band at Welby's Cabaret, until the band went on tour and she decided not to go.

"You know, Mama," she confided in Elizabeth, "I'm glad I've worked in New York and had a career of sorts. But I think I'm ready to settle down now."

Elizabeth's eyes filled with tears. "I'm so happy that you've found a man who can make a home for you, so you won't have to work the way I did."

Burt was traveling a great deal, checking out acts in Chicago, Detroit, New Orleans, and St. Louis, and whenever he was near Kansas City, he'd stop off and see Lynnette's father and her brother. Lynnette missed him while he was away, so much that she stopped seeing other men, even before he asked her.

It was April when Lynnette told him how she felt, and Burt was overjoyed. He gave her a ring, a one-carat, round-cut diamond with a smaller marquise on either side.

"We'll have to find an apartment of our own," Burt said. His bachelor apartment wasn't big enough for the three of them, Lynnette, himself, and his Filipino houseboy.

They set the date for June, as soon as Sid graduated from high school and could join them in New York with his father. Burt's family had all moved to California and were too far away to come to the wedding.

They had made friends with several young couples like themselves who were starting out, but the wedding list would be small. Just Lynnette's family, Burt, and a few acquaintances—not exactly as Lynnette had dreamed, but still lovely nonetheless.

CHAPTER THREE

"Mom, who's at the door?" Both Amy and Miles appeared in the family room at the sound of the doorbell.

"It's Aunt Steffani," I told them. "Now, go finish your homework."

"What's *she* doing here?" Miles asked, echoing the judgmental attitude of his father. Alex used to think Steffani was a bad influence on me, and that being exposed to her lifestyle would corrupt me with drugs, sex, and rock and roll. Even though we were no longer married, Alex's opinion of my sister had caused some problems between Steffi and me over the years—and, that I once had partly agreed with him.

As for Miles, not only was his voice changing at age twelve, seesawing him from childhood to puberty sometimes within the same moment, but his father's absence caused him to seesaw too. Half of him was critical and angry with Alex, the other half longed for his father to be here with us. So, he either imitated or abhorred him. It was difficult to watch. I wanted to protect my son from that kind of pain, and my guilt for getting divorced weighed on me, like a nausea that never left. But my real guilt had its origin in the choice I'd made to love Alex in the first place.

Amy opened the door for Steffani and we crowded around her. She gave the children hugs and kissed me on the cheek, smelling of musk oil perfume. The pupils of her eyes were dilated so that her blue eyes looked black and I wondered if she was on any medication. But otherwise, she looked wonderful. She was tanned an even golden color, wearing a long gypsylike skirt; a fringed shawl was draped across one shoulder, tied at the hip in a rakish fashion, at once bold and yet clever, as it hid her enlarged waist. Under the shawl was an orange scooped-neck T-shirt; her thick and luxuriously curly hair was hanging darkly down her back, picking up highlights from the breakfast room Tiffany fixture. She'd stopped bleaching it years ago. There were bracelets on her wrists, rings on her fingers, and gold hoop earrings in her ears. With her thin, straight patrician nose, long eyelashes, and full sensuous mouth I thought, *All she needs is a crystal ball*. And if she had one, what would it predict for either of us?

She saw my look and tossed her head in that way I had of tossing mine. Then she smiled, looking even more beautiful, dimples piercing her cheeks, exposing the large white teeth that ran in the family, so evenly spaced. "Hi, you guys." To me she said, "You look tired."

"You look vibrant," I acknowledged. Actually she looked like our great-aunt Hilda, done up as Carmen, queen of the stage, ready to challenge a roomful of men. I could never have gotten away with that look, but admired it greatly.

Her greeting was interrupted by a coughing bout. She apologized. "I've had a cold and can't seem to get rid of this cough whatever medicine I take."

"Aunt Steff," Amy said, "I'm reading *Red Badge of Courage*, for English. Can you help me with it?"

"You mean, Henry Fleming's confusion?"

Amy nodded, impressed, but trying not to show it. Her exotic aunt Steffani knew everything about literature. At fifteen, Amy had an investment in *cool*. "Was Henry a coward?"

"What do you think?" Steffi put her arm around Amy's shoulder; they were the same height now, but Amy was still growing and in another month she'd be taller than her aunt.

"I don't think so, but I have to defend my position. And actually, he did run away from the front line of the battle."

"Go get the book and I'll show you passages to support your hypothesis."

Amy left the room and Steffani turned to me. "I have letters from friends of mine who were in Vietnam and fought in hundreds of missions. Some of them still think of themselves as cowards because they didn't lead the pack, or relish what they had to do, or swagger and pretend not to care who they killed, like so many of the men in their units did. Stephen Crane chose to tell Henry Fleming's story but any other character in that war might have told the same one, if we'd been allowed inside their heads instead of Fleming's. I'm glad she's reading that book. I think Crane wrote a brilliant psychological study of how we perceive others, how we project our own shortcomings and longings and fears onto them."

The extended conversation started her coughting again, and I waited for it to be over while trying not to take what she had said personally. *Is she making a dig at the kinds of books I write? So what if my books aren't brilliant psychological studies. I still appreciate writers who write that way, too.* Her comments about other writers made me feel competitive. I calmed myself by thinking, *Someday I'll write a book where the subtle interchanges between characters are as essential to the writing as what happens next. Then, she'll admire me, won't she?*

She held out her hand. "Let me see what you got in the mail."

"Go do your homework, Miles," I said to my older son, not wanting him to hear our conversation. Instead he followed us into the family room.

I pulled out the obnoxious documents from where I'd hidden them under a copy of *Life* magazine and held them against my chest.

"Didn't I tell you to go do your homework?" I asked Miles, who was all eyes.

"What's that, Mom?" he asked, grabbing for the papers, partly to tease, partly to see, as I passed them to Steffani.

"Never mind," I shouted. He flinched and I was immediately sorry.

Just then, Amy came back with her book and noticed Steffani glancing through pages, reading the letter sent to me by the infamous Sherry Fallon. Curiosity prompted Amy to lean over Steffani's shoulder and try to read along with her. This time I didn't shout, I just covered the page with my hand.

"Will you two stay out of this," I said, with great annoyance. "Aunt Steffi came here to talk to me about something, Amy, that's none of your business. She can help you with your homework after we talk, all right? Now, I want both of you to leave us alone for a while, hear me?"

They didn't budge, staring from one of us to the other.

"Go on," Steffani told them. "This is important." She held up the pages in her hand. And before I could stop her, she said, "Someone has done something really disgusting by accusing your mother of plagiarism; you know, when one writer steals from another writer? Well, now your mom and I have to talk about it.''

Too late to slam my hand over her mouth. I shouted again, ''Dammit, Steffani, shut up! I didn't want them to know!'' Instant fury swept through me and I felt my face turn hot and the tendons in my neck stand out. I wanted to throttle her.

Both the children looked at me with that look of fear in their eyes that they'd had off and on ever since the separation. The look that said, *You told us life was wonderful, you even made it wonderful, and now you have destroyed the wonder for us. Bad things can really happen to kids, monsters do exist, and they're in our own closets*!

''What is she talking about, Mom?'' Amy asked, grabbing the pages from Steffani's hand.

I yanked them back so hard I really frightened Amy, and when I saw the fear in her eyes I sank down on the sofa clutching the pages to me. I shouted again, ''God dammit, Steffani. You had no right to bring them into this.'' But I was overreacting, and I put my head in my hands wishing the cushions would open up and swallow me.

A stunned silence followed my outburst and then Miles said, ''Well, now we know, Mom.'' And he came and sat beside me, putting his hand comfortingly on my back.

I almost cringed to think how many times I'd allowed him to comfort me in the past few years. Not this time! I looked at him with what I hoped was a steady gaze but I was furious and ashamed. ''Honey, I asked Aunt Steffi over here to help me, not to drag you children into this.'' I glared up at Steffani again. Her expression was both remorseful and defiant, the way it used to be when she'd accidentally broken something of mine that I considered valuable, or spoiled some special moment in my life. It was as though she were saying, I didn't do it on purpose. It's hard to get satisfaction from that kind of apology.

''Some crackpot who's obviously crazy sent these, Miles,'' I said, hearing my voice stretched so tightly it almost cracked.

"It doesn't mean anything. I'll take care of it. I don't want you or Amy to worry." I uttered a litany of reassurances for myself as well as them, then managed to smile at Amy as I leaned over and kissed Miles's cheek. Miles was at an age where he'd only let me kiss him if no one was around; he ducked his head shyly.

Somehow, I convinced the children to go finish their homework. When they'd left I turned to my sister, anger erupting anew.

"You knew I didn't want them to know. But you never think! Always so wrapped up in your own life. Nobody else suffers but you, is that it? Those children have had a hard enough time lately, without this to worry about. And they will worry, you know. Dammit! Why did you blurt that out?"

She was not about to concede being wrong. "What's so terrible about their knowing, Suze. They're your children, for God's sake. You sound just like Mom and Dad. Don't tell anyone. I hated that! They never wanted me to tell anyone what was wrong with me, like it was the worst thing in the world. I think it's easier to face the truth when nothing's hidden."

"I don't agree," I insisted. I ignored the look of pleading in her eyes that said, *Let this pass.* "I don't want this mess out in the open. If the children find out how this is affecting me, it would upset them terribly. I feel as though everything I've ever stood for has become rotten, poisoned . . . as though my foundations have been eaten away. It's like waking up to find snakes in my bed, or turning on the faucet and having huge spiders crawl out. Can you imagine that? Can you?" I shuddered, wrapping my arms around myself against my own horrors.

"I can imagine even worse," she said, bringing my self-pity into focus by comparison. "I know what it's like to have something fearful and disgusting thrown at you and not be able to duck." She seemed close to tears herself and I realized how thoughtless I'd been. I reached out and clutched her hand, which comforted us both. She continued. "But I still don't think you should keep it a secret. That never does any good. I know, now that my life's an open book.''

"You mean there's nothing in your life you wouldn't want to be kept private?''

She thought for a minute. "Well, maybe a few things.''

"Hah. I thought so.''

"But you're worrying too much about the children. Kids are more resilient than you think. They're not going to brood their lives away on this the way you will. They probably won't even think about it.''

My temper shot up again. "How dare you make light of this? Where do you get off telling me how my children think? Or any children, for that matter?''

I needn't have reminded her that I had children and she didn't, but still I couldn't stop. "You told them on purpose, didn't you?'' I pressed on. "Because you knew I didn't want them to know. You always think you know better, don't you? Let it all hang out, right? Well, you have no right to interfere in my life! Of all people, you should know better!'' My rage toward her was stronger than I'd felt in years. I'd only allowed it to emerge a few times in my life, and when I had, the consequences were disastrous. "You never take anything seriously, do you? That's why all your relationships have been so screwed up.''

We had entered that territory of the soft underbelly, where each of us was the most vulnerable, and because we were sisters we knew exactly where to do the most damage.

"The trouble with you is,'' she said, almost too calmly, "you live in a fairy-tale world where even garbage doesn't smell. Your children cannot become mature adults if you protect them from reality the way you protect yourself. They'll never be prepared to face life if they grow up believing everything is rose colored the way you pretend it is. You're all in for a rude awakening.''

"Now you're a therapist,'' I said, my tone dripping with disgust. "Don't make me laugh. I know damned well about reality, and I know how to embellish it. That's why my books sell.''

"Those glorified romances! I think you hate secrets as much as I do, or why else would you have become a writer. So you could tell the truth. Only you still haven't done it. You're still playing Let's Pretend."

"I don't think we'd better have this argument again, do you?"

"Why not?" She coughed again and had to pause until it stopped.

"Because I'm sick to death of you putting down what I do." Everything I had become, everything I was, culminated in my writing. My anger only covered up the intensity of my pain. In anguish, my heart was crying, *What's wrong with what I do? Why don't you like it? Other people do.*

"I don't put it down," she said, knowing she had been critical when I needed support. All writers need it and grab it greedily whenever we can. I wanted to scream out, *You're just jealous.* I remembered my mother saying wistfully, every time I'd had a book published, "Steffani's always wanted to write." We all figured that someday she'd get around to writing, but until now, she'd had to focus all her attention on surviving, giving her no time for extended creativity. And in spite of my own success, I worried about the competition if she did become a writer, certain that she'd be one of the literary greats immediately and surpass me in an instant. But then, I've always given more power to my family members than anyone else in the world.

She went on, unaware of my thoughts. "I get tired too, you know, of hearing how successful you are, and how much the divorce has wounded your children's delicate psyches. Most of my friend's kids never had two parents to begin with, and they're all just fine."

"How the hell do you know? You don't put them to bed every night, and wake up with them when they have nightmares."

"My friend's kids don't have nightmares. Only your neurotic children do."

We glared at one another while I wondered if my children really were neurotic. Then I thought about what Steffani's

childhood had been like, and all the times she'd suffered at
night with pain wracking her arm or her leg and someone had
comforted her. And the times as a child when I couldn't fall
asleep, and would cry instead, ashamed to call for help,
terrified of letting go, because of fears so deep-rooted I
couldn't even tell anyone what they were. And worse, I
didn't know myself. Thinking about the suffering she'd gone
through as a child, and wanting to protect my own children,
made me ashamed of taking out my anger on her. It certainly
didn't make this sick feeling inside go away.

Suddenly, I knew one of the reasons I was so angry with
her. It wasn't just because she'd told the children and it would
upset them to find out, it was that *anybody* should find out.
Now I suddenly understood one of the reasons my parents
had been so secretive about Steffani. Not only were they
protecting her from being an object of pity, but if no one
knew, it wouldn't be real. Maybe it would just go away.

I had lived most of my life with an unnamed terror in my
soul that lurked in the deepest caverns. It began when I was
a child, but I'd managed to keep it at bay. And now, this
terrible accusation, coming out of the blue as it had, threatened to awaken that monster in the black hole; once awakened, it could erupt at any moment and consume me with its
noxious breath, toss me into the pit of my deepest fears, into
a place of madness introduced to me by my innocent sister's
suffering. The feeling of being out of control was paralyzing.
I felt my insides beginning to crumble. I was near hysteria.

My sister's voice brought me back from my nightmare
journey. With less animosity she said, "As far as I can see,
Suzanne, this accusation is nothing but a crock. Although it
is pretty weird. It looks like it came from a book, doesn't
it?"

"That's what scares me, too," I admitted. "It's so professional, planned out. Can you imagine someone sitting down
and doing this? The letter is so simpering, so nasty."

Steffani put on her glasses and read the letter, then scanned
the Xeroxed pages. "Paco and Luis?" she scoffed, trying for

levity. "Give me a break." With her injection of humor, we had made up without actually saying the words. I guess she understood I had needed to take this out on her and I was relieved that she had been strong enough for it, even though I was now embarrassed by my behavior. For just below the surface of my actions was an enormous well of gratitude toward whatever forces had buffeted her life. At least she had survived to this point and was here with me to offer her understanding and courage when I needed it most.

"Have you told your agent?" she asked, touching my arm.

"She's sailing in the Antilles for a few weeks and can't be reached. Besides, I hate to call her on vacation. I don't know what to do," I said, reaching again for Steffani's hand.

"What about talking to your editor?"

"It was too late to call her today. I guess I'll call her tomorrow. But maybe I shouldn't bring this to her attention. Why worry her? Especially if it's nothing."

"Oh, here we go again. *Don't tell.*"

"Okay, okay. But what if I tell her and she doesn't believe me? What if everybody thinks it's true?" The question made my hands shake, though hers held mine steadily.

"I think you should call the police."

"I did. I spoke to a Detective Lopez in the Van Nuys division. He told me there was nothing the police could do. That there'd been no crime committed and I should forget about it. But if I wanted to pursue it, I'd have to contact the New York police, since the letter was postmarked from New York."

"Not very helpful, was he."

"When I asked him whether this person could be violent, he told me, 'Lady, I've been on the force for twelve years and never in my experience has any violent crime been preceded by someone typesetting a few pages from a well-known lady writer's work and sending them to her.' " Both of us laughed at that.

"Who is this Sherry Fallon, Suzanne? Do you know her?"

"Never heard of her. In fact, I called New York information and got the numbers of all the Sherry, or S. Fallons in the five boroughs. I spent the afternoon calling. There are several listed; some of the numbers were out of order. One was a secretarial service, the other a choreographer in Queens. One was a woman in her eighties and two of the S. Fallons were men. Only one didn't answer. I'll keep trying. But even if I find Sherry Fallon, what would I say to her? Do you think she'd tell me the truth?''

"No, but she might tell the police the truth. And you could sue her for slander, or defamation, or whatever.''

I nodded, knowing somehow that Sherry Fallon was not the name of the person doing this to me.

Steffani read my thoughts. "Who do you think could be doing this?''

"I have no idea,'' I told her honestly. "I've tried to think about who it could be and I can't imagine anyone I know doing such a thing.''

"Yes, but a crazy person would. Who do you know that's crazy?''

"You,'' I joked.

"Besides me. Is there anyone who's been upset with you in the past, maybe on an interview show? Or someone you don't like, a critic?''

"I've been trying to think of who it could be. There have been some negative reviews in my life, but nothing like this. I once wrote a letter to the editor of the book section defending a book by a friend of mine that had gotten a nasty review, but that wouldn't justify this.''

"Did you ever get any hate letters?''

"Never. You know my books. Critics might say they are closer to fantasy than reality, but readers love them.''

"Maybe there are fingerprints on the letter.''

"I thought of that, but now mine and yours and Amy's are all over the pages. And if this person doesn't have a record, what good would having their fingerprints do? Can you even get fingerprints off of paper?''

"I don't think so. Still, why don't you keep the letters in a plastic bag, just in case.''

I agreed to do that.

"You've got to keep thinking about it, trying to come up with who could be doing this. In the meantime, what about talking to a lawyer in case you have to defend yourself, or sue this person. I knew a copyright lawyer when I worked at Plummer Publishing. I can get you his name."

"Did Plummer ever have this kind of problem?"

"No," she hedged. "But they were extra careful to comply with copyright laws. Publishers don't want to get sued. Suzanne, nobody's going to believe this stupidity from a made-up name." She removed her hand from mine and tossed the letters on the coffee table as if to make light of them.

"You think it's a made-up name, too?"

"Nobody would sign a real name to something like this. It's a cowardly act."

I nodded, slightly appeased.

"Do you want me to stay for a while?" she asked.

"No, go ahead." She would have stayed for my sake. "Just give me the name of that lawyer. At least it will feel as though I'm taking action."

"I'll find it and call you tomorrow." She reached over and hugged me and I hugged her back, feeling enveloped by emotion. For the first time all day, I felt comforted. She was about to apologize for what happened earlier, but I stopped her.

"Thanks so much for your help," I said, feeling grateful to have her to turn to. "The next time I need to yell at someone, I'll know just whom to call." And we both smiled and said in unison, "Mom and Dad."

As she left, she called back over her shoulder, "Tell Amy to phone me early in the morning and I'll discuss her homework with her." And she was gone.

That night, lying awake in bed, watching the clock creep along, still hours away from seven (when it would be ten in New York and my editor, Judy Emory, would be at work) I thought, *Worrying doesn't do any good. This mess will straighten itself out eventually. Just concentrate on the posi-*

*tive, on the work you love. You can't let something like this
stop you. You've already spent an afternoon and an evening
being upset; that's enough*! I often give myself pep talks the
way my mother always did. Sometimes it works. But I've
never been able to be as cheerful or optimistic as my mother.
In the face of the most horrendous moments she has the
ability to talk anyone, even herself, out of gloom. My sister's
accomplishments are a testament to that. Eventually, I fell
asleep.

In the morning, I decided not to call my editor, and just
forget the whole thing, when Judy called me.

"Congratulations on making the list!" she said. I listened
for a note of anything else in her voice, but she seemed
perfectly normal, truly happy for me, and I relaxed a bit.

"Everyone's really thrilled for you," she said.

"So am I," I told her. "Yesterday was quite a day."

"Anything else happen?" she asked.

"Why?" I said, instantly alerted.

"Well," she hedged, "I got something in the mail."

"You got one too?" I said, wanting to cry. My hands felt
clammy and my stomach turned over.

"It's just some crackpot, Suzanne," she scoffed. "I
wouldn't have even mentioned it to you, but I was afraid
you'd gotten one too. What a shame to ruin your happy day,
with the best-seller list coming out and all. Try not to worry
about it."

"I'm not worrying, overly," I assured her, lying slightly.
I'd awakened with a feeling of dread, like a morning film on
my teeth that no amount of wiping with my tongue could
remove. "Who is Sherry Fallon? Do you know her?"

There was a pause that made my heart go ga-thump. "Silver's Press has never had an employee by that name. I
checked it out with personnel myself. I suppose it's possible
she worked for a temporary agency or as a summer intern.
But I called some people in other publishing houses. No one's
ever heard of Sherry Fallon. She's a nonperson. I'd just forget
about it, love."

"Have you ever had this happen before to any of your writers?" I asked.

"Hundreds of times."

"*Emis a Torah?*" (swear on the Torah) I asked, needing her assurance badly.

She laughed. "Well, not exactly hundreds."

"Anyone?" My voice shook.

"No," she admitted. "Nobody's ever gone to such lengths before to prove their point, but that doesn't mean anything. We know it's not true; it's ridiculous and it will blow over."

"Judy, when you opened that packet and read that cover letter, didn't you think, just for a moment, that it could be true? That's one of the things I'm most afraid of, that people will believe this thing."

"Oh, no they won't, Suzanne. I never would. Don't forget, I know you. I've seen every draft of the books we've done together. I know how hard you work, how you beat yourself up. Why, we go over those outlines of yours step by step. You won't even take my advice sometimes because you're afraid the ideas won't be entirely yours. You're a total purist, Suzanne. I'd never believe that of you."

I suddenly felt like crying. I hadn't known how crucial her belief in me was until this moment. "Thanks, Judy. That means a lot." I felt my spirits beginning to recover.

"How are you taking it? Are you okay?"

"No." My voice trembled. "I simply can't imagine why anyone would do such a thing."

"Some crazy nut out there," she said, philosophically. "But I'd advise you to get some legal mind working on it right away, just as we will on this end." She paused again.

They're hiring lawyers? My hands were getting all clammy again.

"Now, I don't want to alarm you, but the higher-ups get nervous when this sort of thing happens. Not that we're not behind you one hundred percent, Suze. But just don't let it go on too long, okay?"

"Of course," I assured her, as if I could control it. "It

won't go on beyond this, I'm sure." I spoke with my mother's voice, bolstering Judy the way my mother had done with me and my sister; amazingly, it worked, and my confidence gained strength. "This is the last we've heard from this Fallon person, whoever she is," I insisted. "When she, or he, sees that nothing comes of it, they'll take their marbles and go home." After all, what could an empty accusation really do to me?

"Still, I'd suggest talking to a lawyer," Judy warned.

And as I hung up, I tried not to hear the worried sound in her voice.

CHAPTER FOUR

Our first home, where I was born in New York, had twelve steep steps up from the sidewalk to the front door. I couldn't walk down those steps facing forward until I was nearly three, so I turned around and climbed down backward, counting all the way, one—two—three. There was a bay window in our apartment on the third-floor penthouse, and I would sit on the window seat gazing out onto the tree-lined street watching people pass by, waving to the ones I recognized. That apartment had a piano where my mother taught herself to play so she could practice her singing. And when my father came home from work at night he'd lift me out of my high chair way up in the air. He was so tall, when I was in his arms we both looked down at my mother.

At eighteen months I sat on a lounge swing at my aunt Martha and uncle Sid's house in Long Island and recited all my nursery rhymes for their friends the way my mother had taught me. I knew the last word to every rhyme. Hickory, dickory, *dock*. The mouse ran up the *clock*. I wore organdy dresses with ruffles over the shoulders and big taffeta bows in my golden curls, white leather shoes called Mary Janes and white ankle socks, gold charm bracelets on my chubby little wrists, and I even carried a pocket book with a lace handkerchief inside of it. I remember climbing up on the sofa swing at my aunt Martha's, my feet stretched out in front of me and the book of nursery rhymes in my mother's lap as she read aloud and pointed to the words while I recited the endings. As usual, everybody made a fuss, exclaimed how smart I was, pinched and petted me. I remember the feeling of performing well, of being applauded. How I loved being smart and beautiful, *a regular little doll, a Shirley Temple*.

When I was three, the occasion was marked by a new awareness. Suddenly, my father's mustache, which had never bothered me before, began jabbing me on the cheek or the lips when he kissed me. But I would endure any unpleasantness if I could keep his attention on me. Even at three, I was an expert competitor for the spotlight between two people who never ceased to compete for it as well.

The first time we moved, which was from one apartment to another within the city, I was only in nursery school but I didn't want to leave my friends and my teacher. The idea gave me a sick feeling in my stomach, but like a good girl I didn't say so. My mother told me about the move the way she always described the events in our lives, with a look of rapture in her eyes and a wide infectious smile. "It's going to be wonderful," she'd say. "You'll have a new room and a new closet and we'll have a new kitchen, maybe even a new refrigerator, and Daddy will be closer to his work and everything will be so wonderful." Nobody could paint a picture of ecstasy out of ordinary life the way my mother could. Her words, her expressions, her very being carried me along on her pink cloud of wonder, mesmerizing me. It wasn't until years later that I learned to look beneath the pink clouds she painted with her words to find the solid, sometimes squalid reality there. And yet, even today, I prefer to think that everything will work out for the best in this best of all possible worlds.

When I was three, my mother got pregnant with my sister

and we were so excited about having a baby. My mother told me she was going to the hospital to bring me home a new baby all my own to play with and I truly believed that this baby was mine. One day we were in the shower together and I noticed that her belly was growing. "Mommy," I asked, "how does the baby get in there?" I gave her abdomen a pat.

"Well, you see," she replied, "God plants a seed in the mother and when the father fertilizes it, it grows into a baby. When the baby's ready to be born, the mother goes to the hospital and the doctor helps her give birth."

I pondered that for a long time, five months, probably, because on the day she was in labor and ready to leave for the hospital, I ran to the front door and called to her as she was walking down the stairs, "Wait, Mommy, wait! Isn't it a good thing God didn't plant a lemon seed inside of you, because then you'd be having a lemon tree instead of a baby."

I wondered what the baby would be like, whether it would be a sister or a brother. My great-aunt Hilda, on my father's side, who visited us from California, used to sit me on her knee and sing me a song that said: "Please Mama buy me a baby, a baby with eyes that are blue. I'm tired of my drum and my dolly, the sawdust is all coming through. Johnny Jones got a new sister, I want a sister too."

And that's what I got. The first moment they put her in my arms was the most joyous and wondrous moment of my four-year-old life. I held her and watched her and fell madly in love. Some children, even four-year-olds, love little babies, find them fascinating, love playing with them and cuddling them; and I was one of those children. But then came the betrayal. They only let me hold her for a moment. They took her away and cared for her by themselves even though I knew I was capable. And she cried all the time. Every time I was hungry, she was crying for her dinner. Every time I needed a toy and couldn't find it, no one could help me look because they were taking care of her. And now when my father came home at night, the first thing he did was go to see the baby, not me. My enchantment wore off fast. Especially when my nana came to stay, and even she was preoccupied with the baby. The baby took such a long time to grow up. But I was patient, I didn't complain, because they told me not to. I almost always did what I was told. They expected me to, and I got praise and rewards for being good.

"Look how good Suzanne is with the baby. She sings to her, and talks to her and keeps her amused. I swear, Steffani knows her. Look how she smiles when Suzanne talks to her."

I guess she had her moments.

And then she started to become a person. She'd laugh when I tickled her, reach for my face, nuzzle against my neck. I loved it when she was old enough to sit up in the Tailor-Tot stroller and I could push her along the sidewalks in the company of the nurse or my mother. People stopped to say how beautiful she was and I didn't mind, I was proud. I watched their eyes and waited for them to notice her. When they didn't, I was disappointed.

And when she got to be two and then three, she was even more beautiful and a lot more fun. There was a special way her skin felt, her arms soft like sausages, her back and chest so tender in her T-shirts. Her eyes never left me, she did anything I told her to, watched everything I did and copied me. "Copycat," I'd call her. She didn't mind. But I did. Especially when she did such an excellent job of copying me, even though her plump round body was not as agile as mine and could not master my advanced ballet steps or hopscotch moves. It was scary having that precious, beautiful little usurper around. Half the time I adored her, the other half I resented the hell out of her. I'd learned from my parents and grandparents that I was the center of the universe, that everything I did was miraculous, exceptional, and wondrous. That's the way a child was treated in our house, and that's the way I treated my sister, except when she got in my way.

Vying for the spotlight, I'd sing, "Oh beautiful for spacious skies, for amber waves of grain." And she'd follow, "Oh bootiful for paicha kye, for all da way-da gayne," and we'd laugh until we cried, for she'd do it so seriously, unaware of her mispronunciations. In response to her adorableness, I developed a way of tossing my head, of lifting my chin when I performed some complicated action she couldn't do, which said without words, *Bet you can't do that*! Even now, sometimes I catch myself tossing my head in the same way. Many times in school that attitude got me into trouble. For, though in my family the individual competition for the spotlight had been honed to perfection and it was not only okay, but expected, to tell everyone how wonderful you were, at school if I did that, it was interpreted as defiant superiority, and for whatever reason, that never went off well with other children. I wish I had a nickel for every time I showed my competence and was called a stuck-up snob.

As I grew older, being the responsible bigger sister took its toll. Especially since I had to be so good to get my parents' approval, as opposed to Steffani, who was not such an amenable child. At about age two, we nicknamed her the Grouch, because she always woke up from her nap in a bad mood. And whenever anyone asked her anything, her ready answer was always "No!" (Years later, my mother and I speculated about whether this may have been an early indication of her illness.) As a result, I became attracted to friends who were naughty, who had the nerve to do things I'd never be able to do alone. Their daring gave me permission. But afterward, I always pled innocence. *It wasn't my idea*, I'd swear. Yet I did little to dissuade them.

When I was seven, there was my friend Jasmine. She was half-French, half-Chinese. She lived two doors down from us on Seventy-eighth Street. She had long black hair that hung down her back, olive skin, delicate fingers, and pink fingernails. She picked up her food with two slender fingers and popped it into her mouth. That always fascinated me. I suppose eating with her hands was part of her culture, but it wasn't allowed in my house. Her large brown eyes danced with mischief. She called out nasty names to taxicab drivers and then hid when they slammed on the brakes to see who had insulted them. One time she hid behind the curtains in her living room and her parents thought she'd run away or been kidnapped. They called the police and she could hear them on the phone, but she was so afraid of getting a beating she stayed behind the curtain for fourteen hours, wetting her pants whenever she felt the need.

Jasmine was the one friend Steffani never asked to tag along with and I was relieved, resenting it when she had to come with me. But Steffani wasn't impressed with Jasmine and recognized her as a manipulator, even as a baby. I loved to play with Jasmine because she created fantasies the way I did. We played dress-up, and house, and war—the French against the Arabs, or the Chinese against the Japs. The Japanese were still called Japs in 1947. After Steffani was sick, the game of war lost its fascination and I wanted to play hospital. In my game, the baby always got well.

Jasmine was the champion jump-rope queen of our block and selective over who could be her friend. I wasn't always chosen. When I was, it felt wonderful. Milly Astin was never chosen. Milly Aspirin, as Jasmine called her, lived in the brownstone on our corner, all three floors; her father owned it. They had servants, and a chauffeur. I thought Milly's life was pretty amazing. Jasmine said she was a bourgeoise— a French word.

Milly was chubby, with red curly hair and freckles. Her skin was white and in the summer a roll of fat hung over the sides of her elastic-topped shorts. When Jasmine wasn't around, Milly and I played well together, things like jacks, or trading cards, or Monopoly. But Jasmine stirred things up. She made us choose sides and it was always us against them. Milly was usually them.

Jasmine's attraction for us was powerful. We all wanted to bask in her acceptance, be the one allowed to put a comb through her long silky hair, or be invited into her mother's kitchen to taste the incredible honey-tinged delicacies Madame Aumant could make, combining her Chinese dishes with her husband's French cuisine. Years later, thirty to be exact, when I ate Wolfgang Puck's inventions of French-

Chinese cooking, I remembered the lunches at the Aumants' when I was seven.

Milly had a loose tooth. It was her second. The first one had left a space on the lower center of her smile. Jasmine disdained baby teeth. Baby anything, for that matter. "You're a baby," she told Milly. "You'll never be able to play with us if you're still a baby."

"I can't help it." Milly's lip trembled and her blue eyes filled with tears.

"Grown-ups have their permanent teeth," Jasmine insisted, cutting her with a look. I went cold inside whenever she gave me that look.

"I'll have my big teeth soon," Milly insisted.

"Are any other ones loose?" I asked. I had just lost two uppers and my permanent teeth were beginning to grow in.

Milly nodded defiantly. "Sure they're loose." But I could tell she was lying.

Jasmine knew it too. "If they're loose you can pull them out." It was almost a challenge. She looked down over her pointy, turned-up nose, one hand on her bony hip thrust defiantly forward. It was a sweltering June day; no one had air-conditioning then and the only respite from the heat and the boredom was to play a game or find ways of tormenting one another. Sometimes that turned out to be the same.

"I have seventy-five cents for the movies today," Jasmine announced, pulling her hands out of her pocket and showing us her three quarters. There was nothing more desirable than going to the movies; we did it every Saturday during the school year. But now school was out and if we could, we'd have gone every day. Especially because the movies were refrigerated.

"Can I go?" I said, and then clamped my mouth shut, mortified. No one ever got a favor from Jasmine by asking. She either decided to ask you, or you didn't go. But punishing me was not her plan today.

"Smile," she commanded. I did, a jack-o'-lantern on demand, revealing my empty spaces.

"You're old enough. There's the proof." She pointed to my jagged smile.

Milly looked down at the ground. "I can go too," she insisted. "I have a quarter."

"No baby comes to my movies," Jasmine stated, the generalissimo of our lives.

"Can if I want," Milly insisted, starting to cry again.

"Oh, let her come," I said, risking everything.

"On one condition," Jasmine said.

Milly drew her eyes up from the ground and she gazed at Jasmine. "What?"

"You go in there"—Jasmine pointed to the dark space between our two brownstones where we stored the garbage cans and told each other that spooks and monsters dwelled—"and you pull out your bottom baby tooth and the two top ones and then you can go with us."

"But they're not all—" Milly was about to admit her lie when she caught herself. Jasmine would never forget that. She glanced at me with a helpless expression, but I just shrugged. I was secretly glad at the prospect of having Jasmine to myself. But to my amazement, Milly turned and headed for the alley and stepped into a shadow. We couldn't see her face, but her white T-shirt, stretched over her round tummy, shone in the dark. She was crying quietly.

"Jasmine," I whispered. "Don't make her do that. It's not right."

"Don't be silly. It's good to pull out your baby teeth. Gives the permanent ones a space to grow in. That way they come in straight." She turned and pointed her finger at Milly in the shadow of the alley. "Don't come out until you've done it. I want to see three teeth in your hand. Do you hear me?"

I shuddered at the power of command in her voice. But at the same time, I took great vicarious pleasure in her strength of will. Whatever Jasmine decided she wanted to be in life, she would be; from that moment on, I never doubted it. And then came the harangue. Milly saying she couldn't do it, and Jasmine using every wile she ever had to convince, to cajole, to insist, that Milly could. I knew it was wrong, but Jasmine didn't seem to care. And when my patience ran out, Jasmine wouldn't give up, nor would she let Milly off the hook. Once Milly'd agreed to the bargain, she was going to keep it, by God. Many times she wanted to stop, go home for lunch, but Jasmine wouldn't let her out of the alley until she'd completed her task. Even as a witness I didn't fully comprehend the power of our need for social acceptance. And when the thought of what Milly was actually doing in there crept over me, I'd shut it out by thinking of something else.

The lower tooth wasn't so hard. We tied a string around it and Jasmine gave a yank. But the upper ones were in there solid. Jasmine persevered, and so did Milly.

I never thought she'd do it no matter how much time had gone by. Those teeth weren't even loose. It scared me when I saw all the blood and those two dripping holes in her upper gums. When she came out of the alley with all three teeth in the palm of her hand you could see how pleased Jasmine was. She'd never faltered. I had watched to see if she had doubts, was she doing the right thing, was she truly hurting Milly? But she didn't doubt, and she didn't think about getting into trouble, even though I said many times, "Come on Jasmine, leave her alone. She can't do it. She'll never do it." But my tone wasn't insistent or emphatic. I too was being controlled by Jasmine's purpose and her will. I told myself not to interfere, concerned that Jasmine might turn on me and threaten never to play with me again.

Milly had stopped crying. The tears had made wide paths down her grimy face, her lips were red and swollen, and her fingers were covered with blood. Some had dripped onto her white T-shirt.

The first thing Jasmine did was put her arm around Milly's shoulder. "You did fine," she assured her. "You'll make a fortune tonight when the Tooth Fairy brings you money for three teeth under your pillow." I sensed a new bond between them and it made me jealous. Jasmine had truly conquered Milly—she'd made her do the impossible and she'd proved to herself that she could really control another human being. But Milly was the one who surprised me the most. She was so proud of herself. She may have endured this ordeal only to please Jasmine because Jasmine told her to, but in doing it she had overcome her own pain and fear and weakness. She was by far the greater winner. And then, when Jasmine said, "Let's go to the movies. You've earned it." Milly replied, "I don't feel like going now. I think I'll go home and put my teeth under my pillow."

That day Milly achieved a new stature in my eyes, a rung up the ladder from the basement where I had placed her, to at least street level, where I was. Neither of us had yet reached Jasmine's height on the ladder. As ordinary children, we probably never would.

CHAPTER FIVE

When I was eight, Marilyn Kauffman came to our house to stay for three days while her parents were in Washington testifying before the Senate on what my parents told me was some issue of national security, but they were evasive with details. When I put my ear to their door and listened, I heard them say the word *communism*. Of course, I'd heard it before and knew it was something negative.

Marilyn and Jasmine were alike in many ways, but that didn't make them friends. And Steffani recognized the similarity and kept away from Marilyn too. Marilyn and Jasmine sparred with one another from the moment they met, wary, knowing immediately that they were adversaries. And I, guileless between them, wanting only their approval and acceptance, had no idea what lurked beneath their surfaces, that they each had a cruel streak and a need to control, or I'd never have been so eager to scratch it. I didn't know that they wanted me only as a pawn. Jasmine had the upper hand, she lived here. But Marilyn was more devious, which gave her a slight advantage. And for once, I felt a heady kind of power myself as a member of this threesome. The times I felt most content were when they both wanted me.

Marilyn didn't like me very much, and complained about everything I did when we were alone, but pretended to like me in front of my mother and my friends. Jasmine only liked me when it was convenient, but with someone else threatening her territory, she liked me a lot. What unified Marilyn and Jasmine was Marilyn's instant dislike of Milly.

I must add here that Milly was an easy target. Not only did she have pudgy white skin that puffed out around her waist and puckered her behind like marshmallows, but she bragged about what she had and who her father was. Her mother didn't want her to play with me because I was Jewish, or with Jasmine because she was a half-breed, Milly's mother's word. But there was no one else on our block, so we were stuck with one another after school and on vacations.

One of our favorite pastimes was roller skating. We all had metal skates that fit onto the soles of our shoes with brackets that had to be adjusted into place with a skate key; we wore the key on a string around our necks. The skates were also held on by a leather strap buckled around the ankle, but they rarely stayed on our shoes for more than ten minutes at a time because the natural torque of shoe and the opposing metal dislodged them. Either that, or the vibration of the bumps in the sidewalk loosened the brackets. Right in the middle of a race or a chase, a skate would come off the shoe, leaving the thing attached to the ankle by the leather strap, propelling the wearer forward without wheels, and often causing a fall. It's a wonder more of us didn't break our noses or ankles or newly permanent front teeth.

But when the skates stayed on, it was wonderful. We'd skate along the sidewalk, imagining we were as swift as the wind, listening to the click click of the sidewalk cracks beneath our wheels, dodging pedestrians, baby carriages, dogs on leashes, and other kids playing jump rope or hopscotch.

One Saturday, while Marilyn was staying with me, the four of us skated all morning playing Sonja Henie. Milly and Jasmine left their skates at my house under the front stoop when they went home for lunch. The moment they left Marilyn started complaining about what a slob Milly was. Milly had crashed into her and sent her sprawling, causing Marilyn to scrape both her knees through her corduroy pants. We'd put Mercurochrome on her.

Mrs. Northcote was cleaning the house that day and Steffani was taking her nap. My mother had gone to the market and warned us to be quiet so as not to wake my sister.

I'd never before seen anyone work themselves up by building offense on top of offense the way Marilyn did about Milly. While we ate our Campbell's vegetable soup and tuna sandwiches, she talked about Milly's jiggly fat stomach, the way she talked, her squinting eyes, her freckled face, and her white skin. And of course, her big house.

"I hate her. Don't you just hate her?" she wanted to know.

"She's okay," I said, sensing something happening beyond my control, like the time with Jasmine and the teeth. I was glad Jasmine wasn't here to egg Marilyn on. But she didn't need any help. I felt it was my duty to defuse her, but I wasn't sure how. I tried, by offering to play the games that Jasmine and I played, games that took me out of the everyday like dress-up, but practical Marilyn wasn't interested. She was more adept at dealing directly with people, aggressively, something I found uncomfortable. I wanted everything always to be nice.

After lunch we sat on the stoop and studied Marilyn's red-painted scraped knees, which were already scabbing over. "I hate scraping my knees," she said. "I hear they can leave permanent scars. And I hate Milly for doing this to me."

I tried to change the subject to her parent's trip to Washington. Would they see President Truman? "What are they doing there, exactly?" I wanted to know, asking question after question to get her off the subject that brought a frightened quiver to the pit of my stomach. But she wouldn't be dissuaded.

"My brother got to go with them, 'cause he's fourteen, but not me. I had to be stuck here with a baby like you." She gave my thigh a pinch.

"Oww!" I yelled.

"You're such a baby," she repeated, now pinching my chest. "I bet you'll never grow up, never have breasts like the big girls have."

Being a big girl with breasts was a concept beyond me. I believed her totally, knowing that of course, I would never grow up, except to be a princess in a castle or a movie star like Elizabeth Taylor. Princesses and actresses didn't have breasts, they existed in a state of perfect unreality.

"Let's do something," she suggested, standing up and brushing the dirt off the seat of her pants. She walked down the steps and reached under the stoop to pull out our skates, but all the skates were tangled up together. She tried to shake them apart but Milly's skates (which were labeled with her name in ink on the inside of the leather strap) held on to Marilyn's with a tight grip. In a sudden fit of temper, she slammed the offending skate down on the sidewalk with a loud crash.

"Hey, be careful!" I cautioned, running down the stairs to stop her. People passing by paid no attention to us. As children, we were invisible to the grown-up world unless we did something directly to them and made them notice us.

"She deserves to be punished," Marilyn said, with great conviction, almost the way Jasmine had said, "Pull out those teeth."

As of that moment, Milly's skates didn't have a chance. Carefully, Marilyn untied and untangled Milly's skates from the rest of the pile until she held them by the straps. Then she swung them hard, slamming them against the sidewalk until they were bent and out of shape and coming apart into the two parts that separated the front wheels from the back.

"You'd better stop!" I said. "You'll get in trouble."

But she just handed me a skate and said, "Go ahead. It's what she deserves."

The power of her anger infused me, as much as the justification of her words, "deserves to be punished." I had my own resentment of Milly from all the times she'd made me feel underprivileged, and a wealth of other resentments whose existence I denied like a champ, as all good girls do. In a moment, I too was slamming the skate down on the sidewalk the way Marilyn was doing it. It was amazing how exhilarating the feeling was. It took over. My arm became an extension of this feeling; not exactly *get her*, but close to it. More like *get them*, whoever *they* were. That collection of painful moments in my past when I'd been hurt or angry and never allowed to express it bubbled forth. In my own defense, I only gave the skate a few smashes on the concrete. Marilyn didn't need my help. And it was she who gave Jasmine's skates a few smashes too, not I. Then she decided we'd better smash all the skates, hers and mine too so it would look like someone else had done the deeds.

I loved my skates and didn't want them ruined. But I was suddenly terrified of what would happen when my mother came home. Marilyn never gave it a thought.

Within an hour Milly was back and crying over her ruined skates. Jasmine didn't come back after lunch that day and didn't find out right away. I was more upset over ruining my own skates than I was concerned over covering up what we had done. I examined them to see if they could be made to work again. Then I saw my mother get out of a cab carrying packages and come toward us. She took a look at the carnage and at our faces. I guess she knew at a glance what had happened by Marilyn's lack of concern, and by my red face streaked with dirt and guilt, which I covered by faked unconcern.

Milly's crying got louder until she was wailing and my mother was comforting her. How I longed to be comforted too.

Just then, up from her nap, my sister appeared at the top of the stoop, her round belly protruding out from between her T-shirt and her shorts. Her blue eyes were still glazed looking from being asleep and her braids needed recombing. All this I noticed as she came down the stairs slowly, one step at a time, the way three-year-olds do. Her white high-top shoes were laced up properly. Mrs. Northcote must have put them on for her when she woke up.

"Hi, Mommy," she said, studying the scene at the bottom of the stairs.

"Some boys from another neighborhood came by and smashed all the skates while we were eating lunch," I said, my face losing its red color as I lied.

"That's hard to believe," my mother said, looking from one of us to the other. "What boys? Have we ever seen them here before? Where do they live?"

I'd never felt so caught before. That's all the explanation I had. Some boys. Trying to think of specifics made my stomach churn and my hands turn to ice. I looked at Marilyn, who stared back at me.

"Don't defend her," Marilyn said. And my heart sank. I didn't know what she was talking about.

"Defend who?" my mother asked.

"Her," Marilyn said, pointing at my sister, who had just made it down to the bottom step. Steffani stood there in her blue-striped T-shirt looking at us, her eyes wide with innocence, her upper lip sporting a ring of the red punch she'd just finished drinking. "She did it," Marilyn insisted, "Steffani."

My mother turned and said to my sister, sternly, "Steffani, did you do this?" And she pointed to the bent and broken pile of skates.

Steffani's round eyes went from face to face as she tried to piece together what had happened. She may not have understood what she was being accused of, but whatever it was she knew she hadn't done it. She looked up at our mother and said, in the perfect enunciation of her baby's voice, "I didn't do it. I was taking my nap." And then she turned to Marilyn and said, without missing a beat, "I'm no dope you know."

CHAPTER SIX

When days went by and I didn't receive any more crazy letters from Sherry Fallon, I almost pushed it out of my mind, nearly convincing myself it hadn't happened, except for that vague sense of dread still with me in the mornings when I awoke, obscuring a clarity I usually enjoyed. And Steffani wouldn't let me forget, calling to ask if I'd seen the lawyer yet.

"I'm going today," I told her. Steffani had found out the name of the man who handled copyright cases at Plummer Publishing, and my divorce attorney had given me the same name, Barry Adler, so he came well recommended. Today, Friday, October 15, was the first appointment I was able to get.

"Any new ideas?" she asked.

I hated even thinking about who it might be. "I've made a list of everyone I know, Steffani, and it reads like a social calender. None of my friends would do this to me."

"Well, someone sure has, Suzanne. And I think you should get serious. You called me over there the other night because you were really upset. I broke a date to be with you, so don't sweep it under the rug the way you always do. Face the truth."

"Dammit, I am facing the truth," I insisted. "Simply because I can't believe anyone I know would do this to me doesn't mean I'm sweeping it under the rug. If this happened to you, do you think you could figure it out?"

She laughed. "I'd have a list all right. Mostly women whose boyfriends or husbands I've diddled with."

"Well, I've never diddled with a married man," I told her. "Not even with an engaged one."

"Did you ever fire a housekeeper?" she suggested.

"I've never had one who speaks English, let alone possessed the sophistication to have a section of one of my novels typeset."

Steffani laughed. "Did you ever have an accident?"

"I was rear-ended once. Not my fault."

"What about a workman in your house, or that painter who spilled paint on the terrazzo floor."

"You're grasping at nothing, Steff. I'll call you after the lawyer. I only hope it's not a waste of money."

"You can afford it." She sounded annoyed, underscoring a difference between us. She lived on a salary paid by city government and I earned four times as much. Another inequity in the way things were. I helped her out financially whenever she needed it, gladly. Money was only important to me because it made my life-style possible. I could send the children to private schools because I felt strongly about the quality of their education, and rent a beach house in the summer, because it was the best kind of vacation for a single parent who works at home.

"I'm glad you're not letting this slide," she said. "That would be un-Blacker-like."

I laughed. Our parents had taught us to take care of business.

I brought with me everything I'd received in the mail to the lawyer's office in Century City and was thinking about what I would say to him when I entered the elevator along with several other people. The attorney's office was on the fourteenth floor.

Suddenly, a strange grinding sound filled the elevator. It bounced and then stopped, mid-floor, as the interior lights flickered.

I was near the control panel and pushed all the buttons. But nothing happened. "We're stuck," I announced.

"Oh shit!" a voice behind me said.

Five other people were captive with me: a couple in their fifties, a heavyset woman, a teenager, and a good-looking businessman in a suit.

The heavyset woman, wearing a garishly flowered dress, started to cry. "I can't be stuck, I can't. I have to go to the ladies' room."

The businessman said, "I have an office in this building. Don't worry, there's a computer panel in the basement that buzzes when an elevator gets stuck."

Of all of us, only the heavyset woman was upset, moaning, wiping her hands along her thighs.

I'd better do something, I thought, smiling. I extended my hand, "My name's Suzanne. What's yours?"

"Lillian," she answered, not taking my hand, and looking at me with suspicion. "Oh God, oh God," Lillian cried suddenly, crossing her legs and leaning forward. "I really have to go."

I spoke sharply. "Hold it, Lillian. These nice people don't want to see you embarrass yourself. Tell me, what kind of work do you do?" I tried to get her mind off her fear.

"I'm a legal secretary on the twelfth floor." She was gasping for breath.

"Why don't we sit down," the teenager suggested.

Lillian worked her way down to the floor, propped her back against the paneled wall, and stared at us as we all sat. We were cramped, but polite, moving an ankle or a foot, to accommodate each other.

Lillian closed her eyes and I was afraid she might faint, or empty her bladder.

"Would anyone like me to tell a story?" I asked.

The businessman was studying me with interest. "I would," he said.

But just as I was about to begin, there was a grinding noise, another bump, and the elevator began to move.

We cheered and scrambled to our feet as the door opened onto the tenth floor. Lillian was the first to leave. She pushed her way out and ran down the hall toward the bathroom. We all said good-bye and the others headed for the stairs, except for me and the businessman, who waited for another elevator.

He was taller than I, about five-eight, with curly brown hair and wonderful blue eyes beneath thick eyebrows. I'd describe his face as rugged; his jaw square; his nose long and straight, with a slight deviation at the bridge; his cheekbones formed angles when he smiled, and indented into hollows when at rest; his lips full and sensual. His eyes crinkled at the corners as he smiled at me. Perhaps it was being in a situation together that had caused it, but there was a chemistry between us. From the look in his eyes, I wasn't feeling it alone.

"That was clever of you to offer to tell her a story," he said, as the elevator reached the fourteenth floor and we got out together. Then he turned to me and said, "I'm Barry Adler, your two-thirty appointment." He opened the door to his inner office for me and followed me in.

I was annoyed and then embarrassed. "How did you know who I was?" I asked.

He smiled shyly. "I've seen your pictures before on my wife's books. But when you offered to tell us a story, I was certain of who you were. You were fabulous with Lillian, by the way. Kept her from peeing on all of us. Thank you very much."

I laughed with him, hiding my disappointment.

His wife's books. Darn, I thought, *Why is he giving out these vibrations if he's married?*

The receptionist greeted him. "I'm so glad to see you," she said. "There were some people stuck in the elevator."

He turned and smiled at me. This time I smiled back, his coconspirator. "Hold my calls, Martha," he said, without explanation.

The man doesn't gossip, I thought, following him into a typical lawyer's office: brown desk and chair, paneling, a credenza, bookshelves, swivel chairs for clients, plants, and diplomas. It was rather sterile.

"This is a pleasure," he said, extending his hand, his blue

eyes bright with sparkle, though a touch shy. "You're much more beautiful than your pictures."

His hand felt warm, comfortable, just as being with him felt. There was an ease between us I was finding delightful.

He saw my expression taking everything in as though re-writing it. "I'm not interested enough in my surroundings to decorate them," he said. "Whatever the firm provided was fine with me."

He indicated a chair and I sat down opposite his desk; I was a bit flustered now; watching him watching me I had to resist the urge to touch him. *This is crazy,* I thought. *The man's married.*

"My real love is the comics," he confessed. And he handed me a notebook filled with original cartoon drawings of unusual characters. They were wonderful.

"I'm developing a strip," he explained. "Came that close"—he showed me an inch of space between two fin-gers—"to getting picked up by a newspaper for syndication last year. But then my wife died ten months ago and I stopped drawing for a while. I'm just getting back to it."

"Your wife died? How did that happen?"

"Car," he replied, simply. "Drunk driver, two blocks from our house. She was four months pregnant." We stared at one another and I saw tears in his eyes. I wanted to reach across the desk and hug him. "Creating cartoons takes a kind of ebullient spirit that I'd lost for a long time," he added.

My throat was so constricted that my next words came out slowly, "I'm so sorry," I said, turning away for a moment to blink away my own tears. Imagine what it would be like to get one of those calls: *Mr. Adler, this is fate calling. Your life has just been destroyed.*

Finally, I said, "It's hardly appropriate for me to be telling you my troubles. Maybe we should forget about why I came here," I said, thinking that would suit me fine. "We could go downstairs to the lobby, find a bar, and have a drink." I wasn't usually so bold, but he had that wonderful face and obviously needed diversion as much as I did.

"What a nice invitation," he said, smiling a sweet, vulnerable, lopsided grin, which charmed me. "But I'm not quite ready to drink this early in the day, are you?"

I laughed. "No, I guess not."

He cleared his throat. "I didn't mean to make you feel sorry for me to the point that you couldn't tell me about your trouble. I'm okay about Eileen, now. Though it was difficult at first." I could see what an understatement "difficult" was. "I have my work, which is sometimes fascinating, especially when it allows me to come to the aid of beautiful novelists in distress. I even go out on occasional dates," he said suggestively, making me smile because of the tone in his voice. "And if you haven't guessed, I find you extremely attractive."

"Why thank you," I said. "I couldn't help noticing you either."

We sat there grinning at one another until he said, "So, shall we get on with it?"

The intrusion of reality froze the smile on my face. He sensed my mood change. "May I call you Suzanne?"

I nodded and handed him the documents I had with me. He started to read.

"This is really silly," I insisted. "I shouldn't be wasting your time." He was busy reading and didn't respond.

Finally, when he'd finished the pages, he asked, "Is this Sherry Fallon a real person? Anyone you know?"

I shook my head. "A mystery to me. I've called all the ones listed in New York, even Los Angeles, and no one's been able to verify her existence. I've been reluctant to start calling all the other cities in the country."

"I don't blame you." He smiled. "That would probably be a waste of time and expense. But you might want to check through publishing records and determine that there has never been a book like yours previously published."

"I know there hasn't. Because I know I didn't steal it. I wrote it. It came from me alone. And where would I go to find publishing records from before the war? They no longer exist. I can't disprove that it was ever in print. And I can't connect it to anything viable. I stand accused with no recourse to defend myself."

"Well, there's comfort in the fact that it can't be documented." He leaned back in his chair, arms behind his head, and I saw the tight muscles of his abdomen beneath his shirt as his jacket fell away. No flab at all. "However, the public couldn't care less about that. They believe every word they read in the *Enquirer*."

"The *Enquirer* won't write about this, will they?" The idea was disgusting. I knew the kinds of things they'd printed over the years, way back to using pictures of Jayne Mansfield's bosom on the cover to tell the story of how she'd been beheaded in that fatal car accident. What would they say about me? That I was a liar and a cheat? I supposed so. And that would mean that my work, for which I spread my guts out on the table every day and chopped them into little pieces, was a sham, a worthless effort. If my efforts were worthless, so was I.

Desperation colored my voice. "Aren't you going to tell me to go home and forget about this, that it won't happen again?"

He sighed, brought his arms down from behind his head, and leaned on the desk, looking at me intently. "I wish I could. It's possible that it won't happen again. But I doubt it. This thing is too carefully thought out, too well planned."

My expression showed my dismay. "You think this person is going to persist, don't you? How am I supposed to defend myself against this? What can I do?"

"Look, even though you've been accused, there's no proof. The author of the book you allegedly plagiarized would have to sue you, and that's not going to happen if there's no book. If you can't find out who is doing this to you, you can't do anything to them. You'd have to prove damages."

"What a mess."

"Now, don't worry," he assured me. "There's another way to deal with it. In fact, I have several suggestions. Hire a private investigator. They have avenues of discovery we can't even imagine. And secondly, I'd like to call a press conference, go public with this, and make a statement as your attorney that these accusations are false and unprovable.''

"Go public? I can't do that!" I insisted, feeling my underarms beginning to perspire at the thought of having to defend myself in public, of having my privacy invaded. The reality of the *Enquirer* drew closer and closer.

"But why?" he asked.

The idea frightened me for some reason I couldn't explain so I said, "It's premature. What if I never hear from this person again and I've told the world about it?"

"It's more likely that they won't give up on you," he said, as gently as he could. "And there's an advantage to making an announcement yourself before a hostile reporter hears about it."

I couldn't go public with this, I just couldn't. There had to be another way to fight back. "I know my publisher doesn't want this made public, and neither do I." My voice held a note of pleading.

"Why is that?" he asked, genuinely puzzled.

"Because," I retorted, hotly, angrier than his question warranted. "Going public would lend credence to the accuser. It would give whoever is doing this to me satisfaction that they were getting to me. I can't allow that."

"That's a good point," he said, to my relief. "It's something we can always reserve for later."

I looked away, feeling my heart pound. My next admission was even more difficult. "I'm even afraid to discuss this with the people I know, for fear one of them might have done this to me." I turned back and looked at him, but he wasn't judging me. All I saw was compassion.

"I can see how you might feel that way. But those who really know you won't believe it. Is there anything else?" he asked, gently.

I tried to control it, but my eyes filled with tears. "I

heard what you said, but when someone is accused, there's always a percentage of people who believe it! I couldn't stand seeing that moment of doubt in some people's eyes, that flicker of a shadow which says, Where there's smoke there's fire.''

''But if you go public there's a better chance of discovering the person's identity. Then you can file a libel defamation suit. In a trial, no one would be able to produce a book to demonstrate that you plagiarized. You'd win.''

I shook my head, remembering all the aggravation I'd gone through after my divorce. ''If I had to endure a trial, even if I win I'd lose. I know about emotional stress. The last time it left me nearly unable to function. After my divorce, it took me twice as long to write my next book as the two previous ones had taken. A writer's guts have to be free from the things that eat at them, like stress and lawsuits. We also need a quiet, orderly existence to be prolific. At least I do.''

I had calmed down enough to notice him staring at me, and not as lawyer to client. In spite of our discussion, I felt the color rise to my cheeks. I hadn't been this attracted to a man since Alex.

''I'll respect your wishes,'' he assured me, ''even if I don't agree with you.''

I nodded, getting up to go, still feeling defeated.

He followed me into the reception area. ''Does that quiet and orderly life of a writer include dinner sometimes?''

My heart, which had been sluggishly thumping along, began to hum nicely now. I turned and smiled at him. ''I'd love to,'' I said with a touch too much enthusiasm, then really blushed.

''Great!'' He smiled. ''I'll call you soon.''

We shook hands again and he covered mine with both of his. ''I'm truly sorry that this is happening to you, Suzanne,'' he said. ''But for the first time in a long time, I'm glad to be practicing copyright law, or I'd never have met you.''

''An optimist,'' I commented. ''Even after your own tragedy.''

"Like Johnny Mercer said," he said, smiling, " 'accentu-ate the positive.' Isn't that what we both deserve?"

The sincerity of his reply was definitely reassuring.

CHAPTER SEVEN

"Suzanne. What did you do to your sister?"

"Nothing, Mommy!" My heart beat like crazy whenever I was accused of anything. Yet, accusations were my parents' way: Who turned up the heat? Who left the milk out of the refrigerator? Who left the lights on upstairs? The tone of their questions invited lies, implying, Who could have been this stupid? If I admitted I'd done it, I would be in big trouble. So the stock answer was, "I didn't do it." And the stock behavior was to be diligent, head it off before it got started. Never leave the lights on or forget to put the milk back. In other words, be a *good* girl.

"Then how did she get this bruise?"

We both looked at Steffani's chubby little leg and then at each other. The bruise was the size of a baseball. It made me sick to look at it, to imagine what kind of a blow had caused it.

"How did this happen, honey?" my mother asked my sister.

She shrugged, sat down on the floor, and started playing with blocks. "I dunno."

It wasn't the first time, either. There had been bruises on her arms and on her back, as if some perverse person were pounding on her. But I hadn't done it, I was sure of that. My innocence must have been apparent for my mother didn't question me further.

My mother made an appointment for Steffani with the

pediatrician. I was terrified for her. I cried and begged my mother not to take her.

"Why, Suzanne? He's a good doctor."

"No," I cried. "You can't let him see her." But I was too embarrassed to tell my mother that I was afraid the doctor would examine my sister *down there*, the way he had examined me. How I'd hated that. Last year, during my seventh-year examination, I'd felt mortified when, without any warning, he'd spread the lips of my vagina and looked in, while my mother just sat calmly by. *How can she let him do this to me? Why isn't she stopping him?* I'd wondered, wanting to hit his hands away, shocked by his invasion. I dreaded the same thing happened to my sister and carried on about it, making a nuisance of myself until my mother said, "That's enough!"

All during the examination I waited tensely for Steffani's reaction, but she didn't object at all. In fact, she was a willing patient, giggling when he pressed around her stomach because she was so ticklish.

The doctor and my mother made me leave the exam room and wait in the reception area while they talked in the office about my sister. I colored pictures with the doctor's broken crayons. There were no red ones, only dark pink. The red crayons always got used up first, that and black.

After a while my mother came out of the office carrying my four-year-old sister. She took my hand and we left. But my mother didn't look right. Her face was pasty white and her eye makeup was smudged. "Where are we going?" I asked. She didn't reply, just stared straight ahead. Her behavior scared me so I didn't ask again.

Steffani was getting sleepy; it was her naptime. She curled up in my mother's lap in the backseat of the taxicab, while I sat in the front with the driver. I could just see out of the front window of the cab.

"We're going to see Daddy," she finally told me, as she gave the driver directions.

"At work?" It was a first for me on an ordinary Wednesday. It wasn't a holiday or anything. "Why?" I asked. "Won't he get mad if we go to the office? Isn't he busy?"

"Be quiet!" my mother snapped, and I was. I heard her sigh, and then I heard her crying. I didn't turn around but hearing her made me want to cry too. I wondered if it was something I'd done.

We drove along the bumpy, potholed streets and I distracted myself by watching the people walking on the sidewalks all bundled up in their warm coats. Or I stared at the big buses with signs on them advertising Ipana toothpaste and Oxydol soap.

When we got to my father's office, I held my mother's hand and she squeezed it, too tightly, but I didn't say anything, knowing when not to complain.

My father's office was in a tall building on Forty-eighth Street. We took the elevator up. He was not in his office. The secretary said he'd be right back, then whispered to my mother, "He's in the men's room."

I loved to come to my father's office and see the autographed photographs of his clients hanging on the walls and some of the famous comedians and entertainers he'd known. My favorite was Fanny Brice; I knew her as Baby Snooks. And there was Jack Benny, Burns and Allen, Jimmy Durante, the Three Stooges, and some I didn't recognize. He'd known most of them when he booked vaudeville acts. I wasn't exactly sure what vaudeville was, but it was dead now. And whenever my parents talked about it, they got a sweet kind of smile on their faces and a dreamy look in their eyes. My mother liked to tell me the story of how she met my father after he'd worked for the Orpheum Circuit. He had known all those people in the photographs, then. She insisted he was happier now representing opera singers and famous violinists—a classier caliber of people, she called them—but something in her voice told me there was more to it than she said, like maybe both she and my father were sorry vaudeville was dead. I wished he still knew Baby Snooks.

Steffani was asleep on my mother's shoulder. My mother

put her down on the leather sofa opposite the secretary's desk and I sat on the sofa arm because there wasn't room for me next to her. I was getting tired too. My father's office didn't have any crayons, I went over to the secretary's desk to draw a picture, but first I played with the buttons on the intercom.

"This is the first time Mr. Blacker has had time to breathe all day," Sylvia, the secretary, said, letting me sit in her chair. "That new client, the Italian baritone, has been complaining about his accommodations in Detroit, and the Chamber Quartet missed their train from Chicago last night, so the concert people in St. Louis are worried about whether they'll get there on time." She shook her head. "I don't know how he does it, but your husband always remains calm and smooths everybody's feathers. Somehow it all turns out in the end." Her smile told me she really liked my father. But it didn't surprise me. Everybody liked my father, me most of all. "Is he that way at home?" Sylvia asked.

My mother didn't answer. I poked her so she would wake up from her daydreaming and answer Sylvia, but she looked at me as if she didn't know why I had done that.

I almost said to Sylvia that my father was not calm at all at home, that he had a temper and often gave a *geshrei*, a Yiddish word for *yell*, but my mother wouldn't have wanted Sylvia to know our private family business.

Just then my father came back. He wasn't wearing his jacket, his tie was loose around his neck, his hair needed combing; a curl had gotten loose from his black hair and was hanging down on his forehead. He smoothed it back as he kissed me hello and spun me around in the secretary's chair. Then his blue-gray eyes looked over at my mother. In a worried voice he asked her, "What did he say?"

"Stay here, Suzanne," she said, and was up from the sofa in an instant, pulling him into his office. She closed the door but I saw she was going to cry and that scared me so much.

There was a transom window above my father's door and a ventilation panel near the bottom so I could hear them in the next room even with the door closed. I went back to the sofa and sat next to my sleeping sister, trying not to look at Sylvia so she wouldn't know I was listening.

But my mother was crying so hard I couldn't make out what she was saying and my father was trying to soothe her. They were whispering. I heard the name "Dr. Isaacs"—he was our pediatrician—and then my mother cried even harder.

At one point my father shouted, "My God, is he sure? Does he know?"

"No, he wants to do tests," my mother replied.

The sound of their voices gave me a sick feeling inside, similar to what I'd felt when my nana had died last year. My mother had stopped playing the piano and singing then, and for a long time she didn't sing, until recently. I was afraid this would make her stop for good. Something as awful as my nana dying had invaded my life on this ordinary Wednesday. With all my might I wanted it just to go away and never come back.

Everything was different now because my sister was sick. My parents took her to see doctor after doctor but nobody knew what was wrong. They all had different opinions.

"When are they going to know?" I'd ask my mother, but she'd say, "I wish *I* knew," as if I'd asked something wrong. She snapped at me a lot so that I never knew what was safe to ask. It made me want to cry, but I didn't dare because she was so worried about my sister. Steffani's *condition* was a topic of conversation that took precedence over all others. If I started to talk about something that happened in school my parents just wouldn't hear me. Often, my mother would wave her hand at me, which meant, "Not now, Suzanne, later!" But later never seemed to come.

The one thing the doctors knew was that Steffani had a mass in her abdomen that several of them thought was a tumor, which was really bad. I'd wait for my parents to come home after every doctor's appointment and ask, "Do they know yet?" But they'd just shrug and say, "We're not sure."

Steffani seemed normal to me, except that she had attacks of pain in her arms or legs and big bruises on her body sometimes. When she was in pain, all I wanted to do was hug her and pet her and kiss her and make it all better, the way I did with my dolls—or wave a magic wand. But I was only seven and my magic wasn't very potent.

After every doctor's visit, my mother would call my uncle Sid, who had moved to Long Island, New York, when he became a lawyer, and tell him what happened. I'd sit outside her door listening, afraid she would get angry. But she never noticed. The conversations were full of medical terminology beyond my ken. But what I did understand was the either-or. My mother would say, "Either they're wrong, and she doesn't have cancer or Tay-Sachs, or she does. And if she does, I don't know what I'll do." And then she'd break into sobs.

Once, she said, "Oh God, how I wish Mama was here." And I sat there on the floor, missing my nana with all my heart, barely able to breathe, feeling my mother's agony as my own. My helplessness was an inky blanket of suffocation. And worst of all was the guilt, weighing on my heart and pressing it flat within my chest. How could I be all right when Steffani wasn't? The question clutched my bowels and squeezed so hard that it felt as though I had ropes inside of me.

One day there was a final meeting and all the doctors were going to be there. Maybe we'd finally know what was wrong. Every time I thought of what it could be, I'd get so scared my pulse would pound in my head. I'd run through the apartment to wherever my sister was playing just to look at her. She'd glance up at me from her game on the floor as if nothing was wrong, but I had to see her, be sure she was still there. Often, the discussions I overheard about her didn't seem to be about her at all. For she still had those liquid blue eyes and those round apple cheeks and that way of talking that both infuriated and enchanted me.

Uncle Sid came into the city from Long Island to hear the results of the big meeting and we waited together drinking hot chocolate.

Our attention was riveted on the front door as my parents

came through it that evening, their heads drooping, exhaustion lining their faces, their eyes red from crying. My mother ran to my uncle and put her arms around him as if she'd never let go, and my father hugged me. I felt those knotted ropes inside pulling, as though part of me were hanging from a tree. I clung to my father, needing him to reassure me with my entire being that Steffani was all right, but he just untangled my grasp and patted my cheek.

"It could be worse," my mother told Uncle Sid. "Is Steffani up from her nap yet?" she asked me.

I nodded. "She's playing with her friend Doreen from around the corner."

"Why don't you go and see what they're doing?"

"I don't want to," I said. "I want to hear what happened. You promised you'd tell me."

A look passed between my mother and father and he said, "She might as well hear it now, I guess."

We went into the living room and sat there as if we were company.

My mother started first, her strained voice showing how worried she was. The dark rings under her eyes looked as though her makeup had run. Otherwise she was still my beautiful mother who did her own hair in the newest hairdos and wore suits with matching blouses, shoes, and purse. My father sat next to her and put his arm around her. Lately, he told her often that she had circles under her eyes and ought to get more rest. But he had them too.

"I've been nearly at the end of my patience waiting until all of the results came in," she told us. "But today was Dr. Gaylin's report."

"Which one is Dr. Gaylin?" Uncle Sid asked.

"She's the new hematologist," my mother told him. "Her family originally came from South Africa. Can you imagine?" My mother always described everything in detail. "Gaylin's finally ruled out cancer, thank God," my mother continued. "From the tests they sent to Rochester, they know the mass isn't a malignant tumor, nor does her blood show signs of cancer. The radiologist couldn't find anything either.''

My sister had been sick long enough for me to know that a radiologist was someone who took X rays.

"What about an exploratory?" Uncle Sid asked.

That meant an operation to check things out.

"We talked about it, but they're reluctant to do it on a child so young. Now, we don't have to. She's been through so much," my mother said, her eyes filling with tears. The thought of Steffani's suffering always made her cry and that brought tears to my eyes too.

"No more examinations!" she said. "No more tests!" She spoke as if it were final, the way she talked when she laid down the law to me over some infraction.

"That damned urologist, Dr. Riceman. I'll never forgive him for insisting on that cystoscope, and she didn't even need it. Whoever heard of putting a child through such a thing."

I had had nightmares almost every night since Steffani had that test. Even now, as they talked about it, I wanted to cover my ears. My mother had explained to Steffani what the doctors would do, assuring her it wouldn't hurt. I sat with them on the bed, holding Steffani's hand and listening to the description of everything they would do. They weren't going to use any needles, just put a thin little tube inside of her, *down there*, so they could see if anything was wrong.

"That's not so bad," I told her.

But when the time came for them to insert the catheter into Steffani's tiny body, it must have been excruciatingly painful. I would probably have screamed even if my mother told me not to, but Steffani didn't. Instead she just cried and moaned, begging them to stop; but of course they wouldn't. They strapped her arms and legs to a table so she couldn't move, and then they did it to her. When she told me this later, the thought of it made me want to scream all over again. She'd endured this without kicking or biting the way other children do when someone tortures them. I could barely listen to the description, the thought of it was so horrible. But even worse than that was my helplessness. My precious, beautiful little sister had to suffer so, forced to endure these things for her own good and be brave as well because my parents expected it (I knew all about that). My mother wanted to kill the doctors for hurting Steffani so much, but I couldn't stand even to think about it. If they could do that to my sister, what could they do to me?

"And after all that," my mother was telling my uncle Sid, "they found that nothing was wrong with her urinary tract, that her kidneys were fine."

"Fourteen doctors in six months!" my father exclaimed. "That's how many times they've done blood tests and X rays and examinations. That poor little child," he said, and began to weep. My father's anguish was even harder to endure. Fathers were supposed to be strong and not cry, but I had seen him cry a lot lately. His pain added another dimension to my own, and the tears poured down my cheeks too.

"Dr. Gaylin's only been on the case two weeks, but she knows more than all of them put together," my mother added, patting my father's arm, waiting until he was calmer before she continued. "She sent Steffani's hematology slides to Belgium and they confirmed that the bouts of pain in her arms and legs and the fevers are all part of what she has. It's called Gaucher's disease."

So it finally had a name. It didn't sound as awful as cancer. But my whole body was tense waiting to hear the rest, while those ropes inside tightened.

"What's Gaucher's disease?" Uncle Sid asked the all-important question.

"There's some fancy medical term for it." She turned to my father. "What was it called?" she asked.

"A glycolipid storage disorder," he replied.

I thought my father said, a Jell-O-liquid storage container. I stifled a giggle and didn't dare ask him to repeat it.

"What happens," my mother explained, "is the body's defense cells get swollen."

"How does that affect anything?" my uncle wanted to know.

"Well, you know that the spleen and the liver purify the blood. But if there are Gaucher cells, they jam up in those places making them enlarged, which leads to all sorts of problems. It can also affect her white cell count and her clotting factor. That's why she bruises so easily."

"I see." Uncle Sid nodded.

"It affects the bone marrow too," my father said. "It can cause the bones to fracture more easily, so we have that to worry about as well as the bouts of pain in her joints." The misery in his voice made me shiver. Gone was my moment of amusement; I couldn't look at him.

This sounded horrible to me now, worse than cancer. I pictured one of those skeletons that dangled inside of the closet in an Abbott and Costello movie, only this one was little like my sister and its bones were so brittle they broke and fell apart.

"Is she going to be all right?" Uncle Sid asked. "Can they make her well?"

"*Rednish de kinder*," my father said: *Not in front of the children*. But I knew the answer. *She was not going to be all right*.

My mind floated away. I refused to think of her as anything but perfect. Gone were the moments when I hated her for merely being there, and wished she'd just go away forever and leave me alone with my parents. This disease that threatened her made her more precious to me. How I wanted to be able to do something for her. I pictured Steffani as a fairy princess with wings, the most beautiful fairy in all of the forest. All the birds and animals loved her and she could wave her magic wand and make everything golden and glowing and filled with flowers.

My parents' conversation continued around me but I had tuned them out so that only a part of me heard.

"They're not sure of the prognosis," my mother said. "They don't know a lot about Gaucher's. But Dr. Gaylin told us that it's fairly common. One in two to three hundred Jews of Ashkenazic descent get it as opposed to one in four thousand non-Jews. It occurs in adults too and there is no known cure." My mother was crying now and the sound of it brought me back from the fairy forest, shooting that sick feeling through me again, only worse.

My father went on. "Steffani doesn't have any neurological symptoms, so they think she might outgrow it in time. But there's no one in the city who knows much about it. The only thing we can do is to treat her symptoms. When she's in pain, we have to try and relieve it." He turned and looked directly at me, forcing me to give him all my attention.

"We have to keep a careful watch over her, Suzanne, not let her get bruised or fall down. We're going to need your help in looking after her when we're not around. She mustn't be allowed to do anything dangerous. No skating or bike riding because her bones could break more easily than other childrens'."

"But she loves to run and play with me," I protested. "We fall down all the time." It seemed enormously unfair; the burden of this new responsibility weighed heavily. Not only could she not be allowed to do things, but I would have to keep her from doing them. She wouldn't like that. And what would that mean to me? Not only was my sister sick, but I had lost her as a playmate too. *How could I keep doing the things we both loved when she couldn't? What if I was watching her and she got hurt? How would I feel if they told me I couldn't run and play, or ride a bike, or skate?* There was a lump in my throat I couldn't swallow. I thought about how my sister used to run across the room and fling herself into our arms wildly. Of course her recent attacks of pain had knocked the fearlessness out of her. But I couldn't believe she wouldn't be like that again.

"They told us what to do if she has another attack," my father told my uncle. "Aspirin didn't help at all last time, and they don't like giving drugs to young children, so they recommended Sister Kenny packs, a treatment they use on children with polio."

Uncle Sid nodded, as though he knew what Sister Kenny packs were.

"Can we count on you, Suzanne?" my mother asked.

"I know we can," my father said. "We've always been able to rely on our big girl." His smile sent chills through me. Was he resenting me for not being sick, or was he preferring me because I wasn't?

"I'll try," I promised, giving both my parents a hug. I wanted to curl up in their laps forever, have them tell me it was all a mistake, a bad dream. But when they looked at me, they didn't really see me, they were seeing my sister—a state of existence I would come to know only too well. We were clinging to the fact that there was something practical we could do now; each of us had our jobs. Since the doctors knew best, they were the keepers of hope for my sister's recovery; if they told us to follow a procedure, I was sure it would work and maybe everything would be all right again.

"What are you doing, Mommy?" I asked, when I came home from school to find the gray enameled soup kettle boiling on the stove, my mother stirring some strange concoction that smelled like dirty sheep. The whole apartment smelled of it, and the kitchen was hot and damp from the boiling, steamy brew. I had had a wonderful day at school. We had gone to the Metropolitan Museum and seen the Egyptian exhibit, which had filled me with wonder. I couldn't wait to tell my mother about it. And best of all, David Smith had told me he loved me.

"I'm making a Sister Kenny pack for Steffani."

"Guess what?" I began.

"Not now, Suzanne. Can't you see I'm busy? Steffani is having an attack."

"What happened?"

"They called me from nursery school today and I picked her up. The pain has been getting worse by the hour. So whatever it is you want to tell me will have to wait until later."

I peeked around the corner into the housekeeper's room and saw my sister in the housekeeper's bed; she was there so she'd be nearby while my mother was in the kitchen. Steffani was moaning, "Oh, oh, it hurts." Her round face was contorted in pain, her brow creased. As I watched, she began to cry. I stood in the doorway wanting to talk to her, but she didn't acknowledge me. Finally, I got her attention.

"Hi," I said.

She looked up, glad to see me, and tried to smile, but the pain was too acute.

"Mommy's coming soon. She'll make you feel better," I told her.

Back in the kitchen, my mother was hurrying. The steam from the water was rising to her face, making the dark hair around her forehead curl into tight springy curls. She reached into the pot with two large wooden spatulas and lifted out a large piece of wool. I recognized it as part of a blanket we used for picnics. Then, letting it drip over the boiling cauldron, she twisted it around the wooden spatulas until it was wrung out. It took muscles to lift the heavy, wet wool, and dexterity to keep from burning herself. She made a sucking noise, pulling in short bursts of air between her teeth as she tried not to scald herself: "*Ffff*." It frightened me.

"Stand back," she cried, moving toward the sink; her nerves were taut, her voice shrill. "Move away, Suzanne, for God's sake, I don't want to burn you."

She backed into me, making a sound of exasperated disgust, as her hips touched me. "Can't you see I'm busy," she shouted.

"Can I help?" I asked, wanting to cry from rejection and a frustrated desire to make everyone happy again. I was afraid that she might burn herself, and yet needed to be near her, even to the point of risking her wrath by being where I was obviously in the way.

She held the piece of steaming blanket over the sink and tried to wring it out with her hands, crying out in short little cries as the hot steam touched her skin; she moved it rapidly from one hand to the other. Finally, when she'd gotten as much water out of the wool as she could, she ran out of the kitchen and into the next room where my sister lay moaning.

I could hear Steffani's cries rise several octaves underlined by fear. "No, no, no, *no*," she yelled, as she realized what my mother was going to do. My mother's voice cajoled, trying to soothe, mesmerize, and persuade all at the same time. I couldn't look but stood in the kitchen with my hands clenched into fists and every muscle in my body stiff.

"This is what the doctors said to do, sweetheart. I know it hurts, but this will make it feel better. I promise, Steffani. Just be calm, let me do this to help you. Shall I tell you a story, would you like me to sing you a song?" Soon, Steffani's screams drowned out the sound of my mother's voice.

I stared at that horrible pot boiling on the stove, feeling an emptiness inside like death. I still couldn't watch. Nothing seemed more tortuous to me than to be wrapped in that scalding blanket, yet I yearned for Steffani to be helped, for her to let our mother do what the doctors had said, let the magic be performed even if it was a form of torture. "Oh God, please don't let her hurt anymore. She's only five years old." The words repeated themselves. "Please, God, please," I begged, listening to her cries, which alternated with screaming, as my mother wrapped that scalding cloth around her arm. I stood outside the door, gritting my teeth, waiting for Steffani's screams to subside into whimpers, which they eventually did. From what I surmised, this process had been repeated every few hours, all day long while I was away at school. Had it helped, I wondered?

As it turned out, we never did know if there was any causal relation between the packs and the diminishment of pain, for the pain seemed to wax and wane of its own accord, not influenced or reduced by the Sister Kenny packs, but only by the passage of time. My mother used them for at least a year, every time Steffani had an attack. We never really knew if they helped.

Sister Kenny's treatment, I learned years later, promoted a softening of the atrophied muscles of a polio victim so they could become more pliable and be stretched, hopefully strengthened and restored. Wet wool had the ability to hold in heat for a longer period of time than any other material we had at our disposal in 1949. But it probably didn't help Steffani's condition because she didn't have a muscle disorder.

I never saw a picture of Sister Kenny, but I imagined her as a tall, gray-haired woman in a white nurse's uniform with rimless spectacles and a square, determined jaw. And of course, strong muscles for wringing out scalding wet blankets. Years later, when the Mel Brooks movie, *High Anxiety*, was released and I saw Cloris Leachman's satiric protrayal of a sadistic nurse with a hideous face, I thought, *that's Sister Kenny*.

CHAPTER EIGHT

"I thought only big people have operations, Mommy. Aren't I too little?" Steffani looked up at Lynnette, her blue eyes filling with tears. "Will it hurt?"

"No, honey, 'cause you'll be asleep," Lynnette assured her.

"Then can I ride a bicycle?"

"We'll see."

"All the other kids get to."

"I know," Lynnette replied. There was no end to the deprivation and suffering this child had to endure. Yet, being sick never made her bitter or afraid; she never whined or clung the way some children did. Instead, she was totally filled with life and pursued the normal interests of a child of seven. She never wavered in her determination to follow her sister's lead and do everything Suzanne was doing, like roller skating and high diving, and taking ballet, no matter how they warned her and cautioned her. When she wasn't suffering she skipped through life joyously. Her beauty continued to blossom; each year she got more beautiful, more intelligent, and funnier.

One night at dinner, Burt was telling them a story about one of his clients.

"What's that?" Steffani asked, pointing to the gravy boat on the table.

Burt and Lynnette ignored Steffani's question, too absorbed in conversation.

Lynnette repeated what Burt had just told her. "You mean, Adelaide just stormed off the stage and left the whole cast standing there with their mouths open?"

"And she said she'd never work in that theater again," he told her.

"What's that?" Steffani pointed to the gravy boat again.

"Can you believe it?" Burt said angrily, eating a bite of mashed potatoes.

Nobody answered Steffani.

"But that's childish!" Lynnette commented.

"I know it is," Burt agreed.

And Steffani thought she finally knew what was in the gravy boat. This time she spoke loud enough so everyone could hear her. "Please pass the child*ish*," she said.

But there were other words that Steffani became familiar with, long words with many syllables, such as *hemoglobin, hematocrit, leukocytes,* and *splenectomy*—something the doctors had mentioned might be a possibility for her.

"If we remove her enlarged spleen, Mrs. Blacker, it might arrest the advancement of her disease. But in a child this age, we want to wait and observe her for a while, and see how she does."

"But she's suffering," Lynnette said, trying to be sweet, trying to keep them liking her so as not to offend the sensibilities of these gods she needed so desperately; yet her exasperation showed through because with all the powers of their august positions, they weren't helping worth a damn.

So they waited a year and a half, treating her with those hideously painful Sister Kenny packs whenever Steffani had bouts of pain in her legs or arms (sometimes once a month), until Lynnette and Burt were desperate for anything that would help. By then, removing one of her organs seemed a positive thing to do. "How can one live without a spleen?" Burt had asked, when they started discussing the actual procedure of the surgery.

"The liver takes over the function of the spleen," Dr. Gaylin explained. "Then, Steffani's abdomen won't be so distended."

"It's major surgery, isn't it?" Lynnette wanted to know, thinking of all the things that could go wrong.

"Yes," the surgeon, Dr. Kaye, admitted. "She'll be in the hospital for at least a week, maybe two. It's a long recovery, but afterward, she'll feel better."

"Will the bouts of pain stop?" Lynnette felt her hopes beginning to rise.

"We're hopeful that they will," Dr. Gaylin told her.

"But you don't know?" Hopes were dashed again.

"Mrs. Blacker"—Dr. Gaylin took that tone with her of exasperated largesse, as though Lynnette were some errant child, and not the mother—"there is not much known about Gaucher's disease, how to treat it, or how to predict its advancement. Especially since there is no cure. We can only do the best we can with the knowledge we have." She paused and directed her question to Burt. "Do you have insurance? Because if you don't, we may be able to provide you with some financial assistance."

Burt straightened up to his full height of six feet three, and said icily, "We will be able to pay our own bills, thank you."

"How does he do the operation?" Steffani asked Lynnette after she'd met with her surgeon, Dr. Kaye, an Oriental man with black hair, a pockmarked face, and gentle hands. She was used to having medical procedures explained to her in detail.

"The doctors use special instruments—scissors, and knives called scalpels—used only for surgery, and needles and threads to sew you up afterward." Lynnette made it a game, pretending a sewing motion. "And you'll have a scar right here." She traced a large half-moon across her own abdomen from the top of her rib cage down to the bottom of her stomach while Steffani watched with huge blue eyes, taking it all in. "And everyone will want to see your scar and ask how you got it. And you'll say, 'From an operation.' "

"Will you be there?"

"All the time!"

"Can you sleep in my bed?"

"No, but I can sleep on a cot nearby, if they'll let me."

"Oh please, Mommy, make them let you. I don't want you to be alone without me," she kidded.

If Steffani was worried, she didn't let anyone know. When I asked her how she felt about going to the hospital, she said, "It's going to make me better, Suze. Maybe I won't have 'attacks' anymore"—our family's name for what happened to her much too often. We all looked forward to that with such hope, it was as if we'd found a treasure of gold.

Whenever there was a crisis with my sister, and this one was a doozie, both of us stopped being bratty to one another, I especially. For Steffani never picked a fight with me the way I did with her, but then, I didn't want what she had as much as she wanted what I had. Anticipating the ordeal she was facing made me believe I'd never be angry with her again. (I was wrong of course.) It also made me love her with a kind of desperation that only the fear of loss can bring. She always looked up to me; my parents said so and I could see it was true. She saw the three of us as her support unit, only I was the one who understood what she was going through personally.

Steffani and I prepared for her stay in the hospital. She gave me a list of which dolls I was supposed to feed, which games she would let me play with, and which ones I positively couldn't. I swore and crossed my heart that I wouldn't cheat. I was also supposed to watch every episode of "Cyclone

Malone,'' our favorite television show, so I could tell her about it, and not to watch Hopalong Cassidy movies on Saturday without her.

A few days before the operation, I had an attack of my own, a bout of nighttime terror. I couldn't go to sleep. I lay there thinking about the concept of infinity, how the stars in space just go on and on without end, and how someday I would die like my nana, cease to exist, cease to feel and think, just be no more. And possibly worse, even before that, my parents would die and leave me. I was terrified, but I couldn't explain how I felt to anyone. I knew they couldn't help, there were no answers. Death was inevitable and so was suffering, that much I knew. And an unnamed sadness descended on me, a crushing fear and depression. I cried and stared up at the ceiling in the dark, trying to put these thoughts out of my mind, needing companionship and nurturing with every fiber of my body, but denying myself the comfort because I was nine years old, the big sister, the responsible sister, the good one, the one who wasn't sick. I tossed in bed, bumped against the wall hoping someone might hear me and come and see what was wrong, without my having to go to them and admit it. But no one came. Finally, I got out of bed and went through the kitchen to the den.

My parents never took it kindly when one of us didn't stay in bed. In the Blacker house, once you went to bed, you stayed there.

I was hoping to find my father reading in the den and not sitting with my mother in the living room. My father was more sympathetic when he was alone than when he was with my mother, and easier to approach. She allowed less nonsense than he did. I was in luck: He was smoking his pipe, reading the paper, and listening to *La Bohème* in the wing chair in the corner of the den. That chair had been his special possession in all the places we lived. And *La Bohème* was one of our favorite operas; I knew several of the Italian operas by heart because we played the records over and over.

I stood in the doorway a moment, listening to the music.

I recognized Mimi's aria being sung by Carlotta Strecci, one of Daddy's clients. I had met her before; she was beautiful. A haze of smoke curled over his head, and the room smelled of cherry tobacco. It smelled so good it made my stomach rumble.

He looked up and saw me standing there. "What are you doing here?"

"Daddy, I can't sleep."

"What is it, honey?" he asked, setting aside the paper.

I stood there trembling, thinking that it was from being cold and out of bed without my robe and slippers on. Actually, it was the thought of ever having to go back up to bed in my whole life that made me tremble. If I could have stayed awake forever, and not had bad dreams, and never thought of the terrors that could befall me or my sister, or either of our parents, I'd have been the happiest girl in the world. I thought about my nana, who had often sighed for no reason, and gotten tears in her eyes. When I asked her what was wrong, she hugged me and said, "Mamela, my precious, when I'm holding you close like this, there's nothing bad in the world." But ever since she died, reality had come along and shaken me to the core. Who was going to protect me now? Death existed for me and for my loved ones. During the day I could push it out, but at night, with my sister suffering right across the room, there was no escape. Only, I didn't know what the fear was that terrified me so, only that some unnamed terror had me in its grip and there was no one I could explain it to, no one who knew that I lived in this constant state of dread. After all, I was the *well* one.

I climbed up into my father's lap and curled there, my head on his chest, his arm around me.

"Want to tell Daddy what's wrong?" He could be so wonderfully sweet. All the times he'd rescued me from demons in my sleep, and gotten up in the night with Steffani when she was in pain, and taken us to Coney Island and on the Ferris wheel, and given me piggyback rides when I was younger came rushing back, bringing a lump to my throat.

Suddenly, I couldn't hold back any longer and burst into tears. "I can't say it," I cried.

"Go on, honey." He held me while I sobbed. "You'll feel better, I promise."

"I have to know, but I'm scared to."

He didn't say anything, waiting.

But try as I might, I couldn't put into words what I feared; it was too fearsome, too threatening. And probably too complex.

I could feel his arms stiffen around me. It felt as if he was trying not to cry, too. I was reminded of the time when I was three and overheard someone in the cloakroom at nursery school saying Jews were bad. "Are they?" I'd asked my father. And he'd explained to me that my school friend was only repeating what she'd heard at home.

"Some people don't like Jews, honey," he explained.

"Why?" I wanted to know.

"Because they don't know any better. They need someone to blame for all the problems in the world. In fact, many Jews are being put into camps in Europe right now just for that reason." I knew there was a war on, but even though I was smart, I didn't quite understand about Hitler, or people being killed by bombs. It was too horrible even to think about.

Then he told me I was a Jew, and he was too, and so was Mommy, and all of our family. And none of us were bad, were we? I had such a look of surprise on my face.

"You mean I'm one of those people they're writing about in the news?"

And he nodded. "Don't you remember Passover, and High Holidays, and Hanukkah? Those are Jewish holidays." I hadn't made the connection until now. And for some reason that made me smile. I loved him with all my heart, so anyone who was like him, or me, or Mommy, had to be wonderful. Shortly after that, he enrolled me in religious school.

"Are you worried about Steffani?" he guessed. I nodded. "She's only going to have an operation."

"But she's so sick all the time. And she cries, and I can't help her very much."

"You help more than you know," he assured me. "But the doctors say she might outgrow this condition. As she gets bigger and her bones stop growing, the pain will probably go away."

It made sense. Everyone had heard of growing pains. And no adult had them. His words of comfort and his arms round me made the amorphous terror lose an edge of its hold on my soul, if only for the moment. "I'm going to miss her when she's in the hospital. Can I go and visit her?"

"No," he told me. "Children aren't allowed in the hospital."

"But what about the ones who are sick and having operations? They're allowed to be there. What if she's gone two weeks? Who will I play with?"

"You'll just have to be a big girl and be patient, and soon the time will pass and Steffani will be home again."

"Can she play with me then?" *With limits, with limits*, I repeated to myself.

"Not for a while. She'll have to recover."

It was about what I'd expected. I felt my eyes beginning to get heavy.

"Would you like to go back to bed now?"

"I'm afraid I'll keep *thinking*."

"About what?"

"Nothing." That squirmy, frightened feeling was pressing on me inside again.

"Would you like me to go with you?"

Timidly, I nodded.

My father got up from the chair, still holding me in his arms, and started to carry me back into my room. On the way we passed the living room, where my mother was reading a novel, and she looked up. I could tell she was annoyed that I wasn't asleep yet, but my father shook his head, and she didn't say anything. Then, my father carried me, his big daughter, like a little girl, back to bed. Still, I wasn't ready for sleep.

"Daddy, why did God make Steffani sick?"

"God didn't do that, sweetheart, it just happened."

"But God can make her well with a miracle, can't he?"

My father paused before answering and by that I knew I wouldn't like his answer. I wanted to pull the blankets up over my face, but instead I lay there quietly, waiting.

"God does work miracles, but not the way you think. He works them through us. I believe that all the doctors who take care of Steffani, who do research on her disease, who try to help her and others like her, are performing God's work. And maybe someday there will be a miracle and someone will find a cure for her."

I was deeply disappointed. I'd wanted him to say that if we prayed hard enough and were good enough, God would perform a miracle and make her well, not, God works his miracles through man. What about the Red Sea? I wanted to ask. God did a miracle then, why not now? The way my mother complained about the doctors it was hard to believe they were doing God's work.

"Did you say there are others like Steffani?" This was a new concept for me. "She's not the only one with Gaucher's?"

"No, of course not." His hand on my cheek was so huge it covered the whole side of my face.

"Those poor people," I said, wondering how I had escaped. "We should pray that they get well."

"It would be better to pray for the strength and courage to help Steffani when she needs us, not for favors from God. You wouldn't ask God to bring you a pony, would you?"

I laughed, but I felt my cheeks grow hot. One Hanukkah, years ago, I had prayed for a pony.

The next day, I asked my mother, "Do you believe in God?"

She was preoccupied making potato salad to have in the refrigerator for when Steffani was in the hospital.

"Sometimes I don't know. When I see what people go through it makes me very angry with God."

"Me too," I confessed, trembling slightly, afraid some huge hand would sweep across the kitchen and strike me down. The aroma of hard-boiled eggs overpowered the kitchen, making my stomach contract hungrily.

My mother turned to me then. She was wearing her apron with the pink roses on it that Aunt Anna had made, one hand on her hip, the other holding the chopping knife up like a scepter. "But God has nothing to do with whether or not we do our best, Suzanne. No matter how difficult life may seem, you can be anything in this world you want to be. If you work hard enough, you can do anything you want. You've been born with very special talents. You're beautiful and smart and full of personality. You stand out. Not everybody has what you have. Whatever you set your mind to do, you can do."

Even though it was not what I had asked her about, her words filled me with a joyous excitement. I saw myself up in the clouds on a golden staircase, as a sort of larger-than-life movie star. But then, I had to ask.

"Can Steffani be anything she wants to be, too?"

My mother had gone back to her chopping, this time onions. Maybe it was the onions that made her eyes water, but probably not. "Steffani is special too, though at times she aggravates me like crazy." She gave me a conspiratorial smile. We often allied with one another when Steffani was being stubborn. "And yes, if she wasn't sick, she could be anything she wanted to be too. Maybe someday she won't be sick anymore."

"I guess, until then, I'll have to be something for both of us," I said, feeling slightly triumphant that I could do what my sister couldn't. But then I felt suffocated by my thoughts. How could I be anything in life, if she couldn't; how could I enjoy that? A hot rage boiled up in my stomach and I forced it back. *It's not fair*, I wanted to scream, and my mother saw my expression. I had to hide it from her because it made her furious with me if I got angry with my sister. She'd say things like, "How dare you pick on her, let her have your doll for God's sake, you're so selfish, she's not going to hurt it. Don't you know how much she suffers? How can you be so mean?" And I knew she was right; I was hateful. But, sometimes I just couldn't help it.

Years later, I realized that my mother too had her own rage and resentment for what the intrusion of Steffani's illness did to all our lives, but she couldn't tolerate her feelings of rage against a sick child and so she suppressed them. Therefore, if she saw them in me, she had to squelch my feelings with fervor, lest they cause her own to erupt and pour over all of us, like the scalding waters of the Sister Kenny packs.

The next day, Steffani went to the hospital; she took my Sparkle Plenty doll with her. And the day after that was her operation. Every time I tried to eat, I threw up. In school, the nurse's office wanted to send me home, but they couldn't reach my parents, who were at the hospital with my sister, so I stayed in school. That night, my father called me and told me she was all right. The operation was over and it was a success. He sounded happy, and I'm sure he was relieved, but I heard a kind of anguish in his voice when he said, "It's a good thing she had the operation, Suzanne. Did you know that a spleen in a normal child weighs about two and a half ounces? And when they removed Steffani's spleen it weighed nearly three pounds."

Later that night, alone in the house with the housekeeper, who was in her room behind the kitchen, I eventually managed to fall asleep. But I still couldn't eat. By the time Steffani came home from the hospital, I too had lost three pounds.

Shortly after her surgery we moved again, only this time to California, which caused that sick feeling inside of me to grow even stronger. My father's business was based in the East, and my mother argued that his business would suffer and he'd have to travel more. My father won, because his family was in California and he wanted Steffani to live in a warmer climate. My uncle Sid and aunt Martha had moved there too, he pointed out to my mother, and it was a good idea to unite the family. With that, my mother agreed. Families were the ones who stood by you and supported you when times were bad. I think the family were the only ones my mother could tell about her troubles. With friends, who were often my father's clients, she and my father had to keep up a front and pretend to be as strong and beautiful as ever. They rarely confided in anyone about the status of my father's business, which was only good part of the time, or my sister's illness. I begged not to have to move. I hated the idea of moving, I would miss my friends. And the thought of going so far away only increased my sense of anxiety. Something bad was sure to happen now.

We bought a two-story house in California, a French Normandy style with a circular drive and a turret that made it look like a castle, but I still shared a room with my sister. Part of the time I hated sharing a room with her, and other times I liked it. Since she'd gotten older, I only felt that tenderness and fierce loyalty I'd felt toward her when she was a baby whenever she was sick. The rest of the time, her presence in my life enraged me. I'd be mean to her when no one was around, refuse to play with her and boss her, even hit her, and then hate myself for acting that way. But a rage toward her would grip me sometimes and I'd lash out at her in violent ways, which made her cry. I'd vow each time never to do it again, but when the next time came, I couldn't help it.

While I was in grammar school in California, there were two incidents that stand out. In one of them, my big-sister-overprotectiveness allowed me to be a heroine. In the other one, I wasn't.

"Will you close the bathroom door?" I asked. "The light from the bathroom window is shining in my eyes."

"Close it yourself," Steffani replied. She was half-asleep.

"Now!" I insisted, bullying her, grabbing the opportunity to exercise control and prove who was boss.

It was February and freezing in our bedroom. I didn't want to get out of a warm bed and cross the cold hardwood floor so I could darken the room and fall asleep comfortably. Tomorrow was Saturday, and in the morning the sunlight from the bathroom window would awaken me. On the other hand, Steffani's bed was on the same wall as the bathroom door; she could get to it by crawling to the end of her bed and reaching out, so she ought to close the door. Again, whenever the two of us were at odds, that terrible anger would assail me and all my good-girl behavior would disappear. Of course, I remembered the way Jasmine and Marilyn had been and at these times I felt like them.

"Leave me alone," came the reply. "I'm sleeping."

"I'll never play jacks with you as long as I live," I threatened. "Or let you sit on my side of the car." We always divided up the backseat and I insisted on sitting behind our mother, a much sought-after prize.

"You promised," she whined.

I had promised, but I was capable of treachery. "Too bad," I said.

"Suzanne, you're impossible," she insisted, repeating what she'd heard our parents say about me countless times. She sat up in bed. "I'm not closing the door." She crossed her hands in front of her chest and thrust out her chin. In her stubborn mode nobody could be as inflexible as Steffani. Except me. My temper nearly exploded, with my need to get my way growing all out of proportion.

"Do as I say, now!" I tried for the parental tone of authority. "Crawl down to the end of the bed and close the door. You don't have to get up to do it."

"I'll have to get out of the covers and it's cold in here." She was wearing a flannel nightgown with ruffles at the shoulders and little bears on it; her hair was in braids. But I was immune to her adorableness. "You always want me to do favors for you."

"And what about me?" My voice was shrill, accusing. "I tell you stories. I sit with you when you're sick—and you're always sick."

"I can't help it." Her lower lip quivered and I nearly lost my anger, but not quite.

"I gave you my Sparkle Plenty doll when you had your splenectomy."

"That was ages ago."

The monster within me growled forth and I threatened to

hate her forever. But she resisted. And the more she resisted the harder I fought. If only I could let this go, but at moments like these I had to win. So many times I had to be good to her when I didn't want to, defer to her, understand, and swallow every objection I ever had. My needs were so mundane compared to hers. I don't remember how long it took that night. What seemed like hours was probably twelve minutes. Until finally, slowly, I wore her down.

She climbed out of the covers, crawled to the end of her bed, and reached out for the door.

"I can't reach," she said. "I'll fall."

"No you won't!" I insisted, unwilling to let up for a moment with victory within my grasp. The heady feeling of winning, of getting something back, spurred me on. "Just stretch a little more." The room was only twelve feet wide, the door not that far away from me; by now I could easily have gotten up. But I wouldn't consider it.

She stretched again and nearly fell. "I can't do it." She was close to tears and looked at me for reprieve. But I had been taught by experts, such as Jasmine, what to do. "Yes you can," I said, with authority. "Lie down on your stomach and try once more."

She did. And almost made it, but not quite.

"You'd better do it, or else!" I threatened, growing so tough and menacing no one could have denied me, least of all a little sister who truly wanted to please. Sometimes she drew me pictures at school, or saved me half of her cupcake just to show how special to her I was. But I wasn't thinking about that now.

Finally, she got up on her hands and knees, reached way out for the door, and fell out of bed.

Her screams woke the house. Her arm was broken. Gaucher's disease may have made her bones brittle, but her broken arm was my fault.

"Your sister is in the principal's office," Susan Brown told me with a gloating look on her face.

"I don't believe you," I said.

"See for yourself." She tossed her head, obviously thrilled to be bringing the great Suzanne Blacker, teacher's pet, down a peg. "I heard about it from Leanne, who saw your sister going in there before recess. She was crying."

I flew to Mrs. George's office. The principal was a gray-haired, ancient woman of at least fifty. She ruled the school with an imperious attitude, handing down pronouncements to her "*flock,*" as she called us. The school was in a suburban neighborhood, two teachers per grade. Steffani was in the second, I was in the sixth, and I was feeling quite mature these days. I'd be going to junior high in the fall.

I came into the outer office where the switchboard was located and the teachers' boxes. There was a counter that in other schools used to be too tall for me to see over. Now it came just above my waist. Mrs. Lyons, the school secretary, an underpaid, overworked person whose job it was to answer the telephones, call the parents whenever necessary, write the daily bulletins, and do whatever else it took to run the school, glanced at me with sympathy, then nodded toward the ante-room outside Mrs. George's door. Steffani was sitting there on the bench, her legs too short to reach the floor. One of her shoelaces was untied. She was crying. Her head hung down to her chest; her plump arms were folded in her lap. She was wearing a blue dress with a bow that tied in back at the waist, and a white V-shaped bib in front. Her tears had stained the lap of her blue dress a darker color.

"Steff?" I said, quietly, sitting down next to her and putting my arm around her. She leaned into me and cried so that her body shook.

"It wasn't my fault. Mrs. Pruner hates me."

That was impossible. Nobody could hate her. She was the sweetest, most beautiful, most endearing child in the world. I flashed on a picture of Mrs. Pruner, who looked just like her name, a bony, long-faced woman with dark hair pulled back into a chignon. The most distinctive thing about her was that she applied her lipstick with her fingertip so that her lips never had any definite edge to them, as though she didn't want to admit to wearing lipstick at all. I hadn't gone to this school in the second grade, so I'd never had Mrs. Pruner as a teacher and didn't know what she was like.

"Helen was talking," Steffani explained as she cried, "and she kept turning around to talk to me and I kept shushing her. But Mrs. Pruner said it was my fault. She said I've been absent too much this semester and that's why I'm behind, and now I'm disrupting the class. I can't help it if I'm absent. I try to do my schoolwork at home, but you know," she whispered through her tears, "it's hard when I have an attack." She was whispering because she didn't want anyone to know exactly why she was absent. Since our parents didn't talk about her illness to anyone outside the family, neither did we. Our parents said it was nobody's business, that other people wouldn't understand. Besides, my mother was concerned that people might treat Steffani differently if they knew she had something that didn't go away and kept recurring. She wanted Steffani to be treated just like the other kids. So whenever Steffani was out of school, her excuse notes said she'd had the flu.

Steffani was terrified of being reprimanded by Mrs. George. Good children always feel the shame of that sort of thing, knowing they are letting down parents who don't deserve to be let down. I knew Steffani was a talker, and sometimes didn't pay attention in school. But I also knew what she went through, how brave she was, and how much she suffered. Surely, allowances should be made. Never before had I felt such a fierce protectiveness.

"She's a very mean person," Steffani said, trying to stop crying, but she couldn't. "If I was a teacher when I grow up, I would be nice to the kids."

"What's the worst thing she can say to you?" I asked.

"That I'm bad," Steffani sobbed.

"But you're not, honey. You're good. You're very good. Mrs. Pruner made a mistake. Maybe I can talk to her."

The idea of facing a furious teacher and pleading my sister's case terrified me. But it was less painful than seeing how upset she was.

"Would you talk to her?" My sister turned her huge tear-filled blue eyes on me. "Will you tell her I'm sorry, and I'll be really good from now on, and I won't talk to Helen ever again except at lunch."

I handed her the clean cotton handkerchief from my pocket and she blew her nose.

"I'll talk to her right now," I said, getting up before I lost my nerve.

"No!" Now her terror was even greater. "Don't leave me alone."

"Honey, recess is almost over. The bell is going to ring and I can't be tardy. You want me to talk to Mrs. Pruner, don't you?"

She nodded, torn between the two worst things. Having to face Mrs. Pruner without my talking to her, or having to face Mrs. George alone.

"Listen," I said, trying to put that cheerful tone in my voice our mother used. "Mrs. George isn't so bad. She's not going to do anything to you, I promise. And if you're still upset, I'll see you at lunch. I'll even try to get out of class before lunch and come see you. I'll wave at you through the door to see if you're all right. Can you be brave just until lunch? And then we can be together. I'll eat my lunch with you and I'll give you another hug and you won't be so sad then, okay? And after lunch, you only have an hour before you go home."

"Mom's gonna be so mad."

"No she's not," I assured her, not knowing how our mother would react. One thing I did know, that being good, following orders, doing what you were supposed to do was expected of us at all times.

The clock was moving toward the end of recess and I really had to speak to Mrs. Pruner, make her understand how special my sister was, and how unfair she was being.

I gave her a kiss and wiped her eyes. "Here's what I want you to say to Mrs. George." She was looking at me as though

I was her entire world and all I wanted to do was keep her from having to go through this. "Tell her right away that you're sorry, even before she has a chance to say, 'Steffani, I'm quite disappointed in you.' " I imitated Mrs. George's expression and voice. Steffani gave a little smile. "Say that you understand you were disrupting the class, and that it's very difficult for a teacher to teach when that happens."

She nodded, taking it all in. I asked her to repeat it, which she did perfectly. She was beginning to understand the procedure. For once, her amazing ability to mimic me was coming in handy. "Tell her you want to go back to class and that it won't happen again. And say this, 'I assure you ' When kids use those grown-up words, everyone's impressed," I told her. She nodded again. I could see the wheels turning even though she was still terribly frightened.

I was just about out the door when her little quavering voice called to me, "Suze, what if I cry?" Already her lower lip was trembling again and her eyes were filling with tears.

I turned and smiled. "It's okay if you cry, as long as you apologize like you mean it, even if it wasn't your fault, and say, 'I assure you.' Keep my handkerchief just in case. I'll come back at lunch and talk to Mrs. George too."

Just then, Mrs. George opened her door and saw Steffani on the bench, where all misbehaving students sat. I was still standing in the doorway. "Yes?" she asked, making a point that I had no business here. "Did Mrs. Pruner send you?" she asked my sister.

I watched my little sister push herself off the bench and walk over to Mrs. George's door. "Yes, ma'am," she said, her voice quivering again. "I was talking."

"Well come in," she said, waving me away. I wanted to go in with her, hold her hand, make the speech myself; she was such a little girl. But Mrs. George waved me away. And just as I left to go talk to Mrs. Pruner, I heard my sister's baby voice saying, "I came to apologize for disrupting the class, Mrs. George. I know how difficult it is for a teacher when that happens. I assure you, it won't happen again."

And that's when I burst into tears.

* * *

Eventually it felt as though we'd always lived in California and that Steffani had always been sick, though her illness affected each of us differently.

For instance, my parents lost their tempers with one another more often now and pulled me into their fights. I learned how to circumvent their moods by altering my own depending on the circumstances. Like Emily in *Our Town*, who chose an ordinary birthday to relive, only to find that it was extremely significant in the scope of her life, ordinary days were significant for me too.

One Sunday morning in particular, I remember standing outside the bathroom door listening to my father singing as he shaved, relieved that he was in a good mood.

"Look for the silver lining. Whenever clouds appear in the blue."

I could hear the sound of the water running in between verses as he scraped off his beard and then rinsed his razor. I needed someone to quiz me for my history exam tomorrow, so if I started asking him now, maybe he'd get around to it by evening. He wasn't exactly slow, just methodical. Besides, his mind was on other things: Steffani had been sick all week.

I called through the door. "Daddy. Will you help me with my homework after you shave? I'm going to the movies with Karl in an hour." There was a double bill at the La Reina, Errol Flynn and Dana Andrews, and that would take up most of the day. I wouldn't be sorry to leave my sister sick in bed at home.

"Hold your horses," he called out.

My mother's voice right behind me startled me. "Burt, for God's sake, hurry up. We've got to get those bulbs planted today or they won't come up this spring. You don't have to look gorgeous to work in the garden."

We heard the water shut off and a moment later the door opened. My father stood there, a towel wrapped around his waist, his hairless chest pink from his shower, his hair wet and carefully combed, his face newly smooth, smelling of after-shave. He looked so clean. But the sight of him undressed embarrassed me and filled me with curiosity. I was dying to know what was under that towel.

My mother's hands were on her hips. "You've been in the bathroom for an hour. Now you're going to drive the children to Sherman Oaks, another twenty minutes at least. When were you expecting to work in the yard?" I hated it when she found fault with him; he'd just yell back at her. If I knew what was coming, why didn't she?

"I'll get to it, Lynnette. For Christ's sake." He started to raise his voice. "This is my one day off, will you let me alone? I'll get to it!"

"That's what you always say." Her voice rose to keep up with his. Her temper was shorter than his. "You're not the only one who works hard around here. I take care of the house and the children, and you know what taking care of Steffani means. Can't you help me in the yard? Is that too much to ask?" Her voice rose with each statement, her body grew more tense as she glared at him.

He moved over to his closet and stepped inside. I couldn't see him dressing, though I tried without making it too obvious.

"Daddy." I tried not to sound desperate, but it came out that way. My parents' attention was a precious commodity, one I vied for all the time. My sister usually won. And if this deteriorated into a real fight, it could ruin the whole day. "You promised to help me with my homework." Homework took precedence over planting flower bulbs in my father's agenda. But if Steffani needed him, that would take precedence over everything. And she might, at any minute. Both my mother and I knew that only too well.

"Stay out of this, Suzanne," my mother declared with exaggerated emphasis. "Your father will help you with your homework later. We have planting to do. And don't give me that look! You should be helping me too instead of going to the movies. How many people do you think get to live in a house like this with a garden and a front lawn?"

The count-your-blessings lecture never changed my opinion, I still didn't like gardening. The only reason I got out of it was that my sister couldn't do it, so they didn't make me either.

"*Luz em sei frieden*," my father said in Yiddish: *Leave them alone*. And my expression brightened. The lines had now been drawn, him and me against her. But I didn't want to choose sides—the advantage could shift too readily.

"Don't tell me that," she shouted, her fists clenched. "You're the one who dragged her into this."

"How did I do that?" he insisted.

"By letting her go to the movies instead of helping me the way I asked you to do."

"Maybe we should have a gardener," I suggested, wanting to appease and knowing I shouldn't have said it.

"Ask your father why we don't," my mother said, her tone loaded with censure.

He glared at her as if to say, *How dare you bring this up now in front of Suzanne*.

But I knew my mother dared. There wasn't much sacred within our house that my parents didn't fight about these days, and in front of us. Even though the rule was: Fight about it here, but never tell anyone else our business.

She said things like: "You're the one who *had* to move to California when there are no classical performers on the West Coast. That's why we can't afford a gardener."

And he said things like: "Every time I try to talk to you, you're talking to that goddamned Dr. Levinson." (My sister's orthopedist.)

And she'd reply: "Don't you dare speak about him that way. The man literally saved our lives."

"Okay, okay." My father turned to me. "You're glad we moved to California, aren't you Suzanne?"

I didn't dare say anything. I wasn't glad we'd moved. It had meant getting used to another new house and another new school, starting all over again with friends, finding out who was popular and who wasn't, who would accept me and who wouldn't. And of course, no matter where we lived Steffani was always sick. I found new excuses to explain her absences and new reasons for why my attendance was not always reliable either at after-school functions or Saturday birthday parties. For if my mother had to take care of my sister, I couldn't go to a party, no matter how badly I wanted to or how it affected my new tenuous social life.

"Mommy, don't be mad. I'll stay home and help you in the garden." I would have done anything to make things right again; somehow this fight was all my fault.

"No you won't," my father insisted. "I don't want her working on a Sunday, Lynnette. I told her she could go to the movies and that I'd help you garden," my father shouted. "I stand by my word, for God's sake. Why do you have to keep harping on this over and over."

"I'm not the one harping on it, you are. If we can't afford a gardener the least you can do is help me!" She started to cry.

"Oh for Christ's sake, you always cry and make me out the heavy. Well, I'm not the heavy here. Am I, Suzanne?"

"No, Daddy," I said, feeling tears coming to my eyes too. The only thing I wanted in the whole world was for them to stop yelling at each other and have everything be all right again.

My mother used to be nicer to my father. I noticed it, and he complained about it. He blamed it on her photography hobby, something she'd learned to do in California. Having a car of her own and being able to drive gave her more freedom. Whenever my sister wasn't sick Mother was rarely at home; she'd be out taking pictures. Often, she came home late in the evenings after dark, and I'd be sitting there watching for her headlights, terrified that something had happened to her. My father didn't like not knowing where she was during the day. Recently, people had hired her to take pictures of newborn babies and children's birthday parties, but if my sister was sick, my mother had to cancel the jobs, which truly frustrated her. Not only was Steffani sick and in pain, but my mother couldn't do what she wanted to do, either. My father

called my mother's photography "her little pictures," and
made light of it whenever she had to cancel a session to stay
at home. But I knew how it felt to have to cancel an activity
because of Steffani.

"My photography could work into something steady," she
pleaded.

"I hate that goddamned smelly developing solution," he
yelled. But I think he really objected to her spending time
away from the family.

"If I had my own business, we might be able to afford a
cleaning woman, and certainly a gardener," she threw at him
now.

"Haven't I always provided for you? I resent what you're
implying," he shouted back again, so infuriated I was afraid
something bad might happen.

"Daddy, please don't yell like that," I said, turning from
one to the other.

"Yelling makes him feel more powerful. He doesn't care
who he frightens."

I was crying, and wiped the mucus from my nose with my
sleeve.

"You see what you've done," my mother said, holding
out her arms to me. I felt guilty letting her console me. I was
choosing her side.

"You always put your two cents in, Suzanne. From now
on you can stay out of it." My father felt betrayed and his
anger twisted the pain inside of me.

"You were the one who brought her in," my mother
screamed, all patience lost now.

And just then the phone rang.

I went to answer it, glad for the interruption. Until I heard
who it was. This would make matters worse. They waited,
staring at me.

"Well?" my father said.

"It's Dr. Levinson, for Mom."

"Oh fine!" my father said. "Perfect timing! Go on,
Lynnette, leave in the middle of a fight and talk to your

precious Dr. Levinson who never does anything wrong. And that's another thing I'm sick of, hearing Dr. Levinson's opinion on everything. He's the authority, the final word, isn't he? I told you those goddamned Sister Kenny packs weren't doing any good and we should find something else, but did you listen to me? Only when Levinson suggests ice packs, you think he's a genius." My father's anger was growing to an even more furious pitch over the subject of Dr. Levinson. Though he was nice to Dr. Levinson in person, there was something about the doctor that upset him. I'd watch him shake Dr. Levinson's hand, discuss Steffani's condition, as cordial as could be, and never say the things to his face that he said behind the doctor's back.

My mother held the receiver against her body, motioning for us to be quiet. My father shouted, "I won't be quiet now. We're in the middle of an argument, tell him to call back."

"I can't do that, Burt." My mother's anguish went straight to my heart. "I've been trying to reach him for days. He's taking time out on Sunday to call me, I have to talk to him now."

"Hello, Dr. Levinson," she said, in her best parent-of-the-patient voice. "I'm sorry to bother you, but I had some questions about Steffani's medication. I've been giving her one and a half pills twice a day when the pain is worse, but it doesn't seem to help. Can I increase it?" She waited for his reply.

"I'll bet he doesn't do the gardening on Sunday," my father said, making his voice only a bit lower; we gave each other a conspiratorial look.

"Okay, I'll increase her dosage by half a pill every six hours instead of eight," she said, ignoring my father. "And thank you so much for calling."

"Didn't I tell you to do that?" my father asked, belligerently.

"You're not the doctor," she replied, her anger erupting again.

"Too bad for you," he shouted, stomping out.

"Where are you going?" she screamed, venting frustration and making sure he could hear her.

"To plant some goddamned bulbs before I drive Suzanne to the movies. Come on, Suzanne," he shouted to me. "We'll talk about history, while you help me plant bulbs for an hour, and then we'll go."

I followed meekly after him wondering why my parents' fights were so much worse in California. Maybe it was because my sister hadn't gotten any better. The only thing that was different in California was that here we had Dr. Levinson. And as much as he helped my sister, his presence stirred things up.

The residue of their fight still lingered, making my stomach churn and my head pound. My sister had been in the throes of a painful attack for five days now, and I was worried about my history test tomorrow. But in one hour I would be in a darkened theater next to my friend Karl, with a box of popcorn in my hand, and maybe some jujubes, lost in the magic of the movies. My sister's pain, my parents' fight, and Dr. Levinson's impact on our family would be far behind me.

CHAPTER NINE

"Hiya, Dave," my father said, shaking hands with Dave Chasen as he came up to our table in the green room where all the celebrities sat. "You remember Lynnette?"

Dave Chasen, the owner of Chasen's, remembered my mother, though she commented that few of my father's business associates ever paid her much attention.

"And this is my famous daughter, the author." The restaurateur smiled at me politely. "And my three grandchildren."

Burt introduced each of the children in a row next to my mother. "We're waiting for my other daughter," he explained.

"I hear it's a celebration tonight." Dave Chasen was a short, thin man with dark hair and dark bushy eyebrows, rather unglamorous for someone who entertained the Hollywood elite in his establishment. His wife, Maude, was the pretty one, with well-coiffed strawberry blond hair and an expensive-looking black dress. Both of them were in their restaurant every night greeting their customers, keeping everything running smoothly. My father and Dave Chasen went way back.

"It's my papa's seventieth birthday," Jered offered, thinking this was okay to say. Amy gave him a look, but my father didn't mind. He was proud of his age and I didn't blame him; he didn't look a day over sixty. Sitting next to him on his left, I thought he was as handsome as ever in spite of the fleshier look of his softened chin line and eyelids. His sideburns were gray, but he had all his hair. Tonight, he wore black-rimmed glasses of an Italian design, the kind Cary Grant wore, a shocking pink silk printed tie, and navy suit. More than distinguished, he was rakish. And my mother, in the booth on my father's right, looked wonderful too, certainly better than Myrna Loy or Jane Wyman, her contemporaries, but then she was prettier than either of them. Tonight, her hair was styled into a high wave over her forehead while the rest curled around her face; for the last several years she'd been dying it a lighter shade of auburn than was her natural color. Her face, like my father's, was slightly rounder than it used to be, but she'd hardly aged at all. The black dress she wore tonight, festooned with a splash of red roses down the front, flattered her figure. She was wearing her aunt Anna's diamond necklace.

"You don't look seventy, Burt," Dave Chasen said enviously as he walked away. "We'll take good care of you," he promised. The head waiter took notice of their exchange and I knew we'd get special attention.

My mother gave me a worried look. "How are you, honey? Are you all right?"

I knew instantly. "Steffani told you, didn't she?" I was more exasperated than angry. I'd sworn Steffani to secrecy so my parents wouldn't worry.

"She didn't mean to," my mother said, protecting her.

"Yes, I'm all right. It's just some stupid joke, I'm sure. Let's not talk about it, okay?"

"You mean the plagiarism thing?" Amy said.

"You know too?" my mother said, giving me a look that said, *You told them and not me*?

"Lynnette, stay out of it," my father cautioned, patting my leg as if to say, *You know how she is*.

"That's not what you said in the car on the way over here," she retorted. "You were ready to hire a detective yourself."

"I can't help it if I worry about my children." He was embarrassed that she'd brought it up and defensive at the same time. He often blustered when he was embarrassed.

Just then, we saw my sister coming toward us dressed like Titania from *A Midsummer Night's Dream* in a bottle-green velvet empire-style dress trimmed at the neck, cuffs, and hemline with antique paisley and crocheted lace.

"Sorry I'm late," she sighed, sinking into the corner seat we'd left open for her in the green leather booth. "I thought you said Perino's and I went all the way there and found out you had no reservation."

"You never listen," my mother said. "I told you Chasen's."

"It's all right, she's here now," my father said, reaching over me to kiss her and motioning to the waiter that we were ready to order.

We made our selections and Steffani said, "Happy birthday, Dad," handing him a package that could only have held a tie or handkerchief. Knowing Steffani, it would not be ordinary. I had bought my father a maroon velour pullover shirt with a knitted collar.

"So what's new?" my sister asked me pointedly.

I sighed. "Nothing's new and nothing more has happened, so can we drop it?"

"Everybody knows," Miles said, and Jered nodded wisely.

My father sipped his scotch and water. "What are you doing about this, Suzanne? You can't let it affect your career. I've seen scandals ruin people's lives. I wouldn't want that to happen to you."

"It's not going to be a scandal, Dad," I said. "It's only one letter."

"Who do you think would be doing such a thing?" my mother asked. "It's got to be someone who's jealous of you!" Her standard answer for everything. My sister and I gave each other a smile.

"That's what I've been wondering," Amy said. "In Agatha Christie, Hercule Poirot is always hypothecating over people's motives."

"Hypothesizing," Steffani corrected.

"You don't think it's my dad, do you?" Miles asked quietly.

"Of course not," I assured him. "Anybody who hurts me, hurts you too, and he'd never do that." But it had crossed my mind. I'd rejected it, of course. Alex could never be so diabolical, so disturbed; at least I didn't think so.

"Well, what are you doing about it?" my mother pressed.

"I've spoken to the police, but they weren't very helpful. They said it's nearly impossible to track down. Anybody can get stationery from a publishing company and write a letter on it. It's a civil matter, not criminal—at least not yet. If anyone could help me it would be the New York police. But when I called the New York police they said it was a California matter."

"So nobody wants to deal with it?" my father commented. "Typical."

"I had an appointment with a lawyer yesterday."

"What kind of lawyer?" my father asked.

"Copyright."

"Why didn't you ask me? I know every lawyer in this town."

"He came highly recommended," I assured him.

"What did he say?" Steffani asked.

I told them what Barry had said about hiring a detective.

"You're not just going to leave it to others to find out who's doing this, are you?" my mother asked.

"No," I insisted. "I can't sleep at night thinking of ways I might help myself. Wondering who could want to hurt me this way."

"Can people just do things like that, Mom?" Miles asked. "Make up stuff about another person, lie about them and get away with it?"

"They're not going to get away with it, Miles. Eventually we'll find out who it is. The person probably wants me to know."

"But how?" Amy asked. "How are you supposed to find out who's doing it?" Amy looked as if she was about to cry.

I was filled with fury toward my unknown tormentor, this vile person who was not only hurting me, but my family as well.

"I'm going to the library on Monday and look up all the printers and typesetters in the New York City phone books. Then, I'll send them Xerox copies of the material I received to see if any of them did the work."

"That's really neat detective work, Mom." Jered smiled.

My mother asked, "Couldn't the typesetting have been done in any city in the country? What makes you think it's New York?"

"It was postmarked from New York."

"That doesn't mean anything," Steffani said.

She was right, of course. It did seem hopeless. But I could not let this person, whoever they were, just do this to me without a fight.

"If you need any help, I'll do what I can," my mother offered.

"We both will," my father said.

Just then, I noticed an odd look on my father's face, as though he'd just eaten something disagreeable. But we'd all enjoyed our salads and the toasted cheese crisps they'd served with our drinks. The people at the next table began craning their necks the way they do when a celebrity enters the room. I heard my mother say, "Wouldn't you know."

Amy, who could see who was behind me, announced, "It's Aunt Gloria!"

My heart sank. My ex-sister-in-law, the opera star, and my father's ex-client, was the last person I wanted to see. From the expression on my father's face, he didn't want to see her either. Neither did my sister, because Gloria was with George Ruben.

"Are you still seeing him?" I whispered to my sister.

She replied, with her own facial expression and a shrug of her shoulders, "We're just friends."

Whatever that meant it certainly intrigued me.

I could feel Gloria's eyes boring into my back. I was not one of her favorite people ever since I'd divorced her brother Alex; in the past few years she'd stopped being one of mine. Her presence in this restaurant, tonight of all nights, put a damper on our spirits.

The children didn't know what to do. They could see how uncomfortable we were. My father especially, as though she'd done this on purpose. But then, she couldn't have known where we were going to celebrate tonight. My father and Gloria had parted professional company some months ago and I wondered about it. Even though he'd assured me it had nothing to do with Alex and me, that we were old news, why else would she have left him? My father's business was much more established than it used to be, but still the loss of a major client was never easy.

"Aren't we going to say hello?" Jered asked, making it even worse.

"Oh, you know Aunt Gloria," Amy said, being the diplomat. "When she's in the spotlight, she's not interested in family." A truthful, if unflattering assessment.

Jered raised his hand and waved at his aunt. I saw the happy light in the eyes of my parents and sister fading as they watched to see what she'd do. Either Gloria could ignore Jered's greeting and hurt an innocent child, or come over and embarrass us all.

She approached.

Everybody at the next table stared.

"Hello, hello." Gloria had a way of swooping; partly because she was tall, with all that long dark hair, but mostly because it was more dramatic. Her eyelashes batted at us, her ruby smile glowed. She was behind my chair, which faced into the booth, so I had to turn my head around and crane my neck to see her, a disadvantage. Her bosom and cleavage, sparkling in black sequins, leaned over my shoulder.

"Happy birthday, Burt," she said. "Nice to see you, you too, Lynnette, Steffani." She blew kisses to the children. "You all remember George."

We said hello to George and he leaned over to kiss my sister on the cheek. My sister looked as if she'd swallowed the canary. *She is still seeing him*, I thought. *Good for her.* My mother was wearing her pursed-lip smile, which meant it was killing her to be pleasant.

I thought, *Gloria will never change*. And yet, she'd left my father. I never thought she'd do that, she was so dependent on him, had wanted to be his client ever since we were kids.

"It happens to the best of us, daughter," he'd explained to me when he told me Gloria had gotten another manager. "Besides, I'll be making my ten percent on the contracts I booked for her for the next several years."

"I'm really sorry, Dad," I'd told him.

He'd hugged me then in one of his typical sentimental embraces and said, "Honey, in my business nobody lasts forever." I'd let it go.

"How are you, Suzanne?" Gloria asked me, pointedly.

"Never better," I lied.

"I'm so glad." She was being sarcastic. "Have you seen Alex lately?"

"No, why?" I asked.

"Just wondered." It was as if she knew something I didn't. "Well, enjoy your evening." And she was gone.

We sat there, each absorbed in our own thoughts until my mother spoke. "She was friendlier than the last time we saw her, in Santa Fe."

"Is Aunt Gloria mad at us?" Jered asked.

"No," my father assured him. "She's just being loyal to your father, taking his side."

"I hate divorce," Miles said, and reached for his glass of water angrily, spilling it all across the table into my mother's lap. She gasped from the shock of the cold, and shoved at my father.

"Move, Burt, quickly." She pushed him out of the booth so she could escape some of the water cascading over the edge of the table into the booth.

"Stop shoving me, Lynnette. I can't move that fast," he complained.

"But I'm getting soaked over here," she told him, standing up from a puddle of water.

On the other edge of the booth, Steffani got up quickly so Amy and Jered could move out of the way and I tossed my mother some napkins so she could dry herself and the seat as well.

"Oh, Nana, I'm sorry," Miles said, sliding out after them. *Gloria always leaves a wake of disaster*, I thought.

"It's all right," my mother assured him. "It was an accident." She glared at my father as if it were his fault.

Noticing her expression, Jered said, "I'm sure glad I didn't do it."

I hugged him and laughed. "So am I."

Just then, the waiter arrived with our dinners, two busboys hurried over to help dry the booth, and across the room we could hear Gloria's cultured voice dominating the room with her soprano laughter, ha ha ha ha, as though she were singing an aria from *Aïda*.

Everyone slid back into the booth and my mother tried to

smile but we could see she was still upset—we all were, especially Miles.

And then my sister said, "I thought we were celebrating here tonight. Are we going to let a little spilled water get us down?"

"Everybody's in a bad mood," Amy declared.

"Then, we'll just have to get ourselves out of it," Steffani said.

"How?" Jered asked.

"We'll blame Gloria," she said. And we all laughed.

CHAPTER TEN

"Boy it's hot. Boy, oh boy, oh boy."

"Yes, Dad, we're all hot," Lynnette said to Grandpa Henry, turning around in the front seat and pleading with her eyes for him to stop. He'd made that comment every ten minutes for the past several hours and Steffani could see her mother was nearly out of patience. Since they'd passed through Redlands he'd said it every five minutes.

If Grandpa Henry says that once more, I'll scream, Steffani thought, in the backseat. She was wedged in between her sister and Suzanne's friend Gloria on her left. Grandpa Henry was pressed up against her on the right. Her legs were perspiring in her shorts, sticking to the seat of the car, there was sweat running down the back of her neck, and wherever her body touched someone else's it was wet and uncomfortable. All the windows were open, but the air blowing in was dusty and as hot as a blast from a furnace.

"I've never felt heat like this," Grandpa Henry said again. "Huoy," he exhaled, wiping his pink brow with a handkerchief.

"We can stop in Twentynine Palms and have a cold drink, if you like. We'll be there in about a half an hour. Once we get up to the high desert, it's cooler," Burt announced.

"Stop pushing me," Suzanne complained, giving Steffani a shove with her elbow. "You're on my side."

Steffani moved, giving Suzanne as much room as she could by pressing against Grandpa Henry even more. She hated it when Suzanne got annoyed with her. Ever since Suzanne turned fourteen she got annoyed all the time. She was really growing up and Steffani wanted to be like her more than ever. Suzanne was beautiful, with long blond curly hair and green eyes. She had an answer for everything and Steffani loved to listen to her talk about her friends and the boys she liked in school. Steffani liked boys too. It ran in the family. She thought they were usually more interesting than girls. Suzanne had been kissing boys since she was twelve. Steffani decided she'd start at eleven. But that was just next year.

"Don't hit your sister, Suzanne," Lynnette snapped. "You know how she bruises."

"Is it really cooler in the high desert where we're going, Mr. Blacker," Gloria asked, "or are you just saying that to keep us from forming a revolutionary junta back here?"

Steffani laughed. Gloria had such a mouth. That's why her parents objected to Gloria, especially Lynnette. They tolerated her because Suzanne had invited her on this vacation. Lynnette said Gloria was spoiled and a bad influence on Suzanne, who always chose friends who got her into trouble; that Gloria took advantage and needed her mouth washed out with soap. Burt said Gloria was probably just feeling her oats; he liked a girl with spunk, but not too much. However, it was Suzanne's turn to invite a friend along. Steffani had invited Beth the last time when the family went to Balboa Island.

This time they were going to visit Katy Metrano, one of Burt's opera singer clients who was making a western movie in the high desert in a place called Pioneer Town. They were all excited because they'd get to go on the set and see how

movies were made. In this movie, Katy was going to sing
opera in a saloon. It sounded pretty silly, but Burt was happy
about booking one of his singers in a movie. "It's a new field
for me," he said. They all hoped this would bring him more
business, which he always seemed to need, a bone of con-
tention between him and Lynnette.

"A new field? You mean, instead of growing cabbages,
you're branching out into strawberries?" Steffani'd asked,
teasing him.

"I'll give you a *pow*, right in the kisser," Burt had said,
imitating Jackie Gleason. But instead of a *pow* he'd given her
a hug.

Steffani's cotton T-shirt was riding up over her abdomen.
She could feel the slight cooling of air hitting her waist. She
picked up the material and tried to fan herself. But Gloria
was staring, trying to see *it*. The splenectomy scar. Thirteen
inches long from top to bottom, it curved the full length of
her abdomen, from under her right rib, across her stomach,
down to her left hipbone.

She tugged her shirt down and gave Gloria a dirty look.
Nobody was allowed to see *it* unless she chose. Suzanne
noticed what was going on and gave an exasperated sigh,
then glared at Steffani as if to say, *Why don't you let her see
it, for God's sake*?

It had been three years since the operation, but the attacks
hadn't gone away. The doctors said she was better than before, but she didn't think so. Two years ago February she'd
fallen out of bed and broken her arm trying to close the
bathroom door for Suzanne, and last year she'd bumped into
the dining room table and bruised her rib and had gotten
pleurisy from it. But wearing a cast on her arm or having her
lung filled with liquid was nothing compared to her attacks.
They always came on out of the blue. She never got used to
them and tried to ignore the signs, putting off telling her
parents she was in pain until it hurt so badly she couldn't wait
any longer. For whenever she said, "It's starting to hurt
again," her mother's expression of worry and concern made

it worse. Thank heavens Dr. Levinson had prescribed ice packs for the pain in her legs or arms. The freezing cold ice packs made her bones and muscles ache, but it was better than the boiling blankets. Nothing took the pain away, not even the strongest medicine, though it sometimes made her not care that she had it, and sleep a lot. Another thing she hated was having to drink so much liquid when she was sick. Her mother was afraid she'd get dehydrated and the Cokes, Seven-Up, and juices made her stomach feel too full and sloshed around inside.

Someday, when I'm grown up, I'm only going to drink coffee, she promised herself. It must be the most delicious thing in the world because her parents drank it and wouldn't let her have any.

"Will Gloria and Suzanne be able to ride horses by themselves," Lynnette asked, "or will someone have to go with them?"

"I don't know, honey," Burt said, slightly exasperated. He, too, was hot and tired of driving. They'd been on the road for three hours, and had nearly two more to go. "I've never been there, I don't know what to expect."

"Horses?" Steffani said. "Can I go?"

Lynnette gave her a look. "Only if you promise to take the gentlest horse they have, and make it walk the whole time. Can I trust you to do that?"

"Why put temptation in the child's way?" Burt said. "You know it's more dangerous for her if she falls. We don't want her to have another broken arm, do we?"

"Sometimes we have to let her do the things she wants, Burt. She'll be careful, won't you, sweetheart?" Lynnette said. When her parents had opposing opinions, Steffani sided with the one who let her do what she wanted.

"Oh Dad-dy," she said, with exasperation. "I'll be careful."

"Does she *have* to come." Suzanne's fury filled the car and Steffani felt like crying. Again, Suzanne didn't want her along. *Why not*? she wondered. *Am I so bad?* Most of her friends were treated this way by their older sisters or brothers, but none of them seemed to care the way she did. Why didn't Suzanne like her anymore, the way she used to?

"You know she does," Lynnette insisted. "This is a family weekend, Suzanne. If she doesn't go, you don't go."

"Oh gad!" Suzanne huffed, looking at Gloria for commiseration, who was only too glad to give it to her.

"We'll be staying in a cabin that has no electricity," Lynnette explained to Gloria, changing the subject. "It will be an adventure. We'll use Coleman lamps, and a woodburning stove. The same kind I had when I was a little girl." Lynnette was trying to make the best of things. She hadn't wanted to go on this trip with her father and three children. But whenever Burt had a chance to help his business, she'd do her best to assist. Steffani knew that her father's business problems caused her mother to worry, the way she worried about Steffani. One year her father would have twenty clients working all over the country, and the next year there might be only six. And there were the constant medical bills. Lynnette would have accepted more photography assignments if it weren't for Steffani's illness. That made her wish even more that she wasn't sick.

"Oh look." Lynnette noticed the amazing shapes of the Joshua trees suddenly coming into view, sprinkled in profusion across the desert. "They look like traffic policemen, don't they? Some with their arms up and some with their arms down. Wouldn't it make a great photograph to bring a real traffic cop out here and pose him among the cactus? It looks so different here than it does around Palm Springs, don't you think?" she asked Burt, who was not really listening. "Honey, could we stop the car for a minute? I'd love to take some pictures of this landscape."

Everyone groaned.

"I believe I'll stop too," Grandpa Henry said, reaching for the door handle.

"Dad!" Lynnette shouted, fearing her father was going to open the car door while they were still moving and he and the children would be thrown onto the highway. Once that had almost happened to Suzanne when they were driving in the country. The back door of the car had opened going around a curve and she almost slid out of the car, but Nana was alive then and grabbed her in time. Steffani didn't remember Nana very well, but she knew that Suzanne missed her a lot because she talked about her. Sometimes, when Steffani was in pain, Suzanne would tell her the stories that Nana used to tell. That's when Steffani wished she'd known her better.

Grandpa Henry looked up, startled, as if he didn't know what was happening. He was getting old. His thick curly hair was totally white now, growing like a Brillo pad out of the top of his head. Since Nana had died several years ago, he didn't know what to do with himself. He lived by himself in an apartment, and came over to visit on Sundays. The rest of the week he sat alone listening to the radio, made himself a can of Campbell's soup, and brought her and Suzanne Hershey bars when he visited. Lynnette wanted him to come and live with them, but they didn't have an extra bedroom and he would have had to sleep in the dining room.

"We'd better stop and have those Cokes as soon as possible," Lynnette said to Burt, trying not to let anyone see she was worried about Grandpa Henry, but Steffani could tell. Old people couldn't take the heat very well. Neither did she.

"Well, I suggested it, didn't I?" Burt said, as though to a child.

"Don't talk like that to me," Lynnette snapped. "Especially in front of the children."

"I'll talk any way I like to," Burt retorted.

Suzanne gave Steffani a look that said, *Here they go again.* Their parents had terrible fights all the time where they accused each other of things. If only they wouldn't do that. Steffani hated it. Her mother thought the best way was her way, and Daddy thought his way was best. Neither believed the other knew anything at all. Sometimes Suzanne got into the middle of their fights and tried to stop them, and then they'd end up yelling at her and she'd cry.

Steffani tried to stay out of it, but it wasn't easy when one of them asked her who was right. Usually her mother would end up crying and be so hurt she wouldn't talk to anyone for hours. Whenever Lynnette gave them the silent treatment, as her father called it, it made Steffani feel sick inside, like something really bad was happening.

Sometimes, she'd do something that started the argument, like complaining about one of them to the other. "Daddy left this ice pack too long and it leaked all over the sheets and I can't sleep."

"Burt," Lynnette would yell, "why aren't you taking proper care of her? There's a mess now, and I have to change the sheets."

"I'll change them," he'd yell back.

"Never mind," she'd insist, pulling the sheets out from under Steffani with a yank.

"Nothing I do is ever right," he'd say. "I do the best I can."

"Well, it's not good enough," she'd insist, and they'd be in a fight again, bringing up all the things they usually fought about, like why Burt had gone into such a foolish business as handling concert performers, and why Lynnette was always bellyaching, his word for *complaining*, and why she didn't listen to him when he told her things. The trouble with her mother, according to her father, was that she had her mind on other *things*. And when Lynnette said, "I do not!" with a strange expression on her face, Steffani wondered what those *things* were. If those *things* went away, like Steffani's illness, life would be all right again, and there would be no more fighting.

The place where they stopped for Cokes was a gas station with a soft drink cooler outside. They had to drink their sodas standing in the sun, because they couldn't take the bottles with them in the car, it was crowded enough. Steffani spilled some of the sticky sweet liquid on her T-shirt and Lynnette gave an exasperated sigh.

"Your family is a barrel of laughs," Gloria said to Suzanne, then immediately changed the subject to her most favorite. "I hope there are boys where we're going." She moved Suzanne away so they could talk privately, but Steffani sidled up closer so she could listen to their fascinating teenage talk. It must be the most wonderful thing in the world to be a teenager.

"I'm sure there'll be boys there," Suzanne promised. "And we can make a list of our favorite ones from school and from the movies. How many slam books have you signed this week?"

"About ten," Gloria said. Steffani didn't believe her. Gloria exaggerated, but from the look on Suzanne's face, she believed her.

"I only did four," Suzanne admitted, with disappointment. A slam book was a spiral note pad, with a different question on every page, like Who's your favorite singer? What's your favorite song? and Who would you like to be stuck on a desert island with? The first page in the book had only numbers next to each line. If a girl was asked to sign the book, she put her name next to a free number, and then answered every question on subsequent pages, using the line with her number on it. In order to see who had said what, there was a lot of flipping back and forth of pages. But the anonymity of answering a question without actually writing your name each time, allowed everyone to be more honest. The more books you were asked to sign, the more popular you were.

"Let's make up our own slam books, with really neat questions. And then, we'll ask everyone to sign ours."

Steffani wished they would ask her, but of course they wouldn't. Gloria contemplated the idea of making their own books. It was a good one, but she wouldn't give Suzanne credit for being clever. Steffani watched her sister kissing up to Gloria and it made her angry. Suzanne was worth ten Glorias.

"I'll think about it," Gloria said. Then suddenly, she burst into a song that Jane Powell had sung in *Royal Wedding*, "Too Late Now."

Both Burt and Lynnette stopped to listen. "You have a wonderful voice," Lynnette commented when Gloria was through.

Suzanne seemed embarrassed that her friend had just started singing like that, not caring who was listening, but she complimented her anyway. "That was really wonderful," Suzanne said, echoing Lynnette's praise.

What a show-off, Steffani thought.

Gloria stood taller now, smiling a mysterious smile. Her dark hair was cut in bangs hanging down over her eyebrows and the rest of her hair was in two short pony tails that stuck out of the sides of her head. She had bigger breasts than Suzanne and they protruded from her chest in two points. Steffani guessed she was wearing a Vassarette bra and that she ironed it like Suzanne did. "I'm going to be a singer when I grow up," Gloria announced. "Maybe you can represent me, Mr. Blacker." But Burt had already climbed back into the car and his lack of interest irritated Gloria. Steffani was secretly glad.

"Come on, everybody," Burt said. "Let's get the show on the road."

"Are you all right?" Lynnette asked Steffani, as she usually did twenty times a day.

"Sure!" Steffani insisted, determined to ignore the niggling sensation in her leg that had started about a half hour ago. *It's nothing*, she told herself. *It will go away*. She settled into the backseat, but just as they were about to pull out of the station, Grandpa Henry had to go to the bathroom.

"Oh, brother," Gloria commented. Steffani wanted to hit her for embarrassing Grandpa Henry. What did Suzanne see in this girl?

"I *told* everyone to go, when we first got here," Burt said.

"I didn't have to go then," the old man said, trying to open the car door. But the handle was stuck. So Burt got out and came around and helped him out. Steffani waited in the car, in the hundred-degree heat, while everybody else trooped off to the bathrooms again. Of course, the effects of the cold drinks had totally worn off.

The rest of the way up the mountain Gloria suggested they all sing, which was pretty fun. Steffani especially liked "Don't Fence Me In" and "Always." When they finally pulled into Pioneer Town, it was two in the afternoon and they'd been on the road since nine. The town consisted of one long street, built as a replica of a western town at the middle of the last century, except the houses and stores were real and real people lived in them. They found their cabin and pulled up in front next to a hitching post. Everyone was fascinated, gazing at the sights, enchanted by the old town. To Steffani, it looked unreal, like a movie.

"This is neat!" Suzanne exclaimed, following Gloria out of the car. "Don't you think so?" She turned to Gloria for agreement, who pretended to play it cool by shrugging. Then Suzanne's attention was caught by a real cowboy asleep on a porch across the street, his feet up on a stool, boots crossed, his cowboy hat pulled down over his eyes. "Guy, Gloria, look at that." Suzanne pointed.

Gloria watched for a while and then turned back to Steffani, who was still in the stifling interior of the car. Gloria's smile was sickeningly false, and she spoke low so the rest of them couldn't hear. "I don't want you tagging after us, brat, and your sister doesn't want you either, understand?"

"Get lost," Steffani said, and stuck out her tongue. Gloria turned away in a huff and Steffani glared after her.

The pain was worse. She tried to keep from showing it, but the crease between her eyebrows, and the way her upper lip was pulled back in a slight grimace, gave her away. It hadn't gone away, and for the last two hours she'd endured it, jammed in next to her grandfather and her sister, thinking, *I can't tell them. It will ruin everyone's good time. If I don't think about it, it will go away.* But once it got started, it never went away. She tried not to let her mother see her. One glance would expose her. And her heart pounded with apprehension from each increase of discomfort, which had been getting worse until it was almost an aching pain. Her leg again. *Please, not this time*, she begged. But this particular prayer had never been answered.

"Come on, Steffani, get out of the car." Lynnette turned to look at her daughter and saw the Look. Steffani turned her face away, to try to keep her from knowing, and watched Suzanne.

Suzanne was standing on the porch of the cabin, peeking in the window while Burt tried the key. Gloria was hanging with one hand on a wooden post at the edge of the porch, swinging around it in a circle, singing the theme from the "Carousel Ballet." Grandpa Henry was trying to find some shade, fanning his face with his Panama hat. And Suzanne was looking at the reflection of the car in the window behind her, watching Steffani watching her. Without turning around, she could see her mother climbing into the backseat of the car to talk to Steffani, saw her mother feel Steffani's forehead, look into her eyes. The signs were only too familiar.

Steffani could tell what Suzanne was thinking. *It couldn't be. Not this time. Not now! Not when she'd gotten one of the most popular girls in school here as her friend*. If only Suzanne knew what kind of a person Gloria was.

It wasn't easy for either of them to make friends in California. The kids were different here. When Suzanne entered junior high two years ago, it was the first time that everyone else in her grade started a new school the same time she did. For the first time, she wasn't the newest kid in the room.

Suzanne will hate me if I ruin this weekend for her, Steffani thought. *She'll never forgive me. I wish I could run away. She's not going to take it well this time, I know it*.

Burt finally got the door to the western-style cabin opened, but when he turned around, there was no one behind him waiting to go inside. He looked around in surprise. "Where is everybody?"

"Burt." Lynnette motioned to him from the car. "Will you come here a minute."

Suzanne edged closer to the car so she could hear what they were saying. But she still had her back to them, watching in the reflection of the cabin window—as though by not turning around, she could make it not real.

"I don't want to go home," Steffani said. "Please, can we stay?"

"If you want to stay, I'll help Mommy take care of you, honey," Burt promised. He turned to Lynnette. "I'm not at work now, I can help out. For God's sake, Lynnette, we just got here, the kids are so excited."

Lynnette's nerves were sizzling and raw after the endless hot drive and the close confinement of the car. And now this. "Why do you act as if this is my decision to make? I'm not the boss of this. Do you recall that there are no ice packs here because there is no electricity and no refrigeration? And there's no phonograph. When Steffani's sick she listens to the phonograph all day, or the radio, to distract her. I don't even know if there's a comfortable bed here for her, or any privacy. She certainly can't sleep with Gloria and Suzanne when she's in pain. It's not fair to her or to them." She looked at him as though she wanted him to do something, but there was nothing he could do. "It's impossible to stay here, Burt. We have to take her home before the worst of it starts. This could last two weeks. I can't imagine sitting in the car with all of us and her in the throes of an attack. My father will not be able to stand it. He's never seen her suffer before. I can hardly stand it."

"Calm down, Lynnie," he insisted. "Not in front of the children," he said in Yiddish. Steffani's eyes were huge black saucers in a rim of blue as she looked from one to the other. She was starting to cry. "I don't want to go home." she said. "Please, I don't want to go."

"Honey, we have to," Lynnette insisted. Caring for her child's condition in these primitive surroundings was a nightmare beyond her ken.

"But we haven't even seen the place," Burt said.

"Don't you dare undermine me," Lynnette shouted, losing her temper. "Do you think I want to go back now? Do you? Why do you always make me out to be the bad one? I'm the one who takes care of her day after day. I know what this is like."

"I take care of her too, every night when she's sick," he defended himself. Steffani knew he felt guilty about not being able to stay home and care for her during the day but he made up for it by taking care of her at night. In truth, however, her mother had the brunt of the burden.

Lynnette moved over in the seat and took Steffani on her lap. Gently, she probed the thigh. "Does this hurt?"

Steffani nodded.

"And this?" she probed deeper.

Steffani winced and then moaned.

Lynnette gave a resigned sigh and then looked up at Burt. "We're going home. But first, you go with the girls, take my dad and walk around the town. See if you can find where they're shooting the movie and say hello to Katy. I'll stay here with Steffi, and then we'll leave." Steffani hated herself. She wanted to spend the weekend playing in the cowboy town and riding horses and watching the movie being made more than anything in the world. And it was all her fault that they had to leave. She stared out of the car window and blinked back the tears that rolled down her hot sweaty cheeks.

Burt didn't argue. He just got out of the car, locked up the cabin, and told everyone what had happened.

"We're leaving?" Gloria shouted. "You're kidding, aren't you?" The idea of getting back into that car for another hot five-hour ride home was impossible. She glared at Suzanne, blaming her.

"Oh no!" Suzanne wailed. "It can't be true. We just got here! It's not fair!" Suzanne was too mortified even to look at Gloria.

Steffani could imagine what Gloria would say to the kids in school when she got back. *Suzanne should not have invited Gloria*, Steffani thought. *There were other friends who would have been more understanding*. But Suzanne acted as though she didn't deserve to have any friends when this was the way her family treated them.

Lynnette heard her complaints and shouted furiously, "Suzanne, you come here this minute."

Startled, Suzanne came slowly toward the car. Lynnette was sitting in the backseat with Steffani in her lap. Steffani looked up at Suzanne as if to say, *Please don't hate me. I'm sorry.*

But Suzanne gave her a look of hatred anyway.

"Wipe that expression off your face, young lady," Lynnette insisted, her temper nearly out of control. "I don't ever want to see you look at your sister that way again. I don't care what you want or how unfair it is, we are going home. Do you think it's fair for your sister to have to suffer like this? And I expect you to help us and not complain. None of us wants to leave, but we have to make the best of it. Is that clear? Is it?" she repeated, until her voice was four octaves higher.

Suzanne didn't dare glance around to see if Gloria was listening; she just burned from embarrassment. "I'm sorry," she said, sullenly.

"You can do better than that! Say it as though you mean it!" Lynnette insisted, with a no-nonsense tone, her fury beginning to abate.

"I'm really sorry, Mom," Suzanne said, trying not to cry, knowing she had been selfish again. She glanced at Steffani and showed her remorse. Here Steffani was, about to suffer two weeks of pain, and she was worried about her popularity and the discomfort of a long ride home. She reached out and squeezed Steffani's hand.

"That's better," Lynnette pronounced. "Now go with your father, and see that he hurries."

Suzanne smiled a half smile at Steffani, truly hoping to be forgiven. But Steffani didn't really see her, all her concentration was inward. Steffani knew that as soon as Suzanne was out of her mother's influence, she would feel the same heat of a desperate disappointment that Steffani felt, and she'd have to squelch her anger for there was no way to express it. Suzanne always did what the rest of them wanted her to do, moved aside, or kept out of the way, or put off what she wanted because it wasn't a good time, or because her sister was sick. Would Suzanne ever have her own time? Steffani wondered. When?

CHAPTER ELEVEN

"Haven't you got anyone to fix me up with?" I asked Gloria Winston. "Every possibility of a date has literally dried up."

My friendship with Gloria had survived through junior high all the way to college, in spite of the fiasco of the time she went to Pioneer Town with us. But over the years it had been more off than on because she had a volatile temper and a big mouth. In high school, her nickname was Queen of the Insult. And I, like everyone else, was afraid of her mouth but put up with her because she was so talented and stunningly gorgeous, like Natalie Wood, except taller. And she was outrageously funny, never ordinary. In spite of Gloria's faults, I maintained our friendship because she was one of those people who gave me permission to misbehave. And even if I didn't take advantage of it, I got a vicarious thrill through her. In high school she was forever in detention or sneaking out of the house. I loved hearing about her escapades.

"What about that ZBT you went out with last semester?" Gloria asked. She had a great memory for other people's dates and romances.

"He went back with his girlfriend."

"And Herb Goldman?"

"Never called after our second date. And I really liked him, too."

"Mark Miller?"

"He loves me. You can't go on a date with someone who loves you, when you don't love them."

"So be friends with him."

"He doesn't want to be friends, Gloria."

"You're beginning to piss me off, Blacker. You're a whiny thing, aren't you? What about the guy in your English class?"

"He's never asked me out before. You know I can't ask someone to my biggest sorority formal of the year if he's never even asked me for a coffee date. And I've tried everything I can think of, short of bringing my own thermos of coffee to class."

Gloria mulled it over. "In that whole stuck-up sorority of yours, isn't there anyone else you can ask to fix you up? I don't even go to UCLA." Her third year at college—in her case, Juilliard—ended earlier than mine.

"I swear, I've asked everyone I know. You're my last hope."

"So, now I'm the bottom of the barrel?"

"Come on, you know that's not it."

"I know why you called me," Gloria said, with a sly tone in her voice. "You want my brother, don't you?"

"Alex, the god? He'd never take me out." It was exactly what I did want, why I had called her and risked being put down, but the idea had to come from Gloria. She was even more possessive of him now that he was in law school than when he was in college.

"You're right, he's extremely particular about whom he dates. Only *gorgissimo* women." Gloria used Italian phrases she picked up learning Italian for her opera career. "You know, like Carrie Dayton or Angie Troubeck"—girls from UCLA she knew because Alex had dated them, both Tri Delts and homecoming princesses.

"Forget it," I said. "It was a dumb idea."

"How's your bod lately? I haven't seen you since spring break. Are you thin at the moment? Or fat?"

I wasn't thin, but if I didn't eat a bite of food from now until Saturday, I could lose five pounds. "Thin!" I swore. "Size seven."

"You'd better not be telling one, Suzanne. If you've been pigging out on Barone's pizza, just can it. Alex hates fat girls.

Oh, what's the use. He'll never go to a dumb sorority dance. Not even for me. And besides, what's in it for me? What can you possibly trade me if I get you a date with my extremely gorgeous and eligible brother?''

"He's not that gorgeous," I protested, weakly.

"Oh no?" Both of us knew that was a lie. Alex Winston was extremely good-looking. He'd never agree to a date with me. And what could I possibly offer Gloria as trade for her to intervene on my behalf? *Clothes? No. Money? No. I was broke. The loan of my car? Forget it. She had her own.* There was only one thing I had worth trading for a date with her brother, and we both knew what it was. Gloria was studying opera, and my father was an impresario. I sighed. "I guess I can talk to my father about you. See if he'll give you some advice."

"Oh, no, you don't! Suzanne, you've been dangling that one in front of me since we were kids, promising to get him to come to my recitals. But he hasn't been there yet. So, I'm not going to play the sucker again. And besides, what if I can't deliver what I promised. I mean, how in hell can I convince my brother to take you out if he's going with someone?"

"Is he?" I thought, *Well, this is it.*

"No, he's not!" she retorted.

"Then tell him your career depends on him asking me out."

"My career doesn't depend on anything you do, Suzanne." Haughtiness came naturally to her. "And wouldn't it humiliate you if he said no? Even to me?"

My face flushed. Thank God, she couldn't see me over the phone. "Not exactly." I really wanted to go to that dance. "If you're willing to use a favor to your advantage, so am I," I told her. Something was giving me an unusual amount of confidence at the moment. I was sure if I had the chance with him, Alex would find me appealing. I knew he'd stared at me whenever he saw me at their house.

"You have a wonderful voice, Gloria." I tried flattery.

"I have a great voice."

"And my father will love it, if he listens to you."

"Babyface, your father handles some of the biggest names in classical music. He hasn't got time for me."

"I'll tell him my life depends on it."

"If you get me an audition, Blacker, my brother will take you to the moon."

"Dad, how much do you love me?"

"What a question, daughter. As much as the sky?" He held his long arms out to show how big. They spanned about twelve feet. Ever since I was small, his arm span had amazed me. And he was double-jointed, so his elbows turned the opposite way.

"Do you love me enough to keep me from suffering?"

His head snapped up from the desk where he was writing and he looked at me sharply. I was instantly sorry. How thoughtless of me to have mentioned suffering when we all knew the meaning of the word so intimately. "I mean, could you stand to see me sitting at home and miserable this Saturday night when my sorority is having our major dance of the year?"

"I thought you were going?"

"My date dislocated his knee in a track event and was ordered not to walk, let alone dance."

"Why doesn't someone set you up with a date?"

"I've tried. But this is Thursday, Dad. The dance is Saturday. Everybody has a date."

"Everyone in the entire world?"

"Anyone worth going with."

He gave me a lopsided grin. "Are you asking me to take you?"

I rolled my eyes at the idea. "God no!"

He winced, genuinely hurt. Damn, he was so sensitive.

"I didn't mean it that way."

Now he was losing patience. "What then?"

"Well, you know my friend Gloria Winston?"

"The one who came to Pioneer Town with us that time? The one you've been begging me to listen to ever since you first met her?"

He also had a great memory where my friends were concerned. "Yes . . . but Daddy, she's been attending Juilliard and studying with Andrea Rubeskaya and she's really good. I know you could help her career, discover her."

He had that look again that said, *Nobody understands*. "Honey, I've told you over and over. I don't run a talent school. I book established acts. You know how long it's taken me to build my business, to make a name for myself in classical music. You know what tough times we've had through the years. I can't take some unknown, mediocre friend of my daughter's, with a *peepitzer* voice, and spend my time pushing her along. And I resent that you keep asking me."

"She hasn't got a *peepitzer* voice, Dad." It was his word for "squeaky and untrained." "She's been studying for years. She's appeared in hundreds of recitals and contests. She's won scholarships. And now, her voice is maturing." I was armed with the rhetoric.

He reached into his pocket for the pipe that used to be there, an involuntary movement, almost like scratching a severed limb. He'd stopped smoking a pipe years ago, but still kept his collection on the mantel in the den where they'd always been displayed because he couldn't bear to part with them.

"What's Gloria got to do with any of this?"

"She's willing to fix me up with her brother if you'll just help her a little bit. Just listen to her. Maybe introduce her to someone."

"I don't know anyone who could help her. The only people I know want artists with established names."

I gave him my most pleading look. The dim light in the study underlined the puffiness beneath his eyes, the slightly sagging skin of his upper lids. He was getting older, my handsome daddy, though most of the time I refused to take notice of that.

"Don't look so tragic." He sighed. "I'll listen to her."

I threw my arms around his neck and kissed him. "Oh, thank you!"

"But I'm doing it just so you can get a date for the dance, you understand?"

"Definitely," I declared.

"So, what's this brother of hers like?" he asked. Now that I had the date, out came his protectiveness. He had that sizing-up look on his face. "He'd better not be wild like Gloria. I remember her getting you into trouble. Wasn't there something about cutting Glee Club in junior high? And she's got a fresh mouth."

There never was a transgression he didn't remember. "Alex is nothing like Gloria. He's a doll, in his second year at USC law school, with excellent grades. Just the kind of boy you and Mom want for me. Gloria keeps him away from her friends, protects him like he was made of something that melts. She's always quoting him, talking about him, 'My brother Alex went to Washington, D.C.,' or 'My brother Alex is so funny, he could be a stand-up comic.' I don't know if I'm ready for such responsibility. If he doesn't like me, he'll never let her fix him up again. Not to mention the responsibility of trading her brother for my father."

"Suzanne!" He was embarrassed by the comparison. But as I was leaving his office I saw him turn to look at his reflection in the window next to his desk. He studied his face, turning it this way and that, pulled at the skin around his eyes, ran his fingers through the sides of his hair, then gave a sigh and went back to his contracts.

Alex Winston was good-looking, though not as handsome as my father. However, they were both tall, with dark brown hair and white, even teeth. But Alex's hair was curly and slightly receding, even though he was only twenty-four. His nose was short and straight, his lips full and sensual, his eyes brown; they narrowed to half-moons when he smiled, and they had a direct piercing gaze that unnerved me as I opened the door. His glance took me in from top to toe, making me tingle all over in my dark blue taffeta dress. He handed me a corsage, a wrist orchid. "You did say your dress was blue. I thought white would go well."

A man of details. I thanked him and extended a trembling, pale wrist for him to slip on the elastic bracelet of the corsage next to my pearl one. My mother was thrilled with him. My father eyed him coldly, wondering if this was the one who would eventually deflower his daughter and take her away. My sister was on the upstairs landing, poking her head through the railing. I turned and winked at her. I knew there were times, when we were younger, when I'd hated her, but now I couldn't remember why.

My father exuded animosity as he shook Alex's hand. "Not too late, now," he cautioned, a warning in his voice.

My shoulders stiffened.

"Burt, she's in college," Mother jumped in.

I wanted to run away from embarrassment. "Dad," I said, feeling furious, "don't treat me like a child."

"We'll be home by one-thirty," Alex assured them. "I understand there's a breakfast planned for after the dance at Canter's Deli on Fairfax."

"Fine," my father agreed, one man to another. Between the two of them they'd just settled my fate. My mother handed me my wrap, a white wool stole with a feathered trim, which Alex helped to place over my shoulders, and then we were off.

On the way to the car I stole a glance at him. My palms were moist from nervousness, his hands were cold on my arm. *Where do I begin*, I thought. I had a sudden wild vision of a time in the future when people on dates could say exactly what they were thinking, instead of being on their best behavior. And I would say, "I can't believe that I'm on a date with you, Alex Winston. I've had a crush on you since I was fourteen."

When we were settled in the car he said, "You've certainly grown up nicely. Gloria showed me your picture and I couldn't believe it was the same girl who used to come to our house years ago."

I had seen him many times since junior high, but obviously hadn't made much of an impression so I didn't remind him. "You haven't changed, Alex," I told him, "except to get better." Oh God, my cheeks were getting red. Thank heavens it was dark in the car. "This is kind of awkward. I know you wouldn't be here if Gloria hadn't twisted your arm."

Gallantly, he said, "My arm doesn't hurt a bit." And I relaxed.

We talked about the classes I was taking, professors that he once had, girls he knew in my sorority, and his plans for the future. He was an idealist. "I'm thinking about going into labor law," he said, "but first I'd like to join the Peace Corps." I was impressed.

The dance was being held at the Ambassador Hotel. It was underway when we arrived. As we entered the room I was aware of many pairs of eyes appraising us. The attention brought a glow to my cheeks, a lift to my chin. Alex was a good dancer, socially comfortable. I liked that. He knew almost everyone in the sorority and their dates from when he went to UCLA. I felt important being with him, caught envious glances from my sorority sisters, approval in the eyes of fraternity boys. If Alex Winston thought I was worthy of dating, maybe they'd better take a closer look. So even if this date with Alex didn't turn out too well, my social status had improved.

Later, we managed to go off by ourselves to talk. He talked, that is. He knew about everything. "In submarine warfare," he told me, "the crew members suffer from claustrophobia and skin fungus, or fungi." I wracked my brain for some interesting fact I could quote. He wasn't waiting for me. "Contact lenses are going to get better, more refined. As soon as I save some money, I'm going to buy stock in a company that makes them, though the studies are not in yet about whether or not they can permanently damage your eyes."

After two drinks, he started telling me jokes. And he *was* as good as a stand-up comic. "Did you hear the one about the gorilla who goes into a bar, orders a martini, and gives the bartender twenty bucks. The bartender gives him ninety-eight cents change, thinking the gorilla won't know the difference, and then says, 'Business has been slow lately.' The gorilla says, 'At those prices it's no wonder.' "

He also knew something of Talmudic law. He'd considered being a rabbi when he was in Hebrew School.

"Eclecticism is what excites me—I love differences, crave change. The world is as multifaceted as people are and I want to discover all of it. But not alone. Eventually, I want to get married. That's the way it's supposed to be, you know."

"Yes," I said, wondering if I would ever be the kind of girl he'd consider.

"I don't mean, because it's what our parents want for us, but because it's God's design. When Adam was created and found himself alone in the garden, he had everything; life was complete. God directed that he name the animals, and he tried to have a relationship with them, but he couldn't because he was different from them. There was no other being like him. His aloneness became oppressive. It's not good for the human being to be alone. So God put Adam to sleep, and as the usual interpretation says, took one of his ribs to make a woman. But it wasn't his *rib*. The word is *sides*, that's the meaning of the word in Hebrew. The quote, 'Bone of my bone, flesh of my flesh,' can be interpreted to mean that the first individual was born androgynous, that he contained both aspects of male and female."

"You mean, Adam was a hermaphrodite? That's not in the Bible, is it?"

"It's in the Midrash," he explained. His eyes were partly hidden by the folds of his cheeks as he smiled. "Yes. Adam had both aspects within him. But he was lonely, and so God split him into two parts by taking one of his sides and making it female. Now, there were two beings with separate parts, two halves of a whole. But they didn't know each other. They had to discover one another, get together again in a sexual relationship, which in Hebrew is knowledge. If you love someone, you have to know them. If you don't know them, you can't love them. And that gives the word *knowing* a sexual context, as in, to have knowledge of.''

No one had ever spoken to me of sexual relations before without it being smutty. I nodded, gazing into his eyes, trying to appear sophisticated, as though I discussed these things with boys all the time.

"Man is the only animal who has sex face-to-face. In effect, you have a replaying of the original separation, and the becoming of one flesh. As Martin Buber said, 'In order for there to be betweenness, there must be separateness and distance in which we recognize the otherness of the other.' ''

"I recognize you as other than me," I said, teasingly. I could have listened to him all night. Here was a man who not only appealed to me, but one I could learn from.

"You're very sweet," he said, and then he kissed me.

I felt breathless from that first kiss. His intelligence had gotten to me. He liked me, too. The headiness of having Alex Winston attracted to me was intoxicating. I pressed my breasts against him, ran my fingers through the hair on his neck, and felt his erection growing through the crinolines of my skirt.

We didn't go to the breakfast at Canter's Deli; we came back to my house and necked in the car. He was a gentleman and stopped whenever I said, but we sucked on each other's mouths and necks for over an hour. When he walked me to the door, he said, "I'd like to see you again, Suzanne. I'll call you on Monday." And he did. Alex was always reliable, and compulsive. It was the secret to his success.

We started dating. On Saturday night, we'd go to a party or a movie and have a wonderful time together. But on Monday, Gloria would call. "Don't get your hopes up, Suzanne. He's not really interested in you. There's just no one else in his life right now." My heart, which was on a cloud of euphoria, would be dashed into the depths of sadness and loss. But by Thursday, he'd call again for Saturday night. I was always surprised to hear from him because to hear Gloria tell it, I was the last thing on his mind.

One night we went to the opera, *Madame Butterfly*. He

held my hand and explained every scene to me as it unfolded. I knew the story of Butterfly and her naval officer well, but pretended not to, for his sake.

"The coloratura was adequate," he pronounced when the show was over. "But the tenor stole the performance. Those notes were extraordinary."

The tenor was a client of my father's. He'd been to our house for dinner the week before. I didn't find him extraordinary. But maybe I was wrong. Alex had such excellent taste. "Would you like to meet him?" I asked, wanting to show off, but not certain if knowing the tenor would impress him.

"Sure," he said, not believing me. "And the conductor too, while you're at it."

"That could be arranged," I said, taking him at his word. I led the way backstage and into the dressing room of Fernando Picar, the male star of the night's show.

"Dear girl," Fernando said to me, beckoning for us to join the group gathered to congratulate him. I introduced Alex, proud that I could do such a thing. It wasn't until years later that I discovered what a significant moment that was in Alex's life. He'd never met a celebrity before and he became starstruck, gushing with compliments. Fernando was quite gracious. We stayed for a while, and other members of the cast came in to say hello, including the conductor. Alex introduced himself to every one of them.

When we finally left, Alex turned and hugged me. "You are wonderful, Suzanne. Do you know that? I had no idea you could get us backstage, or that you knew celebrities."

"Fernando isn't exactly famous," I explained. My father's business brought many entertainers into our home over the years. But they were usually known only to small audiences and select groups, certainly to fewer people than who know movie or television stars. I thought of my father's clients as a bit second-rate. But to Alex, they were exciting.

"The next time we go someplace like this," he said, "where we can meet the performers, wear something more special than what you're wearing tonight." I looked down at my gold and rust wool skirt and sweater. "Something that lets them know we've taken care to dress for the occasion, that lets them know, by how we comport ourselves, that we admire them."

"Would you like to look through my closet and pick an outfit yourself?" I asked, amazed at his interest. I'd never known a date who cared what I wore, though I seldom wore the same outfit twice with the same person.

"If you wouldn't mind," he said. "Like that pink dress you wore last week. It's much better on you than what you're wearing now."

My cheeks flushed hotly. How I wanted to please him.

From my earliest memories I'd always been in love. At age three I had a crush on my uncle Sid. I guess I got it from my mother, who loved to flirt. But more than flirting, my feelings toward boys and now young men came from the deepest part of me, filled every corner of my being. I felt a bittersweet, deeply engrossing kind of constant spring fever. Often it was a free-floating longing, and I'd search for an object of my affection, someone to place it on. The need to be completed by another ran through the nucleus of my genes, as basic to me as smiling. It connected me to the entire universe, placed me in the middle of a never-ending, swirling maelstrom, joined me to the universal emotion, and ultimately to the entity, my definition of God. The feelings had to be Godlike, for what else could reach into the center of my soul and run its fingers through the pile of gold dust there, scattering it to the winds of infinity and yet leaving an immense amount still there for me to draw on any time I loved? And now, Alex was my love object. I would pour my love all over him. Somewhere, I dimly saw his faults. I knew he was bossy, needed to be right, had his own way of doing things. But nobody's perfect. And he was such a catch.

Gloria thought we were wrong for each other. She kept telling me he was only using me to meet interesting people. But Alex seemed interested in me for myself. I was afraid to ask him how he felt about me, for fear he'd say Gloria was right. Left to himself, he didn't tell me what he thought of me; consequently, I was on a constant high or low with him. But when we were together, I was the gayest, happiest, friendliest, most affectionate and easy-to-please date any aspiring attorney could want.

CHAPTER TWELVE

The moment I had stepped out of Barry's office last Friday afternoon I'd kept seeing those greenish brown eyes, accompanied by flashing lights signifying danger. *Don't get involved, you've got enough to worry about*. Besides, I couldn't possibly date anyone else now. I was already going out with three different men, though none of them were as appealing to me as Barry Adler. But they were pleasant companions, interesting conversationalists, and acceptable escorts. *Boring*. But safe. Barry, on the other hand, was not safe.

As I'd promised the night before at Chasen's, I spent the better part of the day copying down printers' names from the New York phone book, but it seemed like a waste of time.

I pulled into my street at 2:30 P.M. to see a familiar figure walking up the driveway, wearing a three piece pin-striped suit tailored to fit his newly trim physique. Alex. It wasn't that I didn't recognize him, but everything was different. Bit by bit, I figured it out. No glasses; they'd been replaced by contacts. He was tanned, and as I said, much thinner than before from the gym and playing tennis. The hair transplant he'd had after our divorce had filled in nicely, and his hair was curlier now, obviously a perm, but nicely done. Alex had not only aged well, he'd aged gloriously. Next would probably come plastic surgery. He was a different man from the law student who had wanted to join the Peace Corps.

Seeing him on our doorstep in the middle of the day like this was a surprise.

"Suzanne?" He stopped and turned sideways as I drove into the garage. Smiling that slow knowing smile, he gave a little laugh that said, *I see you.* And I knew he did. One always *sees* one's ex-mate in a certain way, not always flattering.

It's usually difficult for me when confronted by Alex, and today was no exception. Everything came flooding back. How I used to cry when he made love to me, at first because it was so beautiful, and then because it was so seldom, and then because I felt so inadequate. For a moment, coming upon him so suddenly, breathing was difficult; then it eased. It was the second time in just a few days that I felt like a schoolgirl. With Barry I'd had that youthful fluttery feeling, and now, with Alex, it felt as though I wouldn't pass inspection. To compensate, I stood up straighter, held my head higher as I got out of the car.

"I was at a meeting at Warner's in Burbank and thought I'd take a chance and stop by. I called earlier, where were you?"

"At the library," I replied. "What's up?"

"Something we have to discuss."

"What is it?" I picked up a tone in his voice that alerted me. I figured it was about the children.

"In a minute," he said, impatiently. Things usually went at Alex's pace. "How are the kids?"

"They're fine." I unlocked the front door and ushered him in. He tried not to look around, but I could see he was searching for changes. There were very few. "Miles and Amy enjoyed being with you and Dina last weekend. Jered is looking forward to his turn. But I think he'd prefer Hamburger Hamlet to the Bistro."

"Do you still think it's a good idea to split up their visits with me?" Alex asked, following me into the kitchen.

We'd decided on this arrangement for a while, because the older children enjoyed different activities than Jered did, and this gave Alex an opportunity to give them each separate attention. We'd agreed it would be temporary, to see how it worked out. But Alex always discussed everything in minute detail, analyzed it to death before he felt reconciled to a decision, or satisfied that he'd made the right choice. It wasn't that he was indecisive; he was by nature a nudge.

"Yes, it's fine, Alex," I said, immediately falling into the role of reassurer. "It makes Miles and Amy feel special and does the same thing for Jered. It doesn't hurt the three of them to spend some time apart, either." I changed the subject. "I hear Dina's new film starts shooting next month in Australia. How exciting for her. Are you going on location with her?" I sat down at the kitchen table, automatically, the way we always did when we had something to discuss. Then I was sorry we hadn't stayed in the living room, more neutral and less informal.

Alex had married Dina Maitland two years ago, an actress and client of his. She was everything he'd always wanted: glamorous, beautiful, famous. I wondered if he loved her or just the idea of her. Half the time my children liked her, the other half they thought she was a spoiled brat because she competed with them for their father's attention and usually won. I still hadn't gotten used to the idea of another woman influencing my children's lives. In fact, I hated it. I would almost have stayed married to Alex to prevent sharing my children with another mother; almost, but not quite.

"I'll be joining her for part of the time. But it's hard to get away. You know how it is."

I nodded, remembering well.

"How's work?" he asked. He still had an attitude of resentment/admiration about my writing. Especially since I'd been so successful at what he'd decided was my cute little hobby— something temporary about which he could be indulgent. I guess he resented it because without it I might not have had the strength and independence to divorce him. If he'd known how much more my work meant to me than he did, he really would have resented it. Even now, he was patronizing about my career. Whenever people asked him what kind of books

I wrote he said, "Those trashy airport novels." I know, because I once overheard him say it at a party after our divorce. He also knew that nothing hurt me quite as much as my work being referred to as trash.

"Work's fine. I made the *New York Times'* list this week, number three."

"In spite of Brett Slocum's review?" He seemed impressed, even while he rubbed it in.

"Oh, that didn't bother me," I said.

"Sure," he replied. "Don't tell me you wouldn't wish her a case of the hives."

I smiled, wickedly, "Well, maybe."

"So, is being on the best-seller list old hat to you now?"

"It will never be that, Alex. It means everything to me." I forced a smile, realizing how being accused of plagiarism had cast a shadow over my life. Well, I would not let it take the joy out of my triumphs!

"I guess you won't be too worried then, when I tell you what I needed to talk to you about. It's got me worried, though."

Not more bad news, I thought.

"How about a cup of coffee?" he asked.

Now I was truly surprised. Alex knew I didn't drink coffee, and besides, except for our joint investment ventures, he'd avoided socializing with me ever since the post-separation fiasco. Maybe marriage to Dina had mellowed him.

"It depends on how long you plan to be here. I've got to get back to work."

He nodded, as though he'd expected it. "Okay, then," he said, "I'll tell you now." And without even pausing he blurted out, "We lost our appeal with the IRS on the tax shelter deal. We each owe two hundred and twenty-five thousand dollars to the government."

I stared at him for a stunned moment before I found my voice. "You said they would rule in our favor for sure, it was a cinch," I quoted him. I was sure he was joking the way he often did, finding new ways to torment me. Any moment I expected him to chuck me under the chin and say, with a huge guffaw, "Got you this time, didn't I?" But he didn't. Then I saw the white outlines around his mouth from pressing his lips together, and the look of terror in his eyes.

"You're not kidding, are you?" I said, softly. "We lost. Your amazing shelter deal was denied. Good God! So much money." It was the amount of taxes we would have paid over five years without the shelter, plus interest and penalties.

"It's not as if it comes out of the blue, Suzanne. You knew there was a possibility they'd rule against us. I told you so."

Did he tell me? How could I have denied that? It was just that he had been so cocksure of winning. "Will they let us pay it off?" I felt as if I was trapped in that elevator again from last Friday, only this time the cables had snapped and I was hurtling down a shaft. Then I remembered Gloria asking me the other night at dinner whether I'd seen Alex lately. She'd known about this. They'd talked about me. I hated the idea of that, the two of them smirking over my predicament.

"Yes, we can pay it off," Alex said. "The IRS doesn't want to throw you out on the street where you'd just be taking money from another government agency, so they'll give you a payment schedule, but it has to be totally paid back in several months. Look, I'm sorry, Suzanne. It was an amazing write-off, six dollars of tax deduction for every dollar invested. All the investors knew the realities. You think I want to give back all the money and pay the penalties and interest?" He was slightly belligerent.

"But Alex, this will wipe me out." I had just enough to live on for the next nine months. A cold hollow feeling opened up inside me. "I can't pay that money back; I have no income until next September when the paperback of *Mortal Wounds* is published. Almost a year away."

"I suppose you could sell the house." He glanced around, seeming so damned unconcerned, as though it was another disposable commodity. How could he be this flip?

"Sell the house out from under our children? This is our home."

"Look, Suzanne. I've got my troubles too. I have to come up with the same damned money you do. I've been going crazy too."

"You've got a rich wife, Alex," I said, not too fairly.

"And thank God she's not you," he said, getting me back even better.

Alex's vitriol only added to the acid eating in my stomach. My mind drifted to the children. All three of them went to private schools and they'd just started the new semester. I owed their schools a lot of money and my car needed a major overhaul. Alex never paid his full share of child support because I'd always earned good money and didn't ask for it. I would rather depend on myself than press him for what he owed us. He was looking at me now as if I were about to grab him by the throat and shake the money out of him that he'd lost with his can't-lose-sure-thing scheme, as well as back child-support payments. But all I could think about was getting rid of him so I could call my accountant and find out what my finances were. And then Alex said, "I forgot to ask what you were doing at the library."

There was no way I could tell him, especially now, that I was searching for the names of typesetters in New York so I could track down the person who was accusing me of plagiarism, though I longed to unburden myself. One of the things I missed most about marriage was the sharing of problems. But being an object of pity was one thing I couldn't accept from Alex. Nor could I have endured a false masking of his suspicion that the accusation might be true. He would think the worst of me. The kids would tell him eventually, unless I could find some way of keeping them silent. "I was doing research," I said. "Good thing I wasn't shopping since I can't afford to buy anything now."

He gave me a weak smile, "I'm sorry about the deal, Suze. I know it's a hell of a thing to hear. I'm even sorry for my part in it."

"You didn't force me, Alex," I said, gallantly, wondering if it was his fault.

"Tell Jered I'll be by early Saturday." And he got up and left by the kitchen door without looking back.

After Alex left, I had to go and pick up my children at their various after-school activities, Jered at tee-ball practice, Amy at a school rally, and Miles at ice hockey. By the time I got home I felt as if I'd been trudging through sand up to my knees. There were two messages on the answering service that had come in while I was out. My accountant, who had undoubtedly gotten a call from Alex, and my sister, checking up on me. I called my accountant.

"Alex told me," Murray said, when I reached him. "It's going to be tough, honey. I warned you two about this, you know. It didn't sound kosher to me, a six-to-one shelter." Murray Levy had been our accountant for years. After the divorce, we both stayed with him; he was discreet, never telling either of us about the other's finances.

I took the phone over to my desk and sat down, clutching the receiver to keep my hands from shaking. "What's in the account right now?"

"About thirty thousand," he said. "You have one more payment coming next year of eighty grand when the paperback is released. Of course you'll get the usual royalty payments when you've earned out and paid back your advance. But you know it could take them another year before they make royalty payments."

"Murray, I owe the IRS two hundred and twenty-five thousand." The amount was so enormous it sounded like Italian lira, it couldn't possibly be real. Nobody earned that kind of money, let alone owed it. "What am I going to do?" I had visions of myself starving in the street warming my hands over a fire in a trash can.

He sighed. "You're in big trouble, honey. But we'll work it out, don't worry."

"Can I get Alex to pay me the child support he owes?"

"You've spoiled him, Suzanne. It's tough to get money from someone who hasn't had to pay what they owe; it makes an indignant adversary." He paused while I thought about the wisdom of his logic. "You'd have to go back to court," he added. "Do you want to do that right now?"

The thought of it made me shudder. It would hurt the children too much, and even if I didn't tell them about it, Alex would. "Your mother is trying to squeeze me dry," he'd say. Then, there was the other matter—the plagiarism thing—enough stress to deal with at the moment.

"Don't repeat where you heard this, honey," Murray told me, lowering his voice as if someone were listening. "Alex isn't in as good shape as you are, financially, and you've just hit rock bottom."

"But our children are his responsibility too. If I can't pay for their education, he'll have to."

"He'll say put them in public school."

I knew he would do that.

"You can always sell another book."

Of course, I thought. *I can always do that.* Perhaps there was a light at the end of this darkness after all. For the next twenty minutes we discussed my finances and it all came down to this: at best, I'd be able to maintain my existence—in other words, be able to stay in our home—but only if I borrowed against it for all the equity it contained. No more vacations for the next two years, no gifts, no charity contributions, no parties or entertainment other than an occasional movie, and maybe I could keep my kids in private school if I cut down on my business expenses; but I didn't know how I could do that and promote my books.

The bottom line was, at thirty-six years old, I owed more money than I had, even if I sold everything I owned. And that included another book deal at the same level as my last.

My only hope was to get the IRS to allow me twenty-four months to pay off what I owed them, including interest, and make the biggest book deal of my career. Then, at the end of two years, I'd have a zero net worth, but I'd be out of debt and able to start over again.

Quivering with exhaustion, I hung up from Murray. I wandered around my house, touching the tables, running my hands lovingly over the objects I'd collected through the years. The things that I loved were each special mementos, part of a wonderful life. How much money would they bring? Nostalgia was cheap. I had taken a lot for granted: a beautiful home with the latest appliances, spacious rooms, privacy, a bedroom for each child, and my own office off the master bedroom. But what I felt most anxious about losing was my children's bedrooms: I'd always shared with my sister, but they had their own. Amy's white-and-pink gingham, Miles's with its dark woods and formica shelves to hold all his collections, and Jered's red-and-blue plaid, with a pile of toys in the middle. I had worked hard to make a life-style for them different from my own childhood, where there was constancy and stability, where tragedy and suffering wasn't part of the everyday, a life-style where they always lived in the same house and went to the same schools for as long as they wanted. Maybe they didn't know the difference, but I did. I never wanted them to know the feeling of terror in their stomach that I'd known when I entered a new schoolroom in the middle of the semester as the new kid, not knowing anyone, having everyone look at me as if I were a slimy green frog. And once, when the teacher didn't remember my name, I was too mortified to correct her so I went by the name Susan for a whole semester. Yes, I adjusted, but at what price? Now that I look back, I think I married Alex for stability, for the promise of staying in one place, for the security of never being the new kid in the classroom again. And now I was on the brink of total insecurity, once again I was standing in the middle of the room, while the rest of the world stared, or pointed its finger at me and said, You're weird!

With that awful memory in my head, I went to the phone to call the bank and begin the process of refinancing my house.

CHAPTER THIRTEEN

"Hey, you look really cute," Maureen said, giving Steffani the once-over. Steffani was wearing a white blouse with a round collar, a light blue sweater that matched her eyes, a blue plaid skirt, and saddle shoes and socks. Her bleached blond hair was parted on the side, with a wave over one eye, and the lower section curled in fluffy curls.

"You look cute too," Steffani declared, glancing at her friend's navy ensemble. "We're the two cutest girls rushing Pentaliers this semester, don't you think? I'm sure we're going to get in."

They were cute, but not the two cutest, and not the most popular ones either. Girls like Teddy Graves and Lucille McCallister had their pick of clubs to join. Everyone wanted them, especially the Lancelettes and the Bandelles, which were the two top clubs.

"There's some really neat girls in the Pentaliers," Maureen said. The Pentaliers wasn't one of the best clubs; it was in the second category, halfway down.

"Really neat girls," Steffani echoed, knowing there were only a few top-caliber girls in Pentaliers. Suzanne had been a Lancelette, the best club of all, but most of Suzanne's friends who could have helped Steffani get in had graduated. To the newer crop of members, Steffani wasn't what was called "Lancelette material." Those were the student leaders, the cheerleaders, and the most popular girls at MacArthur High, who had steady boyfriends or dates every weekend.

"Even if we don't get in, we'll be okay," Maureen said.

"Don't be a defeatist," Steffani said, something she'd heard her mother say hundreds of times. Then she smiled and waved at three Pentaliers who were walking by. "Hi, you guys."

"Hi." They smiled back. "Good luck tonight."

Steffani felt her heart thud. Tonight was the voting meeting. If you were voted in, the whole club would come to your house after the meeting and take you to Bob's Big Boy, to celebrate and to show you off to the boys' clubs. Then tomorrow would begin Hell Week, where you were required to do anything a member told you to, within reason, for one week, culminating in Hell Night. No one would discuss what went on at Hell Night. Each club's initiation ritual was different, but Suzanne had told her basically what to expect. Suzanne had been popular and sought after when she was in school. She'd held student body offices and was a princess at homecoming. Steffani had been so proud of her, glad to be known as her sister. Sometimes Steffani wished she was like Suzanne and other times she was glad she was different. Suzanne tried to help her learn how to fit in; they had long talks about what the popular kids expected, and Steffani tried. But for Suzanne it came naturally, while Steffani had to force it. She had an independent spirit that put them off; they could tell she thought some of the things they did were silly, yet she still wanted to be accepted by them. Not because she was Suzanne's sister, but for herself. No matter what happened, Suzanne would still love her and think she was special, but *they* had to think so too.

She watched the retreating figures of the three girls who held the fate of her life in their hands. They had shapely hips in their slim wool skirts, which moved in unison as they walked away. Two of them had short dark hair; one had a long ponytail.

"I heard Mary Ann smokes," Maureen said, referring to the girl in the middle.

"So?" Steffani said.

"Do you think she's cheap?" Maureen asked.

"Heck no. Just because someone is willing to experiment with life, doesn't make them cheap, Mo."

Maureen nodded. Steffani knew so much. She was so deep. She aced her schoolwork, whenever she was well enough to be in school. Her frequent absences had kept her grade average down, to an overall C +, but if she were in school all the time, she'd be sure to get all A's. "What do you think of our chances?"

Just then, the noon bell rang, signifying the end of lunch. "We'll go over them on the way to class," Steffani suggested. She enumerated the names of the eight girls she knew who were "going" Pentaliers, and she rattled off the ones who'd get in for sure. Then she discussed the members who she was sure liked her and Maureen, and would fight for them. It only took two votes against you to keep you out. And if one person didn't like you, they'd get their friend to vote against you and you were blackballed. Steffani knew that not every girl in the club liked her, or Maureen either.

"Just remember, we're not a package," Maureen said. "You'll get in for sure, but I may not, and I don't want you to be tied down by me."

"Come on," Steffani assured her. "We'll both make it. We're better than all those other girls who are applying." She'd told herself that every day for the past semester, waiting for spring when new members were voted in.

She could barely eat dinner that night as she watched the clock. At seven o'clock, the meeting was just getting started. At eight-thirty, they were just now discussing their choices. At nine o'clock, she went into the kitchen and stood looking out at the street, wearing her new pink sweater, with her fingers crossed, and her hands crossed and her legs crossed. They could be here any minute now. *Please let them choose me*, she prayed. *I want to belong more than anything. I've missed so many things in school by being sick, but this is my chance to catch up. It would be so wonderful to go to football games with my club, instead of just Maureen, and be able to wear the green jacket to school so everyone will know I'm a Pentalier. There'll be really neat parties, and exchanges with the boys' clubs. I'll do anything to be part of that. I'll be so good. I won't complain. I won't be grouchy to Mom and Dad, or ungrateful to my sister when she loans me her clothes, and I won't cry once, even if I get an attack. Oh, please!*

At ten, she picked up the phone to call Maureen. They'd made a pact not to call one another, just wait and see each other at Bob's later on when they had both been voted in. Maureen's phone was busy. She hung up fast, in case Maureen was calling her.

It was still not too late. She wouldn't start to worry yet.

At ten-thirty, she called Maureen again and Mrs. Simon answered. "She's not here, Steffi. The club picked her up over an hour ago."

It felt as though her heart had just been slammed in a door. Falling off a mountain would have been easier than the feeling of total failure that filled her up to the brim. And even though she was filled with failure there was an emptiness so deep she ached in places she didn't know she had. She burst into tears and ran to her room, throwing the door closed so hard that the house shook.

No one noticed. The television had drowned out her pain. *Will it ever be over*, she wondered, *this wanting something so much, and never having it? Will I ever get what I want?* Tomorrow she'd have to go to school and see Maureen's happy, shining face and the rest of the Frogs in Green—the name the non-orgs gave to the Pentaliers because of their green jackets. She'd have to hold her head up proudly, and congratulate all the girls who'd gotten in and see the sympathy in their eyes, and the secret glee, and know they were thinking, *She's just not Pentalier material, too bad*. How superior they'd feel to be accepted when others were rejected. From now on, she'd always be on the outside. The rest of her life would be different, even more than before. She could see it all ahead of her like a long tunnel of darkness, the aloneness, the separateness, being on the outside, like a black finger pointing at her. Despair overcame her and she sobbed as though something inside of her was breaking.

Her door squeaked as it opened. "Honey? What's the matter?" Lynnette tiptoed across the room and sat down on the bed, pressing the mattress with her weight. Burt was there too, standing in the doorway. Steffani heard him clear his throat.

Her mother's soothing hand on her back almost burned and she flinched, pulling away. She didn't deserve a gentle loving touch. She was nothing. Twenty-eight girls had just said so.

"I didn't get in," she sobbed. "They blackballed me."

Her mother's arm went around her shoulder. "Don't cry so hard, honey, it's not good for you."

"Oh, Mother!" she cried, "I don't give a damn what's good for me anymore."

"I'd like to break every bone in their bodies," her father said, his usual pronouncement for anger. He'd never struck anyone in his life. It almost made her smile, the thought of the Pentaliers in a heap of broken bones and green jackets trying to smile their peppy high school smiles with broken jaws. But then the reality of what life would be like from now on overwhelmed her again, and she sobbed anew.

Behind her, she knew her parents were exchanging glances; their hurt for her was as deep as her own. She'd seen that expression so many times when she was in pain, understood that their commiseration with her was organic, that what they felt when she suffered was as bad or even worse than when her body was throbbing and her head burned with fever. For a brief moment she almost hated them, resented them for encroaching on moments like this. *It's my pain, for God's sake, let me have it*, she wanted to scream. But it was always like that, a competition of whose suffering was worse, hers or theirs. Suzanne said they competed over everything, over whose turn it was to talk, whose career was the more successful, whose artistic expression was the more important. Even to whose choice of a restaurant was better. Now they both wanted to be rejected from the club along with her.

She turned over on her back, shading her eyes from the hallway light that shone in on her. "This is the last time I'm ever going to give those simpering jerks a chance to get to me,'' she said. ''They can take their club and shove it.''

Neither of her parents knew what to say to that. They were quick with righteous indignation, but seldom directed it towards the source of their anger; her mother was too concerned about being nice and that people like her to confront anyone except her husband, and her father rarely yelled at clients who deserved it—instead he took his frustrations out on waiters, gas station attendants, or on Lynnette. Steffani vowed she would not do that. If someone pissed her off, that's who would hear about it.

''I don't understand,'' Lynnette was saying. ''You're so pretty, and so smart. And you have nice clothes. What more do they want?''

Are you kidding, Mother? she wanted to say.

''How many of these girls were Jewish?'' Burt asked.

''Oh Daddy, that has nothing to do with it.''

''I can't imagine Jewish girls acting like this.''

Steffani reached for some Kleenex and blew her nose.

''Have you talked to Suzanne? What does she say?''

''I knew you'd bring her up, Mother. She's different than I am. She got into Lancelettes, the best club. I didn't have a chance with those snobs.''

''They weren't snobs, they were nice girls. They loved it when we used to let them use the house for their parties.''

''You don't understand.'' Her exasperation shot out like steam. ''They're not snobs to each other, or to anyone they think is just like them. But if you're different, forget it. They won't give you the time of day.''

''Well, I say good riddance,'' Burt pronounced. ''You're better off without girls like that. You have your own friends.''

''Sure, the losers and the misfits.''

''That's not true,'' Lynnette said. ''What about Maureen?''

It hurt so badly, Steffani couldn't even tell them that tonight she'd not only been banished into ordinariness for the next three years but she'd also lost her best friend.

''I think I'd like to be alone, now, okay? But I appreciate

your coming in here like this. It helped a lot." She faked a yawn. "I guess I'm kind of tired. Maybe I'll go to sleep."

Soon, they left her alone. She tried not to cry any more, but couldn't help it, sobbing into her pillow, pounding on the mattress. And finally the house was dark and quiet. Her parents had gone to sleep.

She got up from the bed and tiptoed quietly down to the family room. She took the key to the bar cabinet from behind the bottle of rye shaped like a Russian Bear, and unlocked the doors. The bottles glimmered in the moonlight. She reached for the scotch, her favorite, and took a swig. It was harsh at first, burning her throat, and she gasped, trying not to cough or spill any. She looked up at the glasses from where she was sitting on the cold tile floor and thought about using one. But they were too far away to reach, and she didn't want to get up. So she just sat there, taking swig after swig. She thought about Suzanne, wondered if she'd understand what it felt like to be rejected. She'd try, but only the person who'd gone through it would know how it felt. Besides, Suzanne had her own life now in college dating those mature men. Steffani wished things were like they used to be even when they fought instead of Suzanne being so far beyond her. She saw the moon shining through the crack in the curtains, and then studied the horses leaping over stationary hedges in the wallpaper. After a while the horses seemed to actually be jumping and she figured she'd had enough, put the bottle back, locked the cabinet, replaced the key, and went back upstairs to bed.

CHAPTER FOURTEEN

Alex was an odd mixture of components: altruistic, idealistic, practical, and compulsive. If he said he'd do something, by God, he did it—thoroughly and brilliantly, too. He was passionate about politics, wanting to help his fellow man. But from the time we began to date, another side of him emerged, his fascination with glamour.

He and my father became friends because Alex loved to ask about Dad's work and would listen to every story with rapt attention. My father loved to tell about the old days when he'd booked the big vaudeville acts before he met my mother and he'd name-drop about the ones who'd become famous comedians in the movies.

I'd stand by impatiently, while Alex and my father talked. At first I was annoyed because Alex ignored me from the moment he arrived at my door, until I could drag him to the car and get on our way. Gradually, I began to accept that this admiration could bring Alex closer to me. Alex's fascination with famous people surprised me. To me, celebrities were mostly people who let you down when you needed them. I'd seen them do it to my father more times than I cared to remember. Granted, they did create magic on stage, and their voices could fill my heart with longing and a wonder that enriched the soul. But they had no loyalty; my father said so and he was right. And they were users, climbers, insecure people—petty, and sometimes paranoid. Hardly the sort to adore and emulate. Alex didn't know that. Most people don't and wouldn't believe it anyway. They think the characters they see portrayed on the screen or on television are really the people themselves. They rarely remember that a writer created those characters, and the actor or opera singer only interprets the writer's creations. That's what I dreamed of being someday, a writer. Someone who creates lives out of her own head, who peoples a private universe and makes it breathe.

Alex graduated from USC Law School in June of my junior year at UCLA and that summer he studied for the bar. I hardly saw him. When the exam was over in August, he was like someone let out of prison; all he wanted to do was play. But I had my senior year to complete, and couldn't consider going with him on the student tour of Europe he had planned. I couldn't afford it either.

"If we were married, you could go," he said. And my heart stopped. Marrying Alex was my dream. I shook with desire for him, I ate, slept, and drank him with every breath I took. He was everything I wanted in a man. Funny, sexy, authoritative, ambitious, socially conscious, smart, Jewish, and good-looking. He loved my parents, and they loved him. On paper, it looked great. My sister was another matter. She thought he was pompous and jerky, that he wasn't right for me at all, and the worst of it was, he had Gloria for a sister. He thought Steffani was spoiled and smart-mouthed, probably because she didn't like him. Sometimes I agreed with him. Her, I seldom agreed with where Alex was concerned.

"I thought you didn't want to think about marriage until you were established in a practice," I said, crossing my fingers. If I was anything, I was always fair to Alex. And though we'd been dating almost exclusively for a year, he'd never said he loved me.

He took my hands in his. Mine were trembling, the palms moist. I wanted to wipe them but didn't dare move. "You know how I feel about you," he said.

"No, I honestly don't. I know how I feel about you, though." I swallowed the lump in my throat and willed my heart to pound less frantically. "I love you. Very much. I've loved you for a long time, but I never had the courage to say so."

"There, you see," he said, as if that answered the question.

"See what?"

"We both feel the same. You're a beautiful girl, you're smart, you're kind, you're a fantastic listener and a great conversationalist. I'm crazy about your family."

He was reading a laundry list. I wanted to die from humiliation. "What did you mean, we feel the same?"

"You know."

"Say it!" I wanted to shout, but I kept my voice evenly controlled.

"That we feel the same?"

Was he dense, or what? "I said I loved you, and you didn't say it back."

"Of course I love you. Would I want to marry you if I didn't?"

I felt a warmth coursing through my body, a tropical rain washing over me. *He loves me. He wants to marry me.* "Why haven't you ever said so?"

And that's when it happened. Up until that moment, I don't think Alex really did love me, but in that moment he fell in love. I know because of the way he looked at me, deeply into my eyes, as though he were melting. And then his eyes filled with tears. "I do love you, Suzanne," he whispered. "I really love you!" He seemed surprised by his own feelings, by the flood of emotion unleashed within him. I could tell he meant it when he said, "I love you." He kept repeating it and I couldn't hear it enough. "I've listened to my sister tell me I wasn't in love for so long that I believed her. I didn't trust my own instincts. I knew you were the best thing that's ever happened to me, but I told myself, be logical, be practical. And when I was logical and practical, you came out on top. You had all the qualifications. And I measured and weighed you constantly."

So it was Gloria, I thought. *Damn her.*

He saw my expression. "Don't blame my sister. She really likes you. You're one of her best friends."

Her only friend, I thought. *Why would she have tried to*

convince Alex he didn't love me, and told me all those times
that he didn't care about me, when he did? If it wasn't for
Gloria, this might have happened much sooner. I knew she
was strange, but I'd never suspected she could be devious.
That she might be envious of me amazed me. She was so
talented and glamorous.

"Gloria and I have always been close," Alex tried to
explain. "And she's very possessive." He shook his head.
"I can't believe I let myself be fooled into thinking I was
making an intellectual choice when all the time this is what
I wanted to do." And he pulled me to him and kissed me
deeply, passionately, as though he was pouring all his love
for me into that kiss. We were in his car, our most familiar
place, where we were truly alone, and I kissed him back,
feeling my own emotions welling up within me, resolving
never to pay attention to what Gloria said again.

His hands caressed my breasts, fingertips gliding over my
nipples, which sprang erect, yearning for more of him. His
hands claimed my body, allowing our passions to erupt and
continue without stopping. I was on fire. Was this Alex? The
cool kisser, who hardly ever tried anything? I had become
outrageously flirtatious with him; I'd touch his knee, run my
hand up his thigh, sometimes accidentally brush against his
groin, try anything to get a rise out of him, wondering if he
was a homosexual, or if I just didn't appeal to him, wondering
if he would ever want me. And now, there was no doubt of
his virility, or his desire. I could feel his erection pressing
against me, and gently I reached down and stroked him. He
pulled back and gazed at me, not letting me take my eyes
from his as I continued to touch him. Not knowing what he
wanted from me, I started to withdraw my hand.

"Don't stop," he whispered, pressing against my hand,
still looking into my eyes. His facial muscles got all tight,
slightly distorted; his breathing was shallow, panting; he was
rubbing against my hand, harder and harder; and then he came
with a groan, never taking his eyes from mine. I knew he had
given me a gift of love. That he'd wanted me to see how

much he felt for me, how much I made him feel. And then he told me. "This is the only way I could show you that I love you. I've never let myself realize it until now. I'm such a jerk," he said, and then he kissed me again. I was so inexperienced. I'd had boys rub against me until they climaxed, but I rarely helped them along. It wasn't nice to do that. And what they thought of me was so important, I didn't realize they might have thought I was nicer if I had helped. As for letting them touch me, on top of my clothes only, and not under my skirt. It was amazing how excited I could get with all those clothes in between. Imagine what it would be like with bare flesh against flesh? I was trembling all over, wondering if it was my turn now. And it was.

Alex touched me lightly, under my sweater, under my bra, which he reached behind me and unhooked, and at each new place he touched, I gasped and flung my head back, and closed my eyes, but he said, "Look at me, love," and I did. I was so excited that when his hand traveled down to my stomach, and then lightly caressed between my legs, barely brushing me there, I climaxed almost immediately, feeling that amazing warmth flooding through me, as I pulsated inside, out of control. In that moment, gazing at him, giving my deepest emotions to him the way he had given his to me, I felt married to him. Later, when we were finally married, and all the pressures and stresses of a big wedding had taken their toll, there was never again such a sweet pure moment of giving between us as there had been the night we got engaged.

We got married during Christmas vacation of my senior year. Alex had passed the bar and was working at Lloyd, Benson, and Krupp, but he still had to fulfill his armed services requirement, and now that he was out of law school, his student deferment was over. But in 1961, they weren't drafting married men. If there was a need, however, they would draft him, so he decided to join the National Guard, which required him to spend one weekend a month at the base and two weeks a year at camp, for four years. We would hate the weekend separations and knew we'd never have a vacation together until military service was over, but it was better than his being drafted and going to Southeast Asia, where the fighting was heating up all the time. That summer, after graduating from UCLA, I got pregnant with Amy and we decided to take our chances on Alex being drafted. The military wasn't drafting married men with children. After the Cuban missile crisis, when President Kennedy activated the National Guard and we realized that Alex would have had to go into full-time service for eighteen months, we were doubly grateful that we'd had our precious Amy.

One day, when Amy was six months old, Alex came home from the office at eleven o'clock in the morning and went to bed. "Are you sick?" I asked. "Can I get you anything?"

"No, I'm just tired," he mumbled, staring at the walls as he passed me. I heard him in the bathroom and then he got into bed and slept all day. The next morning, he didn't get up for work.

"Alex, what's wrong?" I asked.

"I'm just exhausted," he kept saying, though he'd slept for hours.

"I'm calling the doctor," I insisted.

"No, honey. Just leave me alone. I'll feel better later." That was on a Friday. He slept more or less all weekend. On Monday, I could see the same pattern happening, and was truly alarmed.

But when I went into the bedroom after putting Amy down for her morning nap Alex was sitting up in bed, the drapes still closed, his knees drawn up to his chest and his arms wrapped around his legs.

"Honey, what's wrong with you? You must be sick. Why won't you let me call a doctor? Nobody is tired enough to sleep for four days without something being wrong. I'm sure the office is wondering where you are. Do you want me to call them for you?"

He looked at me then with such guilt on his face. "Did

anybody from the firm call?'' Alex was in the real estate division of a prestigious L.A. law firm, earning a starting salary of fifteen thousand a year, which to us was excellent.

"Nobody called, and I think it's strange, don't you?'' I waited for his reply, staring at him, though I couldn't see his eyes clearly through his glasses. His hair was mussed, the room smelled of stale air, he hadn't changed his pajamas in days, and he needed a shave. This unkempt person couldn't be the fastidious man I married. But then I started realizing that he hadn't been himself for weeks, maybe months. He rarely joked with me anymore, or even smiled, except when he played with Amy.

"Alex, what is it?'' I asked.

"I quit my job, Suze,'' he confessed. "Last Thursday. I just couldn't talk about it until now.''

I was shocked. "You did what? I don't believe it.''

"It's true. I've been unhappy there from almost the first week but I stuck it out because it was a good job.''

"Why didn't you ever tell me?''

"What could you have done?''

"Understood, helped you, listened to you.'' I wanted to cry. Why had he kept this from me?

"I knew how you felt.''

"About what?'' I came and sat on the bed next to him, thinking about all the things I had to do today, especially now, while Amy was napping. Once she was up, I'd never get my work done.

"About show business.''

"What's that got to do with anything?''

"Last week I got the call I've been waiting for. I wanted a job at an entertainment firm, but no one was hiring. And then, last Thursday, I got a call from William Morris. There's an opening in the legal department, and I took it, even though it means a cut in salary. I start next week.''

"How much of a cut?''

"I'll be making twelve-five to start. But I get a raise in six months.''

I just didn't know what to say. "Why did you make this

decision without even talking to me?'' I asked, trying not to let my temper flare, trying to understand.

"I really want this, Suzanne, I knew you wouldn't approve, the way you feel about celebrities. But I'm more alive when I'm around performers and artists, people who make the world go around, the power-brokers, the money men, the stars and the czars.'' His eyes were excited, shining happily, and I realized I hadn't seen him this way ever. "I want to be a part of that life, Suzanne. Can you understand that?'' I nodded, dazed. "I want to know them, and have them know me, be useful to them, even indispensable.''

"I wish you'd told me,'' I said, also wishing he didn't feel this way at all.

"I couldn't. I knew I'd get your standard lecture about how shallow they are, or empty-headed, or self-centered, or cruel. Well, I don't believe it anyway. I think you just spout the tapes you've heard all your life from your parents. Maybe it took your father years to make it big, but that won't happen to me. In the beginning he let people take advantage of him, and he didn't hang on to his name clients because he thought it was beneath him to socialize. Well, I won't make that mistake. I know what it takes to make it, and I'm going to do it.''

I wanted to cry for the way he saw my father, my handsome, compassionate, hardworking, and most of all self-sacrificing father, who had not pursued his own career wholeheartedly, like most men do, because his sick daughter and overworked wife needed him more. He may not have planted bulbs in the garden, but for years he gave up his own dream for Steffani's sake.

"Are you with me in this?'' Alex asked.

I wanted to say yes, but I felt manipulated. He didn't trust me and he hadn't told me something as important as this. Along with feeling bewildered, I felt betrayed and embarrassed. Was I so judgmental that he couldn't confide in me?

He saw my expression. "Now, don't make a case out of it, Suzanne.''

"I just don't understand, Alex. I noticed something was

wrong lately and I didn't know what it was. I thought it would pass, and now I see there's been something festering. Is this the way it's going to be with us? You make the major decisions and tell me about it after the fact?''

"No," he sighed. "This is a one-time thing." He seemed depressed again, as though he too was disappointed. Our inability to reach one another was hurtful, causing an ache inside of me, right between my ribs. I wanted to do something to make this ache go away, but I had no idea what.

The following Monday everything seemed back to normal. He was ebullient as he left for work, and came home at eight o'clock that night whistling. The old Alex was back again. After the first two weeks of such late nights, I mentioned that the hours he put in were above and beyond the call of duty, and he said, cheerily, "That's show biz."

Alex's show biz life was quite different from what I'd known as a child. He was building a career, I'd been born into one. We didn't have the disadvantage of having a sick child. Building a career in show biz is serious business. You have to entertain. Hollywood is a company town. Either you're in the industry, or you're not, and if not, you're not interesting to those who are.

Lawyers entertained clients in the firm, starting with the starlets and bit players, who just might become stars. Also, directors, producers, writers, and—lastly—agents. Entertaining is expensive, so I learned to cook. Alex's favorite kind of entertaining was a formal dinner for eight, just the right amount of people so that everyone could get to know one another. And the guests always talked shop: which films were being packaged, who was hot, who was not, and who was sleeping with whom. The men were obsessed with making deals, and Alex got stars in his eyes talking about 10 percent of 5 million net, 5 million gross.

It was a time of estrangement for me and my sister. If I invited her over, she'd decline. If I asked her why, she'd criticize Alex. I was hurt by her behavior. I wanted her to love the man I loved. She refused. I told myself, two can play that game. Whenever I saw her at home, I ignored her, and though she pretended not to notice, I knew she did. We'd always been so close. I thought she was being a brat; what she was being was scared of losing me.

CHAPTER FIFTEEN

"I like this," Steffani said, trying to be enthusiastic about Suzanne and Alex's new, rustic little house in Beverly Glen— the artsy-craftsy community on the Westside. It had taken her a while, but she'd finally accepted Suzanne's invitation to come and see the house. "In just two years you have all this, and a baby." She tried to keep the sound of envy out of her voice. A picture window in the living room revealed the hill behind the house covered with wild California greenery. *Imagine having a house of your own.* This place was exactly what she would have adored, except that it came with Alex.

"I'm surprised Alex is living here," Steffani commented, "in hippie heaven." Beverly Glen residents held a yearly street fair, and there was a co-op nursery school, plus several communes.

"We both love it here." Suzanne, as usual, was defensive. "We have opossum, skunk, coyote, and even deer wandering around. They warned us to cover the fish pond with chicken wire, or the raccoons will eat the koi."

Steffani tried to seem interested, but all she felt was angry. Here Suzanne was, a married woman with a family. Where did Steffani belong? She never thought she'd feel this way about her own sister, that Suzanne was as far away from Steffani's reality as Grace Kelly.

Suzanne put her arm around Steffani's shoulder and hugged

her, trying to make it seem as though things were the way they used to be. "It's hard to believe, my baby sister is graduating from high school next month. And then what?"

Suzanne's voice held that note of endearment Steffani always responded to, and she began to soften. "I'm going to UCLA for sure, in September. I've been accepted."

Suzanne grinned and Steffani smiled back. Her sister's approval and pride in her always made her feel wonderful.

"And this summer?" Suzanne asked.

"I've decided to have the operation." The idea scared her to death but she hid that from Suzanne so as not to appear weak.

"Then you'll be ready to start school by September. The fraternity boys won't know what hit them when they get a look at you." Suzanne forced her voice to appear cheerful.

"If all goes well," Steffani said, trying to match that cheeriness, but the thought of bone surgery on both legs was terrifying. It was the most painful kind. Her legs had grown crookedly during a growth spurt when she was thirteen; one leg bowed and the other was bent toward it. The result was that she walked at an angle, her body out of alignment. As her mother described it, "One day her legs were straight, and the next day they were not."

Dr. Levinson, her orthopedist, said he could straighten them surgically when she was fully grown. "There's nothing to it," he assured them. Of course, she knew he was minimizing. She'd be in for months of pain, but she trusted Dr. Levinson. She wanted her old self back again without compensations.

The family had met Dr. Levinson when he'd set her arm after she'd fallen out of bed and broken it years ago; so, some good had come out of that episode. David Levinson was one of the few doctors in Los Angeles who knew about Gaucher's disease. He was aware of all the current research and the latest treatments. He also had a daughter with cerebral palsy and knew what it was like to be a parent with exceptional concerns about his child's health. Her mother depended on him, asking his advice about Steffani constantly.

"I'm not surprised Alex is doing well," Steffani said after Suzanne had shown her the house. "Making money is the one thing I knew he'd be good at." They were waiting for Amy to wake up from her nap. "I hear you're going to Spain in May. It's been a dream of mine to go to Europe," Steffani said, longingly.

"I didn't think we could afford it after buying the house," Suzanne confided. "I hate to leave Amy, but our mothers will take care of her."

"I wish I could help," Steffani said wistfully, "but I don't think Alex trusts me with her."

There was an awkward silence when Suzanne finally broached the subject they'd avoided ever since her engagement. "Why don't you like Alex?" she asked.

Steffani was about to let her have it—list all of Alex's faults, describe how he took advantage of Suzanne, how pompous he was, narrow-minded, condescending, and influenced by his sister—but she saw the pleading look in Suzanne's eyes and she was suddenly ashamed. Maybe it wasn't Alex she objected to, except that he was Suzanne's husband. Probably anybody Suzanne might have married would have rubbed Steffani the wrong way. It was strange to realize that but she hadn't seen it before. As her mother would say, she was cutting off her nose to spite her face. Soon she would be facing another terrible ordeal in her life; she needed Suzanne to help her through. Now was not the time for them to be apart. So what if Alex was not the ideal brother-in-law? Her sister loved him.

"I don't dislike him that much," she said, laughing. "I just think he's a bit judgmental."

Suzanne laughed with her. "I guess he is sometimes. But he's a good father and a good husband."

"He makes beautiful babies."

"Amy is beautiful, isn't she? She reminds me of you when you were a baby. I hope she grows up to be as beautiful and as smart."

"You will be home from Spain in time for the surgery,

won't you?'' There was no iciness in her tone now. She was trying to convey to Suzanne she was sorry.

"Of course," Suzanne assured her, softening her own voice to match her sister's. "And I wouldn't miss your graduation, either."

Steffani felt suddenly weepy, grateful that Suzanne would be there. After the way she'd been acting, she didn't deserve it. "I'm so glad," she said, her eyes filling with tears that she wiped at roughly, not wanting them at all. "I was beginning to feel as if I'd be here all alone while the rest of the world was off living their perfect lives, sunbathing and traveling to exotic places."

Suzanne shook her head. "I'll never leave you, Steff. You know that," she said. Her eyes were teary too. "I promise."

The Costa del Sol was as picturesque as I'd expected. White rocky mountains set back from the shore, and a cobalt blue sea. We went to Málaga, Torremolinos, Majorca and Marbella, and even to Tangier for a day. And amazingly, what had started out as a vacation changed my life.

Perhaps it was that I had achieved the basics by twenty-three that enabled me to look outward, beyond myself. After all, I was married and didn't have to worry about finding a mate. I had a child and a home, and someone to support me. I was a lucky woman. Somewhere in the back of my mind, I'd thought eventually it would be a good idea to be a writer and have a legitimate reason to tell myself stories the way I'd always done, sort of formalize my hobby. But it was a fantasy. As an English major I'd been thoroughly intimidated by the literature and the poetry I'd read. To be a writer, one had to be great. I wasn't. But lately I'd thought, perhaps I could entertain. After all, entertainment wasn't such an ignoble occupation. In fact, my husband thought entertainers were the *most* important people, or he wouldn't have been so enamored with them.

It was in Marbella that I got an idea for a book. Alex and I were in the habit of going off on our own, away from the tour whenever we got the chance. Gloria had told us that the Marbella Club was a very *in* place, so we went there. For a few pesetas we gained admission, rented beach chairs, and sat among all the beautiful and wealthy people for an afternoon, letting the waiters bring drinks to us on our lounges, pretending to belong. Joan Crawford was there, and Julie Newmar, and Curt Jurgens. Most of the women wore high heels with their bathing suits, and gold jewelry against their tan skin. The men were either young and darkly handsome or older with silver hair and an air of wealth about them. The men, too, wore gold chains around their necks. Some of them even had their own personal servants waiting on them. Later, we saw those same men aboard enormous yachts docked at the harbor.

I had gotten a glimpse of a life I had never seen before, of European opulence that made a wealthy American life-style seem trivial and mundane by comparison. Just by paying a few dollars' admission and knowing where to go, I'd rubbed elbows with these people. How difficult would it have been to meet them? Not very. Many of the men had looked at me. It would have been easy to flirt.

I got to thinking, what if an American woman decided she wanted to get into the jet set in Europe? Could she do it? Quite possibly, I decided.

On the plane ride home I started to plan my first novel. I didn't tell anybody I was doing it; it was my secret. But in a few weeks the pages started adding up. Alex saw me busily taking notes at odd times and figured I was writing. He humored me. I'll never forget the smile he gave me, the same one he'd give Amy when she did something adorable, the *Isn't she cute, couldn't you just eat her up*? smile.

"When are you going to let me read your story?" Alex asked, belittling its importance by not calling it *my work* or *my novel*.

"Soon," I'd promise, but I didn't think that day would ever come. Alex was a perfectionist, a man who noticed every detail. He wanted me to iron out the fold creases in the tablecloth before setting the table, and he inspected the silverwear for spots. The thought of his scrutiny made me break out in a sweat. Everyone I'd ever heard talk about writing agreed that it took *discipline*. Something I didn't have. So I decided that if I was ever going to do it, I would put no demands on myself. If I wrote, fine; if I didn't, no guilt allowed. I was just telling myself a story that went on and on, the way my grandmother used to tell them to me. I didn't know anything about structure or conflict, just that I was fascinated with what was unfolding on my pages week by week. And since I was never going to send it to a publisher, it didn't matter how good it was. I was only doing it for myself. The only person I told what I was doing was Steffani, just before her graduation.

"You're writing a book?"

I couldn't read her meaning. Either she was laughing at the idea that her sister, the clod, would attempt such a thing, or she was impressed. Either way, her tone made me uncomfortable.

"Hmmm," she said. "What's it about?"

"Well, the basic premise is 'how to catch a count.' I was intrigued with the idea that if a middle-class, fairly sharp American woman really wanted to, and set her mind to it, doing whatever was necessary, she could actually end up marrying a member of European royalty or someone fabulously rich."

"Oh," she said. Not too impressed . . .

"Wallis Simpson did it, and Jenny Jerome, and I'm sure there are many others."

"But who cares, Suze? Why write about something like that when there are much more important things to concern yourself with." I remembered the article she'd written for the school magazine on literary criticism. It won an award.

"Would you prefer me to write about the starving children in Europe?" I teased.

She smiled, recalling the times we'd been told to eat our oatmeal or our liver because there were children starving in

Europe. One time Steffani asked if she could put her oatmeal in a shoe box and send it to them.

"I'm writing about something I find interesting, Steff. It's just a fantasy. I'm not ready for anything important in the beginning," I explained, wanting her to understand, to praise my efforts.

"But once you get to be known as a writer of *that* kind of fiction, that's what you'll be labeled. No one will ever take you seriously."

"Get to be known!" I hooted. "Are you kidding?" The idea was as fantastic as it was outlandish.

Little did I know.

The following week Steffani had the surgery, a nine-hour ordeal, while her bones were cut, reshaped, shortened, lengthened, and restructured as if they weren't made up of tissue and cells and millions of screaming nerve endings.

The hours of that hot summer dragged by, each day longer than the one before because of new and impossible conditions. Steffani lay on a hospital bed in our parents' unair-conditioned family room in a body cast that covered her hips, her waist, both of her legs down to her toes, and her torso all the way up to her armpits, leaving her totally immobile. Only her rear end had been left out so she could go to the bathroom by being lifted, prone, onto a bedpan.

Steffani couldn't tolerate visitors because she was in pain most of the time. Most of her friends stayed away anyway, unable to cope with the torturous situation. Watching her suffer was almost as horrible for us as it was for her. She had no appetite and began wasting away. Just washing her hair was a monumental task. My mother's task. As was most of her care.

I visited as often as I could, as long as Amy didn't have a cold. We couldn't risk infecting Steffani. And I read to her from my book, *To Catch a Count*.

"It's not bad for what it is, Suze," she told me. "The sentence structure is too simplistic and the voice a bit stilted.

I didn't believe a lot of it. I think your situations need work. Your main character is too self-pitying; she loses sympathy. But the other characters are interesting and well delineated. What happens next?''

My heart felt as if it had been stabbed. *Criticism.* The heat of shame and anger washed over me. I fought the need to burst into tears. *How dare you*, I wanted to say, even though I recognized how insightful she was. It came so damned naturally to her. I wanted her to say my book was wonderful, but I knew she'd never say it if she didn't believe it. I swallowed my disappointment and wrote down what she'd said, promising to think about it later when I'd lost the desire to strangle her in her bed. And then I remembered her last question: What happens next? She'd wanted to know! At least I'd hooked her with the story. But right now, with the churning inside of me and this sick feeling in my stomach, I didn't think I could ever write again.

"Do you want me to tell you what happens?" I asked, forcing myself to appear unconcerned.

She was about to say yes, but then a new bout of throbbing pain took her attention and she moaned and gasped, her eyes rolling up in her head. Finally, when the extreme part of the aching had passed, she looked at me with glazed eyes and said, "Don't tell me what happens. Write another chapter and read it to me next time."

And so I kept going, until the pages really began to pile up.

Sometimes Steffani felt as though she were an actress because they were usually immersed in themselves to the exclusion of all else. Nothing existed outside the I-me syndrome. Pain had a way of doing that, it kept you focused on the narrow existence within your own skin where no other consciousness occurred except your own agonizing currents.

When she was able to look beyond her own skin, the entire world consisted of the edge of her bed on the left; the night stand with the clock, the radio, and the glass of water on the right; the foot of the bed, which sometimes extended as far as the television a few feet beyond; and the wall behind her head.

In rare moments she could recall that real life existed outside her room, but that awareness came at odd times. Sometimes it was brought by a visitor who entered the room smelling like the outdoors; perhaps it was the heat of the sun still lingering on their hair, or their perspiration, or newly applied powder, but it brought an instant recall of another reality that sparked an entire memory. Suddenly, with a jolt of recognition, she'd see outside this room, to the world beyond, and even for a brief moment it was wonderful, heady, almost to feel a breeze on her skin or the cool water of a swimming pool as she dived in on a scorching day. But, finally, it was just so tantalizing and so definitely forbidden that she'd slam the door right in her own face; and the realization of exactly how deprived she was of just the simplest pleasures of living would shoot through her like another bolt of unbearable pain. If she'd never experienced the fullness of life, maybe she wouldn't miss it so much, but like the cruelest forms of torture, she'd have it fully, and then it would be snatched away.

All her friends who were eighteen and a half years old were out showing off their bodies at the beach, their senses reeling from erupting hormones, while hers were dormant. Sometimes, when she'd been out of commission for a while—this recovery from surgery being the longest—all that energy, that need to grab life would build up. Once she was free to let it go, it would literally explode into a frenzy of living.

UCLA in September. College! Only that thought kept her going through this summer. To have been accepted at UCLA, with as many absences as she'd had, was a testament to her brains, her friend Lila said. Lila wasn't college material but she was the best friend Steffani had ever had. The only friend who gave back.

She and Maureen had stayed friends, even though Maureen was in a club and she wasn't. Their friendship wasn't as close as it once had been, but Maureen still needed her. All her friends did. She was their voice of reason. She sometimes wondered why she understood the things they didn't, but usually she accepted that she was just more insightful.

"When my mother yells at me and tells me I'm stupid and lazy, I want to kill her. Everything she says drives me up the wall," Maureen had said on the phone just this morning. "But your mother's cool, and beautiful and sweet. She's so good to you, the way she waits on you."

"She gets on my nerves too, Maureen. How would you like to have your mother wiping your ass every day? She's the one I scream at, she's the one I cry to, she's the one who calls the doctor, she's the one who gives me my medication. She feeds me, she bathes me, she plans my goddamned life minute by minute. You think she never loses her temper, you think she's always cheerful and glad to have to take care of me? She pretends to be, but I feel her exasperation. We drive each other crazy sometimes. And she's always telling me what to do. How would you like that?"

There was silence while Maureen thought about what she'd said. Steffani knew she'd made her uncomfortable. Nobody wanted to be reminded of her condition; it made her too different. Illness was scary. Her friends were afraid that maybe they could get it too, or something like it. So they avoided talking about it, and when they said, "How are you?" she just said, "Fine." They didn't like visiting her either. Seeing her forced them to face the reality of her being sick, and that was truly discomforting. Again, if her condition was something that she had all the time, maybe they'd get used to it, accept her for the way she was. But when she was well, she was more beautiful than most of them and she seemed as normal as they were. So, because her condition came and went, whenever she got sick, they felt betrayed. She could see it in their eyes. They couldn't depend on her, know that she'd be there, the way they depended on each other. To compensate, she'd learned how to be the best friend in the world. She listened to their problems, gave them advice, doled out sympathy by the hours. And she did it well. It kept them in her life.

"I'll call you tomorrow," Maureen said, hanging up.

But what Steffani really wanted was for Maureen to come over tomorrow, not call, and tell her about the party she was going to Saturday night and all the other gossip that would have made her feel as though she was part of life, and not the unwanted crusts from someone's sandwich.

UCLA is going to be so wonderful. School starts the second week in September and this is July twenty-third. Hurry up, legs, heal. Bones, in there, mend already. Mend! Bruins, here I come!

That night she was awakened by a pain in her right leg that was so excruciating she couldn't stop screaming as though someone were pounding an iron shaft through her knee. Lynnette and Burt sat with her all night, wiping her brow, putting on cool compresses, doing anything they thought would help. But even an extra half dose of painkillers didn't take away this pain.

"Something's wrong," Steffani kept repeating. "It's pressing against the cast, Mother," she cried. "It's growing in there, my leg is growing."

As soon as it was light, they carried her to the car and rushed her to the hospital where Dr. Levinson met them and removed the cast on the right leg. Steffani's knee had developed a rampant infection inside the cast and it had turned into gangrene.

CHAPTER SIXTEEN

"Mu-thur," Amy said, greeting me at the back door when I came in with my arms full of groceries. "I've been answering the phone all day. Everybody has been calling you. Your publisher said it's urgent if you get home before three-thirty.'' It was now 5:00 P.M. "The *Los Angeles Times* called, the *Herald*, and several reporters from news services. I wrote them all down.''

"Uncle Sid," Jered added. "And Papa too.''

"What did they want?" I asked, feeling a chill go through me. Just then the phone rang and all four of us jumped.

"I'm not getting it again," Amy announced. "It's for you anyway.''

I picked it up. It was my father. "Suzanne, this has got to stop. We've got to do something.''

"Dad, what is it?" I could hear the fury in his voice.

"Your mother and I got one of those letters; it's too disgusting to repeat to you. We're coming over.'' And before I could say anything he hung up. I called him back immediately but my mother answered.

"Don't come over, Mom," I told her. "Let me find out what's going on first and then I'll call you, okay?''

"Suzanne, we're so worried about you. What if this person wants to hurt you more than by just sending letters? You should hire a bodyguard.''

"Mom," I sighed, "I'll call you later.'' And I hung up. But I was truly frightened now. Maybe she was right. *My God*, I thought. *Did everyone I know get one of those letters?* I felt my body start to tremble and I forced myself to go into the kitchen and begin putting away the groceries. Miles came to help me. How stupid I'd been to think I was through with this, that it was a one-time occurrence and would never happen again. I should have protected myself! But how?

I glanced over at the kitchen table. The mail was there. Among it was another brown manila envelope. In that moment I wished I had the power to make that envelope catch fire and burn right there on the table. The children were watching me; I maintained control.

"It's really stupid, isn't it? I can't let this affect my life. I've got other problems to deal with.''

I approached the table and picked up the envelope. This one was postmarked New Jersey, no return address.

With shaking hands I opened it. Inside was another letter on my publisher's stationery, along with the same Xeroxed copies of the pages from the book I was supposed to have plagiarized.

I read:

> *To whom it may concern,*
> *I am enclosing proof positive that Suzanne Winston is a fraud. If she plagiarized one novel, she could have stolen her other ones too. By accident, I discovered the original book she plagiarized in a secondhand bookstore; unfortunately the cover was gone, so I don't know the title. But it was published in 1934 by Obregon Press, Chicago. I'm sending this letter to you and to other members of the press because as an interested party you might help me prove her guilt. I think she should be exposed, don't you?*

It was signed, Sherry Fallon.

The children were watching me. I forced a smile. "This person is crazy. Absolutely nuts."

"Why, Mom?" Miles asked, coming up behind me.

"Sweetheart, I have no idea."

The phone began to ring again. Apparently, this same material had been sent to the press as well. I spent the next half hour trying to convince strange reporters that there was no truth to these accusations.

One woman assured me, "We didn't think it was true, but we have to check these things out. Have you contacted the publisher, Obregon Press?" she asked.

"It's the first I've heard of it," I told her. "But I'd be willing to bet that there's no such publisher, or else they've been out of business for years."

She wished me good luck. But everyone else was accusatory and hostile. Finally, we took the phone off the hook, much to Amy's annoyance. To a teenager, not being able to use the phone was the worst possible punishment.

In my purse was the card Barry Adler had given me of a private detective. Fortunately, he was still in his office and agreed to see me the following morning. But all that night I barely slept, thinking about the damaging articles that were being written about me, possibly ruining my credibility. And I was innocent! How could I convince people? Even more, who in hell was doing this? I was more frightened than I cared to admit. Was someone following me? Would they hurt me physically? What about the children; were they safe? Cars driving behind me, people on the street suddenly became suspect.

The investigator's office was on Wilshire Boulevard near Fairfax Avenue, and his name was Avery Bellows. Fiftyish, portly, with gray hair, he had the appearance of being trustworthy and solid, but who was I to judge? Nothing was as it seemed anymore in my life. As I entered his office all I could see was how expensively it was furnished and how much this was going to cost me when I needed every dollar I had to pay my debts.

Bellows shook my hand and studied me through dark, hooded eyes. We sat on an upholstered sofa across from his desk and he read the letters. "I wouldn't minimize this, Mrs. Winston," he said when he'd finished reading. "These are mean and vicious. They indicate a disturbed individual."

"What I find so hard to believe is that someone took the time and effort to make this look so real. That's the part that scares me the most. Do you think I should get a bodyguard; am I in physical danger?"

"Let me reserve judgment on that," he said, and placed the letters on the teak coffee table in front of us. "I want to help you to get to the bottom of it, though it will be up to you to decide how far you want me to go: to find and identify the criminal, or to prosecute and go all the way to trial, which is more complicated."

"Suppose that, for now, I just want to find and identify the person," I said, feeling hopeful that he could do that. "If I knew who it was, maybe I could get them to stop." I'd also like to wring their neck.

"Unless exposing them would cause them to want to do even greater harm."

"Are you saying we shouldn't try at all, for fear of what we'll uncover?"

"No, we can try and find out who they are." He cleared his throat. "But you'll have to let me have a free hand."

"Of course," I assured him. "Do you think Mr. Adler's suggestion about my going public with this is a good idea?"

"Only if the papers start carrying the story, and we'll know about that in a short time now, I imagine. Otherwise you'll be giving this person just what they want, attention."

"So my instincts were correct."

"Now, as I said, though you don't make a public announcement, I must be given a free hand. Even if it becomes embarrassing to you."

"What do you mean?"

"These kinds of investigations can get rather personal, and even though I maintain the strictest confidence . . . well, you understand."

"No, I don't," I said, hotly. "I have nothing to hide. I'm not guilty of plagiarism, I feel strongly about that. And I didn't do anything in my life to warrant these horrible attacks."

He nodded, reassuringly, but I was afraid he didn't believe me. "Mrs. Winston, more often than not, we find that there's a disgruntled lover somewhere in the past who's the culprit."

"Well, I've been divorced for nearly five years. My ex-husband and I have a friendly relationship. He's remarried." I flashed on all the craziness Alex and I had gone through after the divorce. At one time I'd have suspected him of this, but not now. We'd put that all behind us.

"Anything to do with money?" he asked, as if reading my tea leaves. "Do you owe him any, does he owe you?"

I felt my skin prickle as I avoided his eyes, thinking what a mess my finances were in right now. "We've both lost some money in an investment together recently, but I don't see how that has anything to do with it."

"I need all the details," he said, reaching for a pad of paper and making some notes.

"But I lost as much as Alex did."

"You don't know that for sure, do you? He could be cheating you. This could be a blackmail scheme."

"But I haven't received any demands for money."

"You may and, then again, you may not. How about sex? Any kinky things I should know about, with your ex, or anyone else? Sometimes, kinky people carry that behavior into other parts of their lives."

I studied the little blue horses racing in even rows over the dark red of his tie, feeling as though I were being examined by the KGB. I was suddenly afraid that anything I told him would be used against me. I hated having to tell him intimate, private things about myself that were mine alone. I only told them to my readers when I could give them to a character and pretend they weren't mine at all. To me, writing was an anonymous form of self-revelation.

"There hasn't been anything kinky," I said, knowing that I didn't have anything that would even amuse him, let alone titillate. He made a note of it.

"What about other boyfriends?"

I listed them briefly. Hearing myself, I felt ordinary and uninteresting. Nothing like the stuff of my novels.

"How about your family?"

I described them, our closeness, my sister's illness, my parents' courage, and that made me start to cry. He waited.

The session went on for two hours but each time he brought up a new subject and we examined it, it went nowhere. To his credit, he had amazing patience, explaining, "I'm looking for anyone who could be a hidden connection between the perpetrator and you. Perhaps an envious relative or colleague, or a disgruntled employee, obviously someone bright enough to put together such a manuscript. At least I'll listen to you, which is more than the police will do."

I wracked my brain for more to tell him.

Finally, when he'd completed my history, I asked him, "What now?"

He seemed discouraged; so was I. "Even though we don't have any direct leads to a specific person, I can start out by having a lab analyze the paper that the letters were written on. Once I've narrowed it down to a specific source, I can find the specific time it was shipped. Then I'll go through the records of the retail stores looking for a name that we recognize, maybe someone in your life. It takes time, but we may make headway. I can also have the typewriter analyzed. See if more than one was used and, if so, what kinds. You might trace this person through the typewriter."

It sounded as impossible to me and as much a waste of time, as my trying to find a specific typesetter in the entire country. "What is this going to cost?" I asked.

He handed me a list of his fees, starting at $25 an hour. He saw my expression. "If this is difficult for you, perhaps you'd like to wait awhile, though I must say, the longer you wait the colder the trail becomes. It's always easier to get a witness to remember sooner than later."

I nodded. "I know you're right, but as I explained, my debts are rather large right now. Could we start off in a small way, just find out the source of the paper, maybe, and the kind of typewriter, and then see where we want to go?"

He stood up. "It's up to you; I don't usually work that way. Let me think about it. Whatever I decide, I'll have to charge you for today's session."

I nodded and we shook hands.

"There is one thing I might suggest, based on all that we talked about today. That you make a list of your own, of everyone in your life who could possibly be a suspect, and keep your eyes open. It may be someone you don't know, but my guess is it's someone who knows you, someone closer than you think."

I agreed, thinking about the list I'd had in my mind all this time, comprising everyone I knew. From Alex, to Gloria, to my friends from high school and college, old boyfriends that I hadn't gone to bed with, one girl in junior high named Rosalie who'd started hitting me in the hallway after cooking class because my muffins had risen higher than hers. I'd even considered friends from my childhood, like Jasmine and Marilyn. Once I'd even included my sister on the list, as well as my housekeeper. It was all so ridiculous I might as well include my parents and my cocker spaniel. None of them could have done it, I was sure.

I waited for the story to break in the papers, but only the *Enquirer* carried it, and it didn't make the headlines. The article said someone was out to get me, a popular novelist, by accusing me of plagiarizing one of my novels. I was quoted as saying, "I've never copied from anyone in my life. Who could be doing this to me?" It sounded like me, but I'd never given them an interview. It wasn't as bad as I'd feared.

Shortly after my appointment with Avery Bellows I had to meet with Alex, Murray, the accountant, and Floyd Exner from the IRS to finalize our arrangements for repaying our debt. I had to convince Mr. Exner to let me have twenty-four months to pay back what I owed.

Murray said I'd get the time I needed, but the way things were going lately, I didn't feel I could trust what anyone said.

"You'll help me persuade him, won't you?" I asked Murray.

"You know I will," he said, without much enthusiasm.

For two hours we sat in that office arguing about the IRS ruling but we never made headway; in fact Mr. Exner's patience was gone and I was afraid he would refuse my request.

When I heard Alex and Murray agree to an eighteen-month payment program my heart raced out of control. I had argued, but they ignored me. I felt overruled and ineffective. Murray wouldn't even look at me. Finally, he got my message.

"Floyd," he said with a smooth conciliatory tone, interrupting him as the man gathered his papers. "Mrs. Winston would like a longer pay period than eighteen months. Is there any way you can see fit to allow her more time?"

Mr. Exner had based his decision on Alex's ability to pay, lumping us together in a perverse recap of a once better time.

"We already agreed on eighteen," he pronounced, "and I think that's rather lenient."

"Mr. Exner," I protested, using every ounce of persuasive power I had. "I won't survive without twenty-four months to pay off my debt. Six more months can mean everything to me and my family." Murray was ominously silent while Alex motioned for me to be quiet.

"Mrs. Winston, Mr. Winston is complying. I'm afraid that's final." His lips formed a thin line of determination.

"But Alex makes a steady salary every month. He earns yearly bonuses, while I have an erratic income and the expense of three children." *Dammit, Murray and Alex weren't backing me up.*

"But you're a high earner, Ms. Winston," he said, obviously resenting that I earned more than he did. During the last two hours, I'd found his attitude to be that any woman who wrote about love and sex and business, who thought she could compete with a man, deserved anything that happened to her.

Later, when I told Steffani about it, she said I was being paranoid, but she hadn't been sitting there in Murray's office, watching Mr. Exner wipe his pink bald forehead, which perspired every time he looked at me with a mixture of lust and disgust.

"Twenty months is the most we've ever allowed anyone to pay off their debt, Mr. Levy." He usually spoke to either Murray or Alex, as though I didn't exist.

Twenty months to pay back $225 thousand. I wondered if he'd change his mind if I placed my hands around his throat and choked him until his pink forehead turned red. Probably not. But there was another part of him that if I squeezed tightly enough might make a difference. The thought turned my stomach. I had to do something.

Exner was about to leave. And I was desperate to save my home.

"Please, Mr. Exner, won't you reconsider." I got up from my seat on the opposite side of the table and came around to head him off at the door. "I won't be living frivolously if you grant me this extra time. I'll cut everything to the bare bones. But the extra time would allow me not to lose my home, to keep my family secure."

He looked at me then, with black round eyes under a pink forehead, and I let him see my expression of abject misery. "Please, I'm begging," I said, holding my breath, aware that he was studying my body, which I willed not to perspire, not to intrude, not to entice.

Evidently, he was satisfied that I'd gone as low as possible, for a look of triumph flashed in his eyes briefly and he nodded. "All right, ma'am, twenty-four months." And with that, he hefted his briefcase, opened the door, and left the three of us alone.

Alex turned to me. "That was truly embarrassing to watch, Suzanne. It really wasn't necessary, you know."

"If you'd pay your share of school tuition, I wouldn't have had to grovel, Alex. I'm not kidding. I could lose my home."

The two of us glared at one another but my embarrassment didn't take away my relief. I felt betrayed by the whole male world at the moment, but I'd done it, I'd taken the first step in saving our lives. At least for now we'd have a roof over our heads.

When Alex had gone, I said to Murray, "I expected better of you."

He actually blushed.

"Can you work out a payment schedule for me now?" I asked, coldly.

"It depends on what you make on your next deal, Suzanne. When will that be?"

"Not for several weeks," I guessed. I'd been working

twelve to fourteen hours a day trying to finish more of my new book before I offered it for sale. Ironically, at the moment, my work on *Annica*, the book my grandmother had written so many years ago, and I was now completing, was my only refuge against the harsh realities of life. Losing myself in a sweeter time of history that my grandmother had written about was my only enjoyment. The world of *Annica* was a gentle one, a time when carriages and automobiles shared the roads. It charmed me to be in a time when women's gowns were an essential accessory used to attain the coveted goal of romance, and love at first sight was still a possibility. When I was working on the book, I didn't think about having to do without any luxuries for the next two years. Two years isn't so long when you're living it day by day. But saying no to the children every single time they asked me for something would not be easy. I wondered how they would feel about me when our enforced period of penury was over.

CHAPTER SEVENTEEN

The sound of voices in the next room woke Steffani from her nap. For a moment, upon awakening, she forgot about her plaster prison, and then felt it around her again along with the throbbing pain in both legs. That first moment of awakening, when the realization hit her again, was the most difficult time. Then she became aware of the voices she had heard, a man and woman whispering. Steffani held her breath trying to hear but her heart was pounding too loudly. She was bathed in sweat; often since the surgery she perspired in her sleep, another indignity to endure. Her mother said it was caused by weakness following an infection. Thank God, she hadn't lost her leg. The antibiotics had worked. But she hated being weak. All this time in a cast had drained every ounce of her strength.

The hip cast had been removed last week, and only the leg casts remained. Still, merely sitting up in bed exhausted her. And school was starting in two weeks. All summer she had watched the days go by, counted them moment by moment, everything focused on September 14. Could she be ready in time? *Oh God, please! Let life begin again.*

She felt her body temperature returning to normal and her heart rate slowing. Now she could hear the conversation in the next room. Her mother was talking.

"Sometimes I can't stand it for another minute," Lynnette said. "If I didn't have you to turn to, I couldn't go on. She takes everything out on me. But when I'm just about ready to yell at her or lose my patience, I think about what she's going through and I can't blame her. Thank you for coming over today. I couldn't have handled it alone."

"You have amazing strength, Lynnette. You've always been able to handle the most difficult situations." Steffani recognized Dr. Levinson's voice. "I've seen how you encourage Steffani, time after time, how you keep her spirits up. I never cease to marvel at you. Nobody would blame you if you lost heart now and then."

"Whatever I do is hardly enough. But you, too, keep your spirits up, David, even when we're alone, in spite of your daughter's condition."

"You're my example. No, really. Whenever I get depressed, I think of the way you are."

There was silence for a moment while Steffani held her breath wondering what they were doing; their voices were so personal, intimate. It made her uncomfortable but fascinated.

"How have things been between you and Burt, lately?" the doctor asked.

"We argue all the time. Taking care of Steffani takes up all my attention and I think he resents it. He's jealous of you."

"I was afraid of that."

"But what can I do? I don't have the patience to put up

with him, not now. If only he'd be more understanding. It's as if he waits until I'm exhausted after taking care of her to make demands of me." Lynnette was crying. "It's nothing new. It's been going on for years. Sometimes, I'm so torn. I've never known if we're doing the right thing."

"I am sorry," he said. "But you know she needed the surgery."

"Did she, really? And now, how am I going to tell her this latest news?"

"Do you want me to tell her?" he asked.

"No, it's my responsibility," Lynnette said, starting to cry.

What news? Steffani thought. But the sound of Lynnette's crying was muffled, as if she were crying against him. A mixture of shame and anger and dread rushed through Steffani. She dreaded hearing this latest news, and yet hated her mother for talking about her father to Dr. Levinson, and for leaning on him for comfort. *I'm the one who needs him, not her. Damn her,* Steffani thought. She resented their closeness and in her worst moments suspected her mother of getting more than mere comfort from him over her sick daughter. She even watched the two of them for signs, but all she saw was a kind of heightened awareness when they were together. Most of the time she felt guilty for her unkind thoughts. Her mother may have a perpetually silly expression on her face whenever Dr. Levinson's name came up, or she saw him in person, but that was all.

It seemed that being confined like this, in constant pain, was changing her for the worse, making her suspicious of everyone. But Dr. Levinson was her doctor! Yet, whenever he came over, Lynnette bombarded him with questions, hogged his attention. Dr. Levinson was important to all of them but especially to her, and she wanted him all to herself. His was the only smile that made her feel better even when things were really bad.

"Who's there?" she called out, pretending she didn't know so they wouldn't think she'd been listening.

"Shh, she'll hear us," Lynnette said. The whispering

stopped. Then, the door to the family room, where Steffani had lived for the past nine weeks, opened and Lynnette and Dr. Levinson came in.

Her mother had that look on her face, a cross between guilt and sorrow, her lips kind of pursed, a slight frown between her eyebrows, her cheeks in a sweet semi-smile. Usually it meant, *I'm going to tell you something difficult, you'll hate it, you'll fight it, but there's nothing we can do about it, so you'll just have to accept it.* But sometimes it didn't mean anything at all, except that Dr. Levinson was here. This time, there was a mixture of pain and anguish in Lynnette's eyes Steffani hadn't seen for a while. She knew her mother suffered terribly for her sake, but she ignored that pain or she couldn't have survived.

"Steffani," Lynnette began, softly, gently. "There's something I have to discuss with you; will you hear me out before you interrupt?" Steffani nodded. "Dr. Levinson and I have been talking about your starting college next month. He doesn't think you'll be ready in time. Honey, you're just not strong enough yet. The bones haven't healed . . ."

"Oh God, don't tell me that," Steffani said, turning her face away, holding on so she wouldn't start screaming. Didn't they know? Didn't they understand? She couldn't stand this one more minute! With enormous effort she swallowed the scream that was welling up inside.

Dr. Levinson took over, perching on the edge of the bed. She could not feel his body next to her through the wall of her leg casts, but the bed dipped under his weight. Neither could she look at him, at his curly, graying hair, at his piercing brown eyes, though he took her hand, then touched her arm as he talked, pressing first on her abdomen, then on her upper thighs in that way he had of examining her. He reached down and touched first her right foot and then the left, feeling the skin, testing the movement. She kept her face turned away but she knew his eyes were studying her, seeing the skeleton protruding from her skin at the collarbone, the pointy scarecrow elbows, the chest ribs, thinking she had hardly any flesh left at all.

"Your color is better," he pronounced. She turned and glared at him. "I know you're disappointed, but you can go to UCLA next semester. The important thing is to recover from the surgery first. We had that setback with the infection, and the Gaucher's cells have kept your bones from healing as quickly as I'd hoped."

"Setback. Is that what you call it?" She blamed him, God how she blamed him.

He ignored her accusation, talking on, while every ounce of her was screaming inside, *Not going, not going, damn you!* She felt the tears welling up, spilling over, wasn't even aware she was sobbing, or that he was hugging her and patting her shoulders.

"Honey, don't let yourself get so upset." Lynnette hovered close by her other side. "It doesn't help at all."

"Oh Mother, just shut up! I don't want to hear that anymore!" Steffani cried out, reaching for a Kleenex at her bedside table. "You promised me!" she shouted at Dr. Levinson. His huge brown eyes ringed with the dark lashes stared at her sadly.

"I know I did, Steffani, but sometimes things don't go exactly as we planned. It was a difficult operation; the recovery has been steady, but not as rapid as I'd have liked."

"And gangrene didn't help," Steffani said, trying to hurt him; it was his fault, him with his crazy ideas.

"No, that was something we didn't anticipate. But you're on the road now," he said, with another determined pat. Then he got up and asked Lynnette, "How's she eating? Are you drinking those malteds your mother's making you? That will put some meat on your bones."

She wanted to shove something sharp into his stomach, make him feel the aching disappointment she was feeling. And her mother too, how dare she be so beautiful, so competent, so patient, so kind while Steffani's life was passing by.

Levinson seemed unconcerned, though that was his way. He cared as her parents cared; it just didn't make sense to wallow in her sorrow with her. It never did. She felt her anger start to wane and, instead, that sick feeling of dread filled her up again. More months of boredom, of being at home, of being *out of it*. She thought of what her friends would be doing. New attachments would be formed without her, fall classes would begin and be half-finished by the time she got there. January was a lifetime away. How would she ever get through it? Long weeks, dead hours, months of nothing loomed ahead. And just to give her a reminder, as if she needed one, both of her legs started aching again.

She pressed the electric button on the hospital bed so she could sit up straighter. She was crying again. "Dr. Levinson, the pain is so terrible I can't stand it. The shots aren't holding me, they wear off too soon."

"We have to be careful, Steffani. Your mother knows more about your dosage than I do. She's the one who's been giving you the shots." He was not much taller than her mother, standing next to her. The two of them looked to Steffani like Raggedy Ann and Andy. He turned to Lynnette again. "What do you think?"

"I'd rather not increase the amount, David. She's been on the medication a long time, we don't want her to get addicted."

"If I hear that one more time, I'll scream," Steffani threatened. "People with this kind of pain don't get addicted!"

"Yes they do," Lynnette said, emphatically.

"Oh God, why are you always against me?"

"Honey, I'm not." Lynnette's voice and expression reflected that she'd been injured by the accusation. She looked away and then wiped her eyes.

"Why don't we switch back to the first drug. Sometimes changing after a while is a good idea." He was moving toward the door.

"Dr. Levinson," Steffani called, wanting to detain him, hold him here, not let him leave. He was the one with the knowledge of what would become of her, contained all her hope, all the solutions, all the expertise, and all the answers to her life. And he only stopped by for twenty minutes at a time, spending most of it with her mother. "When can I be up on crutches? When can I walk? If I can't walk, I won't ever get my strength back." The effort of talking made her tremble with weakness.

"Why don't we see how you're doing next week," he said, running his fingers through his hair. He had a deep tan from Sundays in the sun and the kind of skin that didn't need much exposure to retain its color from weekend to weekend.

She thought of his life, the long hours he worked performing complicated surgeries every morning at six, then hospital rounds following that, afternoons of treating patients in the office, evenings lecturing, writing; and then, on Saturdays, he visited his daughter at her special school for children with cerebral palsy in Santa Barbara. His wife was a gourmet cook, wrote cookbooks in fact, but he said he liked Lynnette's cooking better—not as fancy, or saucy as his wife's. He'd tasted it when he came to see them, passing through the kitchen. He always complimented Lynnette on the aromatic smells of stuffed cabbage and chicken paprikash.

"As a matter of fact, I brought a pair of crutches with me in the car, in case you were ready. But, I only want you to practice getting up and standing, before you take any steps, for at least a few days. You'll do as I say, won't you?" And without waiting for her answer, he was out the door.

"See that she takes it slowly," she heard him say to Lynnette, who followed him out of the room. Steffani was sure they would talk more about her and she wanted desperately to hear.

Now that he was gone, Steffani felt bereft, as though not only her energy had been drained, but her hope as well. Dr. Levinson took with him his enthusiasm and his assurance that everything would be all right, leaving her with the knowledge that she wouldn't be able to start college until January. At this moment, she didn't think she could survive one more minute. Oh, the helplessness of being who she was, of being a prisoner within her own body; this hateful betrayer of a body, how it tormented her. Yet, even now, her spirit could soar if only despair wouldn't engulf her again, the damn black cloud of it. She sobbed anew, weakness pressing down on her, steamrolling her flat.

After a while, Lynnette came back, composed enough to give her the pep talk. "Honey, it will be all right. You'll go to college in January. It won't be so bad missing one semester. You'll be much stronger by then and ready for college. This way, it would be too great a risk."

"Oh, will you stop!" Steffani cut her off. "I hate this, I hate it!" Yet her mother's words of encouragement, which she never failed to deliver, were Steffani's lifeline, her oxygen, the only thing that kept pumping new healthy blood, as well as hope, through her veins. She was totally dependent on her mother's constancy, and Lynnette never let her down, no matter how she abused her.

"You know I'm right," Lynnette said, stroking her forehead lovingly. "It won't be so bad to wait until January. It's not as if you're not going at all. And pretty soon you'll be able to get out of bed. Won't that be wonderful? We'll get a wheelchair and take you outside."

The mere thought of feeling fresh air on her skin was exquisite. Steffani stopped crying and wiped her eyes again. There was no use in crying. At least not for long. She'd concentrate on getting her strength back, on getting out of bed. Maybe the next few months would go by more quickly if she had mobility. "Did Dr. Levinson leave the crutches here, Mom?" she asked.

Lynnette nodded. "They're in the other room."

"Will you get them for me."

"Oh honey, not now. You're not ready."

"Yes, I am," she insisted. "I want to stand up. Please, let me try."

Lynnette looked at her and almost shook her head. And Steffani knew why. She was a pitiful sight. Her body was nothing but bones, she had dry flaky skin, there were puffy circles under her eyes, her blond hair had dark roots growing several inches from the scalp, her fingernails were broken and uneven, and her complexion was sallow. But she smiled anyway, even though, at the moment, her straight white teeth—the Blacker family trademark—looked much too large for her small shrunken face.

Lynnette smiled back, a radiant smile that forgave any displays of temper, always looking for ways to encourage in spite of her own trepidation. "I'll go get the crutches, but, honey, there's one condition."

"What?"

"That you'll wait until your father gets home so he can help you up. If you fell, you could injure yourself, and I don't think I'm strong enough to lift you."

Steffani nodded. "Okay, I'll wait till later. But just bring them in here so I can see them, so I can think about walking again. I won't try anything, I promise."

"That's a very good idea," Lynnette agreed, and hurried to get the crutches.

CHAPTER EIGHTEEN

My sister-in-law, Gloria, had her operatic debut during the summer of 1962 at the Spoleto Festival in Italy. We heard about her triumph from my mother-in-law, who had chaperoned her, and of course was prejudiced, though I'm sure Gloria was good. When my father heard her sing in college (in exchange for my first date with Alex), he predicted a successful career for her and kept up on her progress with interest.

At Juilliard she developed into a dramatic coloratura soprano, aspiring to be a spinto soprano. So Alex was delighted when he heard she'd be appearing at the Wilshire Ebell Theater and we'd be able to see her in a recital of operatic excerpts from the festival, along with several other potential stars of the current operatic world.

I had never felt the same toward Gloria since I found out

she had bad-mouthed me to her brother. Even though I'd felt obligated to include her as a bridesmaid, there had been a coolness between us from the time Alex and I got engaged. She and Alex, however, were still quite close and she called him long distance from anywhere in the world to discuss her career and ask his advice.

The longer I was a member of Alex's family the more I learned about them and saw examples of Gloria's true character, which I didn't like. She treated her parents badly. Here they had sacrificed all their lives to pay for her singing lessons and expensive schooling, while Alex paid for his own. And instead of being grateful, she always wanted more. She called her mother the yenta, and her father a milquetoast. Either she used them, or ignored them and nobody but me seemed to mind.

The night of Gloria's performance, my mother had to stay with Steffani, who was still in her cast, and my mother-in-law, who had seen this review in Italy, offered to baby-sit for Amy. So that meant that Alex and I would go with his father and my father. At last, my father would get to see Gloria perform on a stage. He'd heard her sing only when she'd auditioned for him and when she sang at my wedding, "And This Is My Beloved," from *Kismet*.

When she offered to sing at the wedding, I realized it would not be for my benefit, or even as a gift for her brother whom she loved, but to impress my father. I only agreed to let her because Alex would have felt I was slighting her if I'd refused.

The night of the wedding, prior to the procession, she stood on the bimah of the temple and sang directly to my father, as if he were the only member of the audience. My father and I were waiting in the wings to walk down the aisle, and it was truly embarrassing. But my father didn't notice her that day, for there were tears in his eyes. He was giving his baby away in marriage to another man.

As we stood there listening to the song, he turned and smiled at me, clutching my hand in his, and I was overcome by tenderness and longing. My childhood was officially over; I was about to become a married woman with all the responsibilities that entailed. I would have a husband to cleave to instead of my dearest father; and a new mother-in-law, who'd give me mostly unwanted advice; and, of course, a sister-in-law, who immediately after the ceremony came over, and without even congratulating me, wishing me well, or welcoming me to the family, asked, "What did your father think of my song?" As if that was the only thing on my mind during my very own wedding.

"He thought you were excellent," I told her to keep peace, as Alex dragged me away to have our pictures taken by one of my mother's colleagues. But as I smiled for the camera, I knew what I'd said hadn't satisfied her. On the sidelines I could see her questioning my father, gazing up at him, hanging on every word. I wondered if he was telling her she'd been excellent too. Seeing him with her like that, I'd felt uncharacteristically possessive, suddenly realizing that not only was I a member of her family now, but she was a part of mine. I didn't want her having anything to do with my father!

After the formal pictures were taken, I got caught up in the festivities and forgot about Gloria until I heard loud voices shouting at one another and turned to look. "Why won't you?" she was saying to my father in a demanding, embarrassing voice, so that many of our guests stopped with their champagne glasses in midair to look at her.

"Gloria, will you please keep your voice down?" my father said nicely, trying to avoid a scene.

"I will not. Not until you tell me why you won't represent me."

"I told you, dear. I don't think you're ready. You have many years of seasoning ahead of you. I believe I said so last year, when I first heard you. Now, please Gloria, this is my daughter and Alex's wedding, not the place to discuss this."

"You're a fool not to grab me now while you have the chance," she said, her voice dripping with anger. "But then, what else would I expect from someone like you. Someday you'll be sorry," she threatened, childishly. And then, like Rumpelstiltskin, she stamped her foot so hard I thought it might go through the floor, before she turned and ran out of the party to hide herself in the bridesmaids' room. No amount of coaxing would persuade her to come back, not by either of her parents, or by Alex, though they tried several times during the night, leaving me alone to go and talk to her, nearly ruining the wedding for me. Finally, my mother suggested that I go and persuade her, but I refused.

"This is my wedding, Mom, and I'm not going to spend it running after spoiled Gloria," I insisted.

"But Alex and his parents are so unhappy," she said. "You don't want to start out your marriage on the wrong note, do you?"

"Tell Dad to go see her," I said, but my mother didn't like that idea at all, saying that it would be like giving in to a child's tantrum.

Finally, though, it was my father who persuaded her to come back, and later during the evening, I even saw him dancing with her. I nearly felt hatred toward her, or a strong resentment, when she glanced over at me triumphantly as if to say, *See, I won.*

Now, she was finally going to get her chance to dazzle Burt Blacker, the classical artists' agent who she most wanted to represent her in the entire world. Needless to say, I had mixed feelings.

We arrived at the Ebell twenty minutes early. Alex wanted to go backstage and say hello; he hadn't seen Gloria for months.

"Let's wait until after the show," I said as he dragged me backstage. "I'm sure she doesn't want company now."

But Alex couldn't resist basking in whatever limelight there was and disregarded my warning. My father-in-law, Sam, accompanied us backstage, but my father said he'd wait in the lobby until curtain.

Backstage was the usual tumult of people—stagehands moving props, technicians checking cables and lights, and performers getting ready. Gloria had a small private dressing room.

Her eyes lit up with joy when she saw Alex, though she barely gave her father or me a nod.

"Hi brat!" Alex said, giving her a bear hug.

She pulled away and squeezed his face between her fingers so that his mouth puckered, then she gave him a kiss with puckered lips of her own. "Boy, are you gorgeous," she told him, then brushed her father's cheek with her lips. "Daddy!" she exclaimed, as though reprimanding him, "you're so thin."

My father-in-law, a slight, balding man, with Alex's dark eyes and broad smile, hadn't been well lately, suffering from an extreme lack of energy. He said it was nothing and brushed aside our concerns, refusing to see a doctor. My mother, who claimed to practice medicine without a license, thought there was really something wrong with him. Later, it turned out she was right, he had a heart condition.

"Hello, Suzanne," Gloria said, kissing the air next to my cheek. "I see you haven't lost all your weight after Amy was born. Maybe you could give some to my dad."

I felt self-conscious about being scrutinized as Alex and my father-in-law both turned to look at me, in my Courrèges copy from Ohrbach's with the short white boots, to see if I was too fat.

"Yes, I have," I said, defensively. *Only eight pounds overweight isn't so much, considering I gained forty-nine.*

Gloria then noticed that there were just the three of us and it was as if she'd been struck by a blunt instrument. Her expression, always prone to the dramatic, assumed an attitude of horror. "I thought your father was coming," she said to me. "I've been looking forward to having him here."

The timbre of her voice suddenly sounded hoarse, strained. "Are you all right?" I asked, slightly alarmed.

"It's nothing. Just a bit of a strain. It will go away."

But it wasn't going away, in fact she was rasping now, with a voice that sounded as though it came from hell.

"Where is your father?" she repeated.

"He's in the audience," I told her. "He doesn't believe performers should be interrupted before a show." I gave Alex a *"Let's go"* look.

The news that my father was in the audience did not restore her equanimity. Instead, she grew more distracted, staring off into space as if listening to ghostly advice while ignoring us completely. We stood there waiting, not willing to say anything to break her mood for what seemed like a long time, but was probably only seconds. And then, as if waking up, she turned suddenly to me, saying, "Go on, get out of here now," and shoved me toward the door.

"Gloria," her father cautioned, "be careful." He caught my arm as I lost my balance.

But Alex behaved as if everything was normal, and studying her notices taped to the mirror, said, "Boy, these are amazing. Let me read you these rave reviews."

"Alex, not now," I said, nodding my head to Gloria, who was just standing there. "Please."

Alex moved over to his sister and put his arm around her. "Burt is gonna love you tonight, sis," he said, as though oblivious to the undercurrents.

I was getting exasperated; it was as if a mummy from a horror movie had just popped out of a closet in our midst and I was the only one who had noticed.

Finally, my father-in-law timidly intervened, moving us toward the door. "We'd better go now." Evidently he was used to his daughter's behavior.

"We'll see you later, sis," Alex said. But she just stood there staring in some odd state of catatonia.

The moment we were outside in the hall, my father-in-law said, "What do you think? Is she all right?"

"Sure!" Alex insisted, but without great conviction.

"She's got that *expression* again," my father-in-law said. I thought he looked particularly frail himself.

"No, she didn't," Alex said.

"I'm telling you."

"You'd better do something."

"What can I do?" My father-in-law's plaintive tone implied helplessness. "She's never listened to anything I've said in her whole life."

"You're never firm enough with her, Dad." I'd heard Alex complain about this before where his sister was concerned. He'd told me, in rare moments, that his parents were too lenient with Gloria and had spoiled her, catering to her artistic temperament. I wondered which came first, the temperament or the being spoiled.

"Now is not the time for you to give me a lecture in parenting," my father-in-law said. "Your mother should be here. She's the one who handles her."

"Gloria is twenty-five years old, for heaven's sake," I exploded. "You're both acting as if she's twelve. What's the matter with her?"

Alex looked at his father for a beat too long, as though asking for permission to tell me. My father-in-law turned away, abdicating his position. His behavior annoyed me even more. I wanted to say, "You're the father here, Sam, why don't you take control? You're letting your children walk all over you." But to keep peace in the family, I kept my mouth shut. I thought about how my own father would have handled this, instantly and firmly. But then, neither my sister nor I would have ever terrorized our parents, or disrupted our brother's wedding, or accepted financial support as if it were our due. My father wouldn't have allowed it. And in that moment I understood more about Alex by watching his father than I ever knew from what he'd told me. I also wondered if he would be firm enough with our own children.

I repeated my question. "What's going on with her?"

"Once, before a high school recital," Alex explained, "something upset her and she refused to go on. She wouldn't tell us what it was, and we couldn't get her to budge. It was a singing competition, too, in Southgate. We'd all driven two hours to get there and her teacher and the other students from her group needed her to be in the competition. But no amount of coaxing would get her to relent."

"She's strong-minded, my Gloria," my father-in-law said.

As if I didn't know. "You mean, she might not go on, now?" I asked, not believing them.

They just stared at me.

"Perhaps she's just not feeling well. Maybe we should call a doctor." The last thing I wanted to do was go back in there again. Gloria, in one of her vicious moods, was someone to avoid. I had long ago recognized the signs of when she might lash out; anyone in her vicinity had better get out of her way. She could draw blood with her tongue. But I hadn't seen that tonight. Also, I wanted to protect my father-in-law, who seemed terribly pale and short of breath.

Finally, when I recognized that neither of them knew what to do, I opened the door and looked in. Gloria was still standing exactly as we'd left her, staring at some unseen person in the corner of the room, her head tilted to the side as though she was listening. Every now and then she'd nod, almost imperceptibly, as though receiving information. I felt chills run down my arms.

"Gloria, what is wrong? Are you sick?" I used my most soothing tone, the one I used whenever I wanted Amy to let me put Mercurochrome on her scraped knee. I tried to lead her to a chair. But her whole body was stiff, as if in a spasm, or even a kind of catatonia, I thought, remembering abnormal psych in my junior year.

I tried again, but this time as I touched her, she let me have it, an incredibly hard jab with her forearm that caught me right between my ribs and knocked the wind out of me. "Ooof." I exhaled sharply, fell backward, and caught myself against the makeup table. Gloria didn't even acknowledge what she'd done. It was as if she hadn't moved a muscle.

"Gloria!" I raised my voice. "For God's sake, you've got to snap out of this."

Just then, someone knocked on the door and announced, "Five minutes, Miss Winston."

That's when my heart began to race as though I'd just climbed three flights of stairs. I was out of my element. I didn't know what to do. As much as I wanted to keep my father and Gloria apart, I thought I'd better go get him. He could deal with this crazed, temperamental mental case. Then I heard his voice outside the door.

"What are you doing standing around here, you people, they've announced the curtain. It's getting late."

"We're having a little problem with Gloria," I heard my father-in-law explain out in the hall. His breathless voice sounded terrible.

"Can I help?" my father asked. "Where's Suzanne?"

Nobody replied. Then Alex said, "She'll be all right."

Oh, for God's sake, I thought. *It's almost curtain time and Gloria isn't all right!* "Dad," I called, watching Gloria warily, lest she suddenly become violent. "You'd better come in here."

He opened the door, filling the frame with his height. I was so glad to see him. I looked over at Gloria and shrugged, helplessly. He saw her standing there frozen, like some bizarre player in a child's game of statue, and went right into action. First he grabbed her upper arms, covering them with his large hands, and shook her once, to get her attention.

Startled, she came back to herself and looked up at him. Their eyes met, and then her knees just buckled underneath her. But my father's firm grip held her up until she'd regained her balance. A moment went by while she stared at him as though she didn't recognize him. Then, gradually, she realized who he was and a delighted smile spread across her face. "Hello, Burt. I didn't know you'd be here tonight."

I thought, *She did too know. Is this a game?* The idea that she might be playing with us made me both frightened and furious.

Never taking his eyes from hers, as though it was crucial he not break eye contact, he said, "Hello, Gloria. I wouldn't have missed this for the world." Then, still keeping his eyes on her, he tilted his head to let me know that I should leave the room.

As I closed the door, I could hear Gloria saying, in a half-whispered, half-throaty voice, "I'm so happy to see you. I've been looking forward to this moment all my life."

My cheeks were flaming red as though I'd just witnessed a too intimate moment between them, but I recovered my composure and took my father-in-law's arm. "She's going to be all right now. She'll be performing tonight." I was glad to see the relief on his face as we walked him slowly back to our seats.

A few minutes later, just as the curtain was rising for the first singing group, my father rejoined us. I saw lipstick on his cheek and wiped it away. "How is she?" I whispered.

He whispered that she was fine and held a finger to his lips. "What did you say to her?" I whispered again.

But he wouldn't say anything more during the performance, except to indicate to Alex and my father-in-law that everything was all right.

Finally, when the first group had sung, and we had a break before Gloria was due to sing, I asked again, "What did you do?"

He smiled at me and patted my hand and said, "I just told her that enough was enough, and she wasn't allowed to behave like this."

"And that did it?"

"It always worked with you." He smiled.

"I know, but this is different," I replied.

"Honey, I do this sort of thing all the time," he told me, sitting back in the seat with his arms folded across his chest, perfectly composed, as the curtain opened again and Gloria stepped forward with a radiant smile and began to sing. I looked over at my father-in-law, trying not to compare him with my own father, but I couldn't help it. I wondered how different Gloria and Alex would have been if they'd had stronger parents, and then I wondered if that would have any effect on my marriage. Caught by Gloria's performance, I shrugged it off, thinking I had enough strength for the both of us. And then, something else suddenly occurred to me.

"Dad, did you agree to represent her?" I swear, he looked guilty as he nodded.

"I think she's ready now," he said.

And that's when I realized how dangerously manipulative Gloria could be; she'd go to any lengths to get what she wanted. It made me so angry I felt like having a tantrum myself.

CHAPTER NINETEEN

Going back and forth from my grandmother's book to worrying about my finances and the accusation of plagiarism kept me immersed in my own world. I didn't like wrestling with all these problems; I felt fragmented. My concentration was disrupted when I needed it the most. Happily, the work on my grandmother's book absorbed me. There were still 300 pages she hadn't completed, and 250 more that needed editing and plot delineation. My future now depended on this book. It alone could save me. My mother always told me I could do anything in life I set my mind to. That belief has taken me far. I hoped it would take me far enough to get me through this.

Mostly, I felt out of breath from pressure and I kept dreaming I was caught in embarrassing situations: taking a final exam and not having studied, standing in front of my grammar school class without any clothes on. And the worst dream was when I gave a book party for three hundred people and there were no books. I woke up to go to the bathroom, grateful to have interrupted the nightmare, but when I fell back to sleep the nightmare continued. There I stood all dressed up, in a bookstore with empty shelves waiting for my books to arrive, making desperate conversation with people who were leaving. Finally the trucks got there and my new novel was unloaded into the store. Eagerly I passed the books around, until someone exclaimed, "All the pages are blank." I had forgotten to write it.

My researcher had the task of gathering information about

Obregon Press, the supposed publishers of the book I'd allegedly plagiarized. As I suspected, no Obregon Press ever existed. My children were obscenely curious about the
plagiarism letters and made up scenarios.

"I think it's a writer who's jealous of Mom," Miles decided.

"Too easy," Amy claimed. At fifteen, her rampant hormones dictated her thoughts. "It's a male editor about thirty-
eight years old, with gray sideburns, who's been in love with
Mom since he read her first book, but he lives in a New York
penthouse and she lives in California."

"Get out of here," Miles scoffed. "That's not exactly a
cool way to get her attention—accuse her of plagiarism."

"Mom, what exactly is *played-your-isms*?" Jered asked,
trying to pin this down once and for all.

"Plagiarism, goofus," Miles teased, tickling him.

It was the fourth week of my purgatory. We'd just finished
dinner, the time of day when life was comparatively mellow,
before the complaining started.

"Can I watch television tonight? I finished my homework
in school," Miles began with the standard excuse.

I went through the explanation by rote. "If your homework
is done, then read a book. You know the rules, one hour of
television during the week. You've already watched yours."

"Heck, Mom!" Miles tried again. "All the kids get to
watch TV at night but me. There's this really neat show on
in half an hour. It has car chases and everything."

Amy crossed her arms over her narrow, budding chest and
glared at him. "Honestly, Miles, you're such a preadoles-
cent."

"Shut up, fart-face," he retaliated.

"Mu-thur. Are you going to let him get away with that?"

I was adding figures in my head, borrowing from one column
to fortify another. "Miles, don't call your sister names."

"You see what I have to put up with, Mom?"

Mercifully, a phone call for Amy ended the fight. But I
wasn't off the hook yet.

"What does that word mean, Mommy?" Jered asked. There was chocolate pudding on his chin.

"Wipe your face, honey," I told him. "Do you mean *plagiarism*?"

His eyes were huge and round, staring at me, filled with trust. An invisible hand twisted the knife in my guts. I would have given anything not to have to explain this to him. I had a sudden and deep compassion for my parents, who had been required to explain the unexplainable to me and my sister countless times in our lives. "It means, when someone steals the writing of another person, like if you copied your friend Stephen's story and put your name on it as if you wrote it."

"I wouldn't do that."

"Of course not, because you know it's wrong."

"No, 'cause Stephen can't write good stories like you do." I couldn't help laughing. "You write the best ones at night when I go to bed, Mommy. Much better than Miles. He tells the scary ones. I like the beauty."

I remembered my sister saying that to me when we were children and for a moment I couldn't believe I was now a parent with the responsibility of raising three children. Lately, I wasn't doing such a good job of it. Suddenly, all of it was just too much and I started to sob. Jered's arms went around me, his hand patting my back.

"Should I go get Amy?" he asked.

I made myself stop crying. "No," I told him, reaching for a Kleenex at the kitchen desk and blowing my nose.

"What's wrong, Mommy?" he asked, more curious than worried.

"I just have a lot on my mind right now, love. But I'll be fine."

"I know you will," he beamed. " 'Cause you're the mommy and the writer and that's your job."

I smiled then, as my words came back to haunt me. I'd told them their jobs were to be the children and go to school, and play with their friends, and give me lots of hugs and kisses. Mine was to be the mom. I used that rule whenever they didn't want to do what they were supposed to. But I'd been making a mess of my own job lately.

Jered went to his room to play and I went into my office to ponder. No matter how I added and re-added, none of the figures came out right. I was desperate to keep the children in the schools and the home they loved so their lives wouldn't be turned upside down once again. Continuity was crucial for children of divorced parents. Amy was a student body officer now, and Miles was in the science club, the chess club, and on the swim team. What else could I do to ensure their security? Only more of the same; and live each day at a time praying it would all work out somehow.

The first week in November, my agent, Esther Ross, got back from her sailing vacation in the French Antilles and called me. "Suzanne, are you all right? I was shocked when I spoke to my office from St. Bart's and found out what had happened to you. I tried many times to call you from our sloop and especially when we sailed into a port, but I couldn't get a line through. Those islands in the Antilles are maddeningly remote."

"Oh Esther, I'm so glad you're back! What am I going to do?" I hadn't realized how difficult it had been, having her away at this critical time. She was my sounding board and my friend, my ally whenever the world became an armed camp. And the one person who could help me out of my financial dilemma.

"I don't think this plagiarism thing is anything to worry about, love. I saw the article in the *Enquirer*. Where did they get that old picture?"

"You don't know the worst of it." I told her about the IRS ruling, the money I owed, and the bleakness of my future. Even formidable Esther, with the mane of red hair, was thrown by that.

"My God, Suzanne. That's a fortune." It only took her a moment's pause to decide, "Well, we'll just have to get you some more money on your next book. I've been thinking it's time to double our prices."

"I have to, Esther, or I won't survive. I'm worried about losing my home. What if they don't want this book? It's different from my other ones." My writer's insecurity was coming out.

"They'll want it, Suzanne, believe me. You always feel this way when you're working on a new book."

"Do I?" I couldn't recall ever feeling the way I felt lately, as though my skin had been peeled to the flesh and every touch, every brush with another facet of my life made me bleed and scream in pain. "If I could double my advance, I'd have my life back again—in two years, that is." Even a fortune could barely bail me out. "Is it realistic to expect it?"

"We're sure as hell going to try," she insisted.

I could see her shifting her weight in her chair, her pale blue eyes gazing out at the view of Manhattan beyond. Her office was on Sixth Avenue in midtown and you could see two rivers from her window. She had been an agent for twenty-five years, starting as an assistant out of college; after eight months she'd taken over her boss's job. She could read a five-hundred-page manuscript in one evening and sell it the next day. She hung out at a bistro on Seventh Avenue every night where she held court, her current lover in attendance. Playwrights, actors, producers, and authors stopped in to say hello. A daredevil, she had her pilot's license and went mountain climbing with a rope in one hand and a manuscript in the other.

Later that day she called me back, her voice hesitant, concerned. "Suzanne, it's me. I made some calls and spoke to Judy Emory, just to feel her out, let her know you're ready to let her see your new book."

"How did she sound?"

"Not as enthusiastic as I'd expected. It seems after that last batch of letters was sent to the press, your publisher sought their attorney's advice. They're worried they could be sued."

"I don't believe this, Esther." I got up from my chair, still holding the phone, and began to pace my office, around the desk and back again. It's not a large room, and over the years an accumulation of research material, five drafts of each book, and household bills have crammed it to the gills. Especially now, everything was closing in around me. I noticed that my heart beat irregularly, skipping beats. I had ignored it lately, thinking it was nothing, but maybe there was something wrong. *Why not? My body's reacting to stress, isn't that what usually happens? Don't I need something else to worry about?*

"Should I call Judy again and explain that this is some crackpot?"

"If it makes you feel better. But I don't think it would do any good."

"Esther, tell me what to do."

"Send me the manuscript when it's ready, love. We'll decide then."

Just after Thanksgiving, I sent 450 pages to Esther on a Monday. If we could make our deal, my future would at least be secure, if not luxurious. As a reward for myself I called Barry. I hadn't seen him since he'd taken me to dinner earlier in the month. He had wanted to go to L'Escoffier but I couldn't bear the thought of spending that kind of money for a meal when it would have bought us groceries for a week, so we'd had pasta at Mario's in Westwood Village. That night was the first time I'd been to a restaurant in weeks and I felt I'd come back from exile. I'd soaked up the sights of normal people doing normal things; even ordering wine had been a luxury. When he walked me to my car after dinner he'd said, "You're an example of grace under fire, Suzanne," and he'd given me a friendly kiss on the lips as he helped me into my car. Hearing his voice again now made my heart pump with happiness.

"I'm feeling optimistic for the first time in nearly a month," I told him. "I'd love to celebrate. Are you free this evening?"

"I am." I could feel him smiling. "Why don't I stop by and pick you up. I'd like to meet your children. Then, we can eat somewhere nearby in Encino." I was filled with a

teenaged excitement about the evening, though I felt guilty
that the children weren't going out too. But they weren't as
deprived as I; Alex still took them out on weekends.

This "domestic serenade" was playing when the doorbell
rang, the house was in chaos. Amy and Miles were screaming
at one another, something about Miles always forgetting to
unlock the bathroom door and Amy having to go around
through his room to open it—everything about her brother
annoyed her lately. Jered had a croupy-sounding cough I was
afraid he'd caught from my sister, and the older children's
shouting was punctuated by a cough-cough here and a cough-
cough there. I hurried to the door to let Barry in, wishing
everything was calm and peaceful instead of the way it was.
At the moment, I wanted to lock my children in the basement,
except I didn't have one.

Barry's hair looked newly washed, curling over his forehead and combed behind his ears, still wet in places. In his
powder blue shirt and sports coat he looked new and fresh,
as if facing the world for the first time. His boyishness was
appealing. In spite of my personal problems, I was eager to
have fun.

I closed the door at the end of the entry hall to muffle the
children's argument, and opened the front door.

"Hi." We grinned at each other as I let him in.

"Your home is beautiful," he commented, stepping down
into the living room. I saw it from his eyes and felt fiercely
protective of this home where the children and I were safe
and comfortable. I could never have explained it to him,
though he didn't ask, what this collection of rooms meant to
me, nor could I calculate all the precious memories.

"Look at that," he exclaimed, discovering the collection
of antique lion paintings on the living room wall.

"My ex-husband and I bought those in London," I explained, wondering, if I had to sell them, how much they
would bring. "Would you like a drink?"

"It depends on whether or not you're ready to go."

"I'm ready," I assured him. I was wearing a burgundy wool skirt and silk shirt and only had to grab my jacket. "But there's a minor crisis going on with my children and I don't think I can leave at the moment. Why don't I fix you a drink, see if I can arrange a truce among the Indians, and then we can go."

"I would like to meet your children," he reminded me. I was hoping he'd forgotten.

"I don't think this is the best time," I said, leading him down the hall toward the family room door. "They always get like this starting around Halloween. Unfortunately, their monster act often lasts through the holidays."

I entered the bar in the family room. "What would you like?"

"Vodka, rocks," he said, while I fixed one for him and a vodka with Rose's lime for myself.

"Whatever happened with that investigator?" he asked, in a friendly tone.

"We met, didn't I tell you? Oh, I'm sorry, I should have thanked you. I hired him just to do some specific tasks. The way things are, there wasn't much he could do for me. And money is a problem. But he's checking out the kind of type-writer used to write the letters. And the source of the paper, too."

Barry nodded, and we sat down on the sofas at right angles to one another, with the coffee table between us. "I hope you get some positive results." He raised his glass to me and I raised mine too. "To new beginnings," he said.

"I could use a few," I acknowledged, taking a sip.

His expression of sympathy gave me the same feeling of warmth I'd had when we'd first met. Six weeks ago seemed like years. "I recently lost a lot of money in a tax shelter deal with my ex-husband. It wiped out my savings."

"Tax shelters can be risky. They're only as good as the shelter promoters. Some of them look clean, but you never know what they're doing."

"In this case, you're right. The man who invested our

money never really invested it. He's been indicted and is going to jail. So all the deductions we claimed weren't allowed retroactive to the time we were married." I told him how much. "I haven't made a deal on my new book yet, and I'm worried enough about being able to keep my home without paying for a pricy investigator." *Great, Suzanne, financial worries are just what a new date wants to hear.*

"Maybe you've heard the last of those letters," he offered, encouragingly.

"No, each week some new person calls me who has just received one. Several editors at my publishing company, and my agent, got them, even my parents. The press too," I admitted. "You know, it's so crazy to think I have an enemy—me! It's hard to believe. And what if this person gets violent. I never know what's going to happen next. I worry about the children constantly, I'm always looking over my shoulder. And there's nothing I can do, but wait."

"It must be difficult," he agreed.

"But, if I make a new book deal, perhaps I will be able to hire the investigator."

"And you haven't got a clue as to who could be doing this?"

"Not you too! Everybody asks me that, as if I were keeping the truth to myself. Believe me, if there was anybody I suspected, I wouldn't keep it a secret."

"I'm sorry," he said. "This just hasn't been your month, has it?"

It was such an understatement we looked at one another and started to laugh, and the more I thought about it, the more it made me laugh.

"Is there anything I can do?" he asked, kindly.

I shook my head, still amused by what he'd said. "I'll work it out, somehow."

Our conversation was interrupted by the sound of Amy yelling through the door, "And if you don't remember to put down the toilet seat, I'm going to stuff your head into it."

"Oh yeah, says who?" Miles retorted.

I gave Barry an apologetic, helpless smile, left my drink on the table, and went to head off disaster. Barry followed behind me.

When we appeared in the doorway, the sight of a strange man stopped the argument for a minute. Basically, mine were well-mannered, sweet children, but when things got out of hand, I would have liked to pretend not to know them.

I introduced Barry and they shook his hand politely. Then Amy said, "Mother, you've got to make him remember to unlock my bathroom door when he's through and put down the toilet seat. It's so unfair. I get up in the middle of the night to go to the john, and if my door's not locked, I fall in." *Women's complaint since the invention of the toilet seat cover*, I thought.

"If you didn't scarf so many Cokes, you would sleep through the night like I do," Miles answered, and then snorted at her with horrible pig sounds.

She reached out to cuff him, shouting, "You immature brat!" but Barry suddenly stepped in between them.

"Hey, you two. I used to have the same fight with my sisters when I was a kid."

Their hands stopped in midair and they stared at him as if he were a Martian. I too was surprised that he'd intervened. Didn't he know that was part of the territorial imperative? Dates who interacted with one's children were serious contenders for a Relationship, the R word, which led to Commitment, the C word. I watched him with new interest.

"So what if you had the same fight?" Amy breathed, under her breath, trying to keep me from hearing her rude reply.

"Big deal." Miles wasn't as quiet.

I knew they could turn their enmity on him in a moment, and that would be disastrous for anyone, let alone this new man. But when he grinned, disarmingly, it caught them by surprise. "I guess it isn't such earthshaking news, is it? But in my family we solved it in a unique way."

He likes them, I thought. *Amazing.*

Now he had their full attention. Mine too.

"You see," he continued, "I could never remember to

unlock the bathroom door between my room and my sister's or put down the toilet seat, either. My mind was always on much more important matters, such as schoolwork or games or friends. Right?''

Miles nodded. Amy raised her eyebrow and chewed on the corner of her lower lip.

"My folks tried everything: first they punished me, and when that didn't work, they tried rewarding me if I would only remember, but that wasn't fair to my sisters because they weren't getting a reward. I tried leaving notes taped to the door but somehow, I just didn't see them. And I even tied a string around my finger, but I just got used to it. It didn't help.''

"See?'' Miles stuck out his chin, feeling supported by this new ally.

Barry paused, as if he wasn't going to go on, as if that's all he had to say about it while the three of us waited.

Finally, Amy asked, "So, what happened?''

It was then that I realized how clever he was, hooking them into his story, rather than just giving them advice which they'd probably reject. I also realized how starved I was for this kind of interaction with my children. I put up a brave front, but it was difficult being with them alone, making so many decisions without another adult to consult.

"Well,'' he said, sitting on the edge of Amy's bed, bringing me back to the conversation. "My dad, who was pretty strict with us kids, came up with a plan. Every time I forgot to unlock the door to my sister's room, after I'd used the bathroom, or forgot to put down the toilet seat, I got locked out of the bathroom for a whole day.''

"Big deal,'' Miles said. "I could just use Mom's.''

"No,'' Barry told him, "I mean, I was locked out of all the bathrooms in the house. We only had two in our house, ours and my parents'. So that meant I had to hold it in until I went to school.''

"And after school and all night too?'' Miles asked, his eyes narrowing with disbelief.

Barry nodded, keeping a straight face. "Being locked out

of the bathroom just once was all it took. After dinner, I had to sneak out of the house and go in the bushes. That was really embarrassing. I was afraid the neighbors would see me, especially Lucille Wainwright. She was the girl next door who I had a crush on. I would have died if she'd known what I was doing. And that wasn't the hardest part.''

"What was?'' I asked, so caught up in his story, imagining him as a child trying to hold it in all night, that if anyone had asked me if I had any problems of my own I'd have said, absolutely not.

"Not being able to brush my teeth was the hardest,'' he told me. "I'd always hated brushing my teeth before, but when I wasn't allowed to do it, I found that I really wanted to, and I couldn't take a shower, or use my deodorant.''

"No deodorant? Yuk,'' Miles said.

"Why didn't you just brush in the kitchen sink?'' Amy wanted to know, looking for ways around this predicament.

"Because my toothbrush and toothpaste and toiletries were locked up in the bathroom.''

Miles looked at me as if to say, *You're not thinking of doing this to me, are you*?

"But you know what was even harder than all that?'' Barry said.

Both children said, "No, what?''

"Not being able to pick my zits!'' For a moment he kept a straight face while they stared at him, not knowing what to say, and then he laughed, and both of them laughed with him, giving each other a look that said, *This guy's a riot*!

Jered had heard us talking and came into the room, wrapping his arms around my waist, the way he used to do with my thighs when he was smaller and not feeling well, like tonight.

"Why was your father so tough on you?'' Miles asked, sitting on the other side of Barry.

Barry put his hand on Miles's shoulder and looked directly at him with a serious expression. "Because, he knew that remembering to be courteous to others is something that's important to learn, and he also knew that if I could remember things that were important to me, I was capable of remembering what was important to others. And, he thought that not unlocking the door or putting down the toilet seat was my way of annoying my sisters because when they did bad things, nobody seemed to notice. They got away with murder, and I didn't.''

"Yeah," Miles said, gazing up at him with full understanding. "Like, always hogging the phone, and never having time to help you with your homework, and thinking they're so great, and never getting yelled at for leaving a glass on the coffee table. But if I knock it over accidentally, I get hell.''

"Oh, sure," Amy countered. "You never listen to me when I do help you with your homework.''

So that's what this fight is about, I thought, almost wanting to cry with gratitude toward Barry for helping me discover this insight. Sometimes I didn't hear what their subtext was. Wrapped up in my own life, I responded to the name calling and the complaints as if that's all there was.

"And what about sticking your finger in the peanut butter and drinking orange juice from the bottle. Then we all have to catch your germs," Amy retorted.

"Okay, Amy," I said, able to take charge now. "Let's keep to the issue." I turned to Miles. "Do you think you can remember about keeping the bathroom door unlocked and putting the toilet seat down, Miles, without having to be locked out of the bathroom?''

His eyes wouldn't meet mine, but he nodded.

"And Amy, do you think you could find time to help your brother with his homework when he asks you, as long as he gives you some notice?''

She nodded, solemnly.

"Well, I guess that settles it," Barry said, turning to me. "I'm starved.''

"We've got some leftover stew in the fridge," Miles offered, as if Barry was now his personal buddy. I didn't blame him.

"And I could make a salad," Amy said.

This was a first. My children inviting one of my dates to dinner. Usually their resentment was obvious, but then, no one ever took the time to talk to them this way. Though frankly, I was looking forward to getting out of the house for a change, being an adult in an adult setting, ordering something wonderful on the menu.

"We could show you the pinball machine," Jered chimed in, coughing as he talked.

I looked at Barry. "I think Mr. Adler has made reservations for us to go out," I said.

He shrugged. "I love leftover stew and salad," the lovely man said. "And with Jered's cold, wouldn't you feel better staying home?"

Jered nodded in agreement, wiping his runny nose on his hand.

"Are you certain?" I asked, hoping he wasn't being nice for the children's sake, and then wouldn't call me again because I was too domestic. "We can still go out," I offered.

He shook his head no. "Let me cancel my reservation, and then lead me to the pinball machine."

I prepared the leftover meal and served us at the game table in the living room, feeling a kind of floating sensation of delight mixed with hope and laced with excitement.

During dinner we talked again about my problems. I kept saying we should talk about him for a change, but he didn't seem to mind listening to me.

"I'm usually not so self-absorbed," I told him.

"After we've known each other for a while, I'll know if that's true or not," he said, teasing me.

I thought, *If I haven't turned him off by now, maybe there's a chance.*

After the children went to sleep, we sat on the sofa with our coffee mugs (mine contained herb tea), our legs curled up under us knee to knee, and talked about the results of the election—we had both felt neither Carter nor Ford was particularly inspiring. We shared a passion for the movies and had loved the film *Network*; we made a date to go see *Rocky*. And we also had an unfulfilled desire to learn to ski.

"Maybe we can go over the holidays," he suggested. But I knew I couldn't afford even to think about that right now; I nodded noncommittally. He told me about his wife, how they'd met, about their relationship, and I told him about Alex. I longed for him to kiss me but he just played with the ends of my hair.

Finally, I said to him, "Were you just humoring my children by staying home, or did you really like it as much as you seemed to?"

"I really did," he replied. "First of all, it's been entirely too long since we had our first date. And secondly, I didn't know that leftover beef stew would be boeuf Bourguignon with shiitake mushrooms and vegetables al dente. Actually, I miss being part of a family. I eat out almost every night; nobody cooks for me. Most of my married friends would be amazed if they knew how I envy them. They think I have such a great time dating, going out. This is better."

He saw my expression change. "What is it? Are you tired of domesticity?"

"No!" I insisted. "I feel the same way you do. I love being at home, having my family around me, even more since the divorce. It's sort of a cocoon for me now. I was thinking about how I would survive if I ever lost it. It's difficult not to think about."

"I could tell it's been bothering you. You're right to be concerned about keeping the children in their schools. What will you do?"

"Just keep everything in perspective." I heard my own voice repeating the words my mother always used to encourage my sister, to bolster her and keep her going. It could be worse, she'd say, philosophically. And this could be worse too, I kept telling myself. It's not my health or my children's.

Just then, his hand brushed my cheek, sending shivers down my arms. "I'll be glad to listen any time, Suzanne. Maybe it will help to know that you've got somebody on your side, that you don't have to do this all alone.'' And then he leaned over and kissed me.

I melted to him, amazed at how totally he enraptured me. It could have something to do with how long it had been since I'd felt this way, burning with desire, an instant need flooding through me.

Reluctantly, we both pulled away. I guessed he felt uncomfortable being in the house with my children nearby; I know I did. Our next kiss was more tender, while we explored one another with short tender kisses and then, longer deeper ones.

''You take my breath away,'' I whispered, knowing it was unoriginal, but exactly how I felt.

''When can I see you again?'' he asked. ''I don't want to wait so long this time.''

''Anytime you say,'' I offered.

''How's breakfast?'' he asked, and we laughed.

We kept our arms around one another as I walked him to the door, and kissed again, both feeling those incredible feelings of desire, barely able to separate ourselves from one another. *Why did we wait so long for this?* I kept wondering, feeling the ghostlike presence of Alex fading even further away. One more shove, and it would be gone for good along with the other uninteresting dates I'd had lately.

''I have a deposition tomorrow that will probably go into the night,'' he said, being more specific about seeing one another again. ''But I'm free on the weekend, if you are?''

I nodded.

That night I slept wonderfully, without any nightmares at all. Perhaps because I could still feel his arms around me and taste his kisses on my lips.

CHAPTER TWENTY

College, when she finally got there, was everything Steffani had hoped it would be. The freedom of living away from home was intoxicating. And she liked most of her classes, though getting to them on crutches was not easy. But Dr. Levinson wrote a note explaining about her surgery to an administrative official and they issued her a special on-campus parking permit so she didn't have to walk from her dorm, Dykstra Hall, down the hill past the half mile of the practice football field, and up the hundreds of Janss steps. That would have been impossible.

Being a good-looking girl on crutches brought attention, just as her mother said it would. "All they'll see is that I'm a freak!" she'd cried, hating the idea of starting college this way. "Nobody will want to be with me. They'll stare, I'll turn them off!" It had seemed like another end of the world for her. But Lynnette had known better. She could see what Steffani could not, that a cast on her leg did not detract from her beauty or her magnetism. So she soothed and cajoled as usual, allowed her to protest a bit, and then forced her to listen to reason—Lynnette's reason.

"Nobody will think you're a freak, Steffani. Maybe a few people will stare at your cast, but they'll all want to know how you broke your leg. It will be a topic of conversation. You can make up stories about it. You'll see how interested they'll be. And in no time, the cast will finally come off."

Once on campus, she discovered that eye contact with some big tall jock and a dazzling smile brought an offer to carry her books. She devised a dozen different stories about why she was in a cast: a car accident, waterskiing, fell off a horse, caught her leg in a car door while making out, etc. The truth was that her right knee hadn't healed properly after the infection. Recently, she had overheard Dr. Levinson telling her mother that he might want to operate on the right leg again next summer. There was no way she'd allow that, so she wasn't even going to think about it.

On her third day of classes she was having dinner in the cafeteria when she recognized a boy from her American lit class whom she knew only as Mr. Bernfeld. She'd tried to get his attention before, but he hadn't seen her, or wasn't interested. This time she stared at him until he approached her. He had light hair, a strong prominent nose, pale blue eyes, rippling muscles in his arms, and fabulous dimples when he smiled.

"You're Miss Blacker, aren't you?" He took the seat opposite her, putting down his tray, adding, "I'm Ron Bernfeld."

"My name's Steffani," she told him, thinking, *Definite possibilities here.* "I didn't think you'd noticed me."

"You're hard to miss on those things. It must be difficult getting around on crutches." He glanced at the wooden appendages lying under the table.

She nodded, continuing to stare. She guessed him to be an athlete with those muscles, but he was not big enough to play football, though he was tanned, with freckles on his arms and face. She was thinking about what it would feel like to run her hands over his muscles as she put the straw from her Coke between her lips, and ran her tongue around the edge.

Almost immediately he reacted by shifting in his seat. Obviously something below his waist was uncomfortable. She winked and he blushed, and then he laughed, and winked back.

"So, what's your sport?" she asked.

"Baseball," he replied, surprised that she could tell he was an athlete. "I run track too."

"What position do you play?" She said it coquettishly.

He smiled again. "Outfield. We've got a good team this year. Practice has started already, but baseball's not as glamorous as football.'' He was eating the lamb stew on his plate, mixing it with rice.

"You mean, if you were a football player, the girls would all be hot for you?"

Now he was blushing again, but he replied, "Naw, I don't want all the girls. Just one special one." And now he was the one giving the looks.

She laughed. "Are you good enough for the pros?"

"Yeah, I have a batting average of three-forty." His face was clear of guile; she felt he'd give her an honest answer to most any question. "Most guys who have the potential to be a pro go to a farm camp right out of high school. I had an offer, but I wanted my degree, so I went to college instead."

She studied him, wondering whether he was kidding himself or just boasting. If he was really good enough to be a pro baseball player, wouldn't he have gone for it, regardless? "What are you studying to be, an astrophysicist or something?"

He shrugged. "An accountant." He'd finished his stew and was now eating pie. He tilted his head as if offering her a bite, but she didn't want it.

"Do you mean, you gave up baseball for that?" She shook her head. This guy was weird, maybe not for her.

"At least when I graduate I'll have a way to make a living. There's nothing secure about being in professional sports. Guys get injured, they have a few bad years and then they get dropped or traded, anything can happen, it's not sure—at all. Even if you make it."

"But think of how much money professional players can make, and the perks that go along with it. Endorsements, things like that."

"Sure. Can you see me traveling with Bob Hope's variety show, entertaining the troops at Christmas?" He gazed out the window at the lights of the campus beyond the cafeteria where they were sitting. Obviously he'd thought of these things before, had ready answers. And she could see she wasn't going to change his mind. There was nothing she could say he hadn't said to himself, so she decided not to pursue it. But she promised herself she'd go and see him play, when the spring season began, to see if he was really good enough to be a pro.

"An accountant," she said, softly, as though thinking it over. And then she smiled to reassure him that it hadn't turned her off. But in a way, it had. The man she wanted, the one she was looking for, would go for broke. He'd never be satisfied with being an accountant if he could be a professional player, of any kind. But until she found him, Ron was awfully cute.

"And what do you want to do, after college?" he asked.

"I've always wanted to be a teacher. The few good ones I've had in my life have really made a difference. And I understand kids, relate to them." She paused. "But I'd like to write too."

"You could do both," he suggested.

"I'm majoring in English, with a minor in education."

"What do you want to write about?"

"I don't know," she said, thoughtfully. It was a difficult question. Unless she found the answer to that, she'd never be able to do it. "I guess I could write about a person with courage, someone who has a lot to overcome."

"Like going to college with a broken leg?"

"Something like that," she said, wanting to tell him the truth about her illness because he was so easy to talk to, yet she knew she wouldn't. She never told people until she was very close to them, and even then, she never told them everything. "You know, most people just nod when I say I want to be a writer, or they ask if I want to write books or screenplays. You're the only one who's ever asked me what I want to write about. That shows a lot about you."

"Like what?"

"That you're sensitive and you think about things, other than sports. Maybe you do belong in college."

"How nice of you to say so." He sounded offended.

She'd opened her mouth again and turned him off. Damn.

But then he took her by surprise. "Would you like to go out Saturday night?"

Maybe he wasn't as timid as she thought. "That sounds great. What did you have in mind?"

"How about dinner and a play. I hear *Tea and Sympathy* is good. It's playing at the Circle Theater."

"You like the theater?" she asked.

"Yeah," he said. "But I have a feeling I'm going to like it even better if I'm with you."

They went up in the crowded elevator together and he looked at her shyly, "How much longer will you be on crutches?"

"Not too much longer," she said. "I broke my leg in a fall, and had to have surgery on my knee afterwards. It's been giving me trouble."

He nodded, and she wondered if people accepted her explanations or if they could see right through her the way he seemed to do now. Someday, maybe she'd be able to tell the truth about this.

When the elevator reached his floor, the fifth, he mouthed the words, "I'll call you," and got off as she continued on to the eighth. She had planned to fantasize about him in bed that night, but just as she got to her room, she started having a nosebleed.

Stay calm, she told herself, lying on the bed, putting pillows behind her back and tilting her head upward. She put pressure on the bridge of her nose and took deep breaths, but soon she had soaked through one box of Kleenex and was working on another. The taste of her own blood made her stomach recoil as the sticky liquid ran down the back of her throat. She needed ice, but the machine was down the hall and her roommate was out.

Should she call her parents? They were only twenty minutes away. But it aggravated her to think she needed them to come and rescue her at nineteen years old. She was an adult, dammit. She'd ride this one out alone. It was only a nosebleed, she'd had them many times. They were part of her illness because the clotting factor in her blood was abnormal. The problem was, sometimes they didn't stop.

I'll give it an hour, she decided, picking up her Western civilization text and trying to read for the exam tomorrow. But the book was too heavy to hold above her head with one hand. She was afraid she'd drop it on her head and maybe put out her eye. The humor of that got to her and she started to laugh thinking of the article, *Student loses eye when knocked on the head by the whole of Western civilization, while having nosebleed.*

An hour later the bleeding hadn't stopped and she'd gone through all but one of her towels. With resignation, she pulled herself up off the bed, slung her purse over her shoulder, and hobbled on her crutches to the door, trying to keep her head back as she walked. Her only thought was how glad she was that Ron wasn't here to witness this.

Girls in the hallway stared and gasped, asking, "What happened to you?" She couldn't see who they were.

"Nosebleed," she replied.

Someone helped her to the elevator and offered to take her to the hospital.

"I've got my car," she said, just wanting to be alone, hoping she wouldn't pass out before getting to the UCLA Medical Center emergency room across campus.

The sight of so much blood galvanized the receiving staff of the emergency hospital into action and soon she was lying on a gurney in a cubicle with an ice pack on her face while a resident took her history.

"I have an abnormal clotting factor, due to my blood condition," she told him. "Please, call my doctor." And she gave him Levinson's number.

But Dr. Levinson didn't have admitting privileges at UCLA, so they couldn't call him, or else ignored her request thinking they could handle a simple nosebleed. Finally, when they couldn't get the bleeding to stop, and had no authority to use any of the medications she suggested, they decided to pack her nose with cotton packs. She knew that if they'd transfused her with platelets, or given her an IV of vitamin K, she wouldn't have had to endure the painful process of keeping her nose packed for days, but the doctors wouldn't listen to her, so she spent the night in the hospital. It wasn't until three in the morning that the bleeding stopped.

After a few hours' sleep, she got back to the dorm in time to change her clothes and get to class for her exam in Western civ. Her head throbbed, her nose looked like it had been punched, and she was weak from her ordeal, but she'd made a vow to herself when she started college, that only the most excruciating pain would keep her away from class. She wasn't going to miss school anymore. She'd finish each semester on time, and get good enough grades to make it into graduate school! Or die trying.

CHAPTER TWENTY-ONE

Within the next several days there were many messages from Ron Bernfeld. But she couldn't make a date with him because her sinuses were still packed, and then the day they were removed, Dr. Levinson's office called with an appointment to remove the cast on her right leg. Too filled with excitement and apprehension to concentrate on her social life, she decided to postpone her first date with Ron until after she got her cast off.

"I'd really like to see you now," he said, when she told him the reason.

But she convinced him to wait, because she wanted things to be normal between them without the hindrance of a plaster cast.

On the fateful day, Lynnette accompanied her to Dr. Levinson's office and helped Steffani climb up on the table. Together they boosted up the heavy cast so that her leg was stretched out in front of her.

"Steffani, you look wonderful. You've put on all the weight you'd lost, and your face is full again. I'm glad to see it." Dr. Levinson's broad smile made his face seem more youthful in spite of the gray in his curly hair. He caught her staring at him and winked. She nearly blushed from the intimacy in his expression. *He's more of a flirt than I am*, she thought, glancing over at her mother to see if she'd noticed. Steffani wouldn't blame any woman for having a crush on him.

"Shall we get started?" he asked, picking up his saw.

She gripped the sides of the cold metal frame of the table; the saw made a harsh whining noise as it bit through the plaster. And just like the last time, she broke out in cold perspiration fearing that the saw might cut into her flesh. But Dr. Levinson's skill never faltered and he didn't cut her.

He kept up conversation as he drilled through the plaster. "Your mother tells me you're studying literature. That was never my strong subject, I was better in history. But you're a good writer, aren't you? And how's your love life, lately? Any new boys on the horizon?" he asked.

"You know I'm always true to you," she teased.

"I certainly hope so," he said. "Though I suppose I can't expect this to go on forever."

She wasn't sure if he was talking about her or not. And then the feeling of fresh air on her leg captured her attention, a strange sensation, and like a fledgling out of its shell she shivered from the feeling of newness.

Dr. Levinson was in front of her, blocking her view of herself with his back as he examined her leg, probing and pressing, murmuring, "Not bad. Not bad, at all. It's got a ways to go, but it will get there."

His nurse buzzed him on the intercom and requested his presence in the next room.

"I'll be right back," he said, stepping away and walking out of the room with the pieces of the plaster cast.

Steffani was afraid to look at herself, so she looked at Lynnette first. The expression on her mother's face made Steffani's heart plummet; then she looked down.

It was so awful she gasped. The calf muscle was badly atrophied, which made her shin bone seem like the only thing that existed between her knee and her foot. Her knee was three times its normal size, all discolored with shades of purple, gray, green, and yellow. The scar on the side of the knee was red and uneven. This leg belonged to some alien monster who had left it behind, a relic whose ugliness could strike terror in the hearts of men, or a horrible appendage that had somehow attached itself to her. She wanted to crawl into a cave where no one would ever see her again. *I'm a freak*, she thought, wanting to scream. *He's made me a freak.* The more she looked at it, the more her leg seemed to grow, as though it were expanding, throbbing. When she finally found her voice, all she could do was cry out, "Oh, God," and burst into harsh wracking sobs.

Lynnette was by her side in an instant and Steffani didn't even have to look at her to know what her expression was like now. "Steffani," she said, "don't cry like that. You'll only make your eyes red and puffy."

But there was no stopping. *No one will ever want me like this. Oh God, what do I do now? Please, please, don't make this real.* But every time she looked, it was terribly real.

Her mother's face swam though her tears; her expression showed how much she wanted to help and didn't know how, though clearly she was feeling this pain as harshly and intensely as Steffani. But her mother's pain could never penetrate the thick layer of difference that lay between her and her mother now. Steffani had entered a new horrorland, while her mother was still in the real world of whole, nearly perfect people.

Lynnette's lips quivered with tears held in check; her strength was crucial right now. And from her unlimited resource she gathered it up, not questioning God at the moment or railing against him as she longed to do. Instead, she forced her lips not to tremble, straightened her shoulders, and willed the lines in her forehead to smooth away. Her expression softened, underlined by a determination to help her daughter. And though she wanted to kill Dr. Levinson with her bare hands for doing this to Steffani, she'd get to him later.

"Steffani." Lynnette's voice caressed what her hands dared not touch, hovering over the newly revealed knee. "The swelling will go down. Remember how your left leg looked when the cast came off?"

"It didn't look like this," Steffani cried. "Why did Dr. Levinson say it wasn't bad? Is he blind? Or just a natural born liar."

"He sees things differently than we do," Lynnette said, always finding an answer for every question. "He's looking at the way the bone looks, not at the swelling and the bruises. And the bone is straight, isn't it?"

At this point, who cared! Reluctantly, she nodded.

"Your calf muscle will rebuild itself as soon as you start to walk on it, and the scars will fade. Look at how the scar on your stomach faded after the splenectomy, didn't it?"

There was no use comparing; that made her even more frantic. "Mother, the scar across my abdomen has always been smooth, like a long half-moon; this new one is jagged. Look!" It ran from the side of her calf to her mid-thigh and came together at a round, puckered-in place the size of a fifty-cent piece where the infection had been. "How can you even try and compare? This is a disaster." Then her temper flared, shooting through her misery. "You always say things like this, but this time it won't work and you know it! It's worse than horrible, it's disgusting. It's so ugly." And she turned her face away, unable to look anymore. The horror of her own body threatened to suffocate her like a dark cloud of ether, keeping the air from her lungs, making her gasp for breath. And time stretched out in front of her into an endless road, time in which she'd have to face this newest insult in a hundred ways. If she'd been born like this she could have accepted it as part of herself, never known the difference.

But to have it thrust on her, and after enduring so much pain, was an injustice that every ounce of her screamed against, helpless to change.

The suffering she'd experienced already had taught her what stages lay ahead. First came the initial shock when the excruciating pain hit, dragging her into a despair so profound it made her willing to bargain with the devil over her soul just for some relief. And then came the death of hope when the pain wouldn't stop for hours, or days, even weeks. Then, there was resignation and exhaustion when she had to summon up every ounce of patience in the world to deal with it— God, so much patience, until the pain decreased little by little, continuing to torment in a different way by spiking and ebbing, providing just enough hope in the waning stages to be cruel. Yet she never thought of herself as brave simply because she smiled and joked whenever she could. For every joke and every laugh kept the pain at bay for an instant. And if she remained fascinated by life going on around her, in spite of her pain, kept up on the news of her friends, however mundane or impossible it was for her to affect, it was because she was feverish both in her flesh and in her spirit to cling to life. Finally, as the pain ebbed more often than it peaked, her smiles could be sustained for longer than a moment, and she would be almost whole again. But now, with this newest aberration attached to her body, she'd never be free of it again. Now, there was a constant physical reminder that she was different from others; that she was really sick.

She looked into her mother's eyes and saw immense compassion. If her father had been here the compassion would have been doubled. They both gave her as much empathy as anyone who hadn't experienced this for themselves. For a moment she felt comforted, and then, so alone. She was in her own wilderness, her own dry desert with the scorpion's sting draining the life from her. Her mother's gaze held hers for an intense moment, while Steffani drew strength from that well of energy that was always there for her.

It seemed like an eternal moment before Lynnette spoke

again. "You could have lost your leg." They both thought about that for a while. "Let's be thankful for what we have. Be grateful it's not worse."

Steffani thought, *If they had cut off my leg, it wouldn't be this ugly.*

Lynnette's voice soothed, softly cajoled, pulling Steffani's spirits back from that desolate place. "It will be better, you'll see. Aren't I always right about these things? Don't I know what I'm talking about? Come on, now. It doesn't do any good to feel sorry for yourself, even if you're entitled."

That will be my epitaph, Steffani thought, thinking of how many times in her life she'd heard her mother say that. But Lynnette's amazing ability to convince and her will to overcome any obstacle were taking over. A sliver of hope cracked through. After all, they'd been weathering crises like this for as long as Steffani could remember, and it was true, things did always improve, or at least, after a while, she would stop dwelling on them.

Dr. Levinson came back, wisely having left them alone to deal with their realities, confident that Lynnette could console Steffani better than he, and now he was all business, radiating optimism that things would improve.

"I know you're disappointed, Steffani, but then, you're my girl, aren't you? You won't let this discourage you, will you? And you"—he turned to Lynnette—"always give her the help she needs. The two of you are the most remarkable women I've ever known," he said softly.

A look passed between him and her mother and Lynnette's anger softened. Until this moment Lynnette had wanted to kill him on Steffani's behalf, blaming him for this latest result, but his expression begged her to understand. Even Steffani saw it and was moved, though it was not what she'd wanted to feel. "Use the crutches to get around, until the leg feels steadier. And if you need anything for pain, remember that it slows the healing process."

Steffani averted her eyes, almost embarrassed in front of him now, for he'd shown her his own anguish, going against an unwritten law between them that it would not help her at all. She needed him to treat her deformities as though they were not so terrible and eventually she would too. "Will you be okay?" he asked, forcing her to look up now.

"I suppose so," she agreed. "Why don't you show me how to exercise this damn leg. I might as well use it for something, it sure as hell isn't going to win any contests."

He flexed her foot for her, showing her how to gently ease the muscle back to life, while she gritted her teeth against the unbelievable pain that shot through her with just the slightest movement. But, if it meant she'd walk again on two feet, without crutches, be able to hold her own books, not have to keep her head down looking for potholes in the cement and not have calluses and bruises under her arms from the pressure of putting all her weight on her armpits, she'd endure it.

And then, he was gone again, the magician after a performance, not revealing any of his tricks, but leaving them mystified nonetheless and in awe of his prestidigitation. Lynnette helped Steffani down and she hobbled to the door.

For the next week, the feeling of revulsion never left her and she felt too unsteady to even think of going on a date. Her leg throbbed and the knee was like an apex, drawing to it all the fevered heat as well as her animosity. She studied it in fascination, touching it, probing it, the way an animal licks its wound. If her tongue had been long enough or her body able to contort, she too would have licked her wounded knee, but she could not even bend it. The very idea of bending it gave her nightmares and cold sweats. After a while, her noxious knee became a part of her like the gnarls on a tree. Half of her still recoiled from claiming it, but the other half accepted it like a mother would a deformed child. This, now, was her anomaly, her gnarled tree. And if the way she was before haunted her dreams, the way she was now began to integrate, slowly, slowly. Sometimes, she couldn't remember what she had been like before.

Lynnette and Burt spoke to her by phone several times a day, asking how she was doing, checking up on her, encouraging her when she despaired. Suzanne heard about how upset she was and came to take her to lunch, but she couldn't walk because of the swelling and pain, so they ate in the dorm cafeteria.

By the end of that week, her spirits finally began to improve. She still had to use the crutches for support, but little by little, she began to put her weight on both of her legs. And eventually she felt ready to face the world, specifically Ron Bernfeld, for when he asked her out this time, she accepted.

He grinned with approval when he saw her without the cast, wearing a long skirt that covered her deformity. In spite of her apprehension, her heart did a flip when she saw him all bronze and blue-eyed, waiting for her in the lobby of the dorm.

His car was a rattletrap Ford with a broken-down front seat and almost no floorboard, so they took hers. He wanted to see *The Great Escape* with Steve McQueen, and she wanted to see Bergman's new film, *The Silence*, so they compromised on *Lilies of the Field*, with Sidney Poitier.

"How can you go to a movie and not eat popcorn?" he asked, eating his own box and the one he bought for her.

She shrugged. "It doesn't agree with me."

Popcorn sometimes gave her terrible cramps; she couldn't take a chance on eating anything on a date that could cause something like that to happen. Since she'd grown to her full height of five feet three, her attacks of pain had gotten much less and rarely happened. But in the last year, her liver had gotten slightly enlarged from an accumulation of Gaucher's cells, since the liver had taken over the function of the spleen, and that caused certain internal upheavals, like constipation and indigestion.

Ron held her hand during the first part of the movie and then put his arm around her shoulder and snuggled closer. The wooden arm of the seat was pressing against her ribs and it might cause a bruise, but she wouldn't have moved for anything. Then he kissed her, tasting of Coca-Cola, and she breathed in his wholesome, athletic scent. He kissed well, soft and tender, yet passionate. Her heart was pounding crazily and she was out of breath. She felt her body flood with warmth and desire. She reached her hand to his muscular thigh, running her fingers along the taut fabric of his jeans, nearly reaching his groin; but then when she felt him reaching his own hand down her body, almost touching her newly operated knee, she jerked away from him, startling them both.

"I forgot where we were," she said, indicating the people around them by way of an explanation. But that wasn't it. She couldn't bear the idea of someone touching her deformity. And suddenly she realized she might never be able to. It frightened her terribly. She hadn't understood how much this had changed her and, like a turtle, encased her in a permanent shell. Ron tried to kiss her again. He was still breathing heavily, and she was afraid he might suggest they leave, but instead he pulled away, and turned back to watch the movie.

She felt herself trembling and was greatly relieved that the moment had been postponed. She wondered if she'd ever be able to let anyone see her leg.

Fortunately, the movie captured her attention and she was able to set it aside. And after the movie, when they came out of the theater singing, "Amen, a-men, a-men, a-men, a-men," the way Poitier had sung to the nuns, she felt close to normal again.

"Poitier's so gorgeous," she said, and Ron looked at her sideways. They had left the crutches in the car and she was leaning on him, so she couldn't quite see his expression since he was at least six inches taller than she.

"For a Negro," he said.

She stiffened. "What's that supposed to mean?"

He was slightly embarrassed that he'd sounded prejudiced.

They reached her car, and he turned toward her. "What about me?" he said.

"You're gorgeous too," she told him, smiling.

Leaning down to kiss her, he put both his arms around her and pressed himself against her. She kissed him back, reveling in the feeling of her body against his. It had been so long since anyone had kissed her, and she hungered for more. At the moment her knee did not seem to be a problem at all. Instead, the feeling of being alive, truly alive, pulsated within her. And suddenly her knee seemed to be a very small part of her, especially when the rest of her was so enflamed. This new objectivity was a wondrous thing—so relieving. She wanted to shout with the ecstacy of normality. Somebody wanted her despite her flaws. Gratitude overwhelmed her and she wanted to devour him, show him how much she was feeling. But then she realized that she was overreacting because of recent events, and perhaps they should go more slowly. It was she who broke away.

"Maybe we should save this for another time," she whispered in his ear.

"Would you like to go somewhere now?" he asked. "MFK?" offering the traditional after-the-movie cup of coffee, not Mulholland Drive to park.

The coffee shop at the Beverly Wilshire was her least favorite place to go after a movie; too many affluent college kids went there, and they all belonged to sororities or fraternities. But she realized she couldn't suggest to this shy kind of guy that they go and park; besides, she'd decided to go slowly.

"How about the Hamburger Hamlet on Sunset?"

"Hey, great," he said. "I've been wanting to try it."

"You've never been there? They have a wonderful barbecue burger."

He helped her into the car and came around to the driver's side.

The Hamburger Hamlet was crowded with young people waiting to be seated, pressed against the wood-planked walls, leaning against the red-checkered tablecloths, shuffling on the sawdust-covered floor. And then she noticed with disappointment that many of them were the same UCLA fraternity and sorority students she'd wanted to avoid.

"Hey, you guys," Ron called, spotting a group of his friends and waving to them. He seemed delighted to find them here. "Come on," he said, leading her forcefully. "There's some people I'd like you to meet."

They approached the table and she felt her body tensing when the broad welcoming grins of Ron's friends changed to pity as they noticed her leaning on him to walk across the room. These people would be polite to her because Ron had brought her, but she could almost feel them closing ranks because she was different. All her life she'd been different from these kinds of people, and now, since this latest surgery, even more so. She'd learned to resent their happy-go-lucky ways, their belief that they ruled the school simply by their perfection—which was precisely why she wasn't one of them, her own imperfections. If they only felt comfortable with their own kind, then so did she. But in groups where she was accepted there was no requirement to dress like everyone else, talk like everyone else, think like everyone else; you were accepted by an unwritten code of recognition. She assumed that not one of these blond coeds, with the turned-up hair and the blank looks in their eyes, knew anything about real life or cared about contributing to society. And for sure they all had perfectly shaped, tanned legs.

Ron was waiting for her to move forward, and so for his sake she smiled, shook hands, and then squeezed into the booth between two huge guys with enormous muscles who Ron introduced her to as Curtis and Jer, the terrors of the backfield.

"Where you guys been tonight?" Ron asked.

"Basketball playoffs," a girl named Phyllis told him, as if he was the biggest dunce not to have remembered such a crucial college fact as UCLA vying for the championship again this year.

Ron actually blushed and said, "Steffani just got off crutches so I thought she'd better not try the steps at Pauley Pavilion."

Phyllis looked at Steffani, tilting her head with appraisal and then nodding, as if to say, *A cripple, no less*? Phyllis had flawless skin, a short, button nose, smooth blond hair to her shoulders; and she was wearing a crisp white cotton blouse dotted with a sorority pin, with the mandatory string of pearls peeking through the open, round-necked, Peter Pan collar.

"We went to see *Lilies of the Field*," Steffani said.

"Oh." Jer was not impressed. "You gotta see *The Great Escape*, it's so bitchin'! That McQueen is tough."

"I bet he wins the Academy Award for it," Phyllis pronounced. In Los Angeles, everyone talked about an actor's performance in terms of the awards, as though they were experts concerning the biggest party of the year, whether or not they had anything to do with the industry.

"Well, Poitier's performance will be tough to beat," Steffani responded.

"Yeah, he's gorgeous," Phyllis said, seriously, "but not as gorgeous as Belafonte."

Ron looked at Steffani and he winked. That was when she first started to love him.

"I've seen him at the Greek Theater every year since 1956," Phyllis said, raising her estimation in Steffani's eyes. "I love his songs, 'Scarlet Ribbons,' 'Island in the Sun,' 'Day-Oh,' and especially 'Matilda.' "

Jer raised his hands above his head, snapped his fingers, and moved his hips, bumping them between Steffani and Phyllis, as he sang an imitation of Belafonte, "Women over forty," and everyone at the table sang, "Ma-tilda," in reply, following with the chorus about her taking the money and running to Ven-e-zuela.

Steffani joined in and couldn't believe she was actually having a good time. And then, someone at the other end of the table got up to go and said to his date, "Come on baby." And someone else answered back, "Let's do the twist." And someone else added, "And around and around and around we go-o-o." Until the whole table, including Steffani and Ron, began twisting and moving their behinds from side to side in the leatherette booth, and laughing.

Some of the group had already finished eating their burgers while others were just ordering. Steffani asked for an Egg Custard Lulu, thinking that a burger might not agree with her, and Bill, sitting next to Phyllis, called her a "grandma." But when her custard arrived at the table, piled high with whipped cream and sprinkled with cookie crumbs, everyone took spoonfuls until she hardly had any left. But it didn't matter because they all told her she had ordered the best thing of all.

At last the group broke up, paying the bill, each one counting out their quarters for the tip.

"See you around," Phyllis said, and Bill winked at Steffani, and pointed a finger at her in a gesture that meant she was cool.

Then, Ron helped her back to the car and drove them back to campus. "My friends really liked you," he said, gazing at her with such tenderness that she understood how important their approval was to him.

"They're okay," she announced, surprised at herself; she was such a staunch non-org she'd been prepared to dislike them on sight. But then she thought of her sister, Suzanne, who was a lot like them, secure in the belief that whatever she said had value, that she would be liked simply because she was who she was. Steffani had more in common with Ron's fraternity friends than she'd realized, not only because of Suzanne, but because they weren't so bad after all. But still, there was a shallowness to their lives. None of them had experienced the darker side of life the way she had, and that set her apart. It made her care passionately about the world, while they were caring about having a good time and basketball.

"There are so many things I'd like to do with you," he said, when they arrived at the dorm. He handed her the crutches and walked slowly next to her to help her if she needed it. "I want to take you camping, maybe next month when the weather warms up and your leg is stronger. We can go up to the Kern River and sleep out."

"I'd like that," she said, wondering if she'd have the strength to do something so strenuous. If she told him of her limitations, he might be turned off. Better to wait a while until he knew her better, liked her more, the way she usually did with new people in her life.

"And in June there's the Sigma Chi Sweetheart Dance.

This year we're having it in Newport. Would you like to go with me?''

A fraternity formal, her first. She was amazed that this was happening to her, something she'd never expected. ''Why don't we wait and see how things go between us, first?'' she suggested, afraid to commit to a date so far ahead. What if she wasn't feeling well?

''You're a worrier, aren't you?'' he said, pressing the elevator button.

''I've had to be cautious,'' she said. And though he expected her to tell him why, it was clear that she wasn't going to say anything more.

When they were alone in the elevator, he kissed her again, exploring her mouth with his tongue as they ran their hands along each other's bodies feeling one another's instant, fiery response. But when he reached for the emergency button to stop the elevator, she shook her head, not wanting to be one of those girls who comes out of the elevator with mussed clothes and a red face, while everyone stands around the door as it opens, pointing and teasing in singsong voices, ''We know what you're do-ing.''

''I'll see you tomorrow,'' he said, getting off at his floor. ''And the next day, and the next day, and the one after that . . .'' He was still saying it as the elevator door closed, hiding him from sight, and taking her up to her floor, laughing.

There were a trillion stars in the black sky flung there just for them to gaze on. They were sitting on a blanket in front of their campfire on a Thursday night during spring break roasting marshmallows. Everyone else they knew was in Palm Springs or on Balboa Island. But they had chosen to come here to be totally alone, free to indulge their feelings for one another, feelings that had caused Steffani to think in terms of Ron as definite husband material, something she'd vowed not to do for many years yet. It was funny how the right guy at the wrong time could change things. And now, sitting here under the stars with the black sky all around them, there were no roommates to contend with, no gearshift sticking its rodlike presence between them, and no scrounging for money for a motel: just the two sleeping bags awaiting them in the small tent that Steffani had helped Ron assemble. Both of them were nervous. After all the foreplay, the touching and feeling, this was it. And she was both excited and apprehensive, worried about him seeing her leg, wondering whether or not it would turn him off. She'd worn an ace bandage to cover it up, but that had only made her feel uncomfortable, so when she was alone in the bushes, she'd taken it off.

"You hardly ate any of your burger," Ron said. "If we throw it in the trash, it's liable to attract bears."

Her head jerked toward him, making her lose her marshmallow in the fire. "Are there really bears around here?"

"Nah," he laughed, handing her his marshmallow, pleased that he'd gotten the reaction he'd expected.

Her leg was aching, so she moved it out from under her. She should have known better than to go hiking so soon after getting the cast off. Her mother had warned her, but tonight was too important to miss. It sounded wonderful to sleep under the stars, the way she and Suzanne had done when they were kids on hot summer nights on the aluminum chaise longues in the backyard. How she wished she had nothing else to worry about but having a good time, and making love for the first time since before her surgery.

She tried to ignore the throbbing in her leg but it had the familiar pounding of an attack about to happen. It couldn't be, not tonight. Besides, she hadn't had an attack in a long time. They were gone forever, she was certain! She held her breath—and then, it subsided. It was only soreness from the exercise of hiking.

"Maybe tomorrow we'll have trout for lunch," Ron said, putting his arm around her.

"My he-man fisherman," she teased, remembering how every time he'd cast his line that afternoon it had gotten caught in a tree.

She moved closer to him, putting her head on his shoulder,

feeling the hardness of his muscles behind her neck. She'd been waiting for him to make his move all night, but he'd been so busy setting up camp, unpacking the car, starting the fire, and then cooking dinner she felt like she was the last thing on his mind. She'd had no idea that camping took so much equipment or that the bathroom would be the bushes.

She couldn't see the Kern River in the dark but its rushing sound was ever present coming from the bottom of the sloped bank of land where they had set up camp. In the daylight, the water was icy cold and a clear, pale blue-green color at the edges, running over white rocks at the shore bleached by the sun, turning into a dark Prussian blue color at its deepest point. Sitting here like this in the dark made her think of all the adventure books she'd enjoyed as a child where the heroes had battled the elements, *Robinson Crusoe, The Swiss Family Robinson, The Call of the Wild, Huckleberry Finn*, and one in particular about a boy who'd been shipwrecked off the coast of Baja California and made a journey all alone across the desert, finally reaching a northern city. During his journey, he'd learned how to survive on cactus and how to stay clear of rattlesnakes and scorpions. It had amazed her that a mere boy could have accomplished such a feat. And after she'd read that book she was terrified that something like that might happen to her, that she'd find herself stranded somewhere outdoors, lost and removed from civilization. She knew she would die, because she was so vulnerable to any physical crisis. If she had an attack there would be no narcotics to relieve the pain or ice compresses to reduce the fever. And if she cut herself, she'd either die of an infection, without antibiotics, or hemorrhage to death while lying there helpless as the merciless sun beat down on her and the vultures came to pick her bones.

She shuddered at the thought, and Ron, who was sitting there with his arm around her, pressed her closer. "Are you all right?" he asked.

But she wasn't really. She was worried about her very survival, while he was only concerned with getting laid. And how could she keep him from seeing her leg? She'd had nightmares about that. Well, it was now or never. She tilted her head toward him so he might kiss her, letting her breath warm his neck.

"What were you thinking about?" he asked after the kiss.

"Surviving in the wilderness." She traced her fingers along the veins in his forearm, trying not to let her fears get the best of her. "Did you ever read a short story by Herman Melville published in *Putnam's Monthly* magazine about a ship's crew who mutinied and joined forces with the cargo of black slaves? They killed the officers and terrorized the captain."

"Sounds as farfetched as being obsessed with killing a white whale."

"No, Melville based his story on the actual voyage of Amaso Delano. Of course he embellished it." She was pulling conversation out of her repertoire to avoid letting him know how vulnerable she was. She could see through the clear blue portion of his eyes as he stared into the fire and she ran her hand along his thigh up to his knee and back again. But when he tried to do that to her, she moved his hand away from her knee so he wouldn't feel how enlarged it was.

"Melville's style is ponderous," she said to distract him from the fact that she'd changed the path of his caress. "And his sentences have so many subjunctive clauses it drives you crazy, but he's excellent at creating an atmosphere of tension and describing the character's most intimate thoughts."

He turned toward her, his voice deepened by desire. "You make it sound really interesting. You would make a wonderful teacher, better than my American lit professor."

She caressed his cheek with her hand. "You should have taken Nevius, he's the best."

"No, you're the best," he said, leaning over to kiss her.

Her response was immediate, shooting hot desire through her with an energy that was both stimulating and lethargic, a melting sensation like the way the marshmallows had melted, all sweet and syrupy inside. Some part of her felt the cool night air, heard the crickets in the bushes, the sound of rushing water nearby. But the rest of her felt immersed in him. She lay back on the blanket, as he lay on top of her, pressing his groin against her thigh. Her leg was still throbbing and she was only able to ignore it because the rest of her was throbbing too.

"Would you like to go into the tent," he asked, huskily, when their first long kiss had ended.

She nodded.

"We'd better douse the fire first," he said.

"Are you sure you want to?" she asked.

"Are you kidding?" he said, reaching for her hand to stroke the hardness between his legs. Then he put his hand on her bare breast under her sweater, exhaling sharply as his hand touched her flesh. "I'm so lucky I found you," he told her.

His breath was blowing warm air into her hair. Moisture flooded inside her tight jeans.

"I zipped the sleeping bags together into one," he said, pulling away and smiling shyly. "Just in case."

"Very smart." She smiled back. "Why don't you take care of the fire out here, while I start one in the tent." It was a corny comment, but he didn't notice because he was folding the blanket as she climbed into the tent. Quickly she reached into her backpack for a pain pill, swallowing it whole, praying she wouldn't choke on it. But it went down smoothly, and then she pulled off her jeans and climbed into the sleeping bag first so he wouldn't see her leg. In the morning she'd get dressed when he had left the tent. Maybe she could pull it off after all.

CHAPTER TWENTY-TWO

On a Thursday morning, only four days after sending half my manuscript to Esther, she called at 7:15 A.M. "I figured if you're asleep, you wouldn't mind my waking you up to tell you I read the material and I love it." She was right, I didn't mind at all. "It's a departure for you, but I know it will work. They'll die to have it, love. Anyone would. I'm sending it by messenger to Judy Emory with a cover letter today so she can read it over the weekend."

Relief flooded through me and I felt ebullient. "Esther, you don't think it's too sweet?"

"Not at all. Let me read you what I wrote to Judy about it. 'Speaking for myself, I was fascinated by the story of this Romanian peasant girl of such ethereal beauty that she gets a job in a carnival impersonating an angel in a glass box, is kidnapped by gypsies, and ends up a countess, searching for the son the gypsies kidnap from her.' It will sell, Suzanne, you'll see."

"I've got everything banking on it, Esther."

"I'll call you Monday when I hear from Judy, okay?"

Now the weekend loomed ahead, sodden, heavy with expectation yet lightened by hope. Perhaps I would be saved from drowning. I was thankful for the diversion of Barry, who was taking us to the zoo.

I had just gotten the children off to school when the phone rang at 8:15, another New York call.

"Suzanne, it's Michelle." The clipped New York twangy voice was the same as always. Michelle Bryant, my first editor, published my first three books before she left to go to Mansfield Publishing. I was fond of Michelle; owed her a lot.

She'd discovered me, though we hadn't stayed in touch. Usually we saw one another at the American Booksellers Convention over Memorial Day weekend, rarely this time of year. The moment I heard her voice, I knew why she was calling.

"How are you, Michelle?"

"The question is, how are you?" she asked, in her dry, halting way of talking. Quick witted and impatient, she used to say, "Don't give me trouble, Suzanne," when she wanted to bully me into submission. "I know best."

She wouldn't get away with that now, I thought. Over the years my confidence had increased with my success.

"Listen, dear girl. I'll get right to the point. I received some disgusting letters about you the other day. I'd been hearing rumors, but this was really awful."

"You know it's not true," I said, feeling that familiar fury mixed with helplessness. I had learned by now that I couldn't convince anyone of my innocence. Either they believed it or they didn't.

"Of course I know that," she assured me. "I didn't even want to bother you with it."

"Then, why are you calling?" I couldn't help sounding hostile. I hated being the subject of gossip and conjecture. I could just see them dishing me over publishers' lunches.

Michelle heard the tension in my voice. "How long has this been going on?"

"Over two months," I told her, gritting my teeth against the fury. "And I'm no closer to finding out who it is than I was when it first happened. But I will, Michelle. You damned well better know I will."

"So you are doing something about it?"

"Of course I am! I've talked with the police, I've been to a lawyer, and an investigator; I've even done some sleuthing myself. But so far, we really have nothing to go on. I just have to wait it out."

"Well, I've told everyone I know that there's no truth to this, but some of them, well, you know how people are. I recognized that passage from *The Reunion*. Remember all those editorial notes I sent you for your rewrites? There's no way you could have stolen one word of that book and I tell that to everyone. But publishers panic over the possibility of a lawsuit, even if they're not involved. Litigation phobia is in the air after the Clifford Irving hoax.''

"Michelle, I want you to send me the material you received. For whatever good it will do, I'm collecting the evidence. I've had the letters analyzed by an expert and it's been determined that they were all typed on the same typewriter. That might be a way for me to track down this person. Someday this person is going to make a mistake, there will be one goddamned clue that I can use to nail them, and then you're going to see the shit fly. I fall asleep committing the most brutal acts of maiming and killing you can imagine.''

Michelle laughed too. "I don't blame you. But Suzanne''—there was that directive tone again. "The sooner you find this person the better because people are talking, and you know how damaging gossip can be to a writer's career.''

"I thought controversy stimulated the public's appetite and sent book sales skyrocketing," I shot back. *Damn her, didn't she think I knew that!*

"Well, if you're Norman Mailer, perhaps. But scandal doesn't do a writer of women's fiction any good. Women readers will turn off if they get the idea that you're immoral. They could even boycott you.''

"Gee, Michelle, that's exactly what I needed to hear. Maybe you know Sherry Fallon. She claims to have worked at Silver's when you were there.''

"I didn't know her," she insisted.

"Well, she's not using her real name, I've called every Sherry Fallon in the country by now. Michelle, if this happened to you, what would you do?''

"Me? No one cares enough about me to try and get my goat. But . . . I guess I'd have a long look at my life and see if there was anyone in it who could be doing this. And if I found there was, I'd have her legs broken." She gave that one short burst of laughter that was her trademark and I tried to join her, but laughter was hard to come by at the moment.

"Thanks for your concern," I told her. "I'll let you know when I figure it out." And I hung up.

That Saturday morning, a delivery man arrived with a plastic snowman for me and the children filled with enough chocolate chip cookies to cause an overdose. Attached to the snowman was a jingle illustrated with one of Barry's cartoons. Although we had plans to spend time together this weekend, I figured it would be a movie and dinner, like last weekend, and then the zoo on Sunday. I never expected this.

> *Prepare for a fabulous weekend,*
> *Though it won't hurt the fun if you're peekin',*
> *Just remember to smile,*
> *When we're biking for miles,*
> *'Cause life's wonderful treasures we're*
>   *seekin'.*

The children's excitement was contagious. Ever since they'd met Barry only two weeks ago, they talked of him constantly. And now that his invitation included them, they were thrilled. "What do you think we should take?" Jered asked. "Do I need my sneakers?"

"How about tennis rackets?" Amy wondered.

"I bet we're going hiking," Miles guessed, grabbing the phone when it rang before anyone else could get there. He listened to Barry's instructions and repeated them. "Wear jeans, and bring jackets, visors, and a blanket."

"Is it a picnic?" Miles guessed while we crowded around.

"He says I'm partially right," Miles told us. "But where? That is the question." Miles handed me the phone. "He wants to speak to you."

"Can we use your station wagon today?"

"Sure," I told him.

"Is there air in the children's bicycle tires?"

"I think so," I told him.

"Well, if not, we can get them filled when you and I rent our bikes."

"Where are we riding?" I asked, thinking it was a grand idea.

"You'll see," he told me, mysteriously. "I'll be there in about twenty minutes."

At exactly 10:30 A.M. he arrived, we climbed into the car, and Barry headed west. All the way to the coast on the freeway the children and I tried to guess where we were going. Finally, we ended up in the Marina, where Barry and I rented two bikes and made sure the children's tires were in good shape. Our bike ride took us all around the Marina, and up into Venice along the boardwalk where we rode the bike path and stopped to watch the crazy array of peculiar people who paraded there on weekends. Vendors sold all sorts of junk the children had to have. Barry agreed to buy them each one item, so it took hours for them to decide on what that would be. I swallowed the lump in my throat, knowing how special it was to receive a gift when money was so tight these days.

I said to him, "It's wonderful of you to have put so much thought into this day," after we returned our rental bikes and piled the children's bikes into the back of the station wagon.

He took my hand and smiled. "Believe me, I'm having more fun than they are."

When we got back to the house, Barry said good-bye to the children as they all thanked him for a great day. And then he kissed me lightly on the lips. "When we go to the zoo tomorrow, maybe your sister would like to join us?"

I had told Barry all about Steffani and he'd said he wanted to meet her. But to invite her to join us was special, something Alex had rarely done. I kept thinking, this man is too good to be true. "I'll call and ask her," I told him, thanking him for this delightful day.

Sunday was cloudy, not the brilliant sunny day we'd had on Saturday, but it didn't dampen our spirits as we drove over to Griffith Park and entered the zoo. It was more difficult to keep the children together since they each had their favorite animals to visit. But Barry gave them all instructions—the two older ones could go off by themselves, and if we became separated, we'd meet at the gorilla cages. Jered would have to stay with us.

My sister and Barry got into a heated conversation about President Carter. She was a Democrat who believed that Republicans were not only dishonest politicians, as evidenced by Watergate, but wouldn't take a stand on human rights. And he was a Republican who, though he deplored Nixon, still preferred Ford over Carter. I smiled as I listened to Steffani argue. That persistent cough was still hanging on and would not go away. Sometimes, she told me it kept her up all night no matter what kind of cough syrup she took. But today she was as feisty as ever; her eyes sparkled and her skin glowed in the crisp autumn air.

I walked ahead with Jered, listening to his excited exclamations every time he recognized one of his favorite animals. But Steffani and Barry's voices behind me kept me distracted. As loudly and vehemently as they argued, I could tell they respected each other's opinion and now and then they'd laugh at the other's comment.

At one point, when Steffani was buying the children peanuts, Barry told me, ''I really like your sister.'' Gratitude flooded through me because his attitude was so different from the way Alex had always thought of her. (I had promised myself not to compare Barry to Alex, but it was difficult not to.)

''What was it like for you to grow up with a sister who had so many physical problems?'' he asked.

His question stopped me cold. I just stood there, unaware for a moment of where I was, the sights and smells and sounds fading from my consciousness as I thought only of his question.

''What is it?'' he asked, stopping with me. ''Is that too personal?''

"No," I assured him. "It's perfectly logical. Except no one in my whole life has ever asked me that before. Everyone's always so concerned about her, about what she's going through and what's going to happen to her, that my feelings about it were never considered. But you know, it was not easy growing up a witness to her pain, always deferring to her needs. Sometimes I resented the hell out of it. My parents assume I share their concern for her health, and I do. But she's my sister, not theirs. The only one I've got. And God, I worry about her. She's so beautiful, so full of life, and she's been through so much." Tears filled my eyes and I felt an enormous sorrow nearly ready to burst through. It was all I could do to contain it, for if it came flooding out, it might ruin this perfect day.

"She is very beautiful," he said.

I tried to smile, but my smile was all crooked. He just took my hand and squeezed it, and we continued walking until we'd caught up with the rest of them.

I think that moment was when I felt the first stirrings of love toward him, amazed that I could feel it with so much else going on in my life.

For dinner we ended up at Barry's house, on Oriole Drive above Sunset, eating take-out pizza and salad. The children watched television while Barry, Steffani, and I talked. He showed us pictures of Eileen, more of his cartoons, and even his collection of Indian arrowheads he'd saved from his childhood.

Before it was time to go, Jered asked me if I'd tell him more about the story of Annica. "Her mother and sisters hate her because she's beautiful and they're not," he explained to Barry and Steffani.

I continued, "And also because her mother, Katinca, believed she'd been cursed for not having had a son. So, Annica's father raises her in the attic away from the rest of the family and then takes her with him into the fields. When Annica is seven, her grandmother comes to live with them, and for the first time in Annica's life, she experiences the love of a mother."

Jered gazed at me with his large brown eyes. "Like you love me, and Nana and Grandma?"

"Yes, sweetheart, exactly like that."

"Annica's grandmother tells her stories about being governess to the children of Franz Joseph of Austria and living in the palace. She teaches Annica to speak many languages and to play the harp. But then, her dearest grandmother dies. It's a very sad time for her. But with the money she inherits, Annica leaves her father's farm and goes to see the world."

"To seek her fortune?" he asked, remembering the line from other stories.

"Yes," I told him. "And now it's time to go home."

As we left Barry's house Jered said, "I really like this book, Mom." And as I hugged him, I hoped my editor would respond to it in the same way and not think it was merely a fairy tale for children.

On the way home, my sister said, "I'm glad you're writing Nana's book. It meant so much to her and to Mom."

"Thanks for the vote of confidence. I'll probably hear something tomorrow."

"There's one more thing, Suzanne. You ought to marry Barry Adler. He's great."

I felt my cheeks flush hotly and was glad she couldn't see it in the dark. "You and I have never liked the same type of men before," I said, slightly worried about her comment. Did I have to compete with her for Barry?

"You're right, we haven't," she conceded. "You always go for that uptight corporate type."

"Well, Barry is not exactly a hippie."

"But he's got an old soul," she said, teasing me.

"Great. What mumbo-jumbo is that?"

"What I mean is, he's simpatico. And he really likes you, Suze."

"I really like him," I confessed, feeling the heat in my cheeks subsiding. The more I knew him, the better I liked him. Perhaps the next time we spent a weekend together, it would be for adults only.

* * *

On Monday afternoon, Esther still hadn't heard from Judy
Emory. "What do you think it means?" I said.

"Well, they have a sales conference next week, so they
could be gearing up for it, concentrating only on that. Or,
she's submitted your book to the editorial board and is waiting
for approval. After all, we've asked for a hefty sum."

"You talked money already?"

"Of course. I said we're looking to double your last book's
advance. Judy thought it was pretty steep. But I told her your
sales figures warrant it. She knows that's true. I told her you
wanted your money now so you could earn the interest on it,
rather than waiting for royalties."

My heart fell into my stomach at the thought of what was
hanging in the balance here. "Are you worried?" I asked
Esther.

"Not yet."

"When will you be?" I really didn't want to know.

"If they come back with some Chicken-Little amount and
I have to start threatening. Then, I'll worry a little—not a
lot, mind you, but a little."

"Why?" My head was pounding as I tried to concentrate
on what she was saying.

"Because I'll know then, that something about the book
isn't grabbing them the way it should. And since the book
grabs me just right, I'll wonder what else is going on."

"You mean about the plagiarism problem?"

"Yeah," she said, thoughtfully. "I'm sure they'll sign you
in the long run, but I don't want us to have to suffer over it."

There was that spectre again, raising its head from the
muck, leering at me with venom dripping from its jaws. *Who
are you?* I wondered. And then, I clenched imaginary fists
and plowed into its evil oozing snout, yelling, *Damn you to
hell!*

By Thursday, December 16, when I still hadn't heard by 9:00
A.M., which was noon New York time, I was gripped by a
feeling of dread. Something was wrong.

I called Esther and she came right on the line.

"I just got off the phone with Judy," she said. "They want the book!"

"They do?" I shouted, feeling a rush of relief flood through me, glorious, billowing relief, as though the sun had finally broken through a dense fog-shrouded world. I was still in the running. "What did she say?"

"That she cried at least four times. The character of Annica is glorious. The story is a delight and everybody thought so."

"Oh, thank God," I breathed. "That means we're home free, aren't we?" I could see my future stretching out before me, alive and real, golden tinged by brilliant sunlight instead of dark and brooding and falling off the end of the earth into emptiness.

"Not exactly," Esther said, a warning tone in her voice.

My heart clutched again as I asked, "What do you mean?"

"Well, the bad news is they'll only pay ten percent over the last advance—two hundred and seventy-five thousand."

It was as if someone had reached in and squeezed my heart, stopping it mid-beat. "I can't make it on that, Esther," I whispered, my voice unable to muster volume. Most people would consider that much money a fortune, and it was, but I owed every penny of it and more. Fortunes were relative; I was trying to hold my life together. "Is it the plagiarism accusation that's keeping them from giving me more?"

" 'Fraid so. They're worried about a backlash against your books, or of lawsuits you might be involved in, and of adverse publicity. All those things would be detrimental to your career and could definitely affect your sales."

"I have no choice, Esther, I have to turn it down. What should we do?" I asked her, knowing her counsel would be honest and extremely helpful.

"I can ask them to pay us the rest of what we asked for whenever this problem of yours is resolved—in other words, when we find out who the culprit is, they could give us more money."

"But what if I never find out? What if I can't resolve it?

If I accept this offer it will mean total financial disaster for me. We'd lose our home. Where would we go? Where would we live? How would I support us? I might have to give up writing." That scream was welling up inside again and the one word that coalesced was *unfair*! The thought of being shunned, doubted, pitied, avoided as though infested with a disease, enraged and terrified me. Finding out who my tormentor was would hardly compensate for this experience. These disasters had shaken my belief in myself, made me doubt my ability to recover. Like Barry receiving one of those phone calls, *Hello, Mr. Adler, your life has just been destroyed*, I'd gotten letters instead. How did Barry keep from being bitter? I could feel bitterness seeping through me like winter's chill. And then with all my strength, my soul cried out, *I won't let this defeat me, I won't*!

"You can't give up writing, Suzanne. That would be impossible." She paused. "We can always go to another publisher."

"Why would another publisher pay me more than Silver's has offered?"

"To get your contract."

"But wouldn't they be just as concerned about the accusations?"

"Yes. This thing hanging over your head isn't winning you friends in the publishing world."

"I wonder if the person doing this to me knew what the consequences would be."

"Of course, that's why they're doing it."

How diabolical it was. The evil had multiplied, spreading its noxious fumes over all my life, seeping into the layers, into the connective tissue. I couldn't blame my publisher for being cautious; under the circumstances they were acting generously. The miracle I had prayed for, and actually expected, was not coming true. Now, what could I do?

That evening I was supposed to attend a PEN function in Pasadena, a panel discussion of book critics. I had looked forward to going, especially since Brett Slocum, the reviewer who'd disliked *Mortal Wounds,* would be there. I had planned to say a few choice words to her, but feeling the way I did, with my future in the balance, I decided to stay home.

The next morning, Martha, one of my writer friends, a member of PEN, who'd attended the discussion, called to inform me that Brett Slocum hadn't been there after all. She'd had to rush back to New York because her housekeeper was hospitalized in a drug-related incident.

"Anyone who works for her is justified in taking drugs," I quipped to Martha, hoping my sense of humor was returning.

"Yes," Martha admitted. "Several of us last night said the same thing. It's too bad it wasn't Brett Slocum who'd overdosed."

I agreed. I wasn't the only one of my fellow writers whose work had been vilified by Ms. Slocum over the years.

On Saturday afternoon, I received an odd phone call. "Mrs. Suzanne Winston?" a man's voice asked. I could tell he was calling long distance. There was other noise in the background.

"Yes," I replied.

"This is Sergeant Brisco, with the New York City Police Department, narcotics division."

"Yes?" I supposed it had something to do with one of my books, or they wanted me to speak to the police department.

"May I ask you a few questions?"

I was flattered. I often called strangers all over the country to elicit information about their professions when I was doing research for my books, and now someone was calling me. "Of course, Sergeant, go ahead."

"Do you know someone by the name of Brett Slocum?"

My first reaction was to laugh, but I didn't. "No," I told him. "I don't know her personally. I only know her work." I'm sure my voice had an edge to it; I still smarted from her criticism.

"You have no connection with her, whatsoever?"

"No!" I was rather indignant. "Why would I even want to? What's this all about?"

"Well, there was an incident a few days ago with a woman in Ms. Slocum's employ and we're following up on it."

"Why are you calling me? I'm in California." I was truly mystified.

"I know that, ma'am," he said. By his calling me "ma'am," I felt a chill of apprehension.

"And you're telling me you don't know Mrs. Slocum at all and have no reason to be upset with her?"

"That's what I'm telling you," I said, not knowing what to say. When in doubt, say nothing.

"All right, ma'am," he said, again. "Thank you for your time." And that was that.

Why were they calling me? I wondered, trying to shake the sudden feeling of doom that had settled over me. I forced the dire thoughts away, and thought about my future. Judy Emory and Phillip Silver were sure to come up with a better offer. They didn't want to lose me any more than I wanted to leave them. I wondered how long Esther expected us to wait before calling Judy back. Eventually, I forgot about Sergeant Brisco's phone call but the rest of the weekend dragged.

On Tuesday morning, just as the carpool was driving away, I poured myself another cup of tea and turned on the television. This story was on the morning news:

"Literary critic Brett Slocum, in Los Angeles for a speaking engagement last Thursday, returned to New York to attend the bedside vigil of her housekeeper, who ate a box of tainted chocolates sent to Ms. Slocum by a disgruntled writer. The housekeeper, who suffered a mild heart attack, retrieved the candy from the wastebasket where Ms. Slocum, a diabetic, had put it. An unknown poisonous substance had been sprayed or injected into the chocolates, which were from Teuscher's of New York. A spokesman for the chocolatier said the company has no comment at this time. Police are questioning authors all over the country to see who might have sent the chocolates to Ms. Slocum."

So that's why they called me, I thought. *But why me? I'd never do anything like that.* And suddenly the whole room began to spin as it occurred to me, *But I hadn't committed plagiarism either*. I tried to stand, but had to clutch the table to keep from falling.

Tilt.

My whole world was falling out of kilter again. *Don't panic, Suzanne. They're questioning everyone, not just you. Nobody likes that witch, she trashes everyone.* I had to know more about this and reached for the phone to call Martha, when the doorbell rang.

"Yes?" I asked, through the kitchen window that parallels the front door. Two young men stood there, in suits and ties, their hair cut short, military style. Before they told me, I knew they were the police. Thank God, the children had already gone to school.

I was still in my robe; I had a sudden, desperate urge to go to the bathroom and didn't know what to do first: answer the door, put on some clothes, or go to the bathroom.

I went to the door. "What can I do for you?" I asked, clutching at calmness, which never works. I got a glimpse of my own face in the entry hall mirror; it was the color of the pale green chenille robe I was wearing. They showed me their badges.

"I'm Detective Wilkinson, and this is Detective Perez." Perez had large kind eyes, the color of black coffee. Wilkinson had a square Dick Tracy jaw.

"Come in please," I said. "I'll be right back." And I left them there, standing in the entry, while I hurried down the hall to my bedroom, closed the door, and stood there frozen. It was a foreign country. I couldn't remember how to get to the bathroom in a house I had built myself. In that moment, I truly wanted to die, to absolutely vanish from existence rather than face whatever this was, this insanity attacking me at every juncture.

For an insane moment I thought about hiding under my bed, pretending I wasn't home, didn't live here, didn't belong to the human race. But my bladder would give me away. Already the urge to evacuate was so strong I didn't think I could make it to the bathroom.

Somehow I got there, relieved myself, and threw on some clothes, grabbing the first thing I could find, which was what I had worn last night to dinner at my parents', a black wool pantsuit and yellow blouse, much too dressy, festive, and inappropriate for being questioned by the police. I looked guilty already.

Looked guilty, hell, I was guilty. Guilty of being alive.

I came back into the living room and found them standing where I had left them.

"Why didn't you sit down?" I asked them.

"We were waiting for you," the first man said. I know he told me his name, but I didn't remember it now. I remembered Perez and looked to him as somehow familiar. He smiled, politely.

"We're here to ask you some questions about an incident that happened last week in New York," the first man said. I suddenly remembered his name, Wilkinson.

I nodded. "I heard it on the news just as you rang my bell. And a sergeant from narcotics called me, too."

They looked at one another, and that look sent chills through my body. Nothing I'd experienced up to now prepared me for the terror I was feeling. All I could see were the faces of my children as they looked at me with misery. "What have you done now, Mommy?" I could hear them say. And all my protestations of *Nothing!* would only reinforce their doubts. In that moment, I thought the most horrible thing in the world was not to have committed a crime, but to be accused of one. *I'm not accused, I'm not!* I told myself.

"Mrs. Winston, do you know Brett Slocum?"

"Not personally. She's a book reviewer."

"But you know her well enough to send her candy."

"I didn't send her any candy."

"Or the threatening notes, either."

"Did she receive notes?"

"Yes."

"I never sent them." *This is crazy, crazy, crazy*, I screamed silently.

"Mrs. Winston," Detective Perez said, "we're investigating this case because tampering with food is a criminal offense."

"But why have you come to me?"

"Because your name was on the note that came with the candy Ms. Slocum received. The candy had been drugged with LSD and her housekeeper had a pretty bad reaction."

I felt the terrible grip of some monstrous force squeezing the life out of me. *My name was on it?* "But I didn't send it."

"Didn't you tell the officer in New York that you had no reason to be upset with Ms. Slocum?"

"Yes." I felt caught in a trap.

"But Ms. Slocum gave you an unfavorable review, didn't she?"

"Yes."

"Then, that wasn't true, what you told the sergeant in New York, was it?"

"Should I call a lawyer?" I asked them.

"You can call anyone you want, you're not under arrest. We're just trying to get some information."

"But why would I do such a thing and sign my name to it?" I asked.

"That's what New York thought," Wilkinson told me. "We're just following through on every lead."

"I mean, it seems pretty stupid to me, to send someone candy laced with LSD and tell them you've done it."

"That's why Ms. Slocum threw the candy away, because receiving candy from you seemed odd to her. She knew she'd written a rather negative review about your book and you weren't her friend. So why would you send her a gift?"

"Besides, her being diabetic," I added.

"Oh, you knew that?" Detective Wilkinson said.

"I heard it on television," I told him.

"Didn't you tell Sergeant"—he couldn't recall the name and searched through his notes—"Sergeant Brisco, with New York narcotics, that you didn't know Ms. Slocum?"

"Yes, that's what I told him. That I don't know her personally, but I knew her work."

"And at that time you also knew about the review of your book?"

"Yes."

"Did you like the review?"

"No, of course not." I tried to be neutral; my reaction was anything but.

"Have you ever taken drugs, Mrs. Winston?"

"Not illegal ones," I insisted. "The only ones I've taken have been prescribed for me by a doctor."

"Do you mind if we look around your house?" Perez asked.

Now I was in a dilemma. If I said no, would I look more guilty? They sat there looking at me, calmly, waiting. With every ounce of my being I wished I had someone to ask for advice at this moment. My heart was pounding so hard it made my head throb in rhythm with the English clock over the fireplace.

"I don't mind if you look around. I have nothing to hide." The minute I told them that, I regretted it. But I was afraid to withdraw my permission so I bluffed it out.

I showed them around the house, my room and office, the children's rooms, and in each bathroom they opened the medicine chests and scanned the contents, finding nothing other than Clearasil, Pepto Bismol, an old prescription for Valium, and Bufferin. They also ran their hands under the mattresses, and into the sofa cushions. They admired my book covers framed in my office. Detective Perez wanted to know the standard questions: How long did it take me to write a novel? What made me start writing? Had I always wanted to be a writer? They found nothing in the maid's room or bath either, and I began to feel relieved.

"Would either of you like a cup of coffee or tea?" I offered, feeling almost giddy that I'd passed the test. "I have a pot of hot water on the stove."

They smiled congenially and followed me into the kitchen.

"You have a lovely home, Mrs. Winston," Detective Perez said, busying himself by opening cupboards and taking out the coffee cups. I noticed how at ease he seemed in someone else's kitchen.

"I'm having some financial difficulties at the moment," I admitted, "so my house seems quite precious to me."

"I know how that can be," Detective Wilkinson offered.

"There's milk in the refrigerator," I told Detective Perez, who reached in and got it.

"May I?" he asked, friendlily, opening the vegetable drawers.

I nodded, waiting for him to finish. It was then that I realized the search of my house hadn't been completed and my heart started to pound again.

There was nothing in the vegetable drawers.

Wilkinson was opening the cupboards, checking out the pantry closet.

Perez tapped the different containers of leftovers in the refrigerator, opened the sour cream container, and then looked into the top drawer in the refrigerator next to the milk section where I keep cheeses and batteries. I realized there was an old prescription in there for suppositories from when I once had a yeast infection. That embarrassed me. But when he reached into the drawer, it wasn't the suppositories he pulled out. It was a small clear bottle, with a blue liquid in it, the kind of bottle that vanilla or food coloring comes in.

"What's this?" he asked.

I was as mystified as he was. I never kept spices in the refrigerator.

The two of them looked at one another again. "Do we have to wait for a lab report?" Wilkinson asked Perez, who shook his head.

"No, I'm pretty sure what it is."

"Wait a minute," I said, my voice shaking, trying to stave off what was coming next. The water was boiling and just then the teakettle started whistling. I turned it off. "I don't know what that is. I've never seen it before. It doesn't belong to me." For a wild moment, I thought they might have planted it themselves. "I have a statement to make," I told them, rallying to my defense. "Several weeks ago I received letters in the mail, and my publishers received them too, friends of mine and relatives as well as other people in the publishing industry and the press got them too. These letters accused me of plagiarizing my books. The accusation is entirely untrue and it has already caused me a great deal of stress and a loss of income. I am sure that the same person who is tormenting my life also sent that LSD candy to Ms. Slocum and tried to blame it on me. I never sent any candy to her; I don't know where she lives. I would never do anything criminal, and I don't know what that is!" I pointed to the bottle in Perez's hand, my voice rising to a high pitch. "I swear on my life." My lips were trembling with tears held in check. I wanted desperately not to cry, to make sure they had heard me. They both nodded.

"I've never seen that in my life," I repeated.

Perez's kind brown eyes seemed reluctant as he said to me, "I'm sorry to have to do this, Mrs. Winston, but you're under arrest." And he read me my rights.

My knees buckled under me and I sank to the floor right in the kitchen. I didn't have the strength to stand up.

"Why are you arresting me? I told you the truth!" I insisted.

Neither of them replied. Instead, Detective Wilkinson asked, "Are you all right?" And he reached down to help me.

His concern almost made me break down; I was right on the edge of hysteria. Instead I shook my head no.

"Would you like some water?" one of them offered.

Again I shook my head. In the action of replying, my strength returned, and slowly I pushed myself up to a standing position again.

"I'd like to make a phone call," I said.

I went to the phone and called Barry's office, praying he was there.

He wasn't.

I left a message with his secretary that I needed a criminal attorney immediately and would he please find one for me.

The secretary said, "Is this for research, Mrs. Winston?"

My voice shook as I said, "No. I've been arrested. I need someone to defend me." Before she could ask me any more about it, I hung up.

I felt utterly alone.

I thought of calling my parents, but I didn't want to worry them. Oddly, I thought of Alex; although there were no emotional ties between us anymore, old habits live on. I felt sorrier for myself than I ever had in my life and alternated between wanting to scream, or shut my eyes in the hopes that when I opened them, it would all turn out to be a bad dream.

The thoughts that go through one's mind at moments like these are usually stupid. I thought, if I hadn't divorced Alex, maybe none of this would be happening. And then I thought about my sister. What would she do right now? Concentrate on survival, that's for sure. *She's gone through worse than this*, I told myself, and saw her face smiling through her pain, her indomitable sense of humor, the way she'd fought to come back to life each time no matter how badly she'd been knocked down. *Come on, Suzanne*, she'd say, *think of it as an adventure. Something you can write about*. And thinking about her helped me to gather my dignity as I locked the door, waited while they handcuffed me, and let them escort me down the driveway.

CHAPTER TWENTY-THREE

Steffani stood in front of the mirror in her mother's dressing room wearing her sister's blue tulle formal, hating herself and

everyone else too. If her mother would just stop sticking her
with dressmaker's pins maybe she wouldn't be so annoyed.
She tried to hold her temper, but everything Lynnette did
irritated her so that she wanted to hit her. She hated herself
for these feelings even more than she hated her mother at
times. She was the most ungrateful child who ever lived.
Look what her mother had done for her ever since she was a
baby, and look at the way she repaid her, by being sullen,
demanding, nasty, argumentative, ungrateful—all the things
her mother accused her of and she denied vehemently.

"Ouch!" Steffani yelled again, feeling the prick of a pin.
She jerked her body away from where Lynnette was holding
in the waist of the dress. "You're so damned clumsy," Steffani shouted. "You keep sticking me!"

"Honey, I'm sorry." Lynnette's exasperation was at an
edge too. "But this netting is so thick, it's impossible to get
a pin through it." She yanked at the waist, trying to make it
fit over Steffani's waist, but Steffani was larger in the middle
than Suzanne, and smaller in the bust. The bust was miles
too big, in fact.

"This is ugly, Mom, it's never going to work."

"Yes it will," Lynnette insisted, never willing to concede
a mistake as if there was a contest of wills between her and
the rest of the world. Steffani supposed there was. At least
that's how it seemed between the two of them for the past
few years, even before the surgery, as far back as when she
was sixteen: Everything her mother did drove her crazy. And
now, trying to make her body fit into Suzanne's dress was
the last straw.

"This dress is all wrong for me! It's the ugliest thing I've
ever seen. You can't expect me to really wear it, do you?
I'll be laughed at," Steffani insisted. "I should be wearing
something straight, black, and slinky, not this tootsie sweetsie
blue thing." She yanked the dress forward and tried to step
out of it. Didn't her mother know she would never fit into
Suzanne's mold, in any way?

"Steffani," Lynnette yelled. "Will you stop that! I don't

know what to do with you anymore. You waited until the last minute to spring this on me and now we have very little choice. We shopped for a dress, didn't we? And nothing looked good!''

Now, it was Steffani who wouldn't concede the point. ''Well, if we'd gone to Saks instead of May Company, maybe we would have found something.'' Neither of them wanted to say that it was because of Steffani's figure that they hadn't been able to find the right dress.

''I told you we're not made of money! This is the best I can do at the last minute.'' Lynnette indicated the strapless formal. ''If you don't like it, then don't go to the dance.''

But going to the Sigma Chi Spring Formal in Newport Beach with Ron Bernfeld was too exciting to pass up. So if this dress was all there was, it would have to do even though the seams across the bust would never be quite straight, and the flowers that her mother had appliqued catty-corner across the bodice to cover it up looked silly.

''I can't believe how much bigger your waist is than Suzanne's,'' Lynnette said with dismay, trying to make the zipper close. ''Have you gained weight?'' Lynnette placed her hands around Steffani's waist to feel if it was fat.

Steffani's heart thudded with apprehension. For the first time in her life she was hoping that what was wrong with her was an enlarged liver and not something else. Her period was late.

Then Lynnette said, ''I think your liver is getting more enlarged.'' Her tone made it sound unimportant, but Steffani could see she was alarmed. Lynnette always pretended nonchalance, but it was suddenly apparent to both of them, by studying Steffani's image in the mirror of Lynnette's dressing room, that Steffani's body was changing. Where her waist used to go in, in a feminine curve, now there was a much straighter line between her ribs and her hips.

To cover up her dismay, Lynnette would get angry instead. Steffani did the same thing. Lynnette pulled the dress tightly together at the seams, causing Steffani to suck in her breath. But this time she cooperated.

"You know, Dr. Levinson is full of it," Steffani said, knowing she was being provocative, but not caring.

"What do you mean?" Lynnette's voice dripped with curiosity and her hand shook; she stuck Steffani again.

"Ouch!"

"I'm sorry."

"I mean, that if he thinks I'm going to have my right leg reoperated on this summer just for cosmetic reasons, he's crazy."

"When did he tell you that?" Steffani could see Lynnette's face in the mirror and she had that same funny, guilty expression she always got whenever his name was mentioned.

"Yesterday, when I saw him."

"You saw him? Where?"

"At his office, where else?"

"How come?"

"I had to have a check-up, Mom."

"But why didn't you tell me? I would have gone with you."

Steffani could tell she was upset; nothing concerning Dr. Levinson should ever go on without her. Steffani knew that too, and deliberately hadn't told her she was going. "I'm nineteen years old, for God's sake. I don't need my mommy to go to the doctor's with me."

"But I've always gone," Lynnette said, dismayed. Someone had just changed the rules and hadn't told her.

"When I wasn't old enough to drive, I needed you to take me, and when I was in the cast, I needed you to help me. But I'm walking fine now, so I can go by myself." Her tone indicated, *How dumb can you be*?

"Well, what did he say?"

"That if he reoperates, he'll do a better job this time because the right leg hasn't healed as straight as the left."

"What did you tell him?"

"No way! What do you think? I'm not a masochist." Just the thought of it was as if someone was poking her with a hot iron. "I don't care what his reasons are, Mother, I'm not having another operation. I can't go through that again, I can't.'' She felt like bursting into tears but she held on. Finals were coming up, which was enough to cause her tension, and every day that she didn't get her period made her more terrified. First things first. A pregnancy would take precedence. And if Dr. Levinson thought she would allow him to put her through another summer of agony, he was dead wrong. "What's with him, Mom? Why does he think he can just make these kinds of decisions and I'll go along? Just because I've always done it doesn't mean I will now.''

Lynnette, who assumed with her usual tone of explainer, cajoler, and arbiter that the doctor was always right, said, "Don't you want your right leg to be as straight as your left? You know you do. You've complained about the way it looks ever since the cast came off; and there's the lack of mobility. This time he'll have the experience of knowing what went wrong. He can do what he promised in the first place. I knew he shouldn't have done both legs at once, but he is stubborn. And you know how badly he feels about the way it turned out.'' Lynnette was his official interpreter.

Steffani looked at her this moment as the betrayer. "You've talked about this with him already, haven't you?''

"Yes, of course, we discuss everything . . . that has to do with you,'' she added.

"And you always take his side, don't you?''

"No, that's not true!'' Lynnette's eyes were wide and innocent. "I just understand how he feels. Don't forget all the things he's done for you over the years.''

"How could I forget, with you reminding me all the time. He doesn't need you to be his champion with me! I know his value perfectly well.'' Her mother was so damned possessive of him.

Lynnette looked away, injured. "I've maintained a close personal relationship with him over the years to make everything easier for you. I've always done that with every doctor you've ever had. Why do you think I take pictures of their families for free, and find ways to make them like me, always being so nice and smiling and pleasant? So you won't have to wait in their waiting rooms if you're in pain, and you'll get special treatment in the hospital and quick results from the laboratories. I've seen what doctors can be like with people they don't know. Do you think I like spending my time doing all that? I do it for you!''

Steffani didn't know what to say. Over the years, Dr. Levinson had become like some extended family member. No matter what Lynnette asked of him he never turned her down. Very few chronically ill people had such a devoted doctor as Dr. Levinson in their lives, Lynnette had made sure of that. But the reason for that devotion, that Lynnette curried his favor for Steffani's benefit, was only half the truth. The rest of the reasons felt too dangerous to Steffani to discuss with her mother.

"Dr. Levinson may feel badly about botching the results the first time, but what about me?"

"This is your chance to let him make it right." Lynnette put her arm around her daughter's bare shoulders, feeling the bones beneath the flesh, studying the clear olive skin and deep blue eyes. She had always been beautiful, but now there was a grown-up elegance about her, a physical glow that came from maturity. If she could have taken this horrible burden from her daughter onto herself from the very beginning, she would have done so, gladly. Yet Steffani seemed to thrive, no matter what she went through. She had incredible spirit.

"Do you think he could really improve the way my knee looks?"

"I don't know, honey. I just know that if he wants to redo it, it's because he expects to make it better. You don't want to walk with a limp for the rest of your life, do you?"

Suddenly, her mother's words infuriated her and she lashed out, needing to place that fear and rage somewhere. "Why do I always have to do everything you want? I told you I didn't want to wear Suzanne's dress, but you insisted. And I told you I didn't want to do both legs at once last summer, but Dr. Levinson wanted it that way, so you insisted. You always talk me into everything and now the two of you are ganging up on me again. Why can't you just leave me alone? Why do you always have to be in the middle of things, especially with him? It's my leg, and my surgery, and I'll decide what's going to be.''

Lynnette's lip started to quiver and her eyes filled with tears, just as Steffani knew they would. Her mother was an iron butterfly when it came to getting her own way; she would bat her lovely wings until they became steel weapons, but whenever anyone criticized her, she fell apart. Yet, sometimes, the only respite Steffani could find from her own pain and fear was to blame the one person she depended upon the most.

''Fine. That's fine,'' Lynnette said, using her martyr tone. ''You decide. Here I am, doing everything I can for you, trying to help, and this is the thanks I get.'' And she turned and walked away, leaving Steffani standing there in the dress Lynnette had fixed so she could go to the dance, feeling once more like a rotten brat.

''Mom,'' she called. ''I'm sorry.'' But Lynnette didn't come back. It would take a major apology to make things right again, Steffani realized, with a sigh. *Why do I do things like that?*

''Could you pull over at the next gas station?'' Steffani asked, tilting her head back and taking the last swig of beer in the bottle.

''Not again,'' Ron groaned. He was driving her car. Phyllis and Jerry were in the backseat, and whenever Ron complained about what Steffani was doing, Phyllis giggled. She laughed at everything Steffani did, and with Phyllis as her audience, Steffani became more outrageous. There was something about Ron's irritability with her that made her rebellious in spite of her not wanting to get him angry. But lately he'd started to criticize. Her friends were weirdos, he said, and he expected her to act as if she were some prissy sorority girl. That upset her the most. Why couldn't he be happy with her the way she was? In the beginning, he'd thought she was wonderful, couldn't get enough of her, bragged to his friends about how she'd brought culture and an appreciation for literature into his life, what a good sport she was. Now, just to get back at him, she had drunk three beers since they'd left Los Angeles, and they were only at Redondo Beach. It would be another thirty minutes before they reached the Newporter Hotel at Newport Beach where the fraternity formal was being held.

Ron gave her a dirty look and pulled off the highway into a Shell station, reached across her, and opened the door without getting out and without even trying to cop a feel.

Steffani got out of the car and Phyllis followed her into the restroom. Ron and Jerry stayed behind.

"Will you please make it snappy," Ron called. Steffani could hear the exasperation in his voice and it brought a tightening to her chest. *What am I going to say to him?* The question kept repeating over and over in her brain as it had for days. Her period was eleven days late. The thought of being pregnant was the worst fear she had, and yet she'd been very stupid. They'd taken too many chances making love without a rubber; she shouldn't have let him pull out just before coming, but it felt better that way for both of them. *Stupid, that's what you are,* she told herself. *A baby is all you need!*

There was a nauseated feeling in the pit of her stomach that hadn't left for days. She couldn't tell if it was morning sickness, or fear, or something to do with Gaucher's.

She entered the stall next to Phyllis and the two of them emptied their bladders while Phyllis chatted about how Jerry was always trying to get to second base, but she wouldn't let him unless they were pinned. "Don't you think I'm right?" she asked.

"Uh-huh," Steffani replied, checking again with the toilet tissue for any signs of her period. Nothing. *What would Ron do? What would he say?* She could just hear him yell. He'd lose his temper. Yes, sweet Ron had a temper. Sometimes in a game when he missed a pitch, he'd throw his bat. The guys in the fraternity had nicknamed him "Hothead," and his temper had cost him penalties from time to time in the game. What a tantrum he'd throw if he thought she was pregnant. He didn't want to get married; she didn't, either. Maybe never, though she'd never admitted that to anyone before, except to have kids. She loved children. Couldn't wait to have some of her own. But from what she'd seen of marriage, it wasn't so great. Her parents had bickered for years, over everything. She'd come to understand it didn't really mean anything, except that each of them needed to be right about everything. Suzanne appeared to be a kind of love slave to Alex, her perfect mate, who was so stuck on himself he was like a caricature. She was disappointed in Suzanne for being so blind to the kind of person Alex was, as if being with Mr. Wonderful validated her somehow. Didn't she know how special she was on her own? Steffani felt fortunate to know her own worth, in spite of her limitations.

Her parents thought Ron would have been a perfect catch if he were Jewish. In spite of his name, he wasn't and that made her mother tremble at the idea that they might become a permanent pair; she kept pointing out how Steffani was too young to get serious. Her father, on the other hand, thought nobody, especially this kid Ron, was good enough for his angel baby and he'd study Ron with narrowed eyes, while stroking his chin or playing with an imaginary pipe, letting Ron fidget with discomfort whenever they visited her parents. Sometimes she was sure that Ron loved her, and that's when she'd start to feel closed in by his attentions. But when he found fault with her, saying she was too crazy, too spontaneous and erratic, not ladylike enough, it hurt. And that's when she felt a fierce aching love for him. But she wasn't interested in marriage, especially if she *had* to get married.

Phyllis had combed her bouncy hair and was now washing her hands daintily at the sink, pressing the soap dispenser, hygienically cleaning her fingertips. *Such a good girl*, Steffani thought. *She probably washes after sex too—if she has any sex in spite of what she says about not letting Jerry do anything.* All the sorority girls pretended to be virgins. *You should have played hard to get too, and you wouldn't be in this mess, my girl.*

Steffani and Phyllis walked together back to the car and Steffani realized that all that beer had given her gas; she felt it bubbling up inside and tried to control it but her body rarely did what she wanted it to; just as she reached the car the belch came up before she could stop it, a long, low one. Her first reaction was to laugh, except for the look on Ron's face and then, mortified, she felt her cheeks flame with heat. But Jerry gave such an appreciative whoop of laughter, thinking she had done it on purpose, that when Ron started to laugh, she laughed too, mitigating her embarrassment. Only Phyllis was disgusted, making a *tsk-tsk* sound. Evidently, Steffani was no longer so funny.

"I can see I'm going to have some time this weekend with you three animals," Phyllis said, self-righteously.

Steffani could feel that sorority girl disapproval aimed at her like an acid spray and she flinched, almost hunching her shoulders as if to ward it off, but forced herself to toss her head, defiantly. It never failed that at certain times she felt like an outsider. Phyllis and her friends were experts at pointing out the unacceptable differences between themselves and others. *I'll bet she's got a new dress for the formal,* Steffani thought.

For propriety's sake, the girls attending the formal were staying in separate rooms from the boys, four girls to a room to save money. Nobody expected to sleep where they were registered. During these party weekends everyone was flexible, knowing that if there was a do-not-disturb sign on the door you went away and came back later.

Steffani didn't like the idea of rooming with girls she didn't know, especially since the two other girls were sorority sisters of Phyllis: Justine and Linda. She would rather have roomed with Ron, no matter what people said, because at least he was used to her modesty. Even though they'd been together many times, she'd hidden herself from him, only showing him a part at a time. Once she was wearing a skirt and he said, "Come on, let me see." So she pulled it up high enough to show him her knees.

His first reaction was to wince when he looked at those oddly shaped lumps between her thighs and her calves. She'd wanted to die of embarrassment, pull down her skirt, and erase from his memory what he'd just seen. But after the initial shock, he'd said, with concern, "Does it still hurt?"

"Sometimes," she admitted.

"It will go away," he promised. "I understand how an accident can alter your physical ability. I'm always afraid of something like that happening to me. I've known guys who've had terrible football injuries or gotten hit by a baseball and suffered concussions." Being an athlete made him more compassionate than most boys would have been. But still, he avoided looking at her again so she covered herself up. After that he was not curious anymore and let her get dressed and undressed in private. It certainly hadn't affected their sex life.

Now, the thought of undressing in front of other girls had given her nightmares for days. She imagined them staring, asking questions, and then pitying her. How she hated their pity when they were so perfect. Not a blemish on them, their bodies lithe and beautifully shaped, their knees prominent and well sculpted while hers looked like a Quasimodo reject. A pretty face and a good personality could only take you so far before other things started to matter.

In the room she stayed in her robe and pretended to nap while they put on their shorts and bathing suits to go to the beach. Communal outings at the beach had also worried her when she accepted this date. She couldn't be seen in a bathing suit and be the butt of jokes and the object of stares. Ron didn't deserve that. So she pretended to have a headache, which turned into a stomachache, and then actually became an ache in her leg that she wasn't faking.

Within two hours of her arrival in Newport Beach, playground of the blond, blue-eyed, well-muscled gentiles, she had developed a full-blown attack. At first she couldn't believe it; she hadn't had an attack this bad in years. But the stronger the pain got, the more she realized that it was true.

In her suitcase were her pain pills, gotten illegally from someone in the dorm who sold pills to whoever wanted them. She'd bought them just in case, so she wouldn't have to ask her mother, who would tell Dr. Levinson, who monitored her medicines as though she were a child. But if she took them, she'd be out of it, glassy-eyed and drugged, and everyone would notice—especially since she'd drunk so much beer on the drive here. Maybe a half of a pill would do some good.

After her roommates left for the beach, Ron came to the door looking for her but she pretended not to be there. Soon the pain would get better, she promised herself, and she'd get dressed for the dance. But it only got worse. She limped down the hall in her robe to the ice machine and brought back a bucket of ice. Filling the bathtub with a bit of water, she poured the ice in and lowered herself into the freezing water, praying that it would work. The shock of sitting in ice water only made the pain worse and made her shiver uncontrollably. That's when she knew she was getting a fever, too.

Later, Phyllis, Justine, and Linda came back from the beach, pink skinned and perspiring. Each of them took turns in the bathroom and then got dressed for the dance in tight-fitting pastel-colored dresses, cut short at midcalf, while she pretended to doze so they wouldn't know she was in a pain-filled stupor.

"Aren't you getting dressed?" Phyllis asked. "You'll be late."

"It only takes me a few minutes," Steffani said. And one of the girls said, sotto voce, "If I only took a few minutes, I'd look like that too."

Through half-closed eyes she watched them leave, their escorts' corsages at their wrists, their dates at the door in white dinner jackets, and she wanted to cry. How right they all looked with one another, how perfect, their bodies young and smooth and painfree. Here she'd come all this way, and her mother had worked so hard on her dress and it was all going to waste. But even that wasn't as important as being at the dance with Ron. If he didn't show up with a date, he'd be a laughingstock.

When Ron arrived at her door she called out that she'd be ready in twenty minutes.

"Hurry up," he urged. "We don't want to miss the cocktail party."

But now, she'd run out of options; only pain pills would get her to the dance, and she'd waited so long, it probably wouldn't do any good. She swallowed two pills and somehow managed to get dressed, but when she tried to apply her makeup, her hand shook so that she kept smearing it and her eyes wouldn't focus. She looked terrible, with black splotches of eyeliner on her eyelids. She could barely stand up. She didn't know where to turn, where to go. A terrible sense of panic closed in on her as though she were being buried alive with her own pain; it enclosed her in a never-ceasing flow of throbbing. There was no way she could dance—she couldn't even smile, or sit quietly. All she wanted to do was scream with the throbbing in her leg. *You can't go*, she thought. But what could she tell Ron? If she'd been honest with him before and told him about her condition, maybe he'd have understood. But now, there was no way.

She heard his knock at the door and wished the floor would open up and swallow her.

"Steffani," he called. "Come on, will you?"

Holding on to the bed, she lurched from end table to wall to door, the room spinning, the pain throbbing, until finally she reached the doorknob.

Ron was pounding on the door now, both angry and worried. "Are you in there? Where the hell are you?"

She clutched the doorknob and opened the door, swaying so that she had to catch herself on the doorframe or she'd have fallen.

"Ron," she started to say, slurring her words terribly, "I'm not feeling very well." The sight of him, fresh from his shower, dressed in his white dinner jacket, made her want to cry. She controlled it, except for tears that ran down her face. She stood there, ashamed and in pain, not knowing what to say or do.

"What the hell is wrong with you? You're drunk, aren't you? I told you not to drink all that beer this afternoon, and now look at you." He threw his hands up in exasperation.

"No, that's not it," she started to say, but she could barely speak, let alone explain.

"Yeah, sure. And I'm Sandy Koufax! Well, thanks a lot, *date*," he spat. "I should have known better than to invite someone like you to this formal."

"Ron. Let me explain," she called after him, as he strode down the dimly lit hall covered with palm leaf wallpaper. In her altered state of mind, it looked as though the palm fronds were swallowing him up.

"Sure," he called back. "Tell it to Timothy Leary, not to me!"

"Ron, I'm sorry," she tried to call out, barely able to form the words. Turning from the open door, she caught a glimpse of herself in the dresser mirror. Her hair was disheveled, her dress unzipped, her face black from runny mascara, and her pupils so dilated they looked black, not blue. If she disgusted herself, how must she have looked to him? She closed the door to the room and just made it to the bed before she passed out.

Several hours later, she woke up to find that the pain had subsided somewhat, though she still had a fever. Finally able to maneuver, she threw her belongings into a suitcase, called for a bellboy to take it to her car, and drove herself all the way home, stopping now and then at the side of the road when the pain got too bad to travel or she felt too dizzy to stay in her lane.

The rest of the weekend passed in a haze. Ice in the dorm was difficult to get—she had to go down in the elevator to the soft drink machine in the main lobby and she was too sick to do that. She couldn't call her parents because her mother would recognize that she was on drugs and would fly into a tizzy—as she and Suzanne called it. So she called Suzanne and asked her to bring some ice in a bucket, that she was having an attack and didn't want to tell Mom and Dad because they would just worry about her.

"I talked to Dr. Levinson," she lied. "He's sending me a prescription for the pain."

"Shouldn't someone be with you all the time?" Suzanne asked, in alarm. "You can't be alone, Steffani, and I can't stay with you because I have no one to take care of Amy. Why don't I pick you up and bring you here to my house. At least then, I can take care of you." But the thought of her niece's noisy playing and her brother-in-law's scrutiny was more than she could bear, so she declined the offer.

"I'll be fine," Steffani assured her. "This attack isn't as bad as the ones when I was younger. Just bring me the ice." And she hung up.

Ron did not return her calls; even when she wrote him a note apologizing, it did no good. She was so ashamed to face him in person, she avoided running into him. Without telling him the truth, there was no way she could explain what happened. And now, there was no point in telling him about having Gaucher's disease; they'd never see one another again.

Then she looked at the calendar and saw that she was thirteen days late for her period. With everything that had happened, she'd put it out of her mind. There was no getting around it anymore, she was pregnant.

She thought about killing herself, but since the pain in her leg was gone, she felt so good that the thought of dying was just too cruel. *Face the music, Steff. You fucked up*. Despair washed over her, and regret. She could not bring herself to tell her parents. The look of disappointment in their eyes would be more than she could bear. She'd brought them so much anguish, she couldn't add to it. There was only one place to turn.

She got off the elevator on Ron's floor in the dorm and waited outside his door until he finally came home.

He saw her standing in the hall and did an about-face to go the other way.

"Please just let me talk to you," she called out. "Or the whole floor will hear our private business."

Resignedly, he turned around and came back. "I see you're sober," he said, unlocking his door and ushering her in.

"And pregnant," she told him when they were alone.

"How do you know it's mine?" was the first thing he asked. "Maybe it's some other guy's you picked up on the way home from Newport." She'd never seen him deliberately cruel. But she had truly embarrassed him by standing him up. He'd be razzed about that for the rest of his college life.

"Ron, I was really sick that night. I'm sorry for what I did, embarrassing you and leaving you like that. I don't blame you for being pissed at me, but it's over now. I'm sure having too much to drink is something every fraternity brother understands. But we have a more pressing problem than that."

"You don't expect me to marry you, do you?" he scoffed.

"No," she said, meekly.

"Are you going to have an abortion?"

"That's an alternative."

"Well, don't look at me. I don't have any money. I hear they cost over four hundred dollars in Tijuana."

"I couldn't go to Tijuana."

"Why not?"

She couldn't tell him that she had to have a legitimate doctor and the most antiseptic conditions because of her blood disease, so she said, "I'd be too afraid."

"Poor little Steffani, shall I take you to the Med Center and tell them to take care of you 'cause you're too chicken to go to Tijuana?"

She was ashamed, having to ask for his help, especially when he was being so ungenerous. But her parents didn't have the money. Neither did Suzanne and Alex, who were barely making ends meet with a baby and a mortgage. She could just hear her sister; "How could you be so irresponsible; when are you going to learn to take care of yourself? Don't you know you've ruined your reputation?" And Alex would tell Suzanne he didn't want Steffani hanging around their house (not that she did) or taking care of Amy. There was nowhere she could turn but to Ron, and he was being a prick.

"Listen, Ron. You have to help me. Wherever I go for an abortion, I have to have one, and I don't have the money either. Do you want me to have an illegitimate child?"

"No," he agreed.

"Isn't there anyone you can ask for the money? I'll even go to Tijuana if it's less expensive."

He mumbled something.

"What did you say?" she asked, shrilly, losing her patience.

He shouted at her, "I guess I can go to my father."

His parents were divorced and he lived with his mother. The few times he'd mentioned his father, it was clear they didn't get along. "Will he help?" she asked.

He shrugged. "Only one way to find out."

But Ron's father turned them down flat. At first she didn't believe that Ron had really talked to him because all he said was, "My father said no." But when she pressed him about it, he hung his head and mumbled, "My father said we should take responsibility for our own mistakes."

"Is that what you think?" she asked him, feeling her anger growing into desperation.

"No," Ron lashed out at her. "I think you should have been more careful."

"And you shouldn't?" she said. "This is all my fault, now?"

"Maybe my father is right. You said you didn't want to get married. But my father says, they all say that. You could be trying to trap me."

"Into what?" she yelled, her frustration and incredulity spilling over. "You don't think I'd want to marry someone like you, do you?"

He stared at her, wounded. *Well that's too damned bad*, she thought. *He could dish it out but he couldn't take it. And now he'd turned out to be totally unreliable.*

The scary realization began to dawn on her that he really was not going to help her. How could she have loved him? She'd truly believed he had admirable qualities. What a joke. He was the lowest.

"Maybe my dad will come around if we give him some time," Ron said, obviously sorry for what he'd said.

"I don't have any time, Ron." Her heart was slamming against her ribs with fear. "But don't you worry about it. I'll find a way." She held tightly to that sinking feeling in her stomach that threatened to sweep her away, because now she knew she had to go to her family for help. And not to Suzanne, who would judge her, but to her parents. God, she prayed they would understand. How she hated to have to go to them, yet again, for another disaster in her life, one that could have been prevented. They'd be terribly disappointed in her; she could just see the look on her mother's face. And it would only point out so blatantly, how different she was from Suzanne.

CHAPTER TWENTY-FOUR

The next afternoon when she drove to her parents' house to tell Lynnette, her mother said, "Oh Steffani, how could you?" But it was enough to make her feel like she was worthless, the way Ron's father thought of her.

"Don't tell Daddy," she begged, feeling her chest tighten with misery.

"I wouldn't dare tell him," Lynnette said, staring at Steffani's abdomen as if she could see the fetus growing inside. "It would kill your father to know what you've done. It's killing me too." Steffani knew she would tell him; she told him everything. A look of caged panic grew in her mother's eyes that unnerved her even more. "How many times have I told you that you have to be more careful than other people? A hundred thousand times, that's what it seems like! But you never learn, do you? You're going to drive me to an early grave, I swear it. Don't you know? Don't you realize? Oh, what's the use!'' She threw her hands up in despair and then went to the phone.

''What are you doing?'' Steffani asked, but she knew. She should have thought of this herself, had the courage as an adult to take care of her own problems without running home to mommy every time. As usual, she had behaved like a baby.

''Dr. Levinson, please,'' Lynnette was saying. ''Mrs. Burt Blacker calling.'' She listened for a moment while his nurse made some excuse why he couldn't talk to her, then said, ''Tell him to call me right back. It's very important.''

She said to Steffani, ''He'll take care of you. Or he'll find somebody who can.''

''No, he won't, Mother. It's illegal. He can't risk his medical license for me. I couldn't let him.'' She couldn't even say the word *abortion*. It was loaded with derogatory meaning. *He's an abortion*, the kids used to say about a particularly repulsive person. The picture was of a bloody mass of protoplasm thrown in the garbage, or lying in full view in a white enamel hospital pan with the lights focused on it. It could also mean going to jail, or having septicemia, or putting Clorox inside yourself to start a miscarriage and instead burning the tissues beyond repair. Everyone had heard the stories. Bloody coat hangers were a reality. The very word *abortion* was synonymous with death; to have an abortion meant to die.

''Don't worry,'' Lynnette said, her mouth forming a determined line, her arms folded across her chest, one foot tapping nervously up and down. ''He won't let you ruin your life.'' She'd heard those stories too.

Steffani glanced at Lynnette with alarm. Something in her tone had raised an alert. The lines around her mouth, from the aging process of being forty-three years old, looked deeper, the shadows under her eyes more prominent, though she was still beautiful and well dressed. Today she was wearing a mustard yellow lamb's wool sweater and matching cardigan, with a woven pearl collar around her neck, and a full brown skirt. But there was more gray than last year in her rich auburn hair, and a slight drooping of the skin under her chin that upset Steffani to see. Aging meant mortality, and mortality meant Steffani would be without her someday. How could she function without her parents there to take care of her when she needed them desperately? *Grow up, baby!* the voice inside said to her. And then she thought, *Worry has caused the lines in my mother's face to deepen—worry about me.* And then, to counteract her own guilt, a sudden harsh annoyance filled her toward her mother's overbearing concern. The mixture of these same two emotions had tugged at her for years: anger was one of them; the other was deep gratitude and relief that someone was taking care of things. *Fair trade*, she sometimes thought. *If it's my job to suffer, it's theirs to take care of me.* But she never said that to their faces. Gaucher's disease, it was discovered, was genetically inherited from the parents. If two people with the Gaucher gene had offspring, one in four could manifest the symptoms. Suzanne had escaped. But in some families, several of the children had it in varying degrees. And even after all these years, there was still no treatment or cure.

Steffani was getting herself a glass of water from the cooler when the phone rang.

"I'll take it in there," Lynnette said, and went into the den for privacy.

Steffani had a strong desire to eavesdrop, but instead she stood in front of the kitchen sink while the two people on the telephone discussed her fate. She felt a tightening in her chest. Again, she was responsible for bringing those two people together. At first they'd needed the excuse of her illness; now their togetherness had a life of its own. Like a divisive triangle it thrust its points in between the corners of her family square, tearing at its paper-thin fabric the way her membranes sometimes tore and bled. In that moment she felt a huge grip of terror as a terrible insight occurred to her. Someday, she might die, not from a huge moment of pain, or her body breaking in two, or a wrenching, bone-crushing failure of her beating heart or her pumping lungs, but from a paper-thin tear in her membranes that just wouldn't clot.

To flee this reality she stared out of the window at the mountains beyond separating the San Fernando Valley from the area of West Los Angeles, their sharp edges blurred by smoggy sunlight. *Don't think about it!* she told herself.

Lynnette's voice right behind her startled her. "He wants to talk to you."

Steffani walked the length of the kitchen and picked up the wall phone on the service porch. "Hi, Dr. Levinson." She could feel herself blushing because her private affairs were about to become a public topic of conversation. But the tone of his voice was protective, not judgmental.

"How far along do you think you are, Steffani?"

"I'm over fourteen days late."

"Didn't you tell me your periods were fairly irregular, that your cycle could go as long as forty days or more, sometimes?"

"Yes." She was uncomfortable saying this with her mother standing there. "But that was before."

"Before what?"

Don't be so dense, she wanted to yell. "Before I had a steady boyfriend." *And we were doing it day and night*, she thought.

She heard her mother's sharp intake of breath and felt the hairs on her arms bristle.

"Why don't you come in and let me examine you. Maybe you're not pregnant at all."

"Do you think so?" she said. But that voice inside said, *Don't hope. You know what always happens when you hope.* "But what if I am," she insisted.

Her mother was shaking her head, meaning, *Leave well enough alone*.

There was a pause and then he replied, "If you're pregnant, I'll take care of you." He wasn't using *the word* either. "But first, you come on over and let me see you."

"Right now?" she said, turning to her mother with a question.

Lynnette gave a decided nod.

"Okay, we'll be right over," she agreed, hanging up. Then she turned to Lynnette. "You're not staying in the room while he examines me, Mother. Do you promise?"

"Of course," Lynnette said, grabbing her purse. "It's wonderful of him to be willing to help you, isn't it? I knew he would."

But Steffani didn't feel relieved. Instead, the expression on her mother's face made her feel even guiltier, for under the worry was a note of excitement, as if now Lynnette had a legitimate excuse to see him. *How could I be thinking such a thing*, she thought. *I'm the most ungrateful, disgusting person on the face of the earth. Who am I to suspect them or judge them, these people who have devoted their lives to my welfare?* Her cheeks burned with shame. But, sometimes, when her father yelled at her mother or picked a fight with her, or acted unreasonably, she couldn't blame her mother if she'd turned to someone else.

"Dr. Levinson's told me before that he thinks abortions should be legal. Especially if having a baby threatens the life of the mother," Lynnette said, finally stating out loud what was on her mind.

Lynnette's head was turned away as she backed the car out of the driveway, and Steffani couldn't see if her special Dr. Levinson expression was there. Steffani wondered why her mother still called him Dr. Levinson instead of David after all these years.

"Having a baby and not being married isn't exactly threatening my life, Mother. It might ruin my college career and my reputation, but I'd survive."

There was a pause, which made Steffani look at Lynnette more closely. Even in profile, her sadness was apparent.

"What is it?" Steffani asked.

"I'm afraid you wouldn't, Steffani. I was waiting to tell you this when the time was right. Maybe I should have told you before."

"Wouldn't what?" The question echoed through her brain, bouncing off the convoluted canyons of gray matter, *What, what, what?* Silence grew between them until Steffani could feel its palpability as something alive.

"What?" she shouted, making Lynnette jump.

"You wouldn't survive a pregnancy, Steffani. You can't ever have a baby."

"That's crazy! I'm pregnant."

"I didn't say you weren't capable of getting pregnant, but you mustn't ever have a child. You might bleed to death giving birth, and there's no telling whether or not the baby would be all right either. Even a miscarriage could be too dangerous. That's why, from now on, you've got to be very careful."

Her mother's voice came from far away, talking to someone else.

Not have a baby? Ever? But everybody has babies, don't they? My sister has one already. But then, my sister has everything. There was a sledgehammer pounding in her head, pulsing in her chest. She could feel the buttery softness of her sister's child as Amy clung to her, lying in her arms like a lump. The little hands would reach up and touch her cheek with delicate butterfly kisses. Amy's eyelashes lay on her cheeks when she slept. She smelled like a miracle. Steffani had never known such a longing before as when she'd held that baby for the first time. She'd taken it for granted that she'd have her own someday.

So, you got complacent again, didn't you. Thought it was over and then wham, another blow. How does it feel? Huh, huh? She stared straight ahead, her eyes not seeing anything but the thoughts in her head. *Fool! You thought you'd wait until it's convenient to have a child, until you're out of school and married. What a laugh.* She tried to pretend she didn't care. *They're noisy, bratty things anyway*, she told herself. But something inside was dying. Another hope, another part of being normal. And death moved that much closer. How did one live on without children? Ron was better off without her. There were tears on her cheeks before she realized she was crying. And then she looked at her mother and saw the tears running down her cheeks too. She reached out blindly and took her mother's hand. Her mother squeezed her hand back, trying not to break down.

"It's hard to be a parent, isn't it?" Steffani asked. "Maybe I'm lucky never to find out."

"I wouldn't trade you for anything, Steffani," Lynnette said. "Don't ever forget that."

"We've been through a lot, haven't we?" Steffani said.

And Lynnette nodded, removing her hand to wipe her eyes so she could see where she was going.

Poor Mom and Dad, Steffani thought. *Suzanne is the only one who will ever give you grandchildren. But, it's a good thing. Who in their right mind would ever want to pass Gaucher's disease on to their offspring?*

By the time they got to Dr. Levinson's office despair had formed a hardened block around her heart. She hardly cared anymore about the consequences.

But the moment she saw Dr. Levinson her despair turned to an instant fury that slammed through her up from her toes to her head as though she'd just stepped on a nail. He'd known that she couldn't have children all along and never told her. Once again, they hadn't told the truth. He'd let her think everything was fine, that she could reproduce with the best of them, let her get into this situation without any forewarning. Explosive rage poured out of her toward him. Lynnette would get her share later.

"Who the hell do you think you are," she demanded, when they were alone. "God?"

He was shocked, unprepared for this outburst. "What are you talking about, Steffani?"

"You should have told me," she said, trying not to cry, but the sadness burst through anyway, breaking the dam of worry she'd been holding back for such a long time, ever since that day she'd first missed her period, and now it was multiplied by the news she'd just heard. She was gulping back the sobs; crying would make her more vulnerable. It was strange how she'd spent most of her life since she'd been a child dreading the possibility that she might bleed, and now it was all she desired.

"Let me examine you," he said, helping her up on the table. She hated him so in this moment, that when his fingers touched her flesh it burned. And then, after inserting the speculum, he declared, "You're not pregnant. I see no signs of it at all. You'll get your period soon," he predicted. "Worrying about it is what probably kept you from getting it. But perhaps this happened for the best. Now you understand that you must be very careful. I told your mother to explain the seriousness of getting pregnant to you. I think she ought to have told you before, but she wanted to wait."

"Of course," she managed to say. "Where my mother's concerned, lying is always better than the truth."

"She only wants to protect you, Steffani."

Oh God, was there no one to blame? Was swallowing her tears in one enormous gulp the only thing left for her to do, even though they nearly choked her. She stared at him, praying for control, while her blue eyes grew larger, darker, until the rage was completely drained away and all the sadness of her life was contained in that moment.

Gently, he said, "It's not so terrible. People adopt children all the time. Besides, you're too young to worry about having children right now."

She had no choice but to nod, to agree again with her own devastation, accept it. If she tried to speak, those swallowed sobs would escape, pouring forth in a torrent that would surely melt her the way the tigers in "Little Black Sambo" had melted into a puddle of butter.

He helped her up. "You're pretty upset with me, aren't you?"

"Yes," she said, finally able to talk without crying. "I'm sorry for yelling."

"Have you thought about letting me redo your leg this summer? I think I can make quite an improvement, remove some of that cartilage, and the scar tissue caused by the infection that's made this lump." He placed his hand on the side of her knee.

Her temper flared again, up to the end of the thermometer, nearly exploding. "You're just like my mother, aren't you. No wonder the two of you get along. One thing's just barely taken care of, and boom, boom, boom"—she slapped her hands together as if dusting off flour after baking—"on to the next. Steffani's not pregnant, and we've told her she can never have children, so let's operate on her legs again. That's a non sequitur, don't you think?"

He looked at her calmly, his brown eyes boring into her, into her fear and exasperation and straight to her Dread with a capital D. Both of them knew what lay ahead. Not just another summer without swimming or going to the beach or being alive, but of suffering again.

"Will this ever end?" she asked him, feeling those sobs pressing upward.

He ignored the larger question for practical concerns. "It won't be as bad as the last time because I'm only doing one side."

How did I get into this? she wondered. *I came here for a possible abortion, found out I'll never be able to have children, and now I'm facing months of pain plus everything else that goes with it.*

As though it was a most natural question and the misery on her face was a normal state of affairs, he asked, "When are finals over?"

"In three weeks," she said, resignedly.

"Then that's when we'll do it," he pronounced, and he was gone again, leaving her drained of the will to challenge anything. Even a spider would have gone unchecked if it wanted to climb up her leg.

Wearily she got down from the table, and went to tell her

mother the good news—that she wasn't pregnant—and the bad news—that she was having surgery again. What she didn't plan to tell Lynnette was that the world had better watch out, because she was going to cram every moment of living she could into the next few weeks before school was out and she had to face another summer of goddamned pain.

BOOK II

Paperback Writer

CHAPTER TWENTY-FIVE

Handcuffs hurt. They are not shaped or fashioned for comfort; their metallic hardness is unforgiving when encircling the flesh of the wrist. Wristbones become abraded quickly. I find it awkward to sit with my hands behind my back; it makes me slump forward. So as not to think about the indignities being done to me, I focus on those metal rings around my wrists, counting the minutes until they are removed.

The arresting officers don't talk to me now. No one makes small talk. I'm a nonperson. I was nice to them, letting them into my house, showing them around, and they betrayed me. The backseat of the police car smells of french fries, cigarettes, and urine. Whenever we turn a corner, I can't keep my balance and fall sideways.

I keep my head down so no one will see me when we arrive at the Van Nuys courthouse. People see me anyway. I read their thoughts. Waves of shame wash over me as if birds are dropping on my head and animals are using me as a litter box or hydrant.

My immediate reaction is to revert to being a child; I know I've disappointed my parents badly. "We never expected this of you, Suzanne," I hear them saying. "Not our Golden Girl who shines and excels in everything she does. Maybe, some of your fresh-mouthed friends could be arrested, but never you."

The steps of the courthouse are bathed in glaring sunlight that pierces my eyes, which dart about, searching for a place to rest.

I imagine I hear the sounds of prison doors closing on me. *Clang*. Shrill bells are ringing, regulating my every daily act. Taunting voices of inmates shout obscenities at me. Every image or fear I've ever had about prison strobes vividly in my brain, all coming true.

There's a desk. An officer takes my possessions and writes them on a list. I'm allowed to keep certain things I didn't bring, like cigarettes. They take off the handcuffs. I want to cry from relief. The most I can do is try to smile, but it's so inappropriate I discover I can't manage to move the muscles in my face. Nobody smiles.

I'm fingerprinted. The ink is difficult to remove with the solvent and the paper towels they give me, folded in half. They're the same kind of paper towels I used to use in grammar school, institutional. My hands still aren't clean. Maybe, never.

They take my photograph, frontways, sideways. Mug shots. I'm a mug. I should be shot. I think about the retouched publicity photos on a shelf at home; a line next to my cheek was softened, and the folds of skin that crease under my eyes when I smile. Mug shots will not be retouched.

Who will touch me now? Ever again? Only the wrong people for the wrong reasons.

Ollie, ollie, oxen free . . . I hear the sound of a child's voice calling on a warm summer night when we played kick the can with the neighborhood kids. Can I still come home free without being caught in my hiding place? Not anymore.

I step into a room with green painted walls, a sink, a cubicle without a curtain, and hooks for clothes. I'm told to disrobe.

Here, everything has a technical name: arrest, booking, arraignment, body search. That's what she's doing right now, to see if I'm smuggling in narcotics or poison for the candy.

A rubber glove protects her. Nothing protects my shame. I'm starting to feel enraged, but it's a tiny seedling. I want to nurture it, help it grow until it's the size of a giant cabbage. The cabbage that ate the world, or at least Van Nuys. I'm allowed to wipe the lubricant jelly off my privates with a paper towel. It's scratchy against my skin.

I look at the sink, dull from years of standing there, its enamel nearly gone. I long to vomit in it, but I'm too empty. Even the sink wouldn't receive my offering if I could make one.

I get my underwear back and my shoes. No stockings, they're a lethal weapon. I'm given socks.

The prison gown is washed-out blue and has been starched. My cell is a real cell with a cot, which I stand and stare at for a long time, shutting out the noises of the prison, the sound of the door closing. It closes sideways, metallic, with a clang as I'd imagined, electrically operated. Smooth machinery taking away my humanity.

Dear God, what have I done? Is it such a crime not to write great literature? Is this what one deserves for being born less brilliant than Lillian Hellman?

An hour goes by; I count every second, agonizingly slow. I'm allowed to make one phone call. My first priority is for my children.

"If I call information for a number, does that constitute my one call?"

The female officer in charge of me is forty pounds overweight—pudgy cheeks, ample bosom—packed into a brown officer's uniform, top and skirt to match. "Technically, it does."

"Can you call information for me?" I ask.

She holds out her hand for a dime, bored, sarcastic. "Who do you want?"

We are standing in the hall by the on-duty officer's desk outside the cellblock. I've been a jailbird for sixty minutes. "I need the number of Mona Miller, Mrs. Seymore Miller, on Hayvenhurst in Encino." I've never before prayed so hard for anyone to be home in my life. When I hear her voice on the phone I almost cry.

"Mona, it's Suzanne Winston. I have an emergency. Can Jered stay at your house today after school? And will you do me two favors? Call my parents." I give her their number. "And tell them to pick up Jered from you after three o'clock, then go to my house and stay there with my children until they hear from me. And please, one more favor. Could you call a friend of mine, an attorney in Century City named Barry Adler, and tell him to have the lawyer I requested meet me at Van Nuys.''

''What do you mean you're at Van Nuys? Where in Van Nuys?''

I can't say it. What would she think? ''Please, Mona, just give him the message exactly as I said it. Tell him I'm waiting.''

''Suzanne, I'm not a secretary, you know. It's very inconvenient for me to do all these things for you. I have my own phone calls to make this morning. We ordinary people have responsibilities too.''

''I do understand, Mona, and I'm sorry to have to ask you. Perhaps you could ask my mother to call Mr. Adler and give him the message.''

''Yes, I suppose I could do that. It would only be one call, then.''

If there were anyone else I could ask, I would. But Mona is the only mother in the carpool who lives close enough to me to make these arrangements convenient. But she resents my fame.

''Mona, I'll be so grateful if you'd help me,'' I grovel, desperately trying to keep my voice calm. How I want to scream at her in rage.

The officer nods to me to get off the phone.

''Mona, this is truly an emergency. I'll make it up to you.''

''Okay, Suzanne,'' she sighs. ''When will you be home?''

''I don't know. I have to hang up now.''

''Wait!'' she shouts. ''Can I count on you to do five days of traffic duty at the school next week? The mothers are helping out Mrs. Freeman until she gets her cast off.''

''Next week?'' I search for reality among this craziness. Who knows where I'll be next week? But, if I refuse, she might not help me now. ''I'll try, Mona.''

''That's not good enough!'' she snaps. ''Either commit or

don't do it, but I must say, you can't expect to always be the one who takes from others in this life and never gives."

"Yes," I agree, hurrying to say it. "I'll do traffic duty next week. But Wednesday I can't, I have carpool."

She sighs. "I'll find someone for Wednes—"

The guard presses down the receiver cutting us off. "Time's up," she announces, relishing my dismay. Then, she grabs my arm and pulls me back toward the gated door of the cellblock.

It was afternoon when they led me into a conference room furnished with an old oak table and two chairs. At least there was a window and I could see the street outside through the attached grating. Eagerly I looked for Barry, but only my new lawyer, Curtis McCartney, was there. Barry wasn't allowed. I half expected Raymond Burr.

McCartney had dark hair with touches of gray in it, ruddy skin, and droopy eyelids, with tiny moles on them. He held my life in his hands. His lips were full, darkly colored with freckles, and his teeth were yellow, probably from smoking. I saw the package of Camels in his jacket pocket. Nobody smokes Camels anymore. I didn't know they still made them. His suit was expensive and well pressed.

"What have you admitted to, so far?" he asked, after shaking my hand.

I told him what questions the detectives had asked me. "There's nothing to admit, Mr. McCartney," I told him. "I'm not guilty. I would never do such a thing. Can you help me?"

"Mrs. Winston, we'll have bail set, and then get you out of here. I'll look over the written reports of your case and tell you what I can do when I have a chance. But in the meantime, you have to understand, that in here, it's as if you're a prisoner of war and the police are the enemy. You don't give them *any* information at all." He emphasized the word vehemently. "The only thing on their agenda is to clear their paper and go on to the next case, so don't make it any easier for them.

They're not interested in your innocence, only in what they can get on you to expedite it so it can be turned over to the DA's office. Got it?''

I nodded. There was no end to the otherworldliness of this situation. My safe beautiful world existed in a parallel state, next to this one, which was off-color, unclear, and permanently soiled. Somehow I had crossed over into this nightmare place through an invisible shield that separated the two. At the moment, that shield seemed impenetrable, and I doubted that I'd ever get back. Did Mr. McCartney hold the key? I was surprised about his manner and appearance, he wasn't corporate material. But I trusted Barry. He wouldn't have sent anyone who wasn't an expert.

McCartney went out for about twenty minutes while I waited and counted the minutes on the wall clock. He came back in again and said, "I've spoken to the judge, we've played golf together. I explained the details of the case, and who you are. He's allowing you to be released on your own recognizance, so we won't have to post bail. The preliminary hearing is set for about six weeks from now."

"You mean, that's it? I can go home?" I wanted to throw my arms around him in gratitude.

"I just want you to know that the lab report from UCLA done on an infrared spectrophotometer showed a graph curve indicating the sample they took from your house is lysergic acid, LSD."

My shock must have shown because he reached across the table to pat my hand. "I can't imagine how it got there." It was such an awful thought, being invaded, set up.

He nodded, but I suspected he didn't believe me. In his eyes I didn't have to be innocent, only accused, to warrant defending.

"Now, Mrs. Winston," McCartney interrupted my thoughts. "We should discuss my fee. It's fifteen thousand for preliminary work, and if we go to court, it goes up to fifty thousand. I need the first fifteen, cash in advance, by the end of tomorrow. Will that be a problem?"

"Cash?" I whispered, unable to breathe. Fifteen thousand? The walls of my world collapsed. There they went, imploding on themselves, destroyed by the sound of his fee; it reverberated until everything crumbled like the walls of Jericho. I almost laughed at my stupid plans for financial independence, how naive, to think I'd actually believed I'd had a chance to survive. Half the money I borrowed against the house would go to Mr. McCartney now, and to Avery Bellows, the investigator who I would now need full-time. The IRS debt had been moved back several notches in my mind because suddenly a new spore had begun sucking at my resources, draining me of my life's blood. Sherry Fallon was succeeding in ruining my life and I didn't have a clue as to who she was. Or he.

Reporters shouted hurtful inane questions at me as I left the jail; more were waiting for me as I arrived home. The one that really got me in the gut was, "How does it feel to be arrested, Suzanne?" Even though I'm a writer, I couldn't describe my feelings of terror and despair or the depth of my desperate shame. But even worse than that was my overwhelming desire to protect my children from this dreadful reality coupled with the terrible knowledge that I couldn't protect them at all.

I hid my face from the cameras, hating the reporters as a carcass might hate the vermin who devour it.

My children reached to hug me as I came through the door and I melted into their arms, trying not to break down. My parents and my children had been crying.

"Dad called," Amy told me. "He wanted to know what was going on."

"And Barry is on his way over," Miles said.

"Are you all right, Mom?" Amy asked.

"Yes, I'm all right," I told the three of them, wishing that were true.

"Where's Steffani?" I asked, missing her.

"She's on her way," my dad told me. "And Gloria heard about it on the radio." That meant my fall from grace would be on the five o'clock news. This terrible secret couldn't be kept private.

"Did Gloria have a few choice comments to make?" I asked. "I'm sure she thinks I'm guilty."

"No," my father assured me. "She was concerned."

What was he thinking behind those sad eyes? That his golden daughter, who'd always brought glory to the family, except for the divorce, had really fouled the nest this time. I knew Gloria would be gleeful about my downfall despite what my father said.

I introduced Curtis McCartney to my family and the six of us sat down in the living room. I dreaded having my parents and my children find out about my impending financial penury, but I also didn't want to go through this by myself. Even with my family around me, I felt alone.

"There's going to be an arraignment the day after tomorrow," Curtis McCartney began, "where the judge will establish your identity, read the charges into the record, and set a date for the preliminary hearing. That might be in the next two weeks or as long as six weeks away, depending on the calendar. We can always postpone it, if we need to.

"For those of you who don't know," he said, "a preliminary hearing is where the judge decides if there is probable cause to refer Suzanne for a trial. It takes place in the municipal court. The prosecution rarely puts on their whole case at a preliminary, and the defense tries to put on no case at all. We use that time as an opportunity to see what the prosecution has, to find out who their witnesses are. But, at that time, if the judge decides that there is probable cause to hold Suzanne for trial, he'll refer it to the superior court where they try criminal matters such as these."

"My mother is not a criminal," Jered said. His face was flushed red as though he'd been holding his breath or trying to keep from crying, and I could see how upset he was. My inability to protect him was a grinding pain in my guts.

"No, of course not," McCartney assured him. "In fact, we might be able to convince a judge at the preliminary hearing to drop the charges depending on what we come up with in discovery." He turned to me. "I want to get an investigator started on this right away. I know you've worked with Avery Bellows and he's excellent. I'll contact him."

I nodded, thinking about how much that was going to cost.

He continued, his voice a monotone. "Suzanne is accused of a felony; felonies are punishable by imprisonment or death."

My mother's gasp went straight through me.

"Do I have a chance of getting off?" I asked Mr. McCartney, believing for a moment that he could tell the future.

"The chances are pretty good. Juries don't like to convict, especially when the person is sympathetic like you. Nobody likes to decide someone's fate when they have to live with their decision. And no case is ever black or white, there's always doubt."

I felt a tightening grip of fear in my chest again thinking about a jury judging my life. How could I ever get anyone to believe me? My future depended entirely on this man. Could we ever find out the identity of the diabolical person who was ruining my life?

"I'll do my damnedest for you, Suzanne," McCartney assured me.

"What do you need from me?" I asked.

"I need to get paid," he said, quite firmly. "Clients who are faced with this kind of trauma often think these things take care of themselves. But in criminal matters, we collect up front. I'm sure you understand. If money is a problem, I'll take a deed to your house, or any possessions you have that might be worth the equivalent of my fee. Sometimes the family of a client will pitch in to pay the fee, or I've had clients who've had legal-fee parties where everyone comes for wine and cheese and makes a contribution."

I felt my cheeks flush at the idea of asking my friends for handouts. "I can pay you," I insisted, not wanting to air my financial status in front of everyone.

"Are you sure?" my father asked. "We can help out if you need it."

But I could see from the pinched look on my mother's face

that there wasn't much they could afford to offer. And I didn't want to take their money, either. Their savings account would be crucial for them when they both retired. My father might look as good as Rex Harrison, but he was seventy years old, after all. The figures swam around in my head, moving from one column to another. I had earmarked the money in my savings account for so many things, it seemed amusing. I kept moving it from this necessity to that one until finally there was one necessity I couldn't avoid, my defense lawyer's fee. I looked at the children, studying me with such faith. They didn't know that their own world would be changed forever too. I wondered if they'd still believe in me then.

"You'll make a good witness," McCartney assured me. "But you have to tell me everything you know. I can always work with the truth, no matter how damaging it may be. Believe me, I have ways of making the most upsetting facts work in our favor, or at least not hurt us. But I won't countenance any surprises. Surprises will hurt your case the most. You must be honest. All of you," he added, including my family. "Any inconsistencies in your story will be used against you. Like you telling the narcotics officer who called you from New York that you had no reason to be upset with Brett Slocum. He knew that you had a reason, so that lie made them suspicious enough of you to come and question you."

"I shouldn't have let them look through the house, should I?" How I regretted that, now.

"You didn't know there was anything for them to find, did you?"

"I swear, I didn't."

He turned to my family. "I must ask you all, and that means you, young man," he said to Jered, still in my lap. "Did any of you put a bottle of LSD in the refrigerator?"

All of them shook their heads no, and Jered crossed his heart and raised his right hand. "I swear I didn't, sir," he said, solemnly.

"Well, someone did," McCartney said. "And we have to find out who it was."

"It's unbelievable," my mother commented, "to think that someone could come into your house and put that bottle there. If the police hadn't found it, any one of you might have used it. God, I shudder to think of what might have happened."

"Someone's really out to get you, Mom," Miles said. "But I don't understand it." How I wanted to wipe away the fear in his eyes. I knew he was wondering whether this person wanted to get all of us, or just me.

"I'd like to take a look at those letters accusing you of plagiarism," McCartney said. "Obviously, they came from the same person who's gotten you arrested."

"I'll go," Jered said, climbing down off my lap. I didn't know he even knew where they were, but obviously he was more aware than I'd thought. In that moment, a surge of sour hatred shot through me toward my unknown tormentor. It was one thing to hurt me, quite another to hurt my children. If I could have gotten my hands on that person at this very moment, I would have gladly strangled them to death.

Just then the doorbell rang. It was Barry, followed closely by my sister, who was carrying a bag of sandwiches from the deli.

The two of them came over and hugged me. "I figured you wouldn't have thought about dinner," Steffani said. "I'll take this into the kitchen."

"Do you want us to stay, sweetheart?" my father asked.

I shook my head. "No, the children have homework to do, and I'll be talking to Mr. McCartney for a while. You two can leave now." I stood up and hugged them both. "Thank you so much for being here for me when I needed you."

My mother had tears in her eyes. "You know we'd do anything in the world for you," she said. "And for your children. If you need money, we'll find it somehow," she offered.

I nodded, but I knew I couldn't take anything from them. Not unless I was completely desperate.

Barry was talking to McCartney as I walked my parents to the door. My sister came back into the living room. "Why don't I keep the kids out of your hair while you talk to your lawyer," she said. And I nodded gratefully.

Then the three of us, Barry, Curtis, and I, resumed our seats. "Now," Curtis said, "we have to go over every detail of your life, from as far back as you can remember. We're going to be looking for someone who might want to hurt you."

"It can't be anyone I know," I said, not convincing anyone.

"Someone had access to your refrigerator, Suzanne," he said, sharply. "My guess is it wasn't a stranger. We'll have to question everyone who's had access—the children's friends, the housekeeper, anyone you can think of."

Barry could see how this idea terrified me. "Couldn't anyone, even someone she doesn't know, have broken into the house and planted incriminating evidence?" he asked.

"They'd have to know her habits, know when she wasn't at home and the house was deserted. And, they'd have to know a good place to put it."

His statement made me realize all over again that anyone I knew could be a suspect, which was as horrible as the reality.

"Let's start with your friends and acquaintances first," Curtis said. "Was there ever a time when you were going to collaborate with another writer, perhaps, and then you called off the arrangement? That might be a motive for someone to want to hurt you."

I wracked my brain to recall anything like that, but I'd always worked alone, never collaborated. So that wasn't it. "There's no one like that," I told him.

"Then tell me about yourself," Curtis said, reaching into his briefcase for a legal pad.

"I don't know where to start," I said, grateful to feel Barry's hand holding mine. As comforting as it was for him to be with me, I was embarrassed to have him hear the details of my life like this.

"Start with the recent past," Curtis suggested, "with your career as a writer. And don't leave anything out. I want to know all about you, about your ex-husband, your family, and anyone else in your past."

"All right," I sighed, realizing we were in for a long night.

* * *

Finding time to write a novel wasn't easy for someone with a varied degree of discipline, a year-old baby, and one on the way. What had kept me going, since I was writing without an outline, was wondering what would happen next in my story. Once my first draft was completed and I knew the answers, I felt stumped, almost unable to go on. The story seemed to lose its fascination. I rationalized my lack of impetus to raising a child, being pregnant with another one, and catering to my husband's social demands. Really, it was fear; I had no idea what to do next and I knew that my first effort was merely a beginning. (I hesitated to call what I was experiencing writer's block, because at the time I didn't consider myself a writer. I later discovered that a writer is someone who writes. Selling or publishing your work is not really a criterion.)

Then, Steffani elected to have surgery again on her right leg and would be in bed for weeks. My son, Miles, was born in June, and by the middle of July Steffani and I had gotten into the old pattern of my reading chapters to her while she gave me advice. Her cool objectivity was disconcerting, but she knew so damned much about structure that I didn't know.

"It's too simplistic," she kept saying. "Your characters get what they want too easily. You need more conflict."

The concept made no sense to me. "What do you mean, conflict?"

"It's what keeps the reader interested. If you have two characters who fall in love and get married and live happily ever after, that's boring, like a fairy tale, not real life."

"Novels are not real life," I retorted.

"I know that! But you have to have a conflict. Take the love story, for instance. Suppose the count has a business problem, or a health problem, or he can't decide whether or not to marry Anne, or she thinks she might be in love with someone from her past, not Count Allessandro, who is right for her. Those are conflicts. How you resolve them keeps the reader turning the pages. We want to see how the story turns out."

"If you know so much, why don't you write a novel?" I asked, sullenly.

"I'm going to," she stated, as though it was a matter of fact. "When I have something I want to write about. Right now, I'm otherwise occupied," and she gestured to her cast.

"Have you heard from Ron?" I asked, wanting to change the subject.

She raised her chin defensively. "I didn't expect to, and I couldn't care less."

Hearing her admit that she wanted to write a novel made me uncomfortable and competitive. I didn't want her to do the same thing I was doing. All my life, she'd wanted to do everything I did, and often did it better than I. I was intimidated by her brilliance; her mind was keener, her knowledge greater than mine, I thought. And her confidence in her own abilities seemed unshakable, whereas mine was tentative. If she decided to write, I believed she'd be an immediate success, and then what chance would I have? I marveled at her self-confidence. After everything she'd been through in her life, one would think she might be insecure, but not Steffani; she was strong.

"Don't change the subject," she insisted, catching me. "Do you understand what I was trying to tell you?"

I nodded.

"Take Melville, for example. In *Moby Dick*, Captain Ahab's conflict is the whale, man against nature, embodied in the beast who he believes wants to destroy him. Of course, there's other symbolism too. But the reader's interest is riveted by whether or not Ahab will find the whale, and then, whether or not he can destroy it. Same thing in Hemingway's *Old Man and the Sea*. Here, the old fisherman catches the huge fish, big enough to feed his entire village, and not only does he have to battle his own limited strength, but the forces of the weather and the sea, and the sharks who pick it to pieces. Amazing, how Hemingway could create such conflict with only one character."

I nodded, promising myself to read Hemingway's book right away.

"I mean, in your book you've got Anne deciding she wants more out of life than she's had, so in order to get into the jet set, she remolds her figure, has some plastic surgery, and gets everything she wants. It's boring. Put some obstacles in her way."

"Like what?" I asked.

"It's your book," she snapped. "I don't want to write it for you."

"Just give me one example," I asked. "That's not writing the book for me."

"Okay," she said, raising her arms behind her head. I was fascinated to see the luxurious growth of hair under her arms. Everyone I knew shaved their underarms. She saw my expression and smiled that defiant, rebellious smile of hers, ignoring my stare. "Suppose Allessandro's in love with Anne, and he's just the right kind of man for her, but she's spent so much time trying to achieve her goal, that she won't be sidetracked. Besides, her ego's been damaged by the way her husband treated her so she's afraid to trust anyone. And then, someone else enters the picture, someone dangerous."

"Is that conflict?"

"Yes, those are the elements. Now, this new man sidetracks her from her goals. Meanwhile, Allessandro convinces her of his sincerity and that she's worthy of being loved. If she lets the other man go, that's resolving the conflict. You can think of other ways, I'm sure."

It was still confusing to me, but I wouldn't let her know. Instead, I kissed her good-bye, retrieved Amy from my mother's care, and went home to the baby. With a newborn and a toddler, I had very little time to work, an hour here or there, but I began.

By fall I had an even bigger muddle and wished I had someone who could help me. But who? I didn't know anybody who wrote and I needed feedback. It was then that I discovered one of the primary problems of learning to write.

In the beginning, one needs an editor desperately, but no one gets an editor until he knows enough and is good enough to have sold a book. So, I continued writing my *story*, raising two babies, and cooking gourmet meals: veal stuffed with apples, lobster soufflé, baked Alaska, duck à la Chambord. And Alex continued socializing his way into bigger and better circles. Now we knew a lot of near-famous people—supporting actors, television directors, and independent producers. Next would come major movie stars, legendary producers, Oscar-winning writers, and heads of studios.

"We need a bigger house," Alex announced one Sunday when the children were expecting to go to the park. "I've made an appointment with a broker to show us around," he told me.

"But what about the park?" I asked.

"You go with the kids, I'll go with the broker."

I hesitated. Not only was I with the children all week without Alex, but I had to protect my interests. Whenever Alex saw something he wanted, he bought it, often without consulting with me. And I believed, even if he didn't, that the purchase of a new house was something we should share. I called my parents and they happily agreed to take the children to the park.

"Steffani just got a wheelchair, so all three of us will go," my father told me. And I thanked him, not really thinking of what it would be like for him to carry the wheelchair in and out of the house, carry Steffani in and out of the car, wheel her all around Griffith Park with my mother, and take care of my infant in his carriage and Amy in her stroller as well. But then, my parents were always like that, ready and able to do for us both whenever we needed them.

We went from one canyon to another. Nichols, Coldwater, Sunset Plaza, Wrightwood, and Laurel.

"Doesn't anybody live on level ground anymore?" I asked.

The broker and my husband both raised their eyes to the sky. The broker, Joyce, a pert blonde with tanned skin, thin muscular arms, and green eyes, let Alex explain. "You get much more house for your money living in the hills where the property values are not as inflated as in the flats of the city."

He wasn't the one who carpooled the children everywhere. When you lived in the hills, nothing was close to home, not the cleaners or the market or the pediatrician.

"What about the Valley?" I asked, remembering my childhood with fondness.

"Oh gawd," they both pronounced, as though I had suggested Watts. "Anything but that."

The broker hesitated. "There are some nice areas of the Valley," she said, feeling Alex out. "You could buy a lot and build exactly what you want for the same price as a much smaller house in the city."

"Build?" My antennae were quivering, extending themselves as though they belonged to a car radio. "Is that possible?"

"Building a house brings nothing but headaches," Alex pronounced. "A license to steal. It always takes longer than you expect and costs three times more than your budget."

"Not if you have a good builder." The broker had seen my excitement. "My husband is a builder," she said. "He teaches engineering at Valley College, but his real love is construction. Maybe you'd like to see some lots? There's a new subdivision in Encino, right next door to houses costing three hundred and fifty thousand dollars."

"In the Valley?" Alex exclaimed. "This I've got to see."

The area was west of the San Diego Freeway, right around the corner from Richard Crenna's house, not too far from Annette Funicello, near the Clark Gable estate, and George Gobel was building in the very same subdivision. Alex was in his element. We climbed onto the treeless dirt pads with views of the Valley spread out below and smiled at one another. All around us foundations had been poured, framing was going up, gravel piles were waiting for the cement mixers to arrive on Monday. There may have been no trees, but there were streetlights, and underground utilities, and an excellent grammar school in the neighborhood. The houses being built here were mostly owned by private parties, but some of them were being constructed by builders for resale. The lots ranged in price from twenty-eight thousand to forty-two.

"How could we afford this?" I asked Alex, out of our broker's hearing range.

"We've got fifteen thousand saved," he told me. "We could buy the lot and pay the rest over time, and then get a construction loan to build the house. Sometimes you can borrow more than the cost of the house, and it will pay for part of the lot. The construction loan gets converted into a mortgage once the house is completed. Of course, we'd have to sell our house."

"What would it cost to build?"

Alex was always a source of varied information. "I think the going rate is anywhere from nine to twelve dollars a square foot. So, if you build a four-thousand-square-foot house, it will cost you somewhere around fifty thousand dollars, plus the lot."

"Four thousand square feet is a mansion," I declared. Our house was twenty-three hundred square feet and had three bedrooms and a family room.

"Don't think small, Suzanne," he said. And I could see the plans in his head already taking shape. All his former objections to building a home were disappearing as he became more enamored by standing on an empty lot.

And so we began, joining the ranks of middle-class Americans fulfilling the American dream. We scrimped to pay off the lot as we worked on our plans. The square footage of the house grew to five thousand square feet. Each night we took our quarter-inch-scale rulers and measured out additions and changes in the floor plan. The children's bedrooms would be next to ours so I could get to them in the night when they were sick, the garage had to lead directly into the kitchen so I could unload the groceries easily, there had to be a powder room, and separate dining room, and a pantry in the kitchen to store extra china and crystal. Alex wanted a workroom where he could store his fishing gear and tennis trophies, and I insisted on an extra bedroom for guests, which would really be my office. So we laid out our own floorplan within the confines of the lot, and hired a draftsman to design the building plans for the house, avoiding the cost of an architect altogether. To further keep the cost of construction down, the house would have a flat roof and standard windows and doors. However, the size and the heights of the ceilings would make it unusual, as would the interiors, which I designed by poring through home magazines for ideas. Very little conflict occurred between me and Alex while we were building our house. As we made joint decisions, our natural tendency to disagree was set aside. Our builder, Franz, was efficient, honest, and compulsive. The work was completed in four months, something of a building miracle, and at the price we originally planned, because every time I suggested a change or a more expensive door handle, Alex said no.

We moved into the house in September. It had Carrara-G marble fireplaces and champagne wool shag carpeting, a parquet floor in the family room and dining room, and a pull-out island in the kitchen, not to mention the Char-glo barbecue, double electric ovens, and a separate refrigerator and freezer. Alex was now ready to invite the biggies to a housewarming party, black tie. Everyone was impressed. We were so young to have achieved so much. I never saw Alex happier.

But I wasn't. For once the house was completed, we started arguing again. Why didn't he spend more time with the children and me, why did he pick up the phone the moment he came home at night to make business calls, why didn't I want to make love very often, and why did I persist in the foolishness of writing a book? "You've always got that goddamned notepad in your hand, it's so annoying," he'd complain. And I'd be hurt because he had so little interest in what I was doing. Other couples I knew weren't as hostile as we were, always pulling on one another to be different. I wanted more attention, though when I got it from him, it was often criticism. He wanted more attention from me, but I was usually annoyed with him and couldn't give it.

Here I was, twenty-six years old, with two children and a successful husband, living in a veritable mansion, and I felt empty inside. I expected Alex to come home in the evening and fill me up, but he never could. I told him about my day, about problems with the children, and he said I was complaining. I couldn't tell him about my work, because he didn't take it seriously. When I asked him about his day, I'd hear stories about the special clause he added to Gregory Peck's contract, or whether Peter Sellers's newest marriage would make it, and why Steve and Eydie should continue working in Vegas instead of doing a concert tour, and whether or not we could get house seats for *Man of La Mancha* with Richard Kiley at the Music Center. Eventually, he'd lie down on the sofa with the television remote and compulsively change the channels while I went into the guest room to work on my novel at my antique oak table desk. Often, I went to bed alone, but when he found me there he'd get furious that I hadn't said good night.

"Were you trying to get out of making love again?" He'd shake me awake.

That never put me in the mood. "You were watching television," I'd retort. "I didn't want to disturb you."

"And you were locked up in the goddamned guest room all evening. What was I supposed to do?" Both of us were injured, but which came first, his hurt or mine? However, once Alex got started, he seldom stopped. His rage was easily ignited by my behavior, and he'd throw every kitchen sink he could find: "You're spoiled, you let the kids walk all over you, nothing I do is ever enough, and on our honeymoon you did nothing but complain."

I'd fire back: "Listen who's talking about being spoiled, you always want everything your own way. And if I let the kids walk all over me, it's because you're never around. As for complaining on our honeymoon, I had a hundred-and-two fever and the flu and you played tennis all day.'' We had grievances, the two of us. We were both spoiled, unable to compromise. But I was passive-aggressive. I could have said, ''Shut off the TV and give me some attention. I miss you, I need you.'' Or, ''Let's talk about something other than your work and my day's activities.'' But I didn't. I preferred to be injured, to push his temper button, thereby insuring that he'd get furious and we'd fight for hours and nobody would consider making love. Why didn't I see it? Why are poppies red? In my mind, Alex was the one who was wrong, everything was his fault, and he was obviously comfortable in that role. My parents had argued their whole lives about inconsequential things and I guess I thought that's what marriage was. I didn't realize it was like a delicate flowering plant that needed constant attention and nurturing. Perhaps I was justified in feeling unappreciated, but I didn't know how to ask for what I needed, thinking Alex should know what it was by magic. And he was dismayed that the prince, doted on by his mother and sister for his whole life, had met a woman he couldn't please.

CHAPTER TWENTY-SIX

In 1964, her sophomore year in college, Steffani took her first upper-division class, in poetry. The huge auditorium was filled that fall with five hundred eager students, notebooks open, waiting for Jascha Gertsman, the maverick professor who openly defied university policy. Eight minutes, and then ten, passed after the chime, and still no sign of the professor. Necks craned toward the back doors; students fidgeted. Where was he?

Finally, a scarecrow of a man, thin hair pushed back behind

his ears and falling well below his collar, wearing a stained sweat shirt and the baggiest of gray gabardines, came dancing down the aisle. He moved on the balls of his feet, kicking out first one foot and then the other, arms above his head, his fingers snapping as if to a Middle Eastern concert in his head. Some of the students gasped, others snickered, then silence.

Gertsman danced up the stairs onto the stage, coming to rest at the front edge, his arms outstretched before the class. A beautiful smile lit his hollowed cheeks as he commanded, "Everyone touch hands, touch your neighbor's hand, feel the vibration. Give and receive love."

Steffani looked to the right and then to the left at her fellow students. They were as embarrassed and bewildered as she, but no one questioned. Professors were God. She reached out and joined hands with a boy next to her and a girl on the other side. Now the audience was a sea of attached humanity.

Jascha Gertsman seemed delighted at their compliance, nodding his approval. "As many of you know, I spent the summer in Greece with my family. I communed with angels and had the poet's visions. Rilke spoke to me from the heavens and so did the Oracle. I was reborn. I will use this poetry course to transmit my experience to you, as much as it is possible. See you on Wednesday." And he trotted off the stage just ten minutes after class had started, leaving an auditorium filled with awkward hand-holding students.

Jascha didn't reappear that semester. Apparently, the administrators didn't want him transmitting visions to the student body, so he was given a semester's leave. It was rumored that something called LSD was the cause of his erratic behavior. Steffani tried to find out about it; if it made you have visions and see angels, she wanted to try it, especially since it was associated with her new idol, Jascha Gertsman.

Gertsman's spring poetry class was held in a smaller room and this time fewer students attended. A subdued Gertsman, same baggy pants and hawk nose, arrived on time. But underlying this new calm facade was the fire he had shown on that first day last fall. In the first few classes he opened their minds to the I-ching, the philosophy of Jung, and the San Francisco beat poets. Her classmates became her close friends; they read their own poetry to one another in class. She'd thought she was the only one who wrote poetry, but in this class there were kindred souls. On the days when Gertsman wasn't there, class continued as usual, instead of everyone leaving.

On warm days, the class met outdoors in the new sculpture garden where they sat in a huge semicircle on the grass. A flute played; Jascha drummed a rhythmic beat on a hollow sculpture. Someone brought apples and passed them around; everyone held hands, silently feeling the others' presence. And there, on the May lawn, between the austere library and the wary eye of the Political Science Building, something was born. Later, it came to be known as a "love-in" but at the time, Steffani knew she was a part of a new age.

One day in poetry class there was a bear of a man sitting at the end of her row. He was tall and dark, with a beard, older, perhaps a student, perhaps a teacher auditing Gertsman's class. She looked at him and he smiled—white shiny teeth, just like hers, flashed for a moment. He exuded sensuality.

After class started, Gertsman beckoned to him and he came up to the front. "This is my friend Joe Mariano, a writer and poet from New York."

Ever since they'd exchanged smiles, Mariano had been staring at her. Now he continued to stare from the stage. His eyes bore through her, but she didn't flinch, just stared right back.

"Joe has just had his play optioned by a producer for an off-Broadway production; he's here to soak up our atmosphere, become reinspired, and to get ready for rehearsals, which will begin in a few weeks. I asked him to class today as a favor to me. Normally, he's reluctant to talk about his work, prefers to just do it. But I knew this would be a rare opportunity for you to actually speak to a working playwright. He'll take your questions for fifteen minutes, and then we'll continue our discussion of Eliot."

"What's your play about?" someone asked.

"Life," Mariano replied. "What every play is about. Only mine takes place in a ghetto in Harlem."

"How can a white man write about the Negro's experience with honesty?" Hester asked, two seats away from Steffani. She was a heavy young girl, with bushy, curly hair, who always wore jeans and loose cotton blouses.

"Suffering is universal," he told her. "Besides, I am writing about what I know."

"How can you know it if you're not black?" This from Jarnel Walker, one of the black students in the class.

"Take my word for it," Mariano said, harshly. He was the most defiant man she'd ever seen and yet he appealed to her. The city streets that bred him were as much a part of him as the thin film of oil on his swarthy skin. His large hands moved expressively as he talked and she could almost feel those hands on her body.

He told the class it had taken him fifteen months to write this play, but he'd lived in this milieu his whole life. He explained the process of having a play optioned, which was: You had to know someone, who knew somebody else, who was in the market for a play, who knew somebody with enough bread for a production, who had a cousin with an in to a theater—especially if you were doing things on a shoestring.

A real writer who earns his living by writing; awesome. Her eyes took in every inch of his six-feet-two-inch body, in a Mexican hand-woven sweater over a white T-shirt and black cotton pegged pants ending in huge black scuffed boots.

When he stepped off the stage and took his seat she hardly heard the rest of what Gertsman was talking about, aware that he was still watching her. Class was finally over and Mariano waited for her to come out of her aisle, falling into step beside her. They walked out of the building and across the lawn. He smiled down at her.

"You didn't ask me any questions. Why not?"

"I didn't want to feed your enormous ego."

He laughed. "Takes one to know one."

"A real original line for a poet," she shot back.

"Are you one of those tough broads?" He stopped to look at her as though he'd misjudged her. "I came out to California to get away from tough women."

She shook her head, staring up at him; his question had surprised her. She was anything but one of those hard broads. "I'm soft as molasses," she said, quietly, "and twice as sweet."

"Then I'll call you Sugar and eat you all up," he said huskily, gazing deeply into her eyes until she felt her whole body flush in response.

"Are you staying at Jascha's?" she asked.

"Not if you have room for me," he replied, smiling.

"Not I," she said, regretfully. "I live in the dorm."

"Jesus." He whistled. "Jail bait."

"I'm worth it," she said, tossing her now naturally brown long curly hair over her shoulder with a self-satisfied cockiness.

He was grinning as though he'd just won a prize at the fairway. "Sugar, I'll bet you are. So why don't you show me around this place and then we'll have dinner and get to know each other better."

"I think I'd rather read some of your play. You can read my poetry too, then we'll know if we want to waste each other's time. You must have a copy of it somewhere?" she teased. She had seen it sticking out of his pocket and it had made her heart skip. He was the real thing; what she'd dreamed of being her whole life.

He reached into his pocket and almost pulled it out, but didn't. He looked over at the cover of her notebook and read her name. "Look, Steffani, I know I come off as a tough guy, but my work is the best part of me. It's good work because it's honest. I've spent years learning how best to say my piece in a way that lets people hear me. I've learned how to illustrate my philosophy dramatically, how to build a character who's complex enough to seem real while he says what I want him to say and yet he's still a part of me. I've even learned how to structure a play with an eye for the commercial because I know otherwise it won't get done at all, or only a few phony, stoned jerks who go to experimental theater will see it. So I don't want to be judged by anyone, especially a woman I'm attracted to.''

She touched his arm lightly, feeling heat and energy surging through him. "I feel the same way about my poetry, Joe. I don't want to be judged either."

She reached into her book bag and pulled out the dog-eared pages she'd worked on in the early hours of the morning. Stanzas had been rewritten countless times, words scratched over and others put in their place. Sometimes the empty wells of her memory refused to yield as she tried to pull meaning from feelings too raw and painful to express, and other times it overflowed. But whatever it was, it was all her. She handed one to him. Her heart was pounding as she supposed his was.

He reached back into his pocket and handed her his play, a bound Samuel French version.

She looked up at him. "How can this be? I thought it had never been produced."

He seemed embarrassed. "It won a literary prize when I was at Yale, so it's already been published."

She reached out and took it reverently, then sat down on the grass, folding her legs underneath her, and began to read. He stood there awkwardly for a moment before sitting down opposite her and reading her poem.

He read:

So Goes the World

Brothers of my America
I cry for your pain
But you don't feel it
Covered up by cosmetics

It is useless to cry

For someone satisfied by Brut cologne
Or eager for Chanel

Your descent is scented
With the perfume of deception
And you'll asphyxiate in an aromatic haze

My poor sweet-smelling country

She read:

Scene 1 Act 11

Leboe steps out of the darkened corner of the
stage into a single spot. He is older now, his
shoulders stoop, his hair is more gray.

LEBOE

Thelma been sickly. She go to work wit a cough
and come home wit a headache. Henry tole me
to look for some young thang wid a tight ass and
a bigger smile. He would. Hell, he did! They all
did when they's still livin' here. Thelma's all I
got. Wha'd I do wit some young thang? I ain't
no stud. But, I kin git it up wit the best o' 'em.
(He winks.)

A fight starts O.S. We hear shouting, youthful
voices saying, "Don't be no pussy, man, cut him
good! Hear? Get 'im, get 'im."

Leboe's attention turns O.S.

We hear the too-real sounds of someone being
stabbed by a knife. The boys react, and then
yell, "He's daid. Let's split, muther."

Leboe's attention is back to audience.

LEBOE

That's what they do 'roun here now. Nobody
tells 'em different but me. They don't listen.

When she finished reading his scene he was watching her.

"It's sad," Steffani said, "and powerful. You do seem to know about blacks."

"Don't qualify what you feel in your gut with words like 'seem.' Say, 'You know about blacks!' Period!"

"Oh, now you're telling me what to say?"

"Well, there was no equivocation in your poem. The statements were clear, precise."

She nodded, wanting more. "Do you like the poem?"

"Do you?" He threw it back.

"Well, yes. It's fairly good, if pessimistic." She heard herself say "fairly" and wanted to grab it back. So she said, "Yes, it's good. I like it." And almost blushed with her own boldness, thinking someone would disapprove. Yet there was no one to disapprove but herself. A child's voice whispered, *Don't brag, nobody will like you.* She told it to shut up.

"Why do you care what I think about your poem, or what anyone else thinks for that matter? If you think it's good, it is."

"I was merely being polite."

"Bullshit! You're capable of more than politeness."

She chuckled. "Do I get to point out your flaws too?"

The look of surprise on his face amused her. "What flaws?" His eyes were wide, revealing a thin blue circle around the dark brown centers.

"You think it's perfect as it is?" she laughed.

He smiled and shrugged. "So I'm pompous, I admit it."

"What I mean is, that you're the best judge of what works in your play. My opinion, after all, is only mine."

"True." He scratched his cheek. "But I respect your opinion. Input is important."

"That's why I asked you about my poem, for input."

"Touché," he conceded.

She wanted to run her hand over his beard, feel the bristles against her flesh, feel it on her chest and neck, even on her back. She was staring and only came back to herself when he stood up and reached to help her.

"Why don't I drop you off and you can finish the play? I'll read some more of your poetry, and then we can meet for dinner."

"I've got a history midterm on Friday."

"Students." He shook his head.

"Graduates," she mimicked him, shaking her head. He laughed, then threw his arm around her and gave her a hug.

"Are we going to get it on? Or do you play hard to get?"

"If I say yes, I'm easy. If I say no, I'm a fool."

He was staring at her, devouring her with that hot gaze she'd experienced earlier when he was standing in front of the class; her entire body responded. "I was right about you," he said, stepping closer and gazing down. Students walked by, the chimes for the next class rang, and for a moment she couldn't remember whether or not she had a class to go to, but she didn't dare look at her watch and break the spell. She couldn't take her eyes from his.

He ran his hand down her arm and took her fingers in his. Hers were slender, long and brown, the nails unpolished. His were large, thick, with wide clean nails, and dark hair on the back of his hand. He examined her hand, turning it over, tracing the lines with his other hand flat against her palm, as if he were reading things she didn't want revealed; being laid open and bare was a new sensation. Over the years she'd learned to close up, only let someone in when she chose. She wanted to pull away now, but didn't.

He reached up and ran his fingers through her hair, combing it away from her temples on the side, feeling its silkiness almost as if he was learning her through his touch. She wouldn't have been surprised if he'd leaned over and sniffed the fragrance of her body at the side of her neck, but he didn't. She could smell the wool of his Mexican sweater and, now and then, the grass beneath their feet as they shifted their weight, crushing the blades and allowing the fresh aroma to escape.

"First date, my place, top and bottom, possible future, no flings," he said.

Her look of confusion made him smile. "I'm answering your twenty questions."

And so they began.

She was drunk on him, high with the scent of him, the touch, the hunger he made her feel. Their first time together her heart pounded wildly, fearfully. She prayed that her condition would not spoil their lovemaking, and wanted it to remain dark so she could hide her disfigurements. But he had to examine her, limb by limb, scars and all.

"What's this one," he asked, "and this," as his fingers traced the lines and the bumps. His hand on her stomach was so large it covered her, almost like a physician feeling for changes in her anatomy, but he was discovering where he left off and she began.

"It's a chronic illness," she told him. "A blood disorder. It bothered me when I was a child, but now the worst is over." She pushed the truth away, straight-armed it the way a halfback on the Bruins team stopped the defense as he carried the ball cradled to his body. The dark smoking reality that crept up in the night, reminding her of pain, possibilities of getting worse someday, and of other things too terrible to mention, had no place here. She would not let them spill out over her now, darken this moment with their black ink. "I'm lucky," she stated. "My case isn't as serious as it could be. Some people are much worse off than I am." That child's singsong voice repeated in her brain, *Liar, liar, liar*. She straight-armed it too.

He was nuzzling her neck right in the place she'd imagined he would. "My little one," he whispered. "You've lived a lot in such a short time."

"Living is what I do best," she whispered, entwining her legs around him, waiting for him again. She smiled, thinking of him as "The Hard, the Soft, and the Hairy," like an Italian spaghetti western, and almost started to compose a poem about it, but he kissed her again, blotting out everything but the apple taste, the feel of him, the male muskiness, the slippery, dazzling, overwhelming size of him as he filled her up.

CHAPTER TWENTY-SEVEN

"God, you're infuriating!" Steffani yelled. "If you could only hear yourself. I swear I'm hearing Thinkspeak, like in *1984*. Look at the facts. Our troops have no right to be bombing North Vietnam. Johnson is getting us into war!"

"I know what I see, goddamnit! If the government listened to peaceniks like you, the whole country would turn red."

The phone rang, interrupting them, or their fight would have escalated into a brawl. Sometimes they threw things; once, he even hit her. But when he saw how badly she bruised, it brought tears to his eyes and he kissed her arm every day, tenderly touching the evidence of his fury until the last yellow spots of her injury had faded. By that time, she had six more bruises just from ordinary bumps.

But he did infuriate her. Their views were completely opposite. He came from a traditional Italian family where his mama had cooked and cleaned for her four children and his papa raised his fist to keep them in line. Catholicism pervaded everything Joe did, even though he denounced formal religion as superstitious, narrow claptrap. But the behavior and attitudes were ingrained, inescapable. He even said things like, "You screw around with anybody else and you're outta my life, baby." But he looked at every girl who passed by; he even touched and pinched a few when he was drinking, and he was always drinking though he hated her to get high. He had disdain for anyone who used pot, pills, or dope, yet, he drank a bottle of wine, or several scotches, every night.

"I don't want to be tied down to one man," she told him. After Ron, she'd given up the fantasy of true romance in the traditional sense. But he scoffed at her idea of independence. "You love me, I know it," he said. "You don't want anyone else but me."

And she didn't. For now. Sometimes, after they'd made love, and she was still high from something she'd taken, whatever was on hand, since everything was so readily available, she'd feel an ache inside, almost a pain, she loved him so much. But she was afraid to admit it. At those times he was everything she wanted; his body belonged to her as well as his mind. She could twist both of them any way she wanted to, knew where he was vulnerable, knew his mental erogenous zones and played them like musical instruments. But he was fiercely independent, too, in his own way. Only time would test the endurance of their attraction, but somewhere in her heart, she knew that time was the one thing she didn't have.

Joe had an ex-girlfriend named Addie with whom he'd lived a year before. Addie called every day, asking in a sleepy voice, "Is Joseph there?" Her calls came at one in the morning or two in the afternoon, always managing to interrupt them when they were making love. And damn him if he didn't take Addie's calls. Addie had a four-year-old daughter named Heather, who missed Joe and wanted him to come and visit. Steffani suspected it was Addie's way of holding on.

Joe told Addie how to handle Heather, even what to say, though he rolled his eyes in a gesture of impatience, implying that Addie's dependence bothered him. But he enjoyed the hell out of it.

Sometimes, in Steffani's more insightful moments, she glimpsed the truth, that if she were less independent and more amenable to Joe's demands, to his view of what a woman should be, he would love her completely, even bind himself to her in a more permanent way. But she could not be what he wanted, not let him rule her life. And so both her stubbornness and her sense of self worked against her. She told herself she wasn't ready for anything permanent.

Joe's play had been on and off again twice since she'd met him in February. Then in April, he was contacted by someone who wanted to turn it into a Broadway musical. So the avant-garde off-Broadway production was scrapped and the producers' assistants called him every morning at six—nine o'clock New York time—to discuss names of composers and lyricists. Harry Belafonte's name was mentioned for the role of Leboe, and Steffani felt as if she was living on the edge of celebrity. The fact that there had been famous people in her life since she was a child didn't count. Those were her parents' friends; these were people within her own realm.

Finally, Joe announced, "I'll be going back to New York for rehearsals soon." He watched to see her reaction.

"I'll miss you," she said, as if he was just going out for beer.

He wanted her to beg him not to go, or offer to leave school and come with him to prove her love. But she just gave him an encouraging smile and said, "Won't it be wonderful to be in New York again, near your family, especially as a star. How will it feel to go back to the old neighborhood as the writer of a Broadway musical?"

"I'll be too busy for that," he insisted. But the idea pleased him. Through the spring and summer of that year, while Joe worked on his rewrites, Steffani lived at home with her parents, took summer school classes, and worked as a day camp counselor three times a week. In August, Joe went to New York for rewrites and casting and came back to L.A. in September in need of a break after all the hard work. The play was scheduled to open in October. But, just before rehearsals started, the actor playing Leboe left the cast and was replaced by none other than Joe Frazier.

"Joe Frazier!" Steffani hooted. "What does a boxer know about acting and singing?" It was the worst idea she'd ever heard.

Joe was exhausted from weeks of nonstop work and just couldn't argue with the producers anymore, not long distance. "They say he gave a great reading and he's talented." She'd never seen him make excuses before, or allow others to compromise his work.

"They'd be better off getting Cassius Clay," Steffani quipped. "At least he's got a personality."

He glared at her. "Frazier will be good," he insisted. "He's got the right sensibility to play Leboe."

"The only thing he's got going for him is the color of his skin," she stated, and then regretted it when he started shouting.

"Why don't you keep your fucking opinions to yourself, bitch. Who asked you? You're sure as hell no authority on anything." He slammed out of his apartment, leaving her feeling like he was right.

She left Joe a note of apology for sticking in her two cents, and went back to her parents' house, where she waited all evening; but he didn't call. At midnight, she started calling him, but he wasn't home. Finally, by one in the morning, she figured out where he might have gone and drove over to Addie's small house in Van Nuys. Joe's car was parked in front and there were no lights on in the house.

She knew what they were doing and the image of him with Addie tore into her. But before the pain could overwhelm her, she said out loud, as if he could hear, "You can't take the truth, can you, asshole? Too bad. Because the truth is sacred to me. If you want that simpleminded little twit over me, you can have her. 'Joe, what should I do, Joe?' " she whined, imitating Addie's voice. Addie had red hair, worn teased and ratted, and white skin. She looked like a prisoner of war, and she was expert at playing waif-of-the-world. "She can have you, Joseph Francis Mariano," Steffani shouted, feeling every muscle in her body tense with anger. If she relaxed, the anger would give way to sorrow and then to the pain waiting in the wings. She'd be damned if anyone was going to cause her pain. There'd been too much pain in her life that she couldn't control, so this kind was not allowed.

She sat there for nearly an hour to make certain he wasn't coming out. When it was apparent he was in for the night, she decided on a course of action. Dragging him out of there was one possibility, but then she'd have to forgive him and wouldn't have paid him back. "I don't deserve this kind of treatment, you chauvinist pig!" she yelled. What had she done, after all, but speak the truth, truth that he knew perfectly well?

The leading role in his play was miscast and would probably screw it up. But he was only the writer; whatever power he had over his creation was abdicated for fear that if he said no to Joe Frazier the play wouldn't get done. That had to be extremely frustrating. So what does a man do when he feels powerless? He turns to a woman to give him back his sense of power. And if, in the process, he can hurt the woman who made him face the truth, so much the better.

"Two can play that game," she said, starting the car and driving away from Addie's bungalow. And instead of going home, she headed up Van Nuys Boulevard and turned left on Ventura, toward Laurel Canyon, to see what kind of mischief she could find at this hour of the morning.

Even as late as it was, people were out and about on the twisted, narrow, precarious hillside streets of the canyon. Music wafted from stereos here and there as she wound her way up the narrow inclines. Like a concert she heard the Stones, Grace Slick, Janis, and she'd sing along as she caught bits of a song. The air was sweet with the scent of night-blooming jasmine and incense.

There was always a party, a happening, at Melody's, and tonight was no exception. Melody sat on the living room floor in a typical drug circle consisting of Frank, her man of the moment; her sister Opal (their mother was trying to be lyrical when she named them); Davey, who went to Valley College; Sergei, who sold mediocre dope; and Antonio, from Spain, who was hitchhiking through California for the summer. There were two people wrapped up together, sleeping on the sofa, and Ravi Shankar music played on the stereo. A typical Melody scene.

Entering this exotic world brightened her spirits. She stepped over people and sat between Melody and Antonio.

They both kissed her hello as she accepted the toke that was passed to her.

"Hey man, I'm ripped," someone said. It didn't matter who'd said it, they were all ripped. And before the narcotic began to cloud her brain, she got a sudden insight. Most stoned people thought they were talking about profound issues, but what they were really talking about was the state of their stonedness.

"K.C.'s here," Melody said to her, after she'd had her third turn on the toke. It was excellent hash, definitely not from Sergei; already she had a pleasant buzz on.

The initials K.C. didn't mean anything to her because she kept thinking about Addie and Joe doing it in Van Nuys.

"You know, K.C., the gorgeous guy I told you about."

Steffani heard someone come into the room behind her and she turned, looking up at one of the most attractive men she'd ever seen in her life. He stopped in the doorway and leaned against the jamb as if he were Paul Newman in *Hud*, except this dude was black. He wore jeans, nothing else, and the lights of the candles flickered on the muscles of his chest. He looked at her as though appraising and then nodded.

She stared back, until he came over to sit next to her, moving Antonio aside so he could fold his long legs underneath him and make himself comfortable.

"You're Steffani, aren't you?"

"K.C. I presume?" She smiled at him.

"Melody's told me all about you."

"All good, I hope." *God, he's unbelievable.*

"She said not only were you smart, but you were cool. She forgot to say how beautiful or magnetic."

"You're not so bad yourself." *Watch out for this one*, she thought.

"You're at UCLA? I went there for two years."

"And what have you been doing since then, besides standing in doorways looking sexy?"

He shrugged and leaned back on his arms so that the muscles stood out like hard rounded knots. "Little of this, a little of that."

"Don't know what you want, yet?"

"Right on," he conceded.

"That can be tough. I'm lucky, I guess. Since this summer I finally figured out what I want."

"What's that?"

"A combination of two things. One is writing, which won't pay the bills. And teaching, which will."

"Most teachers suck. They don't listen, they don't care."

"But I've had a few in my life who made a difference."

"Yeah," he conceded. "I guess. But it's a grind."

"It can be. I wasn't sure I could stand up there all day and hold their attention. And I'd hate to be one of the bad ones you're thinking about, who bore you to death. But after being a counselor at a day camp, I discovered I'm a natural. I'm good with kids and I love them. I know just how to get them to do as I say; they listen to me without my having to punish them. Some teachers can be s.o.b.'s. I've had a few of those."

"Lucky kids. What will you teach?"

"English," she stated, surprised at how certain she felt. This had been an important summer. She could actually visualize herself in front of a class, see all those teenaged faces watching her, listening, absorbing whatever knowledge she could impart, their hands raised as they called out her name, "Miss Blacker!" If she couldn't have children of her own, she'd have classrooms full of them.

"There's this one boy in my group named James, who is hyperactive. I invented a game for the two of us, called engines. We're engines running as fast as we can, and we make loud engine noises and use our arms like pistons, pumping like crazy—you should see how weird we look—igniting our spark plugs, running in a circle as fast as we can. Then, little by little, we slow down the engines, until they sputter and go out, and we're still. If I play that game with him first thing in the morning, he's okay until lunch. Then we do it again in the afternoon, only we're jet planes. His mother says I'm the only one who's had any control over him since he's been in school." She could feel K.C. staring at her again and she returned his gaze. His eyes reached right inside. There was something about him that invited her to confide, perhaps the way he listened, absorbed. She hadn't even told Joe these things. And even though they'd been talking about work, it felt more intimate.

"You're resourceful, aren't you?" He moved his body closer so they were touching; his movements felt like a caress. "You know what Melody says, don't you?" His voice was low and soothing in her ear. She could feel his breath against her skin.

"What?"

"That we two should get it on."

Steffani felt herself shiver, and then she glanced at Melody, who was too gone to notice. She wished she knew if Melody had really said that or if this was his line, but Melody was smiling dreamily, stroking the fur of her Persian cat as her head nodded to the soothing sounds of Shankar. Melody was one of Jascha Gertsman's teaching assistants; she'd gone with him and his family to Greece on that infamous odyssey, probably slept with him. Steffani was fascinated by her lifestyle, the free way she lived, no conventions, no rules, the antithesis of life with Mom and Dad.

Steffani looked back at K.C. and shrugged. K.C. took hold of her hand, his fingers played lightly with hers, then he ran his up the inside of her arm, extending the growing intimacy between them. Every move he made increased his magnetism. And looking at him was such a pleasure she couldn't help it. His lashes were long; his large dark eyes reflected the flickering lights around the room. His skin was so warm, she felt the heat of it next to her. His nose was short and wide, blending into his cheeks in perfect symmetry, and his mouth was generous and perfectly formed, the skin darker at the outside moving to a light pink tone at the center. He studied her as she studied him, and then smiled, causing dimples to appear in his smooth, round cheeks.

She smiled back, a slow smile that took forever to complete. Her face was getting numb. That hash was powerful.

And then he leaned over and kissed her, touching her body at the same time.

My God, she thought, *I can't do this. He's a stranger*. But she was doing it. She tried to notice if there was anything different about kissing a black man, but there wasn't. Yet when she reached over and touched his skin, it did feel different, so tight over his muscles that it felt like silk to her touch. He sighed with pleasure as she caressed him. She had a sudden thought that she was kissing Melody's Persian cat or a panther and had to open her eyes to ground herself in reality. He sensed that the emotion had changed and pulled away, gazing at her.

"Would you like to go into the other room?" he asked. He moved back so that he was on his knees and able to stand up more easily. He reached for her hand but she hesitated.

Of course she wanted to go with him. He was gorgeous, sensual, and willing. And she wasn't embarrassed about anything, certainly not in this house. People made love around here with strangers all the time. But somewhere the thought of Joe was stopping her. Her heart pounded with desire, and the thrill of doing something she'd always imagined doing, making love to a perfect stranger who would somehow materialize out of the night and be the most romantic lover she'd ever had, and a black man as well. But she had to be sensible. Even though she was floating from the hash and tired from the release of tension over Joe, her better judgment told her no. If Joe found out, he'd kill her. She didn't want to risk losing him, not over a one-night fling that would be over in a few hours. But then, she thought about what those hours would be like, and what Joe was doing this very minute, and her censors faded.

Melody, who was leaning back against the sofa next to her, opened one eye, noticed her hesitation, and whispered, "You'll be sorry if you don't." And closed her eyes again.

As if to convince her further, K.C. leaned over and kissed her again, exploring her mouth with his own in a way that made her shiver with desire. Without breaking the kiss, he helped her up, and only then did he pull away from her to lead her into one of the bedrooms.

Everything moved in slow motion, the way he touched her, the way he removed her clothes, kissing and caressing her all the while. And when they finally got to the bed, it was like dancing with Fred Astaire, effortless, easy, and oh so natural.

The sun streaming into the window and the birds singing in the morning woke her, and then she heard the sounds of the household, people talking, music playing. She'd been dead to the world. K.C. was still asleep, his body wrapped around hers as it had been all night. The darkness of his skin against the sheets made a startling contrast. His skin, in the daylight, was a luscious color of burnished copper tinged with charcoal. What a lover he had been, better than any she'd ever had. But then, he was an expert. He loved to make love, and knew exactly what to do. And he'd had no other purpose in mind but to bring them both pleasure. This had been a unique experience, making love for the sake of it, not because she was interested in a relationship. K.C. might be a fabulous person, and they might have a lot in common, but those factors, which had always been uppermost in her mind, were not important here.

He stirred and smiled at her, kissed her, and stretched, perfectly at ease with the situation, putting her at ease too. In that delightful moment of contentment, she made a decision. She wouldn't tell Joe about this. There was no need. Being with K.C. had given her back her own. Now, when Joe ran off to do whatever he needed to, she would have this night for herself. It wasn't exactly a secret, it was just proof that she could make her own choices. And wasn't that what independence was all about, feeling good about who you are, without doing it at someone else's expense?

She said good-bye to K.C., and they thanked one another for a wonderful night. Then she gathered up her clothes and got dressed and left the house, driving down the canyon, marveling at the glorious day, wanting to embrace the whole world and give back some of the sense of wonder she was feeling. Life was truly glorious and she reveled in being alive. She felt completely in tune with the joy of living, as if she'd been given a priceless gift, one that would last forever. Whenever she needed it, she could conjure this up in the corner of her mind where it would dwell, relive it and recall it when times were not so wonderful. And there would be many other such adventures like this one, too. How fortunate she felt, how special and privileged, and grateful. *Thank you, God*, she thought, *for giving me life, for making me able to appreciate my body, to adore the sensual touch and feel of another human being, and being able to share my self with someone who understands. Thank you for my intellect, and my special gifts, and whatever it is that I am here for. I am humble before the power of your creations*. And then she laughed to herself to realize what it was that had made her feel more religious than any service she'd ever attended. *Oh well, whatever works, works*, she thought, heading back to the Valley for a shower and a change of clothes.

CHAPTER TWENTY-EIGHT

Joe's play proceeded along the circuitous route of stop and go that had been established for it in the beginning and the two of them avoided discussing whether or not Joe Frazier would ruin the play. Addie called often and Joe gave her advice, but he wasn't seeing her as far as Steffani could tell. In fact, he was more devoted and ardent than ever, buoyed by his excitement over the impending opening of his play and news of how rehearsals were going. But now Steffani knew that the attraction between Joe and Addie wasn't all on Addie's part. What had once been a mere annoyance became a thorn in their relationship. Whenever Addie's name came up, or she called on the phone, Steffani would stop whatever it was she was doing, even if they were making love, and leave the room. If Joe noticed, he didn't say anything about it. But then, a man who couldn't face the truth about one issue, had a basic need to deny other things as well.

October came and went and still the play didn't open; now, it was slated for the first week in December, hopefully in time for the holidays. On Thanksgiving, Steffani went to the family dinner at Suzanne's wishing she could have gone instead with Joe and some of their friends to Jascha Gertsman's.

Suzanne's house was decorated with construction paper turkeys that Amy had made in nursery school, and chains made of pieces of red, gold, and brown strips of paper pasted into circles. By the time she got there everyone had arrived and the house smelled of pies baking, turkey roasting, and vegetables simmering. As she came into the entry hall, she was happy to be here. That lasted about five minutes.

In the kitchen, Lynnette was basting the turkey and gave her a cheek to kiss, only shifting her concentration from the turkey baster as she squirted the pan juices over the bird long enough to glance critically at Steffani's outfit, bought at swap meets and secondhand shops on Western Avenue. "Is that a new outfit, honey?"

Steffani ignored the look. "The turkey smells wonderful, Mom." Nobody made a turkey like her mother, even if Lynnette did say so herself. The meat was never dry, always moist and juicy, because of the special way she stuffed it, by putting the stuffing directly under the skin of the breast so that it formed a protective layer over the meat, and not merely filling the cavity of the bird like other people did.

Aunt Sima, her father's sister, who was unwrapping her contribution to the meal, said, "What have you got on, Steffani? My aunt Selena had a skirt like that and I gave it to the Goodwill when she died."

"Maybe this is the same one," Steffani teased.

Steffani left the kitchen and went into the family room greeting everyone: Suzanne, wearing a purple-and-gold striped velvet jumpsuit/hostess outfit, probably the ugliest thing Steffani had ever seen; Alex, behind the bar pouring Bloody Marys; Alex's parents and sister, Gloria; and Steffani's uncle Rausch, and her cousins Elaine and Arlene. Of all of them, only her father embraced her.

"Hi, daughter, long time no see." He was wearing a blue-and-gray argyle sweater vest and gray flannel slacks and a blue linen shirt that matched his eyes. He took her cape and gave her a warm hug and she smelled the bourbon, but he never had more than one drink.

He's getting older, she thought, noticing the extra sag to his skin, the kind of jowliness to his cheeks. His luxurious dark hair had more gray in it than before, and it was getting a little thin on top. It made her sad to see his changes and she felt so much love for him it almost made her cry; but just then, Gloria Winston, who she called the poor man's diva, even though Gloria would probably be a famous singer one day, came up to them and hooked her arm through Burt's, demanding his attention.

"Did I tell you about the rehearsal yesterday?" she asked loudly, confidently.

Steffani felt a rush of jealousy, which she tried to fight. But dammit, it was bad enough having had Suzanne to compete with all her life without this jerk-ess hanging all over her father. She had an intense impulse to just push Gloria away, but her father, bless him, patted Gloria's hand and removed her arm from his.

"Just give me a minute with Steffani, will you, sweetheart, and then I'll hear all about it."

Steffani gave Gloria a sly smile and raised one eyebrow in triumph. Gloria tossed her head, flopped onto a nearby sofa, crossed her legs, wrapped her arms across her chest, and thrust out her lower lip in a pout. "I'm not waiting very long," she threatened.

Steffani almost burst out laughing, but she contained herself. *What a brat*, she thought.

"So what's doing with you?" her father asked, giving her

another hug. She smelled his cologne this time and felt his soft, freshly shaved cheek against hers.

"Nothing much. I got an A on my history midterm, and a B+ on a paper in psych."

"And how's Joe? I hope you understood why we couldn't include him tonight, it was just family."

"Sure," she said, not wanting to get into this again. Her parents didn't like Joe, (a) because he wasn't working; (b) because he wasn't Jewish; and (c) because *she* liked him. When she asked her mother if she could bring him to Thanksgiving, Lynnette had said, "I'll discuss it with your father," who said, "It's Suzanne's party, we'd better ask her," who said, "I think it's only going to be a family affair." By then, she didn't care to push it any longer.

"Joe is getting ready for New York," she replied.

"I thought you were going to be staying at home this Thanksgiving weekend," he said wistfully.

"Oh Dad, you see me all the time. I wanted to stay with Melody." Actually, she was staying at Joe's, but she couldn't tell that to her father.

"I hope we'll see more of you when you come home for Christmas break. I really miss you when you're not there."

She nodded, noncommittally, thinking, *Not if I can help it*. "You know, Joe's play opens next week."

"Really? They've actually got an opening date set?"

"I told you it would happen," she said, defensively.

"Still, I'll believe it when I see it."

"Burt," Gloria called from the sofa, gazing up through her eyelashes like a sorrowful doe, "are you through yet?"

This time he turned and nodded, going over to sit beside her.

"Is there anything I can do to help?" Steffani asked Suzanne. She was putting more small slices of rye bread around the pâté platter.

"I could have used some help this afternoon, setting up," Suzanne told her. "But now, everything is done. We should be ready to eat soon." She looked at Steffani's outfit with the same expression Lynnette had used. The blouse was from the thirties, rayon crepe with rose and yellow flowers on it. The skirt was a patchwork of ruby, black, and brown velvets with touches of brocade here and there. Some of it had come from authentic antique quilts, and she thought the worn places had been mended quite cleverly. She was wearing a lace piano scarf wrapped around her neck a few times because it was very long, and a series of six brooches, pinned across her shoulder, held the scarf in place, hiding some of the holes and mended places in the lace. The high-button, patent leather boots were the only new thing she was wearing, but she wore them so much, they were a bit scuffed. Actually, it was her favorite outfit; she thought it expressed her personality perfectly.

By contrast, Suzanne's sleeveless one-piece horror was molded to her slender body, and had enormous bell-shaped pants that flared at the ankles, managing to wrap around her calves when she walked. She was wearing a gold hip belt, gold square-toed shoes that matched the gold stripe in the outfit, gold modern dangly earrings, and a brass slave bracelet up around her biceps. To Steffani, she looked like an extra from *Cleopatra*, even if the outfit had come from Joseph Magnin's.

In order to get through the rest of the evening she snuck into her sister's bathroom, took a few hits off a joint from her purse, and thought about what dinner would be like at the Gertsmans' tonight. Nobody would have to sneak off to smoke a joint, it would be out in the open. And there would be poetry—Blake, Gibran, Ginsberg—and each person would take turns saying what he or she was grateful for; probably someone would say "orgies," and someone else would say "not getting the clap," and things like that, and of course, they would attack the government's military actions. Here, at Suzanne's, the government would be defended tonight. Her father was a hawk; and though it galled her to hell, she couldn't make him see her point of view. He'd voted for Goldwater, for God's sake (a fact she'd never admitted to any of her friends). The Gertsmans' stereo would be playing loudly, probably the Beatles, Crosby, Stills and Nash, some hard rock, Janis, Kristofferson, and people would sing along. There might even be Greek dancing with Jascha, who was an expert, leading the men. And who would Joe be flirting with? Anyone who'd flirt back, she decided. But she felt mellow enough not to mind.

She heard them calling her name, carefully pinched out her toke, opened the window, and went to join the family.

When Steffani got to the Gertsmans' around ten, the house was in a happy disarray. It was just as she'd envisioned, except that Joe was close to drunk, sitting in a corner by himself, dozing. Melody saw her come in and tried to catch her attention, waving excitedly, making motions for her to be quiet, but she was feeling very little pain herself from all the wine at dinner and the joint she'd finished on the way over, and didn't pick up the message. Instead, she called out loudly, "Happy Thanksgiving, everybody," and Joe woke up.

The look he gave her sent chills down her body.

Steffani glanced at Melody, who shook her head and then shrugged as if to say, "You're in for it," but by then, Joe had taken her arm and was pulling her out the door.

"Hey," she protested, "what gives. I don't want to leave, I just got here."

"Shut up, cunt," he said, growling in her ear as he pulled her down the front stairs of the duplex.

Her heart was slamming against her ribs from the fear that had gripped her with his unexpected fury. All her life, she'd been attacked like this by her own body—suddenly, violently—but never from an outsider. Joe's behavior, coming at her like that out of nowhere, triggered complete terror. But, if she gave in to it, anything might happen.

"What is it?" She heard her own scared voice, almost whining, begging for him not to be angry. It was one thing to have provoked him in a fight when she knew what she'd done, that she could have handled. This was just too frightening.

"You know goddamn well," he insisted, propelling her forward with such force she almost fell. She felt herself giving way, almost ready to scream, to beg him to stop and tell her what was wrong. She would have admitted to anything, pleaded with all her might for this not to be happening. But when he slammed her back against the passenger side of a car parked on the street, something snapped, and instead of falling apart, she became furious.

"Get your hands off me," she shouted, yanking her shoulders away from his grip, her voice filled with as much power as she could manage. "If you touch me like that again, I'll kick you in the balls. I'll scream. I'll have you arrested for assault, you shithead. You'll be spending Christmas in jail instead of in New York at your opening."

He was surprised by her attack, thrown off guard for a moment, long enough for her to push him away. "You damned bully, what the hell do you think you're doing?" The more she defied him, the angrier she got. It seemed to work, for he was calming down.

"We're through, baby," he said. "That's it, I've had it."

Now her heart was pounding again. What kind of a nightmare was this?

"Okay, fine. We're through. Now, for God's sake, will you tell me what's wrong?"

"You know! You know!"

"I don't know!"

A neighbor across the street stuck his head out of an upper-story window and shouted, "Keep it down out there!"

"Shut the fuck up," Joe retorted, "or I'll come up and shut it for you."

The man slammed down the window.

"Joe, calm down," she admonished.

He pulled back his hand as if to hit her, but her glare stopped him. With great effort he lowered his arm. "Don't you—tell—me—to—calm—down." He spoke from between clenched jaws. "You fucking bitch, you no-good tramp."

Then she knew. *K.C.* Somehow, he'd found out about her and K.C. For a moment, she was scared, and then she grew very calm. If only she was sober, she would have been able to think more clearly. Her only consolation was that he was drunk too.

"You going to say it, or do you want me to?" she asked.

"You fucked that nigger, didn't you."

"Oh brother! Don't tell me this is the great liberal playwright, Joe Mariano, speaking? Suddenly his black brothers are niggers, when they do something he doesn't personally like? That's great, Joe. Real liberal, Joe. Real humanitarian, real Catholic."

"You're a whore, you know that?"

"I've been called one before. But I'm not. You sure can dish it out, but you can't take it, can you, big man? What I do when you're out balling your brains out is my business, not yours. If you can't take it, then okay, I guess we're through. I'd be sorry to see that happen, because we're good together."

The thought that they were actually through was too unreal for her at the moment. Life without him was impossible, she'd have to make him see that. But attacking him wouldn't win her any points. Somehow, in all her anger and her need to defend, she knew that.

"What's that supposed to mean, when I'm balling my brains out?" he asked.

"When you're out screwing Addie, or whoever else you're screwing, you have no right to expect me to sit home waiting."

He blinked once, then twice, slowly, the way a drunk reacts, not believing what he'd heard, as though his ears weren't working, and somehow blinking his eyes would clear his hearing. He tried to shake his head, but again his motions were too slow. She knew exactly how he felt.

"I didn't do that."

"And I didn't either," she retorted.

"I know you did, I found out."

"How?"

"I heard Melody talking to that shithead. She brought him here to dinner tonight. They didn't know I was listening. That's some friend you've got, Melody. She wanted to know who was better in bed, you or her, the stupid cunt. He's a real winner," he scoffed. "You sure can pick 'em. He was only too glad to compare. The bastard stood there describing what you do, the way you sound, the things you did."

She hurt inside so badly, it felt like a wound. The humiliation burned like acid in her stomach; she felt her face flush, her eyes fill with tears. There were tears in his eyes too.

"I wanted to tear him apart, first because he was such a bastard, talking about you that way. And second, because I knew what he was saying was true. How could you do those things with him, when you do them with me?"

She wanted to cry, to hide her head in shame, to fall into his arms and have it all be untrue. But instead, she stood there holding his gaze, keeping her composure, learning one of the bitterest lessons of her life. In this new modern age, nothing was sacred.

"I'm sorry you were hurt," she said, reaching for his hand.

He wouldn't let her take it. "I really loved you, babe," he whispered.

"Even when you were fucking Addie?" she asked.

"I didn't know you then," he replied, trying to regain his own defiance, but it was a weak attempt.

"You knew me two weeks ago when I sat outside her house at one in the morning and waited for you to leave and come home to me. But you didn't."

"You followed me?" Now he was incredulous. *Interesting, the gamut he ran*, she thought, *to maintain denial.* "How dare you do that?"

"Gee, I don't know. I guess I really loved you too, babe," she threw back.

He lowered his head as if all the fight was gone out of him, but she knew there'd be more in the morning. "I want to get out of here," he said. "You got your car?"

"Yes," she replied, nodding down the street to where it was parked.

He held out his hand for the keys. "I'll drive," he said.

"I think you're more drunk than I am," she said. "I'll drive."

But he shouted, "Don't argue, goddamnit, will you? Just give me the fucking keys."

She did.

The Gertsmans lived on Holt off of Olympic Boulevard, and Joe lived on Sweetzer Avenue in West Hollywood. They were heading up La Cienega Boulevard when Joe fell asleep at the wheel and the car started to career toward a lamppost. Steffani saw it coming, screamed, "Watch out," and tried to brace herself, but her face slammed into the windshield.

She wrote a lot during that time in the hospital, in between the bad times, letters to Joe trying to explain what had happened, analyzing their relationship, analyzing their future, congratulating him on the opening of his play on Broadway. Right after he was released from the hospital, he was called to New York for final rehearsals. At first, he telephoned every day. He was truly sorry she couldn't be with him, and even sorrier for the accident. Her parents wanted to press charges for negligence, and driving under the influence, but she wouldn't let them. How she regretted that night. But she'd learned another important lesson: never would she turn control of her life over to anyone, ever again, against her better judgment, no matter how they yelled or tried to intimidate her. How easily everything could change, with a snap of a finger or a nod of the head. And now she'd been in the hospital for two weeks and had eight platelet transfusions and vitamin K, and still her broken nose would not stop hemorrhaging. "I might as well be a vampire," she told them every time it started bleeding again. The clotting factor, the white count, the Gaucher's problem, their inability to help her, none of it mattered as much as getting out of here and resuming her life. The only good news was that she would have Christmas break in which to recuperate, take her finals in January on time, and not lose a semester of credits.

Jascha Gertsman and Melody went to the opening and told her the play closed after six performances; the critics hated it. Joe and the producers railed against the critics, insisting there was an Eastern conspiracy against anything from California. She didn't know whether to believe that or not.

By the time the play closed, Joe had stopped calling. She tried him at his hotel but he'd checked out, and his family didn't know where he was. It was the final blow to her flagging spirits, plunging her into greater misery. He wasn't calling because he was terribly disappointed about the play and guilty about the accident, but she needed him, needed the promise of them to keep her going. Her entire being longed for him to be with her, if not in person, then at least long distance. But the phone never rang.

She wasn't supposed to cry, the doctors warned that it would irritate her sinus membranes and exacerbate an already dangerous condition, but she had to do something to ease the ache inside and the fear that never left her for a moment, that the bleeding wouldn't stop. So, she wrote.

> On the X-ray table
> metal, narrow, icy
> pinned under the glaring light,
> a gnat lies, helpless, hopeless, hurting;
> poked at with stainless steel feelers
> by some overpowering giant insect
> a glistening mirrored monster
> equipped with metal magic
>
> Faces behind their masks unreadable,
> designed for facelessness,
> Only mine expresses fear
>
> Oh, help me

> *with your metal magic,*
> *to stop my bleeding flow*
> *the blood-sheets grow*
> *while my soul is leaking,*
> *and metal monsters don't know what to do*
>
> *But suddenly, I know*
> *what dying is*

Eventually she began to heal. The bleeding slowed to an ooze and she was released from the hospital into her parents' care, still with her sinuses packed, and with the warning to curtail her activities, eat the proper foods, and try to keep herself from becoming upset. So there was nothing she could do but put Joseph Mariano out of her mind and concentrate on school. And that's what she did, summoning her indomitable spirit to see her through.

CHAPTER TWENTY-NINE

When Curtis McCartney left it was nearly eleven o'clock. All the time I was talking to the lawyer in the living room, I could hear Steffani coughing in the other room. Eventually she stopped and fell asleep on the family room sofa, for which I was grateful.

After Barry and I said good night to McCartney and closed the door, he put his arms around me and held me, and in that moment, the dam burst and I started to sob. All the memories of my past that I had discussed with the lawyer had been painful, adding weight to the fears I had at the moment. I had not wanted to lose control like this with Barry, but I couldn't help it. He held me until I calmed down.

"You'll get through this, Suzanne," he said, wiping my cheeks, which were streaked with mascara.

I could tell he was speaking from experience of what it was like to suffer excruciating pain and get through it. The pain he'd endured, like Steffani's, one doesn't always survive, yet he was here comforting me and so was she.

I gave him a wan smile and nodded. "I'm not the most romantic date, am I?" I teased. "Wouldn't you prefer someone without traumas in her life?"

"Not at all," he said, giving me a smile filled with courage, but I felt as though I'd touched a nerve. And that really scared me. I realized I shouldn't lean on him so much. We barely knew one another, and I didn't want to turn him off this early in our relationship. But, oh God, I needed someone to lean on. How had the two of them done it? I wondered, both Barry and Steffani. They'd dealt with their traumas alone, relying only on themselves. Of course, Barry had family and friends, and so did Steffani, but that was different than having a mate to share with, someone who was there for you alone. Those thoughts made me miss Alex with an unreasonable ache, even though, during our marriage, I hadn't ever been able to lean on him. Now that we were divorced, it seemed crazy to still be nurturing that same fantasy. *Let it go!* I told myself.

Steffani slept on the sofa all night and I didn't disturb her. But I barely slept myself, reliving the horrible day, remembering what it felt like to be locked in a cell. When I woke from a fitful sleep the next morning she was gone for an early appointment.

The children were quietly subdued at breakfast, pouring their milk and cereal in silence. I longed to liven things up, but no attempt at conversation or humor worked.

Finally, Miles said, "You'd better tell us what to expect, Mom. It's kind of hard on us to keep imagining the worst."

I was brought up short by his demand. I had thought I'd have a much longer time to deal with this, to prepare my speech, to offer alternatives. But since my arrest everything had been speeded up.

I was about to reply to him when the phone rang. It was Esther.

"How are you?" she asked, truly concerned.

"I'm making it at the moment, thanks to my family." I smiled at Amy, who gave me a brave smile back.

"Well, brace yourself," Esther said. "I got a call from Judy this morning. She wanted to know how you are, and whether you were terribly upset about being arrested."

"I guess it was on the national news?" I asked. I had expressly avoided watching television last night, though I knew Amy and Miles had stayed up for the eleven o'clock edition.

"Yes, it was. Everybody's behind you, Suzanne. I've had calls all morning from people anxious to support you, other writers, people in publishing. Nobody believes you did it. It's totally out of character!"

"Thanks, Esther. Now, it's up to my lawyer to prove it."

"I mean, how stupid could you be, to send candy laced with LSD and then sign your name to a note."

I sighed. If this was what conversations with well-meaning friends would be like, I was in for a hard time.

"What else did Judy say? Did you talk about the two-book deal?"

The silence was ominous. "Honey, they've withdrawn their offer. They can't afford to publish you while this other thing is going on."

Oh God, I hadn't realized that could happen. I'd been so busy feeling sorry for myself over being wrongly accused and arrested, I hadn't considered what the results might be. Now, of course it seemed logical, if totally unfair. "Can they do that? Aren't they bound by their word?" I wanted to scream and cry, stamp my foot, shake my fists at the gods, but there were three pairs of eyes watching me.

"Technically, yes. But I doubt that you'd want to sue them over it. That wouldn't make a particularly happy author-publisher relationship."

"But why are they doing this?"

"You have to understand, they're panicked. They don't want adverse publicity if they can avoid it, remember how they were over that book you wanted to do with Sugar Markham? If you're convicted, it would have an effect on your sales. They want to wait and see what happens with your trial, although Judy assured me she's certain you'll be cleared. And of course, as your publisher, they're concerned about being sued too by Brett Slocum."

I hadn't believed anything worse could happen to me, but I was wrong. Without a book deal there was no hope of saving myself. What would the IRS do, I wondered, if I couldn't pay them? What would we live on, if my next book wasn't going to be published? Should I even keep on writing?

The children were staring at me, aware that I'd just received bad news. But I didn't want to burden them or frighten them. Miles was still waiting for the answer to his question.

"Esther, I have to drive carpool today. I'll call you when I get home." And I hung up on her. Somehow, being a parent, the one responsible for those three lives sitting at my kitchen table, gave me the strength to act.

"Miles, you asked me a good question about what we should expect. And I know you want some answers. But, I've got a lot on my mind right now. Why don't we wait until after school. By then, I'll have time to assess everything; maybe we'll even have some good news."

My smile felt as though it were cracking a china mask that adhered to my cheeks.

Jered got up from the table and came over to where I was standing by the phone. He put his arms around my waist and hugged me. "I love you, Mommy," he said.

"I love you too, sweetheart," I told him, choking on the words.

I saw Amy wiping away tears from her cheeks.

"Come on, guys. Let's not give up yet!"

"We've got our health. Right, Mom?" Miles said.

And I nodded. "Darn right, we do." And I went to get my purse and my keys. That's when I remembered something from my conversation with Esther that hadn't registered at the time. *Sugar Markham*. I'd forgotten all about her when I was thinking of possible suspects. Sugar Markham was just crazy enough to have done this. I'd tell Avery Bellows about her as soon as I got home from driving carpool.

Bellows was glad to hear from me. "I'm working on your case right now, Mrs. Winston. Curtis sent everything over to me yesterday afternoon. We're trying to trace the person who bought the candy. Meanwhile I want to interview everybody in your life. Everybody, you hear me?"

"Let's use first names, Avery, okay?"

He agreed.

"I've come up with a possible suspect. Her name is Sugar Markham." I couldn't help feeling excited. "Several years ago I optioned the rights to her life to do a book on her, but my editors didn't like the idea; they thought my readers wouldn't accept a story like that from me. If I'd been a journalist who wrote exposés or someone like Ovid Demaris, they'd consider it. Also, they were worried about the legalities of proving her story; nothing came of it."

"Tell me about it," he said.

"Sugar was a teenaged prostitute in New York. One of her tricks kidnapped her and kept her a sexual prisoner in Japan for two years. I optioned the rights to her life because I wanted to use the actual details. She wanted to expose the Japanese syndicate that had victimized her and was really upset when I told her the project was off. She said I owed her a book, that she had jeopardized her safety by telling me her story and I had taken advantage of her, that I was dead meat. Her exact words were, 'You bitch, you shot me down. You did worse to me than they did.' "

"Did she ever make any threats?"

"Not exactly. But this was several years ago. Maybe she went nuts in the meantime and decided to take it out on me."

"How did you meet her?"

"She was turning tricks in the Oyster Bar at the Plaza in New York and she recognized me when I came in with Alex. She introduced herself and told me I had to write her story.

Now, I hear that from a lot of people. But hers was fascinating. I just realized something. She lives in New York. She could have sent that candy!"

"Do you know how I can reach her?"

"I have her old address, and I know her parents. They live in Brooklyn."

"Give me any information you have on her," he said. "I'll see what I can find out. And Suzanne, this is very encouraging. A real possibility. Good thinking."

"How long do you think this will take?" I asked him.

"There's no way of knowing. You go about your business and leave it to me. If I have anything to report, you'll be the first to know."

Hope. It was a gift of gold and raised my spirits somewhat.

The rest of the day I spent talking to mortgage brokers and real estate agents. It came down to this: If I sold our home and was found innocent, we'd have nothing to go back to. If I leased the house, it would still be there for us. But a sale brought a higher commission so that's what the brokers preferred. I wanted to be able to offer the children hope that temporary measures might stave off disaster. Was I only postponing the inevitable? Or would making a clean break and selling the house be for the best? Who knew how long it would take Bellows to locate Sugar Markham. I had to talk to the children. Every defeat drained my remaining spirit.

"You understand, Mrs. Winston," one of the brokers told me. "Selling or leasing a property can take months, unless you really lower the price of your home." She made that comment while studying a worn place on the carpet of my living room.

The phone rang all the time they were here, but I let the service pick up. When they left the only call I returned was Alex's.

"Jesus, Suzanne, what have you gotten yourself into? How could you let this get so out of control?" I was sorry I'd called him back.

"Don't dump on me, Alex. It's bad enough right now."

"Do you know what this is going to do to the children? This could affect them for the rest of their lives."

"They'll be all right." But I had no idea how they would explain this to their friends.

"All right, my ass. Where are they now?"

"At school," I said, suddenly realizing I might have done the wrong thing by sending them.

"How could you send them to school to face this alone?" he yelled.

"Alex, they wanted to go. They'd have to go eventually anyway. And speaking of school, I won't be able to pay next semester's tuition. Can you help out, just for now?"

I could feel the animosity. "Are you kidding? You know how strapped I am right now, the same as you!"

"Could you borrow it from Dina?"

"No way!" he insisted. "They're not Dina's children. I resent your even asking."

I hated having to ask my ex-husband's wife to keep my children in school. "They don't want to leave their schools, Alex," I admitted. "Especially now."

He began to get the picture. "You mean send them to public school?"

"Yes."

"Are all the LA schools being bused?"

"You know they are."

"And you think sending them to public school so they can drive an hour each way to end up in Watts is an alternative?" His voice rose. "Is that what you want for our kids?"

"What can I do? With my debts, keeping them in private school is impossible."

"Well, I won't have my children bused," he insisted.

"You'll pay the tuition?" There was hope after all.

"I have another solution," he said, almost too quickly, as if he'd just been waiting to spring this on me. "They'll come and live with me and Dina and go to Beverly Hills schools."

The shock of what he'd just said left me nearly speechless. "I don't believe you. With everything that's happened how can you even suggest such a thing? You've never wanted the children before, why now all of a sudden?" I could barely keep from screaming, *You'll never get them, never*! They were my life. My existence revolved around them. I'd give up anything rather than give up my children.

But what if I can't afford to keep them with me? Oh please, don't let this happen, I begged whoever might be listening. It got worse the more I thought about it. I was depriving them of a safe and superior education for my own selfish needs.

I was beginning to hyperventilate. "Alex, I don't want to talk about this now. There's still time to make a decision."

I was about to hang up when he dropped the real bomb. "Think about this, Suzanne. If I have to sue you for custody to keep those kids in a good environment, I will. I'd probably win, too. Family court judges don't take kindly to mothers who are accused of poisoning a critic merely for writing an honest review." And he hung up.

After Alex's call, I acted on impulse—jumped into my car and drove like a demon into Century City. I had no idea what I expected Barry to do for me once I got there, but I couldn't think of anything else. I had no focus, no plan, only a desperate need for advice.

The first lucky thing that had happened to me in days was that Barry didn't have a client with him. But when I arrived unexpectedly at his office with an expression of tragedy in my eyes, his face drained of all its color and he cried out, "For God's sake, what happened?"

"Nothing, nothing," I assured him, not thinking of how he would react to hearing disastrous news. I was filled with remorse for my thoughtlessness.

"I'm so sorry for frightening you," I said, stopping in front of the desk, trying to give a comforting smile. "Everyone's alive, no one's dead."

The color slowly returned to his cheeks as he stared at me, calming down. But then he slumped back in his chair, hid his face in his hands, and I knew he was crying. When he looked up at me again, after he contained himself, he was furious.

"Don't ever do that to me again!" he said, barely able to control his anger.

I wanted to comfort him the way he had comforted me last night, but I just stood there feeling miserable.

"Why are you here?"

I didn't want to tell him, but I felt more foolish refusing. "I've come up with a possible suspect. Bellows is checking it out." Then, I told him what Alex had said about taking the children.

"What do you want me to do, Suzanne?" he asked.

I had really overstepped my bounds. My problems were not so earth-shattering, by comparison to his loss. "I'm sorry I came," I said, sickened by how cold he was. I didn't blame him. Both of us were in a state of shock, brought about by our own need for comfort; neither of us could give it at the moment. "I'm so sorry," I repeated, my voice low, almost a whisper. He was just staring at me with a terrible look on his face. I could see what was replaying in his head, those indescribable moments of pain when he'd been told that Eileen had died.

How selfish I felt, how juvenile, how incapable of independence. This was wrong of me. I'd known it in some part of my brain as I was driving here, but had ignored the warnings. And now, standing here, watching him suffer, realizing that he was only a human being, as I was, that he had no magic solutions for me, I felt as if I'd just been through fire; it forged a new will within me. Never again would I rush to someone else desperate for them to help me. No one else had answers for me. I had to rely only on myself the way my sister did. I felt suddenly free, emancipated.

"Forgive me, Barry," I said, turning to go. "I never meant to hurt you like this."

It wasn't a large office and we had the desk between us, but somehow, as I reached the door, he was there too. His hand closed over mine and he said in my ear, "Don't go. I don't know what came over me. But I don't want you to go."

I turned around to face him and we held one another until both of us felt whole again. I looked up at him, ready to apologize, but there was no need.

Our lips met, quietly at first, a healing kiss. Until it deepened with our hunger, until we were devouring one another, seeking aid, drawing solace, absorbing from one another the knowledge that we were alive, that there was forgiveness in the world, and mercy. I heard the lock on the door click behind me and it was the last real sound I heard, for his urgency matched mine as we pulled at one another's clothing and made love in his office, half on the sofa and half on the floor. Our bodies were so hungry that we were panting, thrusting, grabbing, touching, and merging in a mutuality of passion born of despair. The excitement built and built, and even the realities of sofa arms and scratchy carpet, occasional buttons, zippers, and the constrictions of clothing half-on, half-off, didn't impede our momentum, until we were in sync, enmeshed and entwined, our chemistry firing each other. We both climaxed within moments of one another, and then just lay there panting, out of breath as our frenzy abated. I started to laugh first, and then he joined me, a kind of breathless hilarity.

"Haven't had it for a while, I guess?" I teased.

"You either, I see," he said, smoothing the hair from my brow, where it was stuck by perspiration.

Our bodies were still bound together and neither of us pulled away. He gazed into my eyes and smiled. I smiled back, grateful to be alive in the moment, not allowing myself to think of anything but this, right here, right now.

"Hello," he said.

"Hello, yourself," I replied, reaching up to kiss him, this time slowly and with achingly tender passion. I was so aware of the feel of him, the taste and smell of him, so unique. I wanted to burrow into him like an animal.

He too nuzzled me, learning, enjoying, until carefully we pulled apart and shyly recomposed our clothing.

"What would have happened if the phone had rung?" I asked him.

"My secretary holds my calls in an emergency."

"Does she call a quickie on the office floor an emergency?"

"Definitely." He grinned.

We stood up and put our arms around one another and I wanted to sing with joy. In this one brief moment, I felt that everything would be all right. Sugar Markham would be proven guilty, I would be off the hook, all would be back to normal again, and I'd end up with Barry.

"I'm falling in love with you, Suzanne," he said. "And it scares me. You're not exactly the most stable person to love right now."

"But I'm alive," I told him, so glad to be.

And he nodded. "So am I. And I don't think I have been for the past ten months."

"Will I see you tonight?"

"Can't keep me away," he replied, pressing his groin against my hip. He was already getting hard again.

"How can this be happening in the midst of everything?" I asked him.

"Like my grandmother always said, 'Life goes on.' "

I nodded and kissed him good-bye.

So, I was on the brink of a romance while my life was falling apart, the only bright spot in a world of darkness and gloom.

Later that afternoon when I had dropped off the rest of the children in our carpool, it was time for a talk with my own.

The three of us piled on my bed, our favorite place. Amy lay on her side across the foot of the bed, Miles was on the floor using the bed as a table with his elbows supporting his chin, and Jered curled up next to me against the blue-and-white Delft print pillows.

"I guess you all know, I've had money problems, lately."

"So has Dad," Miles said.

"Yes, well we both owe the government a lot of money because of a bad investment. It wasn't our fault, the man we trusted with our money was a crook."

"That seems to be happening a lot, lately," Miles commented.

I hoped he wasn't referring to me.

"Well, now I have to pay a lawyer so things are going to be even tighter than we thought."

"I can give up my allowance," Jered offered.

I squeezed his hand. "That's really wonderful, sweetie," I said. "But it's more serious than that." I took a deep breath, wishing I could couch this in easier terms, but I just had to say it.

"We'll have to move, won't we?" Amy guessed, glancing at Miles, who kept his face impassive.

"Where will we go?" Jered asked, showing his fear. "To a condo?" Some of his friends lived in condominiums.

"No," I said, swallowing the lump in my throat. "I can't afford a condo." The ones his friends lived in were large and luxurious, with pools and recreation rooms. "It will probably be an apartment."

"What happened really, Mother?" Amy said, her voice beginning to show its panic. At fifteen, appearances were important. What would her friends think if her family was forced to sell their house?

"What do you mean, Amy?" I asked.

"I mean, is this your fault? I mean, whose fault is this?"

"I don't know," I said softly. "You know someone is trying to hurt me and we don't know who it is, yet. For the moment, they're succeeding. That's why it's so important for us four to stick together. If we remain strong, then whatever that sick person does won't affect us as much."

"What do you mean?" her voice had risen two octaves. She wanted a concrete explanation of something inexplicable.

"Amy, you know about the letters; someone accused me of plagiarism, which I didn't do. And probably that same person sent drugged candy to Brett Slocum and signed my name, which is why the police arrested me. My private detective is trying to find out who it is."

"And who planted the drug in our refrigerator," Miles added, good at the details of a mystery.

"But why?" Amy was almost crying. "What did you do to them?"

"I don't know, honey." I was surprisingly calm. "If I knew who was doing it, I'd know why. But most likely, there is no logical reason, only a deranged, sick one."

"Don't they know there are little kids involved," she said, indicating Jered. But she meant herself.

"They know," I said, softly. "They just don't care."

"What are we going to do, Mom?" Miles asked.

"The best we can," I said. "The way we always have. We're a family, and we're here for one another. We'll get through this."

"Are you going to jail?" Jered asked.

"No, Jered," I said, as firmly as I could manage. "That's not going to happen."

"Why not?" Amy asked, her lower lip trembling.

"Because Mr. McCartney and Mr. Bellows are going to see that I don't pay for a crime I didn't commit." How I prayed that would be true.

"When do we have to move?" Miles asked. "Can we wait until after the holidays?"

"I think it might be easier if we moved over vacation, then you can settle in our new home before school starts in January."

"I don't want a new home," Miles said. "I want this one."

I patted his hand in sympathy, but he pulled it away.

"Is an apartment a home?" Jered asked.

"Any place you hang your hat is home," I said, rather lamely.

"It's not," Amy said, "it's little, and cramped, and we'll be on top of each other."

Miles turned his head over so that his face was away from me. He was the one I was most worried about.

"Can we have two bathrooms at least?" Amy continued, aware of the disadvantages.

"I'll try," I told her.

"Well, I'm sure not bringing any of my friends home to visit!" she threatened.

"I'm sure that some of your new friends will live in apartments too," I said, quietly.

"What do you mean?" she was slightly belligerent. "None of my friends at Buckley live in apartments."

"You won't be going to Buckley, honey," I told her. "Or the boys either. I won't be able to afford private schools anymore."

Miles lifted up his head now and looked at me in shock, as though I'd struck him. "But Mom, that's my school. I'm on the team. Next year I'll be in ninth grade. That's the year we go to the science camp. I can't miss that!"

"I know," I told him. "It's going to be hard on all of us."

"What about busing?" Miles said. The dreaded word. Children all over the city had been threatened by that word and what it implied.

"We'll have to take our chances," I said, wishing I could be more reassuring.

"What does Dad say?" Miles asked. "Won't he pay our tuition?"

"It doesn't matter," Amy said, feeling remorse. "We couldn't take the money for private school from Dad when Mom is having such a hard time. I couldn't, at least. I don't know about you."

Miles hung his head. It was clear he would have gladly taken the money.

"Your father had another suggestion," I said, holding my breath. "He can't afford private tuition right now, either, but he said you three could go and live with him and go to school in Beverly Hills. You wouldn't be bused and you'd get a good education. And all of you have friends who go to school there. Maybe it wouldn't be as much of an adjustment for you."

"Live with Daddy?" Jered said, his eyes growing round, and then he started to laugh as though it was a joke. In Jered's world, children didn't live with their father, for he never had.

"That means Dina too," Amy said, holding her nose.

Miles cracked up, laughing hard and inappropriately. It wasn't that funny.

"Would he really want us?" Amy asked.

I tried to nod, but my head wouldn't move. "Yes," I managed to say.

"I want to stay with you," Jered said, throwing himself in my lap.

I grabbed him and half hugged, half wrestled with him. "We don't have to decide this immediately. There's some time left."

Amy shook her head, as if trying to rid it of a pesky bug, bewildered. How could her whole life have changed so drastically inside of fifteen minutes? Then she stood up. "I sure hope I do a better job of being a parent when I grow up," she said snottily, walking out the door.

"I'm never going to have kids," Miles said morosely, and got up and left the room.

I looked at Jered and smiled. But he had tears in his eyes, and as I hugged him he broke down crying even harder. "What's the matter, Mommy?" he cried. "Can't you make it better? I don't want to go away from here, or my school, or live with Daddy. Please, don't make me, please."

And it was all I could do to keep from crying with him as I hushed and soothed him, overwhelmed by helplessness. As I held him in my arms, and later when I put him to bed, I thought about happier times, when my career had first begun and I'd been filled with joyous excitement. How could it have all come to this?

Amy was in kindergarten and Miles was nearly three years old by the time I completed the sixth draft of my first novel on my college typewriter, a portable Smith Corona with a tendency to travel left across the desk every three sentences; half the time I spent pulling it back in front of me. With the sixth draft, I finally had a sense of completion. People have often asked me what it feels like to type "The End," as though the culmination of all the work and accomplishment is contained in those two little words. The truth is that whenever I get to the end of a draft I'm always thinking, *How many more times will I have to do this before it's really finished.*

My sister was the first to read it and she liked it. Maybe it's because she was sick to death of it by now, or maybe because I'd worn her out with draft after draft, but she said, "It's much improved, Suzanne."

I was flying.

Then Alex read it. "Not bad," he said.

High praise, indeed.

"Do you know an agent we could give it to?" I asked.

He stroked his chin. "I can't do that, Suze. Nepotism is frowned on in my company."

I had thought his company thrived on nepotism.

"If I ask a favor of anybody I work with, then I'll owe them one," Alex told me. "Dangerous." He shook his head. "The powers that be wouldn't like it." That's what he called his bosses at William Morris.

"But what good is having a husband in the business, if I can't ask him to help me?" It occurred to me that I knew the same people he knew, they'd eaten food at my table, spilled guacamole on my linen sofa and wine on my rug. But if I asked them for help and they hated the book, I couldn't have taken it.

"Why doesn't your father find you an agent," he suggested. "He knows everybody."

The heat rose to my cheeks. I couldn't ask my father to help me, he'd have to read the book. There were sex scenes in my book. What had I thought? That my father would be the only one not to read it? Or that he didn't know what I was doing with my husband? He must know that my two children hadn't sprung from Alex and me by spontaneous regeneration. My cheeks flushed hotter. The sex scenes were made-up fantasies. What if he thought I had really done them? *You're a jerk, Suzanne. Your father's a sophisticated man. He won't be shocked.*

But I knew he would. So what to do? Not sell my book because I couldn't face my own father's opinion? For a brief moment, I considered putting the novel in a drawer forever. *This should be the most difficult thing I ever face*, I thought. But showing my father my work took more courage than I had imagined.

He was so proud. He read it immediately, didn't keep me waiting for weeks until he got around to it, the way Alex had, and his praise made up for everything Alex hadn't said.

"I know an agent, Suzanne, an old friend of mine, and I called him. He's agreed to read it. I didn't tell him you were my daughter, just a friend. That way, he'll be honest. We wouldn't want him to feel obligated to praise an unpraiseworthy piece, would we?"

Yes, I thought, *I'll take any praise I can get*.

After several weeks, the agent called. A miracle. He agreed to represent the book if I'd make a few changes, soften it a bit here and there, do a minor rewrite. (There is no such thing as a minor rewrite.)

"You're crazy to listen to him," Alex said. "Agents don't know anything about structure or material, they're only salesmen. Who does he think he is, an editor? Tell him no, don't lower yourself like that."

I suspected that Alex was right. The agent wasn't an editor, but he'd been in the business a long time. Maybe he'd refuse to represent the book unless I made changes. I did the rewrite and didn't tell Alex. The agent took the book.

"What happens now?" I asked Alex.

"Nothing, probably," he told me. "Your chances are between none and slim of selling it, one in a thousand. And don't call him all the time. It takes months for a book to be read by an editor and sent back, and then submitted again."

"Don't the agents send it to more than one publisher at a time?"

"Not usually. It's bad form. If an editor takes the time to read a manuscript and consider it, he wants the courtesy of exclusivity. Besides, there may be other people in the company that need to read it. Unless you've got something so hot that the agent knows several houses who might buy it; then, he'll make a multiple submission and hold an auction to the highest bidder. But don't expect that to happen."

Of course I did. I could just see the auctioneer at the podium, gavel raised as he announced, "What am I bid for

Suzanne Winston's book?'' And all the money would shower down on me like in a movie. (Book auctions are done on the phone, with editors standing by, while the agent calls between the interested parties, but I didn't know that then.)

Six months later, my agent called. ''Is this Suzanne Winston?''

''Yes.''

''Chuck Metzger here.''

My heart began to pound. ''Yes?''

''I have good news for you. I sold your book.''

''What?''

''I sold your book. Of course, it's going to be a paperback original, but that's where all the money is, in paperback. The paperback houses support the hardcover houses you know. They're the ones who pay the high prices for reprint rights. The hardcover houses won't last much longer the way the prices of books are going up these days; why a hardcover book is selling for six ninety-five. The average person can't afford that.''

I wasn't listening; angels' voices were singing in my ears, or else the roaring sound of a roller coaster complete with screaming passengers pounded in my head. My body was suddenly ten feet tall. ''Did you say you sold my book? My God, did you say that?''

''Yes, didn't you hear me?''

''That means I'm a writer, a truly bona fide writer!'' *Wait until Alex hears. And my sister!* I couldn't wait to tell them. ''How did it happen? When did it happen?'' I wanted every detail. The thrill, the thrill, it was the greatest thrill I'd ever had.

''Well, there was an editor in from New York a few months ago and she was looking for a certain kind of book for their best-seller category, and I thought of yours but it was being read by someone at Morrow. So I had to wait until Morrow passed, and then I sent it to her. I knew it was what she wanted, and she bought it. Her name is Michelle Bryant, she's with Silver's Press, and you know how big they are.''

"Paperback?" I tried to withold my judgment; after all, they wanted me.

"That's what I said." He was talking to a dunce. "A first-time author in hardcover usually gets a printing of ten thousand copies and no guarantee of a paperback sale. Silver's is going to print three hundred thousand copies of your book, and you can multiply that by two, because most books are read by more than one person. That's half a million readers right there. Not bad for a first novel."

It was dazzling, even if I'd been hoping to be published in hardcover with my picture on the back.

"Oh, there will be reviews, if that's what's worrying you," he assured me, "and they'll put your picture inside the back cover. They want to send you on a media tour. They're serious, they want to build you into a major writer."

I couldn't believe what I was hearing.

"Have you started your next book yet? They want to see it."

I had, but I hadn't gotten very far. "Do they want many changes in *To Catch a Count*?" I asked.

"The editor will call you," he said.

God, the euphoria. I was afraid if I hung up, it would only be a dream, but I was dying to get him off the phone so I could tell my family. "I'm so grateful, Chuck," I gushed. "You're wonderful. The most wonderful agent in the world."

"Well," he laughed, agreeing with me. "It was my knowing exactly where to send this book that got it sold."

"Is there anything else?" I asked.

"Of course there's the money."

"What money?" *Did I owe them anything?* I wondered.

"The money they're paying you, Suzanne."

My God, I get money too? I thought. And then, *Of course I get money. Writers get paid.* "How much is it?"

"Fifteen thousand dollars."

"Oh." It was a staggering amount.

"I know you're not thrilled," his voice soothed, "but it's not bad for a first time. I promise, next time, I'll get you much more."

"Okay," I said, playing it cool and thinking, *I'm rich! Alex's salary for his first year in practice was fifteen thousand dollars*.

"I'll let you know when the contracts arrive, and in the meantime, the editor will call you."

I know I thanked him and hung up the phone and functioned like a normal person, but I was hardly that. I was a writer, about to take my place among the greats. Even a lowly place was a place after all. All my life I'd been intimidated by the literary giants who had inspired me, and the only way I was able to write was to think of them up there, and myself down here. The fact that we all did the same thing, sat alone day after day putting words and story on paper, wrestling with the problems of plot and character, research and point of view, hardly made me their equal. But halfway through my fourth draft, I realized that we are all born with certain abilities; some have more than others. But for those of us with less, we have to work our hardest, struggle to be the best we can, improve with every try, and dedicate ourselves to excellence. Then we are the equal of anyone. Besides, there was a place for my kind of work in the world of books, just as there was for great literature. So I tried to feel proud instead of just lucky and called my husband at the office.

He was in a meeting.

I called my sister. She was not at her apartment, and nobody answered.

My mother's answering service told me she was photographing a family portrait and would call me back.

My father was with a client, but he took my call. "Hi sweetheart, guess who's here with me? Gloria."

My sister-in-law, the opera singer. Her career had grown steadily over the last few years. Her latest contract was with the Cleveland Opera. I didn't know she was in town.

"Hi, Suze," I heard her call out from across the room.

"What's doin with you'n?" my father kidded.

I couldn't tell him with Gloria there. If she found out I'd sold my book before anybody else, she'd tell the world before I had a chance. Since that night at the Wilshire Ebell, my father'd been her agent, and he spent more time on her career than several other of his clients put together. But he said she was on her way, it was only a matter of time. I heard more about Gloria, from both my father and my husband, than I wanted to.

"I have some news for you, Dad," I told him, "but I don't want to share it with Gloria, so why don't you call back when you're alone."

"Oh, tell me now, sweetheart," he insisted, weakening me. But I held firm.

"I'll call you at home tonight so Mom can hear too," I promised, hanging up.

This news was so good it was burning my tongue, but I still hadn't told anyone. It was late, and I had to go to the market, so off I went, my sweet secret bubbling inside of me. When I finally reached the checkout counter I couldn't hold it in any longer and blurted out to the woman at the cash register, "Guess what?" I said. "I sold my novel. It's going to be published. I'm a writer, a real writer."

Verna (her name tag said,) gave me a big grin and patted me on the arm. "Honey, that's somethin'. I never knew a real writer before. They gonna sell your books here in the market?"

"Maybe," I told her, rising again to paradise. And we both smiled at one another the whole time she was adding up my bill.

"Congratulations, you hear?" she said, piling my bags into the cart. And I wheeled it out of the market up the Yellow Brick Road to my car.

The only changes my editor wanted were to shorten the beginning, expand the middle, and change the ending. So I began, trying to make something wonderful out of this book for the seventh time.

Several weeks later, the phone interrupted me. "Hi, it's me." Alex had a cold and sneezed into the receiver. "You working?"

"Yes."

"This is important. Bill Shapiro just called from Wilton Productions. He's interested in optioning your book for a movie. I told him it was only a paperback original, but he's looking for a soapy romance to make on a small budget in Europe and he heard about your novel. I told him to call your agent, but since we're old friends, he thought I could prevail on you to get him an inside track. That's a laugh, inside track."

"What do you mean?"

"I mean, that producers aren't exactly breaking down your door."

"Alex, the book isn't even published yet."

"But that's how it works. If a book has movie potential, the grapevine hears about it and gets hold of a manuscript any way they can, before a book is published."

"How?" I had visions of producers in ski masks breaking into our house at night to pilfer my pages.

"Their best source is the copy store. When a writer has copies made of a manuscript, often the copy store makes extras that you don't know about. Then they peddle it to the indie-prods."

"Everyone's a critic."

"So. Do you have a manuscript you can send him?"

"Why doesn't he just call my copy store and ask them."

"Because your book isn't hot enough to steal." I hated that tone he was using now, like, *How stupid can you get*? He blew his nose. We'd all have colds by the end of the week.

"Alex, I'm still working on the book. Maybe we should wait until I'm finished."

"It's your call, baby, but when you've got a live fish on the line, making him wait is a sure way of losing him. This business runs on enthusiasm."

"And larceny. He just wants to get first crack at something, whether it's good or not."

"You got it; that's the name of the game, the early bird, and all that." All these fishing analogies, Alex must need a vacation.

"What do you think I should do?"

"Send him the most current version you have, and tell him to call your agent. I'll be happy to act as your lawyer, if it ever comes to that."

"You don't think there's a chance?"

"Honey, this business is crazy. Anything's possible. But thousands of properties get optioned and never made. Staggering amounts."

"Alex, the world hunger problem is staggering, not the amount of movies made compared to properties optioned."

"Okay, pick on my semantics. Do what you want."

"I'm not being difficult. It's wonderful that Bill Shapiro is interested. I'll send him a manuscript today, okay?"

"You're sure cool about it."

"But you explained what the odds are, I'm just being practical."

"Sometimes I don't get you, Suzanne."

I could feel my frustration rising. If he didn't *get* me, and I didn't *get* him, where did that leave *us*? "Honey, I'm thrilled about your call. Let's not have a fight."

There was silence on the phone, then he said, "Okay. I don't want to fight either. I'll be home late tonight."

I tried to keep the disappointment out of my voice. "Oh? Why?"

"There's a cocktail party before the screening of Jack Lemmon's new movie, I have to stop by."

"Should I get a sitter and meet you?"

"Naw, it's not worth it for twenty minutes of shmoozing. There's some people I have to say hello to, let them know I've put in an appearance, and then I'll be home."

"Okay," I said, stonily. "Have fun." And I hung up, thinking, *Damn. Here he called with good news, terrific news, and I feel worse than I did before the call. What's the matter with us?*

Then my fantasies took over. Imagine having a film made of a book I'd written, seeing my characters coming to life by some actor, the story perfected by a director, the whole book produced, rewritten, packaged, edited, dressed, coiffed, recorded, and distributed by slews of technicians. It was better than a fairy tale. I wished my grandmother could have been here to see it. She would have taken it in stride; "Of course they want your book," she'd have said, "you're a wonderful writer." The world should have more grandmothers, I decided, forcing myself to get back to work, to a routine I found more difficult now and yet exhilarating. Cocoonlike, my world spun itself around me, and I burrowed into it, wondering if I'd ever emerge a butterfly. Someday soon, people would be reading what I've written, sharing my thoughts, letting me entertain them, titillate them, stimulate them, even instruct them. What a privilege. I'd done research on Italian banking, on methods of plastic surgery, rhinoplasty, on breast augmentation, heroin trafficking in the South of France, and couture designing and manufacturing in Europe. The rest was all my imagination.

"Suz-anne." Bill Shapiro drawled his words slowly with a Bostonian accent, pronouncing all his a's flatly when he *tawked*. "Loved your book. Very hot, very sexy. Lots of adventure, all that romance, and glamour. I think we can make a deal."

My heart was slamming around in my chest, a Ping-Pong ball in a bingo machine.

"Got a development deal with Dino." As in Di Laurentiis, I assumed. "Studio's available in Rome, that's where we'll shoot, at Cinecittà. But honey, I hope you won't be difficult to deal with. After all, this is a low-budget movie, we can't afford to pay a fortune for the book rights. But then, I'm sure it will be reasonable, after all, it's only a paperback original, not some *firecrawker* hardcover.

The way he talked made me feel I should either beg him to option my piddly little book or give it to him for free. "Bill, my agent knows what's fair. I'll take his advice."

"I dunno. That hotshot husband of yours is chomping at the money offers."

"Alex? He's only going to read the contracts. You'll be negotiating with me and Chuck Metzger."

"Hmmm," he drew out. "Okay, I'll get back to you, Suzanne," he promised. And that's the last I heard from him for six months. Then, just before the book was being published, he went into negotiations with my agent and we eventually agreed on his proposal. Later, I discovered that for the past six months, he'd been shopping my book around without paying me any option money, something a more reputable producer wouldn't do. I had a lot to learn about the sleazy game of making movies.

I made my deal with Shapiro-Wilton and went on the road to promote my book.

CHAPTER THIRTY

"Suzanne?" The woman's voice was breathy and low. "This is someone from your past. Can you guess who it is?"

She waited for me to figure it out, while my mind jumped from one annoying blank to another. She sounded familiar, but I couldn't place her. "I'm afraid I don't know," I admitted.

"It's Jasmine, silly."

"Jasmine Aumant! How are you?" It truly was a voice from the past. I got an immediate picture of her as she was at ten years old: the olive skin, the long hair, and those huge black eyes.

"Just fine. I ran into your sister at a party and she told me what you've been doing so I decided to call you up and say hello. It's really exciting." She sounded a touch more bored than excited. "I'd like to come and talk to you, if I may. Why don't we have lunch?"

"What are you doing in Los Angeles? I thought you were living in New York, acting."

"Well, there's acting in LA too, you know," she said.

"How are your parents?"

Her hesitation alerted me. "My mother died last year. Cancer."

"Oh, I'm so sorry." I remembered her mother in their kitchen preparing those exotic French and Chinese dishes that were so delicious. Jasmine had been close to her mother. It must have been hard for her.

"And your dad?"

"Still kicking," she said, without enthusiasm. "He's remarried."

It seemed soon to me. To her, it must have felt like a betrayal.

"How long have you been here?"

"Why don't we answer each other's questions over lunch?"

I sighed. "Jasmine, I don't go out to lunch. In fact, I eat at my desk most days because I only get to work when the children are in school. I have to get as much done as I can while they're not here. But I would like to see you. Maybe you'd like to come to dinner? How about Thursday night?"

"Well," she hesitated. "If that's the only way I can see you." Clearly, she disliked the idea of eating at home with my family. They wouldn't be too thrilled about having her either. Especially, Alex. After all, what could she do for him?

She agreed to come, and we set the date.

Jasmine had turned into a beauty. She was still small, about five three, but her skin was a burnished gold, and her thick dark hair hung like shiny silk down her back. She was wearing a sleeveless dress of a clingy material that was cut in a low vee in front, revealing her cleavage. Then it was gathered under the bust and fell loosely over her well-formed body. Her cleavage was round and umber colored in the middle. I noticed and so did Alex. She wore a small amount of cheek blush and some lip gloss but no other makeup; her thick black lashes framed her huge brown eyes. Her hands caught my attention, beautifully boned, with long tapered fingers and light pink nails. They moved as she talked, like moths skirting our conversation. I remembered how she used to eat with her fingers.

She hugged me, reaching up to do so, then kissed Alex on the cheek and patted Amy and Miles. Nothing this exotic had ever sat at my country French kitchen table before.

Amy was used to meeting actresses, but the ones she'd met were usually famous. "Are you on television?" she wanted to know.

"Not yet, but maybe someday," Jasmine promised. "It takes time to get a break," she told us, almost apologetically. "I've done some small parts. I was in 'That Girl,' and the road company of *West Side Story*."

Amy lost interest when Jasmine wasn't on any of her favorite shows.

"To be honest, I was nervous about calling you," she said to me, sipping her wine. "I'd heard you were living in this beautiful home and married to a big wheel in the entertainment business." She lowered her lashes and looked sideways at Alex, who was wearing his self-satisfied expression. He gave her an appreciative smile. She turned back to me. "You certainly have it all. It was really kind of you to see someone like me, from the past."

I protested. Actually, I was glad to see her after all.

"Well, it's really great that you invited me to dinner. It's so like you, Suzanne, generous to a fault."

This new Jasmine was one I'd never seen before. Not only was she being lady bountiful with her praise, but she was demure, almost insecure. Or was it an act, a performance for Alex's benefit.

Jasmine was seated at the table between Amy and Alex, Miles was next to me. He was an active child and not the neatest eater. I knew Jasmine wouldn't appreciate a glass of milk in her lap. Jasmine listened to Alex talk about the industry and I noted her rapt attention; she even leaned forward now and then so he could check out her cleavage, and check he did. She ate daintily, picking at her food, while the rest of us cleaned our plates. In her honor I had made chicken with cashews, snow peas, and water chestnuts, vegetable fried rice, and scallops in black bean sauce. I might just as well have ordered out instead of cooking for six hours for all the enjoyment she displayed.

"Mommy says you knew her when you were a little girl like me," Amy said, bringing Jasmine's attention away from Alex.

"That's right, Amy. And your mommy was such a good girl too," Jasmine said, shooting me a haughty smile that said, *And I wasn't.* The real Jasmine was alive after all, living inside this imitation of Olivia de Havilland playing Melanie Wilkes.

"Tell us the story about Milly's teeth," Amy said.

"What?" Jasmine's large eyes grew even larger and confusion clouded her face. She'd never expected that story to come back and haunt her. She didn't know how inquisitive Amy was.

I marveled at the way Jasmine's skin glowed, smooth as wax, as though she'd been painted by Botticelli—if he had ever painted Eurasians.

"Mommy told us you made Milly pull out her teeth when they weren't even loose."

"Amy, not at the table, please," I admonished.

"I want to know, too," Miles added.

"I never had anything to do with that," Jasmine said, not looking at me. "That girl's teeth were already loose, hanging by a thread. Why, she must have made a fortune for pulling out all three at once. Do children still do that?" she asked me.

"Yes, there's still a tooth fairy," I told her. "They put their teeth under the pillow." I nodded toward Amy, whose baby teeth had just started to get loose.

"What's this about pulling teeth?" Alex asked.

I'd told him this story before, but Alex didn't often remember what wasn't crucial to his getting ahead.

"Alex." Jasmine turned back to him. "Do you know anybody at William Morris who might be interested in handling me? My current agent isn't doing enough for my career."

There was nothing Alex disliked more than being asked to help someone. If he wouldn't help his own wife get an agent, he certainly wouldn't help a perfect stranger.

But I was amazed when he smiled at her and said, "You know, Harvey Munson might be good for you. He's young, just promoted to agent after being an assistant, and he's open to new clients. Why don't you send me your composite and a credit sheet and I'll see that he gets it."

"Oh, I have it with me," she said, pushing back her chair, which scraped against the floor as she jumped up. "I always carry them in case."

While she was retrieving her credits, I excused the children from the table and they helped me clear the dishes. I raised my eyebrow at Alex, for which he gave me a half smile and a shrug. His helpless *"What can I do?"* look was quite unlike him.

Jasmine was back in a moment, thrusting photos at him of herself in various poses. The one in the diaphanous nightgown, à la George Hurrell, with the light behind her outlining her body was the one he looked at longest.

"These are great," he said enthusiastically. "I'm sure you can do a lot with them."

She gave me a set, and after looking at them I handed them back.

"Oh, keep them, Suzanne. In fact, I was hoping that you could help me get me a part in your movie."

So that's why she called. I couldn't believe how rejected I felt, just like when we were kids and she was nice to me only if she wanted something. "There's nothing I can do about getting you a part, Jasmine. I have no say whatsoever about casting, or any part of the production. They only optioned my book; I didn't even write the screenplay."

"Oh, but you're the author. You know the producer. All

it would take is for you to mention me.'' She was still smiling sweetly, but I could see the steel within her tightening.

"I think the parts have been cast,'' I said, helplessly. "And there aren't any parts for someone like you.'' That sounded offensive, even to me. "I mean with your particular beauty and . . . talents.'' I didn't know how to get out of this gracefully. "Have you read the book?''

"Of course I have. And I know I could play the part of Anne Scott.''

"But that's the lead,'' I said, lamely.

"I know,'' she snapped.

"But you see, the character of Anne is a blank canvas. In the beginning she has to be someone who is not beautiful, but can become beautiful later on.'' She was nodding as though that was her, exactly. "But Jasmine, this is a small-budget production, the lead has to be a star or they won't be able to get financing. I think Barbara Parkins has been cast in the role of Anne.''

"Then what about Brenda?''

I almost laughed; if I'd looked at Alex, I know I would have lost it. "Jasmine, the character of Brenda is a slightly overweight, blond Jewish girl from Brooklyn with curly hair.''

"Haven't you heard of wigs?'' she said, so seriously that I almost laughed again. "And I can do a New York accent,'' she said, adding a heavy Brooklynese twang to her words.

"I'm sure you can,'' I said, looking to Alex for help, but he wasn't giving me any. "That part has been cast too.''

"Then what about Elena? I could play the hell out of that role.''

"Yes, it is a good part.'' I should know, I wrote it. "But, the contessa is being played by Nina Foch. After all, she's a woman in her late thirties, much older than you.''

Jasmine's eyes narrowed as she encountered each obstacle in her way. "I don't know why you're being so obstinate, Suzanne. I never would have believed it of you. I can see that you've really gone Hollywood. It's a sad day when even your friends won't help you," she said. "You want me to believe that your hands are tied, but I know how this business works." The look she gave me made me shudder. As a child, I never wanted her as an enemy, and as an adult she could be an even more vicious adversary.

"Jasmine, I'll speak to the producer," I said. "Maybe there's something for you after all." The idea of calling Bill Shapiro and asking a favor was not something I looked forward to. He rarely returned my calls. In fact, I needed favors from him for myself. I wanted to see the rushes, be invited on the set, invited to the screening, and to get paid my percentage of the gross without having to sue him. I didn't relish using up my favors for Jasmine, who didn't give a damn about me. But here she was, expecting that I would come through for her, or like the queen in *Snow White*, she'd take great pleasure in destroying me. So I agreed to try.

I was surprised to discover how quickly Bill Shapiro returned my call, but when he heard what I wanted there was a subtle shift in his voice.

"I thought you were calling to see how production was going, Suzanne."

"I am, Bill. I'm dying to hear the news. It's like having a child at boarding school, I feel as though I'm missing out on watching him grow up."

"Well, we're scouting locations, talking with Sam Spiegel about using his yacht. And we should start doing some second-camera shooting in Europe next month."

"That sounds wonderful." It didn't seem real to me.

"So," he sighed, "tell me about your friend."

"She's absolutely gorgeous, Bill." I knew if I didn't push hard, he'd never agree to see her so I launched into it. "Her Eurasian blood makes her exotic-looking, but she has a mysterious quality that comes across instantly. She has a special aura that few people possess, but when you see it, you recognize it immediately."

"She sounds wonderful." He was barely paying attention. "Let's have lunch, I'll have my secretary call you."

My heart had been pounding with tension from the moment this conversation began. I truly wanted to say, "Okay, we'll do lunch," and hang up, knowing his secretary would never call me back. But something about Jasmine's determination and her volatile personality stopped me.

"So, when, Bill?" I stammered.

"When, what?"

"Will your secretary call me?"

"Soon, babe," he promised.

"Why not now? Put her on and I'll figure out a time when it's good for you, okay?" There's no defense against a tactless person, Alex always says.

"Okay," he sighed, putting me on hold. The next voice I heard was Bill's secretary, who arranged with me to meet him for lunch at the studio on Thursday and told me passes would be waiting.

We got there at 12:25, for a 12:30 date, picking up our passes from the guard at the gate who allowed peons like us to enter the magical world of moviedom. The moment we arrived on the lot Jasmine seemed to change. Her walk became slinky, her head floated on the top of her neck in a disconnected way that made it look as though she were dancing, her eyes were guided by some inner flame, and I felt mousier by the minute.

Heads turned when we entered the commissary. We took a table in the restaurant instead of the cafeteria.

Bill hadn't arrived yet.

"I have some film clips of myself if he wants to see them," Jasmine said, "or I would be happy to do a test for him, or a reading anytime he wants. You know, I can play an ingenue or an older woman as well. How's your sister-in-law's career going? I read somewhere she's performing in San Francisco this season."

She wasn't interested in my replies.

She rattled on as time passed. It got to be 12:45 and then 1:00.

"I'd better call him," I said, getting halfway up from the table.

But she grabbed my arm and pulled me back. "Don't you dare," she insisted. "It's bad karma to hurry someone when they're late. He's probably finishing up a phone call or something. He'll be here any minute."

By 1:15, after we'd eaten all the bread sticks and drunk two glasses of water, I insisted that we call Bill's office, and she agreed.

There was no answer. *Of course not,* I thought. *He's out having lunch!* I could have killed Bill Shapiro, and when I thought of Jasmine's disappointment I became fearful. The old Jasmine would never have let this pass easily; and this appointment meant so much to her. I tried to appear cheerful as I returned to the table.

"He sends his deepest apologies, Jasmine, but he's stuck in a crisis and can't get away. He suggested that we order lunch and send him the bill, and if he solves the crisis in the next hour, he'll join us for coffee."

That sounded reasonable; I half believed it myself except that my heart was pounding with apprehension. I would call him again in thirty minutes; hopefully he'd be in his office by then and the day wouldn't have been a total loss. But I'm a terrible liar. My left cheek below my eye starts to twitch. My sister, on the other hand, could lie without flinching. Once, my mother was looking for her best lace brassiere and found it under Steffani's bed, still inside the jersey top Steffani had worn it with. Steffani had looked her straight in the eye and said, "I don't know how it got there."

Jasmine's dark eyes were staring through me as I sat back down at the table as though everything was normal, signaling for the waiter to bring us menus.

When I saw her nostrils flare, I knew the smoke was coming next.

"You set me up, didn't you?" she began. "You never arranged this lunch at all, did you? You probably had some flunky get us on the lot so I'd believe you were doing me a favor. What do you think, I was born yesterday? That I don't know all your goodie-two-shoes tricks?" It was like being attacked by Bette Davis at her most vitriolic. "You have no spine. You are a spineless wonder. He's in a crisis, my ass. He's never even heard of me, has he? Because you didn't tell him. Well, you can take your pitiful little commissary lunch and stuff it, Suzanne, Miss Selfish-Bitch Winston. Who the hell needs you, or your half-assed favors."

People were staring. My cheeks were burning red; I wanted to crawl under the tablecloth and hide. Now I remembered how careful one had to be with Jasmine, how she could turn on you in a second and unleash a dragon's breath of insults. "Jasmine, please lower your voice. I'm terribly sorry this has happened. But I did try," I pleaded. "I made this date with Bill."

"And if I call this Bill Shapiro, he'll know who I am, and be happy to meet with me, on your say-so?" Her eyes had narrowed to slits and there were white spots on her cheeks where rage had caused the blood to leave her face. "Haven't you ever heard of the women's movement? Women today are helping one another; we're supposed to be supportive of our sisters in this world of men. If we don't stick together, we'll never get anywhere. But you're the kind of woman who does nothing but take and never gives back. You give the women's movement a bad name. I could see when we were kids that you were a wimpy weasel. And that's exactly what you've grown up to be. You're going to be sorry you ever did this to me, believe me. Your sister was right about you."

I really didn't want to hear what she was going to say next, because even though she was being totally unreasonable, trying to hurt me any way she could, so far she hadn't found her mark. But I knew she'd seen my sister recently, and it was possible that Steffani had said something about me that I didn't want to hear. Whatever it was, Jasmine would be sure to blow it out of proportion. I'd never know which was the exaggeration and which was the truth.

"Jasmine, that's enough!" I said, trying to summon the voice of authority I used with Amy and Miles. "I know you're upset, but I don't appreciate your taking it out on me."

I wanted to get up and go, but it would have been such an impolite thing to do, leave her sitting there.

"Your sister said you got where you are because your husband threatened to blackball Bill Shapiro in the industry if he didn't option your book. And when a big-time executive at a major agency threatens a puny independent producer, what do you think he'll do? Steffani and I both agreed that your book was shit, and it's going to make a stupid shitty little movie. I wouldn't be in it or anything you're ever involved in, if it's the last thing I do."

And she got up and left me sitting there.

CHAPTER THIRTY-ONE

It took me a few days to get up the courage to confront my sister on what she had said to Jasmine. When I finally got her at home, it was on a Tuesday. She was living on Laurel Avenue off of Fountain with her friend Carole, and whoever else might be crashing at their place at the time. Her furniture consisted of a combination of hand-me-downs from Mom's house, a few things I had given her, and some things she'd picked up in thrift shops. It was seedy, yet had a certain sense of charm about it in the way she had hung her collection of antique beaded bags on the wall in an arrangement, strung glass beads at the edges of a lampshade, and used an old Oriental carpet to cover some of the spots on the sofa cushions. There was a vintage Coca-Cola tray on the battered coffee table, with a plant on it, and I remember thinking that the tray was probably the most valuable thing she had, or the only thing I would have wanted out of the whole place. Still, the small apartment was distinctly Steffani, down to the hatrack standing by the door, with her collection of old hats hung there. Today it had a stale smell to it.

"Do you want some tea?" she asked. "I'm brewing some ginseng."

I declined and sat on the sofa, but I had to move over to find a place where the springs didn't poke my behind.

"To what do I owe this visit?"

"Can't I just come and see you if I want?" I was immediately on the defensive, because I was here for another reason. She sat down in a cane armchair with a tapestry cushion and I thought that the chair would have looked better if she'd had the cane repaired. Her hair was piled up on top of her head, casually wound there in the kind of pompadour women wore in the 1890s; the light from the wood-framed windows behind her outlined her silhouette, keeping her face in shadow. I couldn't see her eyes clearly.

"I hear you ran into Jasmine recently," I began.

She didn't respond, just stared off into space.

"Steff? What did you think of her?"

"Who cares."

"She was quoting you all over the place."

"I can't help what she says."

My heartbeat increased as I approached the subject I'd come to discuss. "She said you thought my book was shitty."

I expected a vehement denial, or at least a defiant, *Yeah, I said it, so what*. But Steffani was hardly aware of what I was saying. "I never said anything like that. I said, I was really proud of you, that you've done a hell of a job writing commercial fiction, and that your book is better than a lot of shit being written today. I was using the word as a euphemism for stuff. I guess I wanted to sound tough. But to say I said your work was shitty is a blatant misquote."

"I'm glad to hear it," I said, feeling relieved.

"Jasmine has always been slightly unhinged." Steffani shrugged.

"So, what's new with you?" I asked.

There was a moment before she answered me. "I have an appointment tomorrow with the dean of the School of Education."

"What's that got to do with Jasmine?" I asked.

"It doesn't look too good."

"What doesn't? I thought Jasmine looked beautiful even if she is crazy."

Steffani reached up and wiped at her cheek. She turned her head slightly and I saw there were tears on her face.

"What is it?" I asked, instantly drawn to her concerns. "Are you feeling all right?"

"No." Her voice quavered. "UCLA turned me down for graduate school."

"What!" I couldn't believe what I was hearing. She'd worked toward this goal for four solid years, talked of it constantly. It was a source of pride and gratification for my parents that Steffani was going to be a teacher, that she was going to have a profession, be able to take care of herself, the dream every parent has for their child, that they be independent. Not to mention how much she wanted it. "Are you sure?"

She nodded, sniffling, then reached for a Kleenex in her pocket and blew her nose. "My grades are borderline, I have a three-point-four average. I could have gotten better grades if I hadn't had those surgeries in my first two years. In my freshman year when I was on crutches I got a lot of C's. And then I was hospitalized after the car accident, just before finals in my junior year, which affected my grades too. But it's not only my grades. They don't think my health is good enough to go through graduate school. They said there are only so many graduate school openings, and those places have to be reserved for people without health problems."

"But you've been fine lately. No more attacks. If you're healthy enough to finish four consecutive years of college, you're healthy enough to go to graduate school. How dare they pass judgment on you like that?"

"Oh, they dare all right. Bureaucrats make judgments all the time on people's lives."

"What did Mom and Dad say?"

"Mom wants to go with me tomorrow when I meet with Beverly Goddard. She's the dean who's been handling my appeal. If Dad can get off work, he'll come too, but I don't think it will do any good. Dr. Levinson has already spoken to Mrs. Goddard and assured her I'm capable of doing the work; he's also written a letter to the admissions board. We've even asked Uncle Sid to talk to his friend on the state Supreme Court and see if that will do any good.'' (Our uncle Sid was a judge of the Superior Court in Los Angeles and well connected in political circles.)

''Is there anything I can do?'' I asked, feeling that familiar and terrible mixture of pain, pity, and fierce loyalty I had so often felt for her. The reason I'd come in the first place was to ask her what she'd said to Jasmine. It was unimportant now. My fury at the unfairness of the world grew so that I could barely contain it. I kept thinking, *This can't be happening to her. Something has to be done. Nobody should be asked to endure what she's been through in her life. And now this.*

''There's nothing you can do,'' she said, her voice resonant with despair. Then she lowered her head and began to sob. I got up and went to her and held her against me while she cried. Every ounce of me wanted to reassure her, say the words I say to my own children when they cry: ''Everything's going to be all right.'' But I had never been able to say that to my sister and mean it. For we all knew, where she was concerned, everything was not all right.

Beverly Goddard's office was in the Administration Building on the second floor. Lynnette and Steffani were greeted by Mrs. Goddard's secretary.

''Mrs. Goddard was called into the chancellor's office,'' the secretary told them. ''We've been having problems with demonstrations and sit-ins on many of our campuses, though UCLA students have been less volatile than most. The chancellor needed to see her but she'll be back in a while and wants you to wait, please.''

The wooden bench they sat on reminded Steffani of the time she'd been called into the principal's office in grammar school for talking during class.

''We'll convince her, honey,'' Lynnette said quietly, so

the secretary wouldn't hear. "You know I can talk anyone into anything if I set my mind to it. You'd make such a wonderful teacher, I'm sure she will see that. It wouldn't be right to deprive students of having you as a teacher, not with your dedication."

"I hope so, Mom. They just have to let me in, they just have to."

Lynnette was wearing a gray linen dress with red buttons, and her shoes and purse were red. Steffani was wearing a long cotton skirt and white blouse with a fringed scarf around her shoulders tied at the side. They'd both discussed their outfits today and chosen clothing that would give a proper impression, agreeing that their appearance was important. But Steffani was aware that they were placing importance on their clothing because it was the only thing they could control.

Twenty minutes later Beverly Goddard came hurrying into her office, obviously harassed from her previous meeting. She glanced at Steffani and Lynnette as if they were annoyances in a life already filled with annoyances, then realized who they were and straightened up her posture, looking down at them with an expression that said, "Let's get this over with."

She was a woman in her late fifties with short white hair combed back from her face. She wore fuchsia lipstick, but no other makeup, and her navy suit was institutional. Only the flowered print blouse underneath, with a touch of pink and fuchsia in it, made her seem at all feminine. In fact, she had a way of pursing her lips into a straight line that accented the square jaw of her face, giving her a look of terrible defiance.

Steffani had seen her before, but Lynnette hadn't, and she felt her mother's hand in hers squeeze tightly as they faced the strength of this official person.

"Please sit down," Mrs. Goddard said, indicating the two chairs in front of her desk, and they sat.

Lynnette smiled her lovely, charming smile, trying to get Beverly Goddard to like her, which was her usual approach to anyone who was the least adversarial. "What a lovely blouse you're wearing," Lynnette said.

Beverly Goddard merely nodded.

"My husband wanted to be with us today, but he couldn't get away from work. It was important for us to be here together so that you would know how much it means for Steffani to be admitted to graduate school."

"I'm sure that it does, Mrs. Blacker, but wanting to get in, and having the proper requirements are two different things."

"Oh, but she does meet the requirements. Her test scores were excellent, and her grades are just on the edge of acceptability. We know of other students who were admitted with a three-point-four average."

"But those students had extracurricular activities and no health problem. If you pardon my saying so, Mrs. Blacker, Steffani just isn't teacher material."

"Mrs. Goddard," Steffani spoke for the first time, "I have extracurricular activities too: I was a teaching assistant twice last year, and a counselor at the UCLA camp for underprivileged children. I have excellent letters of recommendation. But even more important than that, I understand children. I know what they're feeling and how to get through to them. And I want to teach with all my heart. Why do you say I'm not teacher material?"

Mrs. Goddard looked slightly discomfited as she leafed through the file on her desk. Then she looked up, her gray eyes cold and unreachable. "Teachers must work within the system, Miss Blacker. It's not enough to just be sympathetic. And they cannot expect to be given special privileges the way you have. Asking your influential friends to intervene on your behalf did not benefit your case at all. In fact, where I'm concerned it made another black mark against you. I don't subscribe to influence peddling. I think it weakens the moral fiber of our country. Now, I have spoken to the doctors at the UCLA medical center about your case and they've told me all about your disease."

"But they're not the ones who treat me. Dr. Levinson and Dr. Asher, my hematologist, are the only ones qualified to discuss my physical condition. Every case of Gaucher's disease is different, in degree and seriousness."

"Miss Blacker, were you not issued a special parking permit so that you could park near your classes on campus because of a medical infirmity?"

"Yes, but that's because I had had bone surgery and couldn't walk long distances. But I've recovered. I can walk for miles now."

"Then why did you continue to have that special parking permit during all four years as an undergraduate?"

Steffani felt her cheeks flush hotly as Lynnette looked at her. She'd forgotten all about the fact that she'd kept her special permit. The healing process had completed itself within months of her second surgery, but the university continued to issue her special permits and she never informed them that she no longer needed them. It was so much more convenient to be able to park on campus. Now, she realized she shouldn't have done it, but it was too late to take it back.

"I don't see what parking permits have to do with anything," Lynnette said, defending her daughter no matter what.

"I think it's extremely important," Beverly Goddard said, glancing away for a moment as though gathering her thoughts. "Because it's indicative of a more grave situation. The state needs teachers desperately, and there are fine young men and women coming through our universities who will fill that need, but we have only so many places available to train them. In all good judgment, I cannot allow one of those valuable spaces to be taken up by someone who I know may not complete the course of learning. And, I'm sorry to say this," she spoke directly to Steffani, "even if you did get your credentials, you may not live long enough to fulfill the job."

Lynnette gasped. "Where did you hear such a thing? That's not true!" she insisted, starting to cry. "You cannot do this to Steffani. She has worked long and hard to get to this place; you can't deny her the opportunity to be a teacher. No one has ever said she wouldn't live a long life. Why, she'll probably teach your great-grandchildren. How can you be so cruel?"

"I'm not being cruel, Mrs. Blacker, just practical. And I'm not denying her the opportunity to be a teacher, there are other schools she can go to."

"But my credits won't apply there," Steffani interrupted. "It will cost me extra time to make up classes and fulfill their requirements before I can even begin graduate courses. And a teaching degree from UCLA would provide me a better chance of employment."

"That part is true, but if you have all the time you say you have, it shouldn't make that much difference. I'm sorry, but there's nothing I can do. The application is denied."

Lynnette and Steffani sat there as if they'd both been punched in the stomach.

Then Steffani got up and picked up her purse. "I'm going to fight you," she said, as she left the room.

"I hope you can't sleep at night after what you have done," Lynnette said as she followed Steffani out.

But Steffani couldn't fight anymore. That limitless source of strength she'd dipped into all her life for needed portions of determination and courage had finally dried up. She had fought from childhood just to get through the next hour, or the next day, or to endure the next bout of pain or physical impairment, or surgery, or minor injury that always became major, because she believed that life would get better, that when this latest test of endurance was over, something better would be waiting. Only now she had reached a place she never believed existed, where after all that struggling and fighting and enduring, the worst possible thing had happened: it had not been worth it. And that was the most devastating blow of all.

But Steffani refused to talk about it and the light in her eyes went out.

That summer I made more progress on my second book, *The Reunion*, while the film they were making of my first book completed shooting and went into post-production. In October, when I saw the first screening of a rough cut, I was filled with the oddest mixture of feelings. It was my creation, and yet not. The characters had a life of their own. No more were they ephemeral creatures in my brain, floating in and out of existence as the mood suited me. Now they were flesh and blood with a physical appearance recognizable anywhere. They were no longer my children, and their lives were being created by other people, a director and screenwriters who had added scenes and changed my story to suit the medium of film. Strangely, it made me look at my own children in a different light. Someday I would be giving them up to the world, to others who would write their stories for them; it was a wrenching thought. I wanted to clutch them to me forever, keep them six and eight, never let them change. I began to have a new sympathy for my parents, for what they'd gone through merely being parents, letting me go without too much guilt. But perhaps, they had been able to let me go because they still had Steffani.

And then she disappeared.

My mother took me aside when I came over for dinner and told me she was gone. There was a terrified edge to her voice. "That bum, Carole, is still living in Steffani's apartment. Carole's on welfare, and pregnant, and doesn't even know who the father is. And a friend of Melody's is moving in with her, a boy named Hank. I think he's a homosexual. They're going to ruin all Steffani's things. They don't care, it's not theirs. I wouldn't have given her my antique table if I'd known those people were going to use it. But there's nothing I can do about it. She gave them permission."

"But where is she, Mom?"

"I don't know, exactly. Somewhere up north, Santa Cruz, I think. She went with some friends who know someone who has a ranch and they're going to stay there for a while. Live off the earth."

"That doesn't sound too bad." I tried to be encouraging.

"Oh, Suzanne, you know she shouldn't just pick up and go. She needs to be monitored by a doctor familiar with her case. What if she gets an infection? Just an ordinary cut can turn into blood poisoning."

During dinner Miles asked where his aunt Steffani was and instead of answering him, my father excused himself from the table.

I followed him into the kitchen where he was scraping the salad plates for the dishwasher. Tears were rolling down his cheeks.

"Dad, she's all right. I'm sure she is."

He shook his head, unconvinced. "Steffani takes chances, Suzanne, she always has. She's not like you. I used to be able to take care of her, but now I can't protect her. Look at how she gets mixed up with the wrong kind of guy. Ron turned out to be a bum and Joe nearly killed her. She thinks you can live on poetry and alfalfa sprouts. Bullshit!"

His vehemence surprised me; my father never cursed.

"I should have done something when that woman refused to admit her to graduate school."

"What could you have done?"

"I don't know. Something!" he insisted.

I put my arms around him and hugged him and said, "It's not your fault, Dad. It's not."

Just then, my mother came into the kitchen and saw us embracing and my father did the oddest thing, he flinched and pulled away from me as if we'd been doing something wrong. And then my mother said, "Well, Burt, I always seem to find you hugging the women, don't I?" And she turned around and walked back out of the kitchen.

CHAPTER THIRTY-TWO

The loan to refinance my house was approved. I paid Curtis McCartney his retainer, set aside enough money in case of a trial and to pay Avery Bellows for several months. I also made a hefty payment to the IRS. Then, I listed the house with a broker, and began looking for an apartment. Lying in bed at the end of each discouraging day, staring at the ceiling, worrying about what would become of us, the jumble of my life tormented me. If only there was some action I could take.

I checked with Avery Bellows every day. So far he hadn't come up with anything. The Markhams were no longer at their Brooklyn address, and looking for a hooker in New York was nearly impossible. But she was the only suspect we had.

While I waited for news from Bellows, I decided to get a holiday job. I needed the money, and besides, I would be setting an example for my children. The book department at Bullock's hired me.

Amy got a job too, wrapping packages. Her willingness to help made me proud. She was still getting her regular allowance from Alex, so she didn't need the money for herself. Instead, she gave it to me. The first time she handed me her paycheck of thirty-one dollars and I realized how many groceries that would buy, I felt a shame so deep inside of me, that I feared I'd never get over it.

Gloria returned from an appearance in Salzburg for the holidays and stopped by the book department in a full-length lynx coat to see me. Her nails were newly lacquered, her dark hair was long and luxuriously curly, her makeup impeccable, and her jewelry huge and chunky. The customers stared at her as if she were a movie star. Her glance let me know she thought I was working in a slum. My body flushed with heat.

"You poor thing," she said. "Alex told me what's been happening."

"I thought you might have read about it," I said.

"What happens in your life is not big news in the world, Suzanne. Europeans are more concerned about nuclear missiles and rising inflation."

Judging from her tone, the mess I'd made of my life was what she'd expected of me. Then, she took my arm and pulled me aside. "I hate to see you like this. Is there anything I can do?"

I was amazed by the offer. I never expected kindness from her. I shook my head and tried to swallow the lump in my throat. Compared to her I felt shabby and bereft.

"Are you sure there's nothing?" she asked. "I know you need money."

"I couldn't borrow from you," I insisted, mortified.

"Don't be proud, for God's sake. If you're thinking of selling your valuables, like artwork, or jewelry, or even silverware, I could take it off your hands."

The thought of having Gloria owning my intimate possessions, my jewelry for instance, was degrading. But, better her than a stranger.

"I wouldn't know what to charge."

"Whatever's fair," she said. "Have your things appraised and I'll give you five percent over the best price you're offered."

I stared at her in amazement. "That's so generous."

"I know you're in a bind, and after all, we've been friends forever, sisters really. That's how I think of you. But let me know soon. I'm leaving for Aspen in a few days and then on to New York for New Year's."

"I'm glad we're friends again. Thank you, Gloria."

"It's nothing," she said, with a wave. "So, how's your investigation going?"

"We've got a real promising lead," I told her.

"Oh?" She was obviously interested.

I described Sugar Markham and told her how encouraged Bellows was for the first time.

She gave me a wonderful smile of encouragement. "I'm sure she's the one, Suzanne. How lucky for you!" And she was off. Her enthusiasm and largesse hung in the air after her as heavy as her scent.

I watched her go down the escalator knowing that if I sold her my jewelry it would be a new low in my life. But I did go to an estate dealer to have everything appraised. There wasn't much to sell, my diamond engagement ring from Alex, an enamel-and-diamond bracelet he'd bought me in Spain, pearls from our tenth anniversary, and a gold choker I'd bought when I sold my second book, plus the silverware from our wedding. I was dismayed to find out how little money it was worth.

"Don't sell it to her," Steffani pleaded. "You won't get enough to keep the children in private school for one semester. I wish I had the money to give you," she said. "Anything's better than taking from Gloria."

"You're right," I agreed, deciding it wasn't worth giving Gloria the satisfaction for the little I'd get in return.

Then, my car transmission died and had to be replaced. There was no available cash to pay for the repair. I had to call Gloria.

The moment I handed her my jewelry and accepted her check, I felt truly poor. There was so much I'd taken for granted in my life that was now either going or gone. I'd thought I would always have my home, always be able to pay my bills, and certainly never fear losing my children. No matter how unsteady my father's income had been when I was growing up, my parents had always managed to provide for us. I was developing a renewed respect for the way they'd managed money as it became more apparent to me every day that I had failed.

The upheaval was having an effect on the children. They were fighting, bickering, slamming more doors than usual. Separately, they were kind and loving to me, but as soon as two of them were in the same room, the arguments started. My patience drained out of me daily in a steady ooze like an oil spill. But their fighting ripped at me even more, making the wounds gush forth.

One by one, each child told me he wanted to stay with me no matter where we lived. But Alex continued his campaign, offering them their own rooms at his house, touting the special qualities of Beverly Hills schools, where there was no threat to their safety. If I were them, I would have been sorely tempted.

I couldn't force them to stay with me; I'd have to do what was best for each of them. So I vacillated between letting

Amy and Miles live with Alex and keeping Jered with me, or just letting the boys live with Alex, and Amy with me. But the thought of losing them overwhelmed me. With every ounce of my being I knew that, no matter what happened, busing or not, the four of us living in one room, I'd never let them go. If only Alex didn't sue me for custody, though he seemed to have let up on that idea.

I had been unable to write ever since I'd gotten the news that my publisher had withdrawn the offer to publish my next book, though I tried all my tricks. I'd sit at my desk, pretending I was writing this book just for myself the way I did fourteen years ago. But the words wouldn't come. It wasn't the same kind of block as when I was trying to work out a plot and couldn't decide what to do next. Rather, it was as if a pile of wet leaves had smothered my creative spirit. When I plumbed my depths there was no well of emotion to draw from, only a hollow emptiness, an echo of what used to be. I, who had always been prolific, who was the most adept of escape artists, couldn't get away from myself.

There was only one bright spot in my life. Barry. He made me smile on my days off. He brought me cartoons and gave me my first nickname, Snooze-N-Boots. I had a pair of boots that came up over my knees and I liked to sleep late in the morning. He called Amy Peaches because of her pale skin; Miles was Racer, after his name; and Jered was Crockett, because he had a raccoon tail tied to his bicycle. The kids called Barry Br'er Rabbit, because he always told them not to throw him in that briar patch. The only time we didn't get along was when the children picked a fight with him. Eventually, I figured out that the children's affection for him competed with their loyalty to their father, which was why they found fault. Just another difficulty in adjusting to divorce. Barry took it in stride.

My preliminary hearing was scheduled to take place just after Christmas. I pressured Avery Bellows to find out about Sugar Markham in the hopes of proving her guilt so I wouldn't have to go to court.

"I couldn't find her parents in Brooklyn," he reported

finally, "so I checked the death records. It's taken me two weeks to learn that the father died and the mother moved to Florida. The mother isn't listed in any city in Florida, and it's a big state. If she's alive, and that's a big if, I'll look for her in retirement homes. If she lives in one, she wouldn't necessarily have a phone."

"What about Sugar herself?"

"Couldn't find her in any of her old haunts. Looking further is really difficult. There's a code of silence on the street."

"She may not be on the street anymore."

"That's what I mean. The best way to find her is through her mother. She probably sends money."

I sighed. There was nothing we could do but wait.

The morning of the preliminary hearing I had diarrhea. I was in the bathroom when Bellows called. When I picked up the phone he said, "I found Sugar's mother, Sybil Markham, in a rest home. The news isn't so good. She's on a cruise that goes to Australia. I've cabled the travel company who booked it, but we probably won't hear from her until she gets home."

I felt my bowels protesting again and that awful grinding feeling inside. I sat down weakly, knowing I had to get dressed and be in court in an hour. "When will she be home?"

"Four weeks," he said.

"Oh God," I said, feeling emptier than I thought possible. I thanked him and hung up, thinking that maybe the hearing would go well and finding Sugar wouldn't matter.

I wore a navy blue wool dress and a magenta scarf to court. The dress was the most conservative thing I owned; the magenta scarf was supposed to lift my spirits. It didn't.

My parents and McCartney were terribly disappointed to hear the news about Sugar Markham. We'd all hoped she might clear me.

The prosecuting attorney assigned to my case was a woman named Blanche Wolcek. In her fifties, with gray hair pulled back into a chignon, she exuded competence. My attorney told me she'd gone to law school only a few years ago when her family had grown, and she was a real zealot. Her self-assurance terrified me. If she thought I was guilty, I didn't have a chance.

My exterior bravado helped me to hold my head up high, but inside I was Jell-O. For weeks, prior to the hearing, I dreamed I had stood before a jury of faceless stone statues who found me guilty over and over.

Occasionally during the proceedings, I was able to detach myself from my inner terror and observe Curtis McCartney. He behaved as if this was nothing extraordinary. *Doesn't he know this is my life, for God's sake!* Whenever I felt like screaming out my frustration, I'd stuff my fist against my mouth like a giant cork.

My parents and Barry sat in the back; knowing they were there helped somewhat. The reporters and news media attended too. I knew I wouldn't remember a thing that went on today. Maybe they would supply the details.

The prosecution paraded proof of my guilt. Exhibit A was the LSD found in my refrigerator; Exhibit B was the lab report proving its chemical makeup. Exhibit C was the typewritten note, with my name on it, sent to Brett Slocum with the candy. Curtis was going to show that the typewriter, a Remington portable with a slanted *P*, used in the accusation letters sent to me and my publishers was the same as the one that typed the note to Slocum. Our fear was that the state would say I had sent those letters to myself for publicity or to cover up what I was planning to do in the future, just to try to throw suspicion on someone else for my own actions.

McCartney had explained that each side, the prosecution and the defense, had a scenario, their own version of what had happened. The outcome, my very fate, depended on whose scenario the judge believed or which side could prove their story the most effectively.

Every time Blanche Wolcek stood and said, "Your Honor, may I call your attention to . . ." my bowels contracted in fear.

There were affidavits: one from Sergeant Brisco in New York that I had lied to him when I said I had no reason to be upset with Brett Slocum; my friend Martha was forced to repeat what I'd said to her, that anyone who works for Brett Slocum couldn't be blamed for overdosing. Even Esther, my agent, quoted me as saying that Brett Slocum ought to endure root canal without Novocaine.

I was amazed at the people they had questioned about my life who could quote what I thought of Slocum's review. The careless comments and off-the-cuff remarks I'd made to friends were convicting me.

Our side didn't have as much testimony in our favor. We'd been concentrating on finding the person who had written the letters so we could prove it was the same one who sent the candy. So far, Sugar Markham was our best suspect, but if I looked at it logically, it might not be Sugar after all. The fact that she lived in New York and had a reason to dislike me were the only facts to make her a suspect. Was she smart enough to concoct this scheme, to type such sophisticated letters about me? And how could she have put the LSD in my house? It costs money to fly back and forth to New York. Would she have spent her money that way? Only if she was really crazy.

The original wrapper from the tainted candy box, which might have provided us with fingerprints or a sample of hand-writing, had been thrown in the incinerator. If Bellows had been on the case sooner, perhaps he would have been able to retrieve that important piece of evidence. According to the doorman at Brett Slocum's apartment, the delivery person had been some kid off the street and couldn't be found either. What did shed some doubt on my guilt was that the candy had been bought locally in New York.

McCartney speculated for the judge, "How could Mrs. Winston have managed to be in New York buying candy, paying a delivery boy, and also here in California with her children?"

Avery Bellows had checked the airline passenger manifests going in and out of New York, to see if there was a name of anyone I knew who had been in New York at the time. But it could be someone who lived there, like Sugar, and hadn't had to travel. Whoever it was had been in two places in a short amount of time. In California in my kitchen, and New York sending candy. I was not encouraged by these details; they made everything seem even more diabolical. One of the worst things for me was hearing who of my friends and acquaintances Bellows had questioned to see if any of them harbored animosity toward me; that made me sick inside.

Finally, the preliminary evidence had all been presented, and we waited anxiously for the ruling.

When the judge came back on the bench, banged his gavel and didn't look at me, I knew it wasn't good news. He believed the state's case. I was bound over for trial, scheduled to take place in three months. *Oh God*, I thought, *this can't be happening. Will it ever end?*

That night, I called in sick to work. I only had enough strength to crawl into bed and sit there shaking. My sister came over to be with me and climbed into bed next to me. She held my hand and the two of us just sat there. My brain whirled, replaying the terrible events of the day and the disappointment over not yet finding Sugar Markham. I kept hearing the judge's pronouncement over and over. "Mrs. Winston, in view of all the state's evidence, you are to be bound over for trial."

Steffani sat quietly, not saying anything. And I thought about all the times I'd sat with her when she'd needed me. My parents and I were worried about her more than usual; her persistent cough had not gone away. But tonight she seemed fine, strong and positive and the only one I could tolerate to be with me at the moment.

"I know that discussing the details right now won't do you any good. God knows, statistics never helped me at times like these," she said, "though we hang on to them as if they were proof of something, as if they could tell us the outcome, as if they were little bits of magic like fairy dust."

"What does help?" I asked, knowing a despair so complete it pervaded my entire being.

"The only thing that helps is to never give up," she said. "Never, never, never!"

I did not want to cry. I had cried my way through the last few weeks, and that too, had not done me any good. "How do you not give up?" I asked her.

She shrugged, her shoulders thin and bony, the covers hiding the rest of her body. "Because life is worth everything, no matter what. As long as you're alive, there's hope. Hope that things will get better."

I thought of all she'd gone through and I marveled at her. "Do you ever give up?" I asked her.

She turned away, hiding what from me? The truth that she'd given up more times than she'd let us know, or that she'd never given up, because she had such a strength of spirit that it was strong enough to keep not only herself going against all odds, but others as well.

She spoke quietly. "When I've given up, there's always been someone in my life I could turn to for strength. To you, or to Mom and Dad." She looked back to me and I could see gratitude shining in her eyes. "I'm here for you now, Suze. I'm here to tell you it will be okay. You'll get through this. I swear you will."

I leaned over and hugged her, feeling her thin body through her sweater, suddenly forgetting how my life was falling apart and thinking only of her, praying that she would be okay too, wondering if I still had the strength to give to her if she needed me and ashamedly glad that, at the moment, she didn't.

Steffani didn't start out from Los Angeles to join a commune or *drop out* that September of her graduation year when she was turned down for graduate school. The reason she'd decided to head north was to see Joe. An article appeared in the LA *Times* that told about the burgeoning little theater groups of San Francisco's East Bay area, and Joe's name was mentioned as director of the Oakland Players Group. One of his plays was being produced that fall along with four other plays he'd chosen for the season.

"It will be a kick to drop in on him," she told Melody, showing her the article.

"If he doesn't kick you first," she said, wryly. Melody was letting her hair grow out from a short shag haircut and it stuck out every which way, neither short nor long.

"I'm not blaming Joe for what happened that night of the accident. He was only doing what he'd done hundreds of times before. I shouldn't have let him drive. But then, who knows what might have happened if I'd been driving. Accidents can happen to anyone." She wanted to say to Melody, *It was more your fault than his.* But she'd never been much good at blaming people. Her family cornered the market on that.

"So, why hasn't he stayed in touch?" Melody asked.

"Could be lots of reasons. But, you should have been more careful about K.C. when he was around."

"It wasn't my fault that he was listening. Maybe you shouldn't have balled K.C.," was the retort.

"You set it up."

"So, I'm a baaad girl, I guess," she said, with a nonchalant wave. "Listen, when you're up north, stop in and see my friends Lyle and Andrea. They're living on this farm outside of Santa Cruz. Remember them?"

Steffani tried, but couldn't.

"She's the hairdresser that did this to me." Melody pulled out a chunk of uneven wisps.

"Oh yes," Steffani recalled, getting a mental picture of Andrea, tall, lanky, brunet, bad complexion, good body, opinionated, and talkative. Her boyfriend, Lyle, was a nondescript dishwater blond who was letting his hair grow long and trying to be hip.

"Well, her old man, Lyle, came upon this place when he was working for Pioneer Paint Company. Nobody was living there, so they moved in. They wanted me to come, but it's not my thing." She drank a long swallow of wine from her glass. "It took me too long to settle in here to think of going away now. But you're rich, white, and twenty-one. You could go."

"Rich? That's a laugh. I've got a hundred and sixty dollars to my name, and then it's get-a-job time."

"So why blow it all on gas to drive up north for that creep, Joe. He won't care."

Steffani's smile was sly. " 'Cause I think he's still crazy about me, and all I have to do to get him back is show up."

Melody stared at her a touch enviously. "How do you know?"

"Signs and portents," she said, with a laugh. "Spells and predictions, sun and moon alliance, and astrological readings."

Melody laughed too, and gave her a shove in the arm. "Then, go girl. I'll draw you a map to Lyle and Andie's place."

Within two days she had packed a bag, loaded her favorite tapes in her car, and decided to go without saying any formal good-byes. Certainly, she didn't expect Suzanne to miss her, and if she'd called her father, he'd have played a guilt trip, so she stopped by to see her mother at her photography studio. Dr. Levinson was there.

"Dr. Levinson just dropped by to see if I was in," Lynnette said, needing to explain his presence. "He wants me to photograph him and Leslie, to surprise Margaret on their anniversary. Isn't he thoughtful? Why, if Burt ever planned a surprise gift like that for me, I'd faint. Burt always goes out the last minute and buys the first thing he sees, and it's usually something I can't return, isn't that right, Steffani?" she asked.

Steffani felt disloyal discussing her father's inadequate gift giving with Dr. Levinson, but she had to agree. Burt never seemed to know what his wife would like and it fell to his two daughters to do it for him.

"I'm going to drive up to Santa Barbara with Dr. Levinson tomorrow to take the pictures. Now, David," she said, turning to him, "I don't want you to worry about Leslie's reaction. I'm sure she'll be all right. I've been shooting pictures of children for years, I know just what to do."

"But not children with cerebral palsy, Lynnette, it's hardly the same thing. She can't focus on anything around her, or stop moving her body even for a moment, and she certainly can't smile on cue."

"I know, David. I'll take candid shots, but I'm sure I'll get some you will love."

"It's Margaret who has to love them," he commented.

"She will, I promise." Lynnette looked at Steffani as if to say, *And we think we've got troubles.*

Steffani had once heard Dr. Levinson confide in Lynnette that even though the chances of a second child being born with cerebral palsy were very small, his wife had refused to have any more children.

"Can't you convince her?" Lynnette had asked.

"No," he said. "No matter what statistics I quote to her, she won't listen. She doesn't have your strength."

He had sounded so sad at the time, Steffani had wanted to hug him, but she figured her mother had comforted him.

"I don't know how long I'll be gone," Steffani told them both when they expressed surprise about her going. She tried to be as noncommittal as possible.

"But how can we reach you?" Lynnette asked.

"I'll let you know," she said, giving Lynnette a kiss on the cheek.

Lynnette reached to embrace her, but she pulled away. The last thing she saw was her mother's disappointed expression.

All during the long drive north, Steffani thought about Joe, something she hadn't allowed herself to do in a long time. The ache of missing him had eventually lessened. Dating other guys helped. But nobody ever meant to her what he had. They'd been really good together in spite of his temper and jealousy—and hers, she admitted. They were opposites, but boy, the attraction had been fabulous. She still got chills thinking of what it was like to be with him, and often she fantasized about him when she was with other men. She knew she shouldn't be going to see him, but the pull was too strong.

When she finally got to Oakland and found the theater it

was nearly eight o'clock at night and she was tired. She stopped and had something to eat at a nearby Italian restaurant and then walked over to the theater. It took up two storefront buildings in a run-down section of the city. A poster of an architectural drawing on the door showed they would be remodeling these stores into a real theater complete with marquee. HERE WE GROW AGAIN, it said.

She pushed open the door and peered in. There were rows of seats set up, and a small stage up front. Adjacent to the lighting booth, a ticket booth stood to the right of the door. Three actors were rehearsing onstage and there were several people scattered throughout the otherwise empty audience. One of them was Joe.

Her heart began to race with excitement when she saw him, and with something else, too. Anger. God, she was angry with him; she hadn't really known that until now.

She closed the door quietly behind her and moved into a back-row seat to listen. The actors were amateurish, the play only mildly interesting. From what she could tell it was about the conflict in a blue-collar Italian family, between a father and his two sons. One son wanted to be a writer.

The autobiographical aspects of Joe's life interested her, but she couldn't concentrate on the play while he sat right in front of her. He kept interrupting the actors, haranguing them to give it more energy, explaining motivation. She felt his frustration. She supposed that these actors were part of a repertory company and, once they joined, the director was stuck with them. After a long time of trying the scene several different ways, they took a break. Joe turned to confer with an older man and a woman sitting nearby, and then the three of them headed up the aisle toward her.

She held her breath. First the woman passed—long, grayish curly hair and dark shapeless clothing—then the man, probably her husband. They suited one another. And then Joe. Their eyes met, but he nearly passed her before he recognized her.

"Steffani?" Shock gave way to incredulity and then that

quirky smile of his. "What are you doing here? Is it really you?" He ran his hand through his thick, dark hair and she saw that he'd shaved his beard. It made him look younger.

There was so much she'd forgotten about him. He wasn't as large as she remembered, and he was much better-looking. The impact of him on her was astounding, especially his eyes. They were mesmerizing, drawing her in. And there was a sweetness about his smile that she hadn't remembered. Her memory had painted him as a big ogre, and now she saw that he wasn't that big, or that frightening, but still intense, and driven. All that happened in an instant.

He reached for her hand and helped her into the aisle. "I can't believe that you're here. How are you?"

"Fine."

"What are you doing here? Are you working? Still in school?"

"I graduated in June. I'm not working. I'm taking some time off. I've had an offer to live on a ranch near Santa Cruz, but I heard you were here, so I thought I'd drop in and say hello."

"What about teaching?" he asked, escorting her out. His hand fit on the small of her back as if it belonged there. She'd forgotten how he took charge, how he assumed everyone wanted what he wanted, how he engineered things his way.

"Doris and Paul are the producers of the theater group." He indicated the middle-aged couple walking on ahead. "We were just going for coffee. Would you like to join us?"

"Sure," she agreed. And then she said, so the other couple couldn't hear her, "I'd rather be alone with you. Any chance of that? Before I head out to Santa Cruz?"

"God, yes," he said, trying to hide a hint of hesitation that flickered in his expression. "If you can stick around until after the rehearsal. I can't get away until then."

She nodded and followed him into the same Italian restaurant where she'd had her soup and salad only an hour before.

Doris and Paul Taubman were polite, smiled at her when he introduced them to her as his good friend, but their agenda was the rehearsal of the play. Steffani listened to them talk shop with Joe, and then the Taubmans said they were tired and were going home.

Doris kissed Joe on the cheek, and Paul patted his arm as they got up to leave.

"Say hi to Addie for us," Paul said as he left. Doris nodded toward Steffani and gave her husband a look to indicate he'd said the wrong thing. He shrugged sheepishly.

"Addie's here with me," Joe explained, trying not to be embarrassed.

Steffani felt her stomach do a flip when he said that. She'd been afraid of that all along, that he'd have someone in his life. But not Addie! *So, that ineffective little nothing had him after all.* "Heather must be a big girl by now." She swallowed the sour taste in her throat, not letting him know she was bothered.

"She'll be five years old next month," he said, glancing away. "We enrolled her in school here." Then he looked back directly at her. "Addie needs me, Steff. You never did."

"Sure, Joe, whatever. You don't owe me an explanation. We haven't been together for a long time. I didn't figure you were alone, I just didn't expect you to be with her. You could do so much better. But then, she's easy, isn't she? You run things, and she doesn't mind. She whines, and you think it's need." She shrugged, making it okay, if disappointing.

"I've got to get back to rehearsal. Do you want to wait?" He put some money down for the coffee and stood up.

"Yes," she said. "It's too late to drive down to Santa Cruz tonight, I'd never find the ranch in the dark. I was hoping you could let me crash with you for the night. But now, I guess not." She followed him back to the theater.

"You're right, that's not such a good idea," he said, opening the door for her. "We'll talk later."

During the rest of rehearsal she digested what he had told her, thought about him objectively. She was still wildly attracted to him, and he was attracted to her, she could tell. But what of the rest of it? Great sex did not make a relationship.

Obviously, he was getting something from Addie, or he wouldn't be with her. Maybe it was a sense of family, probably it was just easier for him to be with her, than to try and fight through a new relationship with someone else. *And where do I fit in?*

In the back of her mind was the expectation that someday they'd get back together. But as impossible as it seemed, mousy Addie had won. *Hang on to this reality*, she told herself. *You've been away from him long enough to see him for what he is: not such a great catch. He's got a terrible temper, he's opinionated, thinks he's always right, thinks he's smarter than most people. Well, he is smart. And I like a man with an ego. But he doesn't know what's best for himself. I'm better for him than she is. And yet, she's got him.* How that rankled.

The rehearsal finally fizzled out because the actors were exhausted and Joe came back to where she was sitting. "It was hard to concentrate knowing you were back here waiting. I've thought so many times about what it would be like to see you, but I never could decide what I would say."

He took her arm and walked her out, turning out the lights and locking the door. "I live close enough to walk from here, so I don't need a car. Shall we take yours?" he asked.

She headed toward the car and took out her keys. He didn't offer to drive. The night was cold. A damp mist from the bay had covered the car with wetness. She cleared the window with a few movements of the wipers so she could see. "Where to?" she asked. "I'm not really hungry."

"There's a bar on Euclid, not far from here." He directed her there. But once they pulled into the parking lot and she shut off the motor, neither one of them made a move to get out of the car.

"You look really wonderful," he said, his voice softer than when he had spoken to his actors. "Have you been feeling well?"

"Yes," she told him. "I haven't had any health problems in a long time. Not since the accident."

"God, I hated myself for what happened that night."

"Is that why you stopped writing or calling?"

"Partly. I couldn't face the guilt."

"It was an accident."

"I was drunk, Steff. You could have been killed."

"I wasn't."

"It made me afraid to be with you. You are so fragile. I had to keep myself in check with you. It was a strain."

"That's a crock." The neon lights from the bar were shining on his face, making a multiple line of color, from red to blue to green to yellow, as though someone had painted a rainbow across his face.

"Why do you say that?" he said, shifting in his seat. Now the colors were up on the top of his head.

"Because you'd use any excuse in the world to get out of facing the truth. For a playwright you certainly do avoid your own motivations. I heard you talking about them all night to the actors, but you haven't got a clue about your own."

"I know myself, baby." Now he was annoyed. She had always been able to get under his skin like that. It felt wonderful to be doing it again, the way an animal must feel if it burrows back into an abandoned but familiar hole in the ground.

"So tell me how you justify spending these precious years of your life with Addie? You haven't married her, have you?"

"No," he admitted.

"Never even thought about it, have you?"

"No. But marriage isn't my thing."

"Bullshit, again, Joseph. You're Catholic. Marriage is a sacrament to you. So is procreating. Even if you don't want to admit it. All your instincts tell you that Addie is only a temporary in your life. But she's been temporary for five years now; without making up your mind, you're making up your mind. Drifting, just drifting."

"So what. It's also been the most productive time of my life."

"Why is that?" The car windows were growing foggy from their conversation, but she didn't want to get out and

go into a bar. She liked the intimate closeness the car provided. And since it was the last place they'd been together,
it was fitting that they end their relationship here too. For
that's what was happening. She tried to fight the sadness she
was feeling, but it wouldn't go away. Endings were always
sad.

"It's been productive because I haven't had to deal with
anyone else's personality but my own."

"Selfish, aren't you. Doesn't she even have a personality?"

"Writers have to be selfish or we'd never get anything
done. We have to shut out the world, dig into ourselves, pick
out the pieces of what we want to write about the way a
squirrel picks out the meat from a walnut, morsel by morsel."

"Oh brother," she said, putting her hands together and
wrinkling her nose like a squirrel, making fun of him.

He laughed. "Okay, so I'm dramatic. But so are you, if I
recall."

"Addie isn't dramatic, is she? She's quiet, passive, but
she comes on steady like a freight train."

"Yes, I guess she's a little like that. But I know what to
expect from her. She's created a peaceful life for us, the kind
that gives me plenty of time to work."

"And what does she do all day, this peacenik?"

"Watches TV, talks to her friends, goes to the store, things
like that."

"Does she clean?"

"She doesn't do windows," they both said, together, and
laughed.

"I don't know how you can stand it," she said.

"I miss the intensity of us," he admitted. "If I were to
compare the two of you, you're Iguaçu Falls, and she's a
quiet pool."

"Don't you know what happens to quiet pools? They stag-
nate."

He didn't have a reply for that.

"Joe, every play you've ever written deals with your past,

the years before you were thirty, because they contain the richest material, the events and people that have obsessed you, the parts of your life that demanded your attention. What will you write about ten years from now, when you've dealt with those conflicts and have only your life with Addie to look back on?''

He glared at her. "Don't be ridiculous, Steffani. I'll have plenty to write about."

"Oh, yeah. What?" She glared back, defiantly.

Finally, after a long time, he said, "I'll write about you."

What else could she say. He'd admitted that he still cared about her, certainly more than Addie. But that wouldn't change anything, and she wasn't sure she wanted it to.

"Shall I drop you off?" she asked.

"Where are you going now?"

"I thought I'd find a motel, since I can't stay with you."

He reached into his pocket and took out some peppermint Lifesavers and offered her one. She declined; he put one in his mouth. "I don't see why you can't sleep on our couch tonight. It's lumpy, but it's long. I've slept there sometimes when I've been working."

"Won't Addie mind?"

"Yes. She's jealous of you. Every time she sees me staring off into space, which I do all the time, she's afraid I'm thinking about you."

"That'll be the day." She laughed, starting the motor and clearing the windshield again with the wiper and the defroster.

"Yeah," he said. But from the way he said it, she realized that he did think about her a lot.

"Maybe it's not a good idea for me to go home with you," she said, reluctant to say good night. It was probably the last time she'd ever see him.

"Why waste your money on a motel. Addie will be asleep by now. You can stay on the sofa and leave in the morning."

"Okay," she agreed.

Their house was just two blocks from the theater, a wooden clapboard with a front porch and peeling paint on the trim.

"We're just renting," he explained. "But the furniture is ours."

It was too dark in the house to see much, but Joe lit a candle so as not to wake anybody up. He showed her where the bathroom was and gave her some blankets and a pillow, and then he whispered good night and disappeared into the bedroom. Watching him close the door gave her a terribly lonely feeling.

Sleep was impossible. The sofa was lumpy and narrow, and not a bed, by any means. She took off her slacks and her boots, but that didn't help. She felt depressed to be in the house of another woman, who Joe was sleeping with in the next room. He was unreachable to her as if he were in another city. What would she say to Addie in the morning? Maybe she'd leave at dawn and not have to see Addie. That sounded like a good idea.

And with that decision made, she actually fell asleep.

It may have been an hour or less when she was awakened by a floorboard creaking near her head. The room was black, but she could tell someone was there. And then she felt Joe's warm hand on her arm as he knelt on the floor beside the sofa.

"What is it?" she whispered. His hand caressed her cheek.

She could see his eyes reflected in the dark. They were gazing at her. And then he laid his head on her chest and put his arms around her. She felt his body shaking. He was crying.

"God, I've missed you," he whispered, wiping his tears on her covers.

She pushed him away for a moment, and he said, "I'm sorry, I'll leave you alone."

But she only had meant to pull back the blankets so he could come under them with her. When he understood that, he gave a sigh of relief.

It was like old times, only more poignant because they were saying good-bye. And all the time they were making love, she kept saying, "Remember this, my love, and this."

And he kept saying, "I will."

And when it was over, he stayed with her and held her, until the first light of dawn appeared. And then, she got up, used the bathroom, got dressed, and left the house, just as the sun was coming up.

She drove away, knowing he was watching her. And when she got around the corner, she turned off the engine, lowered her head to the steering wheel, and cried for a long time. She could still feel his arms around her, his body inside of hers. She was still sore from when he had loved her; her breasts, her arms felt used, but for their best purpose. When she finally stopped crying she felt cleansed, free of the past, and ready for a new adventure.

CHAPTER THIRTY-THREE

So, it's really over, Steffani thought, driving south on the freeway toward the Bay Bridge exit. It didn't seem possible that Joe had no more place for her in his life when there was that deep place inside of her that would always belong to him no matter who she was with. That special world of their own was inviolable. Hopefully, that would make this final separation a bit easier to bear.

The fog was burning off as she crossed the midway point of the bridge and got a glimpse of the city sitting there like a birthday cake dotted with tall wonderful candles. This morning the candles were all lit up for her by the rising sun's reflection in the windows of the buildings. Santa Cruz could wait a few hours while she dropped by the Haight to see what was happening.

It was so easy to get lost in San Francisco. One-way streets came to dead ends at the bases of hills that rose up sharply out of nowhere, and even maps didn't do any good. Steffani knew the general direction of Haight Ashbury, but she couldn't get out of the downtown area because she kept getting caught by the same old trick of ending up on Market Street where many of the downtown streets led. Frustration was getting to her. "If I drive by the Civic Center one more time, I'll scream," she said aloud, realizing that she was talking to herself. "Neat, Steffani, really neat."

And then, after driving by it three times without noticing, she saw that the marquee on the Performing Arts Building said SAN FRANCISCO OPERA PRESENTS IL TROVATORE. How many times had she heard her father singing arias from that opera? He should have been an opera singer himself. If only he'd had a voice, he'd have been great. Thinking about her father gave her a pang. It wasn't that she was homesick, exactly, just confused. Should she go on to Santa Cruz, or turn around and go home?

At that moment, a car parked by the San Francisco Civic Auditorium pulled away from the curb right in front of her and on a whim she parked her car in the empty space, just until she could get her bearings. When she looked up, there was a poster advertising the opera company and she saw Gloria Winston's name listed, singing a minor role.

A sly little smile began forming at the corners of her mouth. *Gloria*! she thought, gleefully. *One of my least favorite people*. Suzanne had to be nice to her for Alex's sake, but Steffani didn't. And she loved tormenting her, just a little bit. Maybe it was the way Gloria monopolized Burt and talked down to Lynnette, or to everyone for that matter, that irritated her. Or it could be the way she criticized anything Suzanne did. But mostly, it was Gloria's attitude. She thought her shit didn't smell, and nobody got away with that when Steffani was around.

She decided to come back later, just before the matinee, and say hello to her dear near relative, Gloria.

The Haight was really happening. Groovy people jammed the sidewalks, the smell of incense wafted in and out, while sitar music, or Beatle music, or Dylan songs came from every open window. She scored some grass, wrote a prescription for downers on some blanks she'd stolen long ago from Dr. Levinson's office, got it filled, and ate a breakfast of muffins, honey, and tea. There was a street artist doing body painting and she considered letting him do her arms, but settled for a flower on her cheek.

And then it was time to go and see Gloria.

Gloria was putting on her makeup in a crowded, communal dressing room when one of the stagehands showed Steffani back. And when he called out, "Gloria, a visitor named Blacker," Gloria turned toward the door with an enormous smile, only to have it freeze on her face when she saw it was Steffani Blacker and not Burt.

"Hi, there," Steffani said, moving through the crowded room of female performers in various stages of dress to Gloria's spot. "I saw your name on the marquee so I thought I'd stop by and say hello."

"I don't have time to visit now, I've got a performance in a little while."

"I know, but it's forty-five minutes till curtain. Plenty of time. In fact, I'm surprised to see you here so early. Dad says you're always late."

"I'm sure he doesn't discuss me with you," she retorted icily, glancing at the way Steffani was dressed with disdain.

"No? Well, I'll have to remind him of that the next time he complains to me about you."

"He does not!" she insisted, knowing Steffani was trying to irritate her but unable to keep her curiosity in check. "He's coming up here in a few days to see me. He takes very good care of me," she said, throwing irritants right back. She was outlining her eyes with a black, wet liner but at the same time managed to watch Steffani's expression.

"I'm sure he does," Steffani conceded, hating the idea that her father had anything at all to do with this witch. She looked around the room. "So, how is everything going? Your career and all?"

Gloria's hand shook slightly as she applied her makeup. "My career is advancing quite well. I have an important role in this opera, even if it is a minor one, but I'm understudying the lead."

"That's fine," Steffani said, unimpressed. What else would Gloria say.

"Your father treats me like a star. Otherwise I wouldn't stay with him. He works for *me*, you know. You ought to remember that. His commission on my earnings helped pay your college tuition." The glint in her eye showed how she'd scored with that comment.

But Steffani had heard it all before. *Being here is a waste of time*, she thought. *She's as impossible as she's always been, not even worth teasing for a little thrill.*

Just then, the same stagehand who had shown Steffani backstage stuck his head in the door and yelled, "Winston, you got another visitor."

And now Gloria began to hurry her makeup in earnest. "Oh, he's early," she said. "Damn." She was putting on her rouge, but the false eyelashes weren't on yet, and neither was her wig. "Listen," she told Steffani, "go outside the dressing room and tell him I'll be out in a few minutes."

"Who is he?" Steffani asked.

"George Ruben, you know, the designer. He's tall and tanned, with dark hair, you can't miss him. He's coming to see the show today and I told him to come at one-thirty."

"It's just one-thirty now," Steffani said, glancing at the clock on the wall.

"It can't be," Gloria said, obviously unnerved.

"Tsk tsk, late again?" Steffani asked.

"Oh, just go," Gloria said, waving her toward the door. "I suppose you want to see the show too?" she called.

"Actually, no," Steffani called back. "But thanks anyway." And she turned her back, so as not to see the daggers Gloria was throwing at her.

George Ruben was waiting right outside the door, looking just as Gloria had described, except she didn't mention how gorgeous he was or how square. He might have been a designer, but he didn't have the arty look at all. He looked more like George Hamilton, in a suit and tie, his ebony eyes darkly twinkling, his tanned complexion bronze against his dazzling smile.

"She's always late," he said with a flirtatious grin, appraising Steffani admiringly.

Steffani gave him a flirtatious smile right back.

"How nice of her to send me you instead."

Steffani introduced herself.

"Blacker," he said, as if it rang a bell. "Isn't her sister-in-law a Blacker, and her manager, too?"

"Yes, my sister is married to her brother."

"Is she as beautiful as you?"

"Of course not," Steffani said, tossing her head.

"Your father's her manager, right? If I didn't know better, I might be jealous of him. She talks of him constantly, won't do a thing without discussing it with him."

"Well, he's good to his clients." Steffani studied Gloria's latest beau. *Definitely not my type. Too mature for me, too suave, too square.* And too something she couldn't put her finger on. *Too phony? Was that it? Maybe.* "How long have you known Gloria?"

"Not long, but I'm fascinated by her. Anyone would be, don't you agree?"

"Not exactly. But if you're so fascinated with her, why are you flirting with me?" She was gazing up into his eyes, and he was gazing back. In fact his eyes had covered her from head to toe the moment she'd walked up to him. His smile implied that he'd have ducked into the nearest closet with her at a moment's notice. Only for the fact that he was Gloria's boyfriend was she tempted.

"It ruins the mystery to discuss why two people are attracted to one another. Don't you think? It's much more fun to flirt," he replied, smiling seductively. And then he leaned forward and kissed her on the cheek, right where she'd had the flower painted earlier that morning. She'd forgotten all about it, and for a moment she was embarrassed because it symbolized how vastly different she was from him, and from Gloria. And then she realized that she had nothing to be embarrassed about.

"So tell me, how do you manage to appear at all those social functions and yet turn out a wonderful line of women's fashions each season? Even I know who you are."

"You're rather well informed, aren't you?"

"You mean, for a hippie," she teased. "My mother and sister wear your clothes."

"And I admire your sense of style. But to answer your question, I have a good publicist who gets my name in the columns, even when I'm not at the parties they say I am."

Steffani was sure there was more to it than that. The responsibilities of this man's life made her momentarily embarrassed that she had none at all whatsoever, and no plans for any in the future.

Just then, Gloria came out of the dressing room in her long costume, wig, false eyelashes, and full makeup. Steffani had to admit she looked imposing. "Well, hello George," Gloria said, extending both hands. "Has my little friend been keeping you company?" She swept past Steffani, nearly pushing her aside, took his arm, and walked him through the backstage area, allowing Steffani to follow.

"Let me point out where your seat will be," she said, leading him to a peekhole in the curtain. And then, as though it was an afterthought, she turned and waved at Steffani. "Say hello to everyone," she called. "I'll see you soon." And she turned back to George, seeking to capture his attention completely.

But George, much to Gloria's annoyance, waved to Steffani, winked. "See you again," he called, and blew her a kiss.

So she blew him one back.

It was midafternoon by the time she got to Santa Cruz, a delightfully quaint old seaside town, with funky shops, outdoor cafés, and college students everywhere, in sandals and Indian print shirts, enjoying the bright sun and the salt sea air. The sun was particularly strong this day, turning the sky to a whitish blue, even though it was late October. She parked the car and walked around the town, checking out the shops, the bookstores, the local small-town paper. It felt as though she'd been liberated from big-city life and she fell in love with the place.

The ranch, or farm (nobody ever could decide what to call it), was a series of migrant cabins, unoccupied for the winter and set back away from any other structures so that nobody could see that they were now occupied. The main house was closer to the highway, down a long driveway bordered by tall eucalyptus trees. It was a rambling old one-story place, with a FOR SALE sign in the front yard, paint peeling off the wood clapboard siding, and a large porch around the front.

You could hardly see any of the cabins from the main house because there were acres of fallow fields between them and anything else in sight. Eucalyptus trees grew between the fields, and a pine forest covered the hills in the distance. Steffani pulled her car in next to an old beat-up Ford truck and turned off the engine. She heard a rooster crow, and saw a few chickens picking in the dirt around the side of the house.

She walked up the cement steps to the front door, which had a window in it, and peered in through a torn curtain. Voices were coming from inside so she knocked, and called, "Hello."

Abruptly, the voices ceased.

"Lyle, Andrea," she called, "it's Steffani Blacker, Melody's friend."

Footsteps sounded from inside, and then someone unlatched the door and opened it. She stepped into a dimly lit, smoky room.

"What are you doing here?" Lyle asked, as he stepped back to let her in.

"Hi, Lyle. Melody gave me directions on how to get here. She thought I might get a kick out of dropping in on you."

"Well, you scared the shit out of us. We're not exactly advertising that we're here."

"Why not?"

" 'Cause it isn't ours," Andrea said, coming in from another room, one Steffani assumed was the kitchen. She was drying her hands on a dishrag. "Hey, Steffani," she said.

Steffani greeted her, then turned to the two other people in the room, a young woman about her age, and a guy also in his midtwenties. They were both sitting on the only piece of furniture in the room, a sofa without any seat cushions. The haze in the room, which made her eyes burn, was caused by smoke coming from the fireplace. Then she smelled the pot and felt right at home.

"I'm Steffani," she said, walking over to take a drag from their joint.

"He's Robin," Lyle said, pointing to the guy, "and this is Felicia."

Felicia, a chunky girl, with long dark straight hair and acne scars on her face, waved hello. Robin just stared.

"So, what's happening?" Steffani asked. "This is some place, isn't it, really beautiful. What's wrong with the fireplace?"

"We don't know," Robin said. He had long hair too, brownish blond, pulled back into a ponytail. His lip sprouted a thin mustache. His eyes were tearing and he kept wiping them. "Every time we light the fire, the smoke comes pouring into the room. But since there's no heat or electricity here, we need it to keep us warm."

"Is the flue open?" she asked.

"What's that?" Andrea said, coming further into the room.

"You know, the little door in the chinmey that you open when you light a fire and close when you're not using it."

They all looked at her in surprise.

"I never heard of that," Robin said.

"Did you ever have a fireplace in your house?" Steffani asked.

"I never lived in a house," Andrea commented.

"Me neither," Lyle said.

Obviously Felicia and Robin were also unfamiliar with fireplaces.

Steffani couldn't tell them that the house she grew up in had three wood-burning fireplaces, one in the den, one in the living room, and one in the family room. Being with people who didn't even know what a flue was reminded her of a night in the dorm when she was visiting Cathy Callahan's room. Several of Cathy's friends were there and they were talking about religion. Every one of them believed that the Jews killed Christ and not one of them had ever eaten a bagel in their lives. It was a real eye-opener.

Steffani went into the kitchen and found a potholder. Then she came back into the living room and reached into the hearth above the smoldering logs, grabbed the handle of the flue, and pushed it hard. They could hear the creaking of the metal door and immediately the smoke from the fire began to flow up the chimney.

"Hey, savior!" Felicia shouted. "I hope you're staying, 'cause there's lots of other things about this rustic life we don't know shit about."

That night, Steffani again slept in her clothes. She lay on the exposed ticking of a lumpy mattress, rough and stained from years of migrant use, thinking about what it would be like to stay here for a while.

They assigned a cabin to her that had no heat, no electricity, and no hot water, but at least the toilet flushed. And she was out of the city, away from the problems of her life. Lyle and Andrea had bought vegetable seed packets and planted a garden—tomatoes, squash, carrots, anything that was easy to grow this time of year. And they'd have eggs from the chickens to eat. They were planning to bake their own bread, if they could get the electric stove to work by buying a used generator. Until then, refrigeration was a problem, so they were using a picnic cooler filled with ice, keeping it outside at night. Judging from the freezing temperature in her cabin, winter would be even colder, good for preserving food, but not people. Maybe she'd buy a sleeping bag and just sleep in the living room by the fire at night. Staying here in this sort of haphazard commune seemed like a challenge and an adventure. The whole country was talking about getting back to nature, and now the opportunity had been given to her. Maybe she'd try it. If only she didn't miss Joe so much.

CHAPTER THIRTY-FOUR

"We've got to get organized," Steffani said. "Divide up the duties, decide what we're going to do—you know, set goals, arrange for seasonal chores, things like that. We can't just sit around getting loaded all the time."

"Why not?" Robin asked, scratching his ankle. He'd stepped in poison oak while walking in the woods and the rash was beginning to spread. He had a way of whining when he talked that had started to grate on her nerves. She'd been here nearly a week and had settled into a routine of sorts, sharing the cooking, helping with the chores, taking walks, getting high. But she could see that unless this group had an organized plan, things would deteriorate rapidly.

"Well, first of all, we'll run out of dope and we won't have the bread to buy more. Second, we'll starve to death if we don't provide a means to feed ourselves."

"That's easy." Robin giggled. "You stick the fork in the food, put it in your mouth, and chew."

Felicia thought that was hysterical. But then, both Robin and Felicia together only had the intelligence of one average sixth-grader. A gay friend of Robin's, Lance, who professed to be a black militant activist and wore army fatigues, had dropped in a few days ago and decided to stay. Robin and Lance were either lying around stoned or making it in the next room, barely able to contain their ardor for aberrant sex. Steffani had never seen two people so turned on to one another as these two boys. And Felicia had several boyfriends who had promised to look her up. One of them was due in that night. That left Steffani as the only single person in the group, an unusual status for her. She attributed her need for organization to this, as well as to her natural leadership ability. None of the others were capable of organizing anything.

"The other day, when I went into town for supplies, I bought the *Whole Earth Catalogue*," she told them. "It's full of useful information about growing crops, sanitation, compost heaps, saving the topsoil, even irrigation. We could turn this place into a utopian community."

Andrea was sitting on the floor in front of the fireplace braiding Lyle's long brownish blond hair into french braids. She'd discovered that being away from hairdressing as a profession had gotten her in touch with the tactile beauty of hair as a symbol of virility and an essential part of humanity. She had a need to touch it, to work with it as something organic, rather than as a commercial experience. Lyle sat there, his long legs crossed Indian style, nodding in a dope haze, while she busily smoothed and plaited, hand over hand. Both their smiles were beatific, as if they'd found total contentment—the need to braid and the need to be braided in perfect coexistence.

They were staring at her as if she'd been swearing in church. "You don't want us to start being farmers, or something like that, do you?" Felicia asked.

"Why not? It wouldn't cost much to feed ourselves. For the price of one order of Kentucky Fried Chicken we could buy enough seed to plant a whole field. Seed is cheap, it's the labor to grow it and the water to irrigate it and the taxes on the land that cost money. But we've got cheap labor among us. We could grow fresh vegetables, maybe even sell them."

"Don't you know how that bullshit works?" Lance stated. "The sale of produce is regulated by the government or a combine. You can't sell food on the marketplace, they won't let you."

"I'm not talking about competing with some large-scale farmer. I'm talking about having our own stand by the side of the road, or supplying a local market," she replied.

"Farmers don't make money," Lance said. "They're exploited by the government, which subsidizes them not to grow food on their land. Instead, they have to sit there with empty fields, while people in Africa are starving."

"It's a question of economics," she told him, not totally agreeing herself with the principle of government subsidy. "If our farmers grow too much food, even for free export, it would drive the price of food down and put other farmers out of business."

"Sounds like another government plot to me," Andrea decided, putting the finishing touches on Lyle's braid. Then she started kissing his neck and kneading his shoulders with her fingers. Obviously this session would deteriorate into something physical between them. Steffani didn't want to watch, so she decided to take a walk.

At the end of three weeks, they had four additions to their group. Felicia's friend Jim, who arrived one night in the cab of his semi. He preferred liquor to drugs, had voted for Goldwater, thought Johnson was a pussy and that anyone who opposed "our" position in Southeast Asia was a commie. Everyone wanted Jim to leave after his frequent drunken outbursts, but Jim was the only one of them who had any mechanical ability, and the used generator they had bought for $125 rarely worked.

The additional three members of the group consisted of a young woman named Kathy and her two children—Justin, six, and Megan, four. Kathy was a heroin addict who needed her fix just to maintain. And Justin and Megan were neglected while their mother nodded out. Steffani assumed immediate control of the children, taking them on nature hikes, teaching them about the plants and animals, and trying to give them a cursory education. Kathy said she didn't believe in formal schooling, but what she meant was, it was too difficult for her to keep her children enrolled anywhere, because she was always moving around looking for dope. She was on welfare, and so was Felicia. Andrea was collecting unemployment.

"Are you starting that again?" Andrea asked, when she found Steffani going over the list of their finances.

"Somebody has to," Steffani said. "The children need proper nutrition and my money is almost gone. You are only entitled to three more weeks of unemployment checks, and Kathy spends every dime on her habit. Lance and Robin are nearly tapped out, which means we have to start taking money from dear old Jim. Even then, we'll all have to leave in a few weeks unless we find a way to make money." She looked up at Andrea. "Could you get some work in Santa Cruz at a local beauty parlor?"

Andrea, whose pale skin was blotchy with a rash that wouldn't go away, put her hands on her hips and cocked her head. She had a heart-shaped face with a pointed chin, full and pudgy around the cheeks, though, from lack of food, she was losing weight. Her eyes were small and close together, but she wasn't unattractive. "Are you kidding? Nobody goes to the hairdresser in Santa Cruz, this is the long-hair capital of the world."

"What about Lyle? Could he get a job?"

"Lyle's hiding out from his old lady, he owes her child support up the wazoo. Any place he works they'll ask for his social security number, and she'll find out where he is. He don't want to go to jail."

"I don't think the government can trace you by your social security number."

"Are you kidding? Of course they can."

"Well, if you'd taken my advice and planted a crop three weeks ago, we would have had something to eat and to sell by now."

"You know we tried," Robin said, coming into the kitchen from the communal room. It had become like a dormitory when Steffani began sleeping by the fire at night. Everybody who was freezing to death out in their cabins thought it was a good idea too, and dragged their mattresses in. Now the place looked like a flop house for derelicts, or a Mafia hide-away. But at least they slept warmly at night. As for sex, nobody cared who was watching or listening, because by the time they got around to screwing everybody was usually stoned.

"The gophers ate the carrots and the birds ate half the seeds before they even sprouted," Robin reminded them. "And then, as soon as the spinach started to sprout, the deer got it. It's fucking hard to grow vegetables!" he said, emphatically. "We need pesticides, or something." And then he giggled as he realized how everyone was into natural food.

It was depressing for Steffani to note how much their personal hygiene had deteriorated. Everyone needed a bath. The first few weeks they'd stayed here, they'd all kept their belongings in their cabins, leaving a minimal amount of possessions and telltale debris in the main house, so that if the realtor showed up unexpectedly, they could clean up the place in an instant and scurry out the back door. But as time went by, they became more and more complacent, so that now, when there might be a need to vacate the premises in a moment's notice, there was so much stuff lying about that only a janitorial service could have gotten rid of it in hours, not minutes. It was a losing battle, Steffani realized, to get this flotsam motivated, and the more she realized how hopeless it was, the more she became aware of how much she missed Joe.

Only Kathy, who was usually dozing on a mattress in the living room, wasn't bothered by the poverty they lived in. What would Joe think if he saw her unkempt clothes, the not-so-neatly combed hair pulled on top of her head, her broken and dirty fingernails. She could just hear him say in his superior way, "Nature giving you guys a rough time?"

With a sudden clarity, she got a glimpse of the things she was in the habit of denying, such as her relationship with her family, her health, her lack of goals. Everything in her life was screwed up. The reality threatened to swallow her up as if she'd stepped into the compost heap outside the kitchen door. But before it could overtake her, she managed to press it back down into its former subdued shape. But her longing for Joe was not so easily denied. She could almost feel him caressing her body, kneading her breasts, sending that wild fire sweeping through her. All those nights of listening to the others panting and moaning in their sleeping bags, witnessing that furtive grabbing between couples, had been playing on her subconscious. And suddenly a fire of desire exploded within her. How she longed to enter that world again that was theirs alone! But Joe was not here with her, would never be with her, and the pain of that tore through her mercilessly.

As time went by, the miserable life she shared with her motley group got only worse. Even the beauty of the surroundings had lost its ability to charm her. She replayed conversations with Joe in her mind, such as the time she'd asked him, "When did you first know you loved me?"

And he'd said, "That first day after Gertsman's class when I read your poem. I could tell more about you from that than anything else, except your scars."

"Do they bother you?" she'd asked, remembering how she'd tensed, waiting for his reply.

"Yes, because they show how much you've suffered."

"Do you mind them, physically?"

"Only because I worry about you. But imperfections don't turn me off."

Maybe that's why the loss of him was so painful. He had loved her for who she was. He'd known her because she'd let him. But ultimately, he hadn't chosen her. She wasn't enough for him, after all.

The only time she could get him out of her mind was when she borrowed something from Kathy and shot up. It was wrong of her to do such a thing herself and she knew it, but it seemed the only alternative. She had to get out of here— this was no place for her—but she couldn't bring herself to leave. There was nothing to go to. She hadn't found herself at all; she'd only been hiding out in a place that belonged to someone else who paid the taxes on it. She was beginning to think of herself as a loser, no different from the others.

Perhaps her despair was exaggerated because she was coming down with a cold; her sinuses were aching and swollen, and her throat hurt when she swallowed. But the cold was only discomfort compared to the pain of loneliness. When she tried to understand why Joe had preferred Addie over her, she just hit a dead end. By evening, she decided she had to speak to him one more time, to ask him why. She drove into Santa Cruz to call him, hoping he would be glad to hear from her, telling herself that her call might be just what he was waiting for.

But she lost her nerve.

That night, her cold got worse and she ran a fever. Everyone had suggestions on what remedies to use, but she knew better than to take medications that could cause unwanted side effects. If only Joe were here she'd feel better.

Then her fever shot up. It was very high; from past experience, even without a thermometer, she could tell. Her glands were swollen and painful, her throat was raw, and she had a dry cough. And now all she could think about was speaking to Joe. She'd drive into Santa Cruz and, this time, she'd call.

"I don't think you should go out feeling as sick as you are," Andrea said.

But Andrea wasn't her mother; she didn't have to obey her. She dragged herself out of bed and into her car, but by then, she was so exhausted and sick, she could barely drive. Finally, she got into town, found a pay phone, and stopped.

The operator gave her the number of Joseph Mariano in Oakland. She dialed the number.

Joe answered the phone.

For a moment she was so happy to hear his voice she couldn't speak. Besides, her throat was so constricted from the painful infection raging there that the words wouldn't come out. She managed to croak out the words, "Joe, it's me. How are you?"

"Steffani?" he said. "Why did you call me? I can't talk right now. Addie's here."

That was all she needed to hear. It was suddenly clear. She felt like a goddamned fool for bothering him. He'd never leave Addie because she let him walk all over her. How could he leave a turn-on like that?

She wanted to scream in his ear, "Stay out of my life, stay out of my heart! Go fuck yourself." But instead, she just hung up. And then she stood there and cried.

Somehow she got back to the ranch and made it into bed. She was sick for ten days. But the flu didn't bother her, and neither did she miss Joe, because whenever either pain got too bad, she borrowed some of Kathy's junk and took the edge off.

CHAPTER THIRTY-FIVE

"How are you, really, honey?" my father asked, folding me into an embrace. For a brief moment in his arms, I felt safe and secure, like a child again. But then the moment passed and I saw reality pressing its hideous face against the window, leering at me.

I sighed and pulled away. "Hanging in there, I guess."

"I have some news."

The way my mind worked lately, the first thing I thought of was Sugar Markham. But I knew that wasn't it. Sugar's mother was due home in a week and we hadn't found Sugar yet.

He held my chin up so he could study my face. I knew what he would see, the same mixture of shell-shocked despair that greeted me whenever I looked in the mirror.

"If it's good news I can use it, Dad." We hadn't moved

into an apartment over the holidays. There wasn't time, with my job and the hearing and all; besides, I couldn't afford to pay rent on two places. Now, it was January 6, 1977, and decisions had to be made. The new semester started on the twentieth and the children wanted to know what schools they were going to attend.

Just today, I'd found a not-so-bad apartment with two bedrooms in Van Nuys, but the neighborhood wasn't exactly prime. I had to place a deposit on it or I'd lose it, and my house wasn't sold or leased. I made the mistake of taking Amy to see the apartment, thinking she ought to have a say in the choice, but she didn't say anything except, "Whatever you want, Mom." And that was all.

"I hope you'll think this is good news," my father said. "One of my clients, Almeida Consalvo, a guest conductor for the Ambassador Auditorium concert series in their winter/ spring session, is looking for a house for himself and his family to lease for a few months while they're here. I told him about your house and he's interested. He'd like to come tomorrow to see it."

It was both good news and bad. It would be a temporary reprieve, and I wouldn't have to rush to sell it. The bad news was, it would force me to move out right away.

"It's great, Dad." I tried to show how much his concern meant to me.

"I thought so," he said. "Almeida can afford to pay a good price, since I got him such an excellent contract. So you won't have a negative cash flow, and since he only needs it for a few months . . ." He noticed my expression. "Maybe by the time his concert season is over, the lawsuit will be settled and you can move back here."

"Or, by then I'll have a bona fide buyer," I couldn't help saying.

He sighed; people did that around me a lot lately. "It's going to be all right, darling," he said. "You'll see."

But somehow, that kind of comforting statement made less and less sense to me.

* * *

I should have stayed home and packed—we were moving in a week—but when Barry offered to take me to Palm Springs for the weekend, I said yes. Alex was glad to have the children—too glad, I thought. They rarely stayed overnight with him and I knew he would take this opportunity to try and convince them to make it permanent by making everything as attractive as he could. Dina had gone back to Australia after her holiday break to complete her filming and I imagined Alex was lonely. I couldn't refuse the children a weekend with him, and I certainly needed some time off.

Barry and I drove down on Friday afternoon, almost early enough to beat the traffic, and my burdens lifted with each passing mile. In spite of everything going wrong in my life, Barry could awaken me to the fullness of enjoyment. We'd had very little time together since we'd become lovers, and both of us were looking forward to this weekend. All the way there, we held hands and touched and stroked one another, so that the minute we checked into the Canyon Country Club, we fell on one another and made love.

Barry is a wonderful lover, not only patient and inventive, but truly enthusiastic. His passion ignited me. There was none of the hesitancy that characterized my sexual relationship with Alex. And above all, no fastidiousness. Barry seemed to like every part of my body, and that was a decidedly new phenomenon for me.

"Mmm," he said, pressing his nose against my neck. We were entwined on the bed, the covers on the floor, our nude bodies moist from exertion. "You taste delicious."

"As good as jamocha almond fudge?" I asked, his favorite.

"Better than a Snickers," he sighed.

And I laughed, remembering that that was his most favorite of all. I wove my fingers through his hair, feeling heavy with contentment, my body floating in a tenuous peace.

"What do you want to do now?" he asked.

"Spend some time outdoors, maybe take a walk in town, have dinner, come back here and do this again."

His hand on my stomach declared his ownership. "I'm dying for a double frozen margarita with a ring of extra salt on the rim," he said.

My mouth watered as I pictured it. The tastes of food and drink were exquisite when I was with him.

"And what about tomorrow?" We had two lovely days ahead of us before I had to go back and face whatever new heartache or disaster was lying in wait.

"Let tomorrow take care of itself," I sighed.

He moved his hand up to my breast, caressing me more out of contentment than eroticism. "If we don't reserve a court we won't be able to play tennis."

"I'd rather go biking."

"We'll do both."

"You'll wear me out." I laughed, feeling a blanket of happiness wrapped around me. *Please let this last*, I begged.

"That's the idea," he agreed. And then he said, "I've been thinking about something I wanted to discuss with you."

I don't know why, but my pulse quickened.

"If things go along the way they have been, maybe you shouldn't move out of the house or lease it to that conductor."

"What do you mean?" I asked, barely able to talk.

"I mean, I could buy your house from you and we could live there with the children," he said.

I sat up in bed and tried to ignore the sensuous glance he was giving my body. "Can you afford it?"

"I think so," he said.

"But it's such a huge step to take, so early in our relationship," I told him. "I don't want to do anything we'll regret. We mustn't rush things or be hasty merely because we're both needy and vulnerable."

"I know," he said, slowly. "You're right. I do have a tendency to want to rush, to make up for lost time. And I'm not saying I would definitely do this, I just wanted to talk to you about it."

Now, I didn't know whether to be happy or not. "I don't want charity, Barry. If you just want to do something nice for me because I've been dragged through an acid pit, don't.

If you love the house and think it's a great investment, and think it's where you'd like to live whether or not anything happens between us, then okay, I'd say yes."

He sighed. "I wasn't thinking of it like that."

"Well, you should. For both our sakes." I was simultaneously elated and deflated. One minute my problems had been solved, and the next they had increased twofold. "What if I'm not cleared of the charges and I couldn't buy the house back, Barry? Would you want to live there alone?"

"I can't imagine that happening," he insisted. "If that hooker from New York is the one doing this to you, you'll be acquitted. And if it's not her, it's got to be someone else, right? But if the worst thing happens and you're found guilty, you'll probably get a suspended sentence and a fine."

"Will you put that in writing?" It would take me the rest of my life to pay back another fine. It was not the first time I'd heard Barry's optimistic prediction, but nobody could guarantee me what was going to happen. "It's a very generous offer," I finally told him. "But I don't expect you to bail me out."

"Nevertheless," he said, pulling me back into his embrace, "I think it's what I should do." And he kissed me, as if sealing the bargain.

All during dinner I was excited. I couldn't help it; I had not wanted to be forced out of my home. And this meant he was declaring himself. The sensible part of me knew I should take this slowly, that we were barely more than strangers, that only time would test our growing affection. But time was a luxury for me right now. I had more immediate concerns. Maybe it was selfish too, but I was thinking about how happy the children would be to be able to stay in our home. They'd get used to public school, and when the case was settled, life could really return to normal. Of course, I knew there were legal ramifications I might not like. In effect, I'd be selling my house to a stranger. If we broke up, he could kick me out. Would I be any better off that way?

We sat on the patio of the Mexican restaurant, under the

outdoor heaters, sipping frozen margaritas and pretending that it was summer. The splashing sounds of the fountain, mingled with the Mariachi music, were romantic. But I couldn't shake the undercurrent between us that had begun when Barry brought up the idea of buying the house. All our politeness and flirting and hand holding couldn't erase the unease in my gut. But by mutual consent, we weren't discussing it.

Saturday was cloudy and cool, with the sun breaking through the clouds to bathe the world in its brilliant glow. We played two sets of tennis, took a swim, and then in the afternoon, as the sun was setting behind Mount San Jacinto, we rode our bikes along the residential streets looking at the tile-roofed houses landscaped with gravel, cactus, and oleanders. Only an occasional house had a lawn.

We went to the Racquet Club that night for dinner and danced to songs from the forties, while we each sang the words to one another from songs like "Embraceable You," "I'll Take Manhattan," "Accentuate the Positive," and "Blue Skies."

"How do you know all those words?" I asked him.

"I love a Gershwin tune," he said, "how about you?"

I laughed. "I love New York in June, how about you?"

"I've always wanted to dance like Fred Astaire," he admitted. "When I was a kid, on Saturday, Laura Lee Fineman and I used to go to the movies and we'd come home and play them all over again. Of course, we'd argue over every detail because her memory was different than mine. But the details didn't matter. I'd be transported into believing I was Roy Rogers on Trigger, or Dana Andrews flying a spitfire in a raid over Germany, or Errol Flynn swordfighting with Basil Rathbone. And if I'd seen a musical, I really thought I could dance. Sometimes I'd hear the songs from the movie again on the radio and I'd always remember the lyrics. One of my favorites is 'All the Things You Are.' What words! 'You are the promised kiss of springtime, that makes the lonely winter seem long,' " he quoted. " 'You are the breathless hush of evening, that trembles on the brink of a lovely song. You are the angel glow, that lights a star, the dearest things I know, are what you are.' "

I looked away to hide the tears that sprang to my eyes while my heart soared, because that's exactly the way I had spent so much of my childhood, going to the movies every Saturday, coming home to reenact what I had seen at the double feature and being completely enamored of the wonderful lyrics to romantic songs; and, of course, wishing I could dance like Leslie Caron or Cyd Charisse.

I felt him touch my chin and pull my face toward him. He was smiling as he wiped away my tears. "That's how I feel about you, Suzanne," he said. "I want all the things you are, to be mine." He kissed me lightly on the lips and I trembled all over.

"I love you," I told him. But for the first time since we'd been saying that to one another, he didn't say it back.

On Sunday, we stayed in bed and read the paper. We had to check out by one o'clock so we decided to go horseback riding. Then we stopped for a lunch about two and headed back to town. It had been a wonderful weekend, but there was something unspoken between us that was making my heart ache. That, and the fact that we hadn't made love on Saturday. After we returned from dinner, we'd gone right to sleep.

"What's wrong?" I asked finally, unable to stand the suspense any longer. We were heading west into the setting sun, which glared into my eyes.

"Nothing's wrong," he said, taking my hand. But I wasn't convinced.

I thought for a moment about what I was going to say, whether or not to broach the subject, but then decided to plunge ahead. "It's the house, isn't it? You're having second thoughts about your offer and you don't know how to take it back. Well, I'm taking it back. It was a wonderful gesture, but let's forget it. Let's just go back to the way things were. Please, Barry, I don't want anything to spoil what we have. It's too important." *Let it alone, Suzanne*, I told myself. *Don't say any more.*

"I care for you very much," he said. "You know that."

"And you got swept away by concern for me. It means a lot to me. Honestly, it does. But I'll be okay in an apartment; so will the kids. When the time is right, if you and I decide there's a future for us, then we can find our own place to live. Okay? Does that make you feel better?" I felt a twisting pain in my guts that almost made me stop breathing. I was saying everything he wanted to hear, but what I wanted to say was, *Yes, buy my house. Rescue me! Rescue my children. Make this awful part of my life go away. You can do it, you have it within your power. Please do it, now!*

"I shouldn't have brought it up," he said, embarrassed.

"Maybe you shouldn't have," I said, suddenly feeling my temper rise. "You raised my hopes. I thought you meant it. I thought you'd come to a decision."

"I never said that." He was getting angry too.

"No, but you certainly implied it." I knew I wasn't being entirely fair, but I felt jerked around.

"I had every intention of going ahead with this thing, Suzanne," he said. "But then, I got to thinking you were right. Maybe I was rushing into it too fast. You've been so preoccupied with this plagiarism thing, you haven't had the time to consider my needs at all. You've been in trouble ever since I met you. I'm not sure I really know who you are. Our relationship has been intense because of your situation. You've needed me in an unusual way, and I've responded to that need. I'd like to know what it would be like if we were just two people, meeting, getting to know one another, without this heightened emotionalism. Would you still want me? Would I still respond to you? I guess what I'm saying is, this may not be the right time for either of us to make a commitment. I'm sorry if I led you on by suggesting I buy the house. It wasn't right of me."

Those twisting sinews inside were being seared by a hot poker. "You mean, I shouldn't take you at your word when you say things like, 'I'm here for you. I want all the things you are to be mine.' Does that mean only the good things?" I couldn't help the sarcasm.

He's not like the others, I told myself. *Nothing like Alex. Not like the men my girlfriends complain about, who say one thing and mean another, or don't mean what they say at all. He can't have been dishonest all this time. And if he was honest, then what's happened to change him?* I screamed silently, feeling as if the bottom was falling out. All I could think about was what my children would say if this didn't work out. They would be devastated, especially with everything else going on. *I should have known better than to trust anyone. I should never have let anyone get so close.* The car was speeding along the highway, tearing up the road; I wanted it to stop, I wanted to press my hands against the dashboard and make the whole thing stop! But inexorably, it kept moving forward.

"I can't say I haven't been there for you, Suzanne," he insisted. "But you're taking what I'm saying the wrong way." His profile, that I usually adored, had suddenly become stonelike.

"How should I take it? It's not as if any of this is my fault. Or is that what you think?"

He glanced at me, trying to soften the moment, but I just glared back. "Of course I don't think it's your fault. You're a victim here. I can see how it torments you."

"But it's not too attractive, is that it? Should I call off what's happening in my life because it's inconvenient for you at this time? You say you want to have things normal—well, for God's sake, so do I! Why don't you tell me what I should do?" I threw up my hands in frustration.

We drove in silence; for a while neither of us spoke. Finally, I said, "Barry, I agree with some of the things you said. Our time together has been under extreme circumstances. But life is full of problems, if it wasn't this, it could have been something else." I paused, suddenly figuring out what this was really about but almost too miserable to say it. "Are you looking for an excuse to get out of this relationship gracefully? Is that it? You're not ready for the C word, especially when you'd be committing yourself to someone as screwed up as I am."

He was ominously silent. Then he said, "I thought I was ready. But maybe I'm not. It's times like these that make me realize we have a lot to learn about each other."

"You mean, nothing like this would ever have happened to Eileen?" I pressed, wanting desperately for him to deny what I'd just said and assure me I was wrong.

"Leave Eileen out of this," he snapped, confirming what I'd thought, that he was clinging to the past, to an ideal, so as not to continue ahead with us. "I just want to see what we'd be like as two normal people, just you and me and your kids, living a normal life."

"But you know I can't do that right now."

"I know you can't," he agreed.

"Barry, what if one of us got sick? How would you deal with that? Would you say that being sick is just too dramatic, that it offers too much heightened drama? Would you blame me for having contracted some disease?"

He gave me a killing glance and refused to answer me. I'd never seen him so angry. Then he shouted, "No I wouldn't! Dammit."

I couldn't help it, I started to cry. And when he reached out to comfort me, I pulled away. *Damn you, Barry Adler*, I thought, *for making me believe in you. I should have known better*. He'd seemed so solid, trustworthy. But life had seemed trustworthy too, and now look at what had happened. What could I do, after all? Force him to love me? No way.

We were silent the rest of the way home. When I took my bag out of the trunk, he offered to carry it up the drive for me, but I wouldn't let him.

"I'll call you," he said.

But I shook my head. "I think we should give it a rest for a while." Every ounce of me was crying for him to get out of the car, put his arms around me, and say this had all been a mistake.

"Whatever you say," he agreed, showing his own hurt.

All I could think about, as I stood there watching him drive away, was that I remembered what this was like, having someone you love turn out to be completely unreliable and eventually turn their back on you, leaving you alone. God, how well I remembered.

Later that week, I finally got a message on my service that Avery had called. This was it! He must have found Sugar or her mother. My heart pounded with excitement as I waited for him to come on the phone. For the first time in days I wasn't thinking about Barry.

"We found Sybil Markham, Suzanne," he began, with none of the excitement I expected.

"Is she coherent? Did you talk to her? Does she know where her daughter is?"

"Slow down and I'll tell you."

"Oh, for God's sake, Avery, spit it out. I can't stand it any longer!"

"Okay, I'm trying. It's not good news, Suzanne."

I grabbed on to the kitchen counter where I was standing. Nothing ever prepares you for bad news.

"She got home from her vacation and returned my call immediately. She remembered you very well and she's in touch with Sugar. But Sugar has been living in Japan for the last three years, working as a paid escort, another word for prostitute. And get this, it's the syndicate she used to work for."

"Those people who kidnapped her?"

"Well, the kidnap part is debatable. But yes. Her mother says she couldn't be happier. I'm quoting now: 'My daughter goes out with some of the top businessmen in Japan.' I guess over there she's special, while here she'd be just another girl on the stroll."

"When was the last time she was home?"

"Not in the last year."

"Oh damn," I said, feeling everything crumbling again. That was that. Back to square one. "Now what?" I said, not caring very much.

"We'll keep looking," he told me. "Nobody's giving up."

"I know," I replied. But at this moment, that's exactly what I felt like doing.

The film of my first novel, *To Catch a Count*, was released on the tenth of November 1968. It wasn't a critical success, but the public liked it and it made a lot of money. Steffani wasn't here for all the excitement. I missed her—we'd always shared every event in each other's lives—but in a way I was glad she wasn't around. Her life had reached a low point, and mine was high with success. It might have been difficult for her to be happy for me; at least it would have been for me, had I been in her place.

Silver's Press rereleased my novel to coincide with the opening of the movie and the book became a best-seller on the *New York Times'* paperback list. I'd had no idea how being on that list could affect my career. For now that my second novel, *The Reunion*, was completed and ready for sale, my price was in a new category. "Fifty thousand, even a hundred might not be unreasonable to expect," my agent told my husband. I was awed by the possibility and looked to Alex to validate my new status.

"I've always loved my wife's literary qualities," Alex started saying to people when they congratulated me. "Especially, her tail and two titties."

The first time he said it, I laughed. But after a while, I didn't think it was funny anymore.

In late November, just before Thanksgiving, Steffani came home from the commune. My mother called me in tears. Steffani had hepatitis.

"She got it from God knows what," my mother said. "Living in those filthy conditions."

I felt sorry for my mother, almost more than I did for my sister. Her worst fears for my sister had come true, that she'd gotten some terrible disease her body couldn't fight. "At least she's home and safe, where you can look after her."

"I don't want her living here, Suzanne," she whispered, in case my father could hear her. "Steffani has lice. I know because I saw her using that blue soap they use to kill parasites. I remember it from when I was a little girl in Kansas City. Can you imagine, a child of mine with such a thing.''

The hepatitis was far more serious than head lice, I thought, but perhaps my mother was focusing on the lesser of two evils so as not to fall into a deeper despair. I didn't know if people recovered from hepatitis, and was afraid to ask. I knew it was dangerous for her, since her liver had to do the work of the spleen too.

''You should see her, she's skin and bones. I think they were all suffering from malnutrition, the fools.'' I could tell she was shaking her head, even over the phone. ''What's gotten into young people these days, can you tell me? I'm so afraid for Amy and Miles growing up in today's world. Who knows what it's going to be like for them?''

''I know,'' I agreed. The fears for what kind of world my children would find were quite real. The Vietnam conflict was worsening every year and there was no end in sight. Street violence, anarchy, splinter groups, marches, protests, anti-nuclear groups—their stories filled the newspapers every day. Columbia University was shut down by the SDS, Martin Luther King had been assassinated in April, and Bobby Kennedy in June, while I stayed isolated in my beautiful house, raising my ideal family and writing about glamour and elegance as if it still existed.

A few years before, when Alex and I went to see Julie Christie in *Darling*, I had been struck by the character's ability to sleep with whomever she chose and not give it a second thought. It truly shocked me. Especially in the scene when she and Laurence Harvey were about to go to bed for the first time, and are in his apartment talking, while she blithely helps him pull down the bedspread so they can do it in the afternoon. That nonchalance about an immoral act amazed me. Alex always had to have the shades drawn, and his eyes closed, and if we ever started to make love outside of the bed, we'd undress each other during the act, as if stopping to remove our clothes was just too clinical and off-putting.

I went over to my mother's house to see Steffani. She looked terrible. Her skin was slightly yellow from the hepatitis and she had an ugly cold sore on her mouth. Her hair was limp and lusterless, half-brown, half-blond, probably from using harsh chemicals on it; but most unsettling of all, her body was different. Her abdomen was enlarged, almost to the point of looking slightly pregnant. Her tiny little waist was gone, and the largeness of her middle made her thin arms and legs look even thinner.

"Her liver is enlarged because of the hepatitis and, of course, the Gaucher's," my mother told me when she was out of the room. "Dr. Levinson is afraid it might never go back to the way it was before. I begged her to be careful, but did she listen to me?"

I took my mother's hand, so like my own, and held it. "You did your best," I assured her. But my heart ached for my sister, who had only been living an adventure that thousands of other young people these days were living. Except for Steffani, normal experimentation had dire consequences.

Eventually, Steffani recovered from her bout of hepatitis, but it left her liver even more damaged and enlarged. She got a job as an assistant manager in a restaurant, but she was really a glorified waitress. My parents were disappointed that she'd given up her dreams of becoming a teacher and tried to encourage her endeavors, but her salary was low and she was on her feet for eight to ten hours at a time and they worried, always worried. *How will she support herself*, they asked, meaning, *if she's sick and we're not here*? I guessed it would become my problem, eventually.

Nineteen sixty-nine was quite a year, highlighted by the event of the century, in my opinion, when we put a man on the moon. How glorious it was to be glued to the television set and witness a feat that blended scientific excellence, with amazing courage and dedication, instead of the killing of soldiers that we saw most of the time. In August, Sharon Tate and some of her friends, including Alex's hairdresser, Jay Sebring, were massacred in their home right off Benedict Canyon, up the block from some friends of ours. Nobody felt safe anymore. And in September, abortions became legal in California. So when, in December, I discovered I was pregnant, for the first time in my life I had a legal choice of whether or not to keep my baby.

"If you really want it," Alex said, "we'll keep it. But, I want to go on record as being opposed, Suzanne. We're just getting to a place where we can enjoy our lives. I don't want to be tied down with a baby right now."

"Why can't we enjoy life, even if we are tied down?" I asked him, wanting him to be delighted so I could express my own doubts, but all I could see was annoyance. "Besides, a baby doesn't stay small for very long. And right now, if we leave the children for any length of time, I don't feel right, so we're tied down anyway, aren't we?"

"That's where you and I differ," he said, as though talking to a not-quite-bright grade-schooler.

"They need us around, Alex, need our supervision. I don't know how they'd get through their homework if I weren't here every day to help them, or at least check it over."

"The children would survive without us for a month, if we wanted to travel more. But you couldn't leave a baby for that long."

"Some people do."

"But not you, right?"

I nodded. Ten days away was my limit. I was most contented when the whole family was together even if we only went to Palm Springs. But Alex wanted us to go to exotic cities on our own where we could eat sophisticated dinners and shop for the perfect antique crystal bowl, or drop in on famous clients who lived there or happened to be on location. I didn't blame him. When we went to London and to Spain, it was romantic. But when we were in London, Miles had come down with tonsilitis and was so sick I couldn't enjoy myself for worrying about him.

Alex's expression was growing more ominous by the moment. There were dark circles under his eyes and a furrow that grew deeper between his eyebrows when he was upset, as he was now. The corners of his mouth turned downward. "You aren't serious, about an abortion, are you? You wouldn't really want me to have one?" I placed my hand on my abdomen, protecting the tiny life inside from its own father. I knew he hadn't meant it.

He looked away without a reply.

"Alex? Would you?" I was beginning to doubt my sense of reality.

"What if I said yes?"

"I think we should talk about it." My heart was beating faster.

"Isn't that what we're doing?" he said. From the tone of his voice, I knew suddenly that he was serious and a part of me felt sick inside, like something poisonous was seeping all through me. "What if I really wanted this baby? You told me that if I really wanted it, we would have it, didn't you?"

He just stared at me. I couldn't believe we were having this discussion. But I remembered back to the other two times I was pregnant. With Amy, he was delighted, but with Miles, it took him a while to get used to the idea. And only when Miles was born, and turned out to be a son, did he fall in love with the baby. Now, whatever we had—a son or a daughter—would be redundant, because he already had one of each. I recalled that joke where the child says to his parents, "I'd rather have a pony than a new baby brother or sister." That's what Alex would have preferred, I bet. And then I had a more sobering thought. "Alex, would you be able to love this baby?"

"I'm not sure, Suzanne," he admitted. The sickness inside was growing worse, pervading every part of me. I wanted to reach out to him, but my husband and I were on opposite shores and the river was widening between us as I stood there helplessly, watching.

He was angry; the edges of his nostrils were white. It seemed that he was looking at me from over a distance that the two of us had created, but he clearly blamed me for it. What a choice: give up my baby, or lose my husband's love.

"Why don't we think about it," I suggested. "Perhaps in a few days or a week, it will resolve itself." I was sure he'd agree. I knew he'd change his mind. He had to!

"What difference do you expect a few days to make? Are you expecting a miscarriage?" he asked. I was stunned by the question. His callousness made me fear he would never come around. Still, my innate optimism refused to admit defeat.

"You might decide you're happy about it," I said, timidly.

The anger and the force he was using to control it battled within him. He clamped his lips together tightly and shook his head from side to side. "I doubt it. Two children are enough for me. I'm not devoted to kids the way you are. You're always complaining that I don't spend enough time with them as it is. A third one won't help. I'm stressed enough already. I don't want this added burden, Suzanne. You know how I feel. How could you let this happen?" He wasn't shouting, but the intensity in his voice made me recoil.

I could barely breathe, my throat was so tight. I felt as if I had been condemned to death along with our baby. I, who had believed that abortion was an essential right of every woman, could never have one myself. Standing there, facing the possibility, I realized that.

"It's not as if you're being forced to keep it anymore," he said, ever the realist.

I could hardly get the words out, "Alex, are we at an impasse? If I can't give up this baby, what will you do?"

With that, he turned on his heel and slammed out of the house.

Alex returned sometime later and I waited for an apology, but none came. We smoothed over the problem by not discussing it. He felt I was being unreasonable about keeping a baby we hadn't planned and that he didn't want. I couldn't believe he wouldn't eventually want it. Who could resist a baby? Alex. At least he could resist it in utero.

I gained more weight this time than I should have. Fearing

what would happen between us made the act of eating more important and necessary for solace. I had always been ravenous during pregnancy, but I was careful about what I ate. This time, I just ate. And Alex never failed to comment. He was fastidious, as I've mentioned, and appearances were important to him. I should have been careful, but I was angry too. I guess it was my way of defying him. It only made things worse.

Our families took sides. My mother-in-law said I was being selfish, putting too much pressure on her son. My sister-in-law, who was supposed to be my friend, said I looked like a cow. "If you think I'm baby-sitting, you're crazy," she told me. "Honestly, Suzanne, you've got the most fabulous husband in the world, why would you deliberately sabotage him?" She thought I was unbalanced and destructive.

My parents became furious with the Winstons for their attitude, and protective of me. At Amy's birthday party neither set of parents would talk to the other.

After an afternoon of watching the grandparents being extremely polite to everyone but each other, making fusses over both the children, and never commenting about the other couple's gifts to Amy, my sister made a speech.

"I think you're all fucked! A new baby is a blessing, a joy to the world. How can you all act as if it were a crime? It's not as if they can't afford this kid, or don't have room for it. Don't you want another grandchild? Don't you have enough love to go around?"

My mother was glad that someone was standing up to *them*, but she was embarrassed by my sister's language. "Steffani!" she said, trying to make her be quiet. "It's none of our business." But her ambivalence showed.

"I'll thank you to keep your two cents to yourself," Alex said. "Your mother's right. This is between Suzanne and me."

My sister's temper flared and she was about to make a retort, but the stone wall of their opinions and the total frustration of it hit her all at once, and instead, her eyes filled with tears. "Have you ever thought of what it would be like not to have any children at all?"

I tried to push myself up from my chair and go to her, but it took me so long she had gone from the room by the time I stood up.

"I still say, it's nobody's business but Suzanne's and mine," Alex repeated.

"And what if your parents thought I was right?" I asked him. "What if they pointed out to you how unreasonable you're being, Alex. Would you still be like this?" In a way, I blamed my in-laws for spoiling him so, for not teaching him the important priorities of life. And even now, when he was being impossibly immature, they were still behind him. "At some point we have to be glad about this, Alex. We have to decide to welcome this child with all our love." It was all I could do to keep from bursting into tears. Never in my life had I expected to be abandoned the way I was now. All my life I'd always found ways of getting my way, if not by asking, then by devious methods, cajoling, pleading, or just not giving up. But this was one time, no matter what I did, I couldn't win. And I wasn't even pleading for myself here. The prospect of bringing a child into a family where only one parent loved it ate at me constantly. And perhaps the baby knew it, for I was sicker than I'd ever been: more headaches, sinus problems, backaches, and other ailments than with both Amy and Miles put together.

Each day for the first few months, I told myself, *Today, he'll come around. Today, when he comes home, he'll smile and hold me, and tell me everything's all right*. And then, when the days turned into weeks, I told myself, *This week, things will be different*. But Alex remained intractable.

"Are you tired of me?" I asked him, at night with the lights out, while we lay there not touching, the baby moving across my abdomen.

"No, not at all," he'd tell me. "I'm trying to make the best of things. If I'm not doing a good-enough job, sue me."

I'd never felt such rage before, but I didn't know what to

do with it. Nothing I could say or do would change his mind. The more I tried, the harder he dug in his heels.

"I don't know what to do," I told my mother. "Would he be satisfied if I told him, okay, I don't want the baby either, I'll ignore it and maybe it will go away. Or, should I offer to give it up for adoption?"

"That's a good idea, call his bluff."

I felt a chill grip my body as I asked her, "What if he says yes?"

Neither of us said it out loud, but we were both thinking, *Steffani would take it in a minute.*

Of course, I would never give up my baby. But it was clear I was losing my husband.

My girlfriends all told me, "He'll get over it, once he sees the baby." And I believed them. I had to.

I went into labor about three in the afternoon, but I waited until Alex came home to tell him. I was not going to disrupt his day with unpopular news. I had notified the baby nurse, told the children what to expect, prepared our housekeeper for my absence, and called my sister. She came over to stay with the children and keep them company while I was away. I wanted their lives to be as normal as possible, and I knew that I couldn't depend on Alex right now. In fact, I didn't even know if he'd want to be with me at the hospital, and that made me desperately unhappy.

But Alex surprised me. He was kind and gentle, a model of control, as he helped me into the car and locked my suitcase into the trunk. He came around and got into the driver's side of the station wagon just as I felt another contraction. My hand was holding on to the armrest and I gripped the end hard until my knuckles turned white. I stared straight ahead, trying not to moan; I didn't want to do anything to enlist his aid or sympathy, but how I longed for the way he used to be, asking me every minute, "How is it, now? Are you all right?" And then I felt his hand steal over mine and hold it there until the pain had passed. His touch, after so long, felt like a wave of warm water washing over me. It was more loving than I could have imagined. I turned to look at him and he was smiling. Not a huge, joyous smile, or even a silly grin, more like a benign professor's smile who's pleased with his class. But it didn't matter, for the smile, benign or not, was meant for me. I raised the armrest between us and leaned over to embrace him and couldn't help it, burst into tears, sobbing with all the pent-up emotions of the past months.

"Oh, God, I've missed you, Alex. I can't stand this distance between us. Please, please, be happy for me. Please," I begged, while he held me.

"It's okay, Suze," he said, soothing me while I cried. "I'm happy, don't worry. Let's just concentrate on getting you to the hospital and having a healthy baby, okay?"

I pulled away to wipe my eyes and blow my nose while he started the engine. I felt such an enormous relief that the tension left my body as if a great rockpile had been lifted and I relaxed in a way I hadn't done in eight and a half months. With that, my water broke, and I screeched, "Oh no! We'd better get there quickly." And so we did.

The labor was long, but the pains came with the contractions, so I could rest in between. And when they wheeled me into the delivery room I saw that my regular obstetrician, Dr. Westland, wasn't there, but his associate Dr. Braun, was.

After they performed the episiotomy and the head started crowning, they discovered that Jered was being born face up, not face down, as babies are supposed to be. Several times, Dr. Braun reached in to unhook the umbilical cord because it was wrapped around the baby's neck. I was terrified for the baby's safety, and tried to shut out the thought that Alex had somehow caused this, that this was the result of nine months of aggravation. I'd never had a problem like this before. By the fourth time they tried to free the baby from possible strangulation, I burst into tears.

"Don't worry, Suzanne," the delivery nurse told me, stroking my cheek. "It will be all right."

"No," I sobbed, "it's not, it's not."

"Hush," she insisted. "You'll only make things harder for yourself. The doctor knows what he's doing."

But I was too ashamed to tell her I was crying because of the fear that my husband would be relieved if this baby died.

Jered was born perfectly healthy, weighing eight pounds, ten ounces, a justification for all my weight gain. And Alex was happy! The miracle had occurred, just as my friends and family predicted. Once he saw the baby, he couldn't resist him. But his eleventh-hour acceptance couldn't possibly undo all the pain I'd suffered for the last nine months. Something within me had changed. I didn't love him anymore.

"He's a bruiser, Suzanne," Alex said, grinning the grin I'd waited so long to see. "He's the biggest baby in the nursery. He already has a double chin." I wanted to open my arms to him and be forgiving, be one of those selfless women I'd read about in the Bible or in frontier novels, who were so long-suffering. But I couldn't. I told myself I was exhausted, but that wasn't it. All those months of needing him, wanting him, longing for his love and support and being denied, of keeping myself going, of pretending to the world that things were normal, of making excuses for him, of never complaining, of being cheerful, of running the house in perfect order so nothing should upset him more than he was already upset came boiling up from inside threatening to choke me. *Now!* I wanted to shout. *Now, you're smiling? Where were you when I needed you? Being a spoiled brat. And I let you.* I didn't know who I was angrier with, myself or Alex. All I knew was that I hated him with every fiber of my being.

I had picked names for the baby; without Alex to argue with, it had been easy. Jessica for a girl, Jered for a boy. "Jered Winston is going to be president," Alex said, using the name as if he'd thought of it himself.

We brought the baby home and tried to adjust to an infant again. The children loved him. That was the good part. And Alex was a new man. Totally gone was the attitude of the last year. It was as if he'd never objected to the baby at all. Jered was amazing. "He's so smart! Look at the way he watches us with his eyes. He hears our voices, Suzanne, you can tell. I know he knows the children. Whenever they're in the room, he gets quiet as though he's trying to find them.''

Alex held the baby, fed him, came home from work early to see him. Yet I couldn't believe how much I resented Alex's very existence.

When Jered was two weeks old, I broke out in huge lumps all over my body, on my scalp, inside my mouth, on my palms, on the bottoms of my feet, as though I was having a toxic reaction to something. And they itched like mad. I was sure it was the anesthetic, but the doctors insisted that it wasn't. I couldn't hold the baby with swollen hands, and I couldn't walk on my swollen, painful feet. It got so bad that at one point I had to crawl to the bathroom, using the backs of my hands for support, and on the way I fainted.

When I came to, I was in bed and overheard the baby nurse speculating with Alex. "Maybe she's allergic to her own milk. I've heard of cases like that.''

"That's an old wives' tale," Alex insisted, having no patience for a sick wife. "She ought to be up and out by now." How guilty I felt for being unable to go places with him and show off his new son. I was a fat, lumpy, ugly mess, and every time Alex looked at me, I knew he thought so too. I wanted to die. I didn't know that the rage I had kept suppressed all these months had found a way to express itself, erupting from me all on its own, without my permission.

They gave me cortizone and made me stop nursing the baby. I had breasts like Jayne Mansfield and enough milk for eight ounces out of each side.

"I nursed both Amy and Miles," I told my sister tearfully, who came every day to keep me company. I was so grateful for her presence; she was the only one who kept me sane. "How can I not nurse Jered? I feel like a failure as a mother," I told her.

"You need to concentrate on yourself, Suzanne. The baby will be all right on a bottle.''

"But he won't get the antibodies from my milk; he won't

need me," I cried. I cried all the time now. "I miss nursing him so much, it's like an ache inside."

She nodded and stroked my hand. "I know how it feels to be sick, to be unable to do what you want."

Thinking about how intimate she was with that aspect of life made me stop crying. And slowly I started to get better.

CHAPTER THIRTY-SIX

It took several weeks before the swollen lumps went away, and left me with just the hives. My weight began to regulate slowly, and I was able to go out with my family and show off our new son, who was the best behaved baby of all. I swear it's true that Jered only cried when he was hungry and smiled the rest of the time. It was as if he was making up to me for all the heartache Alex had caused. I adored him. He was a joyful child who laughed with an adult kind of ha-ha-ha whenever I tickled him by making motor boat sounds on his tummy. And if I didn't mention it before, he was beautiful. He had dark curly hair and huge brown eyes with long lashes, a round face with fat cheeks, and pale skin, like Amy's.

So, when I went to the gynecologist for my one-month check-up I was unnerved to discover I had a problem.

"You have a fistula in the wall of the vagina, Suzanne," Dr. Braun explained. "That's when one of the stitches from the episiotomy has torn a hole through the membrane. It will have to be repaired surgically."

"How did it happen?" I asked him, dismayed by what I was hearing.

Without answering me, he replied, "It's not a difficult procedure. But we'll have to go in and sew you up in two places, both the front and the back. We can't just do it in one place or it won't hold." His expression was placid, unemotional. He blinked, owllike, behind his glasses, and I waited for an acknowledgment that this was his fault. Wasn't he sorry? After all, he'd been the one who'd stitched me up incorrectly. But he said nothing, just stared at me. "Shall I schedule you for next week?"

"Next week? Do I have to do it that soon?"

"The sooner the better. We don't want you to get an infection from possible leakage between the two areas."

Oh God, I thought. *How will I get through this?* My publisher was anxiously awaiting the final chapters of my new book, I itched all over from hives most of the time, the children were having some reactions to the new baby, and my husband and I were living two separate lives under the same roof. If only I could bridge the gap between us, perhaps this would be easier to take.

I was afraid, too. Surgery was no fun. I still believed it was the anesthetic that had caused my allergic reaction and the thought of having it again so soon was terribly upsetting. And there would be pain; surgery was always painful.

Naturally, I thought of my sister and the countless times she'd faced this sort of news. She'd gotten through worse things than this without being defeated. Thinking about her courage gave me hope.

I sighed. "All right, Doctor. Schedule it whenever you think it's best." And I stood up to go.

"It's too bad this had to happen," he said. It was the only conciliatory comment he ever made.

"I'm going to slap a lawsuit on him so fast he won't know what hit him," Alex said, when I told him about it.

"I don't want to sue the man," I said. "I just want to get it over with."

"Suzanne, the man screwed up. He's incompetent! He shouldn't be allowed to get away with this."

"Why don't we wait until afterward, Alex, and see how he handles it. Besides, I insisted that Dr. Westland do the surgery. I wouldn't trust Dr. Braun again."

"Well, at least you're being smart about that. But it's a clear case of malpractice."

"He made an error, Alex. He didn't mean to do it. It was a difficult birth." I didn't want to argue, it only made my hives worse.

"If you don't sue him, you're being as much of an asshole as he is," Alex said.

"I guess it's understandable if I act like an asshole," I admitted, starting to laugh. "After all, I have two of them now."

Strange the way life works. If I had been nursing Jered, I would have had to postpone the surgery. Now he would be fine with a nurse taking care of him. My sister came to stay with Amy and Miles and be their surrogate mother while I was away. That left Alex free to be with me at the hospital.

So I thought.

He was there the day of the surgery, but that night, when I returned to my room suffering with intense postoperative pain, he had to take a client out to dinner. "You know how they are, Suzanne. Eric is in from New York, and Amber has to discuss her deal with Columbia. It's the only time the two of them are available."

Everything below the waist hurt. I was so uncomfortable, I told myself it didn't matter whether he was here or not.

"I'll be by to see you before work in the morning," he said, and he kissed my forehead. I remember being embarrassed because I was perspiring. Amber, the newest film import from Sweden, was five feet seven, with blond hair to her waist, a ski-shaped nose, and a string of lovers across the continent. Why would he pass that up for a postoperative wife, with limp hair, no makeup, and hives? (No, they still hadn't gone away, but, thank God, they hadn't gotten worse after the anesthetic.)

"Alex," I called to him. "Don't forget to see the children before bedtime. They really need you now, after the baby, and my surgery. Your presence assures them that everything is normal, especially because we haven't been getting along."

He nodded, and saluted me, "Yes boss, I go home now, boss." And he smiled an Alex smile.

But when he stopped to call his office from the hospital lobby, Amber needed him early so he didn't go home. Instead, he went right to dinner.

Later, my sister called. "I hate to bother you with this," she said. And immediately my heart began to race. I had just had my shot to go to sleep, and now I was fighting to stay awake so I could listen to her. "Amy is crying and I can't get her to stop. She'll only go to sleep if she talks to you."

"Put her on the phone," I said, hoping to sound coherent to my very bright nine-year-old.

"Mommy?" came the sad, teary voice.

"What is it, honey? What's wrong?"

"I'm sorry to bother you. Are you all right?"

"Yes, sweetheart, I'm all right. It hurts right now, but it will be better in a few days. Why are you so upset, Amy?"

"I wish you were here, Mommy," she said, beginning to cry again. "Only you would understand. I tried to tell Daddy on the phone, but he said to wait until he got home, but then he didn't come home. Aunt Steffi wanted me to tell her, but I couldn't."

How well I remembered what it felt like not to be able to tell anyone how you felt. I was torn between wanting to be there to comfort her and wanting to kill Alex again, for not being where he was supposed to be. He just didn't understand how certain moments in a child's life are crucial, how parents had to maintain a bond with them, especially when one parent was in the hospital, so they'd understand that life was safe and secure, even though every adult knew it wasn't.

"Tell me what happened," I said.

"Robert hit me again when we were on the bus, and gave me a bruise in the arm. I told him to quit it, but he wouldn't. And the bus driver gave me a demerit, and said it was my fault. It wasn't, Mommy, it really wasn't."

Now I wanted to kill Robert *and* the bus driver, *and* Alex. But this was an ongoing problem with Amy; this same boy tormented her several times a week. She had to learn to defend herself, and she knew it. But I was away, and Alex hadn't come home after work, so everything was magnified.

"Amy, what happens when you get a demerit?"

"I don't know, I never had one before. But it's bad. Maybe they can kick me off the bus."

"They won't do that, honey, because you don't deserve such a punishment, and I won't let them." I suddenly recalled that time when my sister had been called to the principal's office. The drug was really working now, and I felt a relief of pain for the first time in hours. I longed to give in to sleep and enjoy this painfree time, but I couldn't at the moment. That was another thing that Alex didn't understand—a child's needs come first, always. Or maybe he did understand it, but he expected to be the child whose needs are always met.

"Amy, remember what we decided you should do when Robert hits you?"

"No, what?" she asked, although we both knew she remembered.

"See if you can tell me," I said.

"I'm supposed to say in a loud voice, 'Robert, stop hitting me, or I'll tell the bus driver.' And then, move my seat."

"That's right, honey. And did you do that?"

"No, but I couldn't move, we were assigned to our seats."

"And what about the letter you were supposed to write to the driver, requesting a new seat?"

"I forgot," she said.

"Then, there is something you can do right now, isn't there? And Aunt Steffi can help you. She's really good at writing letters to officials."

Amy had stopped crying and said in a hopeful voice, "That's right, I remember, you said if I behave maturely, and make my request, the bus driver will probably do as I ask, and if she doesn't, you'll talk to her. But you're in the hospital, Mommy."

"I'll be home in a few days, and then I can talk to her. Okay?"

"Okay," she said.

"Do you feel better?"

"Yes," she whispered. And then, "I love you!"

"Love you too, angel. Let me talk to Aunt Steffi."

My sister got on the phone. "Remember Mrs. Pruner and the time she sent you to the principal's office?" I asked her.

"Oh yeah," she said, imitating a childlike voice, "I apologize for disrupting the class, Mrs. George. I assure you, it won't happen again," she quoted, and we both laughed.

"Well, Amy needs a little of that right now," I told her. "Think you can handle it?"

She sighed. "Not as well as you, Suze. You're really a good mother, you know that? But then, you always were. Sleep well." And she hung up.

Alex was out late that night and overslept, so he didn't come by the hospital in the morning, but we planned to have dinner together that evening. I was feeling somewhat better, enough to put my hair in a ponytail and tie a ribbon around it. But I missed the children terribly, especially my baby. All day, I looked forward to Alex's visit, hoping that we could overcome some of the coldness between us; I acknowledged it was mostly on my part. Alex was only being Alex.

At six, he called to say he was running late. At seven, he was still in the office but on his way out the door. At seven-thirty, I started feeling sorry for myself and then enraged at him, as I waited for the lumps and the hives to erupt. At eight, I called the office; there was no answer, and he wasn't at home either. At nine, the phone rang.

"Hi, hon, it's me. Look, I'm sorry, but I had to get some people into the Robertson Club. You know a member has to be with them to get them in the door. I told these people I'd only stay for a minute, but I was beat, and so I had one drink, and the time just got away from me." He waited for me to say something and when I didn't, he said, "Look, I'm really sorry, Suzanne, but this is business. You're lying there on your back all day, while I'm out here busting my buns."

Still, I didn't say anything. *Lying here on my back?* I thought, steeling myself against a new bout of throbbing pain. Somehow, his comment had made the pain worse. I was thinking, *I earn over double what you make, Alex. You don't have to bust your buns if you don't want to. But if you choose to, it sure as hell isn't my fault.* Suddenly, I saw my whole life ahead of me, exactly what it would be like with him for years to come. More of the same, and I didn't want it. Not one more minute.

"Alex, I'm getting a divorce," I said, bursting into tears. I hung up the phone, and then took the receiver off the hook and sobbed. I cried so hard that the fear of rupturing my stitches was the only thing that helped me calm down. This was a new pain, deeper, more intense than the pain of surgery. As the full force of it hit me, I was afraid it would never heal. Finally, I stopped crying and waited for the hives to break out the way they usually did; I was even poised to scratch. But my skin stayed unblemished. I wiped the tears from my cheeks, blew my nose, and then wrapped my arms around myself for comfort. A sudden thought made me smile through my tears. *Well, that's the second asshole I've gotten rid of in the last twenty-four hours.*

Of course, I didn't get a divorce immediately. In one of my novels, when the heroine says, "I want a divorce," that's the end of it. In real life, things drag on. I had second thoughts, third and fourth thoughts too. Mostly—how could I deprive my children of having their father with them all the time. The idea of being a divorced person was abhorrent to me; it didn't fit my self-image. It said to the world, I'm a failure. I couldn't make this work; no matter what's gone on, I couldn't forgive, couldn't come to terms, couldn't make the necessary changes or influence my spouse to make them, so now my children will pay for my inability to manage my life. But Alex had hurt me badly by his indifference. I didn't think I could get over it.

My mother says love doesn't die, it gets buried under

anger. When you're angry with the one you love, you can't feel the love, until you express the anger. Maybe that is true, but if I expressed my anger to Alex, it wouldn't do any good because he wouldn't change. And what is love, I asked myself, besides passion and excitement. I decided it was this: a basic need for another human being to share your life with, to share your goals and dreams and desires. A particular human being that you prefer above all others, coupled with the desire to be good to them, respectful of them, concerned for them, loyal and devoted. Given that definition, Alex didn't love me. I loved him, and he loved him. I wanted someone to love me. I believed I deserved it. As much as my parents might bicker and find fault with one another, they loved each other too. They were concerned with one another's welfare, not just themselves. Why hadn't I known that when I chose the man I was going to marry? Does anyone? Do many people realize that love includes tolerance, and not pettiness, being *for* someone else no matter what. There's so much to think about when you get married, perhaps that basic rule gets overlooked. I had friends who'd gotten divorced because they had grown apart, or needed excitement, or felt curtailed by the constraints of a monogamous relationship where the glamour had worn off like the plated silver on their wedding presents.

With Alex and me it was different. Alex and I hadn't grown apart, and we really weren't constrained by the demands of monogamy. It was just that Alex wasn't capable of giving me what I needed—first place in his life, the way I gave first place in mine to him. It seemed to me an essential element, and without it the structure fell apart.

When I explained this to him, he listened, nodded, and then said, "I do put you first, Suzanne. Whenever I have to cancel dinner, I call you first. I always think of you if I'm late, or if I'm held up somewhere, don't I?"

His sincere expression showed that he thought he was such a good boy, while I was thinking, *What's the use*? "Alex, it's not that you call me when you cancel, it's that you cancel, period. Whatever I've got planned for the two of us is easily set aside for your work. I don't do that to you with my work."

"That's because your work isn't as demanding as mine."

"Writing a book a year, going on promotional tours, keeping my public and my publishers happy, running a household with three children isn't demanding? If you don't think it is, that's exactly my point. It's because I put you first."

"Well, I can't believe it's a deal-breaker," he said.

And that stopped me for the moment.

I was home from the hospital, trying to recover from the surgery and finding the only place I was comfortable was in a hot bath. But Alex wanted to attend a black-tie event, so he went without me. I don't think a married person should be restricted from attending a function if the husband or wife doesn't want to go, but if the husband or wife is too sick to go, you stay home, right? Not Alex.

"It's business, love. The office bought a table, I can't not go," he said.

Sure.

He couldn't not escort Juliet Prowse, or some other unmarried female client. He wasn't being unfaithful—that I knew—only faithless.

In the next three months, while I completed the final draft of *The Gardener's Daughter*, I tolerated Alex's behavior, telling myself it wasn't a deal-breaker. Until finally, the pain within me was still so intense, even after I'd healed from the surgery, that I was sure I did not want to be married to him any longer. So, I filed for divorce and entered one of the bleakest periods of my life. I never realized how much status a woman relinquishes when she's divorced. Alex had provided us with a lifestyle and a social structure that he took with him. Many of our friends chose to be with him over me, or they chose glamour over normality. Of course, I still had my girlfriends and my family. But Gloria blamed me for the break-up.

"I told you I'd never forgive you if you hurt him," she said, and the sound of naked resentment in her voice sent chills through me.

"Marilyn, I can't talk right now, I'm working." Not one of my most supportive friends, I found her as aggravating as I

had when we were children. Marilyn was more like a bother-
some cousin to me than a friend because of the closeness of
our families. Over the years she'd dropped in and out of my
life, and each time we picked up where we left off. As wacky
as she was, I found her interesting. She brought an element
to my life no one else did. But I never really trusted her,
especially after that incident with the roller skates. I knew
she could turn on me at a moment's notice. Once, we went
to sleep-away camp together and I hated it. It wasn't just
because of Marilyn's presence, but she formed a clique with
three other girls and excluded me. Watching them huddled
together, giggling, glancing at me as if I were a toadstool,
made me so homesick I had to come home before the week
was out. Marilyn stayed, happy in her element with so many
unsuspecting girls to intimidate. And she never let me forget
that I couldn't hack it at camp.

"If you're working, why did you answer the phone?"

"Because the service didn't pick it up and it rang fourteen
times."

"I knew you were there," she said, as determined as ever.
"I never give up, you know that about me by now."

"Are you still with the Students for a Democratic Society?"

"Certainly. But we're having a hell of a time staying alive
since the Weathermen town house blew up."

I'd read about the explosion in Manhattan where three
people were killed. "I thought you said the SDS was nonviolent." She'd been a radical all her life, influenced by her
parents' political philosophy. She'd been a beatnik in the
fifties, and a hippie in the sixties. But by then, she was old
enough to have a voice and she used it.

"We are nonviolent! But you know how many factions
have broken off from our original group, and some of them
advocate violence. I was saying to Bernardine yesterday, we
should get back to our origins, redefine ourselves, issue a
new manifesto. But listen." Her voice rose with excitement.
"I've got this incredible idea on how to infuse us with new
energy."

I had to interrupt. "Marilyn, I really can't talk right now, I'm working. I know this is important, but . . ."

"Okay, okay," she said. "I was just calling to see how you are since the separation and to ask you if I could borrow some money. But, I'll call back later when Her Highness is available."

I was barely able to reconcile both subjects at once. "You heard that Alex moved out two weeks ago today?"

"Yes."

"Well, I'm okay." The truth was that I cried myself to sleep at night. The children were angry and bewildered by the terrible change in their lives. Amy wouldn't let me comfort her, and Miles had retreated into silence. I knew the two of them talked, but not to me. Seeing the pain in their eyes brought home to me how destructive Alex and I had been. I had hurt my children, perhaps irrevocably.

"Maybe we can have dinner one night next week," I offered, anxious to get back to work; at least then I could forget about my problems. And even though Marilyn would talk radical politics at dinner, I'd put up with it for the companionship.

"What about the bread I need, Suzanne?" she said.

"Marilyn, my finances are kind of tight right now, because of the separation. I'm getting a divorce so I don't know what my financial arrangements might be, but . . ."

"Oh, I know that." Her impatience was staccato sharp. "I only want your money, not your body as a volunteer. It's going to cost a fortune to mount the project I have in mind. The mailings alone will be enormous—the SDS had a previous membership of forty thousand—and then there's the press coverage. I want everybody to see how this war is feeding the coffers of corporate America, which in turn finances the election of our leaders, who keep this goddamned war going on for the enormous infusion to our economy. It's sure as hell not for ideological reasons. God, it's going to be so great. A trainload of people singing 'We Shall Overcome.' And then thousands of us lying in the road, using our bodies to stop the munitions trucks from leaving the facility in New

Mexico. So, if you could give us five, or seven, or better yet, ten thousand, it would really be going for a good cause.''

I never knew I had a trapdoor in my solar plexus until this moment, but I swear, cold air suddenly blew through me. I always hated saying no to a friend, especially someone as unstable as she was, but I couldn't possibly say yes to this. "My God, Marilyn, I don't have that kind of money to give away. I thought you wanted a couple of hundred," which now seemed like a real bargain. "There's no way I can contribute anything like that."

Her voice lowered, almost to a growl. "I know how much you make in advances on your books, Suzanne. You can spare some change. The youth of the world is dying, and you're sitting there doing nothing. The SDS needs one big project to bring us back together; our future is at stake. If you say no to me, you're condemning us to oblivion. Can you live with that?"

"Marilyn, please don't make this a condition of our friendship. I can't do it right now."

"Then when can you? When you split the family assets with Alex? When you make three hundred thousand a book, instead of a hundred and fifty? When, Suzanne, next week? Next year? Next life? A measly five thousand dollars is all I'm asking for. A measly ten. If you give me the money, what will it cost you in your life? Nothing! You'll still live in your house, won't you? Your children won't go hungry. Your husband won't die in a rice paddy. You make me sick, you know that? You're a sorry excuse for a friend. Well, don't come running to me when you need something, because I won't forget this stab in the back, Suzanne. You can be damned sure of that. Just think, the next time you see the bodies of dead American boys on the six o'clock news, you could have prevented it. That's right, you! When you look in the mirror, I hope it haunts you. I hope you have nightmares about it. And if I can ever find a way to make you suffer the way you're making other people suffer, I will."

And she slammed the phone down.

CHAPTER THIRTY-SEVEN

"Suzanne, I want you back." Alex sat opposite me at the Four Oaks Café where I had agreed to meet him. When I got there, I realized that the Four Oaks wasn't such a good idea because it used to be our place. It was a rustic house converted into a restaurant; we'd gone there often when we lived in Beverly Glen, and now the sentimentality of the place was playing on me. Alex knew it would.

He had dark circles under his eyes and a gauntness to his cheeks. He was losing weight, which must have pleased him, but it was from not eating properly.

"Alex, nothing has changed. You haven't changed. You should have a different kind of wife than I am, and I need a different kind of husband. Why go over it again? It doesn't do any good."

"I'll be whatever you need," he said, "I swear. Just give me another chance."

I knew what it felt like to be desperate because you couldn't have what you wanted, even if what you wanted wasn't right for you. That's what made Alex want me back, because he couldn't have me. "You'll get used to this after a while," I told him. "It's only hard at first. Soon, you'll see it's the best way."

Seeing him across the table from me, in his custom gray suit, he was dear and familiar. Separating from him was like cutting off a part of myself. But the part no longer functioned for the whole, it had atrophied and now was only a dead weight I didn't want to carry around.

"I'll put you first, Suzanne, I promise."

"Alex, you can't! In some basic part of yourself you don't

know how. It's impossible for you, at least when it comes to me.'' I sighed. ''I'm sorry I've put such demands on you that you feel you're not living up to my standards. That isn't fair of me.'' I was tempted to reach across the table and take his hand, but I didn't. ''Why don't you just think of us as separate but equal, not less than or more than. When you find the woman whose needs are the same as yours, you'll see what I mean.''

''Don't talk to me as if I'm one of the children,'' he snapped. ''I know I'm selfish, but I want to change. Can't you tell that? I want us to make it work. I hate being apart, I hate it. I miss the kids, I miss our life.''

''So do I,'' I admitted. I was tempted, God knows. Sometimes, having the full responsibility of raising three children was overwhelming. There were so many things Alex was good at that I wasn't, like math homework. And the evenings were desperately lonely. I felt as though I was intruding when my married friends invited me to join them, and I couldn't depend on single women, because they'd break a date with me to go out with a man. But every time I wavered, I thought of what it had been like married to Alex. Deep within Alex, there was a core of self-absorption. It defined him, and it would never change. It was wrong for him to even try. Changing it would truly make him unhappy. ''Why don't you come and see the kids more often—I don't mind. They need you.''

''I can't believe you're being so stubborn. You're ruining five lives, do you know that? Not to mention our parents. I'll bet your sister's the only one who thinks you're doing the right thing. Dump the reactionary, she's always said. Well, my sister is offended by what you've done.''

''Gloria is only being protective of her big brother,'' I told him.

''At least she understands.'' He paused a moment. ''You'd tell me if there was anyone else, wouldn't you?''

''Yes, of course.'' I was amazed that he'd think so.

''Who is he?'' I had never seen Alex look so menacing, so stricken. I began to be truly aware of how he was suffering.

"There isn't anybody!" I insisted. "When would I have had time to meet anyone else? I don't even want to. Why would you think such a thing?" And then I knew—Gloria, of course. She always had one boyfriend in the wings and another one out in public. She delighted in intrigue.

"Alex, honestly, there isn't anybody else. Don't even think it."

"Then, for God's sake, why won't you let me come home?"

As he asked me that question, I cast my eyes down and stared into my plate, but the food swam before me in an unfamiliar form. I could not partake of sustenance when there was such pain within me and in Alex. That question hung between us, waiting. I realized that he thought I was punishing him, that this was a temporary state that would eventually be over and we'd resume our normal lives. Until this moment, I guess a part of me had thought that too. But as I raised my eyes to his, I reached a moment of truth. There was no more skirting the issue, or playing with it as a cat plays with a toy, batting it here and there trying to get a response. This issue was sore and bleeding, it deserved to heal, and only I could make that happen. "You can't come home, Alex, because I don't want to be married to you any longer. Our marriage is really over. We both have to make new lives for ourselves from now on, without each other. It's very sad, but it's true. Believe it."

He stared at me until it sunk in. Suddenly he screamed, "I hate you!" His face was red with fury. Then, he grabbed his glass off the table and threw the ice water at me.

I leaped up with the shock, my body stunned by the cold. I was too mortified to look around and see everyone staring at us. Then, he stood up too, his body shaking and out of control. He knocked the table askew, toppling the dishes on our table and the one next to us, threw his napkin down like a gauntlet, and strode out of the room, leaving me to deal with the mess.

The shock of seeing Alex lose his equanimity was much

greater than the freezing ice water in my face. I had unleashed a monster. How I longed to take it all back, to make things right, to make him into a different person, but I couldn't. The desolation I felt stretched before me like an empty highway.

First Alex began following me—I recognized his car almost everywhere I went—then he hired someone to do it. There were phone calls at all hours of the night. I'd be terrified by the shrill ringing at four in the morning, awake in an instant, thinking someone had just died in an accident, my heart slamming against my chest. "Hello," I'd say. Someone would be breathing on the other end, and then, click. It had to be Alex, but I couldn't believe he'd do it, take a chance on disturbing the children, whose lives were so disrupted already. Often they slept through it, except if one of them was sleeping with me. Then, when the phone call came screaming in the night and I'd gasp as I bolted up in bed, grabbing for the receiver until the caller hung up, they'd awaken too. After a while, I wouldn't let them sleep with me any longer, unless they were sick. But the calls kept coming.

One day, I came home from working the book fair at the grammar school to find Antonia, my housekeeper, locked in her room with Jered in her arms. She was shaking, and she'd been crying.

"Señora Winston, I let him in, I'm sorry. But Señor Winston say it's all right. He want to see the baby. But I hear the baby cry and Señor Winston not there. I call him, and I go to see in your room. When he not answer me, I scared."

I put my arms around her to soothe her, feeling my own adrenaline beginning to pump. Jered thought it was amusing to see me embracing the two of them at once. "He must be gone now, Antonia. His car isn't outside."

"*Sí*, he is gone. But it is terrible." She started to cry again.

Holding hands, the two of us walked slowly across the family room and down the hall to the master bedroom. I gasped when I entered my room, our room. My clothes were strewn all about. The drawers in my night table were pulled open as if ransacked by a thief. My lingerie was torn, ripped to pieces, stockings were wrapped around the lamps, costume jewelry thrown with such force there were marks in the wallpaper where it shattered. Beads crunched under my feet on the wooden floor as we walked through the room, and then I saw the really sick things he'd done, holes burned in my dresses, shoes broken in half, the heels smashed, purses open, the linings torn, makeup all over the bathroom.

"My God," I whispered, afraid to speak too loudly, as if I'd awaken the slumbering beast again. But Alex had gone over the edge, I could see. I would have to get a court order barring him from our lives. I motioned for Antonia to take the baby out, and then I sank to the floor in the midst of the ruined effects of my life, stunned beyond comprehension, thoughts reeling in my head: *Should I take him back? Would that heal this sickness? Did I deserve this? Have I been the one who was foolishly destructive? Could I have prevented this? Why is he so enraged at me?* And then I could not think anymore and just sat there, mourning the loss, not so much of my favorite things but of innocence. I had been protected in my marriage. We had been two against the world. Now, there was only me to keep the wolf away from the door, and the wolf had metamorphosed into Alex. It took an hour before I had the strength to get up and go to find boxes to throw away my ruined belongings.

The next night, which was Saturday, about eleven o'clock, as I was getting ready for bed, I heard someone ringing the doorbell and banging on the door. My heart started to pound as I hurried to see who it was and get them to be quiet.

"Suzanne, Suzanne, let me in," Alex called, pounding so hard that the entry hall echoed with the sound.

"Alex," I called through the slit in the center where the double doors met, "be quiet. Get out of here or I'm calling the police!"

"I don't care anymore," he shouted, his voice more despairing than angry, "I want to come home." And then I heard the sound of his body hit the doors with a shout and a thud, and then slide along it to the floor. He was crying; the sounds of his sobs tore through me mingling with my own ache, diffusing my rage against him.

"I want to come home," he cried. "Please, let me in. I shouldn't have done it, I know. I'm so sorry." I couldn't make out all his words.

I was afraid to let him in where the children were sleeping for fear of what destruction he might do. So I hurried around through the kitchen, got the keys to the house, then went out the back door, locking it behind me, and came around to the front. I found him huddled at the front stoop leaning against the doors. I crouched next to him, cradling his body against mine, holding his head to my chest as I would any sick child. "Shh, honey, it's all right," I soothed, feeling more compassionate than frightened of him. I still didn't want to let him into the house, but I couldn't leave him sitting there in pain all by himself. "Alex, Alex, try to calm down. This isn't doing you any good." I rocked him and stroked his hair. "Tell me what's wrong, why are you doing this?"

"I want to come home."

"We're getting a divorce, Alex. But I'm not trying to punish you. Do you understand that?"

Briefly, he nodded. "But you won't let me come home."

I took his face between my hands and turned him toward me so that he had to look at me. "Alex, who am I? Do you know who I am?"

"You're Suzanne, my wife."

"Anything else?"

He took a deep breath then and straightened up, seeming to pull himself together. "Yes," he said, "there's a lot else. I don't know what's come over me lately, but I can't seem to control my emotions. I've never been like this in my life. I think maybe I'm having a nervous breakdown."

"Do you know why?" I asked, expecting him to lash out and say, "Of course, it's because of you, you bitch, it's all your fault."

But instead he nodded and said, "Because for the first time

in my life, I'm not getting my own way, and I can't stand it.'' Tears were rolling down his cheeks.

"And me? Do you miss me so very much?" Now, I was beginning to doubt that I knew what he'd say next.

"Not really. I'm just so ashamed because I lied to you for so long.''

"Lied to me? What about?'' Now, I was truly afraid of his next answer.

He paused for a moment before he spoke. "I don't think I ever loved you. I don't think I've ever loved anyone. The children come closest, and then Gloria, and then my parents and then you. But God, I love this house. I had no idea what it meant to me until I didn't belong here anymore.''

The house? I thought, *He only loves the house*. I almost wanted to laugh, but I was too concerned about his stability. "You love the house that much?" I asked. He nodded. "Do you want us to move out? You can have it, Alex, if you want it that badly. The children won't like giving up their rooms, but I could find someplace close by so they can stay in their schools. The house doesn't mean as much to me now that we don't live here together anymore.''

"Do you really mean that, Suzanne? I could have the house?" His eyes took on a glow of joy that almost made me happy to see, except that it was so upsetting to think of the reason for it.

"Why don't you go back to your apartment now, and we can talk about it tomorrow and then decide.''

He stood up and ran his fingers lovingly across the carved flowers on the front doors. I stood up next to him. "Remember when we had these made," he said. "That Italian guy who made them was only four feet eleven and the doors were eight feet tall. Watching him working on them was like watching someone creating Frankenstein's monster.''

"Alex," I said softly, wrapping my arms around my body against the chill of the night, but mostly to hold myself against the ache inside. "Didn't you really ever love me?''

He shook his head. "I'm really sorry, Suze. But I've been

pretending all this time. I did what I was supposed to do, what I thought everybody expected. I've felt as if I were in jail for the past nine years. I was mean to you and cold, and you took it, like a trooper. And when you started writing and getting famous, I resented you for it. How dare you thrive in this marriage, I thought. But when you got pregnant with Jered, that's when I started hating you. And when you said you wanted the divorce, I was enraged because I thought you'd found me out, and then I thought, damn you for doing what I didn't have the courage to do."

I looked at him, amazed. As much as his words hurt to hear, they were freeing. I had felt like a villain for so long, and I wasn't at all. "Do you really mean what you're saying? Or are you just trying to pay me back?"

"No, it's true, all of it."

"Oh God," I said, feeling my knees giving way. It was as if all the underpinnings of my life had been knocked aside. My marriage was a fraud, a complete fake.

"Then, this is really good-bye," I said.

He nodded, took hold of my shoulders, pulled me toward him and kissed me on the cheek. And then, as he was halfway down the drive, he turned and called out, "I'll have my lawyer call yours about the house." And he was gone.

The children and I were prepared to give Alex the house. We found a condo to rent, north of Ventura Boulevard, full of divorced families. Jered would sleep with Miles and Amy would share a room with Antonia. I'd have a bedroom to myself, which would also serve as my office. And then, just as I was about to sign the lease, Alex announced that he was moving into Beverly Hills, into a duplex on Le Conte, and didn't want the house after all.

"Are you sure?" I asked him, remembering his attachment.

"Yeah," he declared. "I've worked it out of my system. It's too big for a bachelor, and now with my new social life, everything I do is in the city."

We agreed on a buy-out plan where I would pay Alex for his half of the house. The children were ecstatic not to have to move; it helped to replace some of their lost continuity. And I never realized how much the house meant to me. I held on to it fiercely now as the one stable element in my war-torn life.

BOOK III

If I Don't
Have You

CHAPTER THIRTY-EIGHT

I wasn't able to tell Barry about Sugar Markham because I didn't hear from him during the two weeks it took me to make arrangements with Almeida Consalvo and move into the new apartment, though I thought of him constantly. Since I was leasing my house furnished, I couldn't bring anything with me and had to borrow from my parents. The rest I rented.

The apartment was sparse, mix-matched, and decidedly seedy. But the children attempted to be cheerful for my sake, and I for theirs. But that sinking feeling deep in my guts never let up for a moment and weighed like a bellyful of stones. My grandmother used to tell a story about a huge bear that came to a house in the woods looking for something to eat. There were children inside, waiting for their grandmother to come home. When they saw the bear they were terrified and each one found a place to hide. One by one, the bear discovered their hiding places, in the attic, under the stairs, in the grandfather clock, in the cellar, and he gobbled them up. When their grandmother returned to find the children missing, she followed the bear's tracks to its cave where it was hibernating. Making sure he was asleep, she cut open the bear's belly with the scissors in her pocket and freed the children. When the children were safe, she replaced each one with a huge stone, stitched up the bear's belly, and left it to sleep through the winter. The grandmother and the children danced all the way home.

I used to wonder how that bear would feel waking up in the spring with a belly full of stones. Now, I knew.

Alex had tried his best to convince the children to come and live with him, but they'd chosen to stay with me. I knew they'd enjoy school more in Beverly Hills, but the Los Angeles schools weren't so bad. After all, I'd attended them. Besides, I desperately needed them with me. I could live without everything else I'd lost, as long as I had them.

Amy was enrolled at Van Nuys High School, Miles at Van Nuys Junior High, and Jered at Laramie Elementary. We settled down to a cramped but familiar routine, except that nothing was the same, especially with only one bathroom. A family learns to be considerate when the plumbing facilities are so limited.

The children had only been in school four days when I decided to try and work again. I felt no more able than before, but I couldn't put it off forever. I took out my manuscript and reread what I'd done. Within minutes I was transported, through my grandmother's voice, to Annica's world. The innocent story, the purity of the characters, and the love between Annica and her ill-fated Manuel were so ecstatic that each chapter brought me renewed delight and relief from the harsh realities I faced. In this time of need, my grandmother was nurturing me from the grave with the story of the exquisite Annica—with her porcelain skin, her sky-blue eyes as clear as a crystal stream, and her long golden hair the color of wheat (as my grandmother described her)—who joins a carnival and, dressed as an angel with wings, holding a harp, and standing perfectly still, she is displayed in a glass case. People are awestruck as they file by. Some kneel before her to pray.

Tony, the strong man in the circus, whose mother is the queen of a gypsy tribe, falls in love with her, kidnaps her, and forces her to marry him. But the life of a gypsy is not only miserable and unbearable, they are constantly on the road, moving from place to place with no home of their own, exposed to the elements, ruled by superstition and mean spirit. When Annica discovers she's pregnant, she makes her escape into rural France where she meets an artist, Papa Joliet, who paints her portrait as an angel in her carnival costume. The painting, *Angel of My Fate*, wins first prize, the Prix de Paris, at the famous Paris exposition of 1892, and Annica is soon the toast of Paris.

Reading these notes somehow unlocked the bonds that had fettered me, and I was able to work again, even if I couldn't sell what I wrote.

I hadn't seen Curtis McCartney since the preliminary hearing so I was looking forward to our meeting, hoping that he would have made some progress on my behalf. I couldn't help thinking about Barry as I drove downtown to Curtis's office. I missed Barry terribly and had to use all my self-control not to call him. Every time the phone rang I hoped it was he.

Walking into Curtis's office, I felt like a criminal. *Did everyone know*? I wondered. The secretaries who typed up the memos and the briefs knew who the clients were, what they were accused of. I could barely meet anyone's eyes.

Curtis looked even crustier in his own surroundings. The room reeked of cigarettes, but the walls were lined with books. The old-fashioned overstuffed furniture covered in dark reddish brown leather gave off an aura of substance. His many diplomas and awards hung on the wall, along with pictures of him with prominent political figures. I needed Curtis to be the bravest, smartest, and strongest of representatives. Seeing his office gave me confidence.

"Sit down, Suzanne." He indicated the leather sofa across from the desk.

"You know we've got our motion before the Superior Court coming up. I'm going to ask the court to review the municipal findings and dismiss this case."

"Do you think it's possible we can get the dismissal?" He had tried to get the case dismissed at the preliminary hearing on the grounds that the police conducted an illegal search and seizure, but the municipal judge hadn't agreed and I'd been bound over. I didn't have much hope that the Superior Court would dismiss it on those grounds either.

"It doesn't hurt to try." He shrugged. "But what's worrying me is that Avery Bellows hasn't come up with any new information that could help you at the trial from the list of people who might have had access to your house. Of course, we have a lot of character witnesses who'll testify on your behalf that you've never taken drugs and have no drug connections whatsoever. But it would help if you knew someone who did. Then, we might have a real suspect."

The only person I knew with any connection to drugs was my sister, and she hadn't done it. I needed a real suspect, someone's actual features to be placed on that blank face. Often I was so overcome with hatred for this unknown person out there that I could barely stand it and wanted to smash apart the whole world with a sledgehammer. Other times, it hurt so much to think that someone hated me like this that I wanted to crawl under the bed and never come out. But the worst feeling of all was this awful, sickening nagging deep inside that never really left, that maybe I'd brought this on myself.

"If we can't get the case dismissed on a motion," McCartney was saying, "and we have to go to trial, I think we have a good defense. There's the defense of your excellent character, which we will corroborate with witnesses. And all the donations you've made to charity. And there's the defense that someone else is trying to hurt you. I think I can convince a jury that finding a card enclosed with the candy with your name typed on it does more to prove your innocence than your guilt. It's clear that someone's trying to hide their handwriting by using a typewriter, otherwise we could analyze it. And if you were sending letters to publishers accusing yourself of plagiarism, which is really ridiculous, then why would you use the same typewriter to send the drugged candy and sign your name?"

"You know, I thought of something else in my favor," I told him. "I've had negative reviews before in my career, Brett Slocum's isn't the first. And I've never sent anyone else nasty notes or tainted candy. Why should one review send me over the edge?"

"Now you're thinking," he said.

Every little bit helped, but these bits and pieces seemed awfully flimsy if that's all there was to keep me from getting convicted.

"What's the worst that can happen, Curtis? I've never been in trouble with the law, I'm a solid citizen. There's got to be some doubt as to my guilt. Even if a jury convicts me, what would a judge do?"

He paused for a moment, assessing whether or not I could take it, then said, "Probably send you for a psychiatric evaluation at the state hospital. And if you proved out not to be a schizo, you could do time. But I'm going to get you off, Suzanne. We'll find out who's done this to you. I know we will."

If only I could believe him.

That afternoon when I got home from the lawyer's office, Alex was parked outside my building. When Alex was angry he pursed his lips so that a white line appeared around the edges. His grim expression brought that iron fist grabbing at my heart again so that my entire chest was in a vice.

I could barely ask him, "What's wrong?"

"I got a call today from Miles just before school started. He was terrified. He was being bused to Soto Street School in East Los Angeles and begged me to get him out of it. I rushed over there, but I got there too late; the buses had already left. Do you know where Soto Street is? It's in the middle of the barrio, a dangerous neighborhood, Suzanne. But you're so goddamned selfish, what do you care?"

I stood there frozen with too much information to process. "I wasn't notified that he'd be bused."

"Miles has known about it for two days," Alex spat. "But he didn't tell you because you have so much else to worry about. Evidently, he has a mother who needs protecting."

I stared at Alex. *Have I made it impossible for my child to confide in me? I've put him in danger because I couldn't bear to part with him.* "No wonder he was up and out early this morning. He said he was going to a basketball tryout."

"That wasn't it," Alex said. "The buses leave at seven to get across town by eight in time for school."

"He must have worried about this for days and never told me." On the one hand, I was proud of him for having been so brave, but I wished he'd confided in me; I might have been able to allay his fears. Not every child who's bused has difficulties.

"I'm so sorry," I said, knowing it wasn't good enough.

"It's too late for sorry now," Alex said. "This whole thing has gone too far."

"I'm sure when Miles gets home he'll tell us it wasn't so bad." I hastened to assure the both of us, to keep him from his next statement because I was terrified of what it would be. "After all, Miles's test scores put him in the gifted program. The city schools are required to provide that kind of education for him ño matter where he is."

"With a knife in his ribs?" Alex said, through clenched teeth.

"That's not going to happen, merely because he's in a rough neighborhood."

"Oh no? I told him to call me at the nutrition break but he didn't call until noon. It seems that only one of the phones in the school was working, all the others had been ripped off the walls. As you can imagine, there was an enormous line for the one available phone. And besides, he didn't have the money to call and had to go into the office."

"I gave him lunch money."

"A gang of boys cornered him, Suzanne. They were going to beat him up if he didn't give them his money."

"Damn!" I said, thinking it sounded like one of those clichéd stories I'd heard about boys being shaken down in the lavatories. But those things always happened to other people's children, not mine. This time it wasn't a statistic, it was Miles.

"I drove all the way across town to the school," Alex said. "And brought him home with me. Then I went and picked up the other children. Miles is now registered at El Rodeo, and so is Jered. Amy is at Beverly High. The three of them are going to live with me where it's safe, where nobody will shake them down for their lunch money. I just came over to pick up some of their clothing and books for the next few days. I'll buy them whatever else they'll need.''

I couldn't believe what I was hearing; the roaring in my ears distorted his words.

"Don't even try to fight me on this, Suzanne; you'll lose. I'll sue you for custody and you know you can't afford to hire a lawyer to defend yourself, can you?''

"Alex"—I almost screamed against the pain of what he was saying—"they're my babies. They belong with me.'' The searing ache inside of me was so pervasive, so intense, I didn't think I could stand it.

"Not anymore, they don't,'' he said, brushing past me to climb the stairs to the catwalk outside the apartment. He stood there, arms folded across his chest, foot tapping impatiently, waiting for me to come and unlock the door. The foolish thought occurred to me that if I refused to open the door, refused to give him the children's clothes, maybe this all could be prevented, maybe it wouldn't be real. But it was. Finally, I opened the door to our apartment and let him in. Seeing the shabbiness through his eyes shamed me more.

It didn't take him long to pack up some of the children's belongings. "They'll call you tonight,'' he told me. "All three of them were worried about how you'd take this and I assured them you'd be all right.''

I think I nodded.

The sound of the door closing behind Alex was even more devastating than the sound the cell door had made when it locked me in. I sank onto the sofa feeling a despair more encompassing than I'd ever felt before. Somehow, I'd always believed I would come through this. No matter what, there had been a light at the end of my long dark tunnel. But now I knew that the faces, the smiles, and the loving touches of my children had been the only thing keeping me going, giving me the will to go on. There was no reason to fight anymore, no reason at all.

I lay down on the musty foam-rubber cushions of my borrowed sofa and let the flood come. This time, there was nothing to hold it back. And if I drowned in the effluvium of my own making, it would barely matter.

CHAPTER THIRTY-NINE

Clothes were a problem for Steffani working at Plummer Publishing. In 1972, most dress codes had been abolished and people did their own thing, but at Plummer, a publisher of sports magazines for men, the women were expected to wear skirts to work, and not pants. These days, skirts were very short and her legs were definitely not her best feature, her face and bustline were. That's where she preferred to draw attention. She compromised; one day, she'd wear a short skirt, a long vest, and an open-necked blouse, the next day, a long skirt with a closed collar. Her hair was long and dark, parted in the middle, and pulled back over her ears, either tied at the nape of her neck or braided, which gave her almond-shaped blue eyes an exotic look.

Her boss, Morgan Lewis, men's fashion editor, was tall and thin and smoked a pipe. He did layouts of ski wear, surfing gear, tennis clothes, and all the other sportswear of their publications. To work each day, he wore a three-piece suit, the vest carefully buttoned except for the bottom one, and his jacket neatly hung on the coat rack in the corner of his office. Sometimes he wore a foulard instead of a tie.

Morgan had brown eyes, a narrow nose, a soft mustache, and full lips. His cheeks were narrow and his skin was pink, as though rarely exposed to the sun. But in spite of his old-fashioned appearance, Steffani found him attractive and flirted with him every chance she got, mostly because it unnerved him.

It wasn't long before he asked her out. Coffee at first, and
then lunch once or twice, and then he invited her to dinner at
Omar Khayam's on the Sunset Strip, just up the street from
the Plummer Building.

They drank Pimms cups, ate shish kebab, and gazed into
each other's eyes, while she enjoyed the feeling of being the
seducer as she invited him to come home with her. For some
reason he was reluctant. But the more she was with him, the
more she liked him. He was so square, not the kind of man
she expected to be drawn to. He made her imagine that a
whole different kind of life might be possible.

"Maybe, I'll stop in just for a while," he said after their
third date. "It's a long drive home to Anaheim."

Now we're getting somewhere, she thought.

"This is really nice," he said, looking around her apartment at the plants and odd pieces of furniture that moved with
her to every new location. She was living with Maureen,
her old friend from high school, on Orange Grove in West
Hollywood. Maureen, who had never been a good student,
dropped out of Arizona after two years, and eventually Steffani got her a job at Plummer Publishing. They had decided
to room together when Steffani came back from Santa Cruz
and found her apartment nearly trashed by her friend Carole
and whoever else had been living there while Steffani was
gone. Her mother had been right about Carole, but Steffani
would never have admitted it.

"Glad you like it," Steffani said, pulling off her boots and
reaching for a joint. The way he looked at her almost made
her stop, but then she decided that no matter how different
the two of them might be, she had to be herself.

She took a drag and offered him one. Obviously he'd never
smoked dope before and she showed him how to do it, making
the instructions sensual, a part of foreplay. She held the joint
to his lips, showed him how to inhale and hold it in. Tobacco
was familiar to him so he didn't cough.

After a few drags, she could see he was getting high.
"Come on with me," she beckoned, leading him into the

bedroom. He had a silly grin on his face and stood there waiting for her direction while she selected a tape and adjusted the volume on the stereo. Then she put a silk scarf over the lamp next to the bed, and unbuttoned her top. She never wore a bra, and he blushed as he looked at her.

"It's all right," she said, beckoning to him.

She led him to the bed, helped him to lie down, and then sat beside him, indicating that he should fondle her while she unbuttoned his vest one button at a time, taking time to stroke his body in between each button. When he was aroused, she showed him what to do, guiding him so they could make love on their sides. It took a bit of maneuvering, but it was enjoyable. Sex had to be planned more carefully these days because of her enlarged liver. She didn't have the mobility in bed she'd always enjoyed and couldn't tolerate the weight of another body pressing against hers, so sex had to be more imaginative. Morgan didn't seem to mind the instructions or the limits. At all.

"I've never met anyone like you," he told her afterward, gazing at her profile in the scarf-dimmed light.

"In what way?" she asked, tracing the outline of his cheek, running her fingers over his mustache. It was soft, not bristly. She liked the way it felt everywhere he'd kissed her.

"You're unique. So uninhibited. You make everything seem natural. I'm usually not this free," he admitted as though he was telling her something she didn't know.

She shrugged. "What the hell. Life's too short for pretenses. My mother wouldn't agree, but I don't live with her anymore. You know, you could use some letting go. You are a bit uptight."

He nodded. "But not tonight. Could you tell?"

She smiled.

"I feel so damn good right now." He kissed her shoulder, lightly.

"Is there anything you want to know about me?" she asked. "I sense your curiosity, but I can tell you're reluctant to ask, aren't you?"

Even in the dim light, she could see him look away.

"I figured you'd tell me about yourself when you're ready," he said.

"You want to know about this, don't you?" she placed his hand on her moundlike abdomen.

She could feel his fingers tremble, wanting to pull away, but she held him there. "It's okay," she said. "I have a liver disorder. I was born with it. It curtails certain activities, but mostly it doesn't bother me."

"I thought maybe you were pregnant," he said. "A beautiful pregnant woman."

"That's what most people think."

"Will this disorder go away?"

"No," she told him. "It's chronic and progressive."

"What does that mean?"

"That I don't have a terribly long life expectancy, probably."

"How can you say that so calmly?" He was obviously upset.

She gazed at him. "Why not? Who of us knows when he's going to die? I just think I'll die sooner than later. But in the meantime, I intend to live as fully as I can and get as much out of it as possible."

He took her hand and held it. He really was sweet. "I must say, I admire your honesty," he said, softly. "And since you're being so honest with me, I have to be too."

"That's what I want," she said, wondering at his serious tone. "Don't tell me you're a cross-dresser?"

"No," he said, looking away. "It's something else."

"Go ahead, you can tell me." She'd heard some pretty strange confessions from men in bed. Not much shocked her.

"I'm married."

That did. She shot up in bed, almost pushing him off, saw the cloud of her dream going up in smoke. "Goddamn you, Morgan. That stinks! How could you make love to me and not tell me you were married?" The disappointment hurt more than she expected. "I thought you were an honorable man.

But you're a rat, aren't you?'' She smacked her forehead with her palm. "What a dunce! How could I not have known? So that's why you wouldn't come home with me before.'' She thought for a minute. "I've been working for you for four months and I've never heard you make a phone call to your wife. She never calls you either. There aren't any pictures of her in your office. Are you separated?''

His eyes were downcast as he shook his head. "No. I put her picture in the drawer the day I hired you and told her not to call me at work, that I would call her. I do it when you're out on your lunch break.''

"God, is that sneaky. Making secret calls to your wife while your secretary's at lunch.'' She wanted to laugh, but she was too angry and hurt. Angry at him for lying to her, at herself for being such a chump, and for being too easily fooled. *I must have wanted to be*, she thought. Then, something else occurred to her. "You don't have any kids, do you?''

Miserably, he nodded. "Two boys—Morgan Junior, six, and Eric, four.''

"Then what the hell are you doing with me?'' Now, she thought he was crazy. The man had everything; why was he wlling to risk it for sex? It didn't make sense. In her realm of experience sex was a normal function, too good to miss for long. But a home and wife and children were precious. Why would he trade one for the other?

"I know what you're thinking, that I'm disgusting for cheating on my wife. But from the moment I hired you, I've wanted to make love to you. You're the most beautiful, desirable woman I've ever met. Lord, forgive me, but if I didn't take this chance, I knew I'd never have another.''

"But Morgan, you're married. You can have sex with your wife. Can't you?''

"Look at me, Steffani,'' he said, without answering her question. "I'm thirty-seven years old and this is the most exciting thing I've ever done in my life, being here with you. I wasn't going to tell you I was married until we'd been together a few more times. I didn't want you to stop seeing me. But you've been so honest with me, I couldn't lie to you any longer.''

''You know I'd never have gone out with you if I'd known you were married, don't you?''

''Of course. A girl like you. Why would you? I wouldn't blame you if you never spoke to me again. But please don't quit your job. You're the best secretary I've had in ages. In a year or so, you could become an assistant editor.''

Somehow, that thought didn't thrill her. ''What's your wife like?'' Steffani asked, wondering how she would feel if her husband was out cheating. Hell, she knew exactly how she would feel. Shitty.

''Mona? She's all right. But she's nothing like you.''

''We've established that. What do you mean, all right? You mean she's not touched in the head, or anything?''

He laughed, glad she hadn't kicked him out yet. ''She's religious. She goes to church on Sunday and midweek Bible study on Thursdays. She knits sweaters for the boys and won a prize for her cherry cobbler. She doesn't like television, except for classical things like concerts. She's close to her family, keeps the house spotless.''

''Boy, she sounds perfect. No wonder you're uptight,'' Steffani commented. ''And when do the two of you have fun?''

''We get a sitter and go to the movies. Or have people over for dinner.''

''Do the two of you ever send the kids to your mom's and open a bottle of champagne and make love all night?''

He started to laugh to cover his embarrassment. ''That's only in movies or TV. Wives don't do things like that with their husbands.''

''Since when?'' she asked.

''My wife doesn't. She doesn't like sex.'' He sighed. ''Maybe it's my fault.''

''Maybe it is,'' Steffani agreed. ''If both of you are inhibited, who's going to make the moves? Maybe I should lend you a couple of joints to loosen things up a bit at home." She was teasing, but he took her seriously.

"Oh no. Mona would never smoke marijuana. She doesn't drink either."

Oh brother, Steffani thought, raising her eyes to the ceiling. "How did you two meet?"

"At a church social."

"I should have guessed," Steffani sighed, thinking she ought to ask him to leave. What a fool she'd been to think there might have been something between them. "Listen, Morgan. Are you planning to confess to Mona about tonight? Or to your clergyman? Because if you are, I think you'd better go now, before we compound our sin and you'll never get them to forgive you."

"No," he insisted. "I'm not going to confess anything. This was one of the most wonderful nights of my life and I'll be damned if I'll feel guilty."

He leaned over and kissed her, deeply, with intense feeling. It surprised her because, dammit, she liked it so much.

Looking up at him after the kiss she asked, "Now what?"

"I don't know," he said, leaning back on the pillow, his arms behind his head, elbows at right angles. "I'll abide by your decision."

"Abide?" she hooted. "How corny can you get?" And she leaned over and suddenly started tickling him under his arms.

He tried to grab her hands away, but she was too quick and in an instant he was screeching with laughter. "Oh, please stop, don't do that, you don't know how ticklish I am," he gasped, begging for mercy.

She was laughing too as she let up the torturous pressure, and then just as he felt some relief, she began again.

"Oh God, no," he insisted, finally grabbing her wrists and forcing her back on the bed. Now they were in reverse positions, with him holding her down. He kept her hands pinned against the sheets and said, "Now I've got you."

She stared up at him defiantly and said, "Oh yeah? What are you going to do about it?"

They were both out of breath, their chests heaving. Her expression defied him to do something, and he leaned forward and kissed her, keeping her wrists pinned, but being careful not to press his body against her.

What the hell, she thought, as she kissed him back, feeling herself respond. *Everybody's entitled to a fling now and then. Even I.*

This time, it was he who made love to her, and when it was over, he fell asleep with his head buried in the crook of her arm. Finally, about two in the morning, reluctantly she woke him. "You'd better go, lover boy. Mona's waiting."

Startled, he pulled himself up and away from her, then smiled at her with a foolish grin. "God," he said, shaking his head. "You're so beautiful. Thank you for the most wonderful evening of my life."

"And thank you," she said, smiling back, feeling as though they had given each other a wonderful gift. It was rare that a man was as considerate and gentle with her as Morgan had been, or that she inspired such gratitude.

As he was putting on his clothes, she said, "You know, we can't do this again, don't you? I thought I'd better say it, just in case you started to believe I've changed my mind."

He nodded silently, tying his tie. "I understand," he told her. "But couldn't we just leave the decision until tomorrow? I don't want to spoil tonight." He leaned down and kissed her and then left.

The next morning when she arrived at work a dozen red roses were on her desk. Morgan didn't come in until eleven. When he did, he closed the door to the outer office, walked directly to her desk where she was typing an article, and pulled her up out of the chair and kissed her. She was taken off guard for the moment and didn't resist him. But when the kiss ended, she said, "That was for the roses. And now, let's have that discussion you didn't want to have last night."

"After lunch," he said, "okay? I've got a ton of work to do now."

"How was Mona?" she couldn't help asking.

"She was asleep and didn't know what time I got in."

482 Sharleen Cooper Cohen

Sure, Steffani thought, but she didn't say anything.

After lunch, when she came into the office to talk to him, there was an envelope with her name on it on top of her typewriter. In the envelope was a poem.

Steffani Does

If I could renounce
My desk and my chair
And act for just once
As if I don't care

I'd make love to the girl
Who delivers the mail
Round up the executives
And send them to jail

Put LSD in the giant coffee urn
Dance nude down the hall
Screw up every phone call
I'd say, go take a piss
To a secretarial miss

Hang a B.A. for my boss
Empty files with a toss
To the president say
You can keep all your pay

But I just can't get up
From my desk and my chair

Or go flipping my hair
As though less I don't care

But Steffani does . . .

It made her laugh, but it didn't convince her to continue their affair. Not now that she knew he was married.

"Morgan," she said when he came back from lunch, his eyes averted. "The poem is quite a tribute. I think I'm touched to have inspired it. But, that's it, okay? Is that clear? If I find any more flowers or gifts or poems, I'm going to ask to be transferred to another department.''

"Steffani, you don't understand what you mean to me."

"I think I do. But I'm not the one who can set you free. You have to do that for yourself. Do you hear me?"

He wouldn't look at her, but he nodded. And then he turned away. She waited for a few moments for him to turn back to her, but he didn't. She was about to make a smart remark or tease him when she saw him wipe his eyes. He was crying, over her. *Oh, what the hell*, she thought opening her arms to embrace him.

Their affair lasted several months. Each time they made love, she told him it was the last, but he was innovative and dedicated to finding ways to get around her. The gifts and poems wore down her resistance, but more than that, he was so needy she couldn't help responding. Being with him rekindled the dream of having someone in her life who was there for her. Until he became obsessive, wanting to know who else she was seeing, always asking her questions.

"I'll leave Mona and the kids. I just want to be with you," he'd say. But she didn't want to be responsible for him leaving his wife.

"I'm not a homewrecker, Morgan. Your family needs you, your children would miss having a full-time father. You could work it out with Mona if you'd try." The more self-sacrificing she became, the more he wanted her.

"You don't understand," he'd say. And there would be tears in his eyes. "With you I'm alive for the first time in my life. How can you ask me to give that up?"

She asked to be transferred to another department, citing personal reasons. But there were no openings. Office gossip boiled; the executive staff was on one side, the secretaries on the other. Maureen reported the scuttlebutt several times a day.

"Now, there's a bet going on, people are putting two

dollars each into a pool that says he's going to take you to the Christmas party and not his wife. Then, there's another pool that says you two are making it in the office whenever the door's closed. Are you?'' Maureen asked. "Not that I've made a bet, or anything.''

"That's it!'' Steffani declared. "I'm quitting.'' Until now, she hadn't cared about what people were saying. It was silly to her. In the social world she lived in, her behavior was normal, certainly not the stuff of discussion; nobody would have noticed. In the mentality of this middle-class office, the attitudes amazed her; it was as if the sexual revolution had completely passed them by.

"You can't quit and leave me alone here,'' Maureen said, her eyes widening with disbelief. "The rent's due next week and you're still making payments on that dress at the Pleasure Dome. Morgan would die if you quit.''

"He won't die, Maureen. That's the lie that's kept me from saying no to him all this time.''

"You like him,'' Maureen commented. "Don't kid me. He's not the only one keeping this thing going, is he?''

Steffani shook her head. "No, I do like him. But it's got to stop.'' She was finally realizing the truth of that. She should have let it go that first night, not hung on to the impossible.

"What would you do if you quit? You couldn't collect unemployment.''

It was a sobering thought. "I don't want to be anywhere I'm considered a joke, Maureen. If I can't make Morgan understand that it's over, I'll leave this job, compensation or not.''

Maureen stared at her friend and shook her head. "You're really something, you know that? No wonder Morgan loves you.''

Steffani waited until late that evening when most of the staff had gone home and she and Morgan were alone on the sixth floor. He always stayed late these days, hoping she'd agree to see him for dinner. Sometimes, she did. But no more; she'd made a vow and she'd stick to it.

"We have to talk."

"Not tonight, sweetheart," he sighed. "I'm really beat. What do you say we go dancing? The Whiskey? Or that new private club, Pips? You'd like that, wouldn't you? I'm thinking of buying a membership."

"Morgan, that's not the kind of place your wife would like, is it? I think you should consider that first."

"It's not for Mona, it's for me. A place where you and I can go together."

"Morgan, there is no you and I. I've been trying to tell you that all along. As of tonight, whatever we've had is over. If I'm out of your life, you'll work things out with your wife. I know you will."

He didn't believe her. And why should he, she'd said this too many times without meaning it. "What about you, Steffani? Don't you deserve someone to love you?"

"Don't do that," she said, feeling the thrust of pain in her heart. "Sure I deserve that. I believe it, too. But not from you, baby. Not from you."

"I'm beginning to hate her," he said softly, "hate my life. I lie in bed next to her and long for you. Last week I found myself staring at the pills in the medicine cabinet, wondering if any of them were strong enough to put me out of my misery."

"Oh, for God's sake, Morgan. That kind of talk really pisses me off. What the hell have you got to feel sorry about. You want to compare life's miseries with me? Want to trade? Just don't get me started." Her list of physical and emotional ailments was two pages long, starting with hemorrhages that still occurred whenever she didn't want them, particularly from that injury she'd sustained in the car accident with Joe, a permanently enlarged abdomen that seemed to increase with every year, lack of stamina, shortness of breath, skin discolorations, scars, deformities, and, of course, the ever-pervasive knowledge that this was all going to get worse and not better. And to top it off, she was alone, while everyone else around her had someone. Her job was boring, it wasn't going anywhere. Being a secretary or even an assistant editor would never fulfill her. Every time she thought about the dreams she'd had of writing and teaching, it made her sick inside. She was a failure. She hadn't accomplished anything she'd set out to do, except ruin other people's lives, specifically Mona's, her two children's, and Morgan's as well. No wonder she'd hung on to him; he was a perfect way of forgetting.

This job was a dead end, barely tolerable. And Morgan's devotion was all she had going for her. She was using him to forget her aimlessness even more than he was using her to bolster his own life.

"Morgan, have you ever heard that old song, 'Your lips tell me no no, but there's yes yes in your eyes'?"

Her question had taken him off guard. "From when I was a kid. Why?"

"That's what I've been doing to you all this time. I'm not surprised it's been driving you crazy. This time, I really mean it. I'm tendering my resignation as of this moment, unless you'll agree to fire me and let me collect unemployment."

All the color drained from his face, and he sat on the edge of his desk as though his legs wouldn't hold him up any longer.

"No, I guess you wouldn't," she commented.

"I could never fire you. If only for the slightest possibility that you'd stay, I'd never do that."

"There isn't."

"Still, I could never be the one to be responsible for your leaving."

"I really need the money, Morgan."

"Then stay. Please, Steffani, I'm begging you. I don't want to go on without you."

She opened her desk drawer and started putting her personal belongings in her tote bag. "I can send Maureen for the rest," she said, realizing she had to get out of here now before she changed her mind. She thought about what she had in her checkbook at the moment. It was frightening. She barely made ends meet on her salary, and had nothing saved. Now, there wouldn't even be severance pay. He could see her hesitating, and got up from the desk to put his arms around her but she wouldn't be seduced by that one more time. She pushed past him and grabbed her cape, wanting to don it with a flurry, make a dramatic exit, but instead she just walked out the door.

The last thing she heard was his anguished voice calling, "Steffani, please don't go."

"Steffani," Maureen said, before she left for work. "It's been two weeks since you quit Plummer. You've got to get a job. But all you do is sit around here smoking grass. I can't handle the overhead by myself. If you're not going to pull your weight, I'll have to get another roommate. I don't want to be evicted. Steff, are you listening to me?"

But Steffani just sat there cross-legged on the bed staring off into space. Since she'd quit her job, there didn't seem to be any point to getting out of bed. She spent most of her time there, thinking about her past, reviewing it one event at a time, enhanced by the altered state of stonedness. Where was her fighting spirit? she wondered. What had happened to the drive to achieve, to the belief that life was worth living regardless of pain and limitations? *What the fuck's wrong with you, Steffani?* she thought. And then the suffocating blackness threatened to envelop her. She knew the answer. Despair was the sea beneath her dock. On it she stood, feeling its rise and fall, its precarious moorings nearly ripping free. Only her own faith held it fast to the pylons, and merely by a slender thread of hope. *How much time do I have?* she thought. *Not enough to waste one precious moment. But sometimes the fight is so hard, so goddamned hard. I don't want to fight it anymore.* "And what's your alternative?" her mother's voice asked—practical Lynnette. "Sitting there vegetating, stewing in your own marijuana smoke and self-pity? You're better than that. We raised you better. You're worth more! I repeat, life is too precious to throw away. You're alive now. Someday you won't be."

She remembered the woman administrator who'd turned her down for graduate school. How she'd pledged to continue that fight, but she'd been defeated instead.

"Don't let that woman win," her mother's voice insisted.

"You can do anything you set your mind to," her father's voice told her.

"Look at what I've accomplished," her sister's voice egged her on. "And with only half your talent."

And so, in the third week after quitting her job, she spent her first sober day. The next day she dragged herself out of the apartment and went to the Federal Building in Westwood.

"Where do I apply for a student loan to go to graduate school?" she asked at the information desk. They directed her to a loan officer and she was able to get an appointment within an hour.

"I so wanted to go to UCLA," she told the loan officer named Vincent Shepherd. She felt herself starting to cry. "But that's not possible now."

"Northridge State has an excellent graduate school of education," he told her. "And the tuition is far less than at UCLA. If you fulfill the requirements, such as grade points and character references, I think we can help you, Ms. Blacker," he said.

"Is it possible to borrow enough money so I can go to school full time and not have to work?" she asked. "You see, I'll have to fulfill certain undergraduate requirements if I go to Northridge State, which means three years of school. But if I concentrate on my studies, and continue to take classes straight through, I can finish sooner."

"Well, we don't just give money away. I mean, your lifestyle would have to be cut to a minimum if you were to live on your loan without any other income. Most of our loan recipients do work."

"Would I be turned down if I'm not strong enough physically to work and go to school?" she asked.

"Not since the new antidiscrimination laws," the counselor told her.

Her heart had been pounding as she asked him that, and now she felt a smile breaking through that soon turned into a huge grin. "I'm going to make an excellent teacher, Mr. Shepherd," she told him. "You just watch me."

CHAPTER FORTY

"If you're not going to Santa Fe, Suzanne, I'm not going either," Steffani said. "Can you imagine me alone with Mom and Dad for four days? Gads. All they ever do is criticize me. Whoever I date is no good, whatever I wear is no good. You'd think after all this time they'd realize I am who I am and I'm not going to change. They keep trying to fit me into your mold, where I've never wanted to be."

"They don't do that," I countered, weakly, knowing that's exactly what they did. They expected wondrous things from Steffani instead of what she was so good at, being herself. They'd never come to terms with her limitations or appreciated her for who she was. But I couldn't change them either. Steffani's honesty still embarrassed our mother.

"What's so good about being you?" she said, testily. "You're divorced, for God's sake."

"Look, if you interrupted my work to put me down, I'd rather cut this short, okay?"

"No, I'm sorry. I really want to convince you to come to Santa Fe. I won't be able to stand it without you watching Dad make a big deal over Gloria while Mom sits there trying not to mind, with that Cheshire cat smile of hers, pretending to be indulgent, while you know she wants to scratch someone's eyes out."

"Scratch whose eyes out?"

"Gloria's of course, Gloria the impossible," Steffani declared. "I saw her the last time she was in town, when your in-laws were taking care of your kids and I picked them up. Now that she's playing lead roles, she's hell to live with, let me tell you. But, you've got to hand it to Dad, he's hung in there with her through all those lean years and it's finally paid off. Have you listened to her latest album? Gloria Winston sings Italian arias. Even I was impressed."

"I've always wanted to go to Santa Fe. I hear it's romantic. But not with Mom and Dad." I laughed.

"I'll be there," she teased. "We can hold hands and gaze up at the desert sky."

"It might be fun," I agreed. The children could stay with Alex. "But Gloria will hardly be happy to see me," I said. "Since the divorce, I've been on her S list."

"Say it, Suzanne. The S word, s-h-i-t." Steffani spelled it out for me.

"If you know it so well, there's no need for me to say it, is there?" I loved annoying her by playing up to her opinion of me that I'm too prissy for words.

"Come on, Suze, say you'll go. It's my first vacation since graduate school and I deserve it. Besides, Dad's paying for me or I couldn't go."

"I'm paying for myself," I said, thoughtlessly.

"Well, aren't you lucky," she snapped.

"It won't be long now," I told her, trying to make up. "Only nine months to go and you'll graduate."

"A period of gestation," she commented. "Only I'll be acquiring thirty-five kids all at once. Lucky me. If I get a job."

"You will," I assured her. "I just know it."

"So. You coming?"

"I might as well. Are you taking jeans?"

"If I can zip them up over my stomach," she said. "Otherwise it's skirts for me, which is better than curtains."

"Very funny. How have you been feeling lately?" Last month she was hospitalized with a fever of unknown origin— FUO they called it—that lasted for three weeks. And still, even in the hospital she'd kept up with her classes, managing to do all her required work until the fever went away. Every day, one of us would call her doctors to ask what the cause of the fever was, while she lay there, drinking Seven-Up, eating ice chips, and feeling generally awful. But they never found out. If it was unnerving for us, I can imagine how it made her feel. But as usual, she took it in stride, and talked about how she was anxious to get better and be released from the hospital.

My parents made the hour's drive every day to the City of Hope in Duarte where she was being treated, and I was there five days out of seven. I could tell she was lonely and really appreciated the company. If only her friends cared enough about her, but they rarely came. Here she was, in the hospital for weeks this time, and not one—I mean *not one*—of her friends had been there. It depressed them, they said, or it was too far, or their cars were broken, or they couldn't afford the gas. And she was so good to them, so loyal. It infuriated me. I resented the hell out of them for being so self-indulgent, because no matter what was going on in my life, with three children and a career and dating, for God's sake, I was there. And since either I or my parents came there every day, we could easily have brought one of them with us if they didn't have a ride. But no one ever asked. Once, I called her friend Carole and offered to take her with me.

"How long will you be there?" she wanted to know.

"I usually stay a few hours," I told her.

"Plus driving time? Gosh, that's a long time. I don't think I could be stuck in Duarte for that long," she complained. "You know how it is."

If I criticized Carole, or Melody, or Lee, or any of them, she got so defensive. She forgave them, excused them, and only got angry at me or Mom for pointing out the obvious, what scummy people they were. "They're my friends," she'd say. "I accept them for what they are, I don't judge them." Apparently, whatever they did was enough for her. But it sure as hell wasn't enough for me.

"I've been okay," she told me. "Now that I'm finishing with finals. Just tired, as usual, and horny as hell. The other day I almost took one of my fellow classmates home with me, but he was only nineteen and a virgin. That's how desperate I am."

"Steffani!" She said things like that to try to shock me.

"Suzanne!" She copied my tone of exasperation. And then she said, "Gotta go," and hung up.

I didn't speak to her again until we met at the airport and the four of us flew to Albuquerque.

"This is such a treat, having my two girls with me," my father said.

My mother smiled at us, holding first my hand and then Steffani's. We rented a car at the airport and my mother sat in front reading the map, giving my father directions to Santa Fe. Whenever we came to a crosspoint, my father would argue with my mother, "Are you sure this is the way?"

"I'm telling you, go straight here, Burt. This road intersects with the one we want."

"It doesn't seem right. Let the girls read the map, Lynnette." And he'd turn the opposite way.

"I told you to keep going straight, Burt."

"I know where I'm going, Lynnette. This is the highway we're supposed to be on."

"Not according to the map," she insisted.

"We're never going to get there," I whispered to my sister, who laughed and nodded her head. We'd both forgotten what it was like to be with them on a trip. In between arguments my father kept singing, "On the Acheson, Topeka and the Santa Fe." I don't know how we finally got there.

The Santa Fe Opera, where Gloria was appearing for the summer, performed out of doors in a modified amphitheater. Often in the summer it rained and some of the seats were exposed to the sky through the opened-beam construction. But tonight the sky was clear and they were performing Verdi's *Aïda*. Tomorrow, Saturday, they would be doing *The Magic Flute*. Sunday, there was no performance, and Steffani and I were flying back in the evening. My parents were staying on for several more days.

"Are you sure you wouldn't rather return with the girls, Lynnette?" my father asked her for the tenth time. "You know I'll be working while I'm here, planning Gloria's fall appearance schedule. There's nothing much to do in Santa Fe after you've seen the shops and the galleries."

"I'll be fine," my mother told him. "I've brought my camera equipment, and I'll go to Taos and take pictures of the church, and the pueblo, and the desert. Maybe, if I'm lucky, I'll get some wonderful Ansel Adams–type landscapes. Or Edward Weston portraits of craggy-faced Indians."

Burt sighed and shrugged. "Suit yourself. But don't come whining to me that you're bored by Tuesday."

"I don't whine, Burt," Lynnette snapped. "You make me sound as if I'm one of the children. And if it's so boring here, what does Gloria do all day?"

"She practices and rehearses. And I understand there's an active social scene here among the opera patrons, artists, and collectors who entertain visiting celebrities. And since Gloria is a celebrity, she's much in demand."

"Thanks to you," Steffani said.

"Is she still seeing that fashion designer? The one Steffani met in San Francisco?" Lynnette asked.

My sister and I exchanged glances. Over the years, George Ruben was the only one of Gloria's boyfriends who had withstood her tantrums and fickleness. We couldn't figure out why. Especially Steffani, who'd had an affair with him. Our father openly disliked George, called him a flitterbug. "George wastes her time, he's a bad influence on her," Burt insisted.

But Gloria kept him around while the others came and went. Whenever she wanted to upset Burt, she'd threaten to marry George. Burt thought Gloria should not consider marriage until her career was fully established. It looked pretty established to me. Starring in lead roles as a summer headliner for the Santa Fe Opera was quite prestigious. And in the fall, she had a contract with the New York City Opera. There wasn't much further she could go. So I half expected her to announce her engagement any time. But not if Steffani had anything to say about it.

Gloria's performance was inspired. I don't know which was more dazzling, her or the canopy of stars filling the black sky over our heads. Her voice had matured beyond what I had imagined; she commanded the stage as Amneris, the Pharaoh's daughter.

Afterward, when we went to see her, I felt almost shy about meeting a star of her magnitude, as though she was no longer the woman I'd known for so many years.

Gloria's dressing room was crowded with visitors as we arrived. My father maneuvered through the crowd and stood by her side magically as if a hand had reached out and plucked him from among us. There was such a fuss being made over Gloria it was intimidating. I sensed Steffani's impatience. And then, with a determined movement through the crowd, my mother made her way to Gloria and Burt. To Gloria's credit, she was charming. I saw her embrace my mother and introduce her to others.

"Do you want to pay your respects to Her Highness?" my sister asked.

"Not now," I told her. "We'll see her at the party."

We waited outside Gloria's dressing room for our parents, but only my mother joined us. "Your father is going to ride over with Gloria," she told us. "He gave me directions on how to get to the party." So the three of us went by ourselves.

"She was really good," Steffani said. "After a while, even I forgot who she was. She really moved me."

"I thought so too," I said. "The richness of her tone amazed me. And her dramatic performance was superb."

"Do you suppose she's mellowed?" Steffani wondered.

"I'm sure of it," I said. "No one could feel a character's role that deeply and still possess a petty soul."

"I think you're giving her too much credit. It will be interesting to see who's right," Steffani said. Mother didn't say anything.

The party was being held at Peter Jerrold's home, a legendary edifice in Santa Fe. It was just beginning when we arrived and parked our rented car in an enormous graveled circle entryway. As we passed through the hugely tall, thick wooden front doors, I spotted George Ruben standing with a group of people. He was as good-looking as Steffani had described him, tall, tanned, with dark hair and graying temples, wearing an open-collared white shirt, black slacks, and a sweater draped over his shoulders. Steffani saw him then, and made a path directly for him. My father and Gloria hadn't arrived yet. I offered to get my mother a drink.

"I'm going to look around," she told me, when I came back with her gin and tonic. She headed off into another wing of the house. I stayed by the door. That's why I was one of the first people to see Gloria as she came into the party. She was wearing a red suede off-the-shoulder dress, beaded and hand-painted all over the fitted bodice with Indian motif continuing down to the full skirt. Around her waist she wore a huge turquoise conch belt. Her hair was long and thickly rich, curling over her creamy shoulders. She looked stunning as she swept in to be devoured by her fans. My father watched her with an indulgent smile on his face, much the same way he used to watch me and my sister when we'd dive off the diving board yelling, "Watch this," or vie in other ways for his attention.

But for all the adulation, Gloria's eyes searched the room until she spotted Steffani monopolizing George Ruben. He was gazing down at Steffani the way the wolf must have looked at Red Riding Hood. Rather than confront them, Gloria turned away. *She's gotten cool*, I thought. For Steffani was flirting outrageously. If the man had been my boyfriend, I would have been furious. As it was, I was envious of Steffani too, watching her come on like that, take what she wanted and not give a damn who saw, or what they thought.

George Ruben was mesmerized. And then, as I watched, and Gloria pretended not to, he put his arm around Steffani's waist, and with absolute disregard for anyone else, appropriated her out the patio door and into the dark garden beyond. The two of them were so obviously immersed in one another I was sure if I followed them I'd have easily found their red hot footprints smoldering on the terra cotta tile floor.

I don't know why I thought it was my duty to try and smooth things over, but I approached Gloria just then thinking I should distract her. I came at her from the side so that she didn't see me until I put my arm around her shoulder and hugged her to me. "You were incredible," I gushed. "You were so wonderful, I can't find the words to describe it." The group of people she was talking to stopped politely so she could acknowledge me, this woman who'd interrupted them, and she turned to look at me for the first time.

"What are you doing here?" she asked.

"I came with my family," I explained. "We all saw your performance tonight. You were fabulous. I can't get over how amazing you were. I'm so thrilled for you, Gloria, so proud of you."

She just stared ice at me. It was one of those terrible moments when suddenly all is wrong with the world. I removed my arm from her shoulder. The group of people standing there noticed the awkwardness between us and turned away to talk to one another.

Gloria raised her upper lip in a sneer, lowered her lashes, and looked at me through slitted eyes. "How banal of you to say you're proud of me. As if you had something to do with it. Where the hell were you all the years it took me to get where I am. Proud of me? God, you're insufferable. You and that slut of a sister."

If she'd slapped me, it wouldn't have shocked me any more. "What are you talking about? I'm not taking credit for anything you've done. I was complimenting you. You were spectacular."

She kept a fake smile on her face and spoke between

clenched teeth so that only I could hear her. "You don't deserve to wipe my ass, much less enjoy my performance. How dare you come here and assume that you can just walk up to me as if you were a regular person and not the most destructive human being on the face of this earth."

I stared at her, not believing what I was hearing. *Was she crazy?* I wondered. And then in a rush I suddenly remembered all the times she'd behaved bizarrely over the years, reacted inappropriately, or lapsed into catatonia as a prelude to a tantrum. *Dear Lord*, I thought. *What will she do now?* She was capable of anything. I wanted to turn and walk away, but she might scream or grab me or tackle me. I stood there, knowing I was about to get it and unable to stop her.

"You ruined his life, you know. And I blame myself partly, because I fixed you up with my dearest brother. I knew you weren't good enough for him, but I didn't think you'd destroy him. He never loved you, you know. But you are responsible for the only failure in his life. I curse the day I offered you my friendship, you Judas. My brother's life will never be the same because of you. God, the years I've had to listen to my brother or Burt defend you, excuse your stupidity. How a man as fine as Burt could have spawned two such spoors as you and your sister is beyond me. Well, God has punished you through your sister. All that suffering she does is for your sins. I hope you know that. My only regret is that you haven't been the one to suffer for your own actions. But someday you will. Won't that be justice?"

She turned away from me with a flourish, whipping her hair around so that it swiped across my face. Then she walked directly over to my father, took his arm in hers, and insisted that he escort her out of the party.

"Dad!" I called after him, crushed that he would leave with her, especially after her outburst. But he did, and I stared at the empty doorway through which they'd gone hoping it wasn't true, still unable to process what she'd just said.

Just then, someone stepped into my line of vision. It was my mother. First she looked at me, then at the door, as if she couldn't believe it either. Gloria had just insulted me with the worst tirade of my life. And Burt had walked out of the party with her. By his action he taken her side over mine, his own daughter's.

My mother and I exchanged bewildered glances. I felt my face getting hot. And then, without saying a word, she came over to me, took my hand, and the two of us left together.

CHAPTER FORTY-ONE

The party was just getting started when Steffani arrived at Jack and Allison Phillips's house at seven-thirty. Her interview for a teaching job at Hollywood High had gone on longer than she'd expected and so, rather than go back to change at Suzanne's, where she'd been staying to save money, she'd just come right here. Jack Phillips had been one of her education professors at Cal State and she'd gotten friendly with him and his wife when she was studying there. Allison was a teacher at Westlake School for Girls and between the two of them they'd been quite helpful in advising her about job hunting. But it was already late August and school started in just three weeks. If she didn't find something soon, she'd miss out on a job this semester and have to get some other kind of employment. And whether she liked to or not, she had to recognize that she didn't have the stamina she once had. It worried her that even if she got a job, she might not have the strength to stand in front of a class all day. In order to command her students' attention she had to stand in front of them, not sit; and that was not only tiring, but it made her physical condition apparent. Her abdomen was more enlarged than it had ever been, making her look five months pregnant. If only she were, she thought, more often than she liked to admit.

"Hi, Steff," Allison Phillips greeted her at the door. "Any luck with Emily Waterston?"

That was the girls' vice-principal at Hollywood, with whom she'd had her interview. She shook her head. "She was not too encouraging. The most they could offer me was some substitute teaching from time to time. The one opening they thought they'd had in the English Department was taken today when the teacher who was going to leave decided to stay."

Allison patted her arm. "That's too bad. But I'm sure something will turn up soon." She walked with Steffani into the family room where a few early arrivals had congregated around the bar. Jack was behind the bar and he waved to her.

"Hi, beautiful," he called. "Come over here. There's someone who wants to say hello to you."

The song playing on the stereo was "Michelle." Paul McCartney's voice filled the room, bringing back sweet memories. Jack handed her a glass of wine as she arrived at the bar and a man seated there with his back to her turned around.

It was Ron Bernfeld.

She was so surprised to see him she almost dropped her glass. "Ron!" she exclaimed, wanting to shrink up like Alice in Wonderland and totally disappear. Of all the people in the world, he was the last one she ever wanted to see.

"Hi, Steffani," he said, standing up to make room for her at the next stool.

"What are you doing here?" she asked, perching on the edge of the stool.

"Jack's an old fraternity buddy of mine and I call him whenever I'm in town. He mentioned he was having a party, and that you might be here. I really wanted to see you."

She glanced at Jack, who shrugged. "Seems like old times," he sang. "Actually, I'd forgotten that you two dated for a while. Whenever I think of college, I'm embarrassed at what a neanderthal I was, so unenlightened. But you must have been different," he said to Ron. "To appreciate a girl like Steffani, instead of those cheerleaders I went with."

Ron's eyes wouldn't meet hers and she recalled their last

encounter when they'd fought over her being pregnant. How humiliated she'd been.

Just then, another guest ordered a drink and diverted Jack's attention.

"In town from where?" Steffani asked, looking at Ron so he couldn't avoid her. She was beyond caring about the past. If it bothered him, too bad.

"San Francisco," he said, sipping his drink. He had filled out a bit, mostly around the middle. A small spare tire hung over his belt and his blond hair was thin on top. But he had those same sparkling blue eyes and a heavy dusting of blond hair on his forearms. He was wearing a blue-striped short-sleeved shirt and khaki pants. *Some things never change*, she thought, realizing that she no longer hated him for what he had done to her. With a father like his, he couldn't have known any better.

"You're looking good," he said, trying not to stare at her abdomen. "More mature. I like your hair dark, it makes your eyes even bluer."

She smiled, enjoying his awkwardness, and took a sip of wine. She only allowed herself half a glass a week, of any kind of liquor. Alcohol was difficult for her liver to metabolize.

"How have you been?" he asked. "Jack tells me you graduated with honors and that you got an M.A. in education. That's wonderful. It's always been your dream, hasn't it, to teach? Of all the people I've ever known you were certain to follow your dreams."

"I did get sidetracked for a while," she told him. "But things are finally working out. If I could only get a job. I've been trying all summer, and twice I came close. But so far, nothing. I owe my parents money, plus I have a student loan to pay off." Other people could afford to wait until the right job came along, or any job for that matter. But for her, there was no time to waste. If she didn't get it now it might be too late. "What have you been doing since college, Ron?"

"I became a CPA and moved to San Francisco. I work for

a small firm in the city—we do mostly corporate work—and I live in Richmond.'' He was smiling at her, a sweet nostalgic smile, free from any of the bitterness she'd seen the last time they were together. ''I'm glad you're being so nice to me. I don't deserve it after the way I treated you.''

''We were kids,'' she said, making it easier.

''You don't know how many times I've kicked myself for the way I acted back then. I must have been a real ass. The only excuse I can give is that I let my father influence me because I wanted him to love me. I missed him a lot back then because I didn't live with him. I especially resented his other family. I would look for opportunities to be with him. I didn't know where I belonged.'' He gave a short laugh. ''I thought he was someone worth wanting. After that time when he wouldn't help us and told me it was your fault you were pregnant, I began to realize what a horrible man he was. There were other incidents besides that which showed what he was really like. He hates women, especially the ones who stand up to him, like my mom. I'm really sorry about what happened back then.''

''Well, I wasn't pregnant, after all.''

''I've regretted that too.''

''For God's sake, why?'' She reached over and scooped a few cashews out of a bowl and popped them into her mouth, realizing too late that she shouldn't have eaten them and would probably be sorry later.

''Because, if we'd had a baby together, you wouldn't have gone out of my life. A baby would have been a bond between us, something to draw us closer. Maybe, we would have gotten married.''

''You didn't want to marry a Jewish hippie,'' she laughed.

''My dad's father was Jewish,'' he said. ''That's where we got the name of Bernfeld.''

''But your grandmother and your mother weren't Jewish,'' she said. ''Were they?''

''No.'' He shook his head, as if that was something he could never overcome no matter how much he tried. ''Would you like something to eat?'' he offered. ''They're serving dinner in the dining room.''

She nodded, and he helped her up from the stool.

''Who's the lucky guy?'' he asked, nodding to her enlarged middle.

''I'm not pregnant,'' she said, trying not to be annoyed. He was following behind her, leaning forward so he could hear her over the din of the party.

In the dining room she greeted some friends she'd known at Cal State and took her place in the buffet line.

''I just assumed,'' he said, and when she turned to look at him she saw he was blushing so that his ears were bright red.

She smiled and put her hand on his arm. ''It's all right. Everyone thinks that. It's my liver, it's enlarged because of a blood condition I have. You may remember some of the problems I had when we were together? The cast on my leg? Well, I had bone surgery to correct a physical problem, not because I fell off a horse like I used to tell people. And the nosebleeds were part of the same thing.''

He helped her to some turkey and she spooned some potato salad onto their plates. ''Do you remember the Sweetheart Dance in Newport when I left before the party?''

He nodded, offering her a pickle, which she declined.

''I was having an attack of bone pain, but I didn't know how to tell you, so I just split. Wasn't very brave of me, was it?''

''I didn't know,'' he said, shaking his head. ''I was so angry with you. I thought you were being a flake. Boy, was I dense. So wrapped up in myself and my macho image. If I hadn't been like that you could have confided in me.''

''Adolescence is like that,'' she said. ''It's nearly impossible to be honest and still maintain an image. You were more understanding than most. And I was rebellious.'' She laughed. ''I admit it. I made it difficult too, so don't blame yourself. My parents never wanted me to tell anyone. And we expected each other to be perfect. Neither of us was capable of being honest. I thought you should be able to read my mind. You thought I should be exactly the way you wanted. Only, it doesn't work that way, does it?''

He smiled, putting slices of rye bread on their plates and then cole slaw. ''No, I guess not.''

They found the soft drink table and poured themselves two Cokes and then made their way into the living room. There was room on the sofa and they sat there, being careful not to spill their plates.

''Have you been feeling all right?'' he asked. ''I mean, does having an enlarged liver present a lot of problems?''

She glanced away, feeling an amazing desire to just make up a story that would end the questions quickly. If only she could tell him, no, there's no problem, and be done with it. But that's what she'd done when she knew him in college. Now, there was no reason to spare either of them. Truth was always better than a lie, even if truth was bitter.

When she looked back at him, she could see in his eyes that he was prepared for whatever she was going to tell him. So she plunged ahead. ''Yes, it does present problems. The condition is getting worse every year. My liver is so enlarged, that it's causing other malfunctions in my body. But, I've been asked to take part in an experimental program through the City of Hope to try to reduce the size of my liver. The doctors are hopeful that with an enzyme-replacement procedure they can give my body back some of the enzymes I'm lacking and thereby reduce the size of my liver. I've been going into the hospital periodically for transfusions of enzyme, which they purify from human placenta. So far, there's some evidence that it may be reducing the size of my liver. In the meantime, I go along day by day, getting the most I can out of life as it is.''

''And that includes becoming a teacher?''

''Yes,'' she said. ''I want to teach more than anything in the world. I just have to find a job.''

The turkey was dry, or perhaps it was the unshed tears that made her throat constrict, but she was unable to swallow. There were few people in her life with whom she was as honest as she'd just been. Her parents had pinned all their hopes on this enzyme-replacement procedure, so she couldn't express her doubts to them, and nobody in the family ever talked about what would happen if it didn't work.

"Whatever became of that guy you went with during your senior year in college, the playwright?"

"You mean Joe?" Just saying his name brought back his presence in a rush. "I heard he was living in New York, still writing plays, trying to get a hit. He never got married, probably never will."

"He was tough back then. Some of us used to see you two walking on campus like you were in your own world and we'd talk about you. I was envious as hell because he was older and real cool and knew Professor Gertsman. He was the complete opposite of me, Joe College. I knew he was the kind of guy you needed, who could appreciate all your qualities. You couldn't have picked anyone who made me more jealous than he did, unless it was Gertsman himself."

She tried to picture Ron watching her with Joe and it made her smile. She and Joe *had* been in their own world. Sometimes she thought about Joe and it brought an ache to her heart, and then she forced herself to remember what he was really like, not what she'd wanted him to be, and it made the ache easier.

"I really resented you, then, because of what happened between us," she told Ron. "I assumed everyone who was part of the establishment was exactly like you. Rejection has a way of playing to one's deepest insecurities."

He dropped his gaze and nodded, holding on to her hand as if he was desperate to make things different. Neither of them had eaten much of the dinner. She glanced around, noticing that the living room was now filled with people. She'd been so involved in her conversation with Ron, she hadn't noticed the party getting into full swing.

"Is there anyone in your life, right now?" he asked.

"I'm not in love, if that's what you mean. I date different people. One man in particular; but he goes in and out of my life because he lives in New York and also dates a famous singer. We enjoy one another when we're together, no strings. It suits us both. What about you?''

"There is someone," he told her. "But she doesn't mean to me what you did. I've never felt about anyone the way I felt about you," he said. "I've been fooling myself all this time, thinking I loved her." He took her hand suddenly, nearly knocking the plate off her lap, and she grabbed for it. "If you said there was a chance for us, I'd leave her and move down here to be with you."

Gently she disengaged her hand from his. "Ron, you don't mean that. You're just swept up with nostalgia. You've got a whole life and a career up north. You can't give it up on a whim. And besides, I don't know you anymore. I have no idea if we'd be compatible. Even if we were, I can't make any long-range plans. That's a luxury reserved for healthy people."

He leaned forward and kissed her softly, exploring her mouth with his, blending their tongues together. She was touched by the tenderness in his kiss, at how much it awakened in her of lovely memories. She felt his tears on her cheek and pulled away.

"You have no idea how much I've thought about you, how much I regretted losing you. But I never had the courage to come after you, you were so far above me. Every time I'm forced to face a challenge in my life, I think, What would Steffani do? And it gives me the courage I don't have. I guess, when we were in college, I knew something was the matter with you. But if you didn't want to talk about it, I wasn't going to bring it up. That's one of the reasons I let myself be angry with you, not only because I wasn't right for you, couldn't live up to you, but because you were sick and I was helpless to do anything about it. So I blamed you."

She felt her own tears on her cheeks and wiped them away. "I had no idea," she said.

"I swear, I'd get a divorce for you," he told her.

"You're married?" She couldn't help it, her voice rose an octave.

He nodded, embarrassed. "Judy and I were married three

years ago. She knows all about you. She didn't want me to come down here this time, because she guessed that I would try to see you.''

The fantasies some people live with are amazing, she thought. *Here he is, dreaming about me, and I barely think of him at all, except in the context of the past*. What kind of a life did he lead, that he'd had to glamorize her to such a degree? Did he really believe she could infuse his life with whatever was missing? Was that true? Could she? It made her glad to think she had so much power, more than she realized.

''Ron, I don't want you to leave your wife for me. Just think of us fondly, and make the most you can out of what you've got.''

''I knew you would say that, but I hate hearing it.''

She placed her plate on the table in front of her, trailed her hand over his cheek, and gave him a soft, fond smile.

''Steffani, don't go now,'' he said. But she just shook her head and stood up. Then she turned and walked through the crowd of people to the front door and out to the street. She went directly to her car without looking back. But when she got into her car she was smiling. She felt wonderful, as though a terrible weight had been lifted. One she didn't know she'd had.

It was nine-thirty when she pulled her Mazda into Suzanne's carport and climbed out of the car. Her body ached from her exhausting day and the encounter with Ron. Her stomach was rumbling with chronic indigestion and hunger. She'd hardly eaten any dinner at the party. She put her key into the back door, opened it, and gasped. Flashbulbs exploded in her face. Jered, Miles, and Amy were laughing, grabbing at her and yelling, ''Surprise!''

''What surprise?'' she asked Suzanne, when her eyes cleared from the flashbulbs long enough to prepare herself for another one.

''You got a job!'' Suzanne yelled, snapping another picture. "Harrison Junior High in Glendale called. You interviewed with them a few weeks ago. They've had an opening, and you're it! Eighth-grade English, Ms. Blacker!" Suzanne's arms went around her and they hugged. And then Steffani held her sister away and looked at her, and at the joyful faces of her niece and nephews. "This is the happiest moment of my life," she said, feeling emotion well up. And she meant it with all her heart.

CHAPTER FORTY-TWO

The term *going through the motions* had new meaning for me. I had not known that a heart, or a body, or a life could be so empty. And I blamed myself. Who else was there to blame? God? God didn't care what happened to me. I certainly didn't. I was aware of selective things, that the sun came up every day and shone most of the time, but the world had no color, no definition. Days followed days without change.

The children called me after they'd settled in and I pretended to be all right, but when I got off the phone with them I sobbed for hours, missing them with a horrible deathlike ache. I told them not to come over for a while. I couldn't let them see me. If I scared myself when I looked in the mirror, how would I look to them? My skin was gray, the color of my soul. My life was like cold oatmeal, congealing in a chipped bowl, hardening by the minute. I thought of ending it all, but I didn't care enough to make the effort.

Of course, my family tried to encourage me, but my parents' words fell on me like soundless rain on a silent screen. "You should, you mustn't, you ought to," they said.

I tuned them out.

My sister tried too, but I wasn't the expert she was in overcoming despair and hopelessness. I didn't know how the way she did.

"Remember," she said to me in a voice that sounded just like our mother's, "self-pity is poison. It seeps into your soul. First it attacks your blood, then the marrow of your bones, and finally it alters your DNA. Fight it, Suzanne. Don't let yourself be deteriorated by it the way a worm decomposes the flesh. I swear, it will destroy you." She was the expert.

I listened to her more than to the others but then fell back into the warmth of my petri dish life where the mold of despondency grew greenly all over me, changing the shape of me, altering my state of being.

I must have been alive because I got up every day, brushed my teeth, and found time to work toward finishing my grandmother's book. There was a compartment in my brain that turned itself on automatically whenever I flicked on the electric typewriter. I did care about finishing the book. I certainly didn't care about eating. But finishing the book was the final task of things left to do. Perhaps once it was completed I would care about finishing myself. My sister was right about self-pity. When it's eating you, you don't give a damn about stopping it.

I measured time by the event of the children leaving, starting from the night they moved out. The next measurement was the first weekend without them, and then the first week. Each time I saw them it was so painful I feared I wouldn't survive the next encounter. I had never spent this much time away from them before; without them, half of me did not exist.

Three weeks after the children moved out my mother called me. "Steffani's in the hospital again."

"What is it this time?" Steffani's hospitalizations had occurred so often in our lives they were routine. Lately she'd been in for a series of enzyme infusions, designed to reduce the size of her liver. At first we were wildly hopeful that these experimental treatments might reverse the process of her Gaucher's disease, but after six months, there was no apparent difference. Her chronic cough still plagued her, even more than before. It was a vicious cycle. She'd start coughing at night and take syrup with codeine to stop it, which made her so wired she couldn't sleep. Then she'd take a sleeping pill, which knocked her out so that she could barely get up the next day. If she didn't take anything for the cough, she'd cough all night and then not be able to stay awake the next day anyway. The cough was debilitating and the doctors didn't know what was causing it, only that it wasn't bronchitis.

She'd also been having what we euphemistically called nosebleeds, but they were nasal hemorrhages. That's why she was hospitalized at the moment. Twice in the last month she'd been rushed to an emergency room to have her sinuses packed, which made her look as if she'd been hit in the face by Muhammed Ali. Each time she hemorrhaged through the packing.

I wasn't thinking about Steffani when I arrived in Duarte that day. In fact I was resentful that she needed me right now. Her needs had always competed with mine, and this was just another example.

The City of Hope was so familiar that I barely noticed it. Walked right past the acres of blooming roses in the rose garden without smelling a single one. But as I entered the hospital, reality slammed me in the face. I walked by room after room of sick people. In fact, the entire inpatient wing was filled with people who were worse off than I was. It jolted me. I slowed down and looked around, feeling as though I'd been brought here for a reason. Not that other people's misery negated mine—I had a right to my despair—but as bad as things were, as much as I'd lost, I was not physically ill. My problems were surmountable. Most of theirs were not.

I reached my sister's door and stood there in the hall, unable to go in. I remembered her words about self-pity and

I was ashamed of myself. And yet she hadn't berated me. She'd never said, look at me and then tell me how bad your life is. I took a deep breath and pushed open the door.

Steffani was on the phone as I entered her room and she waved hello to me. I tried not to stare at her outlandishly swollen nose and the bloody bandages beneath it.

"Hold on," she said to her caller. "I can't believe you came," she said to me. "You haven't been anywhere in weeks."

I gave her a tentative smile. I'd nearly forgotten how. "I never would have left my house just to go somewhere fun," I said. "But a visit to the hospital seemed appropriate."

We both laughed and she went back to the phone. It was the first time I'd laughed in so long. I was impatient to talk to her but I didn't interrupt, knowing what her caller had gone through to get her on the phone.

It was nearly impossible to get a call through to a patient at this hospital; there were no phones in the rooms. So if I wanted to talk to her, I had to call the hospital switchboard, which then connected me to the nurse's desk on her wing. I'd tell them I wanted to speak to her, and someone at the nurse's station would give me the number of the pay phone. Then, they'd have to find someone else who could put the phone in her room, if it wasn't already in use. When an orderly could finally be located to take the phone into her room and plug it in, then I could call her. But, often the switchboard or the nurse's station would disconnect me before I could even get the number of the pay phone. And sometimes, the pay phone would be busy when I called, or out of order, or in someone else's room because it hadn't been moved to her room yet, or in some other equally frustrating situation. And of course, it was a long-distance toll call. Sort of like calling Algeria. But the worst part of it was not being able to reach her when I needed to, just to hear her voice and assure myself that she was all right, still alive and fighting. Often, the sound of a loved one's voice under those circumstances can help one endure anything.

"I'll only be here a few more days," she said, to whoever was on the line. "Till they get the bleeding under control. So if you can't get out here, I understand. I'll see you when I get home."

It has to be one of her best friends, I thought, as she hung up. *The ones who never come to see her.*

"That was Melody," she told me. "She's having car trouble or she would have come out tonight."

Sure, I thought, but I didn't comment.

"Barry was here last night."

"Barry came to see you?" I was truly surprised. I missed him terribly, needed to share my misery with him, but I couldn't be the one to call him. "That was nice of him," I said, feeling a rush of something I couldn't quite place. Just hearing his name made my heart pound. "How is he?"

"He misses you."

"He knows how to find me."

"That goes both ways, Suzanne. Hand me that manila file, will you?"

I reached it for her. It was filled with student essays. "Where did these come from?"

"Mom and Dad picked them up for me at school. This is an assignment I asked my substitute to give to the class. I promised to grade it myself. I know how the kids always mistreat a substitute. I figured an assignment from me would keep them honest. Besides, I hate to be out of touch."

"Isn't it hard for you to work while you're here?"

"It makes me feel alive," she said, simply. "And in this place, that's a rare commodity. You know, my kids all sent me letters. 'Miss Blacker, we miss you, you're really groovy. Your pal, Mike.' I wrote them all back."

"Steff, you'll be back with them again." She was afraid of not getting out of here. "It must be gratifying to know how much you've given to them," I said.

She looked up and smiled at me. "Some of them are so eager to learn. And when I get through to the toughest ones, it's really something."

"You'll get back again," I assured her. "You always have."

"Do you want to know what we talked about?"

"Who?"

"Come off it, you know who."

"You know damn well I'd like to know."

"Barry said you must be going through hell without the children; he wished he could be of help to you."

I blinked away the tears in my eyes. "I wish he could too."

"Have you seen the children?"

I nodded, unable to trust my voice. But she knew how seldom I'd seen them.

"Suzanne, you've got to get into a regular visiting program with them. The less you see them, the harder it is on all of you. Those children need you, and you need them."

My eyes were filled with despair as I stared at her. "I'm no good for them now, Steff. I failed them. Whenever they look at me they know that. I can barely stand to be with them knowing how I've let them down." The reality of only being able to visit my own children and then leaving them behind was intensely painful.

She held out her hand to me and I came and sat on the edge of her bed. Her hand was hot against my icy fingers. "When they look at you, they'll only be seeing the mommy they love, not a failure. Don't wallow in self-pity, Suzanne. Remember, I warned you."

I heard the strength in her voice and was in awe of it. How could she be saying things like this when she was suffering so? I felt doubly ashamed and lowered my head, unable to meet her gaze.

"Promise me that you'll invite them over for a weekend," she insisted, starting to cough again. "Life is too short," my sick sister said to me.

I could only nod, or I'd burst into tears.

She leaned over to the table by her bed and handed me a folded piece of paper. "Read it later," she instructed.

I put it in my purse and then resumed my seat in the chair opposite the bed. Why are hospital chairs always made of vinyl and torturously uncomfortable, the backs too straight and tall, and the seats lumpy from an out-of-place spring. No matter how I wiggled, there was no good spot.

"Lying here has given me a lot of time to think," she said. "And I've been trying to figure out ways for you to help yourself."

"By doing what?" I asked, defiantly, as if I hadn't thought of every possible way to help myself during all those sleepless nights.

"You told me that your investigator questioned everyone who might have a reason to hurt you?"

"He even questioned those who don't," I told her.

"But, maybe if you talked to certain people, you would see something different than he did. He's a stranger to them. To you they might reveal something more than they did to him."

"Are you suggesting that I go to my friends and say, 'Have you been trying to ruin my life? Just tell me, yes or no?' "

"Okay, fine." She threw up her hands and plopped them down on the sheets. "Forget it, I was only trying to help."

Those inner fingers on my spine scratched on that ever-present chalkboard, causing my adrenaline to pump. "You really think there's someone in my life who could have done this that we overlooked?" She didn't reply. "Do you have any idea who? You?"

"You know I'd never do anything to hurt you."

"Fine, then who?" I folded my arms across my body, holding on to myself, assuming a sarcastic attitude that made me feel as if we were children again having an argument over who was right. "I am," she'd say. "No, I am," I'd insist. But some terrible insidious worm was eating at my guts.

"Why don't we look at it logically." She reached for a pad of paper. "Who doesn't like you? We can rule out Sugar Markham. Does anybody else have a grudge against you?"

"We've gone over this, Steffani. It's not going to help a

bit." My voice was rising and I felt claustrophobic, as though I were being locked in a closet.

"I know it's hard," she said, quietly. "I know what it feels like to be so helpless against insurmountable odds. Believe me. But indulge me, will you? You don't want to be convicted." I could hear a touch of panic in her voice, the sound I heard in my voice when I worried about her.

My eyes filled with tears. "I'm scared to death of what's going to happen," I confessed. "I don't want to go to prison."

"Then let's go over it again," she said, as if she were Quixote mounting Rocinante. Even confined to this narrow perimeter she was willing to fight, limited only by her diseased body, never lacking in spirit. I wondered if I'd ever inspired her this much before. I do know I'd have done anything to take away her pain.

"We'll take it one at a time," she said. "What about Alex? He was unreasonably angry with you once upon a time."

"He certainly has kicked me when I'm down, hasn't he?"

"He was nutso when you two got divorced. I'd say his behavior bordered on the strange and dangerous, wouldn't you?"

"Y-e-s," I hesitated to concede.

"Suppose he's only been suppressing that craziness all this time. Suppose he's still harboring a deep resentment toward you for breaking up his family, for not loving him anymore, for divorcing him. After all, he's the one who's gained directly from your downfall. He's got the children."

"It's impossible," I said. My God, I hated having to doubt the people in my life. Could Alex have done this to me?

Suddenly, I found myself outside her door in the hallway with no recollection of having gotten up from my chair and left. I was halfway down the hall before I realized I had run away in panic. I grabbed on to the wooden railings along the walls of the hallway as if I were an invalid recovering from an injury, too weak to hold myself up. There was a roaring in my ears as my pulse pounded, and the words repeated in my head, *What if it were Alex?* I'd always disregarded the possibility before.

I stood there hyperventilating, too frightened to put a face on my attacker. Then I thought of Steffani waiting for me, willing to help, even though her head throbbed, her nose oozed, and she coughed all night long. I turned around and walked back to her.

"Okay," she said, as though I'd never left.

I sat back down in the vinyl chair, but Alex's face was in front of me, growing into an enormous moon that hung over the horizon, grinning. I blinked to bring him down to size, but his grin filled my brain, turning evil.

"Alex has hurt me more than anyone else," I confessed. "It hardly matters if he's the one."

"Oh, it matters all right," she insisted.

"So what do I do, break into his house, search for a typewriter with a slanted *p*?" That was the one piece of usable evidence we had. "It's so ironic, that a typewriter has turned out to be the instrument of my torture."

"But it's also been the means of your salvation." She handed me a Styrofoam cup of water with an ice cube in it. I drank the water gratefully, trying to push away the hatred that was smothering me.

"Besides Alex," I said, "there's Jasmine, and Marilyn, and Gloria. Even some of your friends might dislike me, like Carole. Remember that time I told her off when she smashed the fender of your new car? I told her she was an irresponsible idiot and didn't deserve to have you for a friend."

"That one time, I agreed with you," Steffani said. "But Carole isn't smart enough to have done this. Now, we know why Gloria doesn't like you, but what about Jasmine. What bone is she picking?"

I told her about the fiasco when I tried to introduce Jasmine to the producer, Bill Shapiro. And then I told her about the time Marilyn wanted me to contribute to her liberal cause. "Both of them reacted inappropriately," I recalled. "I remember thinking, These women are crazy. I would never react the way they had under the same circumstances. As I think of it, either one of them might be capable of doing something crazy. Except for Gloria. When I last saw her, she was syrupy friendly, and she helped me, remember? With the jewelry and silver.''

"She was gloating, Suzanne. I've never trusted her.''

"What would I say to them that Bellows hasn't already said?'' I asked.

She shifted in bed so that her stomach was lying on the right side instead of the left. ''Just talk to them, see if you can find out anything new. And do it in person, not on the phone.''

"But the investigator is the expert; he knew what questions to ask, how to trap them, and he didn't find anything.''

"You'll be able to read them differently,'' she assured me.

I felt a flash of hot and then cold run through my body. ''I wish you were going with me.''

"So do I,'' she said, with a sigh.

I stared at her for a minute, wanting to say the one thing unspoken, but unable to.

"What is it?'' she asked.

It was that unnamed terror again, reappearing from my childhood, the fear that kept me home from school sometimes, the clawing, suffocating feeling that the world was disintegrating before my eyes. ''Why does somebody hate me so much?''

"I don't know,'' she replied.

But in asking the question, an answer occurred to me. I'd avoided it because it was the source of my unnamed fear. Somehow I deserved what was happening to me, deserved this foul wash of hatred spewing over me, because I was guilty. Guilty as hell! Guilty of being well, when my sister wasn't. I was shocked by my revelation, unable to meet her gaze. All I wanted to do was get out of there before she knew what I was thinking. As I kissed her good-bye, it took everything within me not to beg her forgiveness, even as I knew she'd disagree. But there were many things I could never say to my sister.

She caught me at the door. ''Suzanne, if any one of those people are guilty, he or she would cover it up by being extra nice to you, to throw you off. That's what I'd do.''

I nodded. "I'll remember that."

"Good luck," she said.

I forced myself to smile back.

When I got to my car I sat there a while thinking. Facing that fear had made me less afraid. Maybe there was something more I could do. Once again, Steffani had inspired me. I would take her suggestion, but first there were other important things I had to do. I reached in my purse for my keys and found the paper she had given me. It was a poem.

Patient

I

The broom sweeps away another dusty
  day
As gloom seeps under numbered doors,
Settling on sterile hospital floors

The last coughs climb the walls
Ricochet and die
Into echoing whispered snores

Along the soft-footed floors,
Comes the shush of white stockings,
To ease with the silver sleep of the needle,
Day and night
Marking muted clock-ticks
From pin-prick to pin-prick

II

Visitors leave the lighted tomb,
The antiseptic white-walled doom,
And escape into the night,
To crickets and home.

III

Filling the room
Looms the big bed
In it is a shrunken shape
Face pale gray

Flowers and chocolate
Left there to pray

IV
Then again comes the broom
To sweep out the room,
But all that's left to carry away
Are a few fallen petals
And an untouched tray

I told myself I wasn't going to cry, but I couldn't help it. And then, sitting in that parking lot, with the images of her poem still filling my head, I thought, *If she can get through that, I can do whatever it takes.* And I started for home.

CHAPTER FORTY-THREE

I called Barry's office and left a message with his secretary asking him to meet me at the beach after work, in the parking lot north of the Wilshire Boulevard ramp. I hoped he'd show up out of curiosity. I arrived at a quarter to six and waited. Either he'd come, or he wouldn't. But this way he couldn't call and cancel.

Except for the moisture on my palms and the tightness in my chest, I was surprisingly calm. This was my first confrontation in a series of more to come, and one of the more difficult ones.

In April the days were getting longer and the sun was low in the sky, but still above the horizon to my far right. The spring sky was a bright orangeish hue brushed with a few thin wispy clouds. The setting sun tinged them with a brilliant yellow gold light. I breathed in the sea air and in this moment, it felt good to be alive.

At six-thirty, I saw Barry's car as it pulled into the deserted lot; my pulse began to race.

He parked his car next to mine and we both got out, smiling shyly. My eyes drank him in and I felt like a teenager on a first date, fluttery and weak-kneed. He took off his suit coat and put on the leather jacket he kept in the trunk.

"Want to walk on the beach?" I asked him, filled with hope and excitement.

"Sure," he agreed. "But I don't have a lot of time. I have to be at dinner at eight."

"All right," I said. The hope and excitement sank to the pit of my stomach. His life was complete without me. What did I expect?

It was difficult walking on the sand in our shoes, until we got down to the water's edge where the sand was firmer. We used each other for balance while we shook the dry sand out of our shoes, then we headed into the sunset. The surf was calm, lapping at the edge of a rouge-tinted tide. We walked along, aware of an awkwardness between us. I wanted to tell him that I'd missed him, that I needed him in my life and would take him any way I could get him, with limits, without commitments, or just as friends. But where to begin? What if he wasn't interested at all?

"I was surprised that you called me," he began.

"We had unfinished business," I admitted. "After Steffani told me about your visit, I figured you weren't all bad."

He laughed. "I gave her lots of hints. I guess I wanted to see you. Know how you were."

That made me feel slightly better. "Why didn't you call?"

"I didn't think there was any point."

"Oh, come on. I always talk to my ex-boyfriends."

"Is that what I am? An ex?"

"Well, you're not exactly current, are you?" I kept walking, enjoying the chill of the evening, my arms wrapped around my body against the cold. "How have you been?" I asked.

"Pretty well," he said. "I'm sorry about what you've been going through."

"Let's not talk about poor pitiful me, okay? That's what got in our way the last time. I'm handling everything. In fact, I'm hopeful that I can do something about it. If that's what you wanted to know."

"I'm glad to hear it. So, how are the children? They're great kids, Suzanne."

I stiffened against the flash of pain that shot through me whenever I thought about them. "They're fine, doing well in school, glad not to be cramped into my awful apartment."

He glanced at me to see if I was being bitter, but I hadn't meant to be. The only consolation I had was that their surroundings weren't as depressing as mine. Lately, I felt like Stella Dallas.

"Steffani doesn't look well," he commented. I heard the note of anxiety.

"She'll be okay," I assured the both of us. "Once, after a minor surgery, she hemorrhaged for two weeks and had to have fourteen transfusions. But she recovered. This is just a nosebleed."

He reached for my hand and his touch warmed me. I smiled at him. "Who's your eight o'clock date? Some trouble-free young thing?"

"Nobody special, just a social evening."

It hurt anyway. "I guess you're wondering why I called you here like this, so mysteriously?"

"Yeah, kind of."

"I just wanted to see how you were."

"Test the waters, so to speak?" he asked, dipping the toe of his shoe into the surf.

"I guess." This was harder than I'd thought. "Barry, if you felt pressured by me, it wasn't intentional. I'm all right, you know. Having you in my life for a while made the bad times more bearable."

He was silent, listening, not reacting the way I'd wanted him to. I'd been so hoping for a reconciliation. My fantasy was that when he saw me, he'd realize how much I meant to him, throw his arms around me and make everything all right again. Instead, he walked quietly beside me, his profile darkly familiar, blending with the night sky, unreachable.

We walked for a while in silence and when I realized he wasn't going to talk, I said, "We should turn back now, I guess. It's getting late." I fought off my disappointment.

He didn't protest.

Finally I asked him, "Aren't you going to say anything? Why did you come? I mean, you didn't have to show up."

"I wanted to hear what you had to say."

"Well you've heard it. Are you satisfied?" Now, I was bitter.

"Hardly," he said.

"What did you expect?"

"I have no idea," he said coldly.

I felt a chill go through me that wasn't from the night air. Then my temper flared. "You know what disappointed me the most about you? You turned out to be a cliché. All my single girlfriends tell stories about men who say they'll call and then don't, or say things like, 'you're the best thing that's ever happened to me,' and then drop them flat. It's as though men scare themselves or something. Do you all feel obligated to say things like that, even if you don't mean them? I wouldn't have believed it of you, but you led me on and didn't deliver." I felt relieved to say that.

We reached the area of beach opposite to where our cars were parked and started back across the wide stretch of sand. We weren't holding hands anymore.

I had to hurry to keep up with him as he marched back across the beach; he ignored my question. I was gripped by that awful hollowed-out feeling of loss again, and I'd thought I'd gotten over it. What a mistake this had been.

We arrived at the parking lot and stood between our cars as we shook the sand out of our shoes once more. He was wearing loafers and was through before I had retied my sneakers. I looked up at him. The lights from the streetlamps illuminated the cold features of his face in a greenish tinge.

There was an invisible wall between us. If I reached out, I would knock my hand against it.

"Thanks for showing up," I said, thinking, *It's really over now.* "Have a nice dinner and a nice life," I said, waiting for him to go around to the driver's side. I felt like crying, but there had been so much of that lately, I was all cried out.

He reached to unlock the passenger's side of the car, fumbled, and dropped his keys. I picked them up and handed them to him. He took them from me but made no move to go.

"Are you all right?" I asked.

He shook his head. I noticed his fist was clenched around his keys and the tendons in his jaw stood out. His nostrils flared as if he were experiencing some kind of pain.

"What is it?" I asked.

He closed his eyes and I saw tears seeping through the lids, trailing down his cheeks, catching the light from the streetlamps.

"Barry?"

He groaned, and then opened his arms. I stood there dumbfounded for a moment before I stepped into his embrace. His arms folded around me, his body trembling with unshed tears.

"What is it?" I whispered.

"I acted like such a fool. But I was afraid of losing you, Suzanne, afraid that all your problems would pull you away. So I pushed you away myself before that could happen. After losing Eileen, I couldn't take another loss. And every one of your problems meant I could lose you. I felt helpless because I couldn't save you, just as I couldn't save her. I was afraid to love you, Suzanne, but I do. I'm sorry for what I've done. I've missed you so much."

I held him until his trembling subsided, feeling my own strength growing. It was wonderful to have someone to give to, who needed me instead of the other way around. "I understand," I told him, knowing how hard it must have been for him to admit.

He held me away so he could look at me, then he smiled

and touched my face with his hands. "Do you forgive me for putting you through this? I almost let you go again tonight." He searched my face, desperately trying to see if I was strong enough for both of us. I gazed back at him, smiling, letting him know I was. And then, I kissed him.

The next afternoon I parked my car across the street from Alex's duplex, getting up the courage to go in. I saw Amy walking home from school carrying her notebook in her arms the way I used to carry mine in high school. Soon after, a carpool dropped off Miles and Jered. How they were both growing. But as I watched them the tears obscured my vision so that I could barely see them.

I would have sat there until they'd gone into the house but Jered turned and saw me sitting there.

"Mommy's here!" he yelled, running across the lawn.

I jumped out of the car, terrified that he would run into the street, shouting, "Stay there."

He stopped abruptly, his face a mixture of uncertainty, until I reached him and clutched him to me, burying my face in his sweet neck. "Ohhh, baby," I crooned, filling my senses with him.

"Why haven't you been to see us this week?" he asked, squirming away after a moment. "I missed you so much, Mommy. Dina is still mean. She won't let us make a peep in the morning. We have to be so quiet. She's always sleeping."

"Is she here right now?" I asked,

"No, she's at the studio today. You can come in." He pulled on my hand. Usually I picked the kids up and we went someplace, but this time I decided to go in.

Miles stood there, not saying anything. I turned and held out my arms to him, and shyly, with constraint, he came and gave me a hug. I didn't blame him.

Amy had gone into the house and now I saw her face peeking out from the arched picture window above us. When our eyes met, she moved back into the shadows.

"You both look wonderful," I said, ruffling their hair.

"Come see the house," Jered said. "You never saw my room. I share with Miles, and Amy has her own, lucky brat." Jered's defiance was something new.

"Are you all right, Miles?" I asked.

He nodded, noncommittally, and shrugged. The shrug almost made me laugh, because I recognized it as a universal expression that every teenager learns automatically at puberty and uses on all authority figures. It was always maddening.

"How's school?"

"Okay."

"I liked Laramie better," Jered said, for my benefit. "We had live animals there."

I smiled at him gratefully and he beamed.

We entered the duplex. The marble tables, white brocaded upholstery, and the artificial palms were certainly not inviting for children. I hated the paintings on either side of the glittery stone fireplace of huge sad-eyed children with a tear on their cheeks, and especially the fuchsia flowers made of feathers on the game table in the corner. All the room needed to complete it was Barry Manilow singing in the background.

"Amy," I called, "it's Mom. Come say hello." No response.

Jered pulled me into the kitchen. "Want some fresh orange juice? It's supposed to be for Dina, but you can have some."

I sat down at the glass-topped iron table. "I'd love some of Dina's orange juice," I told him, watching him open the refrigerator. It was filled with perfectly shaped fruits from Jurgensens and preroasted chicken on a plate.

"Do you think Amy will join us?" I asked Miles.

Again, the shrug.

"I'll go and get her," I offered, leaving the kitchen and walking down the hall to the only closed door I saw. I knocked.

"Go away." She was trying to be tough, but I could tell she'd been crying.

"Amy, honey, please come and say hello. I have something to tell you."

"Have they let you off?" The hope in her voice leaped forward.

"Not yet," I said. "But please come out and see me. Or, may I come in?"

I heard the bolt on the door being unlocked, and there she stood, my precious daughter, her eyes red and her cheeks streaked with tears. I hugged her while she cried, feeling the shaking of her shoulders and her heartwrenching sobs as if they were my own. "I'm so mad at you," she cried. "We barely ever see you. How could you desert us like this? Do you hate us so much? Just because we didn't want to be bused?"

Is that what they thought, that I was angry with them, that I was punishing them? Oh God.

"Amy darling, that's not it at all. I just miss you so much that I can't bear not having you with me. Every time I see you, I cry afterward for a long time."

"So do I," she confessed.

"Now I see how selfish I've been, protecting myself from my own pain. Please understand, honey. There's nothing I blame you for. I'm grateful that you're safe and in a good school. I just miss you so much."

Her smile was tentative at first, but then got brighter. "Beverly Hills is really snobby, Mom. You wouldn't believe all the rich kids."

I put my arm around her shoulder and led her back into the kitchen where the boys were waiting. Jered sat proudly behind four glasses of orange juice, a small puddle next to each one. I told the boys what I had just told Amy, that I didn't blame them at all for living with Alex and asked them to forgive me if I'd hurt them.

They both hugged me.

"So, what's happening with the case, Mom?" Miles asked. "Is the trial still set for the end of April?"

"Yes. And there's no new evidence so far to help me. But I'm going to talk to a few people who might possibly give me some answers, so I'm very hopeful. And I want you all to be too," I told them. "I saw Barry. Things are better between us."

"That's good, Mom," Amy said.

"When can we go home?" Jered asked, putting his head against my chest.

"I don't know, sweetheart," I told him.

"Have you sold the house?" Amy asked. I could tell how worried she was.

"No, it's still leased. So, if I'm cleared of the charges against me, we can have our house back again, just the way it was before. I'd be able to pay my debts when my books are published, and—"

"We'll all live happily ever after," Jered said, automatically.

The children all laughed, but I could not swallow the lump in my throat.

"Will you tell us some more of *Annica?*" Jered asked, glancing at his brother and sister, who both nodded.

I was thrilled that they wanted to hear. "You recall that Annica's portrait won the Prix de Paris?"

"Dressed like an angel," Jered supplied. "And she meets Count Hugo Zarek and he gives a ball in her honor."

"Yes, and that's where she falls in love with Manuel Tincava."

Miles said, "The mushy stuff."

I continued. "But the young lovers are soon torn apart because Manuel must fight in World War I. Annica travels to Italy to have her portrait painted for the collection of the king and queen of Italy, whom she also met at the party in Paris. And while in Rome, Annica's husband, Tony, and his mother, Baba Angelusha, the queen of the gypsies, steal her two-year-old son Petre from her."

"That's so sad," Jered commented.

I took his hand and held it. "Annica is even more devastated when she gets word that Manuel has married his former childhood sweetheart Sofia."

"Wouldn't you know," Amy commented. I hoped my daughter wasn't becoming cynical about men.

"Soon after that, Manuel is reported missing in action."
All three of them groaned.

"The war continues and each year, on Petre's birthday, Annica paints a portrait of him as she imagines he would look growing up. Meanwhile, her dear friend Count Hugo Zarek uses his resources to find Petre as well as Manuel for her. But in war-torn Europe, a band of gypsies and a missing soldier are impossible to trace.

"Annica returns for a visit to her village in Romania, now a wealthy and famous woman."

"That's great, Mom," Amy declared, imagining herself returning in triumph to Buckley School.

"She also visits Manuel's family where his brother, Theodore, tells her that Manuel only married Sofia because she was dying of tuberculosis, but he loves Annica. Manuel doesn't know about Sofia's death and still believes himself married to the wrong woman."

"When the war ends Annica finds Manuel in a prison camp in Germany, desperately sick. It is too late to save him but she is with him when he dies."

By the end of the story, all three of them were staring at me, enthralled. Then Miles spoke. "Is that the end? Does she ever find her son?"

"Does she marry Count Zarek?" Amy asked.

But before I could reply, we heard a key in the back door and a rotund black woman came in, her arms full of groceries. She saw us sitting there and was startled, until Miles said, "This is our mother, Louise." Then he turned to me. "Louise is the cook. She makes us dinner every night. Dad and Dina go out."

I smiled at Louise, but she didn't smile back. "I don't know," she shook her head. "Mr. Winston don't say nothing about visitors."

I stood up to go. "I don't want to get anyone in trouble."

"You can't leave yet," Amy cried. "Please, Mom. Don't go." She held on to my hand, wringing it so that I had to pry it away.

"It's all right, honey," I assured her. "I don't have Alex's permission to be here, so I'd better go. But this weekend, I want you all to come and be with me. And we'll finish the rest of the story, okay?''

The three of them nodded and I hugged and kissed them good-bye. They clung to me desperately, feeling how much I didn't want to go. It was worse than I'd thought it would be. Finally I wrenched myself away, and hurried down the stairs, giving them a frozen smile as I waved from the lawn. But there were horribly sharp knives making mincemeat of my heart.

Now that the two worst hurdles in my life had been overcome, I had to finish my book. I was close to the end and "finish fever" had taken over. When the end of a project is in sight, I work for hours, pushing myself toward completion. For, as wonderful, as challenging, as fulfilling, as agonizing as it is to write, having written is even better.

During the next ten days, the children spent the weekend with me, Barry and I were reunited, and Steffani was released from the hospital, returned to her classroom and then was hospitalized again with another hemorrhage.

"I'm so worried about her," my mother said, whenever we talked. So was I. These recent troubles had left her terribly thin, which made her enlarged abdomen seem even larger, and she was exhausted, both in spirit and physical strength. We all blamed Joe for her problems. If only she hadn't been in that car accident, she wouldn't be hemorrhaging so much. But if it wasn't that, it might have been something else.

Her moods fluctuated between despair and tolerance, never rallying to the heights of positivity she'd reached in the past. And every time we thought the bleeding had stopped for good, it would start again. The enormous amount of patience and fortitude it took to endure this latest onslaught sapped her strength. And it was no wonder. My parents and I consoled ourselves with the knowledge that she'd overcome much worse bouts in the past and had always survived.

Once again, we talked about her clotting factor, the transfusions, her white count, and the results of the enzyme replacement, holding on to medical information as if it were a talisman against the inevitable.

The completed first draft of *Annica* was eight hundred pages; I'd written over four hundred pages of new material. The most difficult part of it was to write in someone else's style. But Nana had laid a solid foundation and the story almost told itself.

Tony, Annica's gypsy husband, dies in the war and his mother raises her grandson Petre as a gypsy, who barely remembers his other life. After the war, Hugo and Annica search for Petre in band after gypsy band. It takes eight long years to come across a blond, blue-eyed ragamuffin child leading a pack of boys in a pickpocket scheme. Annica sees half of a gold locket around the leader's neck; she wears the other half around her own, given to her by Tony on their wedding day. And so, Annica and her precious son are reunited, and live happily ever after with Count Hugo Zarek, as Amy had guessed.

I sent a copy of the manuscript to Esther in New York with a note that said, "When I'm acquitted, we'll sell it. In the meantime, what do you think?" I also gave a copy to my mother and my sister. But while they were reading it, I had other things to do.

Jasmine was living off Wonderland Park in Laurel Canyon, in the neighborhood Steffani used to haunt. I drove up the street and found the ivy-covered trellis she described that arched over her front gate. The gate was actually a rustic wooden door set into a white, vine-covered brick wall. Beside the gate attached to the wall was an iron bell. It made a pleasant sound, as if the cows were coming home.

A buzzer sounded releasing the electric lock and I pushed open the gate. Inside was an enchanted garden. Everything was overgrown with lush growing plants. Some expert had made it seem as though the profusion was haphazard and it must have taken months. Huge live oak trees, maple, acacia, jacaranda, and olive towered over fern trees, which shaded philodendron, which protected beds of moss and flowers and more delicate ferns. There were elfin statues, and a small stream with stepping stones placed over it, and a view of the city, through a V in the canyon that was just enough to remind me of where I was.

The house was at the end of a winding flagstone path, interspersed with moss and bordered by flowers; I think the house was rustically ranch style, but the vines that covered it made it difficult to tell. I did get a glimpse of dark wood siding, paned windows, shutters, and a shake roof.

Jasmine greeted me at the open door, wearing khaki shorts and a white sweat shirt; her hair, twisted at the nape and draped over her shoulder, hung down one side of her chest. I could see just a few strands of gray in it, but otherwise it was as silky and lustrous as ever. She was slender, wide-eyed, and strikingly lovely.

When I saw the smile that lit up her face, I couldn't imagine her doing anything evil to me even though in our last conversation she'd said my book was shitty.

She held out her hands and took mine. "It's been much too long, Suzanne," she breathed. I heard a cultured tone in her pronunciation of words I'd never noticed before, probably from elocution lessions. But it enhanced her mystique. "It's truly fitting that you came here today to celebrate with me."

"Has something happened?" I asked, surprised by her reception. I followed her into the house, which had polished brick floors, Oriental rugs, and wheat-colored furniture covered with soft down pillows of batik fabrics. There was classical music playing on the stereo; two cats were asleep in a patch of sunlight streaming in from the panoramic windows. I was enveloped by the place, by its sense of peace, obviously garnered by the owner.

"I was sorry to hear about all your troubles. That detective who came to see me asked me some questions, but I wasn't much help. How have you been?" she asked me, plopping down on one of the sofas and tucking her bare feet underneath her.

"I'm holding up," I said. "But my sister's not doing so well. She's been hospitalized off and on for months now with a series of nosebleeds that won't seem to stop." I looked away, trying to concentrate on the beauty of nature outside the window so as not to break down.

"I'm so sorry," Jasmine said. And I could tell by her tone, she meant it.

I turned to look at her. "This place is a miracle," I told her. "Have you done it yourself?"

She smiled that mystical smile of hers and nodded. "I bought it a few years ago when I was on the soap, but since I was living in New York, I couldn't spend much time here. And then, last year, my character was written out, and here I am."

She stretched, reaching up with her long slender arms above her head, and then yawned contentedly, just as one of the cats on the floor did the same thing. I noticed and said, "Look, your cat is psychic."

"No, it's I who am in tune with nature. Everything responds in kind to good vibrations," she said. "I've spent a lot of time trying to get in touch with myself—therapy, yoga, reading the mystics, meditating. And it really works. I have a whole new attitude, Suzanne. I'm really happy, can you tell?"

I nodded, at once envious of her self-containment and embarrassed that I'd suspected her at all. She couldn't be the one. All that anger I'd always sensed below the surface was gone, and a new woman sat opposite me. "What did you do when you left the soap?" I asked. "I'm sorry, but I don't know which one it was, I'm afraid I never saw you."

"That's okay." She smiled. "Millions of other people did. I still get stopped on the street because I played the part of Tawny. People tell me they miss me on the show, and how much they loved to hate me. I played one of those manipulative, scheming women. They're the most fun. I won an Emmy, you know."

I was amazed. "That's wonderful."

"Yes, it is. And even though it's for daytime, it means

the world to me. It's helped me with my career too. To be outstanding in daytime television is not easy, there's a lot of competition. And I learned so much, too.''

''You were telling me what you've been doing lately.''

''Oh yes. Well, first I worked on this place. It was like a vacation for me to be in my own garden without having to be on the set at six A.M. every morning and wear makeup five days a week. I really worked hard to get everything into shape. And then the tough times set in. Last fall, I went through a bad time. All my self-discipline deserted me. I hadn't worked in six months and I was getting panicky. I started to revert to the old Jasmine, you remember, hostile, angry, wanting to lash out at everyone I couldn't control.''

Last fall was when the letters started coming, I thought.

''The holidays were the worst, that's when I hit my low. And one day in mid-January I was sitting in this room, looking out at the view, feeling sorry for myself. My savings had run out, I didn't have an acting job, and I knew I had to get some kind of work in order to keep my house. I couldn't go back to waiting tables again, or selling cars in auto shows, or doing all the things I'd done to stay solvent. And that's when I went into a rampage. I went out and dug up the flowers. I cut off the heads of the stocks and the pansies. I ruined several weeks of work in an hour.''

As I listened, I got a queasy feeling in my stomach. Why was she telling me all this? Was it a confession? Was she going to turn to me in a minute and say, *I'm the one who sent the letters; I did it? While I was on my rampage, I tried to get you, too?*

She waited for me to comment, but I just sat there waiting, afraid to say anything at all.

Finally, she went on. ''It was then that something snapped. I realized how stupid I was being. It didn't matter what kind of job I took to earn a living; I'd act again. If it happened once, it could happen twice. So I made peace with myself, and I went out and got a secretarial job with an acting agent so I'd be in a position to hear about parts as they came along.

In two weeks I had an offer for a movie, which gave me four weeks' work, and now, just this morning, I've been hired as the girlfriend of a police lieutenant on an ensemble TV series called 'Blues at Midnight.' If it goes, I'm set for a whole season." She clapped her hands together with delight, as if a magic genie had just jumped out of her carpet. "Isn't that great?"

I smiled. "Yes, it's wonderful." Now I doubted again that she could have been the one who'd been sending the letters. "Jasmine. Do you still blame me for that time I tried to introduce you to Bill Shapiro?"

She looked at me with complete confusion. Either she honestly didn't remember, or she was a better actress than I gave her credit for. "Who's he?"

"You remember, we had lunch at the studio and he stood us up. You were so angry."

"I honestly don't," she said. "But I was into coke in those days. A lot of what I did then I don't remember. Was I awful to you?"

I nodded, feeling relief begin to flood through me.

"That's really mortifying, Suzanne. You were probably trying to help me and I acted badly. Even though I don't recall it, I can tell by your expression what must have happened. I'm truly sorry."

My pulse was calming down as I tried to keep my mind from leaping to the other people on my list of suspects. "Jasmine, before I go, can I ask you, do you have a type-writer?"

She bounded up from the sofa. "Sure," she said. "It's right here." And she pointed to a desk in a library alcove off the living room. There was an IBM, vintage 1960, sitting on the desk. "Do you want to borrow it? I hardly ever use it, except for correspondence. I write my agent, I write letters to the editor, I correspond with the foster child I support through an East Asian organization, but I could spare it if you need it."

I grinned at her, reaching over to hug her. "No, I don't

need to borrow it. But thanks anyway." She looked at me quizzically because of my strange behavior and then walked me to the gate.

We said our good-byes and agreed to see one another again soon, and as I watched her close her enchanted garden door, I felt as if my heart was floating on a cloud. For the typewriter I was looking for was a Remington portable, not an IBM.

My mother was waiting for me at my apartment and when I saw her a shot of fear ran through me. I rushed over to her. "Mom, is everything all right?"

She got out of her car holding the manuscript in her arms. I could see she'd been crying. "It's so wonderful, honey," she said. "I had no idea there was so much here. I can't believe what you've done with this."

"It's Nana's book," I said simply, leading the way up the stairs and letting us into the apartment.

"I couldn't stop crying," she said. "Not because it was so sad, but because it's such a work of love. I felt her presence so strongly. How I remember all the times she made me listen to this book. All she wanted to do was talk about it and write it. Especially at the end; she wanted me to finish it, you know. But I'm not a writer, even though I transcribed most of it for her."

"I know, Mom, I have all your notes."

She nodded absentmindedly as if she'd forgotten. "Isn't it amazing that you became a writer and that you were the one to finish it. She loved you so much. How did you know all the details of what happens in the end? She didn't write all that, did she?"

"No, I wrote over half of it myself. But I could tell where she was heading."

"What's really amazing is what she accomplished, coming to America all by herself at twelve years old, and getting shipwrecked on the way, and then separated from the family who were bringing her."

"Why did she come by herself?" I asked.

"Because she was the eldest, and my grandmother could

only afford to send one member of the family. That's how they did it back then. One member of the family was sent ahead and had the responsibility of working and saving the money to bring the rest of them to America.''

"Where was your grandfather?''

"Didn't I ever tell you the story?'' she asked.

I shook my head no, because I knew she wanted to tell it again, and I didn't mind listening.

"My grandfather was an architect in his small village in Romania. The local Catholic priest commissioned him to build a new church for the district. It was quite an honor for a Jew to be hired to do such a thing. So he set to work, designing and building a stone church. But every time he asked the priest for money, he was promised that he'd get paid upon completion. He had a pregnant wife and four children, two sons and two daughters, to support. And he trusted the priest's word, and so he spent all his own money and incurred the debts of his subcontractors to build this church. When it was completed, he went to the priest and asked for payment and the priest said, 'I don't have the money. We're a poor parish.'

" 'But you promised to pay me,' my grandfather said. "Isn't the work satisfactory?'

" 'The work is good,' the priest told him. 'But still, I'm not going to pay you.'

" 'You promised,' my grandfather insisted. 'You owe me the money.'

" 'And who do you think people will believe?' the priest said. 'The word of a member of the Catholic clergy, or a Jew?' And he refused to pay my grandfather, who lost everything he owned. Shortly after that, he took sick and died; he left his wife and children nearly destitute. My mother always said he died of a broken heart.''

It was difficult not to hate all Christians after hearing that story.

"You know, the result of his death is what eventually killed Nana too,'' my mother said.

"Why do you say that?'' I asked.

"Because . . ." My mother was reluctant to go on.

"Nana had ulcerative colitis, didn't she?"

My mother nodded, her eyes filling with tears at the memory of her mother's suffering. "She was so sick, poor thing. I knew about the medical theories that said ulcerative colitis could have psychosomatic causes. We tried everything to get her well, but she was wasting away. And one day I said to her, 'Mama, what is it that's eating at you? What is it that makes you so sick that you want to die?'

"She took my hand, and made me swear I would never tell anyone the secret she'd lived with all her life."

"What was it?" I asked.

"Oh, God," my mother sighed. "I can barely think about it, let alone tell you."

"It's all right," I said, holding her hand. "Take your time."

Several times she tried to tell me, but each time she'd start to cry. Finally, she said, "When my grandfather died, he left the family destitute. Soon they lost their home and had to go live with relatives. My grandmother was pregnant at the time and later gave birth to a baby daughter. She was mourning the death of her husband and terrified about how to take care of her family. My mother took on the responsibility of caring for the infant even though she was only eleven. She loved that baby as if it were her own, clung to it even more because of the loss of her father.

"Now, you realize, in those days, when a family was poor with no means of support, they just starved. There was no welfare, or government programs, or anyplace to turn, because the rest of the village was just as bad off. The five of them lived in a hut behind the house of their relative. No heat, no food, close to starvation. My grandmother had to go to work and couldn't take care of the baby, and she wanted her eldest daughter to go to America. That would take lots of money. And though she agonized over what to do, she eventually decided there was only one way out."

My mother couldn't go on. "It's so hard to tell you."

"Mother, Nana's been dead for years. What difference does it make now?"

"I just feel I shouldn't tell you, that it's a sin, or something. I know it's silly."

I waited.

When my mother spoke again a terrible anguish filled her voice. "Faced with no choice but starvation, knowing she had to work, my grandmother could think of no other solution. She put her own child to death. She smothered her."

"My God," I exclaimed. "She killed her own child."

"She was desperate. She saw no other way out. The terror of seeing the rest of her family starve was too much for her. But there were terrible consequences. My mother knew what her mother had done and could never tell anyone. That horrible sin, for which she felt somehow responsible, stayed with her, her whole life. By the time she told me about it, and I convinced her it wasn't her fault, it was too late. She was too sick to recover." My mother was crying now. "And you know, the strangest part of it was, that my grandmother lived a long and happy life in America. She remarried and didn't suffer from guilt. But my mother, who was just a child at the time, felt the terrible responsibility for that act so deeply, it ate her up inside."

As I listened to my mother, I finally understood why she never wanted me to tell people about Steffani. For her, any secret was too terrible to tell.

We were both crying now, as we sat there with the manuscript between us, our hands resting on the pages.

"No wonder you used to tell me that Nana had died from sadness."

"Guilt is a terrible thing," she said. "So are secrets."

And I agreed with all my heart. As I reached over to hug her, I was thinking how proud I was of my heritage. It made me more determined than ever not to let guilt destroy me, and not to give up, but to keep fighting.

CHAPTER FORTY-FOUR

I knew my parents had spent the afternoon with Steffani in the hospital and would not be driving out again tonight, so I planned to go and see her. At five-thirty, they called to report to me about their visit.

"The bleeding is the worst it's ever been," my mother said. She was crying.

I tried to encourage her as best I could. "I'm sure she's going to be all right. Look at what she's gone through before."

My father came on the line. "You know what they've always told us. That someday this might happen, and they won't be able to save her."

"Well, this isn't the time," I insisted, refusing to be drawn into that speculation. "We'll be there for her, just as we've always been, to help her and encourage her."

My mother sighed. "I know you're right, honey." But she didn't sound very sure.

"Good night, daughter," my father said.

Around six o'clock, Steffani called me. Her voice was muffled because of the packing in her sinuses, and the medication made her slur her words.

"I started reading *Annica*, Suze," she said. "And I wanted you to know, I like it. I'm proud of you for doing this. I'll bet Nana is proud too."

I was thrilled. "I know it's not your kind of a book."

"It's good, Suzanne, for exactly what it is. I can't wait to read more tomorrow."

There is no greater compliment for a writer than a reader who is anxious to read more.

"Do you know what you're going to do next?"

The dreaded question. I began asking it of myself halfway through each book, and torturing myself because I didn't always know. It was much easier when I knew what I wanted to write about next. Not knowing came as close to a writer's block as I've ever had.

"First, I have to be able to sell this one."

"You will," she predicted. "You'll see, it will happen."

"How are you feeling?" I asked.

"Pretty awful," she admitted. "I just had a shot, so I'm okay right now, but it was a rough day." She started to cry. "If only it would stop," she said. "I'm so tired of this."

"I know you are." I clutched the receiver, willing all my strength to pass through the phone lines and into her body. As if telepathy worked, I concentrated every ounce of energy in my body across the miles and into her.

"Are you planning to come out tonight?" she asked.

"Yes, I'm leaving soon."

"Maybe you better not. I'm going to sleep now. I think I'd rather rest."

"Are you sure? I wanted to tell you about Jasmine."

"Oh, did you see her?"

"Yes. And she's not the one. Her typewriter is an IBM."

"My sister the sleuth." She managed a laugh. "Who would have known those Nancy Drew books you devoured as a kid would have taught you so much. Did you tell Barry?"

"Yes, why?"

She was drifting off between sentences. "I'm glad you're not being *strubborna*." She imitated our father's way of saying *stubborn* with a Hungarian accent.

"Are you sure you don't want me to come out and see you?" I asked.

"Yeah." She sounded far away. "Suze? I liked this book, but next time, write something real, will you?"

"Okay," I sighed, willing to promise her anything while she was in this state. "I'm glad you like *Annica*."

"What's not to like? I'll assign it to my ninth-graders when it's published. Maybe you'll come and talk to the class."

"I'd love to!" I said, feeling a warm glow fill me. My sister finally approved.

Just then, a man's voice interrupted us, I heard him say, over the phone as he came into her room, "Hi babe." For a moment, I thought maybe it was Barry, but by her response, I could tell it wasn't.

"I didn't want you to see me like this," she said tearfully, still drugged.

"Why not?" he replied. "You're still gorgeous underneath all that, aren't you?"

"I've gotta go, Suze," she said to me. "Talk to you later." And then I heard a clunking sound. She must have dropped the receiver and it hit the floor.

"Hang that up, will you?" she said to her visitor.

I was fascinated, listening, wishing he wouldn't hang up, so I could hear what they were saying, figure out who he was.

He picked up the receiver, and I heard the sound of his hand closing around it.

"I got your telegram," I heard her say.

"I've missed you like hell," he said, and then he hung up, cutting me off.

Damn! I thought. But then I smiled to myself. No wonder she didn't want me to drive out there. She had a much more interesting person to keep her company tonight than me.

I sat there for a moment feeling amazed by her. Here she was, hovering in some terrible twilight zone, physically depleted, fighting to stay alive, and she had mysterious gentlemen coming to see her.

A hot, nauseating rush of envy flooded through me. *How dare she be so full of life at a time when I would have been totally defeated?* Instantly an enormous ton of remorse descended on me. *How could I be envious of her? Look who I am being envious of.* Suddenly, I was sobbing, wracked by guilt. *I'm sorry, Steff, I'm so sorry. Just be well, get better, don't let my stupid, petty thoughts affect you.* As if they could. But with a sick sister, one never knew. As a child, I could never have had the right to wish that my sister would shrivel up and blow away, the way other kids wished about their siblings. With Steffani, it might just have happened.

In order to see Marilyn Kauffman, I had to make an appointment with her secretary. The appointment was arranged at her showroom in the California Clothing Mart. As I entered the modern glass building, and stepped onto the escalator with women who all looked like showroom models, and men who all looked like Jewish or Italian lechers, I couldn't believe that Marilyn, the political activist, would be in a place like this. We'd been out of touch for several years, ever since I declined to loan her money. I'd heard from her mother, through my mother, that she'd gone into business and had become extremely successful. But all mothers say things like that about their children. I didn't really believe it.

"How the hell are you?" she said, hugging me. Of all my friends, Marilyn had made the most amazing changes since I'd seen her last. Gone was the straggly hair and skinny body; she was smooth and voluptuous, wearing a raw silk tailored jacket and gabardine skirt. The jacket alone must have cost two hundred dollars. And were those heels and stockings, and pearls and a silk blouse she was wearing? I looked her up and down, unaware that I was staring. *Her mother told the truth*.

"It's the new me," she exclaimed, holding out her hands and turning around to model. "Did you ever think I'd look like this? I'm the merchandising director for Mystique Fashions." She waved her hand at the clothes that hung on a metal rack jammed with fancy, shiny things. "We have factories in Hong Kong and Taiwan, so I travel all over the world. In fact, I just got back from nearly three months in Europe and Australia. Check out the tan?" She showed me her arm. "The Great Barrier Reef," she exclaimed.

If she'd been out of the country for three months, I thought,

*she couldn't have been sending me those accusatory letters
or done the research necessary to torment me. Could she?*

"I didn't believe it when your mother said you'd been
going to the Far East on business. I'm ashamed to say I
thought you were smuggling drugs, or leading a revolution."

Marilyn laughed. "There was a time when you would have
been right."

"How long have you been doing this?" I asked her.

"Being elegant, or working with Tommy Chen?" she said.

"Both," I shrugged.

"With Tommy, four years. But it took a bit longer to alter
my image. I met Tommy at the Washington, D.C., protest
march that same summer you turned down my idiotic proposition for funds." She laughed. "However did you put up with
me? I was off the wall back then, wasn't I? Nixon could do
that to you. Anyway, I went to Washington to try and revital-
ize the SDS, remember? But things were winding down,
except for the groups who advocated violence like the Weathermen and the Panthers. I didn't want to be a part of that. I
figured they were as bad as or worse than the establishment
they were trying to overthrow. So, there was this good-looking Oriental guy standing next to me, taller than I am, with
black shiny hair, wearing jeans and a jacket. We got to talking, comparing philosophies. By the end of the weekend, we
discovered we were fed up with the protest life and wanted
to try something new. He had studied design in college in
Chicago, and I was an art major. We were both tired of being
one of the unwashed masses."

"When your mother said you had a Chinese boyfriend, I
thought he must be a Maoist."

"Don't even mention Mao around Tommy. He's a Republican, can you believe it?"

That was probably the most incredible thing she'd told me
so far.

"Eventually, Tommy and I discovered what we wanted to
do," she continued. "Be rich! So, we borrowed some seed

money from our parents, and went into the fashion business. Can you believe it? I call myself the merchandising director, but we're really partners. We're grossing fifteen million a year, Suzanne. How about that? Can you believe how I've turned into a capitalist pig?''

"You mean those pearls your mother won't take off are really from you?"

She laughed merrily. "They're huge, aren't they? And I figure I owe my success to you."

"Are you kidding?"

"If you hadn't turned me down when I came to you with my ridiculous proposition, I might be doing time in a federal prison. Instead, I went to Washington, and that's when I met Tommy." And she leaned over and gave me a kiss on my cheek. "Thanks, kiddo. And I'm sorry about the way I treated you at Topanga Camp."

I shrugged, trying to make this whole thing real. I couldn't believe how I'd discounted her mother's stories. Now, I wondered if maybe it was because I wanted to be the only one who was the success out of the two of us. But Marilyn had gotten over those petty childhood rivalries. I believed she was truly grateful to me. Nobody could put on an act like this one. "Marilyn, have you heard anything about what I've been going through, lately?"

She nodded, soberly. "My mom told me about your troubles. I'm really sorry. But your books are still selling like hotcakes, aren't they? Listen, Suzanne, you want some clothes? Wholesale, of course. You can try them on in the bathroom down the hall. We're not supposed to allow try-ons, but all the showrooms do it."

Unfortunately, I couldn't afford to buy any clothes, even at cost. But now I was sure Marilyn wasn't the one I wanted. What cinched it was when she said, "Give my best to your family, will you. I really miss seeing you all. You know, I think of you as my relatives. You were really good to me when my parents were in trouble, and I was such a brat I didn't deserve it." And she hugged me very hard.

When I left Marilyn, I got two dollars' worth of change and called the hospital. A miracle occurred. The phone was already in Steffani's room and they knew the correct number, so in just a few minutes she came on the line.

"It's not Marilyn Kauffman," I told her.

She was drugged and hard to understand. She may have said, "How do you know?"

"She's making a fortune in the *schmatta* business."

I think Steffani laughed, but it was difficult to tell. "The list dwindles down, to a precious few," I said. "I'm going to see Alex this evening when I take the children to McDonald's."

"Call me after," she said.

"How are you?"

"Don't ask." It sounded like "*ash.*"

"I'm coming out," I said, feeling a rush of terror grip me.

"No, it's okay," she said. "I've been sleeping a lot."

"So, you'll let your boyfriends visit you and not me, is that it?" I teased.

"You're—damn—right," she said, enunciating carefully so as to get it all out. "I've never seen you try to cop a feel."

"Steff-ani!"

"Suz-anne!" she mimicked, barely able to say my name. But her sense of humor was still sharp.

"I'll see you tomorrow, then."

"I have to tell you . . ."

"What?" I asked her.

"I love you," she said, and hung up.

Then I realized I hadn't asked her who her visitor was last night.

Alex and Dina were in formal dress when I arrived at their duplex. My three children were so anxious to leave they were waiting on the landing for me. But I had to talk to Alex.

"Suzanne, Dina and I can't be late," he insisted, giving me an impatient look.

"It's all right, lambie," she said, making me slightly ill.

I marveled at the way her skin looked so creamily tan, and her hair was so perfectly coiffed down her bare back. In a ponytail and jeans, I was really the country mouse.

Alex led me into the study, a small room off the master bedroom with its own fireplace. This room was done in green-and-red plaid with dark wood paneling, and there was a country English print over the mantel. Exactly what a study should look like.

"How's your sister?"

"Not good," I told him, refusing to let myself think about that now.

"Steffani has so damned much courage," he said.

His words made the fear inside twist painfully. "This bout has really been a bad one," I said.

"You know why I used to object to her?" he said. "Not because I thought she'd turn you into a hippie, but because she was so self-assured. I thought it might rub off on you and you'd figure out what an incredible person you were and dump me. I was always afraid of that; it came true, didn't it? I guess I had a premonition."

"Which you turned into a self-fulfilling prophecy."

He smiled at the truth of that comment. "How does it look for the trial? Are your lawyers confident of a win?"

"I've been doing some investigating on my own," I said, staring at him, wondering if he had been the one who'd sent me the letters and framed me with that poison candy. But with my sister suffering in the hospital, my problems seemed almost insignificant. Except that she wanted me to find out the truth. For her, I would press on.

"It wasn't me," he said, "if you were wondering." He stared at me, trying to make me see the truth of that. "I know I've done some stupid things in my life, but that's not one of them. Honestly, Suzanne. After the way I trashed our bedroom that time I must have been first on your list."

I couldn't help remembering how awful that had been, and how sick.

"I wanted to reassure you months ago, but I figured, if

you'd suspected me, you'd have accused me. Wouldn't you?''

"I didn't think it was you, Alex.''

"What kind of person would do such a thing?''

"A sick crazy,'' I answered, wondering if I could truly eliminate him from my list.

"I'm not that sick. Besides, I'd never do anything that could jeopardize my life or my career, you know that.''

I almost smiled. If he'd said, *I'd never do anything to hurt you*, I might have doubted him. But as usual, all he was thinking about was himself.

"I swear, Suzanne.''

"What do you swear on, Alex? The lives of our children? That's the only oath that would convince me.''

He raised his right hand and said, "I swear on our children's lives I had nothing to do with this plot against you.''

After my conversation with Alex my brain refused to rest. I lay there sleeplessly, thinking about Steffani, praying she'd be better soon, and about Gloria, the only one left. Was she the person I had been seeking all this time? What would Alex say if it turned out to be his sister who was the sick crazy person trying to ruin my life. Trying, hell—a damned good job had been done so far. Alex would probably defend her. I stared at the ceiling waiting impatiently for tomorrow to come.

Gloria had an apartment at the Shoreham Towers above the Sunset strip. I got there at 10:00 A.M. When she opened the door and found me her charm covered up surprise. "Why Suzanne, come in.'' She grabbed my hand, pulling me in so she could kiss the air around my cheek. "I can't believe you're here. Isn't your sister in critical condition? How is she doing? Poor Steffi.''

Her pity set my teeth on edge. "Your father . . . and your mother,'' she added, "must be so worried. But why are you here, Suzanne? Did you want to visit your jewelry?'' Her eyes were wide, ingenuous, but underneath she was leering.

I shook my head. "I've forgotten all about those things of mine you bought," I said. It seemed to deflate her.

"Really? Well, you're a better woman than I am."

"No argument there," I replied, stepping into the room to look around. The mirrored mantelpiece and coffee table, the laquered side tables, and ebony piano were covered with silver-framed photographs of her in the various roles she had played in her career. The sofas were upholstered in cream satin, trimmed with fringe; the carpet was black, with a red border around the edge; and there were tall plants in the corners. Above the sofa was a Louis Icart lithograph in a red glass frame. The room had a sterile, cold appearance, an expensive look. Just like Gloria.

This was more difficult than I expected. "Sit down," she offered, wrapping her Chinese robe around her and tying the sash more tightly. "Can I get you anything? Coffee? I've got some made."

"No, thanks." I didn't know how to begin. I felt unprepared. If this had been one of my characters, I'd have planned the dialogue to trap her, and she would be giving me clues as to how to proceed. But she just sat there waiting. Her expression was calm, neither guilty nor hostile, and I was unsure. I didn't know which was better, having her be the one, or not be the one.

Just then, I heard the sound of a drawer closing in another room and realized she wasn't alone. I hadn't considered that. In my imagination, the minute I arrived at her door, she would confess everything, or deny it vehemently: "How could you think that I would do such a thing. You're my oldest and dearest friend. I'll never forgive you for accusing me of this," she'd say, with big tears rolling down her cheeks. Instead, I felt myself blushing for intruding on her.

"I'd better go," I said, getting up from the sofa, just as George Ruben came into the room, wearing a charcoal double-breasted suit, pale yellow shirt, and sharper yellow tie. His face was tanned a bronze color, and his dark hair was parted in the middle and slicked back, covering the collar at the back of his neck. He came over to me and kissed both my cheeks.

"How is Steffani? Is she any better?"

"No."

"I saw her at the hospital the night before last."

Gloria's sharp intake of breath startled us both. "You didn't tell me you'd gone to see *her*. I waited for hours."

"I said I was visiting a sick friend." He smiled pleasantly at her.

She was seething. Obviously, as sick as Steffani was, Gloria considered her a threat. It must have been George's voice I heard over the phone saying how he'd missed her. No wonder Gloria felt threatened. *Yea Steff*, I thought, and that made me want to cry; tears filled my eyes. George came over, sat down next to me, and put his arms around me.

"She's a remarkable woman," he said, softly.

"How dare you do this to me," Gloria hissed, on my other side. I pulled away abruptly to look at her.

"I don't think we should have this fight now, do you?" he said.

"You bastard," she retorted, through clenched teeth. Her volume had increased with every word. "What is the fascination with that misshapen little tramp? For the life of me, I can't understand it."

I gasped when she said that.

"In the first place, I see who I wish to see, Gloria. You know that. Steffani is my friend, and she's very sick." George's voice snapped like a whip. "We are all praying for her recovery."

"Don't include me in that," Gloria snapped back. Then she realized she was talking about my sister and stifled her next response. But I'd seen the depth of her hatred, it glowed in her eyes like some malevolent manifestation. The force of it made me almost dizzy.

I turned to George, wanting to ask him so many questions: Are you and Steffani more than friends? Do you care for her, love her? But with Gloria sitting there I didn't dare. George's smile, however, told me most everything. Again, I marveled at my sister. It hadn't mattered to this gorgeous man, a world-famous designer, that she had an imperfect body. Even though glamorous women fawned over him and he traveled in the fanciest circles, he had driven all that way to be with Steffani because of who she was. He'd cared about her enough to infuriate his lover, the beautiful and famous opera star. *My little Steffani*, I thought. *Good for you!*

"This is the worst I've ever seen her," he told me. "But we laughed together and I told her all my news." I saw the pain in his eyes as he recalled the evening. "I didn't stay too long because she kept drifting in and out of sleep. But we were talking about your investigation and I told her something we both thought might be important. She asked me to be sure to tell you. It was the last thing she said to me. 'Promise you'll tell Suzanne.' I'm assuming she told you and that's why you're here."

"George," Gloria called. It was almost a scream.

"Steffani didn't tell me anything." What was Gloria enraged about now? "Maybe she forgot, or she expected to tell me today when I see her. What is it?" I asked, thinking it had something to do with him and Steffani.

"Don't you dare!" Gloria said, with a full scream this time. "I'll kill you, George, I swear I will."

"You're not going to kill anyone, Gloria," he said, crossing over to the entry hall closet and opening the door. He reached inside and pulled out a small blue case and brought it back across the room.

"I told you to throw that away," she said, rising up from her seat to face him. "You told me you threw it away."

At first I thought it was a briefcase, but then I noticed it was too fat and too heavy. It was a typewriter.

"Give me that," Gloria said, lunging for him. But he pushed her away, knocking her back so that she hit the coffee table; several of the framed pictures of her fell over and we heard the sound of shattering glass.

"Steffani told me you were looking for a typewriter to

match the one used to write those letters about you. I told Steffani that I had found one hidden in the back of Gloria's closet the other day. I didn't know what kind it was, but it made me suspect her as the one who's been tormenting you all these months.''

''Don't be ridiculous,'' Gloria said, haughtily. ''That doesn't even belong to me; someone left it here. I told you that, George! Why are you trying to ruin me? It's not mine!''

''I'd check it out if I were you,'' he said, handing it to me. ''I told her I'd thrown it out, but I didn't. It may be the one you're looking for.''

My heart was pounding in my throat so that I could barely speak. I could see that the typewriter was a Remington.

So it was Gloria after all—*Sherry Fallon*!

She glared at me. ''My God, why?'' I cried, finding my voice.

She had moved back to sit on the edge of the sofa as though cornered there by a mad dog, her body iron stiff, the sinews in her neck extended, while her hands gripped themselves so hard in her lap that her nails were digging into the skin. As I watched, several of the places started to bleed.

''I don't believe it, I don't believe it,'' I kept repeating. ''Gloria.'' I said her name, almost as horrified to see her make herself bleed, as to think of what she had done to me. ''They took me to prison. Do you know that? I'm facing a trial. I lost my house, my career has been ruined. Do you realize what you've done to me?'' I started to cry and to scream all at the same time. ''I lost my children! Was that what you wanted? Was that your idea too?'' It was, I could tell. This woman who said she thought of me as a sister had turned into the evil queen, offering a poisoned apple. She'd delivered every killing blow. ''Why did you do this to me?'' I cried again, wanting to grab her hair and rip it from her scalp.

She screamed her reply at me, her face contorted with such rage that saliva sprayed with her words. ''Ask your father!'' she said.

"My father?" I said, dumbly. "You're crazy, you're crazy!" I yelled. "You're going to pay for this, Gloria. I'll see that you pay! There will be criminal charges!"

George took my arm forcefully before we attacked one another and pulled me to the door, opening it for me. "I told your sister about my suspicions the moment I found the typewriter," he said. "If I hadn't been in Europe for the past few months, I might have been able to prevent all of this from happening."

Just then, Gloria leaped off of the sofa and flung herself at us, hitting out, screaming, punching, scratching. George put up his hands, but she managed to rake her fingers over his cheek. Then she turned to me, but I was ready for her. I swung the typewriter to the right, whacking her in the shins so hard that she screamed and doubled over, holding her legs. Then, I swung it back again, hitting her in the thigh, knocking her over. And before she could recover, I hurried out the door, leaving George to deal with this deranged woman.

I sobbed all the way down in the elevator, as much from the relief of finally knowing as from what she'd put me through. But it was going to be over. God, it was over. Finally, finally, I would have my life back again. The elevator door opened in the lobby and I stepped out, unable to stop crying. My emotions were riotous. I wanted to scream and shout for joy, and at the same time, I kept pouring forth these hysterical tears. She'd hurt me so much, God, she'd hurt me. Finally, I gave way and crumpled to the floor, sobbing and clutching the typewriter to me. It was the most precious thing in my life at the moment.

It wasn't until I was in the car that I had a chilling thought. Was it legal for me to have taken this typewriter? If it wasn't found on her premises by a court order, could it be used as evidence against her? I didn't want to jeopardize any case I might have. Then I realized that George was a witness. He'd heard Gloria not only admit her guilt, but say, "Get rid of this typewriter." If I'd left it there, she surely would ha~ thrown it away. Now, at least, we could use it. Barry w

know, my dearest Barry. Wait until I told him! And Steffani.
But Steffani already knew. First I had to see my father and
find out why Gloria had told me to ask him!

"Thank God, it's over, it's over it's over!" I repeated out
loud as I drove to my parents' house.

CHAPTER FORTY-FIVE

"Mom, Dad," I called, using my key to their front door, "I
know who did it. I know."

My father was cleaning out his tackle box and came hurrying in from the garage holding a fishing reel. My mother
was fixing lunch and didn't hear me. I could smell the tuna
salad as I came into the kitchen.

"What did you say?" my father asked.

"Hi, honey," my mother said. "We're going to see Steffani right after lunch. Do you want to come?"

I didn't reply to my mother. "Dad, I found out who's been
ruining my life. I know who sent the letters and the candy
and planted the LSD in my house."

"Who?" my mother asked, drying her hands on her apron.

"Gloria." I was watching my father's face carefully.

He looked as if I'd just stuck a knife in his guts. "That's
impossible. Who told you that?" he said.

"She admitted it. But George Ruben was the one who told
me. He found Gloria's typewriter, the one she used to type
the letters, and he gave it to me. It's in the car. I still can't
believe she did it," I said, thinking how hate-filled her actions
had been. "She studied every detail of my life so she could
destroy me. The poisoned candy, the letters. How she set me
up! She was the one who had access to my refrigerator. Must
have gotten a key from Alex and put the LSD there after she'd

sent the candy to Brett Slocum. If the police hadn't found it on their own, she'd have probably told them where to look. I wonder how long she'd been planning this. Our whole lives, perhaps. I never knew how much she hated me. I asked her why she did it and she said, 'Ask your father.' What did she mean?''

"My God, Burt," my mother said, her lip quivering as she turned away.

"I have no idea," he said, staring out the window into the garden.

"Do you realize what I've been going through for the last six months?" I cried. "If you knew Gloria was doing this to me, how could you let her? You're my father. Where were you? What's wrong with you!"

"I didn't know!" He slammed his fist down on the kitchen table so that the salt and pepper shakers rattled. "If I'd known, do you think I ever would have let her? I would have told you, or the police. Believe me!" he insisted, turning his tear-filled gray-blue eyes to me. The sadness I saw there told me he hadn't known, but that he wasn't surprised.

"Well, I don't believe you," my mother said, turning her dark eyes on him, flashing contempt. "You brought this on your own daughter, Burt Blacker. I hope you're satisfied with yourself. Because of you, Suzanne has suffered for months. Do you know what she's gone through? Isn't it enough that we've had one child suffering all her life! Did we have to have two?"

"Please, Lynnette," he said, "it's not my fault."

"Oh yes it is," she shouted. "I put up with your nonsense for years because I knew what it was, a middle-aged man grabbing for his youth. I knew she'd get tired of you eventually, or you'd get tired of her. I used to laugh at you, the way you preened around her, the way you thought you were getting away with something. And she was so smug. How many times I wanted to slap her face. If she'd been my daughter, I would have. But this is just too much. You're the one who let that nutcase out of her cage. Because of you, she thought she could get away with attacking Suzanne. For all I know, it's because of you she did it in the first place."

"Will one of you tell me what's going on here?" I yelled.

"Your father had an affair with Gloria Winston," my mother stated. "Yes, that's right, don't look at me so surprised, either of you. I've known all along. I even knew when it ended, sometime after she met George Ruben. Am I right? You know I am." She crossed her arms and pursed her lips. She reminded me of Steffani, whenever she was acting stubborn.

My father shook his head once from side to side, and raised his eyes up as if asking for strength.

"An affair, with Gloria?" I was sick inside. The thought of my father doing it with my friend was too graphic, too close, too eminently real. My cheeks burned, my brain reeled with my thoughts. I wanted to bring the blanket of no knowledge up over my head and hide there forever muffled in its wooly warmth. I got a whiff of my mother's Shalimar, thinking Gloria always wore L'Air du Temps. I'd bought it for her myself over the years. Had she worn it with my father? I was feeling so sick and so filled with hatred, I almost understood why Gloria had done it. "If you hadn't kept your affair a secret, I might have known it was Gloria. Don't you see that? I'd have known! It would have saved me months of pain."

"Well, Burt," my mother said, glaring at my father. "How do you feel now?"

"The same as I've always felt," he said, softly. "Like a damned old fool who couldn't help himself." He came toward me to take my hand, but I pulled it away. "I had no idea she was capable of such treachery even though she was always so envious of you, Suzanne. You had everything she wanted. I think she only wanted me because I was your father. And even after she had me, there was no one as important in her life as Alex. I think it was him she was really in love with."

"Her own brother?" I said, disgusted. "That's really sick."

"When you and Alex got divorced, Gloria couldn't understand it. To her, Alex was perfect, and yet you'd rejected him. I guess she's always been a little crazy, but that really did it. And when I stopped seeing her, it didn't help matters. I figured, since she had George in her life, I could back off. But it only made her crazier."

"No shit!" I said. And then, "God, this is sick." I wished Barry was here to breathe some wholesomeness into this sordid arena. I could feel the tentacles of betrayal beginning to tear at me. What would my sister say about all this? My innocent world had been shattered; Humpty Dumpty.

"I only turned to her because of you," my father said, throwing his shame and anger at my mother.

"Oh no, you don't!" she insisted. "Don't try and blame this one on me. You're always blaming me for something." But her voice wasn't as steady as it had been.

"I don't want to hear any more," I shouted. "The two of you have done nothing but blame each other for everything. This is your doing, Dad. Accept it!" I saw the tuna salad in the bowl, the kind my mother always made, with celery and onions and pimientos. I wished it would have been possible to sit down and eat a sandwich at the kitchen table where I'd grown up, and have everything be the way it used to be. *I'm going to get my children back,* I thought, suddenly. *Please God, don't ever let me do anything like this to them.*

"You have to understand it all, Suzanne," my father said, sitting down at the kitchen table. "The only reason I ever turned to Gloria was because of David Levinson."

"Dr. Levinson?" I said, looking at my mother, who was glaring at my father with fury.

"David is my friend," she said. "When I needed him to help me with Steffani, he was there. He was the only one who could help us."

"But you turned to *him*, not to me," my father said, starting to cry. "I felt as helpless as you did over Steffani, but you didn't need me." He turned to me, anguished. "I couldn't help her, my little baby, and Dr. Levinson could. Every time something went wrong, he was the one your mother called."

"He was the doctor," my mother said, starting to cry, too.

"He hardly ever charged us for what he did for us, except for the surgeries. He gave us the medicine we needed, samples from his office. Steffani didn't have the money to pay him all these years."

We were all crying. I didn't know what mattered now. The damage had been done. What must their lives have been like to watch their precious child suffer such a terrible illness? Did they blame themselves? Most parents would. I only knew how I felt about her being sick, how it intruded on everything we did, but I could never get angry because she was so sick. I thought back over those early years when Dr. Levinson had come into our lives, what it must have been like to be so desperate for help and unable to find anyone until he showed up. To me, the doctor was God. To my parents he was savior as well as usurper. So much of my personality had been formed by my sister's illness, and now I saw how it had affected my parents' lives in ways I'd never suspected. The negative consequences had even rippled onto my children's lives as well, though some of it had been positive. (We had all learned how to fight for life, how to keep going, how to achieve and not waste time. How to finish a task, get it done!) Of course, that was the way my parents were, but Steffani's illness had brought it all into focus.

"Were you and Dr. Levinson . . . involved?" I asked my mother. Another secret.

She was crying so hard, she couldn't reply. Finally, she blew her nose and said, "Only so far as I needed him to take care of Steffani. And I needed him desperately," she said. "I see now that it didn't matter what we did or didn't do. If your father thought so, because I'd turned away from him, that's all that counts." She moved away from the sink and approached the table to take my father's hand. "I'm sorry, Burt," she said. "For what it's worth, I'm sorry with all my heart."

"Not as sorry as I am," he said, squeezing her hand back. Then he put his long arm around both of us and the three of us hugged.

The telephone interrupted us and my mother went to answer it. "Yes, this is Mrs. Blacker," she said, and shouted, "Oh my God." She turned to us, her face as white as the apron she wore. "It's Steffani. She suffered a major tear in the nasopharyngeal lining. The surgeon tried to repair it, but the tissue wouldn't hold. She's bleeding badly. They want us to come right away."

"Is this it?" I asked, feeling a scream welling up inside of me. I forced it down before it shattered glass.

Please, fight, Steffi! I begged. *Please, keep fighting.*

It was the longest hour I've ever spent driving all that way. When we got to the hospital, they took us to the ICU. Dr. Mishima, her hematologist, and Dr. Clayburg, her surgeon, came out to talk to us.

"We've done everything we can do," Dr. Clayburg said. "It's just a matter of time. Her tissues won't heal anymore, I'm sorry."

His words were a devastating blow. Disbelief shot through me and I nearly fell. *It can't be. She's always gotten well!*

"Can we see her?" my mother asked.

He nodded. "I must warn you, Mrs. Blacker, she's unconscious. I don't think she'll know you're there."

"I'll know," my mother said. My father took her hand and the two of them went in together.

I was terrified to see her like this. I didn't want to remember this final horror. And my heart was breaking. In a flash I saw her as an infant, and then as a little girl, remembered the way she'd felt in my arms, my baby sister. *I had to tell her about Gloria!*

Sometime later my parents came out, crying in one another's arms. "Don't go in, Suzanne," my father warned me. "That's not our Steff."

But I pushed passed him and went in anyway.

There was a chair by her bed occupied by an attendant who got up when I came in. The packing had been removed from her nose so that she looked like her beautiful self again. Her head was turned to the side away from me so that a basin could catch the life that flowed from her. She was so still. I took her hand and called to her.

"Steff, it's me. Don't be afraid, I'm here. I have so much to tell you. I found out who it was. It was Gloria! I've got the proof I need. George helped me. You forgot to tell me what he told you, but I know it was because you were sick. Everything's going to be all right now."

But as I said it, I knew it would never be all right again. I put my head down on her hand and sobbed. Suddenly, I felt her hand move beneath me; her gentle touch caressed my cheek. Wild hope shot through me and I jerked my head up. "Steffani, can you hear me?"

Just barely, she nodded.

"I love you," I told her.

"Me too," she said. And then she was still.

They had to lead me out of the room because I was so overcome by grief I couldn't find my way. She died at two o'clock that afternoon.

I sobbed in my parents' arms, first my father's and then my mother's. The pain cut so deeply it was as if I'd been cloven in two. So much of me was gone with her, all of our shared memories. There would be no more to come. In that moment, I would have traded places with her not to have felt this pain, this newly raw excruciating part that screamed for relief. *Please forgive me, Steffani,* I begged. *For having had more in life than you did, and for not being sick.*

Steffani's funeral would take place on Friday, in a newly built outdoor mausoleum, near my two uncles. I wanted to be buried in a pine box in the ground. I've always felt that it was better to be returned to the earth's cycle as quickly as possible, rather than keep your bones in a stone or metal casing.

"Why pine?" Steffani had asked me once when we were talking about it.

"Pine is so chic these days," I joked with her. "And if you line my casket with blue-and-white checked linen, and bury me with a bottle of wine and loaf of bread, I'll become a great picnic.'' I could see it now, the way her eyes had crinkled up when she'd laughed at me with her deep hearty infectious laughter.

I contacted her fellow teachers; some of her students were writing a tribute to her to be delivered in a celebration in her honor at the Griffith Park merry-go-round on Sunday, where her friends would read some of her poetry. She'd have loved it. Still, the feeling that I had failed her tormented me. Why had I escaped this illness that had taken her? *Stop wallowing in self-pity,* I told myself. *Steffani didn't.* ''Why waste precious time?'' she'd say. ''Living is too important to spend it complaining.'' I understood that now. Perhaps perspective is the only dividend that results from tragedy.

''Don't be sad, Mommy,'' Jered said. ''She's not sick anymore.'' I stroked his cheek as he sat beside me at the funeral service. Next to me, my father's face was drained of color. The lines in his cheeks had deepened, his expression showed his pain. His tall shoulders were stooped as if the weight of life had finally bowed him. My mother too was in shock. Once, during a prayer, my father covered his eyes with his arm and sobbed, his elbow jutting out in its own peculiar way.

We left the casket open, even though that went against Jewish tradition. I knew she'd want the world to see her courage, even in death. And we'd given permission for an autopsy. Steffani had been a guinea pig all her life; why should it be different in death? Perhaps, the knowledge gained from it might help others. Nothing more hidden.

I don't remember much of the service. There were prayers, and an organ playing, and several people spoke about Steffani, her accomplishments and her courage and her contribution. But I do remember my three children coming up to the podium, Amy in her flowered navy dress, Miles in a new charcoal suit, and Jered in a pink shirt, a gray tie, and slacks. I was filled with such a rush of pride and love for them, I could barely contain it.

Amy began. "Miles and I will read a poem that my aunt Steffani wrote." They each took turns with the stanzas.

> *I wish that I could disappear*
> *Come back again some other year*
> *Would I be different, someone else*
> *Other than just me*
>
> *I find that I am all alone*
> *And usually I'm strong*
> *I rarely cry or scowl or frown*
> *Except when I am down*
> *But not for long*
>
> *Something is wrong with my blood*
> *Though I'm strong*
> *And something is wrong with my bones*
> *Yet I'm strong*
> *And something is wrong with my body*
> *It's not as strong*
>
> *Yet I can withstand many things*
> *Except my suffering, lonely, fellow beings.*

Then, it was Jered's turn. They had to lift him up to the microphone. "My aunt Steffani wrote this," he said.

> *I can smile*
> *Because I am glad*
> *That I am alive*
> *And able to be sad*

It was then, listening to my sister's words, which would be such a wonderful legacy for all of us, just as her life was, that I knew what my next book would be. It would not be a fairy tale, for I was finally ready to keep my promise to her and write something real. My next book would be the story of her life. It would be the truth. And I would call it *Steffani*.